A NORTON CRITICAL EDITION

Rudyard Kipling
KIM

D1319374

AUTHORITATIVE TEXT
BACKGROUNDS
CRITICISM

Edited by

ZOHREH T. SULLIVAN

UNIVERSITY OF ILLINOIS AT URBANA-CHAMPAIGN

W • W • **NORTON & COMPANY** • *New York* • *London*

The text of this book is composed in Fairfield Medium
with the display set in Bernhard Modern.
Composition by Publishing Synthesis, New York.
Manufacturing by the Maple-Vail Book Manufacturing Group.
Book design by Antonina Krass.

Library of Congress Cataloging-in-Publication Data

Kipling, Rudyard, 1865–1936.
Kim : authoritative text, backgrounds, criticism / Rudyard Kipling ;
edited by Zohreh T. Sullivan.
p. cm.— (A Norton critical edition)
Includes bibliographical references.

ISBN 0-393-96650-X (pbk.)

1. Kipling, Rudyard, 1865–1936. Kim. 2. Irish—India—Fiction.
3. Orphans—Fiction. 4. India—Fiction. 5. Lamas—Fiction. 6. Boys—Fiction.
I. Sullivan, Zohreh T. II. Title.

PR4854.K4 2001
823´.8—dc21

2001041045

W. W. Norton & Company, Inc., 500 Fifth Avenue, New York, N.Y. 10010
www.wwnorton.com

W. W. Norton & Company Ltd., Castle House, 75/76 Wells Street, London
W1T 3QT

3 4 5 6 7 8 9 0

Contents

Criticism

Preface

Published in 1901, *Kim* was Kipling's delayed reward for seven years of political and personal crises: the aging of England's imperial enterprise; the bombast of Queen Victoria's Diamond Jubilee (which he refused to celebrate with an ode); the deaths of his closest uncle, Edward Burne-Jones (in 1898), and of his daughter Josephine (in 1899); the deterioration of his sister's mind; and his own depressions. But, for Kipling, the 1890s were also professionally productive years that saw the publication of both Jungle Books (1895, 1896), *The Seven Seas* (1896), *Captains Courageous* (1897), *The Day's Work* (1898), *Stalky and Co.*, and *From Sea to Sea* (both 1899). His letters, diary, and unfinished autobiography, *Something of Myself*, record stages in the conception of the story of *Kim*. His autobiography chooses to place its birth in 1897: "I had a vague notion of an Irish boy, born in India and mixed up with native life. I went as far as to make him the son of a private in an Irish Battalion, and christened him 'Kim of the 'Rishti'—short, that is, for Irish."[1] But an 1892 letter to Mary Mapes Dodge suggests that he had started thinking of the project earlier.

For those who believe "Mother Maturin"—Kipling's projected novel about a half-caste Irish keeper of an opium den in Lahore—to be the source of *Kim*, his work on the novel started even earlier. His diary of March 7, 1885, records its birth: "The idea of 'Mother Maturin' dawned on me today." An 1885 letter to his aunt, Edith Macdonald, announces that he has "really embarked to the tune of 237 foolscap pages on my novel Mother Maturin—an Anglo-Indian episode. Like Topsy 'it growd' while I wrote. . . . It's not one bit nice or proper but it carries a grim sort of a moral with it and tries to deal with the unutterable horrors of lower class Eurasian and native life as they exist outside reports and reports and reports. I haven't got the Pater's verdict on what I've done. He comes up in a couple of Days and will then sit in judgement. Trixie says it's awfully horrid; Mother says its [*sic*] nasty but powerful and I know it to be in large measure true."[2] Truth, however, was not

1. *Something of Myself and Other Autobiographical Writings*, ed. Thomas Pinney (Cambridge: Cambridge University Press, 1990) 81.
2. Charles Carrington, *Rudyard Kipling: His Life and Work* (London: Macmillan, 1986) 103.

an excuse for writing about taboo topics. The journalist-narrator of Kipling's eerie story "A Matter of Fact" concludes with the observation: "Truth is a naked lady, and if by accident she is drawn up from the bottom of the sea, it behoves a gentleman either to give her a print petticoat or to turn his face to the wall, and vow that he did not see."

Both Kipling's letters and his biographers show that his sympathies were passionately entangled with India, that the "magic" readers find in *Kim* is the effect of the range of pleasure in the spiritual, emotional, and visual experiences of India, and that he often felt an outsider in cold England. In a letter to E. K. Robinson in 1886, Kipling writes:

> I am deeply interested in the queer ways and works of the people of the land. I hunt and rummage among 'em; knowing Lahore City—that wonderful, dirty, mysterious ant hill—blind fold and wandering through it like Haroun Al-Raschid in search of strange things. "Section 420. I.P.C." (originally called "In the House of Suddhoo") is the outcome of some of these researches but the bulk of my notes and references goes to enrich a bruised tin tea box where lies—350 f.cp. pages thick— my "Mother Maturin." The novel that is always being written and yet gets no furrarder.

The novel was never published. Biographers such as Angus Wilson and Charles Carrington speculate that Kipling abandoned it because of paternal disapproval. Or perhaps he decided its "truth" was better committed to silence. The unfinished novel returns with a special poignancy in "To Be Filed for Reference," in which the opium addict and Oxford scholar McIntosh Jellaludin calls the narrator to his deathbed to receive his unreadable and unredeemable lifework—"an account of the life and sins and death of Mother Maturin. . . . My only baby! . . . It is a great work and I have paid for it in seven years' damnation" (see p. 257). Similarly, in his autobiography, Kipling describes *Kim* as one of his works inspired by a "daemon."

Parts of the lost novel were retrieved in *Kim*; and Mother Maturin appears as a character in a 1922 "Photo-dramatization" (film script) of his first story, "The Gate of the Hundred Sorrows." This manuscript describes Mother Maturin as a "native woman who becomes MacIntosh's companion. . . . Matronly but attractive and with tragic power."

The original handwritten draft of *Kim*, titled *Kim O' the 'Rishti*, is ms. 44840 in the British Library. Margaret Feeley has written about the differences between that first draft and revised versions that compress scenes, complicate and enrich the characters of the lama

and Mahbub Ali, and satirize the British clergy.[3] *Kim* first appeared in
McClure's Magazine, a New York monthly, from December 1900 to
October 1901, and in *Cassell's Magazine* from January to November
1901. After further revision, the first English edition was published
October 1, 1901; the first U.S. edition was published October 23,
1901. The text of this Norton Critical Edition of *Kim* comes from the
revised English edition of October 1901 (Macmillan) with John
Lockwood Kipling's relief illustrations, although I have referred to
later editions to resolve minor inconsistencies.

Backgrounds and Criticism

I have divided the extratextual material in this edition into two sec-
tions: (1) backgrounds, which include a minute selection of
Kipling's poems, letters, and two early short stories that intersect
with *Kim* (space would not allow room for the Strickland stories
that students interested in the unorthodox strategies of this ethnog-
rapher-policeman-detective should read); a biographical selection
that focuses on his writing of *Kim*; early reviews; two historical
readings of *Kim* in context; and (2) criticism, including a range of
essays from 1960 to the present. Although I have added many new
footnotes, for some of the information in my notes I am indebted,
as are all other editors, to the invaluable work of R. E. Harbord,
Roger Lancelyn Green, Alec Mason, eds., *The Reader's Guide to
Rudyard Kipling's Work*, 8 vols. (Canterbury: Gibbs & Sons;
Bournemouth: Boscombe Printers, 1961–72).

Because space is limited, I have not included extracts from
Edmund Wilson's "The Kipling That Nobody Read" (1942), the first
major essay that, by drawing attention to Kipling's dark psychologi-
cal complexity, jarred readers into another approach to texts they
had written off as the product of an imperial age from whose poli-
tics they wished to disassociate themselves; or from J. M. S.
Tompkins's elegant *The Art of Rudyard Kipling* (1959), which, by
declaring itself as a reading of his "permanent human and moral
themes" rather than his "political relations,"[4] established critical
precedent for splitting Kipling the "artist" from Kipling the "imperi-
alist"; or from Nirad C. Chauduri, who called *Kim* "the finest story
about India in English."

Critical responses to *Kim* have ranged from adulation to con-
demnation, from celebration of its "thorough knowledge" of India,
its charms as an exotic adventure tale and visionary epic, or its use-
fulness as a parable of displacement, homelessness, and rootless

3. Margaret Peller Feeley, "The *Kim* That Nobody Reads," *Studies in the Novel* 13.3 (Fall
1981): 266–81.
4. J. M. S. Tompkins, *The Art of Rudyard Kipling* (London: Methuen, 1959) xi.

modernity to condemnation of its "barbaric" imperial vision. More recently, criticism has focused on the window Kipling opens onto colonial cultural, personal, and gender identities, and onto the constellation of contradictory political values at the heart of the imperial and national enterprise.

The complexity of critical assessment on Kipling moved in the 1960s from Randall Jarrell's paean to Kipling as "a great genius and a great neurotic; and a great professional, one of the most skilled writers who have ever existed," to those who insisted that Kipling be read as a sociologist, as a cultural critic who saw a society that "politically, nervously, physically, and spiritually quivered on the edge of a precipice."[5] Early uncritical celebration of his "knowledge" of India too has shifted along with the critiques of representation that continue to inform anthropology, history, and literary studies. Particularly in the 1980s and 1990s, since the work of John McClure and Edward Said, criticism has struggled to understand how Kipling's aesthetic intersects not only with his psychic wounds but also with the history, politics, and ideology of his age. The selected bibliography directs readers to articles and books that include discussions of *Kim* or that provide the necessary cultural and historical contexts for understanding Kipling's work.

Finally, it gives me pleasure to express my gratitude to the generous responses of my students in English 247 and of my colleagues Robert Parker, Suvir Kaul, and Ania Loomba. But most important, I wish to thank a few people whose sharp eyes and editorial skills saved me from myself: Yvette Koepke-Nelson, who took time from her medical studies and dissertation to assist with questions of matter and form, and my friend and colleague Jim Hurt, who took time away from his own editions and anthologies to offer all manner of help, advice, and criticism. At Norton, I wish to thank my copy editor, Kate Lovelady, for her expert eye, and my editor, Carol Bemis, for her patience, intelligent guidance, and superb editorial expertise.

5. Noel Annan, "Kipling's Place in the History of Ideas," *Victorian Studies* 3 (1959–60): 323–48.

The Text of
KIM

Chapter 1

O ye who tread the Narrow Way
By Tophet-flare to Judgment Day,
Be gentle when 'the heathen' pray
To Buddha at Kamakura!
Buddha at Kamakura.[1]

He sat, in defiance of municipal orders, astride the gun Zam-Zammah[2] on her brick platform opposite the old Ajaib-Gher—the Wonder House, as the natives call the Lahore Museum.[3] Who hold Zam-Zammah, that 'fire-breathing dragon', hold the Punjab,[4] for the great green-bronze piece is always first of the conqueror's loot.

There was some justification for Kim—he had kicked Lala Dinanath's boy off the trunnions—since the English held the Punjab and Kim was English. Though he was burned black as any native; though he spoke the vernacular[5] by preference, and his mother-tongue in a clipped uncertain sing-song; though he consorted on terms of perfect equality with the small boys of the bazar; Kim was white—a poor white of the very poorest. The half-caste[6] woman who looked after him (she smoked opium, and pretended to keep a second-hand furniture shop by the square where the cheap cabs wait) told the missionaries that she was Kim's mother's sister; but his mother had been nurse-maid in a Colonel's family and had married Kimball O'Hara, a young colour-sergeant of the Mavericks,[7] an Irish regiment. He afterwards took a post on the Sind, Punjab, and Delhi Railway, and his Regiment went home without him. The

1. An independent Kipling poem. Kamakura is a center of Buddhist worship in Japan marked by a giant statue of Buddha. Lord Buddha was the title given to Siddhartha Gautama (563–483 B.C.E.), founder of Buddhism, which teaches that suffering is central to life but that one can, through practice of the Four Noble Truths, transcend it and reach enlightenment, knowledge, and nirvana. Kipling's epigraph invites readers to leave the "narrow way" of their conventional religious backgrounds marked by the "Tophet-flare" of ancient punishment and judgment to enter a gentler world of Buddhist spirituality.
2. A huge iron cannon built in Lahore in 1757, used in many battles in the eighteenth century, and later placed where it still stands in Lahore (now in Pakistan).
3. A museum of Indian culture in Lahore. Kipling's father, the artist and illustrator John Lockwood Kipling, was curator there from 1875 to 1894.
4. A province in western India. The word means literally "five waters," the five rivers (the Indus and its four tributaries) that flow south from the Himalayas into the Arabian Sea.
5. Hindustani, a spoken vernacular made up of Hindi, Urdu, Arabic, Punjabi, and other dialects.
6. In the nineteenth century, the term referred to the offspring of a Hindu and a European. The caste system refers to the ancient Vedic hierarchical groupings based on privilege and vocation such as priests and scholars (Brahmins), warriors and rulers (Kshatriyas), farmers and merchants (Vaishyas), and the lowest-caste servants (Sudras). Kim's later confusion on seeing the lama reveals that he knows little of Buddhism.
7. A colour-sergeant's duties involved the flag or regimental "colour." The Mavericks were a fictional Irish regiment in the British army. The name derives from Samuel A. Maverick, an American pioneer and rancher who did not brand his cattle. A maverick is thus an undisciplined nonconformist. Kipling probably learned the word during his stay in America. No actual British regiment had the Maverick's crest of a red bull on a green field.

3

wife died of cholera in Ferozepore,[8] and O'Hara fell to drink and loafing up and down the line with the keen-eyed three-year-old baby. Societies and chaplains, anxious for the child, tried to catch him, but O'Hara drifted away, till he came across the woman who took opium and learned the taste from her, and died as poor whites die in India. His estate at death consisted of three papers—one he called his '*ne varietur*'[9] because those words were written below his signature thereon, and another his 'clearance-certificate'.[1] The third was Kim's birth-certificate. Those things, he was used to say, in his glorious opium-hours, would yet make little Kimball a man. On no account was Kim to part with them, for they belonged to a great piece of magic—such magic as men practised over yonder behind the Museum, in the big blue-and-white Jadoo-Gher—the Magic House, as we name the Masonic Lodge.[2] It would, he said, all come right some day, and Kim's horn would be exalted between pillars—monstrous pillars—of beauty and strength.[3] The Colonel himself, riding on a horse, at the head of the finest Regiment in the world, would attend to Kim—little Kim that should have been better off than his father. Nine hundred first-class devils, whose God was a Red Bull on a green field, would attend to Kim, if they had not forgotten O'Hara—poor O'Hara that was gang-foreman on the Ferozepore line. Then he would weep bitterly in the broken rush chair on the veranda. So it came about after his death that the woman sewed parchment, paper, and birth-certificate into a leather amulet-case[4] which she strung round Kim's neck.

'And some day,' she said, confusedly remembering O'Hara's prophecies, 'there will come for you a great Red Bull on a green field, and the Colonel riding on his tall horse, yes, and'—dropping into English—'nine hundred devils.'

'Ah,' said Kim, 'I shall remember. A Red Bull and a Colonel on a horse will come, but first, my father said, will come the two men making ready the ground for these matters. That is how my father said they always did; and it is always so when men work magic.'

8. A town in the Punjab fifty miles south of Lahore.
9. Appearing at the end of the certificate of membership in a Freemason's lodge, these Latin words mean that the signature "may not vary." The Freemasons are an ancient secret fraternal organization that espouses political and religious tolerance, equality, and liberalism, and whose origins have been traced to the Old Testament and to the medieval guild of stone masons. (Kipling's story "The Man Who Would Be King" connects the organization to Alexander the Great.) For a celebration of the inclusiveness of the lodge to all creeds, colors, and castes, see his poem "The Mother-Lodge."
1. A receipt from a Masonic lodge given to a member before he transfers to another lodge.
2. The model for this lodge was apparently an actual lodge named "Hope and Perseverance, No. 782 E.C.," to which Kipling was admitted at the age of nineteen. "Jadoo-Gher," literally "house of magic," refers to the rituals performed by the Freemasons.
3. The horn is a traditional symbol of power. Pillars are a Masonic symbol deriving from the biblical description of King Solomon's temple.
4. A container traditionally used to hold sacred prayers or charms against evil.

If the woman had sent Kim up to the local Jadoo-Gher with those papers, he would, of course, have been taken over by the Provincial Lodge,[5] and sent to the Masonic Orphanage in the Hills; but what she had heard of magic she distrusted. Kim, too, held views of his own. As he reached the years of indiscretion, he learned to avoid missionaries and white men of serious aspect who asked who he was, and what he did. For Kim did nothing with an immense success. True, he knew the wonderful walled city of Lahore from the Delhi Gate to the outer Fort Ditch; was hand in glove with men who led lives stranger than anything Haroun al Raschid[6] dreamed of; and he lived in a life wild as that of the Arabian Nights, but missionaries and secretaries of charitable societies could not see the beauty of it. His nickname through the wards was 'Little Friend of all the World'; and very often, being lithe and inconspicuous, he executed commissions by night on the crowded housetops for sleek and shiny young men of fashion. It was intrigue, of course—he knew that much, as he had known all evil since he could speak,—but what he loved was the game for its own sake—the stealthy prowl through the dark gullies[7] and lanes, the crawl up a water-pipe, the sights and sounds of the women's world[8] on the flat roofs, and the headlong flight from housetop to housetop under cover of the hot dark. Then there were holy men, ash-smeared *faquirs*[9] by their brick shrines under the trees at the riverside, with whom he was quite familiar— greeting them as they returned from begging-tours, and, when no one was by, eating from the same dish. The woman who looked after him insisted with tears that he should wear European clothes— trousers, a shirt, and a battered hat. Kim found it easier to slip into Hindu or Mohammedan garb when engaged on certain businesses. One of the young men of fashion—he who was found dead at the bottom of a well on the night of the earthquake—had once given him a complete suit of Hindu kit, the costume of a low-caste street boy, and Kim stored it in a secret place under some baulks in Nila Ram's timber-yard, beyond the Punjab High Court, where the fragrant deodar[1] logs lie seasoning after they have driven down the Ravi.[2] When there was business or frolic afoot, Kim would use his properties,[3] returning at dawn to the veranda, all tired out from

5. The Provincial Lodge was superior to and wealthier than the local Masonic lodges.
6. Featured in *The Arabian Nights*, the caliph who ruled over Baghdad in the eighth century.
7. Alleys.
8. Excluded from the public sphere, women lived in a private area of the house referred to as the *zenana*, or woman's space, from which they exerted what influence they could on the world of men.
9. Beggars.
1. Indian cedar.
2. One of the major rivers in the Punjab, a tributary of the Indus River.
3. Kim is a master of "props," or disguises.

shouting at the heels of a marriage procession, or yelling at a Hindu festival. Sometimes there was food in the house, more often there was not, and then Kim went out again to eat with his native friends.

As he drummed his heels against Zam-Zammah he turned now and again from his king-of-the-castle game with little Chota Lal and Abdullah the sweetmeat-seller's son, to make a rude remark to the native policeman on guard over rows of shoes at the Museum door.[4] The big Punjabi grinned tolerantly: he knew Kim of old. So did the water-carrier, sluicing water on the dry road from his goat-skin bag. So did Jawahir Singh, the Museum carpenter, bent over new packing-cases. So did everybody in sight except the peasants from the country, hurrying up to the Wonder House to view the things that men made in their own province and elsewhere. The Museum was given up to Indian arts and manufactures, and anybody who sought wisdom could ask the Curator to explain.

'Off! Off! Let me up!' cried Abdullah, climbing up Zam-Zammah's wheel.

'Thy father was a pastry-cook, Thy mother stole the _ghi_,'[5] sang Kim. 'All Mussalmans fell off Zam-Zammah long ago!'

'Let _me_ up!' shrilled little Chota Lal in his gilt-embroidered cap. His father was worth perhaps half a million sterling, but India is the only democratic land in the world.

'The Hindus fell off Zam-Zammah too. The Mussalmans pushed them off. Thy father was a pastry-cook—'

He stopped; for there shuffled round the corner, from the roaring Motee Bazar,[6] such a man as Kim, who thought he knew all castes, had never seen. He was nearly six feet high, dressed in fold upon fold of dingy stuff like horse-blanketing, and not one fold of it could Kim refer to any known trade or profession. At his belt hung a long open-work iron pencase and a wooden rosary such as holy men wear. On his head was a gigantic sort of tam-o'-shanter.[7] His face was yellow and wrinkled, like that of Fook Shing, the Chinese boot-maker in the bazar. His eyes turned up at the corners and looked like little slits of onyx.

'Who is that?' said Kim to his companions.

'Perhaps it is a man,' said Abdullah, finger in mouth, staring.

'Without doubt,' returned Kim; 'but he is no man of India that _I_ have ever seen.'

'A priest, perhaps,' said Chota Lal, spying the rosary. 'See! He goes into the Wonder House!'

4. Left by Indians who remove them as a sign of respect.
5. Butter clarified by boiling.
6. Pearl bazaar, the jewelry market.
7. A wide, circular woolen Scottish cap with a fitted headband.

'Nay, nay,' said the policeman, shaking his head. 'I do not understand your talk.' The constable spoke Punjabi. 'O Friend of all the World, what does he say?' — *well educated*

'Send him hither,' said Kim, dropping from Zam-Zammah, flourishing his bare heels. 'He is a foreigner, and thou art a buffalo.'

The man turned helplessly and drifted towards the boys. He was old, and his woollen gaberdine still reeked of the stinking artemisia[8] of the mountain passes.

'O Children, what is that big house?' he said in very fair Urdu.[9]

'The Ajaib-Gher, the Wonder House!' Kim gave him no title—such as Lala or Mian.[1] He could not divine the man's creed.

'Ah! The Wonder House! Can any enter?'

'It is written above the door—all can enter.'

'Without payment?'

'I go in and out. *I* am no banker,' laughed Kim.

'Alas! I am an old man. I did not know.' Then, fingering his rosary, he half turned to the Museum.

'What is your caste? Where is your house? Have you come far?' Kim asked.

'I came by Kulu[2]—from beyond the Kailas—but what know you? From the Hills where'—he sighed—'the air and water are fresh and cool.'

'Aha! Khitai (a Chinaman),' said Abdullah proudly. Fook Shing had once chased him out of his shop for spitting at the joss[3] above the boots.

'Pahari (a hillman),' said little Chota Lal.

'Aye, child—a hillman from hills thou'lt never see. Didst hear of Bhotiyal (Tibet)? I am no Khitai, but a Bhotiya (Tibetan), since you must know—a lama[4]—or, say, a *guru* in your tongue.'

'A *guru* from Tibet,' said Kim. 'I have not seen such a man. They be Hindus in Tibet, then?'

'We be followers of the Middle Way,[5] living in peace in our lamasseries, and I go to see the Four Holy Places[6] before I die. Now do you, who are children, know as much as I do who am old.' He smiled benignantly on the boys. — *education*

'Hast thou eaten?'

8. Bitter, aromatic herb.
9. A language introduced at the time of the Moguls that combines Hindi with Persian, written in Arabic script. The fact that the man speaks to Kim in Urdu indicates his ability to cross linguistic boundaries.
1. Titles of respect for a Hindu and a Muslim, respectively.
2. Mountain valley in the lower Himalayas.
3. A Chinese idol.
4. Tibetan word for religious superior.
5. The Buddhist moderate path that avoids either sensuality or asceticism.
6. Sites sacred to Buddhism: where Buddhism was born (the forest at Buddh Gaya), where Buddha delivered his first sermon (the Deer Park), and where he died and is buried (Kusinagara).

He fumbled in his bosom and drew forth a worn wooden begging-bowl. The boys nodded. All priests of their acquaintance begged.

'I do not wish to eat yet.' He turned his head like an old tortoise in the sunlight. 'Is it true that there are many images in the Wonder House of Lahore?' He repeated the last words as one making sure of an address.

'That is true,' said Abdullah. 'It is full of heathen _buts_.[7] Thou also art an idolater.'

'Never mind _him_,' said Kim. 'That is the Government's house and there is no idolatry in it, but only a Sahib[8] with a white beard. Come with me and I will show.'

'Strange priests eat boys,' whispered Chota Lal.

'And he is a stranger and a _but-parast_ (idolater),' said Abdullah, the Mohammedan.

Kim laughed. 'He is new. Run to your mothers' laps, and be safe. Come!'

Kim clicked round the self-registering turnstile; the old man followed and halted amazed. In the entrance-hall stood the larger figures of the Greco-Buddhist sculptures done, savants know how long since, by forgotten workmen whose hands were feeling, and not unskilfully, for the mysteriously transmitted Grecian touch.[9] There were hundreds of pieces, friezes of figures in relief, fragments of statues and slabs crowded with figures that had encrusted the brick walls of the Buddhist _stupas_ and _viharas_[1] of the North Country and now, dug up and labelled, made the pride of the Museum. In open-mouthed wonder the lama turned to this and that, and finally checked in rapt attention before a large alto-relief representing a coronation or apotheosis of the Lord Buddha. The Master was represented seated on a lotus[2] the petals of which were so deeply undercut as to show almost detached. Round Him was an adoring hierarchy of kings, elders, and old-time Buddhas.[3] Below were lotus-covered waters with fishes and water-birds. Two butterfly-winged _dewas_[4] held a wreath over His head; above them another pair supported an umbrella surmounted by the jewelled headdress of the Bodhisat.[5]

7. Idols, which Abdullah, as a Muslim who believes in one God, has been taught to despise.
8. Master or sir—in colonial India, a term used to refer to Europeans.
9. Common Orientalist readings interpreted Greece (and Alexander the Great's invasion of 326 B.C.E.) as the source of accessible and pleasing Indian and Buddhist art. Contemporary Indian historians reject such readings.
1. _Stupas_: Buddhist monuments; _viharas_: Buddhist monasteries; alto-relief (below): a sculpted frieze in which the background has been cut away so the figures protrude.
2. Flower sacred to Buddhism.
3. Gautama taught that four other Buddhas had preceded him.
4. Shining angels.
5. An incarnation of Buddha, a bodhisattva is a saint who prefers to delay entry into nirvana in order to help others attain enlightenment.

'The Lord! The Lord! It is Sakya Muni[6] himself,' the lama half sobbed; and under his breath began the wonderful Buddhist invocation:

> 'To Him the Way—the Law—Apart—
> Whom Maya[7] held beneath her heart
> Ananda's[8] Lord, the Bodhisat.'

'And He is here! The Most Excellent Law is here also. My pilgrimage is well begun. And what work! What work!'

'Yonder is the Sahib,' said Kim, and dodged sideways among the cases of the arts and manufacturers wing. A white-bearded Englishman[9] was looking at the lama, who gravely turned and saluted him and after some fumbling drew forth a note-book and a scrap of paper.

'Yes, that is my name,' smiling at the clumsy, childish print.

'One of us who had made pilgrimage to the Holy Places—he is now Abbot of the Lung-Cho Monastery—gave it me,' stammered the lama. 'He spoke of these.' His lean hand moved tremulously round.

'Welcome, then, O lama from Tibet. Here be the images, and I am here'—he glanced at the lama's face—'to gather knowledge. Come to my office awhile.' The old man was trembling with excitement.

The office was but a little wooden cubicle partitioned off from the sculpture-lined gallery. Kim laid himself down, his ear against a crack in the heat-split cedar door, and, following his instinct, stretched out to listen and watch.

Most of the talk was altogether above his head. The lama, haltingly at first, spoke to the Curator of his own lamassery, the Suchzen, opposite the Painted Rocks, four months' march away. The Curator brought out a huge book of photos and showed him that very place, perched on its crag, overlooking the gigantic valley of many-hued strata.

'Ay, ay!' The lama mounted a pair of horn-rimmed spectacles of Chinese work. 'Here is the little door through which we bring wood before winter. And thou—the English know of these things? He who is now Abbot of Lung-Cho told me, but I did not believe. The Lord—the Excellent One—He has honour here too? And His life is known?'

'It is all carven upon the stones. Come and see, if thou art rested.'

Out shuffled the lama to the main hall, and, the Curator beside him, went through the collection with the reverence of a devotee and the appreciative instinct of a craftsman.

6. Another reverential term for the solitary and wise Buddha.
7. Mother of Gautama (not to be confused with *maya*, the illusion of everyday life as reality).
8. Buddha's cousin and disciple.
9. The curator is based on Kipling's father, John Lockwood Kipling, the architect and first curator of the Lahore Museum.

Incident by incident in the beautiful story he identified on the
blurred stone, puzzled here and there by the unfamiliar Greek con-
vention, but delighted as a child at each new trove. Where the
sequence failed, as in the Annunciation,[1] the Curator supplied it
from his mound of books—French and German, with photographs
and reproductions.

Here was the devout Asita,[2] the pendant of Simeon[3] in the
Christian story, holding the Holy Child on his knee while mother and
father listened; and here were incidents in the legend of the cousin
Devadatta.[4] Here was the wicked woman who accused the Master of
impurity, all confounded; here was the teaching in the Deer-park; the
miracle that stunned the fire-worshippers;[5] here was the Bodhisat in
royal state as a prince; the miraculous birth; the death at Kusinagara,
where the weak disciple fainted; while there were almost countless
repetitions of the meditation under the Bodhi tree;[6] and the adora-
tion of the alms-bowl was everywhere. In a few minutes the Curator
saw that his guest was no mere bead-telling mendicant,[7] but a scholar
of parts. And they went at it all over again, the lama taking snuff, wip-
ing his spectacles, and talking at railway speed in a bewildering mix-
ture of Urdu and Tibetan. He had heard of the travels of the Chinese
pilgrims, Fu-Hiouen and Hwen-Tsiang,[8] and was anxious to know if
there was any translation of their record. He drew in his breath as he
turned helplessly over the pages of Beal and Stanislas Julien.[9] 'Tis all
here. A treasure locked.' Then he composed himself reverently to lis-
ten to fragments hastily rendered into Urdu. For the first time he
heard of the labours of European scholars, who by the help of these
and a hundred other documents have identified the Holy Places of
Buddhism. Then he was shown a mighty map, spotted and traced
with yellow. The brown finger followed the Curator's pencil from
point to point. Here was Kapilavastu,[1] here the Middle Kingdom,[2]
and here Mahabodhi,[3] the Mecca of Buddhism; and here was

1. Buddha's birth was announced when his mother, Maya, dreamed of a star with six rays
 and a white elephant with six tusks.
2. A prophet who foretold a great future for the child Siddhartha.
3. Simeon held up Jesus in the temple in Jerusalem and prophesied the Crucifixion. A pen-
 dant is a counterpart or a "type."
4. King of Benares, sacred Hindu city, and enemy of the Buddha.
5. Persian Zoroastrians.
6. Wisdom tree, the tree under which Buddha achieved enlightenment (it has been identi-
 fied as a jambo, pipal, or fig tree).
7. Religious beggar recognizable by his costume and rosarylike beads.
8. Chinese visitors to India in the fifth and seventh centuries C.E.
9. Samuel Beal (1825–1889) was an Englishman who wrote and translated books on
 Buddhism. Stanislas Julien was the nineteenth-century French translator of the life of the
 seventh-century Chinese scholar Hwen-Thiang.
1. The capital of a state near Nepal where Buddha spent most of his youth.
2. Fo Hian, the fifth-century Chinese scholar who visited India, used this Chinese term to
 refer to the middle states in the plain of the Ganges and Chambal Rivers.
3. Where Buddha received enlightenment and taught his disciples.

Kusinagara, sad place of the Holy One's death. The old man bowed his head over the sheets in silence for a while, and the Curator lit another pipe. Kim had fallen asleep. When he waked, the talk, still in spate, was more within his comprehension.

'And thus it was, O Fountain of Wisdom, that I decided to go to the Holy Places which His foot had trod—to the Birthplace, even to Kapila; then to Mahabodhi, which is Buddh Gaya—to the Monastery—to the Deer-park—to the place of His death.'

The lama lowered his voice. 'And I come here alone. For five— seven—eighteen—forty years it was in my mind that the Old Law[4] was not well followed; being overlaid, as thou knowest, with devil-dom, charms, and idolatry. Even as the child outside said but now. Ay, even as the child said, with *būt-parasti*.'

'So it comes with all faiths.'

'Thinkest thou? The books of my lamassery I read, and they were dried pith;[5] and the later ritual with which we of the Reformed Law have cumbered ourselves—that, too, had no worth to these old eyes. Even the followers of the Excellent One are at feud on feud with one another. It is all illusion. Ay, *maya*, illusion. But I have another desire'—the seamed yellow face drew within three inches of the Curator, and the long forefinger-nail tapped on the table. 'Your scholars, by these books, have followed the Blessed Feet in all their wanderings; but there are things which they have not sought out. I know nothing—nothing do I know but I go to free myself from the Wheel of Things[6] by a broad and open road.' He smiled with most simple triumph. 'As a pilgrim to the Holy Places I acquire merit. But there is more. Listen to a true thing. When our gracious Lord, being as yet a youth, sought a mate, men said, in His father's Court, that He was too tender for marriage. Thou knowest?'

The Curator nodded, wondering what would come next.

'So they made the triple trial of strength against all comers. And at the test of the Bow,[7] our Lord first breaking that which they gave Him, called for such a bow as none might bend. Thou knowest?'

'It is written. I have read.'

'And, overshooting all other marks, the arrow passed for and far beyond sight. At the last it fell; and, where it touched earth, there broke out a stream which presently became a River, whose nature, by our Lord's beneficence, and that merit He acquired ere He freed himself, is that whoso bathes in it washes away all taint and speckle of sin.'

4. The Old Law and the Reformed Law are doctrinal divisions within Buddhism.
5. Sterile and lacking in substance and inspiration.
6. Buddhist symbol of the cycle of birth, death, and rebirth—a wheel that can be escaped through spiritual purification.
7. Siddhartha was required to compete in an archery contest to win the hand of the girl he loved.

'So it is written,' said the Curator sadly.

The lama drew a long breath. 'Where is that River? Fountain of Wisdom, where fell the arrow?'

'Alas, my brother, I do not know,' said the Curator.

'Nay, if it please thee to forget—the one thing only that thou hast not told me. Surely thou must know? See, I am an old man! I ask with my head between thy feet, O Fountain of Wisdom. We *know* He drew the bow! We *know* the arrow fell! We *know* the stream gushed! Where, then, is the River? My dream told me to find it. So I came. I am here. But where is the River?'

'If I knew, think you I would not cry it aloud?'

'By it one attains freedom from the Wheel of Things,' the lama went on, unheeding. 'The River of the Arrow! Think again! Some little stream, maybe—dried in the heats? But the Holy One would never so cheat an old man.'

'I do not know. I do not know.'

The lama brought his thousand-wrinkled face once more a handsbreadth from the Englishman's. 'I see thou dost not know. Not being of the Law,[8] the matter is hid from thee.'

'Ay—hidden—hidden.'

'We are both bound, thou and I, my brother. But I'—he rose with a sweep of the soft thick drapery—'I go to cut myself free. Come also!'

'I am bound,' said the Curator. 'But whither goest thou?'

'First to Kashi (Benares):[9] where else? There I shall meet one of the pure faith in a Jain[1] temple of that city. He also is a Seeker in secret, and from him haply I may learn. Maybe he will go with me to Buddh Gaya. Thence north and west to Kapilavastu, and there will I seek for the River. Nay, I will seek everywhere as I go—for the place is not known where the arrow fell.'

'And how wilt thou go? It is a far cry to Delhi, and farther to Benares.'

'By road and the trains. From Pathânkot, having left the Hills, I came hither in a *te-rain*. It goes swiftly. At first I was amazed to see those tall poles by the side of the road snatching up and snatching up their threads,'—he illustrated the stoop and whirl of a telegraphpole flashing past the train. 'But later, I was cramped and desired to walk, as I am used.'

8. The idea of cosmic and divine law (*dharma*) defines the duties of a Hindu at each stage of life—teaching the sacred law, fighting, laboring, or dancing. The law of Karma (action) declares that action in a past life results in the conditions of present life; the lama's goal is to free himself from being "bound" in the wheel of Karma.

9. Benares, seven hundred miles from Lahore, is a sacred center of Hinduism.

1. Jainism rose, like Buddhism, in the sixth century B.C.E. in reaction against the privileges of Brahmanical dominance. Although Jainism, Buddhism, and Hinduism share a belief in meditation and reincarnation, the Jains are the most ascetic and nonviolent. That the lama is willing to learn from other religions testifies to his tolerance and openmindedness.

'And thou art sure of thy road?' said the Curator.

'Oh, for that one but asks a question and pays money, and the appointed persons despatch all to the appointed place. That much I knew in my lamassery from sure report,' said the lama proudly.

'And when dost thou go?' The Curator smiled at the mixture of old-world piety and modern progress that is the note of India today.

'As soon as may be. I follow the places of His life till I come to the River of the Arrow. There is, moreover, a written paper of the hours of the trains that go south.'

'And for food?' Lamas, as a rule, have good store of money somewhere about them, but the Curator wished to make sure.

'For the journey, I take up the Master's begging-bowl. Yes. Even as He went so go I, forsaking the ease of my monastery. There was with me when I left the hills a *chela* (disciple) who begged for me as the Rule demands, but halting in Kutu awhile a fever took him and he died. I have now no *chela*, but I will take the alms-bowl and thus enable the charitable to acquire merit.' He nodded his head valiantly. Learned doctors of a lamassery do not beg, but the lama was an enthusiast in this quest.

'Be it so,' said the Curator, smiling. 'Suffer me now to acquire merit. We be craftsmen together, thou and I. Here is a new book of white English paper: here be sharpened pencils two and three—thick and thin, all good for a scribe. Now lend me thy spectacles.'

The Curator looked through them. They were heavily scratched, but the power was almost exactly that of his own pair, which he slid into the lama's hand, saying: 'Try these.'

'A feather! A very feather upon the face!' The old man turned his head delightedly and wrinkled up his nose. 'How scarcely do I feel them! How clearly do I see!'

'They be *bilaur*—crystal—and will never scratch. May they help thee to thy River, for they are thine.'

'I will take them and the pencils and the white note-book,' said the lama, 'as a sign of friendship between priest and priest—and now—' He fumbled at his belt, detached the open-work iron pencase, and laid it on the Curator's table. 'That is for a memory between thee and me—my pencase. It is something old—even as I am.'

It was a piece of ancient design, Chinese, of an iron that is not smelted these days; and the collector's heart in the Curator's bosom had gone out to it from the first. For no persuasion would the lama resume his gift.

'When I return, having found the River, I will bring thee a written picture of the Padma Samthora[2] such as I used to make on silk

2. A Buddhist saint known as the founder of Lamaism. The name means lotus-born ("Samthora" is apparently a mistake for "Sambhava").

at the lamassery. Yes—and of the Wheel of Life,' he chuckled, 'for we be craftsmen together, thou and I.'

The Curator would have detained him: they are few in the world who still have the secret of the conventional brush-pen Buddhist pictures which are, as it were, half written and half drawn. But the lama strode out, head high in air, and pausing an instant before the great statue of a Bodhisat in meditation, brushed through the turnstiles.

Kim followed like a shadow. What he had overheard excited him wildly. This man was entirely new to all his experience, and he meant to investigate further, precisely as he would have investigated a new building or a strange festival in Lahore city. The lama was his trove, and he purposed to take possession. Kim's mother had been Irish[3] too.

The old man halted by Zam-Zammah and looked round till his eye fell on Kim. The inspiration of his pilgrimage had left him for awhile, and he felt old, forlorn, and very empty.

'Do not sit under that gun,' said the policeman loftily.

'Huh! Owl!' was Kim's retort on the lama's behalf. 'Sit under that gun if it please thee. When didst thou steal the milk-woman's slippers, Dunnoo?'

That was an utterly unfounded charge sprung on the spur of the moment, but it silenced Dunnoo, who knew that Kim's clear yell could call up legions of bad bazar boys if need arose.

'And whom didst thou worship within?' said Kim affably, squatting in the shade beside the lama.

'I worshipped none, child. I bowed before the Excellent Law.'

Kim accepted this new God without emotion. He knew already a few score.

'And what dost thou do?'

'I beg. I remember now it is long since I have eaten or drunk. What is the custom of charity in this town? In silence, as we do of Tibet, or speaking aloud?'

'Those who beg in silence starve in silence,' said Kim, quoting a native proverb. The lama tried to rise, but sank back again, sighing for his disciple, dead in far-away Kulu. Kim watched—head to one side, considering and interested.

'Give me the bowl. I know the people of this city—all who are charitable. Give, and I will bring it back filled.'

Simply as a child the old man handed him the bowl.

'Rest, thou. *I* know the people.'

3. Kipling is using a familiar English stereotype of the Irish as crafty and clever. His mother's family, though Scots Wesleyan immigrants, had Irish ancestry. For discussion of the politics of Kim's Irishness, see the essays in this volume by A. Michael Matin and Patrick Williams.

He trotted off to the open shop of a *kunjri*, a low-caste vegetable-seller, which lay opposite the belt-tramway[4] line down the Motee Bazar. She knew Kim of old.

'Oho, hast thou turned *yogi*[5] with thy begging-bowl?' she cried.

'Nay,' said Kim proudly. 'There is a new priest in the city—a man such as I have never seen.'

'Old priest—young tiger,' said the woman angrily. 'I am tired of new priests! They settle on our wares like flies. Is the father of my son a well of charity to give to all who ask?'

'No,' said Kim. 'Thy man is rather *yagi* [bad-tempered] than *yogi* [a holy man]. But this priest is new. The Sahib in the Wonder House has talked to him like a brother. O my mother, fill me this bowl. He waits.'

'That bowl indeed! That cow-bellied basket! Thou hast as much grace as the holy bull of Shiv.[6] He has taken the best of a basket of onions already, this morn; and forsooth, I must fill thy bowl. He comes here again.'

The huge, mouse-coloured Brahmini bull of the ward was shouldering his way through the many-coloured crowd, a stolen plantain hanging out of his mouth. He headed straight for the shop, well knowing his privileges as a sacred beast, lowered his head, and puffed heavily along the line of baskets ere making his choice. Up flew Kim's hard little heel and caught him on his moist blue nose. He snorted indignantly, and walked away across the tram-rails, his hump quivering with rage.

'See! I have saved more than the bowl will cost thrice over. Now, mother, a little rice and some dried fish atop—yes, and some vegetable curry.'

A growl came out of the back of the shop, where a man lay.

'He drove away the bull,' said the woman in an undertone. 'It is good to give to the poor.' She took the bowl and returned it full of hot rice.

'But my *yogi* is not a cow,' said Kim gravely, making a hole with his fingers in the top of the mound. 'A little curry is good, and a fried cake, and a morsel of conserve would please him, I think.'

'It is a hole as big as thy head,' said the woman fretfully. But she filled it, none the less, with good, steaming vegetable curry, clapped a fried cake atop, and a morsel of clarified butter on the cake,

4. A system in which trams are powered by a moving underground belt, as in the San Francisco tram line.
5. Religious mendicants bless those who feed them as they meditate their way to union with God. Of the four ideal stages in a Hindu's life, the last is that of the *sanyasi*, or the mendicant wanderer, who, having detached himself from earthly attachments, begs for daily meals.
6. All cattle are sacred to Hindus and must not be killed. The Hindu god Shiv or Shiva represents the principle of destruction and regeneration.

dabbed a lump of sour tamarind conserve at the side; and Kim looked at the load lovingly.

'That is good. When I am in the bazar the bull shall not come to this house. He is a bold beggar-man.'

'And thou?' laughed the woman. 'But speak well of bulls. Hast thou not told me that some day a Red Bull will come out of a field to help thee? Now hold all straight and ask for the holy man's blessing upon me. Perhaps, too, he knows a cure for my daughter's sore eyes. Ask him that also, O thou Little Friend of all the World.'

But Kim had danced off ere the end of the sentence, dodging pariah[7] dogs and hungry acquaintances.

'Thus do we beg who know the way of it,' said he proudly to the lama, who opened his eyes at the contents of the bowl. 'Eat now and—I will eat with thee. Ohé, *bhisti*!' he called to the water-carrier, sluicing the crotons[8] by the Museum. 'Give water here. We men are thirsty.'

'We men!' said the *bhisti*, laughing. 'Is one skinful enough for such a pair? Drink, then, in the name of the Compassionate.'[9]

He loosed a thin stream into Kim's hands, who drank native-fashion; but the lama must needs pull out a cup from his inexhaustible upper draperies and drink ceremonially.

'*Pardesi* (a foreigner),' Kim explained, as the old man delivered in an unknown tongue what was evidently a blessing.

They ate together in great content, clearing the begging-bowl. Then the lama took snuff from a portentous wooden snuff-gourd, fingered his rosary awhile, and so dropped into the easy sleep of age, as the shadow of Zam-Zammah grew long.

Kim loafed over to the nearest tobacco-seller, a rather lively young Mohammedan woman, and begged a rank cigar of the brand that they sell to students of the Punjab University who copy English customs. Then he smoked and thought, knees to chin, under the belly of the gun, and the outcome of his thoughts was a sudden and stealthy departure in the direction of Nila Ram's timber-yard.

The lama did not wake till the evening life of the city had begun with lamp-lighting and the return of white-robed clerks and subordinates from the Government offices. He stared dizzily in all directions, but none looked at him save a Hindu urchin in a dirty turban and Isabella-coloured[1] clothes. Suddenly he bowed his head on his knees and wailed.

'What is this?' said the boy, standing before him. 'Hast thou been robbed?'

7. Stray.
8. Large red and green ornamental plants.
9. One of the attributes of Allah. The *bhisti* (water-carrier) is a Muslim.
1. Gray or yellow.

'It is my new *chela* (disciple) that is gone away from me, and I know not where he is.'

'And what like of man was thy disciple?'

'It was a boy who came to me in place of him who died, on account of the merit which I had gained when I bowed before the Law within there.' He pointed towards the Museum. 'He came upon me to show me a road which I had lost. He led me into the Wonder House, and by his talk emboldened me to speak to the Keeper of the Images, so that I was cheered and made strong. And when I was faint with hunger he begged for me, as would a *chela* for his teacher. Suddenly was he sent. Suddenly has he gone away. It was in my mind to have taught him the Law upon the road to Benares.'

Kim stood amazed at this, because he had overheard the talk in the Museum, and knew that the old man was speaking the truth, which is a thing a native on the road seldom presents to a stranger.

'But I see now that he was but sent for a purpose. By this I know that I shall find a certain River for which I seek.'

'The River of the Arrow?' said Kim, with a superior smile.

'Is this yet another Sending?' cried the lama. 'To none have I spoken of my search, save to the Priest of the Images. Who art thou?'

'Thy *chela*,' said Kim simply, sitting on his heels. 'I have never seen anyone like to thee in all this my life. I go with thee to Benares. And, too, I think that so old a man as thou, speaking the truth to chance-met people at dusk, is in great need of a disciple.'

'But the River—the River of the Arrow?'

'Oh, that I heard when thou wast speaking to the Englishman. I lay against the door.'

The lama sighed. 'I thought thou hadst been a guide permitted. Such things fall sometimes—but I am not worthy. Thou dost not, then, know the River?'

'Not I.' Kim laughed uneasily. 'I go to look for—for a bull—a Red Bull on a green field who shall help me.' Boylike, if an acquaintance had a scheme, Kim was quite ready with one of his own; and, boylike, he had really thought for as much as twenty minutes at a time of his father's prophecy.

'To what, child?' said the lama.

'God knows, but so my father told me. I heard thy talk in the Wonder House of all those new strange places in the Hills, and if one so old and so little—so used to truth-telling—may go out for the small matter of a river, it seemed to me that I too must go a-travelling. If it is our fate to find those things we shall find them—thou, thy River; and I, my Bull, and the Strong Pillars and some other matters that I forget.'

'It is not pillars but a Wheel from which I would be free,' said the lama.

That is all one. Perhaps they will make me a king,' said Kim, serenely prepared for anything.

'I will teach thee other and better desires upon the road,' the lama replied in the voice of authority. 'Let us go to Benares.'

'Not by night. Thieves are abroad. Wait till the day.'

'But there is no place to sleep.' The old man was used to the order of his monastery, and though he slept on the ground, as the Rule decrees, preferred a decency in these things.

'We shall get good lodging at the Kashmir Serai,'[2] said Kim, laughing at his perplexity. 'I have a friend there. Come!'

The hot and crowded bazars blazed with light as they made their way through the press of all the races in Upper India, and the lama mooned through it like a man in a dream. It was his first experience of a large manufacturing city, and the crowded tram-car with its continually squealing brakes frightened him. Half pushed, half towed, he arrived at the high gate of the Kashmir Serai: that huge open square over against the railway station, surrounded with arched cloisters, where the camel and horse caravans put up on their return from Central Asia. Here were all manner of Northern folk, tending tethered ponies and kneeling camels; loading and unloading bales and bundles; drawing water for the evening meal at the creaking well-windlasses; piling grass before the shrieking, wild-eyed stallions; cuffing the surly caravan dogs; paying off camel-drivers; taking on new grooms; swearing, shouting, arguing, and chaffering in the packed square. The cloisters, reached by three or four masonry steps, made a haven of refuge around this turbulent sea. Most of them were rented to traders, as we rent the arches of a viaduct; the space between pillar and pillar being bricked or boarded off into rooms, which were guarded by heavy wooden doors and cumbrous native padlocks. Locked doors showed that the owner was away, and a few rude—sometimes very rude—chalk or paint scratches told where he had gone. Thus: 'Lutuf Ullah is gone to Kurdistan.' Below, in coarse verse: 'O Allah, who sufferest lice to live on the coat of a Kabuli, why hast thou allowed this louse Lutuf to live so long?'

Kim, fending the lama between excited men and excited beasts, sidled along the cloisters to the far end, nearest the railway station, where Mahbub Ali, the horse-trader, lived when he came in from that mysterious land beyond the Passes of the North.[3]

Kim had had many dealings with Mahbub in his little life,—especially between his tenth and his thirteenth year—and the big burly Afghan, his beard dyed scarlet with lime (for he was elderly and did

2. An inn for travelers and caravans (the name is a clipped form of *caravanserai*). The Kashmir Serai is north of Lahore.
3. Afghanistan.

not wish his grey hairs to show), knew the boy's value as a gossip. Sometimes he would tell Kim to watch a man who had nothing whatever to do with horses: to follow him for one whole day and report every soul with whom he talked. Kim would deliver himself of his tale at evening, and Mahbub would listen without a word or gesture. It was intrigue of some kind, Kim knew; but its worth lay in saying nothing whatever to anyone except Mahbub, who gave him beautiful meals all hot from the cookshop at the head of the serai, and once as much as eight annas[4] in money.

'He is here,' said Kim, hitting a bad-tempered camel on the nose. 'Oh, Mahbub Ali!' He halted at a dark arch and slipped behind the bewildered lama.

The horse-trader, his deep, embroidered Bokhariot[5] belt unloosed, was lying on a pair of silk carpet saddle-bags, pulling lazily at an immense silver hookah.[6] He turned his head very slightly at the cry; and seeing only the tall silent figure, chuckled in his deep chest.

'Allah! A lama! A Red Lama! It is far from Lahore to the Passes. What dost thou do here?'

The lama held out the begging-bowl mechanically.

'God's curse on all unbelievers!' said Mahbub. 'I do not give to a lousy Tibetan; but ask my Baltis[7] over yonder behind the camels. They may value your blessings. Oh, horseboys, here is a countryman of yours. See if he be hungry.'

A shaven, crouching Balti, who had come down with the horses, and who was nominally some sort of degraded Buddhist, fawned upon the priest, and in thick gutturals besought the Holy One to sit at the horseboys' fire.

'Go!' said Kim, pushing him lightly, and the lama strode away, leaving Kim at the edge of the cloister.

'Go!' said Mahbub Ali, returning to his hookah. 'Little Hindu, run away. God's curse on all unbelievers! Beg from those of my tail[8] who are of thy faith.'

'Maharaj,'[9] whined Kim, using the Hindu form of address, and thoroughly enjoying the situation; 'my father is dead—my mother is dead—my stomach is empty.'

'Beg from my men among the horses, I say. There must be some Hindus in my tail.'

'Oh, Mahbub Ali, but am *I* a Hindu?' said Kim in English.

4. Equal to about fifty cents.
5. Made in Bokhara, a region that borders Afghanistan, Persia, and Russia. Mahbub Ali is dressed in exotically embroidered clothing.
6. Water pipe.
7. From Baltistan, north of Lahore.
8. My followers.
9. Literally "great ruler," an excessively polite form of address to a stranger.

The trader gave no sign of astonishment, but looked under shaggy eyebrows.

'Little Friend of all the World,' said he, 'what is this?'

'Nothing. I am now that holy man's disciple; and we go a pilgrimage together—to Benares, he says. He is quite mad, and I am tired of Lahore city. I wish new air and water.'

'But for whom dost thou work? Why come to me?' The voice was harsh with suspicion.

'To whom else should I come? I have no money. It is not good to go about without money. Thou wilt sell many horses to the officers. They are very fine horses, these new ones: I have seen them. Give me a rupee,[1] Mahbub Ali, and when I come to my wealth I will give thee a bond and pay.'

'Um!' said Mahbub Ali, thinking swiftly. 'Thou hast never before lied to me. Call that lama—stand back in the dark.'

'Oh, our tales will agree,' said Kim, laughing.

'We go to Benares,' said the lama, as soon as he understood the drift of Mahbub Ali's questions. 'The boy and I, I go to seek for a certain River.'

'Maybe—but the boy?'

'He is my disciple. He was sent, I think, to guide me to that River. Sitting under a gun was I when he came suddenly. Such things have befallen the fortunate to whom guidance was allowed. But I remember now, he said he was of this world—a Hindu.'

'And his name?'

'That I did not ask. Is he not my disciple?'

'His country—his race—his village? Mussalman—Sikh—Hindu—Jain—low caste or high?'

'Why should I ask? There is neither high nor low in the Middle Way. If he is my *chela*—does—will—can anyone take him from me? For, look you, without him I shall not find my River.' He wagged his head solemnly.

'None shall take him from thee. Go, sit among my Baltis,' said Mahbub Ali, and the lama drifted off, soothed by the promise.

'Is he not quite mad?' said Kim, coming forward to the light again. 'Why should I lie to thee, Hajji?'[2]

Mahbub puffed his hookah in silence. Then he began, almost whispering: 'Umballa[3] is on the road to Benares—if indeed ye two go there.'

'Tck! Tck! I tell thee he does not know how to lie—as we two know.'

1. Indian coin, then worth about a dollar.
2. One who has made the pilgrimage to Mecca; here used as a general term of respect.
3. Now called Amballa.

'And if thou wilt carry a message for me as far as Umballa, I will give thee money. It concerns a horse—a white stallion which I have sold to an officer upon the last time I returned from the Passes. But then—stand nearer and hold up hands as begging—the pedigree of the white stallion was not fully established, and that officer, who is now at Umballa, bade me make it clear.' (Mahbub here described the horse and the appearance of the officer.) 'So the message to that officer will be: "The pedigree of the white stallion is fully established." By this will he know that thou comest from me. He will then say "What proof hast thou?" and thou wilt answer: "Mahbub Ali has given me the proof."'

'And all for the sake of a white stallion,' said Kim, with a giggle, his eyes aflame.

'That pedigree I will give thee now—in my own fashion—and some hard words as well.' A shadow passed behind Kim, and a feeding camel. Mahbub Ali raised his voice.

'Allah! Art thou the only beggar in the city? Thy mother is dead. Thy father is dead. So is it with all of them. Well, well—' He turned as feeling on the floor beside him and tossed a flap of soft, greasy Mussalman bread[4] to the boy. 'Go and lie down among my horse-boys for to-night—thou and the lama. Tomorrow I may give thee service.'

Kim slunk away, his teeth in the bread, and, as he expected, he found a small wad of folded tissue-paper wrapped in oilskin, with three silver rupees—enormous largesse. He smiled and thrust money and paper into his leather amulet-case. The lama, sumptuously fed by Mahbub's Baltis, was already asleep in a corner of one of the stalls. Kim lay down beside him and laughed. He knew he had rendered a service to Mahbub Ali, and not for one little minute did he believe the tale of the stallion's pedigree.

But Kim did not suspect that Mahbub Ali, known as one of the best horse-dealers in the Punjab, a wealthy and enterprising trader, whose caravans penetrated far and far into the Back of Beyond, was registered in one of the locked books of the Indian Survey Department[5] as C25 1B. Twice or thrice yearly C25 would send in a little story, baldly told but most interesting, and generally—it was checked by the statements of R17 and M4—quite true. It concerned all manner of out-of-the-way mountain principalities, explorers of nationalities other than English, and the gun-trade—was, in brief, a small portion of that vast mass of 'information received' on which the Indian Government acts. But, recently, five confederated Kings, who had no business to confederate, had been

4. Unleavened flat bread usually called *chapatis*.
5. A department of the British administration, responsible for mapping India, ostensibly for tax purposes; see Ian Baucom's essay in this volume.

informed by a kindly Northern Power[6] that there was a leakage of
news from their territories into British India. So those Kings'
Prime Ministers were seriously annoyed and took steps, after the
Oriental fashion. They suspected, among many others, the bully-
ing, red-bearded horse-dealer whose caravans ploughed through
their fastnesses belly-deep in snow. At least, his caravan that sea-
son had been ambushed and shot at twice on the way down, when
Mahbub's men accounted for three strange ruffians who might, or
might not, have been hired for the job. Therefore Mahbub had
avoided halting at the insalubrious city of Peshawur, and had come
through without stop to Lahore, where, knowing his country-
people, he anticipated curious developments.

And there was that on Mahbub Ali which he did not wish to keep
an hour longer than was necessary—a wad of closely folded tissue-
paper, wrapped in oilskin—an impersonal, unaddressed statement,
with five microscopic pin-holes in one corner, that most scan-
dalously betrayed the five confederated Kings, the sympathetic
Northern Power, a Hindu banker in Peshawur, a firm of gun-
makers in Belgium, and an important, semi-independent
Mohammedan ruler to the south. This last was R17's work, which
Mahbub had picked up beyond the Dora Pass[7] and was carrying in
for R17, who, owing to circumstances over which he had no con-
trol, could not leave his post of observation. Dynamite was milky
and innocuous beside that report of C25; and even an Oriental,
with an Oriental's views of the value of time,[8] could see that the
sooner it was in the proper hands the better. Mahbub had no par-
ticular desire to die by violence, because two or three family blood-
feuds across the Border hung unfinished on his hands, and when
these scores were cleared he intended to settle down as a more or
less virtuous citizen. He had never passed the serai gate since his
arrival two days ago, but had been ostentatious in sending telegrams
to Bombay, where he banked some of his money; to Delhi, where a
sub-partner of his own clan was selling horses to the agent of a
Rajputana state; and to Umballa, where an Englishman was excit-
edly demanding the pedigree of a white stallion. The public letter-
writer, who knew English, composed excellent telegrams, such as:
'*Creighton, Lauel Bank, Umballa. Horse is Arabian as already
advised. Sorrowful delayed pedigree which am translating.*' And later

6. Russia, which in the second half of the nineteenth century extended its territories to the
 northern frontiers of Afghanistan; the five confederated kings are those of semi-indepen-
 dent Indian states.
7. On the frontier between Afghanistan and India about 140 miles north of Peshawar.
8. That the "Oriental" has no sense of time is one of many stereotypes used to categorize
 the East as recognizably different from the West. Because words such as "Orient" and
 "Oriental" refer to no stable reality but are convenient markers of otherness and inferior-
 ity, Edward Said critiques this epistemic strategy as "Orientalism." See Patrick Williams's
 essay in this volume.

to the same address: '*Much sorrowful delay. Will forward pedigree.*' To his sub-partner at Delhi he wired: '*Lutuf Ullah. Have wired two thousand rupees your credit Luchman Narain's bank.*' This was entirely in the way of trade, but every one of those telegrams was discussed and re-discussed, by parties who conceived themselves to be interested, before they went over to the railway station in charge of a foolish Balti, who allowed all sorts of people to read them on the road.

When, in Mahbub's own picturesque language, he had muddied the wells of inquiry with the stick of precaution, Kim had dropped on him, sent from Heaven; and, being as prompt as he was unscrupulous, Mahbub Ali, used to taking all sorts of gutsy chances, pressed him into service on the spot.

A wandering lama with a low-caste boy-servant might attract a moment's interest as they wandered about India, the land of pilgrims; but no one would suspect them or, what was more to the point, rob.

He called for a new light-ball to his hookah, and considered the case. If the worst came to the worst, and the boy came to harm, the paper would incriminate nobody. And he would go up to Umballa leisurely and—at a certain risk of exciting fresh suspicion—repeat his tale by word of mouth to the people concerned.

But R17's report was the kernel of the whole affair, and it would be distinctly inconvenient if that failed to come to hand. However, God was great, and Mahbub Ali felt he had done all he could for the time being. Kim was the one soul in the world who had never told him a lie. That would have been a fatal blot on Kim's character if Mahbub had not known that to others, for his own ends or Mahbub's business, Kim could lie like an Oriental.

Then Mahbub Ali rolled across the serai to the Gate of the Harpies[9] who paint their eyes and trap the stranger, and was at some pains to call on the one girl who, he had reason to believe, was a particular friend of a smooth-faced Kashmiri pundit,[1] who had way-laid his simple Balti in the matter of the telegrams. It was an utterly foolish thing to do; because they fell to drinking perfumed brandy against the Law of the Prophet, and Mahbub grew wonderfully drunk, and the gates of his mouth were loosened, and he pursued the Flower of Delight with the feet of intoxication till he fell flat among the cushions, where the Flower of Delight, aided by a smooth-faced Kashmiri pundit, searched him from head to foot most thoroughly.

About the same hour Kim heard soft feet in Mahbub's deserted stall. The horse-trader, curiously enough, had left his door

9. Prostitutes. In Greek mythology, harpies are female monsters with wings and talons.
1. Learned Brahmin.

unlocked, and his men were busy celebrating their return to India
with a whole sheep of Mahbub's bounty. A sleek young gentleman
from Delhi, armed with a bunch of keys which the Flower had
unshackled from the senseless one's belt, went through every single
box, bundle, mat, and saddle-bag in Mahbub's possession even more
systematically than the Flower and the pundit were searching the
owner.

'And I think,' said the Flower scornfully an hour later, one
rounded elbow on the snoring carcass, 'that he is no more than a pig
of an Afghan horse-dealer, with no thought except women and
horses. Moreover, he may have sent it away by now—if ever there
were such a thing.'

'Nay—in a matter touching Five Kings it would be next his black
heart,' said the pundit. 'Was there nothing?'

The Delhi man laughed and resettled his turban as he entered. 'I
searched between the soles of his slippers as the Flower searched
his clothes. This is not the man but another. I leave little unseen.'

'They did not say he was the very man,' said the pundit thought-
fully. 'They said, "Look if he be the man, since our counsels are
troubled."'

'That North country is full of horse-dealers as an old coat of lice.
There is Sikandar Khan, Nur Ali Beg, and Farrukh Shah—all heads
of *kafilas* (caravans)—who deal there,' said the Flower.

'They have not yet come in,' said the pundit. 'Thou must ensnare
them later.'

'Phew!' said the Flower with deep disgust, rolling Mahbub's head
from her lap. 'I earn my money. Farrukh Shah is a bear, Ali Beg a
swashbuckler, and old Sikandar Khan—yaie! Go! I sleep now. This
swine will not stir till dawn.'

When Mahbub woke, the Flower talked to him severely on the sin
of drunkenness. Asiatics do not wink when they have outmanoeu-
vred an enemy, but as Mahbub Ali cleared his throat, tightened his
belt, and staggered forth under the early morning stars, he came
very near to it.

'What a colt's trick!' said he to himself. 'As if every girl in
Peshawur did not use it! But 'twas prettily done. Now God He
knows how many more there be upon the Road who have orders to
test me—perhaps with the knife. So it stands that the boy must go
to Umballa—and by rail—for the writing is something urgent. I
abide here, following the Flower and drinking wine as an Afghan
coper[2] should.'

He halted at the stall next but one to his own. His men lay there
heavy with sleep. There was no sign of Kim or the lama.

2. An untrustworthy dealer.

'Up!' He stirred a sleeper. 'Whither went those who lay here last even—the lama and the boy? Is aught missing?'

'Nay,' grunted the man, 'the old madman rose at second cockrow saying he would go to Benares, and the young one led him away.'

'The curse of Allah on all unbelievers!' said Mahbub heartily, and climbed into his own stall, growling in his beard.

But it was Kim who had wakened the lama—Kim with one eye laid against a knot-hole in the planking, who had seen the Delhi man's search through the boxes. This was no common thief that turned over letters, bills, and saddles—no mere burglar who ran a little knife sideways into the soles of Mahbub's slippers, or picked the seams of the saddle-bags so deftly. At first Kim had been minded to give the alarm—the long-drawn *cho-or—choor!* (thief! thief!) that sets the serai ablaze of nights; but he looked more carefully, and, hand on amulet, drew his own conclusions.

'It must be the pedigree of that made-up horse-lie,' said he, 'the thing that I carry to Umballa. Better that we go now. Those who search bags with knives may presently search bellies with knives. Surely there is a woman behind this. Hai! Hai!' in a whisper to the light-sleeping old man. 'Come. It is time—time to go to Benares.'

The lama rose obediently, and they passed out of the serai like shadows.

Chapter 2

And whoso will, from Pride released,
Contemning neither creed nor, priest,
May feel the Soul of all the East
About him at Kamakura.
Buddha at Kamakura.[1]

They entered the fort-like railway station, black in the end of night; the electrics sizzling over the goods-yard where they handle the heavy Northern grain-traffic.

'This is the work of devils!' said the lama, recoiling from the hollow echoing darkness, the glimmer of rails between the masonry platforms, and the maze of girders above. He stood in a gigantic stone hall paved, it seemed, with the sheeted dead[2]—third-class passengers who had taken their tickets overnight and were sleeping

1. The Buddhist doctrine in this stanza highlights the search for enlightenment in the chapter and in the book.
2. An allusion to *Hamlet* 1.1.114–16: "A little ere the mightiest Julius fell, / The graves stood tenantless and the sheeted dead / Did squeak and gibber in the Roman streets." Indians who sleep outside cover themselves head to toe with sheets to keep out light and insects.

in the waiting-rooms. All hours of the twenty-four are alike to Orientals, and their passenger traffic is regulated accordingly.

'This is where the fire-carriages come. One stands behind that hole'—Kim pointed to the ticket-office—'who will give thee a paper to take thee to Umballa.'

'But we go to Benares,' he replied petulantly.

'All one. Benares then. Quick: she comes!'

'Take thou the purse.'

The lama, not so well used to trains as he had pretended, started as the 3.25 a.m. south-bound roared in. The sleepers sprang to life, and the station filled with clamour and shootings, cries of water and sweetmeat vendors, shouts of native policemen, and shrill yells of women gathering up their baskets, their families, and their husbands.

'It is the train—only the *te-rain*. It will not come here. Wait!' Amazed at the lama's immense simplicity (he had handed him a small bag full of rupees), Kim asked and paid for a ticket to Umballa. A sleepy clerk grunted and flung out a ticket to the next station, just six miles distant.

'Nay,' said Kim, scanning it with a grin. 'This may serve for farmers, but I live in the city of Lahore. It was cleverly done, Babu.[3] Now give the ticket to Umballa.'

The Babu scowled and dealt the proper ticket.

'Now another to Amritzar,' said Kim, who had no notion of spending Mahbub Ali's money on anything so crude as a paid ride to Umballa. 'The price is so much. The small money in return is just so much. I know the ways of the *te-rain* . . . Never did *yogi* need *chela* as thou dost,' he went on merrily to the bewildered lama. 'They would have flung thee out at Mian Mir but for me. This way! Come!' He returned the money, keeping only one anna in each rupee of the price of the Umballa ticket as his commission—the immemorial commission of Asia.[4]

The lama jibbed at the open door of a crowded third-class carriage. 'Were it not better to walk?' said he weakly.

A burly Sikh[5] artisan thrust forth his bearded head. 'Is he afraid? Do not be afraid. I remember the time when I was afraid of the *te-rain*. Enter! This thing is the work of the Government.'

'I do not fear,' said the lama. 'Have ye room within for two?'

'There is no room even for a mouse,' shrilled the wife of a well-to-do cultivator—a Hindu Jat[6] from the rich Jullundur district. Our

3. A traditional term of respect that took on a derogatory meaning under the British, who applied it to educated Bengalis who often worked as clerks.

4. With sixteen annas in a rupee, one anna per rupee was, as Kipling says, the standard tip.

5. A member of a monotheistic Indian religion influenced by Hinduism in some of its theological concepts, and by Islam in its rejection of caste and multiple gods. Sikhs were valued by the British for their military skills; they are recognizable by their turbans.

6. An ethnic group or subcaste of farmers, most of whose members were Sikhs or Muslims.

night trains are not as well looked after as the day ones, where the sexes are very strictly kept to separate carriages.

'Oh, mother of my son, we can make space,' said the blue-turbaned husband. 'Pick up the child. It is a holy man, see'st thou?'

'And my lap full of seventy times seven bundles! Why not bid him sit on my knee, Shameless? But men are ever thus!' She looked round for approval. An Amritzar courtesan near the window sniffed behind her head drapery.

'Enter! Enter!' cried a fat Hindu money-lender, his folded account-book in a cloth under his arm. With an oily smirk: 'It is well to be kind to the poor.'

'Ay, at seven per cent a month with a mortgage on the unborn calf,' said a young Dogra[7] soldier going south on leave; and they all laughed.

'Will it travel to Benares?' said the lama.

'Assuredly. Else why should we come? Enter, or we are left,' cried Kim.

'See!' shrilled the Amritzar girl. 'He has never entered a train. Oh, see!'

'Nay, help,' said the cultivator, putting out a large brown hand and hauling him in. 'Thus is it done, father.'

'But—but—I sit on the floor. It is against the Rule to sit on a bench,' said the lama. 'Moreover, it cramps me.'

'I say,' began the money-lender, pursing his lips, 'that there is not one rule of right living which these *te-rains* do not cause us to break. We sit, for example, side by side with all castes and peoples.'

'Yea, and with most outrageously shameless ones,' said the wife, scowling at the Amritzar girl making eyes at the young sepoy.[8]

'I said we might have gone by cart along the road,' said the husband, 'and thus have saved some money.'

'Yes—and spent twice over what we saved on food by the way. That was talked out ten thousand times.'

'Ay, by ten thousand tongues,' grunted he.

'The Gods help us poor women if we may not speak. Oho! He is of that sort which may not look at or reply to a woman.' For the lama, constrained by his Rule, took not the faintest notice of her. 'And his disciple is like him?'

'Nay, mother,' said Kim most promptly. 'Not when the woman is well-looking and above all charitable to the hungry.'

'A beggar's answer,' said the Sikh, laughing. 'Thou hast brought it on thyself, sister!' Kim's hands were crooked in supplication.

7. Another ethnic group from Rajputana; its members are highly regarded as soldiers and recognizable by their large turbans. The Dogras formed a major British regiment in 1887.
8. Indian soldier in the British army.

'And whither goest thou?' said the woman, handing him the half
of a cake from a greasy package.

'Even to Benares.'

'Jugglers belike?' the young soldier suggested. 'Have ye any tricks
to pass the time? Why does not that yellow man answer?'

'Because,' said Kim stoutly, 'he is holy, and thinks upon matters
hidden from thee.'

'That may be well. We of the Ludhiana Sikhs'—he rolled it out
sonorously—'do not trouble our heads with doctrine. We fight.'

'My sister's brother's son is *naik* (corporal) in that regiment,' said
the Sikh craftsman quietly. 'There are also some Dogra companies
there.' The soldier glared, for a Dogra is of other caste than a Sikh,
and the banker tittered.

'They are all one to me,' said the Amritzar girl.

'That we believe,' snorted the cultivator's wife malignantly.

'Nay, but all who serve the Sirkar[9] with weapons in their hands
are, as it were, one brotherhood. There is one brotherhood of the
caste, but beyond that again'—she looked round timidly—'the bond
of the *Pulton*—the Regiment—eh?'

'My brother is in a Jat regiment,' said the cultivator. 'Dogras be
good men.'

'*Thy* Sikhs at least were of that opinion,' said the soldier, with a
scowl at the placid old man in the corner. '*Thy* Sikhs thought so
when our two companies came to help them at the Pirzai Kotal in
the face of eight Afridi standards on the ridge not three months
gone.'[1]

He told the story of a Border action in which the Dogra compa-
nies of the Ludhiana Sikhs had acquitted themselves well. The
Amritzar girl smiled; for she knew the tale was to win her approval.

'Alas!' said the cultivator's wife at the end. 'So their villages were
burnt and their little children made homeless?'

'They had marked our dead.[2] They paid a great payment after we
of the Sikhs had schooled them. So it was. Is this Amritzar?'

'Ay, and here they cut our tickets,' said the banker, fumbling at his
belt.

The lamps were paling in the dawn when the half-caste guard
came round. Ticket-collecting is a slow business in the East, where
people secrete their tickets in all sorts of curious places. Kim pro-
duced his and was told to get out.

'But I go to Umballa,' he protested. 'I go with this holy man.'

9. Term for the government of India.
1. "Pirzai Kotal" means literally "the pass of the follower of the saint"; it is the site of an
engagement between British troops and the Afridi tribe, which tried to halt the building
of a road. The appearance of Afridi standards, or flags, was a challenge to battle; each
standard indicated about thirty Afridi warriors.
2. Mutilated them.

'Thou canst go to Jehannum[3] for aught I care. This ticket is only to Amritzar. Out!'

Kim burst into a flood of tears, protesting that the lama was his father and his mother, that he was the prop of the lama's declining years, and that the lama would die without his care. All the carriage bade the guard be merciful—the banker was specially eloquent here—but the guard hauled Kim on to the platform. The lama blinked—he could not overtake the situation—and Kim lifted up his voice and wept outside the carriage window.

'I am very poor. My father is dead—my mother is dead. O charitable ones, if I am left here, who shall tend that old man?'

'What—what is this?' the lama repeated. 'He must go to Benares. He must come with me. He is my *chela*. If there is money to be paid—'

'Oh, be silent,' whispered Kim; 'are we Rajahs to throw away good silver when the world is so charitable?'

The Amritzar girl stepped out with her bundles, and it was on her that Kim kept his watchful eye. Ladies of that persuasion, he knew, were generous.

'A ticket—a little *tikkut* to Umballa—O Breaker of Hearts!' She laughed. 'Hast thou no charity?'

'Does the holy man come from the North?'

'From far and far in the North he comes,' cried Kim. 'From among the hills.'

'There is snow among the pine-trees in the North—in the hills there is snow. My mother was from Kulu. Get thee a ticket. Ask him for a blessing.'

'Ten thousand blessings,' shrilled Kim. 'O Holy One, a woman has given us in charity so that I can come with thee—a woman with a golden heart. I run for the *tikkut*.'

The girl looked up at the lama, who had mechanically followed Kim to the platform. He bowed his head that he might not see her, and muttered in Tibetan as she passed on with the crowd.

'Light come—light go,' said the cultivator's wife viciously.

'She has acquired merit,' returned the lama. 'Beyond doubt it was a nun.'

'There be ten thousand such nuns in Amritzar alone. Return, old man, or the *te-rain* may depart without thee,' cried the banker.

'Not only was it sufficient for the ticket, but for a little food also,' said Kim, leaping to his place. 'Now eat, Holy One. Look. Day comes!'

Golden, rose, saffron, and pink, the morning mists smoked away across the flat green levels. All the rich Punjab lay out in the splen-

3. Urdu or Persian word for hell.

dour of the keen sun. The lama flinched a little as the telegraph-posts swung by.

'Great is the speed of the *te-rain*,' said the banker, with a patronizing grin. 'We have gone farther since Lahore than thou couldst walk in two days: at even, we shall enter Umballa.'

'And that is still far from Benares,' said the lama wearily, mumbling over the cakes that Kim offered. They all unloosed their bundles and made their morning meal. Then the banker, the cultivator, and the soldier prepared their pipes and wrapped the compartment in choking, acrid smoke, spitting and coughing and enjoying themselves. The Sikh and the cultivator's wife chewed *pan*;[4] the lama took snuff and told his beads, while Kim, cross-legged, smiled over the comfort of a full stomach.

'What rivers have ye by Benares?' said the lama of a sudden to the carriage at large.

'We have Gunga,'[5] returned the banker, when the little titter had subsided.

'What others?'

'What other than Gunga?'

'Nay, but in my mind was the thought of a certain River of healing.'

'That is Gunga. Who bathes in her is made clean and goes to the Gods. Thrice have I made pilgrimage to Gunga.' He looked round proudly.

'There was need,' said the young sepoy drily, and the travellers' laugh turned against the banker.

'Clean—to return again to the Gods,' the lama muttered. 'And to go forth on the round of lives anew—still tied to the Wheel.' He shook his head testily. 'But maybe there is a mistake. Who, then, made Gunga in the beginning?'

'The Gods. Of what known faith art thou?' the banker said, appalled.

'I follow the Law—the Most Excellent Law. So it was the Gods that made Gunga. What like of Gods were they?'

The carriage looked at him in amazement. It was inconceivable that anyone should be ignorant of Gunga.

'What—what is thy God?' said the money-lender at last.

'Hear!' said the lama, shifting the rosary to his hand. 'Hear: for I speak of Him now! O people of Hind,[6] listen!'

He began in Urdu the tale of the Lord Buddha, but, borne by his

4. A mild stimulant made of the leaf of a betel vine and other ingredients and chewed like tobacco. It stains the lips red and the teeth black; thus a *pan* user is instantly recognizable.
5. The Ganges, the holy river of the Hindus.
6. One of many local names for what the British called "India," Hind is short for Hindustan—land of the Hindus.

own thoughts, slid into Tibetan and long-droned texts from a Chinese book of the Buddha's life. The gentle, tolerant folk looked on reverently. All India is full of holy men stammering gospels in strange tongues; shaken and consumed in the fires of their own zeal; dreamers, babblers, and visionaries: as it has been from the beginning and will continue to the end.

'Um!' said the soldier of the Ludhiana Sikhs. 'There was a Mohammedan regiment lay next to us at the Pirzai Kotal, and a priest of theirs—he was, as I remember, a *naik*[7]—when the fit was on him, spake prophecies. But the mad all are in God's keeping. His officers overlooked much in that man.'

The lama fell back on Urdu, remembering that he was in a strange land. 'Hear the tale of the Arrow which our Lord loosed from the bow,' he said.

This was much more to their taste, and they listened curiously while he told it. 'Now, O people of Hind, I go to seek that River. Know ye aught that may guide me, for we be all men and women in evil case.'

'There is Gunga—and Gunga alone—who washes away sin,' ran the murmur round the carriage.

'Though past question we have good Gods Jullundur-way,' said the cultivator's wife, looking out of the window. 'See how they have blessed the crops.'

'To search every river in the Punjab is no small matter,' said her husband. 'For me, a stream that leaves good silt on my land suffices, and I thank Bhumia, the God of the Homestead.' He shrugged one knotted, bronzed shoulder.

'Think you our Lord came so far North?' said the lama, turning to Kim.

'It may be,' Kim replied soothingly, as he spat red *pan*-juice on the floor.

'The last of the Great Ones,' said the Sikh with authority, 'was Sikander Julkarn (Alexander the Great). He paved the streets of Jullundur and built a great tank near Umballa. That pavement holds to this day; and the tank is there also. I never heard of thy God.'

'Let thy hair grow long and talk Punjabi,' said the young soldier jestingly to Kim, quoting a Northern proverb. 'That is all that makes a Sikh.' But he did not say this very loud.

The lama sighed and shrank into himself, a dingy, shapeless mass. In the pauses of their talk they could hear the low droning—'*Om mane pudme hum! Om mane pudme hum!*'[8]—and the thick click of the wooden rosary beads.

7. Corporal.
8. A Buddhist mantra, or repeated meditative phrase. It means literally "The jewel is in the lotus!"

'It irks me,' he said at last. 'The speed and the clatter irk me. Moreover, my *chela*, I think that maybe we have overpassed that River.'

'Peace, peace,' said Kim. 'Was not the River near Benares? We are yet far from the place.'

'But—if our Lord came North, it may be any one of these little ones that we have run across.'

'I do not know.'

'But thou wast sent to me—wast thou sent to me?—for the merit I had acquired over yonder at Such-zen. From beside the cannon didst thou come—bearing two faces—and two garbs.'[9]

'Peace. One must not speak of these things here,' whispered Kim. 'There was but one of me. Think again and thou wilt remember. A boy—a Hindu boy—by the great green cannon.'

'But was there not also an Englishman with a white beard—holy among images—who himself made more sure my assurance of the River of the Arrow?'

'He—we—went to the Ajaib-Gher in Lahore to pray before the Gods there,' Kim explained to the openly listening company.

'And the Sahib of the Wonder House talked to him—yes, this is truth—as a brother. He is a very holy man, from far beyond the Hills. Rest, thou. In time we come to Umballa.'

'But my River—the River of my healing?'

'And then, if it please thee, we will go hunting for that River on foot. So that we miss nothing—not even a little rivulet in a field-side.'

'But thou hast a Search of thine own?' The lama—very pleased that he remembered so well—sat bolt upright.

'Ay,' said Kim, humouring him. The boy was entirely happy to be out chewing *pan* and seeing new people in the great good-tempered world.

'It was a bull—a Red Bull that shall come and help thee—and carry thee—whither? I have forgotten. A Red Bull on a green field, was it not?'

'Nay, it will carry me nowhere,' said Kim. 'It is but a tale I told thee.'

'What is this?' The cultivator's wife leaned forward, her bracelets clinking on her arm. 'Do ye both dream dreams? A Red Bull on a green field, that shall carry thee to the heavens—or what? Was it a vision? Did one make a prophecy? *We* have a Red Bull in our village behind Jullundur city, and he grazes by choice in the very greenest of our fields!'

'Give a woman an old wife's tale and a weaver-bird a leaf and a thread, they will weave wonderful things,' said the Sikh. 'All holy

9. Kim had first dressed as an English boy and then had disguised himself as a Hindu-Indian.

men dream dreams, and by following holy men their disciples attain that power.'

'A Red Bull on a green field, was it?' the lama repeated. 'In a former life it may be thou hast acquired merit, and the Bull will come to reward thee.'

'Nay—nay—it was but a tale one told to me—for a jest belike. But I will seek the Bull about Umballa, and thou canst look for thy River and rest from the clatter of the train.'

'It may be that the Bull knows—that he is sent to guide us both,' said the lama, hopefully as a child. Then to the company, indicating Kim: 'This one was sent to me but yesterday. He is not, I think, of this world.'

'Beggars aplenty have I met, and holy men to boot, but never such a *yogi* nor such a disciple,' said the woman.

Her husband touched his forehead lightly with one finger and smiled. But the next time the lama would eat they took care to give him of their best.

And at last—tired, sleepy, and dusty—they reached Umballa City Station.

'We abide here upon a law-suit,' said the cultivator's wife to Kim. 'We lodge with my man's cousin's younger brother. There is room also in the courtyard for thy *yogi* and for thee. Will—will he give me a blessing?'

'O holy man! A woman with a heart of gold gives us lodging for the night. It is a kindly land, this land of the South. See how we have been helped since the dawn!'

The lama bowed his head in benediction.

'To fill my cousin's younger brother's house with wastrels—'the husband began, as he shouldered his heavy bamboo staff.

'Thy cousin's younger brother owes my father's cousin something yet on his daughter's marriage-feast,' said the woman crisply. 'Let him put their food to that account. The *yogi* will beg, I doubt not.'

'Ay, I beg for him,' said Kim, anxious only to get the lama under shelter for the night, that he might seek Mahbub Ali's Englishman and deliver himself of the white stallion's pedigree.

'Now,' said he, when the lama had come to an anchor in the inner courtyard of a decent Hindu house behind the cantonments,[1] 'I go away for a while—to—to buy us victual in the bazar. Do not stray abroad till I return.'

'Thou wilt return? Thou wilt surely return?' The old man caught at his wrist. 'And thou wilt return in this very same shape? Is it too late to look tonight for the River?'

1. Quarters for troops.

'Too late and too dark. Be comforted. Think how far thou art on the road—an hundred miles from Lahore already.'

'Yea—and farther from my monastery. Alas! It is a great and terrible world.'

Kim stole out and away, as unremarkable a figure as ever carried his own and a few score thousand other folk's fate slung round his neck. Mahbub Ali's directions left him little doubt of the house in which his Englishman lived; and a groom, bringing a dog-cart home from the Club, made him quite sure. It remained only to identify his man, and Kim slipped through the garden hedge and hid in a clump of plumed grass close to the veranda. The house blazed with lights, and servants moved about tables dressed with flowers, glass, and silver. Presently forth came an Englishman, dressed in black and white, humming a tune. It was too dark to see his face, so Kim, beggar-wise, tried an old experiment.

'Protector of the Poor!'

The man backed towards the voice.

'Mahbub Ali says—'

'Hah! What says Mahbub Ali?' He made no attempt to look for the speaker, and that showed Kim that he knew.

'The pedigree of the white stallion is fully established.'

'What proof is there?' The Englishman switched at the rose-hedge in the side of the drive.

'Mahbub Ali has given me this proof.' Kim flipped the wad of folded paper into the air, and it fell in the path beside the man, who put his foot on it as a gardener came round the corner. When the servant passed he picked it up, dropped a rupee—Kim could hear the clink—and strode into the house, never turning round. Swiftly Kim took up the money; but for all his training, he was Irish enough by birth to reckon silver the least part of any game. What he desired was the visible effect of action; so, instead of slinking away, he lay close in the grass and wormed nearer to the house.

He saw—Indian bungalows are open through and through—the Englishman return to a small dressing-room, in a corner of the veranda, that was half office, littered with papers and despatch-boxes, and sit down to study Mahbub Ali's message. His face, by the full ray of the kerosene lamp, changed and darkened, and Kim, used as every beggar must be to watching countenances, took good note.

'Will! Will, dear!' called a woman's voice. 'You ought to be in the drawing-room. They'll be here in a minute.'

The man still read intently.

'Will!' said the voice, five minutes later. '*He's* come. I can hear the troopers in the drive.'

The man dashed out bareheaded as a big landau[2] with four native troopers behind it halted at the veranda, and a tall, black-haired man, erect as an arrow, swung out, preceded by a young officer who laughed pleasantly.

Flat on his belly lay Kim, almost touching the high wheels. His man and the black stranger exchanged two sentences.

'Certainly, sir,' said the young officer promptly. 'Everything waits while a horse is concerned.'

'We shan't be more than twenty minutes,' said Kim's man. 'You can do the honours—keep 'em amused, and all that.'

'Tell one of the troopers to wait,' said the tall man, and they both passed into the dressing-room together as the landau rolled away. Kim saw their heads bent over Mahbub Ali's message, and heard the voices—one low and deferential, the other sharp and decisive.

'It isn't a question of weeks. It is a question of days—hours almost,' said the elder. 'I'd been expecting it for some time, but this'—he tapped Mahbub Ali's paper—'clinches it. Grogan's dining here to-night, isn't he?'

'Yes, sir, and Macklin too.'

'Very good. I'll speak to them myself. The matter will be referred to the Council, of course, but this is a case where one is justified in assuming that we take action at once. Warn the Pindi[3] and Peshawur brigades. It will disorganize all the summer reliefs,[4] but we can't help that. This comes of not smashing them thoroughly the first time. Eight thousand should be enough.'[5]

'What about artillery, sir?'

'I must consult Macklin.'

'Then it means war?'

'No. Punishment. When a man is bound by the action of his predecessor—'

'But C25 may have lied.'

'He bears out the other's information. Practically, they showed their hand six months back. But Devenish would have it there was a chance of peace. Of course they used it to make themselves stronger. Send off those telegrams at once—the new code, not the old—mine and Wharton's. I don't think we need keep the ladies waiting any longer. We can settle the rest over the cigars. I thought it was coming. It's punishment—not war.'

As the trooper cantered off, Kim crawled round to the back of the

2. A horse-drawn four-wheeled carriage.
3. Short for Rawalpindi, a British military station northwest of Lahore.
4. Units sent in from the hills to the plains and vice versa.
5. The officers are discussing preparations for the Second Afghan War (1878–80). Russia and Britain struggled for power with the emirs of Afganistan, the land bordering the Punjab and therefore a necessary route to India. See the essays by Blair Kling, A. Michael Matin, and Ann Parry in this volume.

house, where, going on his Lahore experiences, he judged there would be food—and information. The kitchen was crowded with excited scullions, one of whom kicked him.

'Aie,' said Kim, feigning tears. 'I came only to wash dishes in return for a bellyful.'

'All Umballa is on the same errand. Get hence. They go in now with the soup. Think you that we who serve Creighton Sahib need strange scullions to help us through a big dinner?'

'It is a very big dinner,' said Kim, looking at the plates.

'Small wonder. The guest of honour is none other than the Jang-i-Lat Sahib (the Commander-in-Chief).'

'Ho!' said Kim, with the correct guttural note of wonder. He had learned what he wanted, and when the scullion turned he was gone.

'And all that trouble,' said he to himself, thinking as usual in Hindustani, 'for a horse's pedigree! Mahbub Ali should have come to me to learn a little lying. Every time before that I have borne a message it concerned a woman. Now it is men. Better. The tall man said that they will loose a great army to punish someone—some-where—the news goes to Pindi and Peshawur. There are also guns. Would I had crept nearer. It is big news!'

He returned to find the cultivator's cousin's younger brother discussing the family law-suit in all its bearings with the cultivator and his wife and a few friends, while the lama dozed. After the evening meal some one passed him a waterpipe; and Kim felt very much of a man as he pulled at the smooth coconut-shell, his legs spread abroad in the moonlight, his tongue clicking in remarks from time to time. His hosts were most polite; for the cultivator's wife had told them of his vision of the Red Bull, and of his probable descent from another world. Moreover, the lama was a great and venerable curiosity. The family priest, an old, tolerant Sarsut Brahmin,[6] dropped in later, and naturally started a theological argument to impress the family. By creed, of course, they were all on their priest's side, but the lama was the guest and the novelty. His gentle kindliness, and his impressive Chinese quotations, that sounded like spells, delighted them hugely; and in this sympathetic, simple air, he expanded like the Bodhisat's own lotus, speaking of his life in the great hills of Such-zen, before, as he said, 'I rose up to seek enlightenment.'

Then it came out that in those worldly days he had been a master-hand at casting horoscopes and nativities; and the family priest led him on to describe his methods; each giving the planets names that the other could not understand, and pointing upwards as the big stars sailed across the dark. The children of the house tugged unrebuked at his rosary; and he clean forgot the Rule which forbids looking at

6. A priest of Sarasvati, wife of Brahma and goddess of art and learning.

women as he talked of enduring snows, landslips, blocked passes, the remote cliffs where men find sapphires and turquoise, and that wonderful upland road that leads at last into Great China itself.

'How thinkest thou of this one?' said the cultivator aside to the priest.

'A holy man—a holy man indeed. His Gods are not the Gods, but his feet are upon the Way,' was the answer. 'And his methods of nativities, though that is beyond thee, are wise and sure.'

'Tell me,' said Kim lazily, 'whether I find my Red Bull on a green field, as was promised me.'

'What knowledge hast thou of thy birth-hour?' the priest asked, swelling with importance.

'Between first and second cockrow of the first night in May.'

'Of what year?'

'I do not know; but upon the hour that I cried first fell the great earthquake in Srinagar which is in Kashmir.' This Kim had from the woman who took care of him, and she again from Kimball O'Hara. The earthquake had been felt in India, and for long stood a leading date in the Punjab.

'Ai!' said a woman excitedly. This seemed to make Kim's supernatural origin more certain. 'Was not such an one's daughter born then—'

'And her mother bore her husband four sons in four years—all likely boys,' cried the cultivator's wife, sitting outside the circle in the shadow.

'None reared in the knowledge,' said the family priest, 'forget how the planets stood in their Houses upon that night.' He began to draw in the dust of the courtyard. 'At least thou hast good claim to a half of the House of the Bull. How runs thy prophecy?'

'Upon a day,' said Kim, delighted at the sensation he was creating, 'I shall be made great by means of a Red Bull on a green field, but first there will enter two men making all things ready.'

'Yes: thus ever at the opening of a vision. A thick darkness that clears slowly; anon one enters with a broom making ready the place. Then begins the Sight. Two men—thou sayest? Ay, ay. The Sun, leaving the House of the Bull, enters that of the Twins. Hence the two men of the prophecy. Let us now consider. Fetch me a twig, little one.'

He knitted his brows, scratched, smoothed out, and scratched again in the dust mysterious signs—to the wonder of all save the lama, who, with fine instinct, forbore to interfere.

At the end of half an hour, he tossed the twig from him with a grunt.

'Hm! Thus say the stars. Within three days come the two men to make all things ready. After them follows the Bull; but the sign over against him is the sign of War and armed men.'

'There was indeed a man of the Ludhiana Sikhs in the carriage from Lahore,' said the cultivator's wife hopefully.

'Tck! Armed men—many hundreds. What concern hast thou with war?' said the priest to Kim. 'Thine is a red and an angry sign of War to be loosed very soon.'

'None—none,' said the lama earnestly. 'We seek only peace and our River.'

Kim smiled, remembering what he had overheard in the dressing-room. Decidedly he was a favourite of the stars.

The priest brushed his foot over the rude horoscope. 'More than this I cannot see. In three days comes the Bull to thee, boy.'

'And my River, my River,' pleaded the lama. 'I had hoped his Bull would lead us both to the River.'

'Alas, for that wondrous River, my brother,' the priest replied. 'Such things are not common.'

Next morning, though they were pressed to stay, the lama insisted on departure. They gave Kim a large bundle of good food and nearly three annas in copper money for the needs of the road, and with many blessings watched the two go southward in the dawn.

'Pity it is that these and such as these could not be freed from the Wheel of Things,' said the lama.

'Nay, then would only evil people be left on the earth, and who would give us meat and shelter?' quoth Kim, stepping merrily under his burden.

'Yonder is a small stream. Let us look,' said the lama, and he led from the white road across the fields; walking into a very hornets' nest of pariah dogs.

Chapter 3

Yea, voice of every Soul that clung
To life that strove from rung to rung
When Devadatta's rule was young,
 The warm wind brings Kamakura.
 Buddha at Kamakura.[1]

Behind them an angry farmer brandished a bamboo pole. He was a market-gardener, Arain by caste, growing vegetables and flowers for Umballa city, and well Kim knew the breed.

'Such an one,' said the lama, disregarding the dogs, 'is impolite to

1. This stanza, excluded from the Definitive Edition of Kipling's verse, deals, as do the epigraphs to the first and second chapters, with the Buddhist spiritual quest. Buddhists learn not to cling to life. The rungs are those of the ladder to enlightenment; Kim is on the first, the Lama is on the next to last. For Devadatta, see p. 10, n 4.

strangers, intemperate of speech and uncharitable. Be warned by
his demeanour, my disciple.'

'Ho, shameless beggars!' shouted the farmer. 'Begone! Get hence!'

'We go,' the lama returned, with quiet dignity. 'We go from these
unblessed fields.'

'Ah,' said Kim, sucking in his breath. 'If the next crops fail, thou
canst only blame thine own tongue.'

The man shuffled uneasily in his slippers. 'The land is full of beg-
gars,' he began, half apologetically.

'And by what sign didst thou know that we would beg from thee,
O Mali?'[2] said Kim tartly, using the name that a market-gardener
least likes. 'All we sought was to look at that river beyond the field
there.'

'River, forsooth!' the man snorted. 'What city do ye hail from not
to know a canal-cut? It runs as straight as an arrow, and I pay for
the water as though it were molten silver. There is a branch of a
river beyond. But if ye need water I can give that—and milk.'

'Nay, we will go to the river,' said the lama, striding out.

'Milk and a meal,' the man stammered, as he looked at the strange
tall figure. 'I—I would not draw evil upon myself—or my crops. But
beggars are so many in these hard days.'

'Take notice.' The lama turned to Kim. 'He was led to speak
harshly by the Red Mist of anger. That clearing from his eyes, he
becomes courteous and of an affable heart. May his fields be
blessed! Beware not to judge men too hastily, O farmer.'

'I have met holy ones who would have cursed thee from hearth-
stone to byre,' said Kim to the abashed man. 'Is he not wise and
holy? I am his disciple.'

He cocked his nose in the air loftily and stepped across the nar-
row field-borders with great dignity.

'There is no pride,' said the lama, after a pause, 'there is no pride
among such as follow the Middle Way.'

'But thou hast said he was low-caste and discourteous.'

'Low-caste I did not say, for how can that be which is not?
Afterwards he amended his discourtesy, and I forgot the offence.
Moreover, he is as we are, bound upon the Wheel of Things; but he
does not tread the way of deliverance.' He halted at a little runlet
among the fields, and considered the hoof-pitted bank.

'Now, how wilt thou know thy River?' said Kim, squatting in the
shade of some tall sugar-cane.

'When I find it, an enlightenment will surely be given. This, I feel,
is not the place. O littlest among the waters, if only thou couldst tell
me where runs my River! But be thou blessed to make the fields bear!'

2. Gardener.

'Look! Look!' Kim sprang to his side and dragged him back. A yellow-and-brown streak glided from the purple rustling stems to the bank, stretched its neck to the water, drank, and lay still—a big cobra with fixed, lidless eyes.

'I have no stick—I have no stick,' said Kim. 'I will get me one and break his back.'

'Why? He is upon the Wheel as we are—a life ascending or descending—very far from deliverance. Great evil must the soul have done that is cast into this shape.'

'I hate all snakes,' said Kim. No native training can quench the white man's horror of the Serpent.

'Let him live out his life.' The coiled thing hissed and half opened its hood. 'May thy release come soon, brother!' the lama continued placidly. 'Hast *thou* knowledge, by chance, of my River?'

'Never have I seen such a man as thou art,' Kim whispered, overwhelmed. 'Do the very snakes understand thy talk?'

'Who knows?' He passed within a foot of the cobra's poised head. It flattened itself among the dusty coils.

'Come, thou!' he called over his shoulder.

'Not I,' said Kim. 'I go round.'

'Come. He does no hurt.'

Kim hesitated for a moment. The lama backed his order by some droned Chinese quotation which Kim took for a charm. He obeyed and bounded across the rivulet, and the snake, indeed, made no sign.

'Never have I seen such a man.' Kim wiped the sweat from his forehead. 'And now, whither go we?'

'That is for thee to say. I am old, and a stranger—far from my own place. But that the *rêl*-carriage fills my head with noises of devil-drums I would go in it to Benares now . . . Yet by so going we may miss the River. Let us find another river.'

Where the hard-worked soil gives three and even four crops a year—through patches of sugar-cane, tobacco, long white radishes, and nol-kol,[3] all that day they strolled on, turning aside to every glimpse of water; rousing village dogs and sleeping villages at noon-day; the lama replying to the volleyed questions with an unswerving simplicity. They sought a River—a River of miraculous healing. Had any one knowledge of such a stream? Sometimes men laughed, but more often heard the story out to the end and offered them a place in the shade, a drink of milk, and a meal. The women were always kind, and the little children as children are the world over, alternately shy and venturesome. Evening found them at rest under the village tree of a mud-walled, mud-roofed hamlet, talking to the

3. Acorn squash.

headman as the cattle came in from the grazing-grounds and the women prepared the day's last meal. They had passed beyond the belt of market-gardens round hungry Umballa, and were among the mile-wide green of the staple crops.

He was a white-bearded and affable elder, used to entertaining strangers. He dragged out a string bedstead for the lama, set warm cooked food before him, prepared him a pipe, and, the evening ceremonies being finished in the village temple, sent for the village priest.

Kim told the older children tales of the size and beauty of Lahore, of railway travel, and such-like city things, while the men talked, slowly as their cattle chew the cud.

'I cannot fathom it,' said the headman at last to the priest. 'How readest thou this talk?' The lama, his tale told, was silently telling his beads.

'He is a Seeker,' the priest answered. 'The land is full of such. Remember him who came only last month—the *faquir* with the tortoise?'

'Ay, but that man had right and reason, for Krishna[4] Himself appeared in a vision promising him Paradise without the burning-pyre if he journeyed to Prayag.[5] This man seeks no God who is within my knowledge.'

'Peace, he is old: he comes from far off, and he is mad,' the smooth-shaven priest replied. 'Hear me.' He turned to the lama. 'Three *koss* (six miles) to the westward runs the great road to Calcutta.'

'But I would go to Benares—to Benares.'

'And to Benares also. It crosses all streams on this side of Hind. Now my word to thee, Holy One, is rest here till tomorrow. Then take the road' (it was the Grand Trunk Road[6] he meant) 'and test each stream that it overpasses; for, as I understand, the virtue of thy River lies neither in one pool nor place, but throughout its length. Then, if thy Gods will, be assured that thou wilt come upon thy freedom.'

'That is well said.' The lama was much impressed by the plan. 'We will begin tomorrow, and a blessing on thee for showing old feet such a near road.' A deep, sing-song Chinese half-chant closed the sentence. Even the priest was impressed, and the headman feared an evil spell: but none could look at the lama's simple, eager face and doubt him long.

4. Hindu god, an incarnation of Vishnu the Preserver, part of the trinity that includes Brahma and Shiva.
5. The town of Allahabad, seventy-five miles west of Benares.
6. The great communications route constructed by the East India Company, running from Calcutta in east Bengal into northwest India and then south through Agra (see map, p. 245).

'Seest thou my *chela*?' he said, diving into his snuff-gourd with an important sniff. It was his duty to repay courtesy with courtesy.

'I see—and hear.' The headman rolled his eye where Kim was chatting to a girl in blue as she laid crackling thorns on a fire.

'He also has a Search of his own. No river, but a Bull. Yea, a Red Bull on a green field will some day raise him to honour. He is, I think, not altogether of this world. He was sent of a sudden to aid me in this search, and his name is Friend of all the World.'

The priest smiled. 'Ho, there, Friend of all the World,' he cried across the sharp-smelling smoke, 'what art thou?'

'This Holy One's disciple,' said Kim.

'He says thou art a *būt* (a spirit).'

'Can *būts* eat?' said Kim, with a twinkle. 'For I am hungry.'

'It is no jest,' cried the lama. 'A certain astrologer of that city whose name I have forgotten—'

'That is no more than the city of Umballa where we slept last night,' Kim whispered to the priest.

'Ay, Umballa was it? He cast a horoscope and declared that my *chela* should find his desire within two days. But what said he of the meaning of the stars, Friend of all the World?'

Kim cleared his throat and looked around at the village greybeards.

'The meaning of my Star is War,' he replied pompously.

Somebody laughed at the little tattered figure strutting on the brickwork plinth under the great tree. Where a native would have lain down, Kim's white blood set him upon his feet.

'Ay, War,' he answered.

'That is a sure prophecy,' rumbled a deep voice. 'For there is always war along the Border—as I know.'

It was an old, withered man, who had served the Government in the days of the Mutiny[7] as a native officer in a newly raised cavalry regiment. The Government had given him a good holding in the village, and though the demands of his sons, now grey-bearded officers on their own account, had impoverished him, he was still a person of consequence. English officials—Deputy Commissioners even—turned aside from the main road to visit him, and on those occasions he dressed himself in the uniform of ancient days, and stood up like a ramrod.

'But this shall be a great war—a war of eight thousand.' Kim's voice shrilled across the quick-gathering crowd, astonishing himself.

7. The Indian Mutiny of 1857–58 (or the Sepoy Rebellion), later known as the First War of Indian Independence.

'Redcoats[8] or our own regiments?' the old man snapped, as though he were asking an equal. His tone made men respect Kim.

'Redcoats,' said Kim at a venture. 'Redcoats and guns.'

'But—but the astrologer said no word of this,' cried the lama, snuffing prodigiously in his excitement.

'But *I* know. The word has come to me, who am this Holy One's disciple. There will rise a war—a war of eight thousand redcoats. From Pindi and Peshawur they will be drawn. This is sure.'

'The boy has heard bazar-talk,' said the priest.

'But he was always by my side,' said the lama. 'How should he know? *I* did not know.'

'He will make a clever juggler when the old man is dead,' muttered the priest to the headman. 'What new trick is this?'

'A sign. Give me a sign,' thundered the old soldier suddenly. 'If there were war my sons would have told me.'

'When all is ready, thy sons, doubt not, will be told. But it is a long road from thy sons to the man in whose hands these things lie.' Kim warmed to the game, for it reminded him of experiences in the letter-carrying line, when, for the sake of a few pice,[9] he pretended to know more than he knew. But now he was playing for larger things—the sheer excitement and the sense of power. He drew a new breath and went on.

'Old man, give *me* a sign. Do underlings order the goings of eight thousand redcoats—with guns?'

'No.' Still the old man answered as though Kim were an equal.

'Dost thou know who He is, then, that gives the order?'

'I have seen Him.'

'To know again?'

'I have known Him since he was a lieutenant in the *topkhana* (the Artillery).'

'A tall man. A tall man with black hair, walking thus?' Kim took a few paces in a stiff, wooden style.

'Ay. But that anyone may have seen.' The crowd were breathless-still through all this talk.

'That is true,' said Kim. 'But I will say more. Look now. First the great man walks thus. Then He thinks thus.' (Kim drew a forefinger over his forehead and downwards till it came to rest by the angle of the jaw.) 'Anon He twitches his fingers thus. Anon He thrusts his hat under his left armpit.' Kim illustrated the motion and stood like a stork.

The old man groaned, inarticulate with amazement; and the crowd shivered.

8. British infantry, who wore red tunics.
9. Small coins like pennies.

'So—so—so. But what does He when He is about to give an order?'

'He rubs the skin at the back of his neck—thus. Then falls one finger on the table and He makes a small sniffing noise through his nose. Then He speaks, saying: "Loose such and such a regiment. Call out such guns."'

The old man rose stiffly and saluted.

'"For"'—Kim translated into the vernacular the clinching sentences he had heard in the dressing-room at Umballa—'"For," says He, "we should have done this long ago. It is not war—it is a chastisement. Snff!"'

'Enough. I believe. I have seen Him thus in the smoke of battles. Seen and heard. It is He!'

'I saw no smoke'—Kim's voice shifted to the rapt singsong of the wayside fortune-teller. 'I saw this in darkness. First came a man to make things clear. Then came horsemen. Then came He, standing in a ring of light. The rest followed as I have said. Old man, have I spoken truth?'

'It is He. Past all doubt it is He.'

The crowd drew a long, quavering breath, staring alternately at the old man, still at attention, and ragged Kim against the purple twilight.

'Said I not—said I not he was from the other world?' cried the lama proudly. 'He is the Friend of all the World. He is the Friend of the Stars!'

'At least it does not concern us,' a man cried. 'O thou young soothsayer, if the gift abides with thee at all seasons, I have a red-spotted cow. She may be sister to thy Bull for aught I know—'

'Or I care,' said Kim. 'My Stars do not concern themselves with thy cattle.'

'Nay, but she is very sick,' a woman struck in. 'My man is a buffalo, or he would have chosen his words better. Tell me if she recover?'

Had Kim been at all an ordinary boy, he would have carried on the play; but one does not know Lahore city, and least of all the *fakir*s by the Taksali Gate, for thirteen years without also knowing human nature.

The priest looked at him sideways, something bitterly—a dry and blighting smile.

'Is there no priest, then, in the village? I thought I had seen a great one even now,' cried Kim.

'Ay—but—' the woman began.

'But thou and thy husband hoped to get the cow cured for a handful of thanks.' The shot told: they were notoriously the closest-fisted couple in the village. 'It is not well to cheat the temples. Give a

young calf to thine own priest, and, unless thy Gods are angry past recall, she will give milk within a month.'

'A master-beggar art thou,' purred the priest approvingly. 'Not the cunning of forty years could have done better. Surely thou hast made the old man rich?'

'A little flour, a little butter and a mouthful of cardamoms,' Kim retorted, flushed with the praise, but still cautious—'does one grow rich on that? And, as thou canst see, he is mad. But it serves me while I learn the road at least.'

He knew what the *faquirs* of the Taksali Gate were like when they talked among themselves, and copied the very inflection of their lewd disciples.

'Is his Search, then, truth or a cloak to other ends? It may be treasure.'

'He is mad—many times mad. There is nothing else.'

Here the old soldier hobbled up and asked if Kim would accept his hospitality for the night. The priest recommended him to do so, but insisted that the honour of entertaining the lama belonged to the temple—at which the lama smiled guilelessly. Kim glanced from one face to the other, and drew his own conclusions.

'Where is the money?' he whispered, beckoning the old man off into the darkness.

'In my bosom. Where else?'

'Give it me. Quietly and swiftly give it me.'

'But why? Here is no ticket to buy—'

'Am I thy *chela*, or am I not? Do I not safeguard thy old feet about the ways? Give me the money and at dawn I will return it.' He slipped his hand above the lama's girdle and brought away the purse.

'Be it so—be it so.' The old man nodded his head. 'This is a great and terrible world. I never knew there were so many men alive in it.'

Next morning the priest was in a very bad temper, but the lama was quite happy; and Kim had enjoyed a most interesting evening with the old man, who brought out his cavalry sabre and, balancing it on his dry knees, told tales of the Mutiny and young captains thirty years in their graves, till Kim dropped off to sleep.

'Certainly the air of this country is good,' said the lama. 'I sleep lightly, as do all old men; but last night I slept unwaking till broad day. Even now I am heavy.'

'Drink a draught of hot milk,' said Kim, who had carried not a few such remedies to opium-smokers of his acquaintance. 'It is time to take the Road again.'

'The long Road that overpasses all the rivers of Hind,' said the lama gaily. 'Let us go. But how thinkest thou, *chela*, to recompense these people, and especially the priest, for their great kindness?

Truly they are *bŭt-parast*, but in other lives, maybe, they will receive enlightenment. A rupee to the temple? The thing within is no more than stone and red paint, but the heart of man we must acknowledge when and where it is good.'

'Holy One, hast thou ever taken the Road alone?' Kim looked up sharply, like the Indian crows so busy about the fields.

'Surely, child: from Kulu to Pathânkot—from Kulu, where my first *chela* died. When men were kind to us we made offerings, and all men were well-disposed throughout all the Hills.'

'It is otherwise in Hind,' said Kim drily. 'Their Gods are many-armed and malignant. Let them alone.'

'I would set thee on thy road for a little, Friend of all the World— thou and thy yellow man.' The old soldier ambled up the village street, all shadowy in the dawn, on a gaunt, scissor-hocked[1] pony. 'Last night broke up the fountains of remembrance in my so-dried heart, and it was a blessing to me. Truly there is war abroad in the air. I smell it. See! I have brought my sword.'

He sat long-legged on the little beast, with the big sword at his side—hand dropped on the pommel—staring fiercely over the flat lands towards the North. 'Tell me again how He showed in thy vision. Come up and sit behind me. The beast will carry two.'

'I am this Holy One's disciple,' said Kim, as they cleared the village-gate. The villagers seemed almost sorry to be rid of them, but the priest's farewell was cold and distant. He had wasted some opium on a man who carried no money.

'That is well spoken. I am not much used to holy men, but respect is always good. There is no respect in these days—not even when a Commissioner Sahib comes to see me. But why should one whose Star leads him to war follow a holy man?'

'But he *is* a holy man,' said Kim earnestly. 'In truth, and in talk and in act, holy. He is not like the others. I have never seen such an one. We be not fortune-tellers, or jugglers, or beggars.'

'*Thou* art not. That I can see. But I do not know that other. He marches well, though.'

The first freshness of the day carried the lama forward with long, easy, camel-like strides. He was deep in meditation, mechanically clicking his rosary.

They followed the rutted and worn country road that wound across the flat between the great dark-green mango-groves, the line of the snow-capped Himalayas faint to the eastward. All India was at work in the fields, to the creaking of well-wheels, the shouting of ploughmen behind their cattle, and the clamour of the crows. Even

1. Weak-legged (a term coined by Kipling).

the pony felt the good influence and almost broke into a trot as Kim laid a hand on the stirrup-leather.

'It repents me that I did not give a rupee to the shrine,' said the lama on the last bead of his eighty-one.[2]

The old soldier growled in his beard, so that the lama for the first time was aware of him.

'Seekest thou the River also?' said he, turning.

'The day is new,' was the reply. 'What need of a river save to water at before sundown? I come to show thee a short lane to the Big Road.'

'That is a courtesy to be remembered, O man of good will. But why the sword?'

The old soldier looked as abashed as a child interrupted in his game of make-believe.

'The sword,' he said, fumbling it. 'Oh, that was a fancy of mine— an old man's fancy. Truly the police orders are that no man must bear weapons throughout Hind, but'—he cheered up and slapped the hilt—'all the constabeels hereabout know me.'

'It is not a good fancy,' said the lama. 'What profit to kill men?'

'Very little—as I know; but if evil men were not now and then slain it would not be a good world for weaponless dreamers. I do not speak without knowledge who have seen the land from Delhi south awash with blood.'

'What madness was that, then?'

'The Gods, who sent it for a plague, alone know. A madness ate into all the Army, and they turned against their officers. That was the first evil, but not past remedy if they had then held their hands. But they chose to kill the Sahibs' wives and children. Then came the Sahibs from over the sea and called them to most strict account.'

'Some such rumour, I believe, reached me once long ago. They called it the Black Year,[3] as I remember.'

'What manner of life hast thou led, not to know The Year? A rumour indeed! All earth knew, and trembled!'

'Our earth never shook but once—upon the day that the Excellent One received Enlightenment.'

'Umph! I saw Delhi shake at least; and Delhi is the navel of the world.'

'So they turned against women and children? That was a bad deed, for which the punishment cannot be avoided.'

'Many strove to do so, but with very small profit. I was then in a regiment of cavalry. It broke. Of six hundred and eighty sabres stood fast to their salt—how many, think you? Three. Of whom I was one.'

2. A significant number because prayer-beads in Indic religions come in multiples of nine.
3. The year of the Mutiny, 1857.

'The greater merit.'

'Merit! We did not consider it merit in those days. My people, my friends, my brothers fell from me. They said: "The time of the English is accomplished. Let each strike out a little holding for himself." But I had talked with the men of Sobraon, of Chilianwallah, of Moodkee and Ferozeshah.[4] I said: "Abide a little and the wind turns. There is no blessing in this work." In those days I rode seventy miles with an English Memsahib and her babe on my saddlebow. (Wow! That was a horse fit for a man!) I placed them in safety, and back came I to my officer—the one that was not killed of our five. "Give me work," said I, "for I am an outcast among my own kind, and my cousin's blood is wet on my sabre." "Be content," said he. "There is great work forward. When this madness is over there is a recompense."'

'Ay, there is a recompense when the madness is over, surely?' the lama muttered half to himself.

'They did not hang medals in those days on all who by accident had heard a gun fired. No! In nineteen pitched battles was I; in six-and-forty skirmishes of horse; and in small affairs without number. Nine wounds I bear; a medal and four clasps and the medal of an Order, for my captains, who are now generals, remembered me when the Kaisar-i-Hind[5] had accomplished fifty years of her reign, and all the land rejoiced. They said: "Give him the Order of Berittish India." I carry it upon my neck now. I have also my *jaghir* (holding) from the hands of the State—a free gift to me and mine. The men of the old days—they are now Commissioners—come riding to me through the crops—high upon horses so that all the village sees—and we talk out the old skirmishes, one dead man's name leading to another.'

'And after?' said the lama.

'Oh, afterwards they go away, but not before my village has seen.'

'And at the last what wilt thou do?'

'At the last I shall die.'

'And after?'

'Let the Gods order it. I have never pestered Them with prayers. I do not think They will pester me. Look you, I have noticed in my long life that those who eternally break in upon Those Above with complaints and reports and bellowings and weepings are presently sent for in haste, as our Colonel used to send for slack-jawed down-country men who talked too much. No, I have never wearied the Gods. They will remember this, and give me a quiet place where I

4. Four battles of the Sikh Wars (1845–49).
5. Empress of India (Queen Victoria).

can drive my lance in the shade, and wait to welcome my sons: I have no less than three—Rissaldar-majors[6] all—in the regiments.'

'And they likewise, bound upon the Wheel, go forth from life to life—from despair to despair,' said the lama below his breath, 'hot, uneasy, snatching.'

'Ay,' the old soldier chuckled. 'Three Rissaldar-majors in three regiments. Gamblers a little, but so am I. They must be well mounted; and one cannot take the horses as in the old days one took women. Well, well, my holding can pay for all. How thinkest thou? It is a well-watered strip, but my men cheat me. I do not know how to ask save at the lance's point. Ugh! I grow angry and I curse them, and they feign penitence, but behind my back I know they call me a toothless old ape.'

'Hast thou never desired any other thing?'

'Yes—yes—a thousand times! A straight back and a close-clinging knee once more; a quick wrist and a keen eye; and the marrow that makes a man. Oh, the old days—the good days of my strength!'

'That strength is weakness.'

'It has turned so; but fifty years since I could have proved it otherwise,' the old soldier retorted, driving his stirrup-edge into the pony's lean flank.

'But I know a River of great healing.'

'I have drank Gunga-water to the edge of dropsy. All she gave me was a flux,[7] and no sort of strength.'

'It is not Gunga. The River that I know washes from all taint of sin. Ascending the far bank one is assured of Freedom. I do not know thy life, but thy face is the face of the honourable and courteous. Thou hast clung to thy Way, rendering fidelity when it was hard to give, in that Black Year of which I now remember other tales. Enter now upon the Middle Way which is the path to Freedom. Hear the Most Excellent Law, and do not follow dreams.'

'Speak, then, old man,' the soldier smiled, half saluting. 'We be all babblers at our age.'

The lama squatted under the shade of a mango, whose shadow played checkerwise over his face; the soldier sat stiffly on the pony; and Kim, making sure that there were no snakes, lay down in the crotch of the twisted roots.

There was a drowsy buzz of small life in hot sunshine, a cooing of doves, and a sleepy drone of well-wheels across the fields. Slowly and impressively the lama began. At the end of ten minutes the old soldier slid from his pony, to hear better as he said, and sat with the reins round his wrist. The lama's voice faltered—

6. The highest rank available to Indian officers.
7. Diarrhea.

the periods lengthened. Kim was busy watching a grey squirrel. When the little scolding bunch of fur, close pressed to the branch, disappeared, preacher and audience were fast asleep, the old officer's strong-cut head pillowed on his arm, the lama's thrown back against the tree-bole, where it showed like yellow ivory. A naked child toddled up, stared, and, moved by some quick impulse of reverence, made a solemn little obeisance before the lama—only the child was so short and fat that it toppled over sideways, and Kim laughed at the sprawling, chubby legs. The child, scared and indignant, yelled aloud.

'Hai! Hai!' said the soldier, leaping to his feet. 'What is it? What orders? . . . It is . . . a child! I dreamed it was an alarm. Little one—little one—do not cry. Have I slept? That was discourteous indeed!'

'I fear! I am afraid!' roared the child.

'What is it to fear? Two old men and a boy? How wilt thou ever make a soldier, Princeling?'

The lama had waked too, but, taking no direct notice of the child, clicked his rosary.

'What is that?' said the child, stopping a yell midway. 'I have never seen such things. Give them me.'

'Aha,' said the lama, smiling, and trailing a loop of it on the grass:

> This is a handful of cardamons,
> This is a lump of *ghi*:
> This is millet and chillies and rice,
> A supper for thee and me!

The child shrieked with joy, and snatched at the dark, glancing beads.

'Oho!' said the old soldier. 'Whence hadst thou that song, despiser of this world?'

'I learned it in Pathânkot—sitting on a doorstep,' said the lama shyly. 'It is good to be kind to babes.'

'As I remember, before the sleep came on us, thou hadst told me that marriage and bearing were darkeners of the true light, stumbling-blocks upon the Way. Do children drop from Heaven in thy country? Is it the Way to sing them songs?'

'No man is all perfect,' said the lama gravely, recoiling the rosary. 'Run now to thy mother, little one.'

'Hear him!' said the soldier to Kim. 'He is ashamed for that he has made a child happy. There was a very good householder lost in thee, my brother. Hai, child!' He threw it a pice. 'Sweetmeats are always sweet.' And as the little figure capered away into the sunshine: 'They grow up and become men. Holy One, I grieve that I slept in the midst of thy preaching. Forgive me.'

'We be two old men,' said the lama. 'The fault is mine. I listened to thy talk of the world and its madness, and one fault led to the next.'

'Hear him! What harm do thy Gods suffer from play with a babe? And that song was very well sung. Let us go on and I will sing thee the song of Nikal Seyn[8] before Delhi—the old song.'

And they fared out from the gloom of the mango tope,[9] the old man's high, shrill voice ringing across the field, as wail by long-drawn wail he unfolded the story of Nikal Seyn (Nicholson)—the song that men sing in the Punjab to this day. Kim was delighted, and the lama listened with deep interest.

'*Ahi! Nikal Seyn is dead—he died before Delhi! Lances of the North, take vengeance for Nikal Seyn.*' He quavered it out to the end, marking the trills with the flat of his sword on the pony's rump.

'And now we come to the Big Road,' said he, after receiving the compliments of Kim; for the lama was markedly silent.[1] 'It is long since I have ridden this way, but thy boy's talk stirred me. See, Holy One—the Great Road which is the backbone of all Hind. For the most part it is shaded, as here, with four lines of trees; the middle road—all hard—takes the quick traffic. In the days before rail-carriages the Sahibs travelled up and down here in hundreds. Now there are only country-carts and such like. Left and right is the rougher road for the heavy carts—grain and cotton and timber, folder, lime and hides. A man goes in safety here—for at every few *koss* is a police-station. The police are thieves and extortioners (I myself would patrol it with cavalry—young recruits under a strong captain), but at least they do not suffer any rivals. All castes and kinds of men move here. Look! Brahmins and chumars,[2] bankers and tinkers, barbers and bunnias,[3] pilgrims and potters—all the world going and coming. It is to me as a river from which I am withdrawn like a log after a flood.'

And truly the Grand Trunk Road is a wonderful spectacle. It runs straight, bearing without crowding India's traffic for fifteen hundred miles—such a river of life as nowhere else exists in the world. They looked at the green-arched, shade-flecked length of it, the white breadth speckled with slow-pacing folk; and the two-roomed police-station opposite.

8. John Nicholson, commander of the British forces in the assault on Delhi in 1857, during which he was killed. The fiery-tempered Nicholson became the mythic embodiment of British power and heroism. See Lewis D. Wurgraft, *The Imperial Imagination* (Middletown, Conn.: Wesleyan University Press, 1983), for more on this controversial figure.

9. Grove.

1. The pacifist lama would not approve of a song of war.

2. Low-caste leather workers.

3. Shopkeepers.

'Who bears arms against the law?' a constable called out laughingly, as he caught sight of the soldier's sword. 'Are not the police enough to destroy evil-doers?'

'It was because of the police I brought it,' was the answer. 'Does all go well in Hind?'

'Rissaldar Sahib, all goes well.'

'I am like an old tortoise, look you, who puts his head out from the bank and draws it in again. Ay, this is the Road of Hindustan. All men come by this way . . .'

'Son of a swine, is the soft part of the road meant for thee to scratch thy back upon? Father of all the daughters of shame and husband of ten thousand virtueless ones, thy mother was devoted to a devil, being led thereto by her mother. Thy aunts have never had a nose for seven generations![4] Thy sister—What owl's folly[5] told thee to draw thy carts across the road? A broken wheel? Then take a broken head and put the two together at leisure!'

The voice and a venomous whip-cracking came out of a pillar of dust fifty yards away, where a cart had broken down. A thin, high Kathiawar mare, with eyes and nostrils aflame, rocketed out of the jam, snorting and wincing as her rider bent her across the road in chase of a shouting man. He was tall and grey-bearded, sitting the almost mad beast as a piece of her, and scientifically lashing his victim between plunges.

The old man's face lit with pride. 'My child!' said he briefly, and strove to rein the pony's neck to a fitting arch.

. 'Am I to be beaten before the police?' cried the carter. 'Justice! I will have Justice—'

'Am I to be blocked by a shouting ape who upsets ten thousand sacks under a young horse's nose? That is the way to ruin a mare.'

'He speaks truth. He speaks truth. But she follows her man close,' said the old man. The carter ran under the wheels of his cart and thence threatened all sorts of vengeance.

'They are strong men, thy sons,' said the policeman serenely, picking his teeth.

The horseman delivered one last vicious cut with his whip and came on at a canter.

'My father!' He reigned back ten yards and dismounted.

The old man was off his pony in an instant, and they embraced as do father and son in the East.

4. They have had their noses cut as punishment for unfaithfulness.
5. Translates best as "idiot-child" because in India the owl is regarded as not wise but stupid.

Chapter 4

Good Luck, she is never a lady,
But the cursedest quean[1] alive,
Tricksy, wincing, and jady[2]—
Kittle to lead or drive.[3]
Greet her—she's hailing a stranger!
Meet her—she's busking[4] to leave!
Let her alone for a shrew to the bone
And the hussy comes plucking your sleeve!
 Largesse! Largesse, O Fortune!
 Give or hold at your will.
 If I've no care for Fortune,
 Fortune must follow me still!
 The Wishing-Caps.[5]

Then, lowering their voices, they spoke together. Kim came to rest under a tree, but the lama tugged impatiently at his elbow.

'Let us go on. The River is not here.'

'*Hai mai!* Have we not walked enough for a little? Our River will not run away. Patience, and he will give us a dole.'

'This,' said the old soldier suddenly, 'is the Friend of the Stars. He brought me the news yesterday. Having seen the very man Himself, in a vision, giving orders for the war.'

'Hm!' said his son, all deep in his broad chest. 'He came by a bazar-rumour and made profit of it.'

His father laughed. 'At least he did not ride to me begging for a new charger, and the Gods know how many rupees. Are thy brothers' regiments also under orders?'

'I do not know. I took leave and came swiftly to thee in case—'

'In case they ran before thee to beg. O gamblers and spendthrifts all! But thou hast never yet ridden in a charge. A good horse is needed there, truly. A good follower and a good pony also for the marching. Let us see—let us see.' He thrummed on the pommel.

'This is no place to cast accounts in, my father. Let us go to thy house.'

'At least pay the boy, then: I have no pice with me, and he brought auspicious news. Ho! Friend of all the World, a war is toward as thou hast said.'

'Nay, as I know, *the* war,' returned Kim composedly.

'Eh?' said the lama, fingering his beads, all eager for the road.

1. Unreliable woman.
2. Playful, shrinking, and worthless.
3. Hard to control.
4. Getting ready.
5. The third and last stanza of a poem by Kipling; it was included in *Songs from Books* in a slightly different version.

'My master does not trouble the Stars for hire. We brought the news—bear witness, we brought the news, and now we go.' Kim half-crooked his hand at his side.

The son tossed a silver coin through the sunlight, grumbling something about beggars and jugglers. It was a four-anna piece, and would feed them well for days. The lama, seeing the flash of the metal, droned a blessing.

'Go thy way, Friend of all the World,' piped the old soldier, wheeling his scrawny mount. 'For once in all my days I have met a true prophet—who was not in the Army.'

Father and son swung round together: the old man sitting as erect as the younger.

A Punjabi constable in yellow linen trousers slouched across the road. He had seen the money pass.

'Halt!' he cried in impressive English. 'Know ye not that there is a *takkus*[6] of two annas a head, which is four annas, on those who enter the Road from this side-road? It is the order of the Sirkar, and the money is spent for the planting of trees and the beautification of the ways.'

'And the bellies of the police,' said Kim, slipping out of arm's reach. 'Consider for a while, man with a mud head. Think you we came from the nearest pond like the frog, thy father-in-law? Hast thou ever heard the name of thy brother?'

'And who was he? Leave the boy alone,' cried a senior constable, immensely delighted, as he squatted down to smoke his pipe in the veranda.

'He took a label from a bottle of *belaitee-pani* (soda-water), and, affixing it to a bridge, collected taxes for a month from those who passed, saying that it was the Sirkar's order. Then came an Englishman and broke his head. Ah, brother, I am a town-crow, not a village-crow!'

The policeman drew back abashed, and Kim hooted at him all down the road.

'Was there ever such a disciple as I?' he cried merrily to the lama. 'All earth would have picked thy bones within ten mile of Lahore city if I had not guarded thee.'

'I consider in my own mind whether thou art a spirit, sometimes, or sometimes an evil imp,' said the lama, smiling slowly.

'I am thy *chela*.' Kim dropped into step at his side—that indescribable gait of the long-distance tramp all the world over.

'Now let us walk,' muttered the lama, and to the click of his rosary they walked in silence mile upon mile. The lama, as usual, was deep in meditation, but Kim's bright eyes were open wide. This broad,

6. Tax.

smiling river of life, he considered, was a vast improvement on the cramped and crowded Lahore streets. There were new people and new sights at every stride—castes he knew and castes that were altogether out of his experience.

They met a troop of long-haired, strong-scented Sansis[7] with baskets of lizards and other unclean food on their backs, their lean dogs sniffing at their heels. These people kept their own side of the road, moving at a quick, furtive jog-trot, and all other castes gave them ample room; for the Sansi is deep pollution. Behind them, walking wide and stiffly across the strong shadows, the memory of his leg-irons still on him, strode one newly released from the jail; his full stomach and shiny skin to prove that the Government fed its prisoners better than most honest men could feed themselves. Kim knew that walk well, and made broad jest of it as they passed. Then an Akali, a wild-eyed, wild-haired Sikh devotee in the blue-checked clothes of his faith, with polished-steel quoits glistening on the cone of his tall blue turban, stalked past, returning from a visit to one of the independent Sikh States, where he had been singing the ancient glories of the Khalsa[8] to College-trained princelings in top-boots and white-cord breeches. Kim was careful not to irritate that man; for the Akali's temper is short and his arm quick. Here and there they met or were overtaken by the gaily dressed crowds of whole villages turning out to some local fair; the women, with their babes on their hips, walking behind the men, the older boys prancing on sticks of sugar-cane, dragging rude brass models of locomotives such as they sell for a half-penny, or flashing the sun into the eyes of their betters from cheap toy mirrors. One could see at a glance what each had bought; and if there were any doubt it needed only to watch the wives comparing, brown arm against brown arm, the newly purchased dull glass bracelets that come from the North-West. These merrymakers stepped slowly, calling one to the other and stopping to haggle with sweetmeat-sellers, or to make a prayer before one of the wayside shrines—sometimes Hindu, sometimes Mussalman—which the low-caste of both creeds share with beautiful impartiality. A solid line of blue, rising and falling like the back of a caterpillar in haste, would swing up through the quivering dust and trot past to a chorus of quick cackling. That was a gang of *changars*—the women who have taken all the embankments of all the Northern railways under their charge—a flat-footed, big-bosomed, strong-limbed, blue-petticoated clan of earth-carriers, hurrying north on news of a job, and wasting no time by the road. They belong to the caste whose men do not count, and they walked

7. Gypsies of the untouchable caste who were reputed to eat dogs.
8. An inclusive term for the Sikhs, meaning "pure."

with squared elbows, swinging hips, and heads on high, as suits
women who carry heavy weights. A little later a marriage procession
would strike into the Grand Trunk with music and shoutings, and a
smell of marigold and jasmine stronger even than the reek of the
dust. One could see the bride's litter, a blur of red and tinsel, stag-
gering through the haze, while the bridegroom's bewreathed pony
turned aside to snatch a mouthful from a passing fodder-cart. Then
Kim would join the Kentish-fire[9] of good wishes and bad jokes,
wishing the couple a hundred sons and no daughters, as the saying
is. Still more interesting and more to be shouted over it was when a
strolling juggler with some half-trained monkeys, or a panting, fee-
ble bear, or a woman who tied goats' horns to her feet, and with
these danced on a slack-rope, set the horses to shying and the
women to shrill, long-drawn quavers of amazement.

The lama never raised his eyes. He did not note the money-lender
on his goose-rumped[1] pony, hastening along to collect the cruel
interest; or the long-shouting, deep-voiced little mob—still in mili-
tary formation—of native soldiers on leave, rejoicing to be rid of
their breeches and puttees,[2] and saying the most outrageous things
to the most respectable women in sight. Even the seller of Ganges-
water he did not see, and Kim expected that he would at least buy a
bottle of that precious stuff. He looked steadily at the ground, and
strode as steadily hour after hour, his soul busied elsewhere. But
Kim was in the seventh heaven of joy. The Grand Trunk at this point
was built on an embankment to guard against winter floods from the
foothills, so that one walked, as it were, a little above the country,
along a stately corridor, seeing all India spread out to left and right.
It was beautiful to behold the many-yoked grain and cotton wagons
crawling over the country roads: one could hear their axles, com-
plaining a mile away, coming nearer, till with shouts and yells and
bad words they climbed up the steep incline and plunged on to the
hard main road, carter reviling carter. It was equally beautiful to
watch the people, little clumps of red and blue and pink and white
and saffron, turning aside to go to their own villages, dispersing and
growing small by twos and threes across the level plain. Kim felt
these things, though he could not give tongue to his feelings, and so
contented himself with buying peeled sugar-cane and spitting the
pith generously about his path. From time to time the lama took
snuff, and at last Kim could endure the silence no longer.

'This is a good land—the land of the South!' said he. 'The air is
good; the water is good. Eh?'

9. Hubbub. The term originates from the noisy conduct adopted in Kent, England, during
 debates opposing the Catholic Relief Bill (1828–29).
1. Weak in the hindquarters.
2. Leggings.

'And they are all bound upon the Wheel,' said the lama. 'Bound from life after life. To none of these has the Way been shown.' He shook himself back to this world.

'And now we have walked a weary way,' said Kim. 'Surely we shall soon come to a *parao* (a resting-place). Shall we stay there? Look, the sun is sloping.'

'Who will receive us this evening?'

'That is all one. This country is full of good folk. Besides'—he sunk his voice beneath a whisper—'we have money.'

The crowd thickened as they neared the resting-place which marked the end of their day's journey. A line of stalls selling very simple food and tobacco, a stack of firewood, a police-station, a well, a horse-trough, a few trees, and, under them, some trampled ground dotted with the black ashes of old fires, are all that mark a *parao* on the Grand Trunk; if you except the beggars and the crows—both hungry.

By this time the sun was driving broad golden spokes through the lower branches of the mango-trees; the parakeets and doves were coming home in their hundreds; the chattering, grey-backed Seven Sisters,[3] talking over the day's adventures, walked back and forth in twos and threes almost under the feet of the travellers; and shufflings and scufflings in the branches showed that the bats were ready to go out on the night-picket.[4] Swiftly the light gathered itself together, painted for an instant the faces and the cart-wheels and the bullocks' horns as red as blood. Then the night fell, changing the touch of the air, drawing a low, even haze, like a gossamer veil of blue, across the face of the country, and bringing out, keen and distinct, the smell of wood-smoke and cattle and the good scent of wheaten cakes cooked on ashes. The evening patrol hurried out of the police-station with important coughings and reiterated orders; and a live charcoal ball in the cup of a wayside carter's hookah glowed red while Kim's eye mechanically watched the last flicker of the sun on the brass tweezers.

The life of the *parao* was very like that of the Kashmir Serai on a small scale. Kim dived into the happy Asiatic disorder which, if you only allow time, will bring you everything that a simple man needs.

His wants were few, because, since the lama had no caste scruples,[5] cooked food from the nearest stall would serve; but, for luxury's sake, Kim bought a handful of dung-cakes[6] to build a fire. All about, coming and going round the little flames, men cried for oil, or grain, or sweetmeats, or tobacco, jostling one another while they

3. Small birds.
4. Night guard duty.
5. The Hindu requirement that one's food be cooked by a member of one's own caste.
6. Dry cow dung used as fuel.

waited their turn at the well; and under the men's voices you heard from halted, shuttered carts the high squeals and giggles of women whose faces should not be seen in public.

Nowadays, well-educated natives are of opinion that when their womenfolk travel—and they visit a good deal—it is better to take them quickly by rail in a properly screened compartment; and that custom is spreading. But there are always those of the old rock[7] who hold by the use of their forefathers; and, above all, there are always the old women—more conservative than the men—who toward the end of their days go on a pilgrimage. They, being withered and undesirable, do not, under certain circumstances, object to unveiling. After their long seclusion, during which they have always been in business touch with a thousand outside interests, they love the bustle and stir of the open road, the gatherings at the shrines, and the infinite possibilities of gossip with like-minded dowagers.[8] Very often it suits a long-suffering family that a strong-tongued, iron-willed old lady should disport herself about India in this fashion; for certainly pilgrimage is grateful to the Gods. So all about India, in the most remote places, as in the most public, you find some knot of grizzled servitors in nominal charge of an old lady who is more or less curtained and hid away in a bullock-cart. Such men are staid and discreet, and when a European or a high-caste native is near will net their charge with most elaborate precautions; but in the ordinary haphazard chances of pilgrimage the precautions are not taken. The old lady is, after all, intensely human, and lives to look upon life.

Kim marked down a gaily ornamented *ruth* or family bullock-cart, with a broidered canopy of two domes, like a double-humped camel, which had just been drawn into the *parao*. Eight men made its retinue, and two of the eight were armed with rusty sabres—sure signs that they followed a person of distinction, for the common folk do not bear arms. An increasing cackle of complaints, orders, and jests, and what to a European would have been bad language, came from behind the curtains. Here was evidently a woman used to command.

Kim looked over the retinue critically. Half of them were thin-legged, grey-bearded Ooryas[9] from down country. The other half were duffle-clad, felt-hatted hillmen of the North; and that mixture told its own tale, even if he had not overheard the incessant sparring between the two divisions. The old lady was going south on a visit—probably to a rich relative, most probably to a son-in-law, who had sent up an escort as a mark of respect. The hillmen would be

7. Conservative beliefs.
8. Widows of wealthy landowners.
9. Members of a servant caste from Orissa, a province west of Bengal.

of her own people—Kulu[1] or Kangra folk. It was quite clear that she was not taking her daughter down to be wedded, or the curtains would have been laced home[2] and the guard would have allowed no one near the car. A merry and a high-spirited dame, thought Kim, balancing the dung-cake in one hand, the cooked food in the other, and piloting the lama with a nudging shoulder. Something might be made out of the meeting. The lama would give him no help, but, as a conscientious *chela*, Kim was delighted to beg for two.

He built his fire as close to the cart as he dared, waiting for one of the escort to order him away. The lama dropped wearily to the ground, much as a heavy fruit-eating bat cowers, and returned to his rosary.

'Stand farther off, beggar!' The order was shouted in broken Hindustani by one of the hillmen.

'Huh! It is only a *pahari* (a hillman),' said Kim over his shoulder. 'Since when have the hill-asses owned all Hindustan?'

The retort was a swift and brilliant sketch of Kim's pedigree for three generations.

'Ah!' Kim's voice was sweeter than ever, as he broke the dung-cake into fit pieces. 'In *my* country[3] we call that the beginning of love-talk.'

A harsh, thin cackle behind the curtains put the hillman on his mettle for a second shot.

'Not so bad—not so bad,' said Kim with calm. 'But have a care, my brother, lest we—*we*, I say—be minded to give a curse or so in return. And our curses have the knack of biting home.'

The Ooryas laughed; the hillman sprang forward threateningly. The lama suddenly raised his head, bringing his huge tam-o'-shanter hat into the full light of Kim's new-started fire.

'What is it?' said he.

The man halted as though struck to stone. 'I—I—am saved from a great sin,' he stammered.

'The foreigner has found him a priest at last,' whispered one of the Ooryas.

'*Hai!* Why is that beggar-brat not well beaten?' the old woman cried.

The hillman drew back to the cart and whispered something to the curtain. There was dead silence, then a muttering.

'This goes well,' thought Kim, pretending neither to see nor hear.

'When—when—he has eaten'—the hillman fawned on Kim— 'it—it is requested that the Holy One will do the honour to talk to one who would speak to him.'

1. Another word for Kangra, an area north of the Punjab in the lower Himalayas.
2. Laced up.
3. Punjab. Kim thinks of himself as a Punjabi rather than as an Englishman, at least when he is exchanging good-humored insults.

'After he has eaten he will sleep,' Kim returned loftily. He could not quite see what new turn the game had taken, but stood resolute to profit by it. 'Now I will get him his food.' The last sentence, spoken loudly, ended with a sigh as of faintness.

'I—I myself and the others of my people will look to that—if it is permitted.'

'It is permitted,' said Kim, more loftily than ever. 'Holy One, these people will bring us food.'

'The land is good. All the country of the South is good—a great and a terrible world,' mumbled the lama drowsily.

'Let him sleep,' said Kim, 'but look to it that we are well fed when he wakes. He is a very holy man.'

Again one of the Ooryas said something contemptuously.

'He is not a *faquir*. He is not a down-country beggar,' Kim went on severely, addressing the stars. 'He is the most holy of holy men. He is above all castes. I am his *chela*.'

'Come here!' said the flat thin voice behind the curtain; and Kim came, conscious that eyes he could not see were staring at him. One skinny brown finger heavy with rings lay on the edge of the cart, and the talk went this way:

'Who is that one?'

'An exceedingly holy one. He comes from far off. He comes from Tibet.'

'Where in Tibet?'

'From behind the snows—from a very far place. He knows the stars; he makes horoscopes; he reads nativities. But he does not do this for money. He does it for kindness and great charity. I am his disciple. I am called also the Friend of the Stars.'

'Thou art no hillman.'

'Ask him. He will tell thee I was sent to him from the Stars to show him an end to his pilgrimage.'

'Humph! Consider, brat, that I am an old woman and not altogether a fool. Lamas I know, and to these I give reverence, but thou art no more a lawful *chela* than this my finger is the pole of this wagon. Thou art a casteless Hindu—a bold and unblushing beggar, attached, belike, to the Holy One for the sake of gain.'

'Do we not all work for gain?' Kim changed his tone promptly to match that altered voice. 'I have heard'—this was a bow drawn at a venture[4]—'I have heard—'

'What hast thou heard?' she snapped, rapping with the finger.

'Nothing that I well remember, but some talk in the bazars, which is doubtless a lie, that even Rajahs—small Hill Rajahs—'

'But none the less of good Rajput blood.'

4. A biblical phrase meaning a speculative attempt. See 1 Kings 22.34.

'Assuredly of good blood. That these even sell the more comely of their womenfolk for gain. Down south they sell them—to zemindars[5] and such—all of Oudh.'[6]

If there be one thing in the world that the small Hill Rajahs deny it is just this charge; but it happens to be one thing that the bazars believe, when they discuss the mysterious slave-traffics of India. The old lady explained to Kim, in a tense, indignant whisper, precisely what manner and fashion of malignant liar he was. Had Kim hinted this when she was a girl, he would have been pommelled to death that same evening by an elephant. This was perfectly true.

'Ahai! I am only a beggar's brat, as the Eye of Beauty has said,' he wailed in extravagant terror.

'Eye of Beauty, forsooth! Who am I that thou shouldst fling beggar-endearments at me?' And yet she laughed at the long-forgotten word. 'Forty years ago that might have been said, and not without truth. Ay, thirty years ago. But it is the fault of this gadding up and down Hind that a king's widow must jostle all the scum of the land, and be made a mock by beggars.'

'Great Queen,' said Kim promptly, for he heard her shaking with indignation, 'I am even what the Great Queen says I am; but none the less is my master holy. He has not yet heard the Great Queen's order that—'

'Order? I order a Holy One—a Teacher of the Law—to come and speak to a woman? Never!'

'Pity my stupidity. I thought it was given as an order—'

'It was not. It was a petition. Does this make all clear?'

A silver coin clicked on the edge of the cart. Kim took it and salaamed[7] profoundly. The old lady recognized that, as the eyes and the ears of the lama, he was to be propitiated.

'I am but the Holy One's disciple. When he has eaten perhaps he will come.'

'Oh, villain and shameless rogue!' The jewelled forefinger shook itself at him reprovingly; but he could hear the old lady's chuckle.

'Nay, what is it?' he said, dropping into his most caressing and confidential tone—the one, he well knew, that few could resist. 'Is—is there any need of a son in thy family? Speak freely, for we priests—' That last was a direct plagiarism from a *faquir* by the Taksali Gate.

'We priests! Thou art not yet old enough to—' She checked the joke with another laugh. 'Believe me, now and again, we women, O

5. Landowners.
6. Norther.1 province between the Ganges River and Nepal. The rumors of slave-traffic in the following paragraph were persistently associated with Oudh.
7. A salaam is an Arabic greeting: "Peace," accompanied by a hand raised to bowed head.

priest, think of other matters than sons. Moreover, my daughter has borne her man-child.'

'Two arrows in the quiver are better than one; and three are better still.' Kim quoted the proverb with a meditative cough, looking discreetly earthward.

'True—oh, true. But perhaps that will come. Certainly those down-country Brahmins are utterly useless. I sent gifts and monies and gifts again to them, and they prophesied.'

'Ah,' drawled Kim, with infinite contempt, 'they prophesied!' A professional could have done no better.

'And it was not till I remembered my own Gods that my prayers were heard. I chose an auspicious hour, and—perhaps thy Holy One has heard of the Abbot of the Lung-Cho lamassery. It was to him I put the matter, and behold in the due time all came about as I desired. The Brahmin in the house of the father of my daughter's son has since said that it was through his prayers—which is a little error that I will explain to him when we reach our journey's end. And so afterwards I go to Buddh Gaya, to make *shraddha*[8] for the father of my children.'

'Thither go we.'

'Doubly auspicious,' chirruped the old lady. 'A second son at least!'

'O Friend of all the World!' The lama had waked, and, simply as a child bewildered in a strange bed, called for Kim.

'I come! I come, Holy One!' He dashed to the fire, where he found the lama already surrounded by dishes of food, the hillmen visibly adoring him and the Southerners looking sourly.

'Go back! Withdraw!' Kim cried. 'Do we eat publicly like dogs?' They finished the meal in silence, each turned a little from the other, and Kim topped it with a native-made cigarette.

'Have I not said an hundred times that the South is a good land? Here is a virtuous and high-born widow of a Hill Rajah on pilgrimage, she says, to Buddh Gaya. She it is sends us those dishes; and when thou art well rested she would speak to thee.'

'Is this also thy work?' The lama dipped deep into his snuff-gourd.

'Who else watched over thee since our wonderful journey began?' Kim's eyes danced in his head as he blew the rank smoke through his nostrils and stretched him on the dusty ground. 'Have I failed to oversee thy comforts, Holy One?'

'A blessing on thee.' The lama inclined his solemn head. 'I have known many men in my so long life, and disciples not a few. But to none among men, if so be thou art woman-born, has my heart gone

8. A ceremony to honor ancestors, performed at the holy Buddhist site of the Tree of Wisdom.

out as it has to thee—thoughtful, wise, and courteous; but something of a small imp.'

'And I have never seen such a priest as thou.' Kim considered the benevolent yellow face wrinkle by wrinkle. 'It is less than three days since we took the road together, and it is as though it were a hundred years.'

'Perhaps in a former life it was permitted that I should have rendered thee some service. Maybe'—he smiled—'I freed thee from a trap; or, having caught thee on a hook in the days when I was not enlightened, cast thee back into the river.'

'Maybe,' said Kim quietly. He had heard this sort of speculation again and again, from the mouths of many whom the English would not consider imaginative. 'Now, as regards that woman in the bullock-cart, I think she needs a second son for her daughter.'

'That is no part of the Way,' sighed the lama. 'But at least she is from the Hills. Ah, the Hills, and the snow of the Hills!'

He rose and stalked to the cart. Kim would have given his ears to come too, but the lama did not invite him; and the few words he caught were in an unknown tongue, for they spoke some common speech of the mountains. The woman seemed to ask questions which the lama turned over in his mind before answering. Now and again he heard the sing-song cadence of a Chinese quotation. It was a strange picture that Kim watched between drooped eyelids. The lama, very straight and erect, the deep folds of his yellow clothing slashed with black in the light of the *parao* fires precisely as a knotted tree-trunk is slashed with the shadows of the low sun, addressed a tinsel and lacquered *ruth* which burned like a many-coloured jewel in the same uncertain light. The patterns on the gold-worked curtains ran up and down, melting and re-forming as the folds shook and quivered to the night wind; and when the talk grew more earnest the jewelled forefinger snapped out little sparks of light between the embroideries. Behind the cart was a wall of uncertain darkness speckled with little flames and alive with half-caught forms and faces and shadows. The voices of early evening had settled down to one soothing hum whose deepest note was the steady chumping of the bullocks above their chopped straw, and whose highest was the tinkle of a Bengali dancing-girl's *sitar*.[9] Most men had eaten and pulled deep at their gurgling, grunting hookahs, which in full blast sound like bull-frogs.

At last the lama returned. A hillman walked behind him with a wadded cotton-quilt and spread it carefully by the fire.

'She deserves ten thousand grandchildren,' thought Kim. 'None the less, but for me, those gifts would not have come.'

9. Indian long-necked lute with a varying number of strings.

'A virtuous woman—and a wise one.' The lama slackened off, joint by joint, like a slow camel. 'The world is full of charity to those who follow the Way.' He flung a fair half of the quilt over Kim.

'And what said she?' Kim rolled up in his share of it.

'She asked me many questions and propounded many problems— the most of which were idle tales which she had heard from devil-serving priests who pretend to follow the Way. Some I answered, and some I said were foolish. Many wear the Robe, but few keep the Way.'

'True. That is true.' Kim used the thoughtful, conciliatory tone of those who wish to draw confidences.

'But by her lights she is most right-minded. She desires greatly that we should go with her to Buddh Gaya; her road being ours, as I understand, for many days' journey to the southward.'

'And?'

'Patience a little. To this I said that my Search came before all things. She had heard many foolish legends, but this great truth of my River she had never heard. Such are the priests of the lower hills! She knew the Abbot of Lung-Cho, but she did not know of my River—nor the tale of the Arrow.'

'And?'

'I spoke therefore of the Search, and of the Way, and of matters that were profitable; she desiring only that I should accompany her and make prayer for a second son.'

'Aha! "We women" do *not* think of anything save children,' said Kim sleepily.

'Now, since our roads run together for a while, I do not see that we in any way depart from our Search if so be we accompany her— at least as far as—I have forgotten the name of the city.'

'*Ohé!*' said Kim, turning and speaking in a sharp whisper to one of the Ooryas a few yards away. 'Where is your master's house?'

'A little behind Saharunpore,[1] among the fruit gardens.' He named the village.

'That was the place,' said the lama. 'So far, at least, we can go with her.'

'Flies go to carrion,' said the Oorya, in an abstracted voice.

'For the sick cow a crow; for the sick man a Brahmin.'[2] Kim breathed the proverb impersonally to the shadow-tops of the trees overhead.

The Oorya grunted and held his peace.

'So then we go with her, Holy One?'

1. Some fifty miles southeast of Umballa (Ambala). The woman's home is only slightly off their route.
2. The proverb means that as a crow picks out a sick cow's eyes, so a Brahmin will take what he can from a sick man.

'Is there any reason against? I can still step aside and try all the rivers that the road overpasses. She desires that I should come. She very greatly desires it.'

Kim stifled a laugh in the quilt. When once that imperious old lady had recovered from her natural awe of a lama he thought it probable that she would be worth listening to.

He was nearly asleep when the lama suddenly quoted a proverb: 'The husbands of the talkative have a great reward hereafter.' Then Kim heard him snuff thrice, and dozed off, still laughing.

The diamond-bright dawn woke men and crows and bullocks together. Kim sat up and yawned, shook himself, and thrilled with delight. This was seeing the world in real truth; this was life as he would have it—bustling and shouting, the buckling of belts, and beating of bullocks and creaking of wheels, lighting of fires and cooking of food, and new sights at every turn of the approving eye. The morning mist swept off in a whorl of silver, the parrots shot away to some distant river in shrieking green hosts: all the well-wheels within ear-shot went to work. India was awake, and Kim was in the middle of it, more awake and more excited than anyone, chewing on a twig that he would presently use as a toothbrush; for he borrowed right- and left-handedly from all the customs of the country he knew and loved. There was no need to worry about food—no need to spend a cowrie[3] at the crowded stalls. He was the disciple of a holy man annexed by a strong-willed old lady. All things would be prepared for them, and when they were respectfully invited so to do they would sit and eat. For the rest—Kim giggled here as he cleaned his teeth—his hostess would rather heighten the enjoyment of the road. He inspected her bullocks critically, as they came up grunting and blowing under the yokes. If they went too fast—it was not likely—there would be a pleasant seat for himself along the pole; the lama would sit beside the driver. The escort, of course, would walk. The old lady, equally of course, would talk a great deal, and by what he had heard that conversation would not lack salt. She was already ordering, haranguing, rebuking, and, it must be said, cursing her servants for delays.

'Get her her pipe. In the name of the Gods, get her her pipe and stop her ill-omened mouth,' cried an Oorya, tying up his shapeless bundles of bedding. 'She and the parrots are alike. They screech in the dawn.'

'The lead-bullocks! *Hai!* Look to the lead-bullocks!' They were backing and wheeling as a grain-cart's axle caught them by the horns. 'Son of an owl, where dost thou go?' This to the grinning carter.

3. Small white shell used as currency.

'*Ai! Yai! Yai!* That within there is the Queen of Delhi going to pray for a son,' the man called back over his high load. 'Room for the Queen of Delhi and her Prime Minister the grey monkey climbing up his own sword!'[4] Another cart loaded with bark for a down-country tannery followed close behind, and its driver added a few compliments as the *ruth*-bullocks backed and backed again.

From behind the shaking curtains came one volley of invective. It did not last long, but in kind and quality, in blistering, biting appropriateness, it was beyond anything that even Kim had heard. He could see the carter's bare chest collapse with amazement, as the man salaamed reverently to the voice, leaped from the pole, and helped the escort haul their volcano on to the main road. Here the voice told him truthfully what sort of wife he had wedded, and what she was doing in his absence.

'Oh, *shabash!*'[5] murmured Kim, unable to contain himself, as the man slunk away.

'Well done, indeed? It is a shame and a scandal that a poor woman may not go to make prayer to her Gods except she be jostled and insulted by all the refuse of Hindustan—that she must eat *gâli* (abuse) as men eat *ghi*. But I have yet a wag left to my tongue—a word or two well spoken that serves the occasion. And *still* am I without my tobacco! Who is the one-eyed and luckless son of shame that has not yet prepared my pipe?'

It was hastily thrust in by a hillman, and a trickle of thick smoke from each corner of the curtains showed that peace was restored.

If Kim had walked proudly the day before, disciple of a holy man, today he paced with tenfold pride in the train of a semi-royal procession, with a recognized place under the patronage of an old lady of charming manners and infinite resource. The escort, their heads tied up native-fashion, fell in on either side the cart, shuffling enormous clouds of dust.

The lama and Kim walked a little to one side; Kim chewing his stick of sugar-cane, and making way for no one under the status of a priest. They could hear the old lady's tongue clack as steadily as a rice-husker. She bade the escort tell her what was going on on the road; and so soon as they were clear of the *parao* she flung back the curtains and peered out, her veil a third across her face. Her men did not eye her directly when she addressed them, and thus the proprieties were more or less observed.

A dark, sallowish District Superintendent of Police, faultlessly uni-

4. The carter's scurrilous reference is to rumors regarding the relationship between the pre-Mutiny queen of Delhi, Zeenat Mahal, wife of the elderly king, Bahadur Shah, and the younger prime minister.
5. Well done.

formed, an Englishman, trotted by on a tired horse, and, seeing from her retinue what manner of person she was, chaffed her.

'O mother,' he cried, 'do they do this in the zenanas?[6] Suppose an Englishman came by and saw that thou hadst no nose?'

'What?' she shrilled back. 'Thine own mother has no nose? Why say so, then, on the open road?'

It was a fair counter. The Englishman threw up his hand with the gesture of a man hit at sword-play. She laughed and nodded.

'Is this a face to tempt virtue aside?' She withdrew all her veil and stared at him.

It was by no means lovely, but as the man gathered up his reins he called it a Moon of Paradise, a Disturber of Integrity, and a few other fantastic epithets which doubled her up with mirth.

'That is a *nut-cut* (rogue),' she said. 'All police-constables are *nut-cuts*; but the police-wallahs are the worst. *Hai*, my son, thou hast never learned all that since thou camest from *Belait* (Europe). Who suckled thee?'

'A *pahareen*—a hillwoman of Dalhousie,[7] my mother. Keep thy beauty under a shade—O Dispenser of Delights,' and he was gone.

'These be the sort'—she took a fine judicial tone, and stuffed her mouth with *pan*—'These be the sort to oversee justice. They know the land and the customs of the land. The others, all new from Europe, suckled by white women and learning our tongues from books, are worse than the pestilence. They do harm to Kings.' Then she told a long, long tale to the world at large, of an ignorant young policeman who had disturbed some small Hill Rajah, a ninth cousin of her own, in the matter of a trivial land-case, winding up with a quotation from a work by no means devotional.

Then her mood changed, and she bade one of the escort ask whether the lama would walk alongside and discuss matters of religion. So Kim dropped back into the dust and returned to his sugarcane. For an hour or more the lama's tam-o'-shanter showed like a moon through the haze; and, from all he heard, Kim gathered that the old woman wept. One of the Ooryas half apologized for his rudeness overnight, saying that he had never known his mistress of so bland a temper, and he ascribed it to the presence of the strange priest. Personally, he believed in Brahmins, though, like all natives, he was acutely aware of their cunning and their greed. Still, when Brahmins but irritated with begging demands the mother of his master's wife, and when she sent them away so angry that they cursed the whole retinue (which was the real reason of the second off-side bullock going lame, and of the pole breaking the night

6. Women's quarters.
7. A hill station in northern Punjab. The English policeman implies that he got his toughness from his Indian wet nurse.

before), he was prepared to accept any priest of any other denomination in or out of India. To this Kim assented with wise nods, and bade the Oorya observe that the lama took no money, and that the cost of his and Kim's food would be repaid a hundred times in the good luck that would attend the caravan henceforward. He also told stories of Lahore city, and sang a song or two which made the escort laugh. As a town-mouse well acquainted with the latest songs by the most fashionable composers—they are women for the most part— Kim had a distinct advantage over men from a little fruit-village behind Saharunpore, but he let that advantage be inferred.

At noon they turned aside to eat, and the meal was good, plentiful, and well-served on plates of clean leaves, in decency, out of drift of the dust. They gave the scraps to certain beggars, that all requirements might be fulfilled, and sat down to a long, luxurious smoke. The old lady had retreated behind her curtains, but mixed most freely in the talk, her servants arguing with and contradicting her as servants do throughout the East. She compared the cool and the pines of the Kangra and Kulu hills with the dust and the mangoes of the South; she told a tale of some old local Gods at the edge of her husband's territory; she roundly abused the tobacco which she was then smoking, reviled all Brahmins, and speculated without reserve on the coming of many grandsons.

Chapter 5

> Here come I to my own again—
> Fed, forgiven, and known again—
> Claimed by bone of my bone again,
> And sib[1] to flesh of my flesh!
> The fatted calf is dressed for me,
> But the husks have greater zest for me . . .
> I think my pigs will be best for me,
> So I'm off to the styes afresh.
> *The Prodigal Son.*[2]

Once more the lazy, string-tied, shuffling procession got under way, and she slept till they reached the next halting-stage. It was a very short march, and time lacked an hour to sundown, so Kim cast about for means of amusement.

1. Related.
2. Published with revisions in *Songs from Books*. Kipling's poem alludes to Jesus' parable of the Prodigal Son in Luke 15. In this story, a son wastes his inheritance and ends up eating out of a trough with pigs. He returns home and his forgiving father kills a fatted calf in his honor. By placing the poem as an epigraph to this chapter, Kipling suggests a link between Kim and his version of the prodigal son, who prefers the pigsty to the fatted calf.

'But why not sit and rest?' said one of the escort. 'Only the devils and the English walk to and fro without reason.'

'Never make friends with the Devil, a Monkey, or a Boy. No man knows what they will do next,' said his fellow.

Kim turned a scornful back—he did not want to hear the old story how the Devil played with the boys and repented of it—and walked idly across country.

The lama strode after him. All that day, whenever they passed a stream, he had turned aside to look at it, but in no case had he received any warning that he had found his River. Insensibly, too, the comfort of speaking to someone in a reasonable tongue,[3] and of being properly considered and respected as her spiritual adviser by a well-born woman, had weaned his thoughts a little from the Search. And further, he was prepared to spend serene years in his quest; having nothing of the white man's impatience, but a great faith.

'Where goest thou?' he called after Kim.

'Nowhither—it was a small march, and all this'—Kim waved his hands abroad—'is new to me.'

'She is beyond question a wise and a discerning woman. But it is hard to meditate when—'

'All women are thus.' Kim spoke as might have Solomon.[4]

'Before the lamassery was a broad platform,' the lama muttered, looping up the well-worn rosary, 'of stone. On that I have left the marks of my feet—pacing to and fro with these.' He clicked the beads, and began the *Om mane pudme hum*'s of his devotion; grateful for the cool, the quiet, and the absence of dust.

One thing after another drew Kim's idle eye across the plain. There was no purpose in his wanderings, except that the build of the huts near by seemed new, and he wished to investigate.

They came out on a broad tract of grazing-ground, brown and purple in the afternoon light, with a heavy clump of mangoes in the centre. It struck Kim as curious that no shrine stood in so eligible a spot: the boy was observing as any priest for these things. Far across the plain walked side by side four men, made small by the distance. He looked intently under his curved palms and caught the sheen of brass.

'Soldiers. White soldiers!' said he. 'Let us see.'

'It is always soldiers when thou and I go out alone together. But I have never seen the white soldiers.'

'They do no harm except when they are drunk. Keep behind this tree.'

3. The hill-people speak a dialect of the lama's native language.
4. Wise king of the ancient Hebrews. The biblical books of Proverbs and Ecclesiastes, traditionally attributed to Solomon, are full of generalizations like Kim's.

They stepped behind the thick trunks in the cool dark of the mango-tope. Two little figures halted; the other two came forward uncertainly. They were the advance-party of a regiment on the march, sent out, as usual, to mark the camp. They bore five-foot sticks with fluttering flags, and called to each other as they spread over the flat earth. At last they entered the mango-grove, walking heavily.

'It's here or hereabouts—officers' tents under the trees, I take it, an' the rest of us can stay outside. Have they marked out for the baggage-wagons behind?'

They cried again to their comrades in the distance, and the rough answer came back faint and mellowed.

'Shove the flag in here, then,' said one.

'What do they prepare?' said the lama, wonderstruck. 'This is a great and terrible world. What is the device on the flag?'

A soldier thrust a stave within a few feet of them, grunted discontentedly, pulled it up again, conferred with his companion, who looked up and down the shaded cave of greenery, and returned it.

Kim stared with all his eyes, his breath coming short and sharp between his teeth. The soldiers stamped off into the sunshine.

'O Holy One!' he gasped. 'My horoscope! The drawing in the dust by the priest at Umballa! Remember what he said. First come two— *ferashes*[5]—to make all things ready—in a dark place, as it is always at the beginning of a vision.'

'But this is not vision,' said the lama. 'It is the world's Illusion, and no more.'

'And after them comes the Bull—the Red Bull on the green field. Look! It is he!'

He pointed to the flag that was snap-snapping in the evening breeze not ten feet away. It was no more than an ordinary camp marking-flag; but the regiment, always punctilious in matters of millinery, had charged it with the regimental device, the Red Bull, which is the crest of the Mavericks—the great Red Bull on a background of Irish green.

'I see, and now I remember,' said the lama. 'Certainly it is thy Bull. Certainly, also, the two men came to make all ready.'

'They are soldiers—white soldiers. What said the priest? "The sign over against the Bull is the sign of War and armed men." Holy One, this thing touches my Search.'

'True. It is true.' The lama stared fixedly at the device that flamed like a ruby in the dusk. 'The priest at Umballa said that thine was the sign of War.'

'What is to do now?'

'Wait. Let us wait.'

5. Servants or couriers.

'Even now the darkness clears,' said Kim. It was only natural that the descending sun should at last strike through the tree-trunks, across the grove, filling it with mealy gold light for a few minutes; but to Kim it was the crown of the Umballa Brahmin's prophecy.

'Hark!' said the lama. 'One beats a drum—far off!'

At first the sound, carrying diluted through the still air, resembled the beating of an artery in the head. Soon a sharpness was added.

'Ah! The music,' Kim explained. He knew the sound of a regimental band, but it amazed the lama.

At the far end of the plain a heavy, dusty column crawled in sight. Then the wind brought the tune:[6]

> We crave your condescension
> To tell you what we know
> Of marching in the Mulligan Guards
> To Sligo Port below!

Here broke in the shrill-tongued fifes:

> We shouldered arms,
> We marched—we marched away.
> From Phoenix Park
> We marched to Dublin Bay.
> The drums and the fifes,
> Oh, sweetly they did play,
> As we marched—marched—marched—with the
> Mulligan Guards!

It was the band of the Mavericks playing the regiment to camp; for the men were route-marching with their baggage. The rippling column swung into the level—carts behind it—divided left and right, ran about like an ant-hill, and . . .

'But this is sorcery!' said the lama.

The plain dotted itself with tents that seemed to rise, all spread, from the carts. Another rush of men invaded the grove, pitched a huge tent in silence, ran up yet eight or nine more by the side of it, unearthed cooking-pots, pans, and bundles, which were taken possession of by a crowd of native servants; and behold the mango-tope turned into an orderly town as they watched!

'Let us go,' said the lama, sinking back afraid, as the fires twinkled and white officers with jingling swords stalked into the Mess-tent.

'Stand back in the shadow. No one can see beyond the light of a fire,' said Kim, his eyes still on the flag. He had never before watched the routine of a seasoned regiment pitching camp in thirty minutes.

6. The tune is "The Mulligan Guards," the title song from an operetta by the Americans Harrigan and Hart. Their comic marching song links the Mavericks to stage Irishness, or the stereotyped representation of Irishness on the popular stage.

'Look! look! look!' clucked the lama. 'Yonder comes a priest.' It was Bennett, the Church of England Chaplain of the regiment, limping in dusty black. One of his flock had made some rude remarks about the Chaplain's mettle; and to abash him Bennett had marched step by step with the men that day. The black dress, gold cross on the watch-chain, the hairless face, and the soft, black wideawake hat[7] would have marked him as a holy man anywhere in all India. He dropped into a camp-chair by the door of the Mess-tent and slid off his boots. Three or four officers gathered round him, laughing and joking over his exploit.

'The talk of white men is wholly lacking in dignity,' said the lama, who judged only by tone. 'But I considered the countenance of that priest and I think he is learned. Is it likely that he will understand our talk? I would talk to him of my Search.'

'Never speak to a white man till he is fed,' said Kim, quoting a well-known proverb. 'They will eat now, and—and I do not think they are good to beg from. Let us go back to the resting-place. After we have eaten we will come again. It certainly was a Red Bull—*my* Red Bull.'

They were both noticeably absent-minded when the old lady's retinue set their meal before them; so none broke their reserve, for it is not lucky to annoy guests.

'Now,' said Kim, picking his teeth, 'we will return to that place; but thou, O Holy One, must wait a little way off, because thy feet are heavier than mine and I am anxious to see more of that Red Bull.'

'But how canst thou understand the talk? Walk slowly. The road is dark,' the lama replied uneasily.

Kim put the question aside. 'I marked a place near to the trees,' said he, 'where thou canst sit till I call. Nay,' as the lama made some sort of protest, 'remember this is my Search—the Search for my Red Bull. The sign in the Stars was not for thee. I know a little of the customs of white soldiers, and I always desire to see some new things.'

'What dost thou not know of this world?' The lama squatted obediently in a little hollow of the ground not a hundred yards from the hump of the mango-trees dark against the star-powdered sky.

'Stay till I call.' Kim flitted into the dusk. He knew that in all probability there would be sentries round the camp, and smiled to himself as he heard the thick boots of one. A boy who can dodge over the roofs of Lahore city on a moonlight night, using every little patch and corner of darkness to discomfit his pursuer, is not likely to be checked by a line of well-trained soldiers. He paid them

7. A hat with a wide brim and a small nap; hence, "wideawake."

the compliment of crawling between a couple, and, running and halting, crouching and dropping flat, worked his way toward the lighted Mess-tent where, close pressed behind the mango-tree, he waited till some chance word should give him a returnable lead.[8]

The one thing now in his mind was further information as to the Red Bull. For aught he knew, and Kim's limitations were as curious and sudden as his expansions, the men, the nine hundred thorough devils of his father's prophecy, might pray to the beast after dark, as Hindus pray to the Holy Cow. That at least would be entirely right and logical, and the padre with the gold cross would be therefore the man to consult in the matter. On the other hand, remembering sober-faced padres whom he had avoided in Lahore city, the priest might be an inquisitive nuisance who would bid him learn. But had it not been proven at Umballa that his sign in the high heavens portended War and armed men? Was he not the Friend of the Stars as well as of all the World, crammed to the teeth with dreadful secrets? Lastly—and firstly as the undercurrent of all his quick thoughts— this adventure, though he did not know the English word, was a stupendous lark—a delightful continuation of his old flights across the housetops, as well as the fulfilment of sublime prophecy. He lay belly-flat and wriggled towards the Mess-tent door, a hand on the amulet round his neck.

It was as he suspected. The Sahibs prayed to their God; for in the centre of the Mess-table—its sole ornament when they were on the line of march—stood a golden bull fashioned from old-time loot of the Summer Palace at Pekin[9]—a red-gold bull with lowered head, ramping upon a field of Irish green. To him the Sahibs held out their glasses and cried aloud confusedly.

Now the Reverend Arthur Bennett always left Mess after that toast, and being rather tired by his march his movements were more abrupt than usual. Kim, with slightly raised head, was still staring at his totem on the table, when the Chaplain stepped on his right shoulder-blade. Kim flinched under the leather, and, rolling sideways, brought down the Chaplain, who, ever a man of action, caught him by the throat and nearly choked the life out of him. Kim then kicked him desperately in the stomach. Mr Bennett gasped and doubled up, but without relaxing his grip, rolled over again, and silently hauled Kim to his own tent. The Mavericks were incurable practical jokers; and it occurred to the Englishman that silence was best till he had made complete inquiry.

'Why, it's a boy!' he said, as he drew his prize under the light of the tent-pole lantern, then shaking him severely cried: 'What were

8. A phrase borrowed from card-playing: something he can respond to.
9. An international force that included British regiments looted the Chinese Summer Palace in 1860.

you doing? You're a thief. *Choor? Mallum?*[1] His Hindustani was
very limited, and the ruffled and disgusted Kim intended to keep to
the character laid down for him. As he recovered his breath he was
inventing a beautifully plausible tale of his relations to some scul-
lion, and at the same time keeping a keen eye on and a little under
the Chaplain's left arm-pit. The chance came; he ducked for the
doorway, but a long arm shot out and clutched at his neck, snapping
the amulet-string and closing on the amulet.

'Give it me. O, give it me. Is it lost? Give me the papers.'

The words were in English—the tinny, saw-cut English of the
native-bred, and the Chaplain jumped.

'A scapular,'[2] said he, opening his hand. 'No, some sort of heathen
charm. Why—why, do you speak English? Little boys who steal are
beaten. You know that?'

'I do not—I did not steal.' Kim danced in agony like a terrier at a
lifted stick. 'Oh, give it me. It is my charm. Do not thieve it from
me.'

The Chaplain took no heed, but, going to the tent door, called
aloud. A fattish, clean-shaven man appeared.

'I want your advice, Father Victor,' said Bennett. 'I found this boy
in the dark outside the Mess-tent. Ordinarily, I should have chas-
tised him and let him go, because I believe him to be a thief. But it
seems he talks English, and he attaches some sort of value to a
charm round his neck. I thought perhaps you might help me.'

Between himself and the Roman Catholic Chaplain of the Irish
contingent lay, as Bennett believed, an unbridgeable gulf, but it was
noticeable that whenever the Church of England dealt with a
human problem she was very likely to call in the Church of Rome.
Bennett's official abhorrence of the Scarlet Woman[3] and all her
ways was only equalled by his private respect for Father Victor.

'A thief talking English, is it? Let's look at his charm. No, it's not
a scapular, Bennett.' He held out his hand.

'But have we any right to open it? A sound whipping—'

'I did *not* thieve,' protested Kim. 'You have hit me kicks all over my
body. Now give me my charm and I will go away.'

'Not quite so fast. We'll look first,' said Father Victor, leisurely
rolling out poor Kimball O'Hara's *'ne varietur'* parchment, his
clearance-certificate, and Kim's baptismal certificate. On this last
O'Hara—with some confused idea that he was doing wonders for his
son—had scrawled scores of times: *'Look after the boy. Please look
after the boy'*—signing his name and regimental number in full.

1. Thief? Do you know?
2. A religious medal worn around the neck.
3. The Catholic Church.

'Powers of Darkness below!' said Father Victor, passing all over to Mr Bennett. 'Do you know what these things are?'

'Yes,' said Kim. 'They are mine, and I want to go away.'

'I do not quite understand,' said Mr Bennett. 'He probably brought them on purpose. It may be a begging trick of some kind.'

'I never saw a beggar less anxious to stay with his company, then. There's the makings of a gay mystery here. Ye believe in Providence, Bennett?'

'I hope so.'

'Well, I believe in miracles, so it comes to the same thing. Powers of Darkness! Kimball O'Hara! and his son! But then he's a native, and I saw Kimball married myself to Annie Shott. How long have you had these things, boy?'

'Ever since I was a little baby.'

Father Victor stepped forward quickly and opened the front of Kim's upper garment. 'You see, Bennett, he's not very black. What's your name?'

'Kim.'

'Or Kimball?'

'Perhaps. Will you let me go away?'

'What else?'

'They call me Kim Rishti ke. That is Kim of the Rishti.'

'What is that—"Rishti"?'

'*Eye*-rishti—that was the Regiment—my father's.'

'Irish—oh, I see.'

'Yess. That was how my father told me. My father, he has lived.'

'Has lived where?'

'Has lived. Of *course* he is dead—gone-out.'

'Oh! That's your abrupt way of putting it, is it?'

Bennett interrupted. 'It is possible I have done the boy an injustice. He is certainly white, though evidently neglected. I am sure I must have bruised him. I do not think spirits—'

'Get him a glass of sherry, then, and let him squat on the cot. Now, Kim,' continued Father Victor, 'no one is going to hurt you. Drink that down and tell us about yourself. The truth, if you've no objection.'

Kim coughed a little as he put down the empty glass, and considered. This seemed a time for caution and fancy. Small boys who prowl about camps are generally turned out after a whipping. But he had received no stripes; the amulet was evidently working in his favour, and it looked as though the Umballa horoscope and the few words that he could remember of his father's maunderings fitted in most miraculously. Else why did the fat padre seem so impressed, and why the glass of hot yellow drink from the lean one?

'My father, he is dead in Lahore city since I was very little. The woman, she kept *kabarri*[4] shop near where the hire-carriages are.' Kim began with a plunge, not quite sure how far the truth would serve him.

'Your mother?'

'*No!*'—with a gesture of disgust. 'She went out when I was born. My father, he got these papers from the Jadoo-Gher—what do you call that?' (Bennett nodded) 'because he was in—good-standing. What do you call that?' (again Bennett nodded). 'My father told me that. He said, too, and also the Brahmin who made the drawing in the dust at Umballa two days ago, *he* said, that I shall find a Red Bull on a green field and that the Bull shall help me.'

'A phenomenal little liar,' muttered Bennett.

'Powers of Darkness below, what a country!' murmured Father Victor. 'Go on, Kim.'

'I did *not* thieve. Besides, I am just now disciple of a very holy man. He is sitting outside. We saw two men come with flags, making the place ready. That is *always* so in a dream, or on account of a—a—prophecy. So I knew it was come true. I saw the Red Bull on the green field, and my father he said: "Nine hundred *pukka*[5] devils and the Colonel riding on a horse will look after you when you find the Red Bull!" I did not know what to do when I saw the Bull, but I went away and I came again when it was dark. I wanted to see the Bull again, and I saw the Bull again with the—the Sahibs praying to it. I think the Bull shall help me. The holy man said so too. He is sitting outside. Will you hurt him, if I call him a shout now? He is very holy. He can witness to all the things I say, and he knows I am not a thief.'

'"Sahibs praying to a bull!" What in the world do you make of that?' said Bennett. '"Disciple of a holy man!" Is the boy mad?'

'It's O'Hara's boy, sure enough. O'Hara's boy leagued with all the Powers of Darkness. It's very much what his father would have done—if he was drunk. We'd better invite the holy man. He may know something.'

'He does not know anything,' said Kim. 'I will show you him if you come. He is my master. Then afterwards we can go.'

'Powers of Darkness!' was all that Father Victor could say, as Bennett marched off, with a firm hand on Kim's shoulder.

They found the lama where he had dropped.

'The Search is at an end for me,' shouted Kim in the vernacular. 'I have found the Bull, but God knows what comes next. They will not hurt you. Come to the fat priest's tent with this thin man and

4. Junk.
5. Thoroughgoing.

see the end. It is all new, and they cannot talk Hindi. They are only uncurried[6] donkeys.'

'Then it is not well to make a jest of their ignorance,' the lama returned. 'I am glad if thou art rejoiced, *chela*.'

Dignified and unsuspicious, he strode into the little tent, saluted the Churches as a Churchman, and sat down by the open charcoal brazier. The yellow lining of the tent reflected in the lamplight made his face red-gold.

Bennett looked at him with the triple-ringed uninterest of the creed that lumps nine-tenths of the world under the title of 'heathen'.

'And what was the end of the Search? What gift has the Red Bull brought?' The lama addressed himself to Kim.

'He says, "What are you going to do?"' Bennett was staring uneasily at Father Victor, and Kim, for his own ends, took upon himself the office of interpreter.

'I do not see what concern this *faquir* has with the boy, who is probably his dupe or his confederate,' Bennett began. 'We cannot allow an English boy—Assuming that he is the son of a Mason, the sooner he goes to the Masonic Orphanage the better.'

'Ah! That's your opinion as Secretary to the Regimental Lodge,' said Father Victor; 'but we might as well tell the old man what we are going to do. He doesn't look like a villain.'

'My experience is that one can never fathom the Oriental mind. Now, Kimball, I wish you to tell this man what I say—word for word.'

Kim gathered the import of the next few sentences and began thus:

'Holy One, the thin fool who looks like a camel says that I am the son of a Sahib.'

'But how?'

'Oh, it is true. I knew it since my birth, but *he* could only find it out by rending the amulet from my neck and reading all the papers. He thinks that once a Sahib is always a Sahib, and between the two of them they purpose to keep me in this Regiment or to send me to a *madrissah* (a school). It has happened before. I have always avoided it. The fat fool is of one mind and the camel-like one of another. But that is no odds. I may spend one night here and perhaps the next. It has happened before. Then I will run away and return to thee.'

'But tell them that thou art my *chela*. Tell them how thou didst come to me when I was faint and bewildered. Tell them of our Search, and they will surely let thee go now.'

6. Ungroomed.

'I have already told them. They laugh, and they talk of the police.'

'What are you saying?' asked Mr Bennett.

'Oah. He only says that if you do not let me go it will stop him in his business—his ur-gent private af-fairs.' This last was a reminiscence of some talk with a Eurasian clerk in the Canal Department, but it only drew a smile, which nettled him. 'And if you *did* know what his business was you would not be in such a beastly hurry to interfere.'

'What is it then?' said Father Victor, not without feeling, as he watched the lama's face.

'There is a River in this country which he wishes to find so verree much. It was put out by an Arrow which—' Kim tapped his foot impatiently as he translated in his own mind from the vernacular to his clumsy English. 'Oah, it was made by our Lord God Buddha, you know, and if you wash there you are washed away from all your sins and made as white as cotton-wool.' (Kim had heard mission-talk in his time.) 'I am his disciple, and we *must* find that River. It is so verree valuable to us.'

'Say that again,' said Bennett. Kim obeyed, with amplifications.

'But this is gross blasphemy!' cried the Church of England.

'Tck! Tck!' said Father Victor sympathetically. 'I'd give a good deal to be able to talk the vernacular. A river that washes away sin! And how long have you two been looking for it?'

'Oh, many days. Now we wish to go away and look for it again. It is not here, you see.'

'I see,' said Father Victor gravely. 'But he can't go on in that old man's company. It would be different, Kim, if you were not a soldier's son. Tell him that the Regiment will take care of you and make you as good a man as your—as good a man as can be. Tell him that if he believes in miracles he must believe that—'

'There is no need to play on his credulity,' Bennett interrupted.

'I'm doing no such thing. He must believe that the boy's coming here—to his own Regiment—in search of his Red Bull is in the nature of a miracle. Consider the chances against it, Bennett. This one boy in all India, and our Regiment of all others on the line o' march for him to meet with! It's predestined on the face of it. Yes, tell him it's *Kismet*.[7] *Kismet, mallum?* (Do you understand?)'

He turned towards the lama, to whom he might as well have talked of Mesopotamia.

'They say,'—the old man's eye lighted at Kim's speech—'they say that the meaning of my horoscope is now accomplished, and that being led back—though as thou knowest I went out of curiosity—to these people and their Red Bull I must needs go to a *madrissah* and

7. Fate.

be turned into a Sahib. Now I make pretence of agreement, for at the worst it will be but a few meals eaten away from thee. Then I will slip away and follow down the road to Saharunpore. Therefore, Holy One, keep with that Kulu woman—on no account stray far from her cart till I come again. Past question, my sign is of War and of armed men. See how they have given me wine to drink and set me upon a bed of honour! My father must have been some great person. So if they raise me to honour among them, good. If not, good again. However it goes, I will run back to thee when I am tired. But stay with the Rajputni,[8] or I shall miss thy feet . . . Oah yess,' said the boy, 'I have told him everything you tell me to say.'

'And I cannot see any need why he should wait,' said Bennett, feeling in his trouser-pocket. 'We can investigate the details later— and I will give him a ru—'

'Give him time. Maybe he's fond of the lad,' said Father Victor, half arresting the clergyman's motion.

The lama dragged forth his rosary and pulled his huge hat-brim over his eyes.

'What can he want now?'

'He says'—Kim put up one hand. 'He says: Be quiett. He wants to speak to me by himself. You see, you do not know one little word of what he says, and I think if you talk he will perhaps give you very bad curses. When he takes those beads like that, you see, he always wants to be quiett.' - what nes leaned

The two Englishmen sat overwhelmed, but there was a look in Bennett's eye that promised ill for Kim when he should be relaxed to the religious arm.

'A Sahib and the son of a Sahib—' The lama's voice was harsh with pain. 'But no white man knows the land and the customs of the land as thou knowest. How comes it this is true?'

'What matter, Holy One?—but remember it is only for a night or two. Remember, I can change swiftly. It will all be as it was when I first spoke to thee under Zam-Zammah the great gun—'

'As a boy in the dress of white men—when I first went to the Wonder House. And a second time thou wast a Hindu. What shall the third incarnation be?' He chuckled drearily. 'Ah, *chela*, thou hast done a wrong to an old man because my heart went out to thee.'

'And mine to thee. But how could I know that the Red Bull would bring me to this business?'

The lama covered his face afresh, and nervously rattled the rosary. Kim squatted beside him and laid hold upon a fold of his clothing.

8. A female Rajput, sometimes called the woman of Kulu, widow of the Rajput raja. The feminine of a Raja, the term Rani flatters by addressing a woman as Queen.

'Now it is understood that the boy is a Sahib?' he went on in a muffled tone. 'Such a Sahib as was he who kept the images in the Wonder House.' The lama's experience of white men was limited. He seemed to be repeating a lesson. 'So then it is not seemly that he should do other than as the Sahibs do. He must go back to his own people.'

'For a day and a night and a day,' Kim pleaded.

'No, ye don't!' Father Victor saw Kim edging towards the door, and interposed a strong leg.

'I do not understand the customs of white men. The Priest of the Images in the Wonder House in Lahore was more courteous than the thin one here. This boy will be taken from me. They will make a Sahib of my disciple? Woe to me! How shall I find my River? Have *they* no disciples? Ask.'

'He says he is very sorree that he cannot find the River now any more. He says, Why have you no disciples, and stop bothering him? He wants to be washed of his sins.'

Neither Bennett nor Father Victor found any answer ready.

Said Kim in English, distressed for the lama's agony: 'I think if you will let me go now we will walk away quietly and not steal. We will look for that River like before I was caught. I wish I did not come here to find the Red Bull and all that sort of thing. I do not want it.'

'It's the very best day's work you ever did for yourself, young man,' said Bennett.

'Good heavens, I don't know how to console him,' said Father Victor, watching the lama intently. 'He can't take the boy away with him, and yet he's a good man—I'm sure he's a good man. Bennett, if you give him that rupee he'll curse you root and branch!'

They listened to each other's breathing—three—five full minutes. Then the lama raised his head, and looked forth across them into space and emptiness.

'And I am a Follower of the Way,' he said bitterly. 'The sin is mine and the punishment is mine. I made believe to myself—for now I see it was but make-belief—that thou wast sent to me to aid in the Search. So my heart went out to thee for thy charity and thy courtesy and the wisdom of thy little years. But those who follow the Way must permit not the fire of any desire or attachment, for that is all Illusion. As says . . .' He quoted an old, old Chinese text, backed it with another, and reinforced these with a third. 'I stepped aside from the Way, my *chela*. It was no fault of thine. I delighted in the sight of life, the new people upon the roads, and in thy joy at seeing these things. I was pleased with thee who should have considered my Search and my Search alone. Now I am sorrowful

because thou art taken away and my River is far from me. It is the Law which I have broken!'

'Powers of Darkness below!' said Father Victor, who, wise in the confessional, heard the pain in every sentence.

'I see now that the sign of the Red Bull was a sign for me as well as for thee. All Desire is red—and evil. I will do penance and find my River alone.'

'At least go back to the Kulu woman,' said Kim, 'otherwise thou wilt be lost upon the roads. She will feed thee till I run back to thee.'

The lama waved a hand to show that the matter was finally settled in his mind.

'Now,'—his tone altered as he turned to Kim,—'what will they do with thee? At least I may, acquiring merit, wipe out past ill.'

'Make me a Sahib—so they think. The day after tomorrow I return. Do not grieve.'

'Of what sort? Such an one as this or that man?' He pointed to Father Victor. 'Such an one as those I saw this evening—men wearing swords and stamping heavily?'

'Maybe.'

'That is not well. These men follow desire and come to emptiness. Thou must not be of their sort.'

'The Umballa priest said that my Star was War,' Kim interjected. 'I will ask these fools—but there is truly no need. I will run away this night, for all I wanted to see the new things.'

Kim put two or three questions in English to Father Victor, translating the replies to the lama.

Then: 'He says, "You take him from me and you cannot say what you will make him." He says, "Tell me before I go, for it is not a small thing to make a child."'

'You will be sent to a school. Later on, we shall see. Kimball, I suppose you'd like to be a soldier?'

'Gorah-log (white-folk). No-ah! No-ah!' Kim shook his head violently. There was nothing in his composition to which drill and routine appealed. 'I will not be a soldier.'

'You will be what you're told to be,' said Bennett; 'and you should be grateful that we're going to help you.'

Kim smiled compassionately. If these men lay under the delusion that he would do anything that he did not fancy, so much the better.

Another long silence followed. Bennett fidgeted with impatience, and suggested calling a sentry to evict the faquir.

'Do they give or sell learning among the Sahibs? Ask them,' said the lama, and Kim interpreted.

'They say that money is paid to the teacher—but that money the Regiment will give . . . What need? It is only for a night.'

'And—the more money is paid the better learning is given?' The lama disregarded Kim's plans for an early flight. 'It is no wrong to pay for learning. To help the ignorant to wisdom is always a merit.' The rosary clicked furiously as an abacus. Then he faced his oppressors.

'Ask them for how much money do they give a wise and suitable teaching? And in what city is that teaching given?'

'Well,' said Father Victor in English, when Kim had translated, 'that depends. The Regiment would pay for you all the time you are at the Military Orphanage; or you might go on the Punjab Masonic Orphanage's list (not that he or you 'ud understand what that means); but the best schooling a boy can get in India is, of course, at St Xavier's in Partibus[9] at Lucknow.' This took some time to interpret, for Bennett wished to cut it short.

'He wants to know how much?' said Kim placidly.

'Two or three hundred rupees a year.' Father Victor was long past any sense of amazement. Bennett, impatient, did not understand.

'He says: "Write that name and the money upon a paper and give it him." And he says you must write your name below, because he is going to write a letter in some days to you. He says you are a good man. He says the other man is a fool. He is going away.'

The lama rose suddenly. 'I follow my Search,' he cried, and was gone.

'He'll run slap into the sentries,' cried Father Victor, jumping up as the lama stalked out; 'but I can't leave the boy.' Kim made swift motion to follow, but checked himself. There was no sound of challenge outside. The lama had disappeared.

Kim settled himself composedly on the Chaplain's cot. At least the lama had promised that he would stay with the Rajput woman from Kulu, and the rest was of the smallest importance. It pleased him that the two padres were so evidently excited. They talked long in undertones, Father Victor urging some scheme on Mr Bennett, who seemed incredulous. All this was very new and fascinating, but Kim felt sleepy. They called men into the tent—one of them certainly was the Colonel, as his father had prophesied—and they asked him an infinity of questions, chiefly about the woman who looked after him, all of which Kim answered truthfully. They did not seem to think the woman a good guardian.

After all, this was the newest of his experiences. Sooner or later, if he chose, he could escape into great, grey, formless India, beyond tents and padres and colonels. Meantime, if the Sahibs were to be impressed, he would do his best to impress them. He too was a white man.

9. "Partibus" means literally "the country of the unbelievers."

After much talk that he could not comprehend, they handed him over to a sergeant, who had strict instructions not to let him escape. The Regiment would go on to Umballa, and Kim would be sent up, partly at the expense of the Lodge and in part by subscription, to a place called Sanawar.[1]

'It's miraculous past all whooping, Colonel,' said Father Victor, when he had talked without a break for ten minutes. 'His Buddhist friend has levanted[2] after taking my name and address. I can't quite make out whether he'll pay for the boy's education or whether he is preparing some sort of witchcraft on his own account.' Then to Kim: 'You'll live to be grateful to your friend the Red Bull yet. We'll make a man of you at Sanawar—even at the price o' making you a Protestant.'

'Certainly—most certainly,' said Bennett.

'But you will not go to Sanawar,' said Kim.

'But we *will* go to Sanawar, little man. That's the order of the Commander-in-Chief, who's a trifle more important than O'Hara's son.'

'You will not go to Sanawar. You will go to thee War.'

There was a shout of laughter from the full tent.

'When you know your own Regiment a trifle better you won't confuse the line of march with line of battle, Kim. We hope to go to "thee War" sometime.'

'Oah, I know all thatt.' Kim drew his bow again at a venture. If they were not going to the war, at least they did not know what he knew of the talk in the veranda at Umballa.

'I know you are not at thee war now; but I tell *you* that as soon as you get to Umballa you will be sent to the war—the new war. It is a war of eight thousand men, besides the guns.'

'That's explicit. D'you add prophecy to your other gifts? Take him along, sergeant. Take up a suit for him from the Drums, an' take care he doesn't slip through your fingers. Who says the age of miracles is gone by? I think I'll go to bed. My poor mind's weakening.'

At the far end of the camp, silent as a wild animal, an hour later sat Kim, newly washed all over, in a horrible stuff suit that rasped his arms and legs.

'A most amazin' young bird,' said the sergeant. 'He turns up in charge of a yellow-headed buck-Brahmin priest, with his father's Lodge certificates round his neck, talkin God knows what all of a red bull. The buck-Brahmin evaporates without explanations, an' the bhoy sets cross-legged on the Chaplain's bed prophesyin' bloody war to the men at large. Injia's a wild land for a God-fearin' man. I'll

1. Site of a military orphanage.
2. Run away.

just tie his leg to the tent-pole in case he'll go through the roof. What did ye say about the war?'

'Eight thousand men, besides guns,' said Kim. 'Very soon you will see.'

'You're a consolin' little imp. Lie down between the Drums an' go to bye-bye. Those two boys will watch your slumbers.'

Chapter 6

Now I remember comrades—
　　Old playmates on new seas—
Whenas we traded orpiment[1]
　　Among the savages.
Ten thousand leagues to southward,
　　And thirty years removed—
They knew not noble Valdez,
　　But me they knew and loved.
　　　　　Song of Diego Valdez.[2]

Very early in the morning the white tents came down and disappeared as the Mavericks took a side-road to Umballa. It did not skirt the resting-place, and Kim, trudging beside a baggage-cart under fire of comments from soldiers' wives, was not so confident as overnight. He discovered that he was closely watched—Father Victor on the one side, and Mr Bennett on the other.

In the forenoon the column checked. A camel-orderly handed the Colonel a letter. He read it, and spoke to a Major. Half a mile in the rear, Kim heard a hoarse and joyful clamour rolling down on him through the thick dust. Then someone beat him on the back, crying: 'Tell us how ye knew, ye little limb of Satan? Father dear, see if ye can make him tell.'

A pony ranged alongside, and he was hauled on to the priest's saddle-bow.

'Now, my son, your prophecy of last night has come true. Our orders are to entrain at Umballa for the Front tomorrow.'

'What is thatt?' said Kim, for 'front' and 'entrain' were newish words to him.

'We are going to "thee War," as you called it.'

'Of course you are going to thee War. I said last night.'

'Ye did; but, Powers o' Darkness, how did ye know?'

Kim's eyes sparkled. He shut his lips, nodded his head, and looked unspeakable things. The Chaplain moved on through the

1. Yellow dye.
2. Part of Kipling's fourteen-stanza poem about a captain in the Spanish Armada. His brother Pedro, also a sea captain, was captured and held for ransom in England.

dust, and privates, sergeants, and subalterns[3] called one another's attention to the boy. The Colonel, at the head of the column, stared at him curiously. 'It was probably some bazar rumour,' he said; 'but even then—' He referred to the paper in his hand. 'Hang it all, the thing was only decided within the last forty-eight hours.'

'Are there many more like you in India?' said Father Victor, 'or are you by way o' being a *lusus naturae?*'[4]

'Now I have told you,' said the boy, 'will you let me go back to my old man? If he has not stayed with that woman from Kulu, I am afraid he will die.'

'By what I saw of him he's as well able to take care of himself as you. No. Ye've brought us luck, an' we're goin' to make a man of you. I'll take ye back to your baggage-cart and ye'll come to me this evening.'

For the rest of the day Kim found himself an object of distinguished consideration among a few hundred white men. The story of his appearance in camp, the discovery of his parentage, and his prophecy, had lost nothing in the telling. A big, shapeless white woman on a pile of bedding asked him mysteriously whether he thought her husband would come back from the war. Kim reflected gravely, and said that he would, and the woman gave him food. In many respects, this big procession that played music at intervals— this crowd that talked and laughed so easily—resembled a festival in Lahore city. So far, there was no sign of hard work, and he resolved to lend the spectacle his patronage. At evening there came out to meet them bands of music, and played the Mavericks into camp near Umballa railway station. That was an interesting night. Men of other regiments came to visit the Mavericks. The Mavericks went visiting on their own account. Their pickets[5] hurried forth to bring them back, met pickets of strange regiments on the same duty; and, after a while, the bugles blew madly for more pickets with officers to control the tumult. The Mavericks had a reputation for liveliness to live up to. But they fell in on the platform next morning in perfect shape and condition; and Kim, left behind with the sick, women, and boys, found himself shouting farewells excitedly as the trains drew away. Life as a Sahib was amusing so far; but he touched it with a cautious hand. Then they marched him back in charge of a drummer-boy to empty, lime-washed barracks, whose floors were covered with rubbish and string and paper, and whose ceilings gave back his lonely footfall. Native-fashion, he curled himself up on a stripped cot and went to sleep. An angry man stumped down the veranda, woke him up, and said he was a schoolmaster. This was

3. Junior officers.
4. Freak of nature (Latin).
5. Sentries.

enough for Kim, and he retired into his shell. He could just puzzle
out the various English Police notices in Lahore city, because they
affected his comfort; and among the many guests of the woman who
looked after him had been a queer German who painted scenery for
the Parsee[6] travelling theatre. He told Kim that he had been 'on the
barricades in 'Forty-eight,'[7] and therefore—at least that was how it
struck Kim—he would teach the boy to write in return for food. Kim
had been kicked as far as single letters, but did not think well of
them.

'I do not know anything. Go away!' said Kim, scenting evil.
Hereupon the man caught him by the ear, dragged him to a room in
a far-off wing where a dozen drummer-boys were sitting on forms,
and told him to be still if he could do nothing else. This he managed
very successfully. The man explained something or other with white
lines on a black board for at least half an hour, and Kim continued
his interrupted nap. He much disapproved of the present aspect of
affairs, for this was the very school and discipline he had spent two-
thirds of his young life in avoiding. Suddenly a beautiful idea
occurred to him, and he wondered that he had not thought of it
before.

The man dismissed them, and first to spring through the veranda
into the open sunshine was Kim.

''Ere, you! 'Alt! Stop!' said a high voice at his heels. 'I've got to
look after you. My orders are not to let you out of my sight. Where
are you goin'?'

It was the drummer-boy who had been hanging round him all the
forenoon—a fat and freckled person of about fourteen, and Kim
loathed him from the soles of his boots to his cap-ribbons.

'To the bazar—to get sweets—for you,' said Kim, after thought.

'Well, the bazar's out o' bounds. If we go there we'll get a dressing-
down. You come back.'

'How near can we go?' Kim did not know what bounds meant, but
he wished to be polite—for the present.

''Ow near? 'Ow far, you mean! We can go as far as that tree down
the road.'

'Then I will go there.'

'All right. I ain't goin'. It's too 'ot. I can watch you from 'ere. It's
no good your runnin' away. If you did, they'd spot you by your
clothes. That's regimental stuff you're wearin'. There ain't a picket
in Umballa wouldn't 'ead you back quicker than you started out.'

This did not impress Kim as much as the knowledge that his rai-
ment would tire him out if he tried to run. He slouched to the tree

6. Parsees are descendants of the Zoroastrians who fled from Persia to India after the inva-
sion of the Muslim Arabs.
7. He had participated in the political riots in Paris.

at the corner of a bare road leading towards the bazar, and eyed the natives passing. Most of them were barrack-servants of the lowest caste. Kim hailed a sweeper, who promptly retorted with a piece of unnecessary insolence, in the natural belief that the European boy could not follow it. The low, quick answer undeceived him. Kim put his fettered soul into it, thankful for the late chance to abuse somebody in the tongue he knew best. 'And now, go to the nearest letter-writer in the bazar and tell him to come here. I would write a letter.'

'But—but what manner of white man's son art thou to need a bazar letter-writer? Is there not a schoolmaster in the barracks?'

'Ay; and Hell is full of the same sort. Do my order, you—you Od![8] Thy mother was married under a basket! Servant of Lal Beg' (Kim knew the God of the sweepers), 'run on my business or we will talk again.'

The sweeper shuffled off in haste. 'There is a white boy by the barracks waiting under a tree who is not a white boy,' he stammered to the first bazar letter-writer he came across. 'He needs thee.'

'Will he pay?' said the spruce scribe, gathering up his desk and pens and sealing-wax all in order.

'I do not know. He is not like other boys. Go and see. It is well worth.'

Kim danced with impatience when the slim young Kayeth[9] hove in sight. As soon as his voice could carry he cursed him volubly.

'First I will take my pay,' the letter-writer said. 'Bad words have made the price higher. But who art thou, dressed in that fashion, to speak in this fashion?'

'Aha! That is in the letter which thou shalt write. Never was such a tale. But I am in no haste. Another writer will serve me. Umballa city is as full of them as is Lahore.'

'Four annas,' said the writer, sitting down and spreading his cloth in the shade of a deserted barrack-wing.

Mechanically Kim squatted beside him—squatted as only the natives can—in spite of the abominable clinging trousers.

The writer regarded him sideways.

'That is the price to ask of Sahibs,' said Kim. 'Now fix me a true one.'

'An anna and a half. How do I know, having written the letter, that thou wilt not run away?'

'I must not go beyond this tree, and there is also the stamp to be considered.'

'I get no commission on the price of the stamp. Once more, what manner of white boy art thou?'

8. Member of a low caste of manual laborers.
9. Member of a caste of scribes and accountants.

'That shall be said in the letter, which is to Mahbub Ali, the horse-dealer in the Kashmir Serai, at Lahore. He is my friend.'

'Wonder on wonder!' murmured the letter-writer, dipping a reed in the inkstand. 'To be written in Hindi?"

'Assuredly. To Mahbub Ali then. Begin! *I have come down with the old man as far as Umballa in the train. At Umballa I carried the news of the bay mare's pedigree.*' After what he had seen in the garden, he was not going to write of white stallions.

'Slower a little. What has a bay mare to do . . . Is it Mahbub Ali, the great dealer?'

'Who else? I have been in his service. Take more ink. Again. *As the order was, so I did it. We then went on foot towards Benares, but on the third day we found a certain regiment.* Is that down?'

'Ay, *pulton*,'[1] murmured the writer, all ears.

'*I went into their camp and was caught, and by means of the charm about my neck, which thou knowest, it was established that I was the son of some man in the regiment: according to the prophecy of the Red Bull, which thou knowest was common talk of our bazar.*' Kim waited for this shaft to sink into the letter-writer's heart, cleared his throat, and continued: '*A priest clothed me and gave me a new name . . . One priest, however, was a fool. The clothes are very heavy, but I am a Sahib and my heart is heavy too. They send me to a school and beat me. I do not like the air and water here. Come then and help me, Mahbub Ali, or send me some money, for I have not sufficient to pay the writer who writes this.*'

'"Who writes this." It is my own fault that I was tricked. Thou art as clever as Husain Bux that forged the Treasury stamps at Nucklao.[2] But what a tale! What a tale! Is it true by any chance?'

'It does not profit to tell lies to Mahbub Ali. It is better to help his friends by lending them a stamp. When the money comes I will repay.'

The writer grunted doubtfully, but took a stamp out of his desk, sealed the letter, handed it over to Kim, and departed. Mahbub Ali's was a name of power in Umballa.

'That is the way to win a good account with the Gods,' Kim shouted after him.

'Pay me twice over when the money comes,' the man cried over his shoulder.

'What was you bukkin'[3] to that nigger about?' said the drummer-boy when Kim returned to the veranda. 'I was watchin' you.'

'I was only talkin' to him.'

'You talk the same as a nigger, don't you?'

1. Regiment. (The scribe repeats the last word he wrote.)
2. Lucknow (facetious mispronunciation).
3. Chatting idly; from the Urdu "bukkwas."

'No-ah! No-ah! I onlee speak a little. What shall we do now?'

'The bugles'll go for dinner in arf a minute. My Gawd! I wish I'd gone up to the Front with the Regiment. It's awful doin' nothin' but school down 'ere. Don't you 'ate it?'

'Oah yess!'

'I'd run away if I knew where to go to, but, as the men say, in this bloomin' Injia you're only a prisoner at large. You can't desert without bein' took back at once. I'm fair sick of it.'

'You have been in Be[4]—England?'

'W'y, I only come out last troopin' season with my mother. I should think I 'ave been in England. What a ignorant little beggar you are! You was brought up in the gutter, wasn't you?'

'Oah yess. Tell me something about England. My father he came from there.'

Though he would not say so, Kim of course disbelieved every word the drummer-boy spoke about the Liverpool suburb which was his England. It passed the heavy time till dinner—a most unappetizing meal served to the boys and a few invalids in a corner of a barrack-room. But that he had written to Mahbub Ali, Kim would have been almost depressed. The indifference of native crowds he was used to; but this strong loneliness among white men preyed on him. He was grateful when, in the course of the afternoon, a big |soldier took him over to Father Victor, who lived in another wing across another dusty parade-ground. The priest was reading an English letter written in purple ink. He looked at Kim more curiously than ever.

'An' how do you like it, my son, as far as you've gone? Not much, eh? It must be hard—very hard on a wild animal. Listen now. I've an amazin' epistle from your friend.'

'Where is he? Is he well? Oah! If he knows to write me letters, it is all right.'

'You're fond of him then?'

'*Of* course I am fond of him. He was fond of me.'

'It seems so by the look of this. He can't write English, can he?'

'Oah no. Not that I know, but *of* course he found a letter-writer who can write English verree well, and so he wrote. I *do* hope you understand.'

'That accounts for it. D'you know anything about his money affairs?' Kim's face showed that he did not.

'How can I tell?'

'That's what I'm askin'. Now listen if you can make head or tail o' this. We'll skip the first part . . . It's written from Jagadhir Road . . . "*Sitting on wayside in grave meditation, trusting to be favoured*

4. Kim is about to say the Hindi word for England: Belait.

with your Honour's applause of present step, which recommend your Honour to execute for Almighty God's sake. Education is greatest blessing if of best sorts. Otherwise no earthly use." Faith, the old man's hit the bull's-eye that time! "*If your Honour condescending giving my boy best educations Xavier*" (I suppose that's St Xavier's in Partibus) "*in terms of our conversation dated in your tent 15th instant*" (a business-like touch there!) "*then Almighty God blessing your Honour's suc-ceedings to third an' fourth generation and*"—now listen!—"*confide in your Honour's humble servant for adequate remuneration per hoondi*[5] *per annum three hundred rupees a year to one expensive edu-cation St Xavier, Lucknow, and allow small time to forward same per hoondi sent to any part of India as your Honour shall address yourself. This servant of your Honour has presently no place to lay crown of his head, but going to Benares by train on account of persecution of old woman talking so much and unanxious residing Saharunpore in any domestic capacity.*" Now what in the world does that mean?'

'She has asked him to be her *puro*—her clergyman—at Saharunpore, *I* think. He would not do that on account of his River. She *did* talk.'

'It's clear to you, is it? It beats me altogether. "*So going to Benares, where will find address and forward rupees for boy who is apple of eye, and for Almighty God's sake execute this education, and your peti-tioner as in duty bound shall ever awfully pray. Written by Sobrao Satai, Failed Entrance Allahabad University, for Venerable Teshoo Lama the priest of Such-zen looking for a River, address care of Tirthankars*[6] *Temple, Benares. P.M.—Please note boy is apple of eye, and rupees shall be sent per hoondi three hundred per annum. For God Almighty's sake.*" Now, is that ravin' lunacy or a business propo-sition? I ask you, because I'm fairly at my wits' end.'

'He says he will give me three hundred rupees a year? So he will give me them.'

'Oh, that's the way you look at it, is it?'

'*Of* course. If he says so!'

The priest whistled; then he addressed Kim as an equal.

'I don't believe it; but we'll see. You were goin' off today to the Military Orphanage at Sanawar, where the Regiment would keep you till you were old enough to enlist. Ye'd be brought up to the Church of England. Bennett arranged for that. On the other hand, if ye go to St Xavier's ye'll get a better education an'—an' can have the religion. D'ye see my dilemma?'

Kim saw nothing save a vision of the lama going south in a train with none to beg for him.

5. By check.
6. Jain priests'.

'Like most people, I'm going to temporize. If your friend sends the money from Benares—Powers of Darkness below, where's a street-beggar to raise three hundred rupees?—ye'll go down to Lucknow and I'll pay your fare, because I can't touch the subscription-money if I intend, as I do, to make ye a Catholic. If he doesn't, ye'll go to the Military Orphanage at the Regiment's expense. I'll allow him three days' grace, though I don't believe it at all. Even then, if he fails in his payments later on . . . but it's beyond me. We can only walk one step at a time in this world, praise God! An' they sent Bennett to the Front an' left me behind. Bennett can't expect everything.'

'Oah yess,' said Kim vaguely.

The priest leaned forward. 'I'd give a month's pay to find what's goin' on inside that little round head of yours.'

'There is nothing,' said Kim, and scratched it. He was wondering whether Mahbub Ali would send him as much as a whole rupee. Then he could pay the letter-writer and write letters to the lama at Benares. Perhaps Mahbub Ali would visit him next time he came south with horses. Surely he must know that Kim's delivery of the letter to the officer at Umballa had caused the great war which the men and boys had discussed so loudly over the barrack dinner-tables. But if Mahbub Ali did not know this, it would be very unsafe to tell him so. Mahbub Ali was hard upon boys who knew, or thought they knew, too much.

'Well, till I get further news'—Father Victor's voice interrupted the reverie. 'Ye can run along now and play with the other boys. They'll teach ye something—but I don't think ye'll like it.'

The day dragged to its weary end. When he wished to sleep he was instructed how to fold up his clothes and set out his boots; the other boys deriding. Bugles waked him in the dawn; the schoolmaster caught him after breakfast, thrust a page of meaningless characters under his nose, gave them senseless means, and whacked him without reason. Kim meditated poisoning him with opium borrowed from a barrack-sweeper, but reflected that, as they all ate at one table in public (this was peculiarly revolting to Kim, who preferred to turn his back on the world at meals), the stroke might be dangerous. Then he attempted running off to the village where the priest had tried to drug the lama—the village where the old soldier lived. But far-seeing sentries at every exit headed back the little scarlet figure. Trousers and jacket crippled body and mind alike, so he abandoned the project and fell back, Oriental-fashion, on time and chance. Three days of torment passed in the big, echoing white rooms. He walked out of afternoons under escort of the drummer-boy, and all he heard from his companions were the few useless words which seemed to make two-thirds of the white man's abuse.

Kim knew and despised them all long ago. The boy resented his
silence and lack of interest by beating him, as was only natural. He
did not care for any of the bazars which were in bounds. He styled
all natives 'niggers'; yet servants and sweepers called him abom-
inable names to his face, and, misled by their deferential attitude,
he never understood. This somewhat consoled Kim for the beatings.

On the morning of the fourth day a judgement overtook that
drummer. They had gone out together towards Umballa racecourse.
He returned alone, weeping, with news that young O'Hara, to
whom he had been doing nothing in particular, had hailed a scarlet-
bearded nigger on horseback; that the nigger had then and there
laid into him with a peculiarly adhesive quirt,[7] picked up young
O'Hara, and borne him off at full gallop. These tidings came to
Father Victor, and he drew down his long upper lip. He was already
sufficiently startled by a letter from the Temple of the Tirthankars
at Benares, enclosing a native banker's note of hand for three hun-
dred rupees, and an amazing prayer to 'Almighty God'. The lama
would have been more annoyed than the priest had he known how
the bazar letter-writer had translated his phrase 'to acquire merit'.

'Powers of Darkness below! Father Victor fumbled with the note.
'An' now he's off with another of his peep-o'-day[8] friends. I don't
know whether it will be a greater relief to me to get him back or to
have him lost. He's beyond my comprehension. How the Divil—yes,
he's the man I mean—can a street-beggar raise money to educate
white boys?'

Three miles off, on Umballa racecourse, Mahbub Ali, reining a
grey Kabuli[9] stallion with Kim in front of him, was saying:

'But, Little Friend of all the World, there is my honour and rep-
utation to be considered. All the officer-Sahibs in all the regi-
ments, and all Umballa, know Mahbub Ali. Men saw me pick thee
up and chastise that boy. We are seen now from far across this
plain. How can I take thee away, or account for thy disappearing
if I set thee down and let thee run off into the crops? They would
put me in jail. Be patient. Once a Sahib, always a Sahib. When
thou art a man—who knows?—thou wilt be grateful to Mahbub
Ali.'

'Take me beyond their sentries where I can change this red. Give
me money and I will go to Benares and be with my lama again. I do
not want to be a Sahib, and remember I *did* deliver that message.'

The stallion bounded wildly. Mahbub Ali had incautiously driven
home the sharp-edged stirrup. (He was not the new sort of fluent

7. Whip.
8. The Peep o' Day Boys were a Protestant secret society in eighteenth-century Ireland.
 They searched Catholic homes for arms.
9. From Kabul, capital of Afghanistan, famous for its horses.

horse-dealer who wears English boots and spurs.) Kim drew his own conclusions from that betrayal.

'That was a small matter. It lay on the straight road to Benares. I and the Sahib have by this time forgotten it. I send so many letters and messages to men who ask questions about horses, I cannot well remember one from the other. Was it some matter of a bay mare that Peters Sahib wished the pedigree of?'

Kim saw the trap at once. If he had said 'bay mare' Mahbub would have known by his very readiness to fall in with the amendment that the boy suspected something. Kim replied therefore:

'Bay mare. No. *I* do not forget my messages thus. It was a white stallion.'

'Ay, so it was. A white Arab stallion. But thou didst write "bay mare" to me.'

'Who cares to tell truth to a letter-writer?' Kim answered, feeling Mahbub's palm on his heart.

'Hi! Mahbub, you old villain, pull up!' cried a voice, and an Englishman raced alongside on a little polo-pony. 'I've been chasing you half over the country. That Kabuli of yours can go. For sale, I suppose?'

'I have some young stuff coming on made by Heaven for the delicate and difficult polo-game. He has no equal. He—'

'Plays polo and waits at table. Yes. We know all that. What the deuce have you got there?'

'A boy,' said Mahbub gravely. 'He was being beaten by another boy. His father was once a white soldier in the big war.[1] The boy was a child in Lahore city. He played with my horses when he was a babe. Now I think they will make him a soldier. He has been newly caught by his father's Regiment that went up to the war last week. But I do not think he wants to be a soldier. I take him for a ride. Tell me where thy barracks are and I will set thee there.'

'Let me go. I can find the barracks alone.'

'And if thou runnest away who will say it is not my fault?'

'He'll run back to his dinner. Where has he to run to?' the Englishman asked.

'He was born in the land. He has friends. He goes where he chooses. He is a *chabuk sawai* (a sharp chap). It needs only to change his clothing, and in a twinkling he would be a low-caste Hindu boy.'

'The deuce he would!' The Englishman looked critically at the boy as Mahbub headed towards the barracks. Kim ground his teeth. Mahbub was mocking him, as faithless Afghans will; for he went on:

'They will send him to a school and put heavy boots on his feet

1. The Second Afghan War (1878–80).

and swaddle him in these clothes. Then he will forget all he knows. Now, which of the barracks is thine?'

Kim pointed—he could not speak—to Father Victor's wing, all staring white near by.

'Perhaps he will make a good soldier,' said Mahbub reflectively. 'He will make a good orderly at least. I sent him to deliver a message once from Lahore. A message concerning the pedigree of a white stallion.'

Here was deadly insult on deadlier injury—and the Sahib to whom he had so craftily given that war-waking letter heard it all. Kim beheld Mahbub Ali frying in flame for his treachery, but for himself he saw one long grey vista of barracks, schools, and barracks again. He gazed imploringly at the clear-cut face in which there was no glimmer of recognition; but even at this extremity it never occurred to him to throw himself on the white man's mercy or to denounce the Afghan. And Mahbub stared deliberately at the Englishman, who stared as deliberately at Kim, quivering and tongue-tied.

'My horse is well trained,' said the dealer. 'Others would have kicked, Sahib.'

'Ah,' said the Englishman at last, rubbing his pony's damp withers with his whip-butt. 'Who makes the boy a soldier?'

'He says the Regiment that found him, and especially the Padre-sahib of that regiment.'

'There is the Padre!' Kim choked as bare-headed Father Victor sailed down upon them from the veranda.

'Powers o' Darkness below, O'Hara! How many more mixed friends do you keep in Asia?' he cried, as Kim slid down and stood helplessly before him.

'Good morning, Padre,' the Englishman said cheerily. 'I know you by reputation well enough. Meant to have come over and called before this. I'm Creighton.'

'Of the Ethnological Survey?'[2] said Father Victor. The Englishman nodded. 'Faith, I'm glad to meet ye then; an' I owe you some thanks for bringing back the boy.'

'No thanks to me, Padre. Besides, the boy wasn't going away. You don't know old Mahbub Ali.' The horse-dealer sat impassive in the sunlight. 'You will when you have been in the station a month. He sells us all our crocks. That boy is rather a curiosity. Can you tell me anything about him?'

'Can I tell you?' puffed Father Victor. 'You'll be the one man that could help me in my quandaries. Tell you! Powers o' Darkness, I'm bursting to tell someone who knows something o' the native!'

A groom came round the corner. Colonel Creighton raised his

2. Government organization responsible for the mapping of India. Creighton is director of the survey and of British intelligence in India. See the essays by Edward Said and Ian Baucom in this volume.

voice, speaking in Urdu. 'Very good, Mahbub Ali, but what is the use of telling me all those stories about the pony? Not one pice more than three hundred and fifty rupees will I give.'

'The Sahib is a little hot and angry after riding,' the horse-dealer returned, with the leer of a privileged jester. 'Presently, he will see my horse's points more clearly. I will wait till he has finished his talk with the Padre. I will wait under that tree.'

'Confound you!' The Colonel laughed. 'That comes of looking at one of Mahbub's horses. He's a regular old leech, Padre. Wait, then, if thou hast so much time to spare, Mahbub. Now I'm at your service, Padre. Where is the boy? Oh, he's gone off to collogue[3] with Mahbub. Queer sort of boy. Might I ask you to send my mare round under cover?'

He dropped into a chair which commanded a clear view of Kim and Mahbub Ali in conference beneath the tree. The Padre went indoors for cheroots.

Creighton heard Kim say bitterly: 'Trust a Brahmin before a snake, and a snake before an harlot, and an harlot before a Pathan,[4] Mahbub Ali.'

'That is all one.' The great red beard wagged solemnly. 'Children should not see a carpet on the loom till the pattern is made plain. Believe me, Friend of all the World, I do thee great service. They will not make a soldier of thee.'

'You crafty old sinner!' thought Creighton. 'But you're not far wrong. That boy mustn't be wasted if he is as advertised.'

'Excuse me half a minute,' cried the Padre from within, 'but I'm gettin' the documents in the case.'

'If through me the favour of this bold and wise Colonel Sahib comes to thee, and thou art raised to honour, what thanks wilt thou give Mahbub Ali when thou art a man?'

'Nay, nay! I begged thee to let me take the Road again, where I should have been safe; and thou hast sold me back to the English. What will they give thee for blood-money?'

'A cheerful young demon!' The Colonel bit his cigar, and turned politely to Father Victor.

'What are the letters that the fat priest is waving before the Colonel? Stand behind the stallion as though looking at my bridle!' said Mahbub Ali.

'A letter from my lama which he wrote from Jagadhir Road, saying that he will pay three hundred rupees by the year for my schooling.'

'Oho! Is old Red Hat of that sort? At which school?'

'God knows. I think in Nucklao.'

'Yes. There is a big school there for the sons of Sahibs—and half-

3. Conspire.
4. Or Pashtun, an ethnic group of Muslims living between Afghanistan and the Punjab, distinctive through language (Pushto) and dress.

Sahibs. I have seen it when I sell horses there. So the lama also loved the Friend of all the World?'

'Ay; and *he* did not tell lies, or return me to captivity.'

'Small wonder the Padre does not know how to unravel the thread. How fast he talks to the Colonel Sahib!' Mahbub Ali chuckled. 'By Allah!'—the keen eyes swept the veranda for an instant— 'thy lama has sent what to me looks like a note of hand. I have had some few dealings in *hoondis*. The Colonel Sahib is looking at it.'

'What good is all this to me?' said Kim wearily. 'Thou wilt go away, and they will return me to those empty rooms where there is no good place to sleep and where the boys beat me.'

'I do not think that. Have patience, child. All Pathans are not faithless—except in horseflesh.'

Five—ten—fifteen minutes passed, Father Victor talking energetically or asking questions which the Colonel answered.

'Now I've told you everything that I know about the boy from beginnin' to end; and it's a blessed relief to me. Did ye ever hear the like?'

'At any rate, the old man has sent the money. Gobind Sahai's notes of hand are good from here to China,' said the Colonel. 'The more one knows about natives the less can one say what they will or won't do.'

'That's consolin'—from the head of the Ethnological Survey. It's this mixture of Red Bulls and Rivers of Healing (poor heathen, God help him!) an' notes of hand and Masonic certificates. Are you a Mason, by any chance?'

'By Jove, I am, now I come to think of it. That's an additional reason,' said the Colonel absently.

'I'm glad ye see a reason in it. But as I said, it's the mixture o' things that's beyond me. An' his prophesyin' to our Colonel sitting on my bed with his little shimmy torn open showing his white skin; an' the prophecy comin' true! They'll cure all that nonsense at St Xavier's, eh?'

'Sprinkle him with holy water,' the Colonel laughed.

'On my word, I fancy I ought to sometimes. But I'm hoping he'll be brought up as a good Catholic. All that troubles me is what'll happen if the old beggar-man—'

'Lama, lama, my dear sir; and some of them are gentlemen in their own country.'

'The lama, then, fails to pay next year. He's a fine business head to plan on the spur of the moment, but he's bound to die some day. An' takin' a heathen's money to give a child a Christian education—'

'But he said explicitly what he wanted. As soon as he knew the boy was white he seems to have made his arrangements accordingly. I'd give a month's pay to hear how he explained it all at the Tirthankars' Temple at Benares. Look here, Padre, I don't pretend to know much about natives, but if he says he'll pay, he'll pay—dead or alive. I mean, his heirs will assume the debt. My advice to you is,

send the boy down to Lucknow. If your Anglican Chaplain thinks you've stolen a march on him—'

'Bad luck to Bennett! He was sent to the Front instead o' me. Doughty certified me medically unfit. I'll excommunicate Doughty if he comes back alive! Surely Bennett ought to be content with—'

'Glory, leaving you the religion. Quite so! As a matter of fact I don't think Bennett will mind. Put the blame on me. I—er—strongly recommend sending the boy to St Xavier's. He can go down on pass as a soldier's orphan, so the railway fare will be saved. You can buy him an outfit from the Regimental subscription. The Lodge will be saved the expense of his education, and that will put the Lodge in a good temper. It's perfectly easy. I've got to go down to Lucknow next week. I'll look after the boy on the way—give him in charge of my servants, and so on.'

'You're a good man.'

'Not in the least. Don't make that mistake. The lama has sent us money for a definite end. We can't very well return it. We shall have to do as he says. Well, that's settled, isn't it? Shall we say that, Tuesday next, you'll hand him over to me at the night train south? That's only three days. He can't do much harm in three days.'

'It's a weight off my mind, but—this thing here?'—he waved the note of hand—'I don't know Gobind Sahai: or his bank, which may be a hole in a wall.'

'You've never been a subaltern in debt. I'll cash it if you like, and send you the vouchers in proper order.'

'But with all your own work too! It's askin'—'

'It's not the least trouble indeed. You see, as an ethnologist, the thing's very interesting to me. I'd like to make a note of it for some Government work that I'm doing. The transformation of a regimental badge like your Red Bull into a sort of fetish that the boy follows is very interesting.'

'But I can't thank you enough.'

'There's one thing you can do. All we Ethnological men are as jealous as jackdaws of one another's discoveries. They're of no interest to anyone but ourselves, of course, but you know what book-collectors are like. Well, don't say a word, directly or indirectly, about the Asiatic side of the boy's character—his adventures and his prophecy, and so on. I'll worm them out of the boy later on and—you see?'

'I do. Ye'll make a wonderful account of it. Never a word will I say to anyone till I see it in print.'

'Thank you. That goes straight to an ethnologist's heart. Well, I must be getting back to my breakfast. Good Heavens! Old Mahbub here still?' He raised his voice, and the horse-dealer came out from under the shadow of the tree, 'Well, what is it?'

'As regards that young horse,' said Mahbub, 'I say that when a colt is born to be a polo-pony, closely following the ball without teaching—when such a colt knows the game by divination—then I say it is a great wrong to break that colt to a heavy cart, Sahib!'

'So say I also, Mahbub. The colt will be entered for polo only. (These fellows think of nothing in the world but horses, Padre.) I'll see you tomorrow, Mahbub, if you've anything likely for sale.'

The dealer saluted, horseman-fashion, with a sweep of the off hand. 'Be patient a little, Friend of all the World,' he whispered to the agonized Kim. 'Thy fortune is made. In a little while thou goest to Nucklao, and—here is something to pay the letter-writer. I shall see thee again, I think, many times,' and he cantered off down the road.

'Listen to me,' said the Colonel from the veranda, speaking in the vernacular. 'In three days thou wilt go with me to Lucknow, seeing and hearing new things all the while. Therefore sit still for three days and do not run away. Thou wilt go to school at Lucknow.'

'Shall I meet my Holy One there?' Kim whimpered.

'At least Lucknow is nearer to Benares than Umballa. It may be thou wilt go under my protection. Mahbub Ali knows this, and he will be angry if thou returnest to the Road now. Remember—much has been told me which I do not forget.'

'I will wait,' said Kim, 'but the boys will beat me.'

Then the bugles blew for dinner.

Chapter 7

> Unto whose use the pregnant suns are poised
> With idiot moons and stars retracing stars?
> Creep thou betweene—thy coming's all unnoised.
> Heaven hath her high, as Earth her baser, wars.
> Heir to these tumults, this affright, that fraye
> (By Adam's, fathers', own, sin bound alway);
> Peer up, draw out thy horoscope and say
> Which planet mends thy threadbare fate or mars![1]
> Sir John Christie.[2]

In the afternoon the red-faced schoolmaster told Kim that he had been 'struck off the strength',[3] which conveyed no meaning to him

1. Kim's future, too, hangs by such distant and fragile threads as those determined by "pregnant suns," "idiot moons," earthly wars, and other planetary signs of the horoscope. The relevance of the verse is to this particular moment in Kim's life, when, for the first time, he reaches a state of confusion about his identity. Will he take up assigned roles or transform himself through disguise?
2. No information is available on Sir John Christie; Kipling may have chosen to conflate a Scottish poet and an astronomer, both named Christie.
3. Military term for dismissal from the regiment.

till he was ordered to go away and play. Then he ran to the bazar, and found the young letter-writer to whom he owed a stamp.

'Now I pay,' said Kim royally, 'and now I need another letter to be written.'

'Mahbub Ali is in Umballa,' said the writer jauntily. He was, by virtue of his office, a bureau of general misinformation.

'This is not to Mahbub, but to a priest. Take thy pen and write quickly. *To Teshoo Lama, the Holy One from Bhotiyal*[4] *seeking for a River, who is now in the Temple of the Tirthankars at Benares.* Take more ink! *In three days I am to go down to Nucklao to the school at Nucklao. The name of the school is Xavier. I do not know where that school is, but it is at Nucklao.*'

'But I know Nucklao,' the writer interrupted. 'I know the school.'

'Tell him where it is, and I give half an anna.'

The reed pen scratched busily. 'He cannot mistake.' The man lifted his head. 'Who watches us across the street?'

Kim looked up hurriedly and saw Colonel Creighton in tennis-flannels.

'Oh, that is some Sahib who knows the fat priest in the barracks. He is beckoning me.'

'What dost thou?' said the Colonel, when Kim trotted up.

'I—I am not running away. I send a letter to my Holy One at Benares.'

'I had not thought of that. Hast thou said that I take thee to Lucknow?'

'Nay, I have not. Read the letter, if there be a doubt.'

'Then why hast thou left out my name in writing to that Holy One?' The Colonel smiled a queer smile. Kim took his courage in both hands.

'It was said once to me that it is inexpedient to write the names of strangers concerned in any matter, because by the naming of names many good plans are brought to confusion.'

'Thou hast been well taught,' the Colonel replied, and Kim flushed. 'I have left my cheroot-case in the Padre's veranda. Bring it to my house this even.'

'Where is the house?' said Kim. His quick wit told him that he was being tested in some fashion or another, and he stood on guard.

'Ask anyone in the big bazar.' The Colonel walked on.

'He has forgotten his cheroot-case,' said Kim, returning. 'I must bring it to him this evening. That is all my letter except, thrice over, *Come to me! Come to me! Come to me!* Now I will pay for a stamp

4. Tibet and Nepal.

and put it in the post.' He rose to go, and as an afterthought asked: 'Who is that angry-faced Sahib who lost the cheroot-case?'

'Oh, he is only Creighton Sahib—a very foolish Sahib, who is a Colonel Sahib without a regiment.'

'What is his business?'

'God knows. He is always buying horses which he cannot ride, and asking riddles about the works of God—such as plants and stones and the customs of people. The dealers call him the father of fools, because he is so easily cheated about a horse. Mahbub Ali says he is madder than most other Sahibs.'

'Oh!' said Kim, and departed. His training had given him some small knowledge of character, and he argued that fools are not given information which leads to calling out eight thousand men besides guns. The Commander-in-Chief of all India does not talk, as Kim had heard him talk, to fools. Nor would Mahbub Ali's tone have changed, as it did every time he mentioned the Colonel's name, if the Colonel had been a fool. Consequently—and this set Kim to skipping—there was a mystery somewhere, and Mahbub Ali probably spied for the Colonel much as Kim had spied for Mahbub. And, like the horse-dealer, the Colonel evidently respected people who did not show themselves to be too clever.

He rejoiced that he had not betrayed his knowledge of the Colonel's house; and when, on his return to barracks, he discovered that no cheroot-case had been left behind, he beamed with delight. Here was a man after his own heart—a tortuous and indirect person playing a hidden game. Well, if he could be a fool, so could Kim.

He showed nothing of his mind when Father Victor, for three long mornings, discoursed to him of an entirely new set of Gods and Godlings—notably of a Goddess called Mary, who, he gathered, was one with Bibi Miriam[5] of Mahbub Ali's theology. He betrayed no emotion when, after the lecture, Father Victor dragged him from shop to shop buying articles of outfit, nor when envious drummer-boys kicked him because he was going to a superior school did he complain, but awaited the play of circumstances with an interested soul. Father Victor, good man, took him to the station, put him into an empty second-class next to Colonel Creighton's first, and bade him farewell with genuine feeling.

'They'll make a man o' you, O'Hara, at St Xavier's—a white man, an', I hope, a good man. They know all about your comin', an' the Colonel will see that ye're not lost or mislaid anywhere on the road. I've given you a notion of religious matters,—at least I hope so,—and you'll remember, when they ask you your religion, that

5. Muslim term for the Virgin Mary.

you're a Cath'lic. Better say Roman Cath'lic, tho' I'm not fond of the word.'

Kim lit a rank cigarette—he had been careful to buy a stock in the bazar—and lay down to think. This solitary passage was very different from that joyful down-journey in the third-class with the lama. 'Sahibs get little pleasure of travel,' he reflected. '*Hai mai!* I go from one place to another as it might be a kick-ball. It is my *Kismet*. No man can escape his *Kismet*. But I am to pray to Bibi Miriam, and I am a Sahib.' He looked at his boots ruefully. 'No; I am Kim. This is the great world, and I am only Kim. Who is Kim?' He considered his own identity, a thing he had never done before, till his head swam. He was one insignificant person in all this roaring whirl of India, going southward to he knew not what fate.

Presently the Colonel sent for him, and talked for a long time. So far as Kim could gather, he was to be diligent and enter the Survey of India as a chain-man.[6] If he were very good, and passed the proper examinations, he would be earning thirty rupees a month at seventeen years old, and Colonel Creighton would see that he found suitable employment.

Kim pretended at first to understand perhaps one word in three of this talk. Then the Colonel, seeing his mistake, turned to fluent and picturesque Urdu and Kim was contented. No man could be a fool who knew the language so intimately, who moved so gently and silently, and whose eyes were so different from the dull fat eyes of other Sahibs.

'Yes, and thou must learn how to make pictures of roads and mountains and rivers—to carry these pictures in thine eye till a suitable time comes to set them upon paper. Perhaps some day, when thou art a chain-man, I may say to thee when we are working together: "Go across those hills and see what lies beyond." Then one will say: "There are bad people living in those hills who will slay the chain-man if he be seen to look like a Sahib." What then?'

Kim thought. Would it be safe to return the Colonel's lead?

'I would tell what that other man had said.'

'But if I answered: "I will give thee a hundred rupees for knowledge of what is behind those hills—for a picture of a river and a little news of what the people say in the villages there"?'

'How can I tell? I am only a boy. Wait till I am a man.' Then, seeing the Colonel's brow clouded, he went on: 'But I think I should in a few days earn the hundred rupees.'

'By what road?'

6. The lowest position on a surveying team, the chain man carried a sixty-six-foot chain for measuring distances.

Kim shook his head resolutely. 'If I said how I would earn them, another man might hear and forestall me. It is not good to sell knowledge for nothing.'

'Tell now.' The Colonel held up a rupee. Kim's hand half reached towards it, and dropped.

'Nay, Sahib; nay. I know the price that will be paid for the answer, but I do not know why the question is asked.'

'Take it for a gift, then,' said Creighton, tossing it over. 'There is a good spirit in thee. Do not let it be blunted at St Xavier's. There are many boys there who despise the black men.'

'Their mothers were bazar-women,' said Kim. He knew well there is no hatred like that of the half-caste for his brother-in-law.

'True; but thou art a Sahib and the son of a Sahib. Therefore, do not at any time be led to contemn the black men. I have known boys newly entered into the service of the Government who feigned not to understand the talk or the customs of black men. Their pay was cut for ignorance. There is no sin so great as ignorance. Remember this.'

Several times in the course of the long twenty-four hours' run south did the Colonel send for Kim, always developing this latter text.

'We be all on one lead-rope, then,' said Kim at last, 'the Colonel, Mahbub Ali, and I—when I become a chain-man. He will use me as Mahbub Ali employed me, I think. That is good, if it allows me to return to the Road again. This clothing grows no easier by wear.'

When they came to the crowded Lucknow station there was no sign of the lama. He swallowed his disappointment, while the Colonel bundled him into a *ticca-gharri*[7] with his neat belongings and despatched him alone to St Xavier's.

'I do not say farewell, because we shall meet again,' he cried. 'Again, and many times, if thou art one of good spirit. But thou art not yet tried.'

'Not when I brought thee'—Kim actually dared to use the *tum*[8] of equals—'a white stallion's pedigree that night?'

'Much is gained by forgetting, little brother,' said the Colonel, with a look that pierced through Kim's shoulder-blades as he scuttled into the carriage.

It took him nearly five minutes to recover. Then he sniffed the new air appreciatively. 'A rich City,' he said. 'Richer than Lahore. How good the bazars must be! Coachman, drive me a little through the bazars here.'

7. A four-wheeled carriage.
8. Familiar term of address comparable to the French "tu" as opposed to "vous." The more formal term would be "aap."

'My order is to take thee to the school.' The driver used the 'thou', which is rudeness when applied to a white man. In the clearest and most fluent vernacular Kim pointed out his error, climbed on to the box-seat and, perfect understanding established, drove for a couple of hours up and down, estimating, comparing, and enjoying. There is no city—except Bombay, the queen of all—more beautiful in her garish style than Lucknow, whether you see her from the bridge over the river, or from the top of the Imambara[9] looking down on the gilt umbrellas of the Chutter Munzil,[1] and the trees in which the town is bedded. Kings have adorned her with fantastic buildings, endowed her with charities, crammed her with pensioners, and drenched her with blood. She is the centre of all idleness, intrigue, and luxury, and shares with Delhi the claim to talk the only pure Urdu.

'A fair city—a beautiful city.' The driver, as a Lucknow man, was pleased with the compliment, and told Kim many astounding things where an English guide would have talked of the Mutiny.

'Now we will go to the school,' said Kim at last. The great old school of St Xavier's in Partibus, block on block of low white buildings, stands in vast grounds over against the Gumti River, at some distance from the city.

'What like of folk are they within?' said Kim.

'Young Sahibs—all devils. But to speak truth, and I drive many of them to and fro from the railway station, I have never seen one that had in him the making of a more perfect devil than thou—this young Sahib whom I am now driving.'

Naturally, for he was never trained to consider them in any way improper, Kim had passed the time of day with one or two frivolous ladies at upper windows in a certain street, and naturally, in the exchange of compliments, had acquitted himself well. He was about to acknowledge the driver's last insolence, when his eye—it was growing dusk—caught a figure sitting by one of the white plaster gate-pillars in the long sweep of wall.

'Stop!' he cried. 'Stay here. I do not go to the school at once.'

'But what is to pay me for this coming and re-coming?' said the driver petulantly. 'Is the boy mad? Last time it was a dancing-girl. This time it is a priest.'

Kim was in the road headlong, patting the dusty feet beneath the dirty yellow robe.

'I have waited here a day and a half,' the lama's level voice began. 'Nay, I had a disciple with me. He that was my friend at the Temple of the Tirthankars gave me a guide for this journey. I came from

9. The tomb of a Muslim saint.
1. Umbrella House, used as the women's quarters of the court. The umbrellas signify royalty.

Benares in the *te-rain*, when thy letter was given me. Yes, I am well fed. I need nothing.'

'But why didst thou not stay with the Kulu woman, O Holy One? In what way didst thou get to Benares? My heart has been heavy since we parted.'

'The woman wearied me by constant flux of talk and requiring charms for children. I separated myself from that company, permitting her to acquire merit by gifts. She is at least a woman of open hands, and I made a promise to return to her house if need arose. Then, perceiving myself alone in this great and terrible world, I bethought me of the *te-rain* to Benares, where I knew one abode in the Tirthankars' Temple who was a Seeker, even as I.'

'Ah! Thy River,' said Kim. 'I had forgotten the River.'

'So soon, my *chela*? I have never forgotten it. But when I had left thee it seemed better that I should go to the Temple and take counsel, for, look you, India is very large, and it may be that wise men before us, some two or three, have left a record of the place of our River. There is debate in the Temple of the Tirthankars on this matter; some saying one thing, and some another. They are courteous folk.'

'So be it; but what dost thou do now?'

'I acquire merit in that I help thee, my *chela*, to wisdom. The priest of that body of men who serve the Red Bull wrote me that all should be as I desired for thee. I sent the money to suffice for one year, and then I came, as thou seest me, to watch for thee going up into the Gates of Learning. A day and a half have I waited—not because I was led by any affection towards thee—that is no part of the Way—but, as they said at the Tirthankars' Temple, because, money having been paid for learning, it was right that I should oversee the end of the matter. They resolved my doubts most clearly. I had a fear that, perhaps, I came because I wished to see thee—misguided by the Red Mist of affection. It is not so . . . Moreover, I am troubled by a dream.'

'But surely, Holy One, thou hast not forgotten the Road and all that befell on it. Surely it was a little to see me that thou didst come?'

'The horses are cold, and it is past their feeding-time,' whined the driver.

'Go to Jehannum and abide there with thy reputationless aunt!' Kim snarled over his shoulder. 'I am all alone in this land; I know not where I go nor what shall befall me. My heart was in that letter I sent thee. Except for Mahbub Ali, and he is a Pathan, I have no friend save thee, Holy One. Do not altogether go away.'

'I have considered that also,' the lama replied, in a shaking voice. "It is manifest that from time to time I shall acquire merit—if before

that I have not found my River—by assuring myself that thy feet are set on wisdom. What they will teach thee I do not know, but the priest wrote me that no son of a Sahib in all India will be better taught than thou. So from time to time, therefore, I will come again. Maybe thou wilt be such a Sahib as he who gave me these spectacles'—the lama wiped them elaborately—'in the Wonder House at Lahore. That is my hope, for he was a Fountain of Wisdom—wiser than many abbots . . . Again, maybe thou wilt forget me and our meetings.'

'If I eat thy bread,' cried Kim passionately, 'how shall I ever forget thee?'

'No—no.' He put the boy aside. 'I must go back to Benares. From time to time, now that I know the customs of letter-writers in this land, I will send thee a letter, and from time to time I will come and see thee.'

'But whither shall I send my letter?' wailed Kim, clutching at the robe, all forgetful that he was a Sahib.

'To the Temple of the Tirthankars at Benares. That is the place I have chosen till I find my River. Do not weep; for, look you, all Desire is Illusion and a new binding upon the Wheel. Go up to the Gates of Learning. Let me see thee go . . . Dost thou love me? Then go, or my heart cracks . . . I will come again. Surely I will come again.'

The lama watched the *ticca-garri* rumble into the compound, and strode off, snuffing between each long stride.

'The Gates of Learning' shut with a clang.

· · · · ·

The country–born and bred boy has his own manners and customs, which do not resemble those of any other land; and his teachers approach him by roads which an English master would not understand. Therefore, you would scarcely be interested in Kim's experiences as a St Xavier's boy among two or three hundred precocious youths, most of whom had never seen the sea. He suffered the usual penalties for breaking out of bounds when there was cholera in the city. This was before he had learned to write fair English, and so was obliged to find a bazar letter-writer. He was, of course, indicted for smoking and for the use of abuse more full-flavoured than even St Xavier's had ever heard. He learned to wash himself with the Levitical[2] scrupulosity of the native-born, who in his heart considers the Englishman rather dirty. He played the usual tricks on the patient coolies pulling the punkahs[3] in the sleeping-rooms where

2. Fastidious, as in the Hebrew laws in the book of Leviticus.
3. Indian fans: a screen hung from the ceiling and attached to a string pulled back and forth by a laborer (coolie) to keep the air moving.

the boys threshed through the hot nights telling tales till the dawn; and quietly he measured himself against his self-reliant mates.

They were sons of subordinate officials in the Railway, Telegraph, and Canal Services; of warrant-officers, sometimes retired and sometimes acting as commanders-in-chief to a feudatory Rajah's army; of captains of the Indian Marine Government pensioners, planters, Presidency shopkeepers, and missionaries. A few were cadets of the old Eurasian houses that have taken strong root in Dhurrumtollah—Pereiras, De Souzas, and D'Silvas.[4] Their parents could well have educated them in England, but they loved the school that had served their own youth, and generation followed sallow-hued generation at St Xavier's. Their homes ranged from Howrah of the railway people to abandoned cantonments like Monghyr and Chunar; lost tea-gardens Shillongway; villages where their fathers were large landholders in Oudh or the Deccan; Mission-stations a week from the nearest railway line; seaports a thousand miles south, facing the brazen Indian surf; and cinchona-plantations[5] south of all. The mere story of their adventures, which to them were no adventures, on their road to and from school would have crisped a Western boy's hair. They were used to jogging off alone through a hundred miles of jungle, where there was always the delightful chance of being delayed by tigers; but they would no more have bathed in the English Channel in an English August than their brothers across the world would have lain still while a leopard snuffed at their palanquin.[6] There were boys of fifteen who had spent a day and a half on an islet in the middle of a flooded river, taking charge, as by right, of a camp of frantic pilgrims returning from a shrine. There were seniors who had requisitioned a chance-met Rajah's elephant, in the name of St Francis Xavier, when the Rains once blotted out the cart-track that led to their father's estate, and had all but lost the huge beast in a quicksand. There was a boy who, he said, and none doubted, had helped his father to beat off with rifles from the veranda a rush of Akas[7] in the days when those head-hunters were bold against lonely plantations.

And every tale was told in the even, passionless voice of the native-born, mixed with quaint reflections, borrowed unconsciously from native foster-mothers, and turns of speech that showed they had been that instant translated from the vernacular. Kim watched, listened, and approved. This was not insipid, single-word talk of drummer-boys. It dealt with a life he knew and in part understood.

4. Portuguese names of mixed European and Indian families. Dhurrumtollah was an area of Calcutta popular with Anglo-Indians.
5. Areas planted with trees whose bark is used for quinine.
6. An enclosed litter carried on the shoulders of men.
7. Members of a mountain tribe in northern India against whom the English sent an expedition in 1883.

The atmosphere suited him, and he throve by inches. They gave him a white drill suit as the weather warmed, and he rejoiced in the new-found bodily comforts as he rejoiced to use his sharpened mind over the tasks they set him. His quickness would have delighted an English master; but at St Xavier's they know the first rush of minds developed by sun and surroundings, as they know the half-collapse that sets in at twenty-two or twenty-three.

None the less he remembered to hold himself lowly. When tales were told of hot nights, Kim did not sweep the board with his reminiscences; for St Xavier's looks down on boys who 'go native all-together.' One must never forget that one is a Sahib, and that some day, when examinations are passed, one will command natives. Kim made a note of this, for he began to understand where examinations led.

Then came the holidays from August to October—the long holidays imposed by the heat and the Rains. Kim was informed that he would go north to some station in the hills behind Umballa, where Father Victor would arrange for him.

'A barrack-school?' said Kim, who had asked many questions and thought more.

'Yes, I suppose so,' said the master. 'It will not do you any harm to keep you out of mischief. You can go up with young De Castro as far as Delhi.'

Kim considered it in every possible light. He had been diligent, even as the Colonel advised. A boy's holiday was his own property—of so much the talk of his companions had advised him,—and a barrack-school would be torment after St Xavier's. Moreover—this was magic worth anything else—he could write. In three months he had discovered how men can speak to each other without a third party, at the cost of half an anna and a little knowledge. No word had come from the lama, but there remained the Road. Kim yearned for the caress of soft mud squashing up between the toes, as his mouth watered for mutton stewed with butter and cabbages, for rice speckled with strong-scented cardamons, for the saffron-tinted rice, garlic and onions, and the forbidden greasy sweetmeats of the bazars. They would feed him raw beef on a platter at the barrack-school, and he must smoke by stealth. But again, he was a Sahib and was at St Xavier's, and that pig Mahbub Ali . . . No, he would not test Mahbub's hospitality—and yet . . . He thought it out alone in the dormitory, and came to the conclusion he had been unjust to Mahbub.

The school was empty; nearly all the masters had gone away; Colonel Creighton's railway pass lay in his hand, and Kim puffed himself that he had not spent Colonel Creighton's or Mahbub's money in riotous living. He was still lord of two rupees seven annas.

His new bullock-trunk, marked 'K. O'H.', and bedding-roll lay in the empty sleeping-room. 'Sahibs are always tied to their baggage,' said Kim, nodding at them. 'You will stay here.' He went out into the warm rain, smiling sinfully, and sought a certain house whose outside he had noted down some time before . . .

'Arré! Dost thou know what manner of women we be in this quarter? Oh, shame!'

'Was I born yesterday?' Kim squatted native-fashion on the cushions of that upper room. 'A little dyestuff and three yards of cloth to help out a jest. Is it much to ask?'

'Who is *she*? Thou art full young, as Sahibs go, for this devilry.'

'Oh, she? She is the daughter of a certain schoolmaster of a regiment in the cantonments. He has beaten me twice because I went over their wall in these clothes. Now I would go as a gardener's boy. Old men are very jealous.'

'That is true. Hold thy face still while I dab on the juice.'

'Not too black, *Naikan*.[8] I would not appear to her as a *hubshi* (black African).'

'Oh, love makes nought of these things. And how old is she?'

'Twelve years, I think,' said the shameless Kim. 'Spread it also on the breast. It may be her father will tear my clothes off me, and if I am piebald—' he laughed.

The girl worked busily, dabbing a twist of cloth into a little saucer of brown dye that holds longer than any walnut-juice.

'Now send out and get me a cloth for the turban. Woe is me, my head is all unshaved! And he will surely knock off my turban.'

'I am not a barber, but I will make shift. Thou wast born to be a breaker of hearts! All this disguise for one evening? Remember, the stuff does not wash away.' She shook with laughter till her bracelets and anklets jingled. 'But who is to pay me for this? Huneefa[9] herself could not have given thee better stuff.'

'Trust in the Gods, my sister,' said Kim gravely, screwing his face round as the stain dried. 'Besides, hast thou ever helped to paint a Sahib thus before?'

'Never indeed. But a jest is not money.'

'It is worth much more.'

'Child, thou art beyond all dispute the most shameless son of Shaitan[1] that I have ever known to take up a poor girl's time with this play, and then to say: "Is not the jest enough?" Thou wilt go very far in this world.' She gave the dancing-girls' salutation in mockery.

'All one. Make haste and rough-cut my head.' Kim shifted from foot to foot, his eyes ablaze with mirth as he thought of the fat days

8. Here, a dancing girl or prostitute.
9. We will meet Huneefa in Chapter 10.
1. Satan.

before him. He gave the girl four annas, and ran down the stairs in the likeness of a low-caste Hindu boy—perfect in every detail. A cookshop was his next point of call, where he feasted in extravagance and greasy luxury.

On Lucknow station platform he watched young De Castro, all covered with prickly-heat, get into a second-class compartment. Kim patronized a third, and was the life and soul of it. He explained to the company that he was assistant to a juggler who had left him behind sick with fever, and that he would pick up his master at Umballa. As the occupants of the carriage changed, he varied this tale, or adorned it with all the shoots of a budding fancy, the more rampant for being held off native speech so long. In all India that night was no human being so joyful as Kim. At Umballa he got out and headed eastward, plashing over the sodden fields to the village where the old soldier lived.

About this time Colonel Creighton at Simla was advised from Lucknow by wire that young O'Hara had disappeared. Mahbub Ali was in town selling horses, and to him the Colonel confided the affair one morning cantering round Annandale racecourse.

'Oh, that is nothing,' said the horse-dealer. 'Men are like horses. At certain times they need salt, and if that salt is not in the mangers they will lick it up from the earth. He has gone back to the Road again for a while. The *madrissah* wearied him. I knew it would. Another time, I will take him upon the Road myself. Do not be troubled, Creighton Sahib. It is as though a polo-pony, breaking loose, ran out to learn the game alone.'

'Then he is not dead, think you?'

'Fever might kill him. I do not fear for the boy otherwise. A monkey does not fall among trees.'

Next morning, on the same course, Mahbub's stallion ranged alongside the Colonel.

'It is as I had thought,' said the horse-dealer. 'He has come through Umballa at least, and there he has written a letter to me, having learned in the bazar that I was here.'

'Read,' said the Colonel, with a sigh of relief. It was absurd that a man of his position should take an interest in a little country-bred vagabond; but the Colonel remembered the conversation in the train, and often in the past few months had caught himself thinking of the queer, silent, self-possessed boy. His evasion, of course, was the height of insolence, but it argued some resource and nerve.

Mahbub's eyes twinkled as he reined out into the centre of the cramped little plain, where none could come near unseen.

'"*The Friend of the Stars, who is the Friend of all the World—*"'

'What is this?'

'A name we give him in Lahore city. *"The Friend of all the World
takes leave to go to his own places. He will come back upon the
appointed day. Let the box and the bedding-roll be sent for; and if
there has been a fault, let the Hand of Friendship turn aside the Whip
of Calamity."* There is yet a little more, but—'

'No matter, read.'

'*"Certain things are not known to those who eat with forks. It is bet-
ter to eat with both hands for a while. Speak soft words to those who
do not understand this that the return may be propitious."* Now the
manner in which that was cast is, of course, the work of the letter-
writer, but see how wisely the boy has devised the matter of it so
that no hint is given except to those who know!'

'Is this the Hand of Friendship to avert the Whip of Calamity?'
laughed the Colonel.

'See how wise is the boy. He would go back to the Road again, as
I said. Not knowing yet thy trade—'

'I am not all sure of that,' the Colonel muttered.

'He turns to me to make a peace between you. Is he not wise? He
says he will return. He is but perfecting his knowledge. Think, Sahib!
He has been three months at the school. And he is not mouthed to
that bit. For my part, I rejoice. The pony learns the game.'

'Ay, but another time he must not go alone.'

'Why? He went alone before he came under the Colonel Sahib's
protection. When he comes to the Great Game[2] he must go alone—
alone, and at peril of his head. *Then*, if he spits, or sneezes, or sits
down other than as the people do whom he watches, he may be
slain. Why hinder him now? Remember how the Persians say: The
jackal that lives in the wilds of Mazanderan can only be caught by
the hounds of Mazanderan.'[3]

'True. It is true, Mahbub Ali. And if he comes to no harm, I do
not desire anything better. But it is great insolence on his part.'

'He does not tell me, even, whither he goes,' said Mahbub. 'He is
no fool. When his time is accomplished he will come to me. It is
time the healer of pearls[4] took him in hand. He ripens too quickly—
as Sahibs reckon.'

This prophecy was fulfilled to the letter a month later. Mahbub
had gone down to Umballa to bring up a fresh consignment of
horses, and Kim met him on the Kalka road at dusk riding alone,
begged an alms of him, was sworn at, and replied in English. There
was nobody within earshot to hear Mahbub's gasp of amazement.

'Oho! And where hast thou been?'

2. The cold war between the British Empire and Russia for control over southern and west-
ern Asia.
3. A province to the north of Iran near the Caspian Sea.
4. Specially gifted jewelers can "heal" pearls and other gemstones when they lose their color.

'Up and down—down and up.'

'Come under a tree, out of the wet, and tell.'

'I stayed for a while with an old man near Umballa; anon with a household of my acquaintance in Umballa. With one of these I went as far as Delhi to the southward. That is a wondrous city. Then I drove a bullock for a *teli* (an oilman) coming north; but I heard of a great feast forward in Patiala, and thither went I in the company of a firework-maker. It was a great feast' (Kim rubbed his stomach). 'I saw Rajahs, and elephants with gold and silver trappings; and they lit all the fireworks at once, whereby eleven men were killed, my firework-maker among them, and I was blown across a tent but took no harm. Then I came back to the *rêl* with a Sikh horseman, to whom I was groom for my bread; and so here.'

'*Shabash!*' said Mahbub Ali.

'But what does the Colonel Sahib say? I do not wish to be beaten.'

'The Hand of Friendship has averted the Whip of Calamity; but another time, when thou takest the Road it will be with me. This is too early.'

'Late enough for me. I have learned to read and to write English a little at the *madrissah*. I shall soon be altogether a Sahib.'

'Hear him!' laughed Mahbub, looking at the little drenched figure dancing in the wet. 'Salaam—Sahib,' and he saluted ironically. 'Well, art tired of the Road, or wilt thou come on to Umballa with me and work back with the horses?'

'I come with thee, Mahbub Ali.'

Chapter 8

> Something I owe to the soil that grew—
> More to the life that fed—
> But most to Allah Who gave me two
> Separate sides to my head.
>
> I would go without shirts or shoes,
> Friends, tobacco or bread
> Sooner than for an instant lose
> Either side of my head.
> *The Two-Sided Man.*[1]

'Then in God's name take blue for red,' said Mahbub, alluding to the Hindu colour of Kim's disreputable turban.

1. The first and last verses of Kipling's poem "The Two-Sided Man," collected in *Songs from Books*. Its acknowledgment of split identity is central to understanding not only the split between Kim's ethnically British and culturally Indian identity, but other Kipling stories split between the daytime work of colonial discipline and a nighttime world of desire and freedom.

Kim countered with the old proverb, 'I will change my faith and my bedding, but *thou* must pay for it.'

The dealer laughed till he nearly fell from his horse. At a shop on the outskirts of the city the change was made, and Kim stood up, externally at least, a Mohammedan.

Mahbub hired a room over against the railway station, sent for a cooked meal of the finest with the almond-curd sweetmeats (*balushai* we call it) and fine-chopped Lucknow tobacco.

'This is better than some other meat that I ate with the Sikh,' said Kim, grinning as he squatted, 'and assuredly they give no such victuals at my *madrissah*.'

'I have a desire to hear of that same *madrissah*.' Mahbub stuffed himself with great boluses of spiced mutton fried in fat with cabbage and golden-brown onions. 'But tell me first, altogether and truthfully, the manner of thy escape. For, O Friend of all the World,'—he loosed his cracking belt—'I do not think it is often that a Sahib and the son of a Sahib runs away from there.'

'How should they? They do not know the land. It was nothing,' said Kim, and began his tale. When he came to the disguisement and the interview with the girl in the bazar, Mahbub Ali's gravity went from him. He laughed aloud and beat his hand on his thigh.

'*Shabash! Shabash!* Oh, well done, little one! What will the healer of turquoises say to this? Now, slowly, let us hear what befell afterwards—step by step, omitting nothing.'

Step by step then, Kim told his adventures between coughs as the full-flavoured tobacco caught his lungs.

'I said,' growled Mahbub Ali to himself, 'I *said* it was the pony breaking out to play polo. The fruit is ripe already—except that he must learn his distances and his pacings, and his rods and his compasses.[2] Listen now. I have turned aside the Colonel's whip from thy skin, and that is no small service.'

'True.' Kim pulled serenely. 'That is true.'

'But it is not to be thought that this running out and in is any way good.'

'It was my holiday, Hajji. I was a slave for many weeks. Why should I not run away when the school was shut? Look, too, how I, living upon my friends or working for my bread, as I did with the Sikh, have saved the Colonel Sahib a great expense.'

Mahbub's lips twitched under his well-pruned Mohammedan moustache.

'What are a few rupees'—the Pathan threw out his open hand carelessly—'to the Colonel Sahib? He spends them for a purpose, not in any way for love of thee.'

2. Items used in surveying, mapping, and spying.

'That,' said Kim slowly, 'I knew a very long time ago.'

'Who told?'

'The Colonel Sahib himself. Not in those many words, but plainly enough for one who is not altogether a mud-head. Yea, he told me in the *te-rain* when we went down to Lucknow.'

'Be it so. Then I will tell thee more, Friend of all the World, though in the telling I lend thee my head.'

'It was forfeit to me,' said Kim, with deep relish, 'in Umballa, when thou didst pick me up on the horse after the drummer-boy beat me.'

'Speak a little plainer. All the world may tell lies save thou and I. For equally is thy life forfeit to me if I chose to raise my finger here.'

'And this is known to me also,' said Kim, readjusting the live charcoal-ball on the weed. 'It is a very sure tie between us. Indeed, thy hold is surer even than mine; for who would miss a boy beaten to death, or, it may be, thrown into a well by the roadside? Most people here and in Simla and across the passes behind the Hills would, on the other hand, say: "What has come to Mahbub Ali?" if he were found dead among his horses. Surely, too, the Colonel Sahib would make inquiries. But again,'—Kim's face puckered with cunning,—'he would not make overlong inquiry, lest people should ask: "What has this Colonel Sahib to do with that horse-dealer?" But I—if I lived—'

'As thou wouldst surely die—'

'Maybe; but I say, *if* I lived, I, and I alone, would know that one had come by night, as a common thief perhaps, to Mahbub Ali's bulkhead in the serai, and there had slain him, either before or after that thief had made a full search into his saddle-bags and between the soles of his slippers. Is that news to tell to the Colonel, or would he say to me—(I have not forgotten when he sent me back for a cigar-case that he had not left behind him)—"What is Mahbub Ali to me?"?'

Up went a gout of heavy smoke. There was a long pause: then Mahbub Ali spoke in admiration: 'And with these things on thy mind, dost thou lie down and rise again among all the Sahibs' little sons at the *madrissah* and meekly take instruction from thy teachers?'

'It is an order,' said Kim blandly. 'Who am I to dispute an order?'

'A most finished Son of Eblis,'[3] said Mahbub Ali. 'But what is this tale of the thief and the search?'

'That which I saw,' said Kim, 'the night that my lama and I lay next thy place in the Kashmir Serai. The door was left unlocked, which I think is not thy custom, Mahbub. He came in as one assured that thou wouldst not soon return. My eye was against a

3. Leading satanic figure in Muslim mythology.

knot-hole in the plank. He searched as it were for something—not a rug, not stirrups, nor a bridle, nor brass pots—something little and most carefully hid. Else why did he prick with an iron between the soles of thy slippers?'

'Ha!' Mahbub Ali smiled gently. 'And seeing these things, what tale didst thou fashion to thyself, Well of the Truth?'

'None. I put my hand upon my amulet, which lies always next to my skin, and, remembering the pedigree of a white stallion that I had bitten out of a piece of Mussalmani bread, I went away to Umballa perceiving that a heavy trust was laid upon me. At that hour, had I chosen, thy head was forfeit. It needed only to say to that man, "I have here a paper concerning a horse which I cannot read." And then?' Kim peered at Mahbub under his eyebrows.

'Then thou wouldst have drunk water twice—perhaps thrice, afterwards. I do not think more than thrice,' said Mahbub simply.

'It is true. I thought of that a little, but most I thought that I loved thee, Mahbub. Therefore I went to Umballa, as thou knowest, but (and this thou dost not know) I lay hid in the garden-grass to see what Colonel Creighton Sahib might do upon reading the white stallion's pedigree.'

'And what did he?' for Kim had bitten off the conversation.

'Dost *thou* give news for love, or dost thou sell it?' Kim asked.

'I sell and—I buy.' Mahbub took a four-anna piece out of his belt and held it up.

'Eight!' said Kim, mechanically following the huckster instinct of the East.

Mahbub laughed, and put away the coin. 'It is too easy to deal in that market, Friend of all the World. Tell me for love. Our lives lie in each other's hand.'

'Very good. I saw the Jang-i-Lat Sahib (the Commander-in-Chief) come to a big dinner. I saw him in Creighton Sahib's office. I saw the two read the white stallion's pedigree. I heard the very orders given for the opening of a great war.'

'Hah!' Mahbub nodded with deepest eyes afire. 'The game is well played. That war is done now, and the evil, we hope, nipped before the flower—thanks to me—and thee. What didst thou later?'

'I made the news as it were a hook to catch me victual and honour among the villagers in a village whose priest drugged my lama. But I bore away the old man's purse, and the Brahmin found nothing. So next morning he was angry. Ho! Ho! And I also used the news when I fell into the hands of that white Regiment with their Bull!'

'That was foolishness.' Mahbub scowled. 'News is not meant to be thrown about like dung-cakes, but used sparingly—like *bhang*.'[4]

4. A strong opiate.

'So I think now, and moreover, it did me no sort of good. But that was very long ago,'—he made as to brush it all away with a thin brown hand—'and since then, and especially in the nights under the punkah at the *madrissah*, I have thought very greatly.'

'Is it permitted to ask whither the Heaven-born's thought might have led?' said Mahbub, with an elaborate sarcasm, smoothing his scarlet beard.

'It is permitted,' said Kim, and threw back the very tone. 'They say at Nucklao that no Sahib must tell a black man that he has made a fault.'

Mahbub's hand shot into his bosom, for to call a Pathan a 'black man' (*kala admi*) is a blood-insult. Then he remembered and laughed. 'Speak, Sahib. Thy black man hears.'

'But,' said Kim, 'I am *not* a Sahib, and I say I made a fault to curse thee, Mahbub Ali, on that day at Umballa when I thought I was betrayed by a Pathan. I was senseless; for I was but newly caught, and I wished to kill that low-caste drummer-boy. I say now, Hajji, that it was well done; and I see my road all clear before me to a good service. I will stay in the *madrissah* till I am ripe.'

'Well said. Especially are distances and numbers and the manner of using compasses to be learned in that game. One waits in the Hills above to show thee.'

'I will learn their teaching upon a condition—that my time is given to me without question when the *madrissah* is shut. Ask that for me of the Colonel.'

'But why not ask the Colonel in the Sahibs' tongue?'

'The Colonel is the servant of the Government. He is sent hither and yon at a word, and must consider his own advancement. (See how much I have already learned at Nucklao!) Moreover, the Colonel I know since three months only. I have known one Mahbub Ali for six years. So! To the *madrissah* I will go. At the *madrissah* I will learn. In the *madrissah* I will be a Sahib. But when the *madrissah* is shut, then must I be free and go among my people. Otherwise I die!'

'And who are thy people, Friend of all the World?'

'This great and beautiful land,' said Kim, waving his paw round the little clay-walled room where the oil-lamp in its niche burned heavily through the tobacco-smoke. 'And, further, I would see my lama again. And, further, I need money.'

'That is the need of everyone,' said Mahbub ruefully. 'I will give thee eight annas, for much money is not picked out of horses' hooves, and it must suffice for many days. As to all the rest, I am well pleased, and no further talk is needed. Make haste to learn, and in three years, or it may be less, thou wilt be an aid—even to me.'

'Have I been such a hindrance till now?' said Kim, with a boy's giggle.

'Do not give answers,' Mahbub grunted. 'Thou art my new horse-boy. Go and bed among my men. They are near the north end of the station, with the horses.'

'They will beat me to the south end of the station if I come without authority.'

Mahbub felt in his belt, wetted his thumb on a cake of Chinese ink, and dabbed the impression on a piece of soft native paper. From Balkh to Bombay men know that tough-ridged print with the old scar running diagonally across it.

'That is enough to show my headman. I come in the morning.'

'By which road?' said Kim.

'By the road from the city. There is but one, and then we return to Creighton Sahib. I have saved thee a beating.'

'Allah! What is a beating when the very head is loose on the shoulders?'

Kim slid out quietly into the night, walked half round the house, keeping close to the walls, and headed away from the station for a mile or so. Then, fetching a wide compass, he worked back at leisure, for he needed time to invent a story if any of Mahbub's retainers asked questions.

They were camped on a piece of waste ground beside the railway, and, being natives, had not, of course, unloaded the two trucks in which Mahbub's animals stood among a consignment of country-breds bought by the Bombay tram-company. The headman, a broken-down, consumptive-looking Mohammedan, promptly challenged Kim, but was pacified at sight of Mahbub's sign-manual.

'The Hajji has of his favour given me service,' said Kim testily. 'If this be doubted, wait till he comes in the morning. Meantime, a place by the fire.'

Followed the usual aimless babble that every low-caste native must raise on every occasion. It died down, and Kim lay out behind the little knot of Mahbub's followers, almost under the wheels of a horse-truck, a borrowed blanket for covering. Now a bed among brickbats and ballast-refuse on a damp night, between overcrowded horses and unwashed Baltis, would not appeal to many white boys; but Kim was utterly happy. Change of scene, service, and sur-roundings were the breath of his little nostrils, and thinking of the neat white cots of St Xavier's all arow under the punkah gave him joy as keen as the repetition of the multiplication-table in English.

'I am very old,' he thought sleepily. 'Every month I become a year more old. I was very young, and a fool to boot, when I took Mahbub's message to Umballa. Even when I was with that white Regiment I was very young and small and had no wisdom. But now I learn every day, and in three years the Colonel will take me out of the *madrissah* and let me go upon the Road with Mahbub hunting

for horses' pedigrees, or maybe I shall go by myself; or maybe I shall find the lama and go with him. Yes; that is best. To walk again as a *chela* with my lama when he comes back to Benares.' The thoughts came more slowly and disconnectedly. He was plunging into a beautiful dreamland when his ears caught a whisper, thin and sharp, above the monotonous babble round the fire. It came from behind the iron-skinned horse-truck.

'He is not here, then?'

'Where should he be but roystering in the city. Who looks for a rat in a frog-pond? Come away. He is not our man.'

'He must not go back beyond the Passes a second time. It is the order.'

'Hire some woman to drug him. It is a few rupees only, and there is no evidence.'

'Except the woman. It must be more certain; and remember the price upon his head.'

'Ay, but the police have a long arm, and we are far from the Border. If it were in Peshawur, now!'

'Yes—in Peshawur,' the second voice sneered. 'Peshawur, full of his blood-kin—full of bolt-holes and women behind whose clothes he will hide. Yes, Peshawur or Jehannum would suit us equally well.'

'Then what is the plan?'

'O fool, have I not told it a hundred times? Wait till he comes to lie down, and then one sure shot. The trucks are between us and pursuit. We have but to run back over the lines and go our way. They will not see whence the shot came. Wait here at least till the dawn. What manner of *faquir* art thou, to shiver at a little watching?'

'Oho!' thought Kim, behind close-shut eyes. 'Once again it is Mahbub. Indeed a white stallion's pedigree is not a good thing to peddle to Sahibs! Or maybe Mahbub has been selling other news. Now what is to do, Kim? I know not where Mahbub houses, and if he comes here before the dawn they will shoot him. That would be no profit for thee, Kim. And this is not a matter for the police. That would be no profit for Mahbub; and'—he giggled almost aloud—'I do not remember any lesson at Nucklao which will help me. Allah! Here is Kim and yonder are they. First, then, Kim must wake and go away, so that they shall not suspect. A bad dream wakes a man—thus—'

He threw the blanket off his face, and raised himself suddenly with the terrible, bubbling, meaningless yell of the Asiatic roused by nightmare.

'Urr-urr-urr-urr! Ya-la-la-la-la! *Narain*![5] The *churel*! The *churel*!'

5. An exclamation of the name of one of the Hindu gods, analogous to the Muslim exclamation below, "Allah kerim."

A *churel* is the peculiarly malignant ghost of a woman who has died in child-bed. She haunts lonely roads, her feet are turned backwards on the ankles, and she leads men to torment.

Louder rose Kim's quavering howl, till at last he leaped to his feet and staggered off sleepily, while the camp cursed him for waking them. Some twenty yards farther up the line he lay down again, taking care that the whisperers should hear his grunts and groans as he recomposed himself. After a few minutes he rolled towards the road and stole away into the thick darkness.

He padded along swiftly till he came to a culvert,[6] and dropped behind it, his chin on a level with the coping-stone. Here he could command all the night-traffic, himself unseen.

Two or three carts passed, jingling out to the suburbs; a coughing policeman and a hurrying foot-passenger or two who sang to keep off evil spirits. Then rapped the shod feet of a horse.

'Ah! This is more like Mahbub,' thought Kim, as the beast shied at the little head above the culvert.

'Ohé, Mahbub Ali,' he whispered, 'have a care!'

The horse was reined back almost on its haunches, and forced towards the culvert.

'Never again,' said Mahbub, 'will I take a shod horse for night-work. They pick up all the bones and nails in the city.' He stooped to lift its forefoot, and that brought his head within a foot of Kim's. 'Down—keep down,' he muttered. 'The night is full of eyes.'

'Two men wait thy coming behind the horse-trucks. They will shoot thee at thy lying down, because there is a price on thy head. I heard, sleeping near the horses.'

'Didst thou see them? . . . Hold still, Sire of Devils!' This furiously to the horse.

'No.'

'Was one dressed belike as a *faquir*?'

'One said to the other, "What manner of *faquir* art thou, to shiver at a little watching?"'

'Good. Go back to the camp and lie down. I do not die tonight.'

Mahbub wheeled his horse and vanished. Kim tore back down the ditch till he reached a point opposite his second resting-place, slipped across the road like a weasel, and recoiled himself in the blanket.

'At least Mahbub knows,' he thought contentedly. 'And certainly he spoke as one expecting it. I do not think those two men will profit by tonight's watch.'

An hour passed, and, with the best will in the world to keep awake all night, he slept deeply. Now and again a night train roared along

6. Drainage ditch.

the metals within twenty feet of him; but he had all the Oriental's indifference to mere noise, and it did not even weave a dream through his slumber.

Mahbub was anything but asleep. It annoyed him vehemently that people outside his tribe and unaffected by his casual amours[7] should pursue him for the life. His first and natural impulse was to cross the line lower down, work up again, and, catching his well-wishers from behind, summarily slay them. Here, he reflected with sorrow, another branch of the Government, totally unconnected with Colonel Creighton, might demand explanations which would be hard to supply; and he knew that south of the Border a perfectly ridiculous fuss is made about a corpse or so. He had not been troubled in this way since he sent Kim to Umballa with the message, and hoped that suspicion had been finally diverted.

Then a most brilliant notion struck him.

'The English do eternally tell the truth,' he said, 'therefore we of this country are eternally made foolish. By Allah, I will tell the truth to an Englishman! Of what use is the Government police if a poor Kabuli be robbed of his horses in their very trucks. This is as bad as Peshawur! I should lay a complaint at the station. Better still, some young Sahib on the Railway! They are zealous, and if they catch thieves it is remembered to their honour.'

He tied up his horse outside the station, and strode on to the platform.

'Hullo, Mahbub Ali!' said a young Assistant District Traffic Superintendent who was waiting to go down the line—a tall, tow-haired, horsey youth in dingy white linen. 'What are you doing here? Selling weeds[8]—eh?'

'No; I am not troubled for my horses. I come to look for Lutuf Ullah. I have a truck-load up the line. Could anyone take them out without the Railway's knowledge?'

'Shouldn't think so, Mahbub. You can claim against us if they do.'

'I have seen two men crouching under the wheels of one of the trucks nearly all night. *Faquirs* do not steal horses, so I gave them no more thought. I would find Lutuf Ullah, my partner.'

'The deuce you did? And you didn't bother your head about it? 'Pon my word, it's just almost as well that I met you. What were they like, eh?'

'They were only *faquirs*. They will no more than take a little grain, perhaps, from one of the trucks. There are many up the line. The State will never miss the dole. I came here seeking for my partner, Lutuf Ullah—'

7. Love affairs.
8. Thin, undernourished horses.

'Never mind your partner. Where are your horse-trucks?'

'A little to this side of the farthest place where they make lamps for the trains.'

'The signal-box! Yes.'

'And upon the rail nearest to the road upon the right-hand side— looking up the line thus. But as regards Lutuf Ullah—a tall man with a broken nose, and a Persian greyhound—Aie!'

The boy had hurried off to wake up a young and enthusiastic policeman; for, as he said, the Railway had suffered much from depredations in the goods-yard. Mahbub Ali chuckled in his dyed beard.

'They will walk in their boots, making a noise, and then they will wonder why there are no *faquirs*. They are very clever boys—Barton Sahib and Young Sahib.'

He waited idly for a few minutes, expecting to see them hurry up the line girt for action. A light engine slid through the station, and he caught a glimpse of young Barton in the cab.

'I did that child an injustice. He is not altogether a fool,' said Mahbub Ali. 'To take a fire-carriage for a thief is a new game!'

When Mahbub Ali came to his camp in the dawn, no one thought it worth while to tell him any news of the night. No one, at least, but one small horseboy, newly advanced to the great man's service, whom Mahbub called to his tiny tent to assist in some packing.

'It is all known to me,' whispered Kim, bending above saddle-bags. 'Two Sahibs came up on a *te-rain*. I was running to and fro in the dark on this side of the trucks as the *te-rain* moved up and down slowly. They fell upon two men sitting under this truck—Hajji, what shall I do with this lump of tobacco? Wrap it in paper and put it under the salt-bag? Yes—and struck them down. But one man struck at a Sahib with a *faquir*'s buck's horn' (Kim meant the con-joined black-buck horns, which are a *faquir*'s sole temporal weapon)—'the blood came. So the other Sahib, first smiting his own man senseless, smote the stabber with a short gun which had rolled from the first man's hand. They all raged as though mad together.'

Mahbub smiled with heavenly resignation. 'No! That is not so much *dewanee* (madness, or a case for the civil court—the word can be punned upon both ways) as *nizamut* (a criminal case). A gun, sayest thou? Ten good years in jail.'

'Then they both lay still, but I think they were nearly dead when they were put on the *te-rain*. Their heads moved thus. And there is much blood on the line. Come and see?'

'I have seen blood before. Jail is the sure place—and assuredly they will give false names, and assuredly no man will find them for a long time. They were unfriends of mine. Thy fate and mine seem on one string. What a tale for the healer of pearls! Now swiftly with

the saddle-bags and the cooking-platter. We will take out the horses and away to Simla.'[9]

Swiftly—as Orientals understand speed—with long explanations, with abuse and windy talk, carelessly, amid a hundred checks for little things forgotten, the untidy camp broke up and led the half-dozen stiff and fretful horses along the Kalka road in the fresh of the rain-swept dawn. Kim, regarded as Mahbub Ali's favourite by all who wished to stand well with the Pathan, was not called upon to work. They strolled on by the easiest of stages, halting every few hours at a wayside shelter. Very many Sahibs travel along the Kalka road; and, as Mahbub Ali says, every young Sahib must needs esteem himself a judge of a horse, and, though he be over head in debt to the money-lender, must make as if to buy. That was the reason that Sahib after Sahib, rolling along in a stage-carriage, would stop and open talk. Some would even descend from their vehicles and feel the horses' legs; asking inane questions, or, through sheer ignorance of the vernacular, grossly insulting the imperturbable trader.

'When first I dealt with Sahibs, and that was when Colonel Soady Sahib was Governor of Fort Abazai and flooded the Commissioner's camping-ground for spite,' Mahbub confided to Kim as the boy filled his pipe under a tree, 'I did not know how greatly they were fools, and this made me wroth. As thus—' and he told Kim a tale of an expression, misused in all innocence, that doubled Kim up with mirth. 'Now I see, however,'—he exhaled smoke slowly—'that it is with them as with all men—in certain matters they are wise, and in others most foolish. Very foolish it is to use the wrong word to a stranger; for though the heart may be clean of offence, how is the stranger to know that? He is more like to search truth with a dagger.'

'True. True talk,' said Kim solemnly. 'Fools speak of a cat when a woman is brought to bed, for instance. I have heard them.'

'Therefore, in one situate as thou art, it particularly behoves thee to remember this with both kinds of faces. Among Sahibs, never forgetting thou art a Sahib; among the folk of Hind, always remembering thou art—' He paused, with a puzzled smile.

'What am I? Mussalman, Hindu, Jain, or Buddhist? That is a hard knot.'

'Thou art beyond question an unbeliever, and therefore thou wilt be damned. So says my Law—or I think it does. But thou art also my Little Friend of all the World, and I love thee. So says my heart. This matter of creeds is like horse-flesh. The wise man knows

9. Hill station and seat of the imperial government in the summer, about seven thousand feet above sea level in the foothills of the Himalayas; a popular summer vacation place for the British, who needed to escape the heat of the plains.

horses are good—that there is a profit to be made from all; and for myself—but that I am a good Sunni[1] and hate the men of Tirah—I could believe the same of all the Faiths. Now manifestly a Kathiawar mare taken from the sands of her birthplace and removed to the west of Bengal founders—nor is even a Balkh stallion (and there are no better horses than those of Balkh, were they not so heavy in the shoulder) of any account in the great Northern deserts beside the snow-camels I have seen. Therefore I say in my heart the Faiths are like the horses. Each has merit in its own country.'

'But my lama said altogether a different thing.'

'Oh, he is an old dreamer of dreams from Bhotiyal. My heart is a little angry, Friend of all the World, that thou shouldst see such worth in a man so little known.'

'It is true, Hajji; but that worth do I see, and to him my heart is drawn.'

'And his to thine, I hear. Hearts are like horses. They come and they go against bit or spur. Shout Gul Sher Khan yonder to drive in that bay stallion's pickets more firmly. We do not want a horse-fight at every resting-stage, and the dun and the black will be locked[2] in a little . . . Now hear me. Is it necessary to the comfort of thy heart to see that lama?'

'It is one part of my bond,' said Kim. 'If I do not see him, and if he is taken from me, I will go out of that madrissah in Nucklao and, and—once gone, who is to find me again?'

'It is true. Never was colt held on a lighter heel-rope than thou.' Mahbub nodded his head.

'Do not be afraid.' Kim spoke as though he could have evanished on the moment. 'My lama has said that he will come to see me at the madrissah—'

'A beggar and his bowl in the presence of those young Sa—'

'Not all!' Kim cut in with a snort. 'Their eyes are blued[3] and their nails are blackened with low-caste blood, many of them. Sons of mehteranees[4]—brothers-in-law to the bhungi (sweeper).'

We need not follow the rest of the pedigree; but Kim made his little point clearly and without heat, chewing a piece of sugar-cane the while.

'Friend of all the World,' said Mahbub, pushing over the pipe for the boy to clean, 'I have met many men, women, and boys, and not

1. An orthodox Muslim. An early schism in Islam occurred between Sunnis, who believed that Islam should continue to choose its leaders (caliphs) through majority vote, and Shi'as, who believed its leaders (imams) should continue to be direct descendants of the Prophet, Muhammad, and Ali, the first imam. Most Indian Muslims are Sunni; most Persian Muslims are Shi'a; the Tirah, a tribe west of Peshawar, are Shi'a.
2. Mated.
3. Not blue irises, but a bluish tinge to the whites, a sign of racial hybridity.
4. Sweeper-women.

a few Sahibs. I have never in all my days met such an imp as thou art.'

'And why? When I always tell thee the truth.'

'Perhaps the very reason, for this is a world of danger to honest men.' Mahbub Ali hauled himself off the ground, girt in his belt, and went over to the horses.

'Or sell it?'

There was that in the tone that made Mahbub halt and turn. 'What new devilry?'

'Eight annas, and I will tell,' said Kim, grinning. 'It touches thy peace.'

'O Shaitan!' Mahbub gave the money.

'Rememberest thou the little business of the thieves in the dark, down yonder at Umballa?'

'Seeing they sought my life, I have not altogether forgotten. Why?'

'Rememberest thou the Kashmir Serai?'

'I will twist thy ears in a moment—Sahib.'

'No need—Pathan. Only, the second *faquir*, whom the Sahibs beat senseless, was the man who came to search thy bulkhead at Lahore. I saw his face as they helped him on the engine. The very same man.'

'Why didst thou not tell before?'

'Oh, he will go to jail, and be safe for some years. There is no need to tell more than is necessary at any one time. Besides, I did not then need money for sweetmeats.'

'*Allah kerim!*' said Mahbub Ali. 'Wilt thou some day sell my head for a few sweetmeats if the fit takes thee?'

• • • • •

Kim will remember till he dies that long, lazy journey from Umballa, through Kalka and the Pinjore Gardens near by, up to Simla. A sudden spate in the Gugger River swept down one horse (the most valuable, be sure), and nearly drowned Kim among the dancing boulders. Farther up the road the horses were stampeded by a Government elephant, and being in high condition of grass food, it cost a day and a half to get them together again. Then they met Sikandar Khan coming down with a few unsaleable screws[5]—remnants of his string—and Mahbub, who has more of horse-coping in his little fingernail than Sikandar Khan in all his tents, must needs buy two of the worst, and that meant eight hours' laborious diplomacy and untold tobacco. But it was all pure delight—the wandering road, climbing, dipping, and sweeping about the growing spurs;[6] the flush of the morning laid along the distant snows; the branched

5. Slang for poor-quality horses.
6. Mountain ridges.

cacti, tier upon tier on the stony hillsides; the voices of a thousand water-channels; the chatter of the monkeys; the solemn deodars, climbing one after another with down-drooped branches; the vista of the Plains rolled out far beneath them; the incessant twanging of the tonga-horns[7] and the wild rush of the led horses when a tonga swung round a curve; the halts for prayers (Mahbub was very religious in dry-washings and bellowings when time did not press); the evening conferences by the halting-places, when camels and bullocks chewed solemnly together and the stolid drivers told the news of the Road—all these things lifted Kim's heart to song within him.

'But, when the singing and dancing is done,' said Mahbub Ali, 'comes the Colonel Sahib's, and that is not so sweet.'

'A fair land—a most beautiful land is this of Hind—and the land of the Five Rivers[8] is fairer than all,' Kim half chanted. 'Into it I will go again if Mahbub Ali or the Colonel lift hand or foot against me. Once gone, who shall find me? Look, Hajji, is yonder the city of Simla? Allah, what a city!'

'My father's brother, and he was an old man when Mackerson Sahib's well was new at Peshawur,[9] could recall when there were but two houses in it.'

He led the horses below the main road into the lower Simla bazar—the crowded rabbit-warren that climbs up from the valley to the Town Hall at an angle of forty-five. A man who knows his way there can defy all the police of India's summer capital, so cunningly does veranda communicate with veranda, alley-way with alley-way, and bolt-hole with bolt-hole. Here live those who minister to the wants of the glad city—*jhampanis* pull the pretty ladies' rickshaws[1] by night and gamble till the dawn; grocers, oil-sellers, curio-vendors, firewood-dealers, priests, pickpockets, and native employees of the Government. Here are discussed by courtesans the things which are supposed to be profoundest secrets of the India Council; and here gather all the sub-sub-agents of half the Native States. Here, too, Mahbub Ali rented a room, much more securely locked than his bulkhead at Lahore, in the house of a Mohammedan cattle-dealer. It was a place of miracles, too, for there went in at twilight a Mohammedan horseboy, and there came out an hour later a Eurasian lad—the Lucknow girl's dye was of the best—in badly-fitting shop-clothes.

'I have spoken with Creighton Sahib,' quoth Mahbub Ali, 'and a second time has the Hand of Friendship averted the Whip of Calamity. He says that thou hast altogether wasted sixty days upon

7. *Tonga*: small carriage pulled by horses.
8. The Punjab.
9. Colonel Mackerson was a British commissioner of Peshawar; he was assassinated in 1853.
1. Small hooded carriages pulled by one man, the *jhampani*.

the Road, and it is too late, therefore, to send thee to any Hill-school.'

'I have said that my holidays are my own. I do not go to school twice over. That is one part of my bond.'

'The Colonel Sahib is not yet aware of that contract. Thou art to lodge in Lurgan Sahib's house till it is time to go again to Nucklao.'

'I had sooner lodge with thee, Mahbub.'

'Thou dost not know the honour. Lurgan Sahib himself asked for thee. Thou wilt go up the hill and along the road atop, and there thou must forget for a while that thou hast ever seen or spoken to me, Mahbub Ali, who sells horses to Creighton Sahib, whom thou dost not know. Remember this order.'

Kim nodded. 'Good,' said he, 'and who is Lurgan Sahib? Nay'— he caught Mahbub's sword-keen glance—'indeed I have never heard his name. Is he by chance'—he lowered his voice—'one of us?'

'What talk is this of *us*, Sahib?' Mahbub Ali returned, in the tone he used towards Europeans. 'I am a Pathan; thou art a Sahib and the son of a Sahib. Lurgan Sahib has a shop among the European shops.[2] All Simla knows it. Ask there . . . and, Friend of all the World, he is one to be obeyed to the last wink of his eyelashes. Men say he does magic, but that should not touch thee. Go up the hill and ask. Here begins the Great Game.'

Chapter 9

> S'doaks was son of Yelth the wise—
> Chief of the Raven clan.
> Itswoot the Bear had him in care
> To make him a medicine-man.
>
> He was quick and quicker to learn—
> Bold and bolder to dare:
> He danced the dread Kloo-Kwallie Dance
> To tickle Itswoot the Bear!
> *Oregon Legend.*[1]

Kim flung himself wholeheartedly upon the next turn of the wheel. He would be a Sahib again for a while. In that idea, so soon as he had reached the broad road under Simla Town Hall, he cast about

2. The character is based on a real person, Alexander M. Jacob, who ran a jewelry store in Simla. He was an adventurer who gave several different exotic accounts of his life.
1. This Native American "legend" is the invention of the Irish-American dramatist Dion Boucicault (1822–1890) and thus is one of the few chapter epigraphs not by Kipling. S'doaks and Itswoot parallel Kim and Lurgan Sahib.

for one to impress. A Hindu child, some ten years old, squatted under a lamp-post.

'Where is Mr Lurgan's house?' demanded Kim.

'I do not understand English,' was the answer, and Kim shifted his speech accordingly.

'I will show.'

Together they set off through the mysterious dusk, full of the noises of a city below the hillside, and the breath of a cool wind in deodar-crowned Jakko,[2] shouldering the stars. The house-lights, scattered on every level, made, as it were, a double firmament. Some were fixed, others belonged to the rickshaws of the careless, open-spoken English folk, going out to dinner.

'It is here,' said Kim's guide, and halted in a veranda flush with the main road. No door stayed them, but a curtain of beaded reeds that split up the lamplight beyond.

'He is come,' said the boy, in a voice little louder than a sigh, and vanished. Kim felt sure that the boy had been posted to guide him from the first, but, putting a bold face on it, parted the curtain. A black-bearded man, with a green shade over his eyes, sat at a table, and, one by one, with short, white hands, picked up globules of light from a tray before him, threaded them on a glancing silken string, and hummed to himself the while. Kim was conscious that beyond the circle of light the room was full of things that smelt like all the temples of all the East. A whiff of musk, a puff of sandalwood, and a breath of sickly jessamine-oil caught his opened nostrils.

'I am here,' said Kim at last, speaking in the vernacular: the smells made him forget that he was to be a Sahib.

'Seventy-nine, eighty, eighty-one,' the man counted to himself, stringing pearl after pearl so quickly that Kim could scarcely follow his fingers. He slid off the green shade and looked fixedly at Kim for a full half-minute. The pupils of the eye dilated and closed to pin-pricks, as if at will. There was a *faquir* by the Taksali Gate who had just this gift and made money by it, especially when cursing silly women. Kim stared with interest. His disreputable friend could further twitch his ears, almost like a goat, and Kim was disappointed that this new man could not imitate him.

'Do not be afraid,' said Lurgan Sahib suddenly.

'Why should I fear?'

'Thou wilt sleep here tonight, and stay with me till it is time to go again to Nucklao. It is an order.'

'It is an order,' Kim repeated. 'But where shall I sleep?'

'Here, in this room.' Lurgan Sahib waved his hand towards the darkness behind him.

2. The eight-thousand-foot mountain peak near Simla.

'So be it,' said Kim composedly. 'Now?'

He nodded and held the lamp above his head. As the light swept them, there leaped out from the walls a collection of Tibetan devil-dance masks, hanging above the fiend-embroidered draperies of those ghastly functions—horned masks, scowling masks, and masks of idiotic terror. In a corner, a Japanese warrior, mailed and plumed, menaced him with a halberd, and a score of lances and *khandas* and *kuttars*[3] gave back the unsteady gleam. But what interested Kim more than all these things—he had seen devil-dance masks at the Lahore Museum—was a glimpse of the soft-eyed Hindu child who had left him in the doorway, sitting cross-legged under the table of pearls with a little smile on his scarlet lips.

'I think that Lurgan Sahib wishes to make me afraid. And I am sure that that devil's brat below the table wishes to see me afraid. This place,' he said aloud, 'is like a Wonder House. Where is my bed?'

Lurgan Sahib pointed to a native quilt in a corner by the loath-some masks, picked up the lamp, and left the room black.

'Was that Lurgan Sahib?' Kim asked as he cuddled down. No answer. He could hear the Hindu boy breathing, however, and, guided by the sound, crawled across the floor, and cuffed into the darkness, crying: 'Give answer, devil! Is this the way to lie to a Sahib?'

From the darkness he fancied he could hear the echo of a chuckle. It could not be his soft-fleshed companion, because he was weeping. So Kim lifted up his voice and called aloud: 'Lurgan Sahib! O Lurgan Sahib! Is it an order that thy servant does not speak to me?'

'It is an order.' The voice came from behind him and he started.

'Very good. But remember,' he muttered, as he resought the quilt, 'I will beat thee in the morning. I do not love Hindus.'

That was no cheerful night; the room being overfull of voices and music. Kim was waked twice by someone calling his name. The second time he set out in search, and ended by bruising his nose against a box that certainly spoke with a human tongue, but in no sort of human accent. It seemed to end in a tin trumpet and to be joined by wires to a smaller box on the floor—so far, at least, as he could judge by touch. And the voice, very hard and whirring, came out of the trumpet. Kim rubbed his nose and grew furious, thinking, as usual, in Hindi.

'This with a beggar from the bazar might be good, but—I am a Sahib and the son of a Sahib and, which is twice as much more beside, a student of Nucklao. Yess' (here he turned to English), 'a

3. Both short swords.

boy of St Xavier's. Damn Mr Lurgan's eyes!—It is some sort of machinery like a sewing-machine. Oh, it is a *great* cheek of him—we are not frightened that way at Lucknow—No!' Then in Hindi: 'But what does *he* gain? He is only a trader—I am in his shop. But Creighton Sahib is a Colonel—and I think Creighton Sahib gave orders that it should be done. *How* I will beat that Hindu in the morning! What is this?'

The trumpet-box was pouring out a string of the most elaborate abuse that even Kim had ever heard, in a high uninterested voice, that for a moment lifted the short hairs of his neck. When the vile thing drew breath, Kim was reassured by the soft, sewing-machine-like whirr.

'*Chûp!* (Be still)' he cried, and again he heard a chuckle that decided him. '*Chûp*—or I break your head.'

The box took no heed. Kim wrenched at the tin trumpet and something lifted with a click. He had evidently raised a lid. If there were a devil inside, now was its time, for—he sniffed—thus did the sewing-machines of the bazar smell. He would clean that *shaitan*. He slipped off his jacket, and plunged it into the box's mouth. Something long and round bent under the pressure, there was a whirr and the voice stopped—as voices must if you ram a thrice-doubled coat onto the wax cylinder and into the works of an expensive phonograph. Kim finished his slumbers with a serene mind.

In the morning he was aware of Lurgan Sahib looking down on him.

'Oah!' said Kim, firmly resolved to cling to his Sahib-dom. 'There was a box in the night that gave me bad talk. So I stopped it. Was it your box?'

The man held out his hand.

'Shake hands, O'Hara,' he said. 'Yes, it was my box. I keep such things because my friends the Rajahs like them. That one is broken, but it was cheap at the price. Yes, my friends, the Kings, are very fond of toys—and so am I sometimes.'

Kim looked him over out of the corners of his eyes. He was a Sahib in that he wore Sahib's clothes; the accent of his Urdu, the intonation of his English, showed that he was anything but a Sahib. He seemed to understand what moved in Kim's mind ere the boy opened his mouth, and he took no pains to explain himself as did Father Victor or the Lucknow masters. Sweetest of all—he treated Kim as an equal on the Asiatic side.

'I am sorry you cannot beat my boy this morning. He says he will kill you with a knife or poison. He is jealous, so I have put him in the corner and I shall not speak to him today. He has just tried to kill me. You must help me with the breakfast. He is almost too jealous to trust, just now.'

Now a genuine imported Sahib from England would have made a great to-do over this tale. Lurgan Sahib stated it as simply as Mahbub Ali was used to record his little affairs in the North.

The back veranda of the shop was built out over the sheer hillside, and they looked down into their neighbours' chimney-pots, as is the custom of Simla. But even more than the purely Persian meal cooked by Lurgan Sahib with his own hands, the shop fascinated Kim. The Lahore Museum was larger, but here were more wonders—ghost-daggers[4] and prayer-wheels from Tibet; turquoise and raw amber necklaces; green jade bangles; curiously packed incense-sticks in jars crusted over with raw garnets; the devil-masks of overnight and a wall full of peacock-blue draperies; gilt figures of Buddha, and little portable lacquer altars; Russian samovars[5] with turquoises on the lid; egg-shell china sets in quaint octagonal cane boxes; yellow ivory crucifixes—from Japan of all places in the world, so Lurgan Sahib said; carpets in dusty bales, smelling atrociously, pushed back behind torn and rotten screens of geometrical work; Persian water-jugs for the hands after meals; dull copper incense-burners neither Chinese nor Persian, with friezes of fantastic devils running round them; tarnished silver belts that knotted like raw hide; hairpins of jade, ivory, and plasma;[6] arms of all sorts and kinds, and a thousand other oddments were cased, or piled, or merely thrown into the room, leaving a clear space only round the rickety deal table, where Lurgan Sahib worked.

'Those things are nothing,' said his host, following Kim's glance. 'I buy them because they are pretty, and sometimes I sell—if I like the buyer's look. My work is on the table—some of it.'

It blazed in the morning light—all red and blue and green flashes, picked out with the vicious blue-white spurt of a diamond here and there. Kim opened his eyes.

'Oh, they are quite well, those stones. It will not hurt them to take the sun. Besides, they are cheap. But with sick stones it is very different.' He piled Kim's plate anew. 'There is no one but *me* can doctor a sick pearl and re-blue turquoises. I grant you opals—any fool can cure an opal—but for a sick pearl there is only me. Suppose I were to die! Then there would be no one . . . Oh no! *You* cannot do anything with jewels. It will be quite enough if you understand a little about the Turquoise—some day.'

He moved to the end of the veranda to refill the heavy, porous clay water-jug from the filter.

'Do you want drink?'

4. Used by Tibetan exorcists to stab demons.
5. Double-decked urns with taps at the bottom used to boil water for tea.
6. Green quartz.

Kim nodded. Lurgan Sahib, fifteen feet off, laid one hand on the jar. Next instant, it stood at Kim's elbow, full to within half an inch of the brim—the white cloth only showing, by a small wrinkle, where it had slid into place.

'Wah!' said Kim in most utter amazement. 'That is magic.' Lurgan Sahib's smile showed that the compliment had gone home.

'Throw it back.'

'It will break.'

'I say, throw it back.'

Kim pitched it at random. It fell short and crashed into fifty pieces, while the water dripped through the rough veranda boarding.

'I said it would break.'

'All one. Look at it. Look at the largest piece.'

That lay with a sparkle of water in its curve, as it were a star on the floor. Kim looked intently. Lurgan Sahib laid one hand gently on the nape of his neck, stroked it twice or thrice, and whispered: 'Look! It shall come to life again, piece by piece. First the big piece shall join itself to two others on the right and the left—on the right and the left. Look!'

To save his life, Kim could not have turned his head. The light touch held him as in a vice, and his blood tingled pleasantly through him. There was one large piece of the jar where there had been three, and above them the shadowy outline of the entire vessel. He could see the veranda through it, but it was thickening and darkening with each beat of his pulse. Yet the jar—how slowly the thoughts came!—the jar had been smashed before his eyes. Another wave of prickling fire raced down his neck, as Lurgan Sahib moved his hand.

'Look! It is coming into shape,' said Lurgan Sahib.

So far Kim had been thinking in Hindi, but a tremor came on him, and with an effort like that of a swimmer before sharks, who hurls himself half out of the water, his mind leaped up from a darkness that was swallowing it and took refuge in—the multiplication-table in English!

'Look! It is coming into shape,' whispered Lurgan Sahib.

The jar had been smashed—yess, smashed—not the native word, he would not think of that—but smashed—into fifty pieces, and twice three was six, and thrice three was nine, and four times three was twelve. He clung desperately to the repetition. The shadow-outline of the jar cleared like a mist after rubbing eyes. There were the broken shards; there was the spilt water drying in the sun, and through the cracks of the veranda showed, all ribbed, the white house-wall below—and thrice twelve was thirty-six!

'Look! Is it coming into shape?' asked Lurgan Sahib.

'But it *is* smashed—smashed,' he gasped—Lurgan Sahib had been

muttering softly for the last half-minute. Kim wrenched his head aside. 'Look! *Dekho!*[7] It is there as it was there.'

'It is there as it was there,' said Lurgan, watching Kim closely while the boy rubbed his neck. 'But you are the first of many who has ever seen it so.' He wiped his broad forehead.

'Was that more magic?' Kim asked suspiciously. The tingle had gone from his veins; he felt unusually wide awake.

'No, that was not magic. It was only to see if there was—a flaw in a jewel. Sometimes very fine jewels will fly all to pieces if a man holds them in his hand, and knows the proper way. That is why one must be careful before one sets them. Tell me, did you see the shape of the pot?'

'For a little time. It began to grow like a flower from the ground.'

'And then what did you do? I mean, how did you think?'

'Oah! I knew it was broken, and so, I think, that was what I thought—and it *was* broken.'

'Hm! Has anyone ever done that same sort of magic to you before?'

'If it was,' said Kim, 'do you think I should let it again? I should run away.'

'And now you are not afraid—eh?'

'Not now.'

Lurgan Sahib looked at him more closely than ever. 'I shall ask Mahbub Ali—not now, but some day later,' he muttered. 'I am pleased with you—yes; and I am pleased with you—no. You are the first that ever saved himself. I wish I knew what it was that . . . But you are right. You should not tell that—not even to me.'

He turned into the dusky gloom of the shop, and sat down at the table, rubbing his hands softly. A small, husky sob came from behind a pile of carpets. It was the Hindu child obediently facing towards the wall. His thin shoulders worked with grief.

'Ah! He is jealous, so jealous. I wonder if he will try to poison me again in my breakfast, and make me cook it twice.'

'*Kubbee—kubbee nahin* (Never—never. No!)', came the broken answer.

'And whether he will kill this other boy?'

'*Kubbee—kubbee nahin.*'

'What do *you* think he will do?' He turned suddenly on Kim.

'Oah! I do not know. Let him go, perhaps. Why did he want to poison you?'

'Because he is so fond of me. Suppose you were fond of someone, and you saw someone come, and the man you were fond of was more pleased with him than he was with you, what would you do?'

7. Look!

Kim thought. Lurgan repeated the sentence slowly in the vernacular.

'I should not poison that man,' said Kim reflectively, 'but I should beat that boy—*if* that boy was fond of my man. But first, I would ask that boy if it were true.'

'Ah! He thinks everyone must be fond of me.'

'Then I think he is a fool.'

'Hearest thou?' said Lurgan Sahib to the shaking shoulders. 'The Sahib's son thinks thou art a little fool. Come out, and next time thy heart is troubled, do not try white arsenic quite so openly. Surely the Devil Dasim was lord of our table-cloth that day! It might have made me ill, child, and then a stranger would have guarded the jewels. Come!'

The child, heavy-eyed with much weeping, crept out from behind the bale and flung himself passionately at Lurgan Sahib's feet, with an extravagance of remorse that impressed even Kim.

'I will look into the ink-pools[8]—I will faithfully guard the jewels! Oh, my Father and my Mother, send *him* away!' He indicated Kim with a backward jerk of his bare heel.

'Not yet—not yet. In a little while he will go away again. But now he is at school—at a new *madrissah*—and thou shalt be his teacher. Play the Play of the Jewels against him. I will keep tally.'

The child dried his tears at once, and dashed to the back of the shop, whence he returned with a copper tray.

'Give me!' he said to Lurgan Sahib. 'Let them come from thy hand, for he may say that I knew them before.'

'Gently—gently,' the man replied, and from a drawer under the table dealt a half-handful of clattering trifles into the tray.

'Now,' said the child, waving an old newspaper. 'Look on them as long as thou wilt, stranger. Count and, if need be, handle. One look is enough for *me*.' He turned his back proudly.

'But what is the game?'

'When thou hast counted and handled and art sure that thou canst remember them all, I cover them with this paper, and thou must tell over the tally to Lurgan Sahib. *I* will write mine.'

'Oah!' The instinct of competition waked in his breast. He bent over the tray. There were but fifteen stones on it. 'That is easy,' he said after a minute. The child slipped the paper over the winking jewels and scribbled in a native account-book.

'There are under that paper five blue stones—one big, one smaller, and three small,' said Kim, all in haste. 'There are four green stones, and one with a hole in it; there is one yellow stone that I can see through, and one like a pipe-stem. There are two red

8. Held in the palm of the hand to facilitate hypnotism.

stones, and—and—I made the count fifteen, but two I have forgotten. No! Give me time. One was of ivory, little and brownish; and—and—give me time . . .'

'One—two'—Lurgan Sahib counted him out up to ten. Kim shook his head.

'Hear my count!' the child burst in, trilling with laughter. 'First, are two flawed sapphires—one of two ruttees[9] and one of four as I should judge. The four-ruttee sapphire is chipped at the edge. There is one Turkestan turquoise, plain with black veins, and there are two inscribed—one with a Name of God in gilt, and the other being cracked across, for it came out of an old ring, I cannot read. We have now all five blue stones. Four flawed emeralds there are, but one is drilled in two places, and one is a little carven—'

'Their weights?' said Lurgan Sahib impassively.

'Three—five—five—and four ruttees as I judge it. There is one piece of old greenish pipe amber, and a cut topaz from Europe. There is one ruby of Burma, of two ruttees, without a flaw, and there is a balas-ruby,[1] flawed, of two ruttees. There is a carved ivory from China representing a rat sucking an egg; and there is last—ah ha!—a ball of crystal as big as a bean set on a gold leaf.'

He clapped his hands at the close.

'He is thy master,' said Lurgan Sahib, smiling.

'Huh! He knew the names of the stones,' said Kim, flushing. 'Try again! With common things such as he and I both know.'

They heaped the tray again with odds and ends gathered from the shop, and even the kitchen, and every time the child won, till Kim marvelled.

'Bind my eyes—let me feel once with my fingers, and even *then* I will leave thee open-eyed behind,' he challenged.

Kim stamped with vexation when the lad made his boast good.

'If it were men—or horses,' he said, 'I could do better. This playing with tweezers and knives and scissors is too little.'

'Learn first—teach later,' said Lurgan Sahib. 'Is he thy master?'

'Truly. But how is it done?'

'By doing it many times over till it is done perfectly—for it is worth doing.'

The Hindu boy, in highest feather, actually patted Kim on the back.

'Do not despair,' he said. 'I myself will teach thee.'

'And I will see that thou art well taught,' said Lurgan Sahib, still speaking in the vernacular, 'for except my boy here—it was foolish of him to buy so much white arsenic when, if he had asked, I could

9. Seeds used as weights in a balance scale, each approximately one carat.
1. A red stone from Afghanistan, not truly a ruby.

have given it—except my boy here I have not in a long time met with one better worth teaching. And there are ten days more ere thou canst return to Lucknao where they teach nothing—at the long price. We shall, I think, be friends.'

They were a most mad ten days, but Kim enjoyed himself too much to reflect on their craziness. In the morning they played the Jewel Game—sometimes with veritable stones, sometimes with piles of swords and daggers, sometimes with photographs of natives. Through the afternoons he and the Hindu boy would mount guard in the shop, sitting dumb behind a carpet-bale or a screen and watching Mr Lurgan's many and very curious visitors. There were small Rajahs, escorts coughing in the veranda, who came to buy curiosities—such as phonographs and mechanical toys. There were ladies in search of necklaces, and men, it seemed to Kim—but his mind may have been vitiated by early training—in search of the ladies; natives from independent and feudatory Courts whose ostensible business was the repair of broken necklaces—rivers of light poured out upon the table—but whose true end seemed to be to raise money for angry Maharanees[2] or young Rajahs. There were Babus to whom Lurgan Sahib talked with austerity and authority, but at the end of each interview he gave them money in coined silver and currency notes. There were occasional gatherings of long-coated theatrical natives who discussed metaphysics in English and Bengali, to Mr Lurgan's great edification. He was always interested in religions. At the end of the day, Kim and the Hindu boy—whose name varied at Lurgan's pleasure—were expected to give a detailed account of all that they had seen and heard—their view of each man's character, as shown in his face, talk, and manner, and their notions of his real errand. After dinner, Lurgan Sahib's fancy turned more to what might be called dressing-up, in which game he took a most informing interest. He could paint faces to a marvel; with a brush-dab here and a line there changing them past recognition. The shop was full of all manner of dresses and turbans, and Kim was apparelled variously as a young Mohammedan of good family, an oilman, and once—which was a joyous evening—as the son of an Oudh landholder in the fullest of full dress. Lurgan Sahib had a hawk's eye to detect the least flaw in the make-up; and lying on a worn teakwood couch, would explain by the half-hour together how such and such a caste talked, or walked, or coughed, or spat, or sneezed, and, since 'hows' matter little in this world, the 'why' of everything. The Hindu child played this game clumsily. That little mind, keen as an icicle where tally of jewels was concerned, could not temper itself to enter another's soul; but a demon in Kim woke

2. Princesses, the feminine of Maharaja.

up and sang with joy as he put on the changing dresses, and changed speech and gesture therewith.

Carried away by enthusiasm, he volunteered to show Lurgan Sahib one evening how the disciples of a certain caste of *faquir*, old Lahore acquaintances, begged doles by the roadside; and what sort of language he would use to an Englishman, to a Punjabi farmer going to a fair, and to a woman without a veil. Lurgan Sahib laughed immensely, and begged Kim to stay as he was, immobile for half an hour—cross-legged, ash-smeared, and wild-eyed, in the back room. At the end of that time entered a hulking, obese Babu whose stockinged legs shook with fat, and Kim opened on him with a shower of wayside chaff. Lurgan Sahib—this annoyed Kim— watched the Babu and not the play.

'I think,' said the Babu heavily, lighting a cigarette, 'I am of opee-nion that it is most extraordinary and effeecient performance. Except that you had told me I should have opined that—that—that you were pulling my legs. How soon can he become approximately effeecient chain-man? Because *then* I shall indent for him.'

'That is what he must learn at Lucknow.'

'Then order him to be jolly-dam'-quick. Good-night, Lurgan.' The Babu swung out with the gait of a bogged cow.

When they were telling over the day's list of visitors, Lurgan Sahib asked Kim who he thought the man might be.

'God knows!' said Kim cheerily. The tone might almost have deceived Mahbub Ali, but it failed entirely with the healer of sick pearls.

'That is true. God, He knows; but I wish to know what you think.'

Kim glanced sideways at his companion, whose eye had a way of compelling truth.

'I—I think he will want me when I come from the school, but'— confidentially, as Lurgan Sahib nodded approval—'I do not under-stand how *he* can wear many dresses and talk many tongues.'

'Thou wilt understand many things later. He is a writer of tales for a certain Colonel. His honour is great only in Simla, and it is notice-able that he has no name, but only a number and a letter—that is a custom among us.'[3]

'And is there a price upon his head too—as upon Mah[4]—all the others?'

'Not yet; but if a boy rose up who is now sitting here and went— look, the door is open!—as far as a certain house with a red-painted veranda, behind that which was the old theatre in the Lower Bazar,

3. Indian employees of the Indian Survey Department were collectively known as Pundits and assigned codes, each made up of a letter and a number, for their own safety in case of discovery.
4. Kim almost says "Mahbub."

and whispered through the shutters: "Hurree Chunder Mookerjee
bore the bad news of last month", that boy might take away a belt
full of rupees.'

'How many?' said Kim promptly.

'Five hundred—a thousand—as many as he might ask for.'

'Good. And for how long might such a boy live after the news was
told?' He smiled merrily at Lurgan Sahib's very beard.

'Ah! That is to be well thought of. Perhaps if he were very clever,
he might live out the day—but not the night. By no means the
night.'

'Then what is the Babu's pay if so much is put upon his head?'

'Eighty—perhaps a hundred—perhaps a hundred and fifty
rupees; but the pay is the least part of the work. From time to time,
God causes men to be born—and thou art one of them—who have
a lust to go abroad at the risk of their lives and discover news—today
it may be of far-off things, tomorrow of some hidden mountain, and
the next day of some near-by men who have done a foolishness
against the State. These souls are very few; and of these few, not
more than ten are of the best. Among these ten I count the Babu,
and that is curious. How great, therefore, and desirable must be a
business that brazens the heart of a Bengali!'[5]

'True. But the days go slowly for me. I am yet a boy, and it is only
within two months I learned to write Angrezi.[6] Even now I cannot
read it well. And there are yet years and years and long years before
I can be even a chain-man.'

'Have patience, Friend of all the World'—Kim started at the title.
'Would I had a few of the years that so irk thee. I have proved thee
in several small ways. This will not be forgotten when I make my
report to the Colonel Sahib.' Then, changing suddenly into English
with a deep laugh:

'By Jove! O'Hara, I think there is a great deal in you; but you must
not become proud and you must not talk. You must go back to
Lucknow and be a good little boy and mind your book, as the
English say, and perhaps, next holidays if you care, you can come
back to me!' Kim's face fell. 'Oh, I mean *if* you like. I know where
you want to go.'

Four days later a seat was booked for Kim and his small trunk at
the rear of a Kalka tonga. His companion was the whale-like Babu,
who, with a fringed shawl wrapped round his head, and his fat
openwork-stockinged left leg tucked under him, shivered and
grunted in the morning chill.

5. Hardens the heart. Hurree Chunder, "the Babu," both uses and subverts the British car-
 icature of the Bengali as passive and cowardly.
6. English.

'How comes it that this man is one of *us*?' thought Kim consider-
ing the jelly back as they jolted down the road; and the reflection
threw him into most pleasant day-dreams. Lurgan Sahib had given
him five rupees—a splendid sum—as well as the assurance of his
protection if he worked. Unlike Mahbub, Lurgan Sahib had spoken
most explicitly of the reward that would follow obedience, and Kim
was content. If only, like the Babu, he could enjoy the dignity of a
letter and a number—and a price upon his head! Some day he
would be all that and more. Some day he might be almost as great
as Mahbub Ali! The housetops of his search should be half India; he
would follow Kings and Ministers, as in the old days he had fol-
lowed *vakils*[7] and lawyers' touts across Lahore city for Mahbub Ali's
sake. Meantime, there was the present, and not at all unpleasant,
fact of St Xavier's immediately before him. There would be new boys
to condescend to, and there would be tales of holiday adventures to
hear. Young Martin, son of the tea-planter at Manipur, had boasted
that he would go to war, with a rifle, against the head-hunters. That
might be, but it was certain young Martin had not been blown half
across the forecourt of a Patiala palace by an explosion of fireworks;
nor had he . . . Kim fell to telling himself the story of his own
adventures through the last three months. He could paralyse St
Xavier's—even the biggest boys who shaved—with the recital, were
that permitted. But it was, of course, out of the question. There
would be a price upon his head in good time, as Lurgan Sahib had
assured him; and if he talked foolishly now, not only would that
price never be set, but Colonel Creighton would cast him off—and
he would be left to the wrath of Lurgan Sahib and Mahbub Ali—for
the short space of life that would remain to him.

'So I should lose Delhi for the sake of a fish,' was his proverbial
philosophy. It behoved him to forget his holidays (there would
always remain the fun of inventing imaginary adventures) and, as
Lurgan Sahib had said, to work.

Of all the boys hurrying back to St Xavier's, from Sukkur in the
sands to Galle beneath the palms, none was so filled with virtue as
Kimball O'Hara, jiggering down to Umballa behind Hurree
Chunder Mookerjee, whose name on the books of one section of the
Ethnological Survey was R17.

And if additional spur were needed, the Babu supplied it. After a
huge meal at Kalka, he spoke uninterruptedly. Was Kim going to
school? Then he, an MA of Calcutta University, would explain the
advantages of education. There were marks to be gained by due
attention to Latin and Wordsworth's *Excursion* (all this was Greek
to Kim). French, too, was vital, and the best was to be picked up in

7. Lawyers.

Chandernagore a few miles from Calcutta. Also a man might go far, as he himself had done, by strict attention to plays called *Lear* and *Julius Caesar*, both much in demand by examiners. *Lear* was not so full of historical allusions as *Julius Caesar*; the book cost four annas, but could be bought second-hand in Bow Bazar for two. Still more important than Wordsworth, or the eminent authors, Burke and Hare,[8] was the art and science of mensuration. A boy who had passed his examination in these branches—for which, by the way, there were no cram-books—could, by merely marching over a country with a compass and a level and a straight eye, carry away a picture of that country which might be sold for large sums in coined silver. But as it was occasionally inexpedient to carry about measuring-chains a boy would do well to know the precise length of his own foot-pace, so that when he was deprived of what Hurree Chunder called 'adventitious aids' he might still tread his distances. To keep count of thousands of paces, Hurree Chunder's experience had shown him nothing more valuable than a rosary of eighty-one or a hundred and eight beads, for 'it was divisible and sub-divisible into many multiples and sub-multiples'. Through the volleying drifts of English, Kim caught the general trend of the talk, and it interested him very much. Here was a new craft that a man could tuck away in his head and by the look of the large wide world unfolding itself before him, it seemed that the more a man knew the better for him.

Said the Babu when he had talked for an hour and a half, 'I hope some day to enjoy your offeecial acquaintance. *Ad interim*, if I may be pardoned that expression, I shall give you this betel-box, which is highly valuable article and cost me two rupees only four years ago.' It was a cheap, heart-shaped brass thing with three compartments for carrying the eternal betel-nut, lime and *pan*-leaf; but it was filled with little tabloid-bottles. 'That is reward of merit for your performance in character of that holy man. You see, you are so young you think you will last for ever and not take care of your body. It is great nuisance to go sick in the middle of business. I am fond of drugs myself, and they are handy to cure poor people too. These are good Departmental drugs—quinine and so on. I give it you for souvenir. Now good-bye. I have urgent private business here by the roadside.'

He slipped out noiselessly as a cat, on the Umballa road, hailed a passing cart and jingled away, while Kim, tongue-tied, twiddled the brass betel-box in his hands.

• • • • •

The record of a boy's education interests few save his parents,

8. An in-joke. Hurree Babu refers to Edmund Burke, the Irish statesman and writer, and Augustus Hare, an English travel-writer; but the juxtaposition of the names recalls William Burke and William Hare, early-nineteenth-century serial killers.

and, as you know, Kim was an orphan. It is written in the books of St Xavier's in Partibus that a report of Kim's progress was forwarded at the end of each term to Colonel Creighton and to Father Victor, from whose hands duly came the money for his schooling. It is further recorded in the same books that he showed a great aptitude for mathematical studies as well as map-making, and carried away a prize (*The Life of Lord Lawrence*, tree-calf,[9] two vols., nine rupees, eight annas) for proficiency therein; and the same term played in St Xavier's eleven[1] against the Alighur Mohammedan College, his age being fourteen years and ten months. He was also re-vaccinated (from which we may assume that there had been another epidemic of smallpox at Lucknow) about the same time. Pencil notes on the edge of an old muster-roll record that he was punished several times for 'conversing with improper persons', and it seems that he was once sentenced to heavy pains for 'absenting himself for a day in the company of a street beggar'. That was when he got over the gate and pleaded with the lama through a whole day down the banks of the Gumti to accompany him on the Road next holidays—for one month—for a little week; and the lama set his face as a flint against it, averring that the time had not yet come. Kim's business, said the old man as they ate cakes together, was to get all the wisdom of the Sahibs and then he would see. The Hand of Friendship must in some way have averted the Whip of Calamity, for six weeks later Kim seems to have passed an examination in elementary surveying 'with great credit', his age being fifteen years and eight months. From this date the record is silent. His name does not appear in the year's batch of those who entered for the subordinate Survey of India, but against it stand the words 'removed on appointment'.

Several times in those three years, cast up at the Temple of the Tirthankars in Benares the lama, a little thinner and a shade yellower, if that were possible, but gentle and untainted as ever. Sometimes it was from the South that he came—from south of Tuticorin, whence the wonderful fire-boats go to Ceylon where are priests who know Pali;[2] sometimes it was from the wet green West and the thousand cotton-factory chimneys that ring Bombay; and once from the North, where he had doubled back eight hundred miles to talk for a day with the Keeper of the Images in the Wonder House. He would stride to his cell in the cool, cut marble—the priests of the Temple were good to the old man,—wash off the dust of travel, make prayer, and depart for Lucknow, well accustomed now to the way of the rail, in a third-class carriage. Returning, it was noticeable, as his friend the Seeker

9. Bound in calfskin with a motif of trees. Lawrence was governor-general of India, 1864–69.
1. Cricket team.
2. Ancient language of Buddhist scriptures.

pointed out to the head-priest, that he ceased for a while to mourn the loss of his River, or to draw wondrous pictures of the Wheel of Life, but preferred to talk of the beauty and wisdom of a certain mysterious *chela* whom no man of the Temple had ever seen. Yes, he had followed the traces of the Blessed Feet throughout all India. (The Curator has still in his possession a most marvellous account of his wanderings and meditations.) There remained nothing more in life but to find the River of the Arrow. Yet it was shown to him in dreams that it was a matter not to be undertaken with any hope of success unless that seeker had with him the one *chela* appointed to bring the event to a happy issue, and versed in great wisdom—such wisdom as white-haired Keepers of Images possess. For example (here came out the snuff-gourd, and the kindly Jain priests made haste to be silent):

'Long and long ago, when Devadatta was King of Benares—let all listen to the *Jâtaka!*[3]—an elephant was captured for a time by the king's hunters and, ere he broke free, beringed with a grievous leg-iron. This he strove to remove with hate and frenzy in his heart, and hurrying up and down the forests, besought his brother-elephants to wrench it asunder. One by one, with their strong trunks, they tried and failed. At the last they gave it as their opinion that the ring was not to be broken by any bestial power. And in a thicket, new-born, wet with moisture of birth, lay a day-old calf of the herd whose mother had died. The fettered elephant, forgetting his own agony, said: "If I do not help this suckling it will perish under our feet." So he stood above the young thing, making his legs buttresses against the uneasily moving herd; and he begged milk of a virtuous cow, and the calf throve, and the ringed elephant was the calf's guide and defence. Now the days of an elephant—let all listen to the *Jâtaka!*— are thirty-five years to his full strength, and through thirty-five Rains the ringed elephant befriended the younger, and all the while the fetter ate into the flesh.

'Then one day the young elephant saw the half-buried iron, and turning to the elder said: "What is this?" "It is even my sorrow," said he who had befriended him. Then that other put out his trunk and in the twinkling of an eyelash abolished the ring, saying: "The appointed time has come." So the virtuous elephant who had waited temperately and done kind acts was relieved, at the appointed time, by the very calf whom he had turned aside to cherish—let all listen to the *Jâtaka!*—for the Elephant was Ananda,[4] and the Calf that broke the ring was none other than The Lord Himself . . .'

Then he would shake his head benignly, and over the ever-clicking rosary point out how free that elephant-calf was from the

3. A fable based on an event in Buddha's life.
4. Buddha's faithful disciple.

sin of pride. He was as humble as a *chela* who, seeing his master sit-
ting in the dust outside the Gates of Learning, over-leapt the gates
(though they were locked) and took his master to his heart in the
presence of the proud-stomached city. Rich would be the reward of
such a master and such a *chela* when the time came for them to
seek freedom together!

So did the lama speak, coming and going across India as softly as
a bat. A sharp-tongued old woman in a house among the fruit-trees
behind Saharunpore honoured him as the woman honoured the
prophet,[5] but his chamber was by no means upon the wall. In an
apartment of the forecourt overlooked by cooing doves he would sit,
while she laid aside her useless veil and chattered of spirits and
fiends of Kulu, of grandchildren unborn, and of the free-tongued
brat who had talked to her in the resting-place. Once, too, he
strayed alone from the Grand Trunk Road below Umballa to the
very village whose priest had tried to drug him; but the kind Heaven
that guards lamas sent him at twilight through the crops, absorbed
and unsuspicious, to the Rissaldar's door. Here was like to have
been a grave misunderstanding, for the old soldier asked him why
the Friend of the Stars had gone that way only six days before.

'That may not be,' said the lama. 'He has gone back to his own
people.'

'He sat in that corner telling a hundred merry tales five nights
ago,' his host insisted. 'True, he vanished somewhat suddenly in the
dawn after foolish talk with my granddaughter. He grows apace, but
he is the same Friend of the Stars as brought me true word of the
war. Have ye parted?'

'Yes—and no,' the lama replied. 'We—we have not altogether
parted, but the time is not ripe that we should take the Road
together. He acquires wisdom in another place. We must wait.'

'All one—but if it were not the boy how did he come to speak so
continually of thee?'

'And what said he?' asked the lama eagerly.

'Sweet words—an hundred thousand—that thou art his father
and mother and such all. Pity that he does not take the Queen's ser-
vice. He is fearless.'

This news amazed the lama, who did not then know how reli-
giously Kim kept to the contract made with Mahbub Ali, and per-
force ratified by Colonel Creighton . . .

'There is no holding the young pony from the game,' said the
horse-dealer when the Colonel pointed out that vagabonding over
India in holiday time was absurd. 'If permission be refused to go and

5. In 2 Kings 4.8–10, a woman gives charity to the prophet Elisha. Here as elsewhere in
 Kim, Kipling combines religious traditions.

come as he chooses, he will make light of the refusal. Then who is to catch him? Colonel Sahib, only once in a thousand years is a horse born so well fitted for the game as this our colt. And we need men.'

Chapter 10

> Your tiercel's too long at hack, Sire. He's no eyass[1]
> But a passage-hawk that footed[2] ere we caught him,
> Dangerously free o' the air. Faith! were he mine
> (As mine's the glove he binds to for his tirings[3])
> I'd fly him with a make-hawk. He's in yarak[4]
> Plumed to the very point—so manned, so weathered[5] . . .
> Give him the firmament God made him for,
> And what shall take the air of him?
>
> *Old Play.*[6]

Lurgan Sahib did not use as direct speech, but his advice tallied with Mahbub's; and the upshot was good for Kim. He knew better now than to leave Lucknow city in native garb, and if Mahbub were anywhere within reach of a letter, it was to Mahbub's camp he headed, and made his change under the Pathan's wary eye. Could the little Survey paint-box that he used for map-tinting in term-time have found a tongue to tell of holiday doings, he might have been expelled. Once Mahbub and he went together as far as the beautiful city of Bombay, with three truckloads of tram-horses, and Mahbub nearly melted when Kim proposed a sail in a dhow across the Indian Ocean to buy Gulf Arabs,[7] which, he understood from a hanger-on of the dealer Abdul Rahman, fetched better prices than mere Kabulis.

He dipped his hand into the dish with that great trader when Mahbub and a few co-religionists were invited to a big Haj dinner.[8] They came back by way of Karachi by sea, when Kim took his first experience of sea-sickness sitting on the fore-hatch of a coasting-steamer, well persuaded he had been poisoned. The Babu's famous drug-box proved useless, though Kim had restocked it at Bombay. Mahbub had business at Quetta, and there Kim, as Mahbub admitted, earned his keep, and perhaps a little over, by spending four

1. A nestling hawk. *Tiercel*: male falcon. *At hack*: partial liberty given a trained hawk.
2. Killed its prey. *Passage-hawk*: hawk captured during migration.
3. Food given as a treat. *Binds to*: perches on.
4. Good condition. *Make-hawk*: trained hawk used to teach younger hawks.
5. Used to the open air. *Plumed*: fully feathered. *Manned*: used to strangers.
6. An uncompleted five-act play by Kipling titled *Gow's Watch*.
7. Horses from the Persian Gulf.
8. Celebratory dinner for those making the pilgrimage to Mecca.

curious days as scullion in the house of a fat Commissariat
sergeant, from whose office-box, in an auspicious moment, he
removed a little vellum ledger which he copied out—it seemed to
deal entirely with cattle and camel sales—by moonlight, lying
behind an outhouse, all through one hot night. Then he returned
the ledger to its place, and, at Mahbub's word, left that service
unpaid, rejoining him six miles down the road, the clean copy in his
bosom.

'That soldier is a small fish,' Mahbub Ali explained, 'but in time
we shall catch the larger one. He only sells oxen at two prices—one
for himself and one for the Government—which I do not think is a
sin.'

'Why could not I take away the little book and be done with it?'

'Then he would have been frightened, and he would have told his
master. Then we should miss, perhaps, a great number of new rifles
which seek their way up from Quetta to the North. The Game is so
large that one sees but a little at a time.'

'Oho!' said Kim, and held his tongue. That was in the monsoon
holidays, after he had taken the prize for mathematics. The
Christmas holidays he spent—deducting ten days for private amuse-
ments—with Lurgan Sahib, where he sat for the most part in front
of a roaring wood-fire—Jakko road was four feet deep in snow that
year—and—the small Hindu had gone away to be married—helped
Lurgan to thread pearls. He made Kim learn whole Chapters of the
Koran by heart, till he could deliver them with the very roll and
cadence of a mullah.[9] Moreover, he told Kim the names and prop-
erties of many native drugs, as well as the runes[1] proper to recite
when you administer them. And in the evenings he wrote charms on
parchment—elaborate pentagrams crowned with the names of
devils—Murra, and Awan the Companion of Kings—all fantastically
written in the corners. More to the point, he advised Kim as to the
care of his own body, the cure of fever-fits, and simple remedies of
the Road. A week before it was time to go down, Colonel Creighton
Sahib—this was unfair—sent Kim a written examination-paper that
concerned itself solely with rods and chains and links and angles.

Next holidays he was out with Mahbub, and here, by the way,
he nearly died of thirst, plodding through the sand on a camel to
the mysterious city of Bikanir, where the wells are four hundred
feet deep, and lined throughout with camel-bone. It was not an
amusing trip from Kim's point of view, because—in defiance of the
contract—the Colonel ordered him to make a map of that wild,
walled city; and since Mohammedan horse-boys and pipe-tenders

9. Muslim cleric.
1. Incantations.

are not expected to drag Survey-chains round the capital of an
independent Native State, Kim was forced to pace all his distances
by means of a bead rosary. He used the compass for bearings as
occasion served—after dark chiefly, when the camels had been
fed—and by the help of his little Survey paint-box of six colour-
cakes and three brushes, he achieved something not remotely
unlike the city of Jeysulmir. Mahbub laughed a great deal, and
advised him to make up a written report as well; and in the back
of the big account-book that lay under the flap of Mahbub's pet
saddle Kim fell to work.

'It must hold everything that thou hast seen or touched or con-
sidered. Write as though the Jung-i-Lat Sahib himself had come by
stealth with a vast army outsetting to war.'

'How great an army?'

'Oh, half a lakh[2] of men.'

'Folly! Remember how few and bad were the wells in the sand.
Not a thousand thirsty men could come near by here.'

'Then write that down—also all the old breaches in the walls—
and whence the firewood is cut—and what is the temper and dis-
position of the King. I stay here till all my horses are sold. I will hire
a room by the gateway, and thou shalt be my accountant. There is a
good lock to the door.'

The report in its unmistakable St Xavier's running script, and the
brown, yellow, and lake-daubed map, was on hand a few years ago
(a careless clerk filed it with the rough notes of E23's second
Seistan[3] survey), but by now the pencil characters must be almost
illegible. Kim translated it, sweating under the light of an oil-lamp,
to Mahbub, the second day of their return-journey. The Pathan rose
and stooped over his dappled saddle-bags.

'I knew it would be worthy a dress of honour, and so I made one
ready,' he said, smiling. 'Were I Amir of Afghanistan (and some day
we may see him), I would fill thy mouth with gold.' He laid the gar-
ments formally at Kim's feet. There was a gold-embroidered
Peshawur turban-cap, rising to a cone, and a big turban-cloth end-
ing in a broad fringe of gold. There was a Delhi embroidered waist-
coat to slip over a milky white shirt, fastening to the right, ample
and flowing; green pyjamas with twisted silk waist-string; and that
nothing might be lacking, russia-leather slippers, smelling divinely,
with arrogantly curled tips.

'Upon a Wednesday, and in the morning, to put on new clothes is
auspicious,' said Mahbub solemnly. 'But we must not forget the
wicked folk in the world. So!'

2. Fifty thousand.
3. A contested area between Persia and Afghanistan.

He capped all the splendour, that was taking Kim's delighted breath away, with a mother-of-pearl, nickel-plated, self-extracting .450 revolver.

'I had thought of a smaller bore, but reflected that this takes Government bullets. A man can always come by those—especially across the Border. Stand up and let me look.' He clapped Kim on the shoulder. 'May you never be tired,[4] Pathan! Oh, the hearts to be broken! Oh, the eyes under the eyelashes, looking sideways!'

Kim turned about, pointed his toes, stretched, and felt mechanically for the moustache that was just beginning. Then he stooped towards Mahbub's feet to make proper acknowledgment with fluttering, quick-patting hands; his heart too full for words. Mahbub forestalled and embraced him.

'My son,' said he, 'what need of words between us? But is not the little gun a delight? All six cartridges come out at one twist. It is borne in the bosom next the skin, which, as it were, keeps it oiled. Never put it elsewhere, and please God, thou shalt some day kill a man with it.'

'*Hai mai!*' said Kim ruefully. 'If a Sahib kills a man he is hanged in the jail.'

'True: but one pace beyond the Border, men are wiser. Put it away; but fill it first. Of what use is a gun unfed?'

'When I go back to the *madrissah* I must return it. They do not allow little guns. Thou wilt keep it for me?'

'Son, I am wearied of that *madrissah*, where they take the best years of a man to teach him what he can only learn upon the Road. The folly of the Sahibs has neither top nor bottom. No matter. Maybe thy written report shall save thee further bondage; and God He knows we need men more and more in the Game.'

They marched, jaw-bound against blowing sand, across the salt desert to Jodhpur, where Mahbub and his handsome nephew Habib Ullah did much trading; and then sorrowfully, in European clothes, which he was fast outgrowing, Kim went second-class to St Xavier's. Three weeks later, Colonel Creighton, pricing Tibetan ghost-daggers at Lurgan's shop, faced Mahbub Ali openly mutinous. Lurgan Sahib operated as support in reserve.

'The pony is made—finished—mouthed and paced, Sahib! From now on, day by day, he will lose his manners if he is kept at tricks. Drop the rein on his back and let go,' said the horse-dealer. 'We need him.'

'But he is so young, Mahbub—not more than sixteen—is he?'

'When I was fifteen, I had shot my man and begot my man, Sahib.'

4. A traditional Pathan greeting.

'You impenitent old heathen!' Creighton turned to Lurgan. The black beard nodded assent to the wisdom of the Afghan's dyed scarlet.

'*I* should have used him long ago,' said Lurgan. 'The younger the better. That is why I always have my really valuable jewels watched by a child. You sent him to me to try. I tried him in every way: he is the only boy I could not make to see things.'

'In the crystal—in the ink-pool?' demanded Mahbub.

'No. Under my hand, as I told you. That has never happened before. It means that he is strong enough—but you think it skittles,[5] Colonel Creighton—to make anyone do anything he wants. And that is three years ago. I have taught him a good deal since, Colonel Creighton. I think you waste him now.'

'Hmm! Maybe you're right. But, as you know, there is no Survey work for him at present.'

'Let him out—let him go,' Mahbub interrupted. 'Who expects any colt to carry heavy weight at first? Let him run with the car-avans—like our white camel-colts—for luck. I would take him myself, but—'

'There is a little business where he would be most useful—in the South,' said Lurgan, with peculiar suavity, dropping his heavy blued eyelids.

'E23 has that in hand,' said Creighton quickly. 'He must not go down there. Besides, he knows no Turki.'

'Only tell him the shape and the smell of the letters we want and he will bring them back,' Lurgan insisted.

'No. That is a man's job,' said Creighton.

It was a wry-necked matter of unauthorized and incendiary cor-respondence between a person who claimed to be the ultimate authority in all matters of the Mohammedan religion throughout the world, and a younger member of a royal house who had been brought to book for kidnapping women within British territory. The Moslem Archbishop had been emphatic and over-arrogant; the young prince was merely sulky at the curtailment of his privileges, but there was no need he should continue a correspondence which might some day compromise him. One letter indeed had been pro-cured, but the finder was later found dead by the roadside in the habit of an Arab trader, as E23, taking up the work, duly reported.

These facts, and a few others not to be published, made both Mahbub and Creighton shake their heads.

'Let him go out with his Red Lama,' said the horse-dealer with vis-ible effort. 'He is fond of the old man. He can learn his paces by the rosary at least.'

5. Nonsense.

'I have had some dealings with the old man—by letter,' said Colonel Creighton, smiling to himself. 'Whither goes he?'

'Up and down the land, as he has these three years. He seeks a River of Healing. God's curse upon all—' Mahbub checked himself. 'He beds down at the Temple of the Tirthankars or at Buddh Gaya when he is in from the Road. Then he goes to see the boy at the *madrissah*, as we know, for the boy was punished for it twice or thrice. He is quite mad, but a peaceful man. I have met him. The Babu also has had dealings with him. We have watched him for three years. Red Lamas are not so common in Hind that one loses track.'

'Babus are very curious,' said Lurgan meditatively. 'Do you know what Hurree Babu really wants? He wants to be made a member of the Royal Society[6] by taking ethnological notes. I tell you, I tell him about the lama everything which Mahbub and the boy have told me. Hurree Babu goes down to Benares—at his own expense, I think.'

'I don't,' said Creighton briefly. He had paid Hurree's travelling expenses, out of a most lively curiosity to learn what the lama might be.

'And he applies to the lama for information on lamaism, and devil-dances, and spells and charms, several times in these few years. Holy Virgin! I could have told him all that yee-ars ago. I think Hurree Babu is getting too old for the Road. He likes better to collect manners and customs information. Yes, he wants to be an FRS.'[7]

'Hurree thinks well of the boy, doesn't he?'

'Oh, very indeed—we have had some pleasant evenings at my little place—but I think it would be waste to throw him away with Hurree on the Ethnological side.'

'Not for a first experience. How does that strike you, Mahbub? Let the boy run with the lama for six months. After that we can see. He will get experience.'

'He has it already, Sahib—as a fish controls the water he swims in. But for every reason it will be well to loose him from the school.'

'Very good, then,' said Creighton, half to himself. 'He can go with the lama, and if Hurree Babu cares to keep an eye on them so much the better. He won't lead the boy into any danger as Mahbub would. Curious—his wish to be an FRS. Very human, too. He *is* best on the Ethnological side—Hurree.'

No money and no preferment would have drawn Creighton from his work on the Indian Survey, but deep in his heart also lay the ambition to write 'FRS' after his name. Honours of a sort he knew could be obtained by ingenuity and the help of friends, but, to the best of his belief, nothing save work—papers representing a life of

6. Founded by Charles II in 1662 for the advancement of science.
7. Fellow of the Royal Society.

it—took a man into the Society which he had bombarded for years
with monographs on strange Asiatic cults and unknown customs.
Nine men out of ten would flee from a Royal Society soirée in
extremity of boredom; but Creighton was the tenth, and at times his
soul yearned for the crowded rooms in easy London where silver-
haired, bald-headed gentlemen who know nothing of the Army
move among spectroscopic experiments, the lesser plants of the
frozen tundras, electric flight-measuring machines, and apparatus
for slicing into fractional millimetres the left eye of the female mos-
quito. By all right and reason, it was the Royal Geographical that
should have appealed to him, but men are as chancy as children in
their choice of playthings. So Creighton smiled, and thought the
better of Hurree Babu, moved by like desire.

He dropped the ghost-dagger and looked up at Mahbub.

'How soon can we get the colt from the stable?' said the horse-
dealer, reading his eyes.

'Hmm! If I withdraw him by order now—what will he do, think
you? I have never before assisted at the teaching of such an one.'

'He will come to me,' said Mahbub promptly. 'Lurgan Sahib and
I will prepare him for the Road.'

'So be it, then. For six months he shall run at his choice: but who
will be his sponsor?'

Lurgan slightly inclined his head. 'He will not tell anything, if that
is what you are afraid of, Colonel Creighton.'

'It's only a boy, after all.'

'Ye-es; but first, he has nothing to tell; and secondly, he knows what
would happen. Also, he is very fond of Mahbub, and of me a little.'

'Will he draw pay?' demanded the practical horse-dealer.

'Food and water allowance only. Twenty rupees a month.'

One advantage of the Secret Service is that it has no worrying
audit. That Service is ludicrously starved, of course, but the funds are
administered by a few men who do not call for vouchers or present
itemized accounts. Mahbub's eyes lighted with almost a Sikh's love of
money. Even Lurgan's impassive face changed. He considered the
years to come when Kim would have been entered and made to the
Great Game that never ceases day and night, throughout India. He
foresaw honour and credit in the mouths of a chosen few, coming to
him from his pupil. Lurgan Sahib had made E23 what E23 was, out
of a bewildered, impertinent, lying, little North-West Province man.

But the joy of these masters was pale and smoky beside the joy of
Kim when St Xavier's Head called him aside, with word that Colonel
Creighton had sent for him.

'I understand, O'Hara, that he has found you a place as an assis-
tant chain-man in the Canal Department: that comes of taking up
mathematics. It is great luck for you, for you are only sixteen; but of

course you understand that you do not become *pukka* (permanent)
till you have passed the autumn examination. So you must not think
you are going out into the world to enjoy yourself, or that your for-
tune is made. There is a great deal of hard work before you. Only, if
you succeed in becoming *pukka*, you can rise, you know, to four
hundred and fifty a month.' Whereat the Principal gave him much
good advice as to his conduct, and his manners, and his morals; and
others, his elders, who had not been wafted into billets, talked as
only Anglo-Indian lads can, of favouritism and corruption. Indeed,
young Cazalet, whose father was a pensioner at Chunar, hinted very
broadly that Colonel Creighton's interest in Kim was directly pater-
nal; and Kim, instead of retaliating, did not even use language. He
was thinking of the immense fun to come, of Mahbub's letter of the
day before, all neatly written in English, making appointment for
that afternoon in a house the very name of which would have
crisped the Principal's hair with horror . . .

Said Kim to Mahbub in Lucknow railway station that evening,
above the luggage-scales: 'I feared lest, at the last, the roof would
fall upon me and cheat me. It is indeed all finished, O my father?'

Mahbub snapped his fingers to show the utterness of that end,
and his eyes blazed like red coals.

'Then where is the pistol that I may wear it?'

'Softly! A half-year, to run without heel-ropes. I begged that much
from Colonel Creighton Sahib. At twenty rupees a month. Old Red
Hat knows that thou art coming.'

'I will pay thee *dustoorie* (commission) on my pay for three
months,' said Kim gravely. 'Yea, two rupees a month. But first we
must get rid of these.' He plucked his thin linen trousers and
dragged at his collar. 'I have brought with me all that I need on the
Road. My trunk has gone up to Lurgan Sahib's.'

'Who sends his salaams to thee—Sahib.'

'Lurgan Sahib is a very clever man. But what dost thou do?'

'I go North again, upon the Great Game. What else? Is thy mind
still set on following old Red Hat?'

'Do not forget he made me that I am—though he did not know it.
Year by year, he sent the money that taught me.'

'I would have done as much—had it struck my thick head,'
Mahbub growled. 'Come away. The lamps are lit now, and none will
mark thee in the bazar. We go to Huneefa's house.'

On the way thither, Mahbub gave him much the same sort of
advice as his mother gave to Lemuel,[8] and curiously enough,
Mahbub was exact to point out how Huneefa and her likes
destroyed kings.

8. In Proverbs 31.1–9, Lemuel's mother counsels him on chastity and temperance.

'And I remember,' he quoted maliciously, 'one who said, "Trust a snake before an harlot, and an harlot before a Pathan, Mahbub Ali." Now, excepting as to Pathans, of whom I am one, all that is true. Most true is it in the Great Game, for it is by means of women that all plans come to ruin and we lie out in the dawning with our throats cut. So it happened to such a one.' He gave the reddest particulars.

'Then why—?' Kim paused before a filthy staircase that climbed to the warm darkness of an upper chamber, in the ward that is behind Azim Ullah's tobacco-shop. Those who know it call it The Birdcage— it is so full of whisperings and whistlings and chirrupings.

The room, with its dirty cushions and half-smoked hookahs, smelt abominably of stale tobacco. In one corner lay a huge and shapeless woman clad in greenish gauzes, and decked, brow, nose, ear, neck, wrist, arm, waist, and ankle with heavy native jewellery. When she turned it was like the clashing of copper pots. A lean cat in the balcony outside the window mewed hungrily. Kim checked, bewildered, at the door-curtain.

'Is that the new stuff, Mahbub?' said Huneefa lazily, scarce troubling to remove the mouthpiece from her lips. 'O Buktanoos!'—like most of her kind, she swore by the Djinns—'O Buktanoos! He is very good to look upon.'

'That is part of the selling of the horse,' Mahbub explained to Kim, who laughed.

'I have heard that talk since my Sixth Day,' he replied, squatting by the light. 'Whither does it lead?'

'To protection. Tonight we change thy colour. This sleeping under roofs has blanched thee like an almond. But Huneefa has the secret of a colour that catches. No painting of a day or two. Also, we fortify thee against the chances of the Road. That is *my* gift to thee, my son. Take out all metals on thee and lay them here. Make ready, Huneefa.'

Kim dragged forth his compass, Survey paint-box, and the new-filled medicine-box. They had all accompanied his travels, and boy-like he valued them immensely.

The woman rose slowly and moved with her hands a little spread before her. Then Kim saw that she was blind. 'No, no,' she muttered, 'the Pathan speaks truth—my colour does not go in a week or a month, and those whom I protect are under strong guard.'

'When one is far off and alone, it would not be well to grow blotched and leprous of a sudden,' said Mahbub. 'When thou wast with me I could oversee the matter. Besides, a Pathan is a fair-skin. Strip to the waist now and look how thou art whitened.' Huneefa felt her way back from an inner room. 'It is no matter, she cannot see.' He took a pewter bowl from her ringed hand.

The dye-stuff showed blue and gummy. Kim experimented on the back of his wrist, with a dab of cotton-wool; but Huneefa heard him.

'No, no,' she cried, 'the thing is not done thus, but with the proper ceremonies. The colouring is the least part. I give thee the full protection of the Road.'

'*Jadoo*? (magic),' said Kim, with a half start. He did not like the white, sightless eyes. Mahbub's hand on his neck bowed him to the floor, nose within an inch of the boards.

'Be still. No harm comes to thee, my son. I am thy sacrifice!'[9]

He could not see what the woman was about, but heard the clish-clash of her jewellery for many minutes. A match lit up the darkness; he caught the well-known purr and fizzle of grains of incense. Then the room filled with smoke—heavy, aromatic, and stupefying. Through growing drowse he heard the names of devils—of Zulbazan, Son of Eblis, who lives in bazars and *paraos*, making all the sudden lewd wickedness of wayside halts; of Dulhan, invisible about mosques, the dweller among the slippers of the faithful, who hinders folk from their prayers; and Musboot, Lord of lies and panic. Huneefa, now whispering in his ear, now talking as from an immense distance, touched him with horrible soft fingers, but Mahbub's grip never shifted from his neck till, relaxing with a sigh, the boy lost his senses.

'Allah! How he fought! We should never have done it but for the drugs. That was his white blood, I take it,' said Mahbub testily. 'Go on with the *dawut* (invocation). Give him full Protection.'

'*O Hearer! Thou that hearest with ears, be present. Listen, O Hearer!*' Huneefa moaned, her dead eyes turned to the west. The dark room filled with moanings and snortings.

From the outer balcony, a ponderous figure raised a round bullet head and coughed nervously.

'Do not interrupt this ventriloquial necromanciss, my friend,' it said in English. 'I opine that it is very disturbing to you, but no enlightened observer is jolly-well upset.'

'. . . *I will lay a plot for their ruin! O Prophet, bear with the unbelievers. Let them alone awhile!*' Huneefa's face, turned to the northward, worked horribly, and it was as though voices from the ceiling answered her.

Hurree Babu returned to his notebook, balanced on the window-sill, but his hand shook. Huneefa, in some sort of drugged ecstasy, wrenched herself to and fro as she sat cross-legged by Kim's still head, and called upon devil after devil, in the ancient order of the ritual, binding them to avoid the boy's every action.

9. A common Persian and Puslato idiom of hyperbolic endearment.

'With Him are the keys of the Secret Things! None knoweth them besides Himself. He knoweth that which is in the dry land and in the sea!' Again broke out the unearthly whistling responses.

'I—I apprehend it is not at all malignant in its operation?' said the Babu, watching the throat-muscles quiver and jerk as Huneefa spoke with tongues. 'It—it is not likely that she has killed the boy? If so, I decline to be witness at the trial . . . What was the last hypothetical devil mentioned?'

'Babuji,'[1] said Mahbub in the vernacular. 'I have no regard for the devils of Hind, but the Sons of Eblis are far otherwise, and whether they be *jumalee* (well-affected) or *jullalee* (terrible) they love not Kafirs.'[2]

'Then you think I had better go?' said Hurree Babu, half rising. 'They are, of course, dematerialized phenomena. Spencer[3] says—'

Huneefa's crisis passed, as these things must, in a paroxysm of howling, with a touch of froth at the lips. She lay spent and motionless beside Kim, and the crazy voices ceased.

'Wah! That work is done. May the boy be better for it; and Huneefa is surely a mistress of *dawut*. Help haul her aside, Babu. Do not be afraid.'

'How am I to fear the absolutely non-existent?' said Hurree Babu, talking English to reassure himself. It is an awful thing still to dread the magic that you contemptuously investigate—to collect folk-lore for the Royal Society with a lively belief in all Powers of Darkness.

Mahbub chuckled. He had been out with Hurree on the Road ere now. 'Let us finish the colouring,' said he. 'The boy is well protected if—if the Lords of the Air have ears to hear. I am a *Sufi* (free-thinker), but when one can get blind-sides of a woman, a stallion, or a devil, why go round to invite a kick? Set him upon the way, Babu, and see that old Red Hat does not lead him beyond our reach. I must get back to my horses.'

'All raight,' said Hurree Babu. 'He is at present curious spectacle.'

• • • • •

About third cockcrow, Kim woke after a sleep of thousands of years. Huneefa, in her corner, snored heavily, but Mahbub was gone.

'I hope you were not frightened,' said an oily voice at his elbow. 'I superintended entire operation, which was most interesting from ethnological point of view. It was high-class *dawut*.'

'Huh!' said Kim, recognizing Hurree Babu, who smiled ingratiatingly.

1. The suffix *-ji* indicates friendliness and respect.
2. Muslim term for unbelievers.
3. Herbert Spencer (1820–1903), British sociologist and psychologist who, as a major popularizer of Darwin, justified the evolutionary legitimacy of imperialism. That an Indian should cast himself as a "Herbert Spencerian" is ironic.

'And also I had honour to bring down from Lurgan your present costume. I am not in the habit offeecially of carrying such gauds to subordinates, but'—he giggled—'your case is noted as exceptional on the books. I hope Mr Lurgan will note my action.'

Kim yawned and stretched himself. It was good to turn and twist within loose clothes once again.

'What is this?' He looked curiously at the heavy duffle-stuff loaded with the scents of the far North.

'Oho! That is inconspicuous dress of *chela* attached to service of lamaistic lama. *Com*plete in every particular,' said Hurree Babu, rolling into the balcony to clean his teeth at a goglet.[4] 'I am of opee-nion it is not your old gentleman's precise releegion, but rather sub-variant of same. I have contributed rejected notes to *Asiatic Quarterly Review* on these subjects. Now it is curious that the old gentleman himself is totally devoid of releegiosity. He is not a dam' particular.'

'Do you know him?'

Hurree Babu held up his hand to show he was engaged in the pre-scribed rites that accompany tooth-cleaning and such things among decently bred Bengalis. Then he recited in English an Arya-Somaj[5] prayer of a theistical nature, and stuffed his mouth with *pan* and betel.

'Oah yes. I have met him several times at Benares, and also at Buddh Gaya, to interrogate him on releegious points and devil-worship. He is pure agnostic—same as me.'

Huneefa stirred in her sleep, and Hurree Babu jumped nervously to the copper incense-burner, all black and discoloured in morning-light, rubbed a finger in the accumulated lamp-black and drew it diagonally across his face.

'Who has died in thy house?' asked Kim in the vernacular.

'None. But she may have the Evil Eye—that sorceress,' the Babu replied.

'What dost thou do now, then?'

'I will set thee on thy way to Benares, if thou goest thither, and tell thee what must be known by Us.'

'I go. At what hour runs the *te-rain*?' He rose to his feet, looked round the desolate chamber and at the yellow-wax face of Huneefa as the low sun stole across the floor. 'Is there money to be paid that witch?'

'No. She has charmed thee against all devils and all dangers—in the name of her devils. It was Mahbub's desire.' In English: 'He is

4. Water-jug.
5. Noble Knowledge, a modern Hindu reformist movement, many of whose followers were anti-British.

highly obsolete, *I* think, to indulge in such supersteetion. Why, it is all ventri*lo*quy. Belly-speak—eh?'

Kim snapped his fingers mechanically to avert whatever evil— Mahbub, he knew, meditated none—might have crept in through Huneefa's ministrations; and Hurree giggled once more. But as he crossed the room he was careful not to step in Huneefa's blotched, squat shadow on the boards. Witches—when their time is on them—can lay hold of the heels of a man's soul if he does that.

'Now you must well listen,' said the Babu when they were in the fresh air. 'Part of these ceremonies which we witnessed they include supply of effeecient amulet to those of our Department. If you feel in your neck will find one small silver amulet, verree cheap. That is *ours*. Do you understand?'

'Oah yes, *hawa-dilli* (a heart-lifter),' said Kim, feeling at his neck.

'Huneefa she makes them for two rupees twelve annas with—oh, all sorts of exorcisms. They are quite common, except they are par-tially black enamel, and there is a paper inside each one full of names of local saints and such things. *Thatt* is Huneefa's look-out, you see? Huneefa makes them onlee for us, but in case she does not, when we get them we put in, before issue, one small piece of turquoise. Mr Lurgan he gives them. There is no other source of supply; but it was me invented all this. It is strictly unoffeecial of course, but convenient for subordinates. Colonel Creighton he does not know. He is European. The turquoise is wrapped in the paper . . . Yes, that is road to railway station . . . Now suppose you go with the lama, or with me, I hope, some day, or with Mahbub. Suppose we get into a dam'-tight place. I am a fearful man—most fearful—but I tell you I have been in dam'-tight places more than hairs on my head. You say: "I am Son of the Charm." Verree good.'

'I do not understand quite. We must not be heard talking English here.'

'That is all raight. I am only Babu showing off my English to you. All we Babus talk English to show off,' said Hurree, flinging his shoulder-cloth jauntily. 'As I was about to say, "Son of the Charm" means that you may be member of the *Sat Bhai*—the Seven Brothers,[6] which is Hindi *and* Tantric.[7] It is popularly supposed to be extinct Society, but I have written notes to show it is still extant. You see, it is all my invention. Verree good. *Sat Bhai* has many mem-bers, and perhaps before they jolly-well-cut-your-throat they may give you just a chance of life. That is useful, anyhow. And moreover, these foolish natives—if they are not too excited—they always stop to think before they kill a man who says he belongs to any speecific

6. A Hindu secret society.
7. Pertaining to a Hindu sect associated with magic and mysticism.

organization. You see? You say then when you are in tight place, "I am Son of the Charm", and you get—perhaps—ah—your second wind. That is only in extreme instances, or to open negotiations with a stranger. Can you quite see? Verree good. But suppose now, I, or any one of the Department, come to you dressed quite different. You would not know me at all unless I choose, I bet you. Some day I will prove it. I come as Ladakhi trader—oh, anything—and I say to you: "You want to buy precious stones?" You say: "Do I look like a man who buys precious stones?" Then I say: "Even verree poor man can buy a turquoise or *tarkeean*." '[8]

'That is *kichree*—vegetable curry,' said Kim.

'Of course it is. You say: "Let me see the *tarkeean*." Then I say: "It was cooked by a woman, and perhaps it is bad for your caste." Then you say: "There is no caste when men go to—look for *tarkeean*." You stop a little between those words, "to—look". That is thee whole secret. The little stop before the words.'

Kim repeated the test-sentence.

'That is all right. Then I will show you my turquoise if there is time, and then you know who I am, and then we exchange views and documents and those-all things. And so it is with any other man of us. We talk sometimes about turquoises and sometimes about *tarkeean*, but always with that little stop in the words. It is verree easy. First, "Son of the Charm", if you are in a tight place. Perhaps that may help you—perhaps not. Then what I have told you about the *tarkeean*, if you want to transact offeecial business with a strange man. Of course, at present, you have no offeecial business. You are—ah ha!—supernumerary on probation. Quite unique specimen. If you were Asiatic of birth you might be employed right off; but this half-year of leave is to make you de-Englishized, you see? The lama he expects you, because I have demi-offeecially informed him you have passed all your examinations, and will soon obtain Government appointment. Oh ho! You are on acting-allowance, you see: so if you are called upon to help Sons of the Charm mind you jolly-well try. Now I shall say good-bye, my dear fellow, and I hope you—ah—will come out top-side all raight.'

Hurree Babu stepped back a pace or two into the crowd at the entrance of Lucknow station and—was gone. Kim drew a deep breath and hugged himself all over. The nickel-plated revolver he could feel in the bosom of his sad-coloured robe, the amulet was on his neck; begging-gourd, rosary, and ghost-dagger (Mr Lurgan had forgotten nothing) were all to hand, with medicine, paint-box, and compass, and in a worn old purse-belt embroidered with porcupine-quill patterns lay a month's pay. Kings could be no richer. He bought

8. Sautéed vegetables.

sweetmeats in a leaf-cup from a Hindu trader, and ate them with
glad rapture till a policeman ordered him off the steps.

Chapter 11

Give the man who is not made
　　To his trade
Swords to fling and catch again,
Coins to ring and snatch again,
Men to harm and cure again,
Snakes to charm and lure again—
He'll be hurt by his own blade,
By his serpents disobeyed,
By his clumsiness bewrayed,
By the people mocked to scorn—
　　So 'tis not with juggler born!
Pinch of dust or withered flower,
　　Chance-flung fruit or borrowed staff,
Serve his need and shore his power,
　　Bind the spell, or loose the laugh!
　　　　But a man who, etc., Op. 15.[1]

Followed a sudden natural reaction.

'Now am I alone—all alone,' he thought. 'In all India is no one so
alone as I! If I die today, who shall bring the news—and to whom?
If I live and God is good, there will be a price upon my head, for I
am a Son of the Charm—I, Kim.'

A very few white people, but many Asiatics, can throw themselves
into a mazement as it were by repeating their own names over and
over again to themselves, letting the mind go free upon speculation
as to what is called personal identity. When one grows older, the
power, usually, departs, but while it lasts it may descend upon a man
at any moment.

'Who is Kim—Kim—Kim?'

He squatted in a corner of the clanging waiting-room, rapt from
all other thoughts; hands folded in lap, and pupils contracted to pin-
points. In a minute—in another half-second—he felt he would
arrive at the solution of the tremendous puzzle; but here, as always
happens, his mind dropped away from those heights with a rush of
a wounded bird, and passing his hand before his eyes, he shook his
head.

A long-haired Hindu *bairagi* (holy man), who had just bought a
ticket, halted before him at that moment and stared intently.

1. The second verse of a Kipling poem, "The Juggler's Song," collected in *Songs from Books*.
 The juggler's act anticipates the performative quality of Kim's actions in this chapter.

'I also have lost it,' he said sadly. 'It is one of the Gates to the Way, but for me it has been shut many years.'

'What is the talk?' said Kim, abashed.

'Thou wast wondering there in thy spirit what manner of thing thy soul might be. The seizure came of a sudden. I know. Who should know but I? Whither goest thou?'

'Toward Kashi (Benares).'

'There are no Gods there. I have proved them. I go to Prayag (Allahabad) for the fifth time—seeking the Road to Enlightenment. Of what faith art thou?'

'I too am a Seeker,' said Kim, using one of the lama's pet words. 'Though'—he forgot his Northern dress for the moment—'though Allah alone knoweth what I seek.'

The old fellow slipped the *bairagi's* crutch under his armpit and sat down on a patch of ruddy leopard's skin as Kim rose at the call for the Benares train.

'Go in hope, little brother,' he said. 'It is a long road to the feet of the One;[2] but thither do we all travel.'

Kim did not feel so lonely after this, and ere he had sat out twenty miles in the crowded compartment, was cheering his neighbours with a string of most wonderful yarns about his own and his master's magical gifts.

Benares struck him as a peculiarly filthy city, though it was pleasant to find how his cloth was respected. At least one-third of the population prays eternally to some group or other of the many million deities, and so reverse every sort of holy man. Kim was guided to the Temple of the Tirthankars, about a mile outside the city, near Sarnath, by a chance-met Punjabi farmer—a Kamboh from Jullundur-way who had appealed in vain to every God of his homestead to cure his small son, and was trying Benares as a last resort.

'Thou art from the North?' he asked, shouldering through the press of the narrow, stinking streets much like his own pet bull at home.

'Ay, I know the Punjab. My mother was a *pahareen*,[3] but my father came from Amritzar—by Jandiala,' said Kim, oiling his ready tongue for the needs of the Road.

'Jandiala—Jullundur? Oho! Then we be neighbours in some sort, as it were.' He nodded tenderly to the wailing child in his arms. 'Whom dost thou serve?'

'A most holy man at the Temple of the Tirthankars.'

'They are all most holy and—most greedy,' said the Jat[4] with bitterness. 'I have walked the pillars and trodden the temples till my

2. The singular universal spirit toward which Hindus meditate.
3. Hill-woman.
4. Earlier referred to as the Punjabi farmer, a Kamboh, or a Jat (a subcaste of farmers).

feet are flayed, and the child is no whit better. And the mother being sick too . . . Hush, then, little one . . . We changed his name when the fever came. We put him into girl's clothes.[5] There was nothing we did not do, except—I said to his mother when she bundled me off to Benares she should have come with me—I *said* Sakhi Sarwar Sultan[6] would serve us best. We know His generosity, but these down-country Gods are strangers.'

The child turned on the cushion of the huge corded arms and looked at Kim through heavy eyelids.

'And was it all worthless?' Kim asked, with easy interest.

'All worthless—all worthless,' said the child, lips cracking with fever.

'The Gods have given him a good mind, at least,' said the father proudly. 'To think he should have listened so cleverly. Yonder is thy Temple. Now I am a poor man—many priests have dealt with me— but my son is my son, and if a gift to thy master can cure him—I am at my very wits' end.'

Kim considered for a while, tingling with pride. Three years ago he would have made prompt profit on the situation and gone his way without a thought; but now, the very respect the Jat paid him proved that he was a man. Moreover, he had tasted fever once or twice already, and knew enough to recognize starvation when he saw it.

'Call him forth and I will give him a bond on my best yoke, so that the child is cured.'

Kim halted at the carved outer door of the temple. A white-clad Oswal[7] banker from Ajmir, his sins of usury new wiped out, asked him what he did.

'I am *chela* to Teshoo Lama, an Holy One from Bhotiyal—within there. He bade me come. I wait. Tell him.'

'Do not forget the child,' cried the importunate Jat over his shoulder, and then bellowed in Punjabi: 'O Holy One—O disciple of the Holy One—O Gods above all the Worlds—behold affliction sitting at the gate!' That cry is so common in Benares that the passers never turned their heads.

The Oswal, at peace with mankind, carried the message into the darkness behind him, and the easy, uncounted Eastern minutes slid by; for the lama was asleep in his cell, and no priest would wake him. When the click of his rosary again broke the hush of the inner court where the calm images of the Arhats[8] stand, a novice whispered, 'Thy *chela* is here,' and the old man strode forth, forgetting the end of that prayer.

5. To keep the evil eye away (because girls are less valued than boys).
6. Famous Muslim shrine in Benares.
7. A subcaste of money-lenders.
8. Buddhist saints.

Hardly had the tall figure shown in the doorway than the Jat ran before him, and, lifting up the child, cried: 'Look upon this, Holy One; and if the Gods will, he lives—he lives!'

He fumbled in his waist-belt and drew out a small silver coin.

'What is now?' The lama's eyes turned to Kim. It was noticeable he spoke far clearer Urdu than long ago, under Zam-Zammah; but the father would allow no private talk.

'It is no more than a fever,' said Kim. 'The child is not well fed.'

'He sickens at everything, and his mother is not here.'

'If it be permitted, I may cure, Holy One.'

'What! Have they made thee a healer? Wait here,' said the lama, and he sat down by the Jat upon the lowest step of the temple, while Kim, looking out of the corner of his eyes, slowly opened the little betel-box. He had dreamed dreams at school of returning to the lama as a Sahib—of chaffing the old man before he revealed himself—boy's dreams all. There was more drama in this abstracted, brow-puckered search through the tabloid-bottles, with a pause here and there for thought and a muttered invocation between whiles. Quinine he had in tablets, and dark brown meat-lozenges—beef most probably, but that was not *his* business. The little thing would not eat, but it sucked at a lozenge greedily, and said it liked the salt taste.

'Take then these six.' Kim handed them to the man. 'Praise the Gods, and boil three in milk; other three in water. After he has drunk the milk give him this' (it was the half of a quinine pill), 'and wrap him warm. Give him the water of the other three, and the other half of this white pill when he wakes. Meantime, here is another brown medicine that he may suck at on the way home.'

'Gods, what wisdom!' said the Kamboh, snatching.

It was as much as Kim could remember of his own treatment in a bout of autumn malaria—if you except the patter that he added to impress the lama.

'Now go! Come again in the morning.'

'But the price—the price,' said the Jat, and threw back his sturdy shoulders. 'My son is my son. Now that he will be whole again, how shall I go back to his mother and say I took help by the wayside and did not even give a bowl of curds in return?'

'They are alike, these Jats,' said Kim softly. 'The Jat stood on his dunghill and the King's elephants went by. "O driver," said he, "what will you sell those little donkeys for?"'

The Jat burst into a roar of laughter, stifled with apologies to the lama. 'It is the saying of my own country—the very talk of it. So are we Jats all. I will come tomorrow with the child; and the blessing of the Gods of the Homesteads—who are good little Gods—be on you both . . . Now, son, we grow strong again. Do not spit it out, little

Princeling! King of my Heart, do not spit it out, and we shall be strong men, wrestlers and club-wielders, by morning.'

He moved away, crooning and mumbling. The lama turned to Kim, and all the loving old soul of him looked out through his narrow eyes.

'To heal the sick is to acquire merit; but first one gets knowledge. That was wisely done, O Friend of all the World.'

'I was made wise by thee, Holy One,' said Kim, forgetting the little play just ended; forgetting St Xavier's; forgetting his white blood; forgetting even the Great Game as he stooped, Mohammedan-fashion, to touch his master's feet in the dust of the Jain temple. 'My teaching I owe to thee. I have eaten thy bread three years. My time is finished. I am loosed from the schools. I come to thee.'

'Herein is my reward. Enter! Enter! And is all well?' They passed to the inner court, where the afternoon sun sloped golden across. 'Stand that I may see. So!' He peered critically. 'It is no longer a child, but a man, ripened in wisdom, walking as a physician. I did well—I did well when I gave thee up to the armed men on that black night. Dost thou remember our first day under Zam-Zammah?'

'Ay,' said Kim, 'Dost thou remember when I leapt off the carriage the first day I went to—'

'The Gates of Learning? Truly. And the day that we ate the cakes together at the back of the river by Nucklao. Aha! Many times hast thou begged for me, but that day I begged for thee.'

'Good reason,' quoth Kim. 'I was then a scholar in the Gates of Learning, and attired as a Sahib. Do not forget, Holy One,' he went on playfully. 'I am still a Sahib—by thy favour.'

'True. And a Sahib in most high esteem. Come to my cell, *chela*.'

'How is that known to thee?'

The lama smiled. 'First by means of letters from the kindly priest whom we met in the camp of armed men; but he is now gone to his own country, and I sent the money to his brother.' Colonel Creighton, who had succeeded to the trusteeship when Father Victor went to England with the Mavericks, was hardly the Chaplain's brother. 'But I do not well understand Sahibs' letters. They must be interpreted to me. I chose a surer way. Many times when I returned from my Search to this Temple, which has always been a nest to me, there came one seeking Enlightenment—a man from Leh—that had been, he said, a Hindu, but wearied of all those Gods.' The lama pointed to the Arhats.

'A fat man?' said Kim, a twinkle in his eye.

'Very fat; but I perceived in a little his mind was wholly given up to useless things—such as devils and charms and the form and fashion of our tea-drinkings in the monasteries, and by what road we initiated the novices. A man abounding in questions; but he was a

friend of thine, *chela*. He told me that thou wast on the road to much honour as a scribe. And I see thou art a physician.'

'Yes, that am I—a scribe, when I am a Sahib, but it is set aside when I come as thy disciple. I have accomplished the years appointed for a Sahib.'

'As it were a novice?' said the lama, nodding his head. 'Art thou freed from the schools? I would not have thee unripe.'

'I am all free. In due time I take service under the Government as a scribe—'

'Not as a warrior. That is well.'

'But first I come to wander—with thee. Therefore I am here. Who begs for thee, these days?' he went on quickly. The ice was thin.[9]

'Very often I beg myself; but, as thou knowest, I am seldom here, except when I come to look again at my disciple. From one end to another of Hind have I travelled afoot and in the *te-rain*. A great and a wonderful land! But here, when I put in, is as though I were in my own Bhotiyal.'

He looked round the little clean cell complacently. A low cushion gave him a seat, on which he had disposed himself in the cross-legged attitude of the Bodhisat emerging from meditation; a black teak-wood table, not twenty inches high, set with copper tea-cups, was before him. In one corner stood a tiny altar, also of heavily carved teak, bearing a copper-gilt image of the seated Buddha and fronted by a lamp, an incense-holder, and a pair of copper flower-pots.

'The Keeper of the Images in the Wonder House acquired merit by giving me these a year since,' he said, following Kim's eye. 'When one is far from one's own land such things carry remembrance; and we must reverence the Lord for that He showed the Way. See!' He pointed to a curiously-built mound of coloured rice crowned with a fantastic metal ornament. 'When I was Abbot in my own place— before I came to better knowledge—I made that offering daily. It is the Sacrifice of the Universe to the Lord. Thus do we of Bhotiyal offer all the world daily to the Excellent Law. And I do it even now, though I know that the Excellent One is beyond all pinchings and pattings.' He snuffed from his gourd.

'It is well done, Holy One,' Kim murmured, sinking at ease on the cushions, very happy and rather tired.

'And also,' the old man chuckled, 'I write pictures of the Wheel of Life. Three days to a picture. I was busied on it—or it may be I shut my eyes a little—when they brought word of thee. It is good to have thee here: I will show thee my art—not for pride's sake, but because thou must learn. The Sahibs have not all this world's wisdom.'

9. Kim is on "thin ice" because he has lied to the lama.

He drew from under the table a sheet of strangely scented yellow Chinese paper, the brushes, and slab of Indian ink. In cleanest, severest outline he had traced the Great Wheel with its six spokes, whose centre is the conjoined Hog, Snake, and Dove (Ignorance, Anger, and Lust), and whose compartments are all the Heavens and Hells, and all the chances of human life. Men say that the Bodhisat Himself first drew it with grains of rice upon dust, to teach His disciples the cause of things. Many ages have crystallized it into a most wonderful convention crowded with hundreds of little figures whose every line carries a meaning. Few can translate the picture-parable; there are not twenty in all the world who can draw it surely without a copy: of those who can both draw and expound are but three.

'I have a little learned to draw,' said Kim. 'But this is a marvel beyond marvels.'

'I have written it for many years,' said the lama. 'Time was when I could write it all between one lamp-lighting and the next. I will teach thee the art—after due preparation; and I will show thee the meaning of the Wheel.'

'We take the Road, then?'

'The Road and our Search. I was but waiting for thee. It was made plain to me in a hundred dreams—notably one that came upon the night of the day that the Gates of Learning first shut—that without thee I should never find my River. Again and again, as thou knowest, I put this from me, fearing an illusion. Therefore I would not take thee with me that day at Lucknow, when we ate the cakes. I would not take thee till the time was ripe and auspicious. From the Hills to the Sea, from the Sea to the Hills have I gone, but it was vain. Then I remembered the *Jâtaka*.'

He told Kim the story of the elephant with the leg-iron, as he had told it so often to the Jain priests.

'Further testimony is not needed,' he ended serenely. 'Thou wast sent for an aid. That aid removed, my Search came to naught. Therefore we will go out again together, and our Search is sure.'

'Whither go we?'

'What matters, Friend of all the World? The Search, I say, is sure. If need be, the River will break from the ground before us. I acquired merit when I sent thee to the Gates of Learning, and gave thee the jewel that is Wisdom. Thou didst return, I saw even now, a follower of Sakyamuni, the Physician, whose altars are many in Bhotiyal. It is sufficient. We are together, and all things are as they were—Friend of all the World—Friend of the Stars—my *chela!*'

Then they talked of matters secular; but it was noticeable that the lama never demanded any details of life at St Xavier's, nor showed the faintest curiosity as to the manners and customs of Sahibs. His mind moved all in the past, and he revived every step of their won-

derful first journey together, rubbing his hands and chuckling, till it pleased him to curl himself up into the sudden sleep of old age.

Kim watched the last dusty sunshine fade out of the court, and played with his ghost-dagger and rosary. The clamour of Benares, oldest of all earth's cities awake before the Gods, day and night, beat round the walls as the sea's roar round a breakwater. Now and again, a Jain priest crossed the court, with some small offering to the images, and swept the path about him lest by chance he should take the life of a living thing. A lamp twinkled, and there followed the sound of a prayer. Kim watched the stars as they rose one after another in the still, sticky dark, till he fell asleep at the foot of the altar. That night he dreamed in Hindustanee, with never an English word . . .

'Holy One, there is the child to whom we gave the medicine,' he said, about three o'clock in the morning, when the lama, also waking from dreams, would have fared forth on pilgrimage. 'The Jat will be here at the light.'

'I am well answered. In my haste I would have done a wrong.' He sat down on the cushions and returned to his rosary. 'Surely old folk are as children,' he said pathetically. 'They desire a matter—behold, it must be done at once, or they fret and weep! Many times when I was upon the Road I have been ready to stamp with my feet at the hindrance of an ox-cart in the way, or a mere cloud of dust. It was not so when I was a man—a long time ago. None the less it is wrongful—'

'But thou art indeed old, Holy One.'

'The thing was done. A Cause was put out into the world, and, old or young, sick or sound, knowing or unknowing, who can rein in the effect of that Cause? Does the Wheel hang still if a child spin it—or a drunkard? *Chela*, this is a great and a terrible world.'

'I think it good,' Kim yawned. 'What is there to eat? I have not eaten since yesterday even.'

'I had forgotten thy need. Yonder is good Bhotiyal tea and cold rice.'

'We cannot walk far on such stuff.' Kim felt all the European's lust for flesh-meat, which is not accessible in a Jain temple. Yet, instead of going out at once with the begging-bowl, he stayed his stomach on slabs of cold rice till the full dawn. It brought the farmer, voluble, stuttering with gratitude.

'In the night the fever broke and the sweat came,' he cried. 'Feel here his skin is fresh and new! He esteemed the salt lozenges, and took milk with greed.' He drew the cloth from the child's face, and it smiled sleepily at Kim. A little knot of Jain priests, silent but all-observant, gathered by the temple door. They knew, and Kim knew that they knew, how the old lama had met his disciple. Being cour-

teous folk, they had not obtruded themselves overnight by presence, word, or gesture. Wherefore Kim repaid them as the sun rose.

'Thank the Gods of the Jains, brother,' he said, not knowing how those Gods were named. 'The fever is indeed broken.'

'Look! See!' The lama beamed in the background upon his hosts of three years. 'Was there ever such a *chela*? He follows our Lord the Healer.'

Now the Jains officially recognize all the Gods of the Hindu creed, as well as the Lingam[1] and the Snake. They wear the Brahminical thread;[2] they adhere to every claim of Hindu caste-law. But, because they knew and loved the lama, because he was an old man, because he sought the Way, because he was their guest, and because he collogued long of nights with the head-priest—as free-thinking a metaphysician as ever split one hair into seventy—they murmured assent.

'Remember,'—Kim bent over the child—'this trouble may come again.'

'Not if thou hast the proper spell,' said the father.

'But in a little while we go away.'

'True,' said the lama to all the Jains. 'We go now together upon the Search whereof I have often spoken. I waited till my *chela* was ripe. Behold him! We go North. Never again shall I look upon this place of my rest, O people of good will.'

'But I am not a beggar.' The cultivator rose to his feet, clutching the child.

'Be still. Do not trouble the Holy One,' a priest cried.

'Go,' Kim whispered. 'Meet us again under the big railway bridge, and for the sake of all the Gods of our Punjab, bring food—curry, pulse, cakes fried in fat, and sweetmeats. Specially sweetmeats. Be swift!'

The pallor of hunger suited Kim very well as he stood, tall and slim, in his sand-coloured, sweeping robes, one hand on his rosary and the other in the attitude of benediction, faithfully copied from the lama. An English observer might have said that he looked rather like the young saint of a stained-glass window, whereas he was but a growing lad faint with emptiness.

Long and formal were the farewells, thrice ended and thrice renewed. The Seeker—he who had invited the lama to that haven from far-away Tibet, a silver-faced, hairless ascetic—took no part in it, but meditated, as always, alone among the images. The others were very human; pressing small comforts upon the old man—a betel-box, a fine new iron pencase, a food-bag, and such-like—

1. Phallus, sacred symbol of Shiva, god of creation.
2. Brahmins wear a sacred thread (*sutra*) around their necks that symbolizes their link to learning.

warning him against the dangers of the world without, and proph-
esying a happy end to the Search. Meantime Kim, lonelier than
ever, squatted on the steps, and swore to himself in the language of
St Xavier's.

'But it is my own fault,' he concluded. 'With Mahbub, I ate
Mahbub's bread, or Lurgan Sahib's. At St Xavier's, three meals a day.
Here I must jolly-well look out for myself. Besides, I am not in good
training. *How* I could eat a plate of beef now! . . . Is it finished,
Holy One?'

The lama, both hands raised, intoned a final blessing in ornate
Chinese. 'I must lean on thy shoulder,' said he, as the temple gates
closed. 'We grow stiff, I think.'

The weight of a six-foot man is not light to steady through miles
of crowded streets, and Kim, loaded down with bundles and pack-
ages for the way, was glad to reach the shadow of the railway bridge.

'Here we eat,' he said resolutely, as the Kamboh, blue-robed and
smiling, hove in sight, a basket in one hand and the child in the
other.

'Fall to, Holy Ones!' he cried from fifty yards. (They were by the
shoal under the first bridge-span, out of sight of hungry priests.)
'Rice and good curry, cakes all warm and well scented with *hing*
(asafoetida), curds and sugar. King of my fields,'—this to the small
son—'let us show these holy men that we Jats of Jullundur can pay
a service . . . I had heard the Jains would eat nothing that they
had not cooked, but truly'—he looked away politely over the broad
river—'where there is no eye there is no caste.'

'And we,' said Kim, turning his back and heaping a leafplatter for
the lama, 'are beyond all castes.'

They gorged themselves on the good food in silence. Nor till he
had licked the last of the sticky sweetstuff from his little finger did
Kim note that the Kamboh too was girt for travel.

'If our roads lie together,' he said roughly, 'I go with thee. One
does not often find a worker of miracles, and the child is still weak.
But *I* am not altogether a reed.' He picked up his *lathi*—a five-foot
male-bamboo ringed with bands of polished iron—and flourished it
in the air. 'The Jats are called quarrelsome, but that is not true.
Except when we are crossed, we are like our own buffaloes.'

'So be it,' said Kim. 'A good stick is a good reason.'

The lama gazed placidly up-stream, where in long, smudged per-
spective the ceaseless columns of smoke go up from the burning-
ghats[3] by the river. Now and again, despite all municipal regula-
tions, the fragment of a half-burned body bobbed by on the full
current.

3. Funeral pyres.

'But for thee,' said the Kamboh to Kim, drawing the child into his hairy breast, 'I might today have gone thither—with this one. The priests tell us that Benares is holy—which none doubt—and desirable to die in. But I do not know their Gods, and they ask for money; and when one has done one worship a shaved-head vows it is of none effect except one do another. Wash here! Wash there! Pour, drink, lave, and scatter flowers—but always pay the priests. No, the Punjab for me, and the soil of the Jullundur-*doab*[4] for the best soil in it.'

'I have said many times—in the Temple, I think—that if need be, the River will open at our feet. We will therefore go North,' said the lama, rising. 'I remember a pleasant place, set about with fruit-trees, where one can walk in meditation—and the air is cooler there. It comes from the Hills and the snow of the Hills.'

'What is the name?' said Kim.

'How should I know? Didst thou not—no, that was after the Army rose out of the earth and took thee away. I abode there in meditation in a room against the dovecot—except when she talked eternally.'

'Oho! the woman from Kulu. That is by Saharunpore.' Kim laughed.

'How does the spirit move thy master? Does he go afoot, for the sake of past sins?' the Jat demanded cautiously. 'It is a far cry to Delhi.'

'No,' said Kim. 'I will beg a *tikkut* for the *te-rain*.' One does not own to the possession of money in India.

'Then, in the name of the Gods, let us take the fire-carriage. My son is best in his mother's arms. The Government has brought on us many taxes, but it gives us one good thing—the *te-rain* that joins friends and unites the anxious. A wonderful matter is the *te-rain*.'

They all piled into it a couple of hours later, and slept through the heat of the day. The Kamboh plied Kim with ten thousand questions as to the lama's walk and work in life, and received some curious answers. Kim was content to be where he was, to look out upon the flat North-Western landscape, and to talk to the changing mob of fellow-passengers. Even today, tickets and ticket-clipping are dark oppression to Indian rustics. They do not understand why, when they have paid for a magic piece of paper, strangers should punch great pieces out of the charm. So, long and furious are the debates between travellers and Eurasian ticket-collectors. Kim assisted at two or three with grave advice, meant to darken counsel and to show off his wisdom before the lama and the admiring Kamboh. But at Somna Road the Fates sent him a matter to think upon. There

4. Two waters (rivers) that run through Jullundar.

tumbled into the compartment, as the train was moving off, a mean, lean little person—a Mahratta,[5] so far as Kim could judge by the cock of the tight turban. His face was cut, his muslin upper-garment was badly torn, and one leg was bandaged. He told them that a country-cart had upset and nearly slain him: he was going to Delhi, where his son lived. Kim watched him closely. If, as he asserted, he had been rolled over and over on the earth, there should have been signs of gravel-rash on the skin. But all his injuries seemed clean cuts, and a mere fall from a cart could not cast a man into such extremity of terror. As, with shaking fingers, he knotted up the torn cloth about his neck he laid bare an amulet of the kind called a keeper-up of the heart. Now, amulets are common enough, but they are not generally strung on square-plaited copper wire, and still fewer amulets bear black enamel on silver. There were none except the Kamboh and the lama in the compartment, which, luckily, was of an old type with solid ends. Kim made as to scratch in his bosom, and thereby lifted his own amulet. The Mahratta's face changed altogether at the sight, and he disposed the amulet fairly on his breast.

'Yes,' he went on to the Kamboh, 'I was in haste, and the cart, dri-ven by a bastard, bound its wheel in a water-cut, and besides the harm done to me there was lost a full dish of *tarkeean*. I was not a Son of the Charm (a lucky man) that day.'

'That was a great loss,' said the Kamboh, withdrawing interest. His experience of Benares had made him suspicious.

'Who cooked it?' said Kim.

'A woman.' The Mahratta raised his eyes.

'But all women can cook *tarkeean*,' said the Kamboh. 'It is a good curry, as I know.'

'Oh yes, it is a good curry,' said the Mahratta.

'And cheap,' said Kim. 'But what about caste?'

'Oh, there is no caste where men go to—look for *tarkeean*,' the Mahratta replied, in the prescribed cadence. 'Of whose service art thou?'

'Of the service of this Holy One.' Kim pointed to the happy, drowsy lama, who woke with a jerk at the well-loved word.

'Ah, he was sent from Heaven to aid me. He is called the Friend of all the World. He is also called the Friend of the Stars. He walks as a physician—his time being ripe. Great is his wisdom.'

'And a Son of the Charm,' said Kim under his breath, as the Kamboh made haste to prepare a pipe lest the Mahratta should beg.

'And who is *that*?' the Mahratta asked, glancing sideways nervously.

5. A member of a Hindu warrior sect of Maharashtra in central India.

'One whose child I—we have cured, who lies under great debt to us.—Sit by the window, man from Jullundur. Here is a sick one.'

'Humph! I have no desire to mix with chance-met wastrels. My ears are not long. I am not a woman wishing to overhear secrets.' The Jat slid himself heavily into a far corner.

'Art thou anything of a healer? I am ten leagues deep in calamity,' cried the Mahratta, picking up the cue.

'This man is cut and bruised all over. I go about to cure him,' Kim retorted. 'None interfered between thy babe and me.'

'I am rebuked,' said the Kamboh meekly. 'I am thy debtor for the life of my son. Thou art a miracle-worker—I know it.'

'Show me the cuts.' Kim bent over the Mahratta's neck, his heart nearly choking him; for this was the Great Game with a vengeance. 'Now, tell thy tale swiftly, brother, while I say a charm.'

'I come from the South, where my work lay. One of us they slew by the roadside. Hast thou heard?' Kim shook his head. He, of course, knew nothing of E23's predecessor, slain down South in the habit of an Arab trader. 'Having found a certain letter which I was sent to seek, I came away. I escaped from the city and ran to Mhow.[6] So sure was I that none knew, I did not change my face. At Mhow a woman brought charge against me of theft of jewellery in that city which I had left. Then I saw the cry was out against me. I ran from Mhow by night, bribing the police, who had been bribed to hand me over without question to my enemies in the South. Then I lay in old Chitor city a week, a penitent in a temple, but I could not get rid of the letter which was my charge. I buried it under the Queen's Stone, at Chitor, in the place known to us all.'

Kim did not know, but not for worlds would he have broken the thread.

'At Chitor, look you, I was all in Kings' country; for Kotah to the east is beyond the Queen's law,[7] and east again lie Jaipur and Gwalior. Neither love spies, and there is no justice. I was hunted like a wet jackal; but I broke through at Bandakui, where I heard there was a charge against me of murder in the city I had left—of the murder of a boy. They have both the corpse and the witnesses waiting.'

'But cannot the Government protect?'

'We of the Game are beyond protection. If we die, we die. Our names are blotted from the book. That is all. At Bandakui, where lives one of Us, I thought to slip the scent by changing my face, and so made me a Mahratta. Then I came to Agra, and would have turned back to Chitor to recover the letter. So sure I was I had

6. A military station in central India in Mahratta country.
7. Queen Victoria's rule (or British India) as opposed to "King's country," or native states.

slipped them. Therefore I did not send a *tar* (telegram) to any one saying where the letter lay. I wished the credit of it all.'

Kim nodded. He understood that feeling well.

'But at Agra, walking in the streets, a man cried a debt against me, and approaching with many witnesses, would hale me to the courts then and there. Oh, they are clever in the South! He recognized me as his agent for cotton. May he burn in Hell for it!'

'And wast thou?'

'O fool! I was the man they sought for the matter of the letter! I ran into the Fleshers' Ward[8] and came out by the House of the Jew, who feared a riot and pushed me forth. I came afoot to Somna Road—I had only money for my *tikkut* to Delhi—and there, while I lay in a ditch with a fever, one sprang out of the bushes and beat me and cut me and searched me from head to foot. Within earshot of the *te-rain* it was!'

'Why did he not slay thee out of hand?'

'They are not so foolish. If I am taken in Delhi at the instance of lawyers, upon a proven charge of murder, my body is handed over to the State that desires it. I go back guarded, and then—I die slowly for an example to the rest of Us. The South is not my country. I run in circles—like a goat with one eye. I have not eaten for two days. I am marked'—he touched the filthy bandage on his leg—'so that they will know me at Delhi.'

'Thou art safe in the *te-rain*, at least.'

'Live a year at the Great Game and tell me that again! The wires will be out against me at Delhi, describing every tear and rag upon me. Twenty—a hundred, if need be—will have seen me slay that boy. And thou art useless!'

Kim knew enough of native methods of attack not to doubt that the case would be deadly complete—even to the corpse. The Mahratta twitched his fingers with pain from time to time. The Kamboh in his corner glared sullenly; the lama was busy over his beads; and Kim, fumbling doctor-fashion at the man's neck, thought out his plan between invocations.

'Hast thou a charm to change my shape? Else I am dead. Five—ten minutes alone, if I had not been so pressed, and I might—'

'Is he cured yet, miracle-worker?' said the Kamboh jealously. 'Thou hast chanted long enough.'

'Nay. There is no cure for his hurts, as I see, except he sit for three days in the habit of a *bairagi*.' This is a common penance, often imposed on a fat trader by his spiritual teacher.

'One priest always goes about to make another priest,' was the

8. The meat-slaughtering quarters.

retort. Like most grossly superstitious folk, the Kamboh could not keep his tongue from deriding his Church.

'Will thy son be a priest, then? It is time he took more of my quinine.'

'We Jats are all buffaloes,' said the Kamboh, softening anew.

Kim rubbed a finger-tip of bitterness on the child's trusting little lips. 'I have asked for nothing,' he said sternly to the father, 'except food. Dost thou grudge me that? I go to heal another man. Have I thy leave—Prince?'

Up flew the man's huge paws in supplication. 'Nay—nay. Do not mock me thus.'

'It pleases me to cure this sick one. Thou shalt acquire merit by aiding. What colour ash is there in thy pipe-bowl? White. That is auspicious. Was there raw turmeric[9] among thy food-stuffs?'

'I—I—'

'Open thy bundle!'

It was the usual collection of small oddments: bits of cloth, quack medicines, cheap fairings, a clothful of *atta*—greyish, rough-ground native flour—twists of down-country tobacco, tawdry pipe-stems, and a packet of curry-stuff, all wrapped in a quilt. Kim turned it over with the air of a wise warlock, muttering a Mohammedan invocation.

'This is wisdom I learned from the Sahibs,' he whispered to the lama; and here, when one thinks of his training at Lurgan's, he spoke no more than the truth. 'There is a great evil in this man's fortune, as shown by the Stars, which—which troubles him. Shall I take it away?'

'Friend of the Stars, thou hast done well in all things. Let it be at thy pleasure. Is it another healing?'

'Quick! Be quick!' gasped the Mahratta. 'The train may stop.'

'A healing against the shadow of death,' said Kim, mixing the Kamboh's flour with the mingled charcoal and tobacco ash in the red-earth bowl of the pipe. E23, without a word, slipped off his turban and shook down his long black hair.

'That is my food—priest,' the Jat growled.

'A buffalo in the temple! Hast thou dared to look even thus far?' said Kim. 'I must do mysteries before fools; but have a care for thine eyes. Is there a film before them already? I save the babe, and for return thou—oh, shameless!' The man flinched at the direct gaze, for Kim was wholly in earnest. 'Shall I curse thee, or shall I—' He picked up the outer cloth of the bundle and threw it over the bowed head. 'Dare so much as to think a wish to see, and—and—even I cannot save thee. Sit! Be dumb!'

9. A yellow spice and dye that was thought to protect the body against bacteria and to heal wounds.

'I am blind—dumb. Forbear to curse! Co—come, child; we will play a game of hiding. Do not, for my sake, look from under the cloth.'

'I see hope,' said E23. 'What is thy scheme?'

'This comes next,' said Kim, plucking the thin body-shirt. E23 hesitated, with all a North-West man's dislike of baring his body.

'What is caste to a cut throat?' said Kim, rending it to the waist. 'We must make thee a yellow Saddhu all over. Strip—strip swiftly, and shake thy hair over thine eyes while I scatter the ash. Now, a caste-mark on thy forehead.' He drew from his bosom the little Survey paint-box and a cake of crimson lake.

'Art thou only a beginner?' said E23, labouring literally for the dear life, as he slid out of his body-wrappings and stood clear in the loin-cloth while Kim splashed in a noble caste-mark on the ash-smeared brow.

'But two days entered to the Game, brother,' Kim replied. 'Smear more ash on the bosom.'

'Hast thou met—a physician of sick pearls?' He switched out his long, tight-rolled turban-cloth and, with swiftest hands, rolled it over and under about his loins into the intricate devices of a Saddhu's cincture.

'Hah! Dost thou know his touch, then? He was my teacher for a while. We must bare thy legs. Ash cures wounds. Smear it again.'

'I was his pride once, but thou art almost better. The Gods are kind to us! Give me *that*.'

It was a tin box of opium pills among the rubbish of the Jat's bundle. E23 gulped down a half handful. 'They are good against hunger, fear, and chill. And they make the eyes red too,' he explained. 'Now I shall have heart to play the Game. We lack only a Saddhu's tongs. What of the old clothes?'

Kim rolled them small, and stuffed them into the slack folds of his tunic. With a yellow-ochre paint cake he smeared the legs and the breast, great streaks against the background of flour, ash, and turmeric.

'The blood on them is enough to hang thee, brother.'

'Maybe; but no need to throw them out of the window . . . It is finished.' His voice thrilled with a boy's pure delight in the Game. 'Turn and look, O Jat!'

'The Gods protect us,' said the hooded Kamboh, emerging like a buffalo from the reeds. 'But—whither went the Mahratta? What hast thou done?'

Kim had been trained by Lurgan Sahib; E23, by virtue of his business, was no bad actor. In place of the tremulous, shrinking trader there lolled against the corner an all but naked, ash-smeared, ochre-barred, dusty-haired Saddhu, his swollen eyes—opium takes quick

effect on an empty stomach—luminous with insolence and bestial lust, his legs crossed under him, Kim's brown rosary round his neck, and a scant yard of worn, flowered chintz on his shoulders. The child buried his face in his amazed father's arms.

'Look up, Princeling! We travel with warlocks, but they will not hurt thee. Oh, do not cry . . . What is the sense of curing a child one day and killing him with fright the next?'

'The child will be fortunate all his life. He has seen a great healing. When I was a child I made clay men and horses.'

'I have made them too. Sir Banás,[1] he comes in the night and makes them all alive at the back of our kitchen-midden,' piped the child.

'And so thou art not frightened at anything. Eh, Prince?'

'I was frightened because my father was frightened. I felt his arms shake.'

'Oh, chicken-man!' said Kim, and even the abashed Jat laughed. 'I have done a healing on this poor trader. He must forsake his gains and his account-books, and sit by the wayside three nights to overcome the malignity of his enemies. The Stars are against him.'

'The fewer money-lenders the better, say I; but, Saddhu or no Saddhu, he should pay for my stuff on his shoulders.'

'So? But that is thy child on thy shoulder—given over to the burning-ghat not two days ago. There remains one thing more. I did this charm in thy presence because need was great. I changed his shape and his soul. None the less, if, by any chance, O man from Jullundur, thou remeberest what thou hast seen, either among the elders sitting under the village tree, or in thine own house, or in company of thy priest when he blesses thy cattle, a murrain[2] will come among the buffaloes, and a fire in thy thatch, and rats in the corn-bins, and the curse of our Gods upon thy fields that they may be barren before thy feet and after thy ploughshare.' This was part of an old curse picked up from a *faquir* by the Taksali Gate in the days of Kim's innocence. It lost nothing by repetition.

'Cease, Holy One! In mercy, cease!' cried the Jat. 'Do not curse the household. I saw nothing! I heard nothing! I am thy cow!' and he made to grab at Kim's bare foot beating rhythmically on the carriage floor.

'But since thou hast been permitted to aid me in the matter of a pinch of flour and a little opium and such trifles as I have honoured by using in my art, so will the Gods return a blessing,' and he gave it at length, to the man's immense relief. It was one that he had learned from Lurgan Sahib.

1. A folk figure who transforms clay models into living animals, men, and women.
2. Infectious disease.

The lama stared through his spectacles as he had not stared at the business of disguisement.

'Friend of the Stars,' he said at last, 'thou hast acquired great wisdom. Beware that it do not give birth to pride. No man having the Law before his eyes speaks hastily of any matter which he has seen or encountered.'

'No—no—no, indeed,' cried the farmer, fearful lest the master should be minded to improve on the pupil. E23, with relaxed mouth, gave himself up to the opium that is meat, tobacco, and medicine to the spent Asiatic.

So, in a silence of awe and great miscomprehension, they slid into Delhi about lamp-lighting time.

Chapter 12

Who hath desired the Sea—the sight of salt-water unbounded?
The heave and the halt and the hurl and the crash of the comber[1] wind-hounded?
The sleek-barrelled swell before storm—grey, foamless, enormous, and growing?
Stark calm on the lap of the Line[2]—or the crazy-eyed hurricane blowing?
His Sea in no showing the same—his Sea and the same 'neath all showing—
 His Sea that his being fulfils?
So and no otherwise—so and no otherwise hill-men desire their Hills!
 The Sea and the Hills.[3]

'I have found my heart again,' said E23, under cover of the platform's tumult. 'Hunger and fear make men dazed, or I might have thought of this escape before. I was right. They come to hunt for me. Thou hast saved my head.'

A group of yellow-trousered Punjab policemen, headed by a hot and perspiring young Englishman, parted the crowd about the carriages. Behind them, inconspicuous as a cat, ambled a small fat person who looked like a lawyer's tout.

'See the young Sahib reading from a paper. My description is in his hand,' said E23. 'They go carriage by carriage, like fisher-folk netting a pool.'

When the procession reached their compartment, E23 was counting his beads with a steady jerk of the wrist; while Kim jeered at him for being so drugged as to have lost the ringed fire-tongs which are the Saddhu's distinguishing mark. The lama, deep in

1. A smooth wave that precedes a sea storm.
2. The belt of calm that surrounds the equator or that precedes a storm at sea is like the peace and silence that draws hill-people (like the lama) back to the hills.
3. This stanza is the first verse of Kipling's poem, which was collected in *The Five Nations.*

meditation, stared straight before him; and the farmer, glancing furtively, gathered up his belongings.

'Nothing here but a parcel of holy-bolies,' said the Englishman aloud, and passed on amid a ripple of uneasiness; for native police mean extortion to the native all India over.

'The trouble now,' whispered E23, 'lies in sending a wire as to the place where I hid that letter I was sent to find. I cannot go to the *tar*-office[4] in this guise.'

'Is it not enough I have saved thy neck?'

'Not if the work be left unfinished. Did never the healer of sick pearls tell thee so? Comes another Sahib! Ah!'

This was a tallish, sallowish District Superintendent of Police— belt, helmet, polished spurs and all—strutting and twirling his dark moustache.

'What fools are these Police Sahibs!' said Kim genially.

E23 glanced up under his eyelids. 'It is well said,' he muttered in a changed voice. 'I go to drink water. Keep my place.'

He blundered out almost into the Englishman's arms, and was bad-worded in clumsy Urdu.

'*Tum mut?* You drunk? You mustn't bang about as though Delhi station belonged to you, my friend.'

E23, not moving a muscle of his countenance, answered with a stream of the filthiest abuse, at which Kim naturally rejoiced. It reminded him of the drummer-boys and the barrack-sweepers at Umballa in the terrible time of his first schooling.

'My good fool,' the Englishman drawled. '*Nickle-jao!*[5] Go back to your carriage.'

Step by step, withdrawing deferentially, and dropping his voice, the yellow Saddhu clomb back to the carriage, cursing the D.S.P. to remotest posterity by—here Kim almost jumped—by the curse of the Queen's Stone, by the writing under the Queen's Stone, and by an assortment of Gods with wholly new names.

'I don't know what you're saying,'—the Englishman flushed angrily—'but it's some piece of blasted impertinence. Come out of that!'

E23, affecting to misunderstand, gravely produced his ticket, which the Englishman wrenched angrily from his hand.

'Oh, *zoolum*![6] What oppression!' growled the Jat from his corner. 'All for the sake of a jest too.' He had been grinning at the freedom of the Saddhu's tongue. 'Thy charms do not work well today, Holy One!'

4. Telegraph office.
5. Get out!
6. Cursed oppression!

The Saddhu followed the policeman, fawning and supplicating. The ruck[7] of passengers, busy with their babies and their bundles, had not noticed the affair. Kim slipped out behind him; for it flashed through his head that he had heard this angry, stupid Sahib discoursing loud personalities to an old lady near Umballa three years ago.

'It is well,' the Saddhu whispered, jammed in the calling, shouting, bewildered press—a Persian greyhound between his feet and a cageful of yelling hawks under charge of a Rajput falconer in the small of his back. 'He has gone now to send word of the letter which I hid. They told me he was in Peshawur. I might have known that he is like the crocodile—always at the other ford. He has saved me from present calamity, but I owe my life to thee.'

'Is he also one of Us?' Kim ducked under a Mewar camel-driver's greasy armpit and cannoned off a covey of jabbering Sikh matrons.

'Not less than the greatest. We are both fortunate! I will make report to him of what thou hast done. I am safe under his protection.'

He bored through the edge of the crowd besieging the carriages, and squatted by the bench near the telegraph-office.

'Return, or they take thy place! Have no fear for the work, brother—or my life. Thou hast given me breathing-space, and Strickland Sahib[8] has pulled me to land. We may work together at the Game yet. Farewell!'

Kim hurried to his carriage: elated, bewildered, but a little nettled in that he had no key to the secrets about him.

'I am only a beginner at the Game, that is sure. *I* could not have leaped into safety as did the Saddhu. He knew it was darkest under the lamp. *I* could not have thought to tell news under pretence of cursing . . . and how clever was the Sahib! No matter, I saved the life of one . . . Where is the Kamboh gone, Holy One?' he whispered, as he took his seat in the now crowded compartment.

'A fear gripped him,' the lama replied, with a touch of tender malice. 'He saw thee change the Mahratta to a Saddhu in the twinkling of an eye, as a protection against evil. That shook him. Then he saw the Saddhu fall sheer into the hands of the *polis*—all the effect of thy art. Then he gathered up his son and fled; for he said that thou didst change a quiet trader into an impudent bandier of words with the Sahibs, and he feared a like fate. Where is the Saddhu?'

'With the *polis*,' said Kim . . . 'Yet I saved the Kamboh's child.' The lama snuffed blandly.

7. Crowd.
8. The idealized English policeman whose power lies in his knowledge of Indian culture and his ability to disguise and pass as native. Strickland also appears in such Kipling stories as "Miss Youghal's Sais," "The Return of Imray," "To Be Filed for Reference," and "The Mark of the Beast."

'Ah, *chela*, see how thou art overtaken! Thou didst cure the Kamboh's child solely to acquire merit. But thou didst put a spell on the Mahratta with prideful workings—I watched thee—and with sidelong glances to bewilder an old old man and a foolish farmer: whence calamity and suspicion.'

Kim controlled himself with an effort beyond his years. Not more than any other youngster did he like to eat dirt or to be misjudged, but he saw himself in a cleft stick.[9] The train rolled out of Delhi into the night.

'It is true,' he murmured. 'Where I have offended thee I have done wrong.'

'It is more, *chela*. Thou hast loosed an Act upon the world, and as a stone thrown into a pool so spread the consequences thou canst not tell how far.'

This ignorance was well both for Kim's vanity and for the lama's peace of mind, when we think that there was then being handed in at Simla a code-wire reporting the arrival of E23 at Delhi, and, more important, the whereabouts of a letter he had been commissioned to—abstract. Incidentally, an over-zealous policeman had arrested, on charge of murder done in a far southern State, a horribly indignant Ajmir cotton-broker, who was explaining himself to a Mr Strickland on Delhi platform, while E23 was paddling through byways into the locked heart of Delhi city. In two hours several telegrams had reached the angry minister of a southern State reporting that all trace of a somewhat bruised Mahratta had been lost; and by the time the leisurely train halted at Saharunpore the last ripple of the stone Kim had helped to heave was lapping against the steps of a mosque in far-away Roum[1]—where it disturbed a pious man at prayers.

The lama made his in ample form near the dewy bougainvillea-trellis near the platform, cheered by the clear sunshine and the presence of his disciple. 'We will put these things behind us,' he said, indicating the brazen engine and the gleaming track. 'The jolting of the *te-rain*—though a wonderful thing—has turned my bones to water. We will use clean air henceforward.'

'Let us go to the Kulu woman's house,' said Kim, and stepped forth cheerily under the bundles. Early morning Saharunporeway is clean and well scented. He thought of the other mornings at St Xavier's, and it topped his already thrice-heaped contentment.

'Where is this new haste born from? Wise men do not run about like chickens in the sun. We have come hundreds upon hundreds of *koss* already, and, till now, I have scarcely been alone with thee an

9. Caught between a lie and its consequences.
1. Constantinople, or Istanbul (Turkey)—implying the ripple effects of Kim's actions on the courts of the Ottoman Empire and its pious caliph.

instant. How canst thou receive instruction all jostled of crowds? How can I, whelmed by a flux of talk, meditate upon the Way?'

'Her tongue grows no shorter with the years, then?' the disciple smiled.

'Nor her desire for charms. I remember once when I spoke of the Wheel of Life'—the lama fumbled in his bosom for his latest copy— 'she was only curious about the devils that besiege children. She shall acquire merit by entertaining us—in a little while—at an after-occasion—softly, softly. Now we will wander loose-foot, waiting upon the Chain of Things. The Search is sure.'

So they travelled very easily across and among the broad bloomful fruit-gardens—by way of Aminabad, Sahaigunge, Akrola of the Ford, and little Phulesa—the line of the Sewaliks[2] always to the north, and behind them again the snows. After long, sweet sleep under the dry stars came the lordly, leisurely passage through a waking village—begging-bowl held forth in silence, but eyes roving in defiance of the Law from sky's edge to sky's edge. Then would Kim return soft-footed through the soft dust to his master under the shadow of a mango-tree or the thinner shade of a white Doon *siris*,[3] to eat and drink at ease. At mid-day, after talk and a little wayfaring, they slept; meeting the world refreshed when the air was cooler. Night found them adventuring into new territory—some chosen village spied three hours before across the fat land, and much discussed upon the road.

There they told their tale—a new one each evening so far as Kim was concerned—and there were they made welcome, either by priest or headman, after the custom of the kindly East.

When the shadows shortened and the lama leaned more heavily upon Kim, there was always the Wheel of Life to draw forth, to hold flat under wiped stones, and with a long straw to expound cycle by cycle. Here sat the Gods on high—and they were dreams of dreams. Here was our Heaven and the world of the demi-Gods—horsemen fighting among the hills. Here were the agonies done upon the beasts, souls ascending or descending the ladder and therefore not to be interfered with. Here were the Hells, hot and cold, and the abodes of tormented ghosts. Let the *chela* study the troubles that come from over-eating—bloated stomach and burning bowels. Obediently, then, with bowed head and brown finger alert to follow the pointer, did the *chela* study; but when they came to the Human World, busy and profitless, that is just above the Hells, his mind was distracted; for by the roadside trundled the very Wheel itself, eating, drinking, trading, marrying, and quarrelling—all warmly alive.

2. A range of foothills about fifty miles long that precedes the Himalayas.
3. An acacialike bush that grows in the valleys of Doon.

Often the lama made the living pictures the matter of his text, bid-
ding Kim—too ready—note how the flesh takes a thousand shapes,
desirable or detestable as men reckon, but in truth of no account
either way; and how the stupid spirit, bond-slave to the Hog, the
Dove, and the Serpent[4]—lusting after betel-nut, a new yoke of oxen,
women, or the favour of kings—is bound to follow the body through
all the Heavens and all the Hells, and strictly round again.
Sometimes a woman or a poor man, watching the ritual—it was
nothing less—when the great yellow chart was unfolded, would
throw a few flowers or a handful of cowries upon its edge. It suf-
ficed these humble ones that they had met a Holy One who might
be moved to remember them in his prayers.

'Cure them if they are sick,' said the lama, when Kim's sporting
instincts woke. 'Cure them if they have fever, but by no means work
charms. Remember what befell the Mahratta.'

'Then all Doing is evil?' Kim replied, lying out under a big tree at
the fork of the Doon road, watching the little ants run over his
hand.

'To abstain from action is well—except to acquire merit.'

'At the Gates of Learning we were taught that to abstain from
action was unbefitting a Sahib. And I am a Sahib.'

'Friend of all the World,'—the lama looked directly at Kim—'I am
an old man—pleased with shows as are children. To those who fol-
low the Way there is neither black nor white, Hind nor Bhotiyal. We
be all souls seeking escape. No matter what thy wisdom learned
among Sahibs, when we come to my River thou wilt be freed from
all illusion—at my side. *Hai!* my bones ache for that River, as they
ached in the *te-rain*; but my spirit sits above my bones, waiting. The
Search is sure!'

'I am answered. Is it permitted to ask a question?'

The lama inclined his stately head.

'I ate thy bread for three years—as thou knowest. Holy One,
whence came—?'

'There is much wealth, as men count it, in Bhotiyal,' the lama
returned with composure. 'In my own place I have the illusion of
honour. I ask for that I need. I am not concerned with the account.
That is for my monastery. *Ai!* The black high seats in the monastery,
and novices all in order!'

And he told stories, tracing with a finger in the dust, of the
immense and sumptuous ritual of avalanche-guarded cathedrals; of
processions and devil-dances; of the changing of monks and nuns
into swine; of holy cities fifteen thousand feet in the air; of intrigue

4. Representing greed, ignorance, and hatred as the roots of evil, these figures are drawn at
 the center of the Wheel of Life.

between monastery and monastery; of voices among the hills, and of that mysterious mirage that dances on dry snow. He spoke even of Lhassa[5] and of the Dalai Lama,[6] whom he had seen and adored.

Each long, perfect day rose behind Kim for a barrier to cut him off from his race and his mother-tongue. He slipped back to thinking and dreaming in the vernacular, and mechanically followed the lama's ceremonial observances at eating, drinking, and the like. The old man's mind turned more and more to his monastery as his eyes turned to the steadfast snows. His River troubled him nothing. Now and again, indeed, he would gaze long and long at a tuft or a twig, expecting, he said, the earth to cleave and deliver its blessing; but he was content to be with his disciple, at ease in the temperate wind that comes down from the Doon. This was not Ceylon, nor Buddh Gaya, nor Bombay, nor some grass-tangled ruins that he seemed to have stumbled upon two years ago. He spoke of those places as a scholar removed from vanity, as a Seeker walking in humility, as an old man, wise and temperate, illumining knowledge with brilliant insight. Bit by bit, disconnectedly, each tale called up by some wayside thing, he spoke of all his wanderings up and down Hind; till Kim, who had loved him without reason, now loved him for fifty good reasons. So they enjoyed themselves in high felicity, abstaining, as the Rule demands, from evil words, covetous desires; not over-eating, not lying on high beds, nor wearing rich clothes. Their stomachs told them the time, and the people brought them their food, as the saying is. They were lords of the villages of Aminabad, Sahaigunge, Akrola of the Ford, and little Phulesa, where Kim gave the soulless woman a blessing.

But news travels fast in India, and too soon shuffled across the crop-land, bearing a basket of fruits with a box of Kabul grapes and gilt oranges, a white-whiskered servitor—a lean, dry Oorya—begging them to bring the honour of their presence to his mistress, distressed in her mind that the lama had neglected her so long.

'Now do I remember'—the lama spoke as though it were a wholly new proposition. 'She is virtuous, but an inordinate talker.'

Kim was sitting on the edge of a cow's manger, telling stories to a village smith's children.

'She will only ask for another son for her daughter. I have not forgotten her,' he said. 'Let her acquire merit. Send word that we will come.'

They covered eleven miles through the fields in two days, and were overwhelmed with attentions at the end; for the old lady held a fine tradition of hospitality, to which she forced her son-in-law, who was

5. The capital of Tibet.
6. The spiritual and worldly head of the lamas and of Tibet; believed to be the living Buddha.

under the thumb of his women-folk and bought peace by borrowing of the money-lender. Age had not weakened her tongue or her memory, and from a discreetly barred upper window, in the hearing of not less than a dozen servants, she paid Kim compliments that would have flung European audiences into unclean dismay.

'But thou art still the shameless beggar-brat of the *parao*,' she shrilled. 'I have not forgotten thee. Wash ye and eat. The father of my daughter's son is gone away awhile. So we poor women are dumb and useless.'

For proof, she harangued the entire household unsparingly till food and drink were brought; and in the evening—the smoke-scented evening, copper-dun and turquoise across the fields—it pleased her to order her palanquin to be set down in the untidy fore-court by smoky torchlight; and there, behind not too closely drawn curtains, she gossiped.

'Had the Holy One come alone, I should have received him otherwise; but with this rogue, who can be too careful?'

'Maharanee,' said Kim, choosing as always the amplest title, 'is it my fault that none other than a Sahib—a *polis*-Sahib—called the Maharanee whose face he—'

'Chutt! That was on the pilgrimage. When we travel—thou knowest the proverb.'

'Called the Maharanee a Breaker of Hearts and a Dispenser of Delights?'

'To remember that! It was true. So he did. That was in the time of the bloom of my beauty.' She chuckled like a contented parrot above the sugar lump. 'Now tell me of thy goings and comings—as much as may be without shame. How many maids, and whose wives, hang upon thine eyelashes? Ye hail from Benares? I would have gone there again this year, but my daughter—we have only two sons. Phaii! Such is the effect of these low plains. Now in Kulu men are elephants. But I would ask thy Holy One—stand aside, rogue—a charm against most lamentable windy colics that in mango-time overtake my daughter's eldest. Two years back he gave me a powerful spell.'

'Oh, Holy One!' said Kim, bubbling with mirth at the lama's rueful face.

'It is true. I gave her one against wind.'

'Teeth—teeth—teeth,' snapped the old woman.

'"Cure them if they are sick,"' Kim quoted relishingly, ' "but by no means work charms. Remember what befell the Mahratta."'

'That was two Rains ago; she wearied me with her continual importunity.' The lama groaned as the Unjust Judge had groaned before him. 'Thus it comes—take note, my *chela*—that even those who would follow the Way are thrust aside by idle women. Three days through, when the child was sick, she talked to me.'

'*Arré!* and to whom else should I talk? The boy's mother knew nothing, and the father—in the nights of the cold weather it was— "Pray to the Gods," said he, forsooth, and turning over, snored!'

'I gave her the charm. What is an old man to do?'

'"To abstain from action is well—except to acquire merit."'

'Ah *chela*, if thou desertest me, I am all alone.'

'He found his milk-teeth easily at any rate,' said the old lady. 'But all priests are alike.'

Kim coughed severely. Being young, he did not approve of her flippancy. 'To importune the wise out of season is to invite calamity.'

'There is a talking *mynah*[7]—the thrust came back with the well-remembered snap of the jewelled fore-finger—'over the stables which has picked up the very tone of the family priest. Maybe I forget honour to my guests, but if ye had seen *him* double his fists into his belly, which was like a half-grown gourd, and cry: "Here is the pain!" ye would forgive. I am half minded to take the *hakim's*[8] medicine. He sells it cheap, and certainly it makes him fat as Shiv's own bull. *He* does not deny remedies, but I doubted for the child because of the inauspicious colour of the bottles.'

The lama, under cover of the monologue, had faded out into the darkness towards the room prepared.

'Thou hast angered him, belike,' said Kim.

'Not he. He is wearied, and I forgot, being a grandmother. (None but a grandmother should ever oversee a child. Mothers are only fit for bearing.) Tomorrow, when he sees how my daughter's son is grown, he will write the charm. Then, too, he can judge of the new *hakim's* drugs.'

'Who is the *hakim*, Maharanee?'

'A wanderer, as thou art, but a most sober Bengali from Dacca[9]— a master of medicine. He relieved me of an oppression after meat by means of a small pill that wrought like a devil unchained. He travels about now, vending preparations of great value. He has even papers, printed in Angrezi, telling what things he has done for weak-backed men and slack women. He has been here four days; but hearing ye were coming (*hakims* and priests are snake and tiger the world over) he has, as I take it, gone to cover.'

While she drew breath after this volley, the ancient servant, sitting unrebuked on the edge of the torchlight, muttered: 'This house is a cattle-pound, as it were, for all charlatans and—priests. Let the boy stop eating mangoes . . . but who can argue with a grand-

7. A small Indian bird resembling a starling that, like a parrot, can be trained to talk.
8. Doctor.
9. Town in Bengal about 150 miles from Calcutta, the nineteenth-century capital of British India.

mother?' He raised his voice respectfully: 'Sahiba, the *hakim* sleeps after his meat. He is in the quarters behind the dovecot.'

Kim bristled like an expectant terrier. To outface and down-talk a Calcutta-taught Bengali, a voluble Dacca drug-vendor, would be a good game. It was not seemly that the lama, and incidentally himself, should be thrown aside for such an one. He knew those curious bastard English advertisements at the backs of native newspapers. St Xavier's boys sometimes brought them in by stealth to snigger over among their mates; for the language of the grateful patient recounting his symptoms is most simple and revealing. The Oorya, not unanxious to play off one parasite against the other, slunk away towards the dovecot.

'Yes,' said Kim, with measured scorn. 'Their stock-in-trade is a little coloured water and a very great shamelessness. Their prey are broken-down kings and overfed Bengalis. Their profit is in children—who are not born.'

The old lady chuckled. 'Do not be envious. Charms are better, eh? I never gainsaid it. See that thy Holy One writes me a good amulet by the morning.'

'None but the ignorant deny'—a thick, heavy voice boomed through the darkness, as a figure came to rest squatting—'None but the ignorant deny the value of charms. None but the ignorant deny the value of medicines.'

'A rat found a piece of turmeric. Said he: "I will open a grocer's shop,"' Kim retorted.

Battle was fairly joined now, and they heard the old lady stiffen to attention.

'The priest's son knows the names of his nurse and three Gods. Says he: "Hear me, or I will curse you by the three million Great Ones."' Decidedly this invisible had an arrow or two in his quiver. He went on: 'I am but a teacher of the alphabet. I have learned all the wisdom of the Sahibs.'

'The Sahibs never grow old. They dance and they play like children when they are grandfathers. A strong-backed breed,' piped the voice inside the palanquin.

'I have, too, our drugs which loosen humours of the head in hot and angry men. *Siná* well compounded when the moon stands in the proper House; yellow earths I have—*arplan* from China that makes a man renew his youth and astonish his household; saffron from Kashmir, and the best salep[1] of Kabul. Many people have died before—'

'That I surely believe,' said Kim.

'They knew the value of my drugs. I do not give *my* sick the mere

1. *Sina, arplan*, and salep are drugs made from roots.

ink in which a charm is written, but hot and rending drugs which descend and wrestle with the evil.'

'Very mightily they do so,' sighed the old lady.

The voice launched into an immense tale of misfortune and bankruptcy, studded with plentiful petitions to the Government. 'But for my fate, which overrules all, I had been now in Government employ. I bear a degree from the great school at Calcutta—whither, maybe, the son of this House shall go.'

'He shall indeed. If our neighbour's brat can in a few years be made an F A' (First Arts—she used the English word, of which she had heard so often), 'how much more shall children clever as some that I know bear away prizes at rich Calcutta.'

'Never,' said the voice, 'have I seen such a child! Born in an auspicious hour, and—but for that colic which, alas! turning into black cholers, may carry him off like a pigeon—destined to many years, he is enviable.'

'Hai mai!' said the old lady. 'To praise children is inauspicious, or I could listen to this talk. But the back of the house is unguarded, and even in this soft air men think themselves to be men, and women we know . . . The child's father is away too, and I must be chowkedar (watchman) in my old age. Up! Up! Take up the palanquin. Let the hakim and the young priest settle between them whether charms or medicine most avail. Ho! worthless people, fetch tobacco for the guests, and—round the homestead go I!'

The palanquin reeled off, followed by straggling torches and a horde of dogs. Twenty villages knew the Sahiba—her failings, her tongue, and her large charity. Twenty villages cheated her after immemorial custom, but no man would have stolen or robbed within her jurisdiction for any gift under heaven. None the less, she made great parade of her formal inspections, the riot of which could be heard half-way to Mussoorie.

Kim relaxed, as one augur must when he meets another. The hakim, still squatting, slid over his hookah with a friendly foot, and Kim pulled at the good weed. The hangers-on expected grave professional debate, and perhaps a little free doctoring.

'To discuss medicine before the ignorant is of one piece with teaching the peacock to sing,' said the hakim.

'True courtesy,' Kim echoed, 'is very often inattention.'

These, be it understood, were company-manners, designed to impress.

'Hi! I have an ulcer on my leg,' cried a scullion. 'Look at it!'

'Get hence! Remove!' said the hakim. 'Is it the habit of the place to pester honoured guests? Ye crowd in like buffaloes.'

'If the Sahiba knew—' Kim began.

'Ai! Ai! Come away. They are meat for our mistress. When her

young Shaitan's colics are cured perhaps we poor people may be suffered to—'

'The mistress fed thy wife when thou wast in jail for breaking the money-lender's head. Who speaks against her?' The old servitor curled his white moustaches savagely in the young moonlight. '*I am* responsible for the honour of this house. Go!' and he drove the underlings before him.

Said the *hakim*, hardly more than shaping the words with his lips: 'How do you do, Mister O'Hara? I am jolly glad to see you again.'

Kim's hand clenched about the pipe-stem. Anywhere on the open road, perhaps, he would not have been astonished; but here, in this quiet backwater of life, he was not prepared for Hurree Babu. It annoyed him, too, that he had been hoodwinked.

'Ah ha! I told you at Lucknow—*resurgam*—I shall rise again and you shall not know me. How much did you bet—eh?'

He chewed leisurely upon a few cardamon seeds, but he breathed uneasily.

'But why come here, Babuji?'

'Ah! *Thatt* is the question, as Shakespeare hath it. I come to congratulate you on your extraordinary effeecient performance at Delhi. Oah! I tell you we are all proud of you. It was verree neat and handy. Our mutual friend, he is old friend of mine. He has been in some dam'-tight places. Now he will be in some more. He told me; I tell Mr Lurgan; and he is pleased you graduate so nicely. All the Department is pleased.'

For the first time in his life, Kim thrilled to the clean pride (it can be a deadly pitfall, none the less) of Departmental praise—ensnaring praise from an equal of work appreciated by fellow-workers. Earth has nothing on the same plane to compare with it. But, cried the Oriental in him, Babus do not travel far to retail compliments.

'Tell thy tale, Babu,' he said authoritatively.

'Oah, it is nothing. Onlee I was at Simla when the wire came in about what our mutual friend said he had hidden, and old Creighton—' He looked to see how Kim would take this piece of audacity.

'The Colonel Sahib,' the boy from St Xavier's corrected.

'*Of* course. He found me at a loose string, and I had to go down to Chitor to find that beastly letter. I do not like the South—too much railway travel; but I drew good travelling allowance. Ha! Ha! I meet our mutual at Delhi on the way back. He lies quiett just now, and says Saddhu-disguise suits him to the ground. Well, there I hear what you have done so well, so quickly, upon the instantaneous spur of the moment. I tell our mutual you take the bally bun, by Jove! It was splendid. I come to tell you so.'

'Umm!'

The frogs were busy in the ditches, and the moon slid to her setting. Some happy servant had gone out to commune with the night and to beat upon a drum. Kim's next sentence was in the vernacular.

'How didst thou follow us?'

'Oah. Thatt was nothing. I know from our mutual friend you go to Saharunpore. So I come on. Red Lamas are not inconspicuous persons. I buy myself my drug-box, and I am very good doctor really. I go to Akrola of the Ford, and hear all about you, and I talk here and talk there. All the common people know what you do. I knew when the hospitable old lady sent the *dooli*.[2] They have great recollections of the old lama's visits here. I know old ladies cannot keep their hands from medicines. So I am a doctor, and—you hear my talk? *I* think it is verree good. My word, Mister O'Hara, they know about you and the lama for fifty miles—the common people. So I come. Do you mind?'

'Babuji,' said Kim, looking up at the broad, grinning face, 'I am a Sahib.'

'My dear Mister O'Hara—'

'And I hope to play the Great Game.'

'You are subordinate to me departmentally at present.'

'Then why talk like an ape in a tree? Men do not come after one from Simla and change their dress, for the sake of a few sweet words. I am not a child. Talk Hindi and let us get to the yolk of the egg. Thou art here—speaking not one word of truth in ten. Why art thou here? Give a straight answer.'

'That is so verree disconcerting of the Europeans, Mister O'Hara. You should know a heap better at your time of life.'

'But I want to know,' said Kim, laughing. 'If it is the Game, I may help. How can I do anything if you *bukh* (babble) all round the shop?'

Hurree Babu reached for the pipe, and sucked it till it gurgled again.

'Now I will speak vernacular. You sit tight, Mister O'Hara . . . It concerns the pedigree of a white stallion.'

'Still? That was finished long ago.'

'When everyone is dead the Great Game is finished. Not before. Listen to me till the end. There were Five Kings who prepared a sudden war three years ago, when thou wast given the stallion's pedigree by Mahbub Ali. Upon them, because of that news, and ere they were ready, fell our Army.'

'Ay—eight thousand men with guns. I remember that night.'

'But the war was not pushed. That is the Government custom. The troops were recalled because the Government believed the Five

2. A bamboo litter.

Kings were cowed; and it is not cheap to feed men among the high Passes. Hilás and Bunár—Rajahs with guns—undertook for a price to guard the Passes against all coming from the North. They protested both fear and friendship.' He broke off with a giggle into English: 'Of course, I tell you this unoffeecially to elucidate political situation, Mister O'Hara. Offeecially, I am debarred from criticizing any action of superiors. Now I go on.—This pleased the Government, anxious to avoid expense, and a bond was made for so many rupees a month that Hilás and Bunár should guard the Passes as soon as the State's troops were withdrawn. At that time—it was after we two met—I, who had been selling tea in Leh, became a clerk of accounts in the Army. When the troops were withdrawn, I was left behind to pay the coolies who made new roads in the Hills. This road-making was part of the bond between Bunár, Hilás, and the Government.'

'So? And then?'

'I tell you, it was jolly-beastly cold up there too, after summer,' said Hurree Babu confidentially. 'I was afraid these Bunár men would cut my throat every night for thee pay-chest. My native sepoy-guard, they laughed at me! By Jove! I was such a fearful man. Nevar mind thatt. I go on colloquially . . . I send word many times that these two Kings were sold to the North; and Mahbub Ali, who was yet farther North, amply confirmed it. Nothing was done. Only my feet were frozen, and a toe dropped off. I sent word that the roads for which I was paying money to the diggers were being made for the feet of strangers and enemies.'

'For?'

'For the Russians. The thing was an open jest among the coolies. Then I was called down to tell what I knew by speech of tongue. Mahbub came South too. See the end! Over the Passes, this year after snow-melting'—he shivered afresh—'come two strangers under cover of shooting wild goats. They bear guns, but they bear also chains and levels and compasses.'

'Oho! The thing gets clearer.'

'They are well received by Hilás and Bunár. They make great promises; they speak as the mouthpiece of a Kaisar with gifts. Up the valleys, down the valleys go they, saying, "Here is a place to build a breastwork; here can ye pitch a fort. Here can ye hold the road against an army"—the very roads for which I paid out the rupees monthly. The Government knows, but does nothing. The three other Kings, who were *not* paid for guarding the Passes, tell them by runner of the bad faith of Bunár and Hilás. When all the evil is done, look you—when these two strangers with the levels and the compasses make the Five Kings to believe that a great army will sweep the Passes tomorrow or the next day—Hill-people are all

fools—comes the order to me, Hurree Babu, "Go North and see what those strangers do." I say to Creighton Sahib, "This is not a lawsuit, that we go about to collect evidence."' Hurree returned to his English with a jerk: '"By Jove," I said, "why the dooce do you not issue demi-offeecial orders to some brave man to poison them, for an example? It is, if you permit the observation, most reprehensible laxity on your part." And Colonel Creighton, he laughed at me! It is all your beastly English pride. You think no one dare conspire! That is all tommy-rott.'

Kim smoked slowly, revolving the business, so far as he understood it, in his quick mind.

'Then thou goest forth to follow the strangers?'

'No. To meet them. They are coming in to Simla to send down their horns and heads to be dressed at Calcutta. They are exclusively sporting gentlemen, and they are allowed special faceelities by the Government. Of course, we always do that. It is our British pride.'

'Then what is to fear from them?'

'By Jove, they are not black people. I can do all sorts of things with black people, of course. They are Russians, and highly unscrupulous people. I—I do not want to consort with them without a witness.'

'Will they kill thee?'

'Oah, thatt is nothing. I am good enough Herbert Spencerian,[3] I trust, to meet little thing like death, which is all in my fate, you know. But—but they may beat me.'

'Why?'

Hurree Babu snapped his fingers with irritation. 'Of *course* I shall affeeliate myself to their camp in supernumerary capacity as perhaps interpreter, or person mentally impotent and hungree, or some such thing. And then I must pick up what I can, I suppose. That is as easy for me as playing Mister Doctor to the old lady. Onlee—onlee—you see, Mister O'Hara, I am unfortunately Asiatic, which is serious detriment in some respects. And *all*-so I am Bengali—a fearful man.'

'God made the Hare and the Bengali. What shame?' said Kim, quoting the proverb.

'It was process of Evolution, *I* think, from Primal Necessity, but the fact remains in all the *cui bono*.[4] I am, oh, awfully fearful!—I remember once they wanted to cut off my head on the road to Lhassa. (No, I have never reached to Lhassa.) I sat down and cried, Mister O'Hara, anticipating Chinese tortures. I do not suppose these two gentlemen

3. See p. 152, n. 3.
4. To whom the good (Latin).

will torture me, but I like to provide for possible contingency with European assistance in emergency.' He coughed and spat out the cardamoms. 'It is purely unoffeecial indent, to which you can say "No, Babu". If you have no pressing engagement with your old man—perhaps you might divert him; perhaps I can seduce his fancies—I should like you to keep in Departmental touch with me till I find those sporting coves. I have great opeenion of you since I met my friend at Delhi. And also I will embody your name in my offeecial report when matter is finally adjudicated. It will be a great feather in your cap. That is why I come really.'

'Humph! The end of the tale, I think, is true; but what of the forepart?'

'About the Five Kings? Oah! there is ever so much truth in it. A lots more than you would suppose,' said Hurree earnestly. 'You come—eh? I go from here straight into the Doon. It is verree verdant and painted meads. I shall go to Mussoorie—to good old Munsoorie Pahar, as the gentlemen and ladies say. Then by Rampur into Chini. That is the only way they can come. I do not like waiting in the cold, but we must wait for them. I want to walk with them to Simla. You see, one Russian is a Frenchman, and I know my French pretty well. I have friends in Chandernagore.'

'*He* would certainly rejoice to see the Hills again,' said Kim meditatively. 'All his speech these ten days past has been of little else. If we go together—'

'Oah! We can be quite strangers on the road, if your lama prefers. I shall just be four or five miles ahead. There is no hurry for Hurree—that is an Europe pun, ha! ha!—and you come after. There is plenty of time; they will plot and survey and map, of course. I shall go tomorrow, and you the next day, if you choose. Eh? You go think on it till morning. By Jove, it is near morning now.' He yawned ponderously, and with never a civil word lumbered off to his sleeping-place. But Kim slept little, and his thoughts ran in Hindustani:

'Well is the Game called great! I was four days a scullion at Quetta, waiting on the wife of the man whose book I stole. And that was part of the Great Game! From the South—God knows how far came up the Mahratta, playing the Great Game in fear of his life. Now I shall go far and far into the North playing the Great Game. Truly, it runs like a shuttle throughout all Hind. And my share and my joy'—he smiled to the darkness—'I owe to the lama here. Also to Mahbub Ali—also to Creighton Sahib, but chiefly to the Holy One. He is right—a great and a wonderful world—and I am Kim—Kim—Kim—alone—one person—in the middle of it all. But I will see these strangers with their levels and chains . . .'

'What was the upshot of last night's babble?' said the lama, after his orisons.

'There came a strolling seller of drugs—a hanger-on of the Sahiba's. Him I abolished by arguments and prayers, proving that our charms are worthier than his coloured waters.'

'Alas, my charms! Is the virtuous woman still bent upon a new one?'

'Very strictly.'

'Then it must be written, or she will deafen me with her clamour.' He fumbled at his pencase.

'In the Plains,' said Kim, 'are always too many people. In the Hills, as I understand, there are fewer.'

'Oh! the Hills, and the snows upon the Hills.' The lama tore off a tiny square of paper fit to go in an amulet. 'But what dost thou know of the Hills?'

'They are very close.' Kim thrust open the door and looked at the long, peaceful line of the Himalayas flushed in morning-gold. 'Except in the dress of a Sahib, I have never set foot among them.'

The lama snuffed the wind wistfully.

'If we go North,'—Kim put the question to the waking sunrise— 'would not much mid-day heat be avoided by walking among the lower hills at least? . . . Is the charm made, Holy One?'

'I have written the names of seven silly devils—not one of whom is worth a grain of dust in the eye. Thus do foolish women drag us from the Way!'

Hurree Babu came out from behind the dovecot, washing his teeth with ostentatious ritual. Full-fleshed, heavy-haunched, bull-necked, and deep-voiced, he did not look like 'a fearful man'. Kim signed almost imperceptibly that matters were in good train, and when the morning toilet was over, Hurree Babu, in flowery speech, came to do honour to the lama. They ate, of course, apart, and after-wards the old lady, more or less veiled behind a window, returned to the vital business of green-mango colics in the young. The lama's knowledge of medicine was, of course, sympathetic only. He believed that the dung of a black horse, mixed with sulphur, and carried in a snakeskin, was a sound remedy for cholera; but the sym-bolism interested him far more than the science. Hurree Babu deferred to these views with enchanting politeness, so that the lama called him a courteous physician. Hurree Babu replied that he was no more than an inexpert dabbler in the mysteries; but at least—he thanked the Gods therefore—he knew when he sat in the presence of a master. He himself had been taught by the Sahibs, who do not consider expense, in the lordly halls of Calcutta; but, as he was ever first to acknowledge, there lay a wisdom behind earthly wisdom— the high and lonely lore of meditation. Kim looked on with envy. The Hurree Babu of his knowledge—oily, effusive, and nervous— was gone; gone, too, was the brazen drug-vendor of overnight. There

remained—polished, polite, attentive—a sober, learned son of experience and adversity, gathering wisdom from the lama's lips. The old lady confided to Kim that these rare levels were beyond her. She liked charms with plenty of ink that one could wash off in water, swallow, and be done with. Else what was the use of the Gods? She liked men and women, and she spoke of them—of kinglets she had known in the past; of her own youth and beauty; of the depredations of leopards and the eccentricities of love Asiatic; of the incidence of taxation, rack-renting,[5] funeral ceremonies, her son-in-law (this by allusion, easy to be followed), the care of the young, and the age's lack of decency. And Kim, as interested in the life of this world as she soon to leave it, squatted with his feet under the hem of his robe, drinking all in, while the lama demolished one after another every theory of body-curing put forward by Hurree Babu.

At noon the Babu strapped up his brass-bound drug-box, took his patent-leather shoes of ceremony in one hand, a gay blue-and-white umbrella in the other, and set off northwards to the Doon, where, he said, he was in demand among the lesser kings of those parts.

'We will go in the cool of the evening, *chela*,' said the lama. 'That doctor, learned in physic and courtesy, affirms that the people among these lower hills are devout, generous, and much in need of a teacher. In a very short time—so says the *hakim*—we come to cool air and the smell of pines.'

'Ye go to the Hills? And by Kulu road? Oh, thrice happy!' shrilled the old lady. 'But that I am a little pressed with the care of the homestead I would take palanquin . . . but that would be shameless, and my reputation would be cracked. Ho! Ho! I know the road—every march of the road I know. Ye will find charity throughout—it is not denied to the well-looking. I will give orders for provision. A servant to set you forth upon your journey? No . . . Then I will at least cook ye good food.'

'What a woman is the Sahiba!' said the white-bearded Oorya, when a tumult rose by the kitchen quarters. 'She has never forgotten a friend: she has never forgotten an enemy in all her years. And her cookery—wah!' He rubbed his slim stomach.

There were cakes, there were sweetmeats, there was cold fowl stewed to rags with rice and prunes—enough to burden Kim like a mule.

'I am old and useless,' she said. 'None now love me—and none respect—but there are few to compare with me when I call on the Gods and squat to my cooking-pots. Come again, O people of good will. Holy One and disciple, come again. The room is always prepared; the welcome is always ready . . . See the women do not fol-

5. The charging of exorbitant rents.

low thy *chela* too openly. *I* know the women of Kulu. Take heed, *chela*, lest he run away when he smells his Hills again . . . *Hai!* Do not tilt the rice-bag upside down . . . Bless the household, Holy One, and forgive thy servant her stupidities.'

She wiped her red old eyes on a corner of her veil, and clucked throatily.

'Women talk,' said the lama at last, 'but that is a woman's infirmity. I gave her a charm. She is upon the Wheel and wholly given over to the shows of this life, but none the less, *chela*, she is virtuous, kindly, hospitable—of a whole and zealous heart. Who shall say she does not acquire merit?'

'Not I, Holy One,' said Kim, reslinging the bountiful provision on his shoulders. 'In my mind—behind my eyes—I have tried to picture such an one altogether freed from the Wheel—desiring nothing, causing nothing—a nun, as it were.'

'And, O imp?' The lama almost laughed aloud.

'I cannot make the picture.'

'Nor I. But there are many, many millions of lives before her. She will get wisdom a little, it may be, in each one.'

'And will she forget how to make stews with saffron upon that road?'

'Thy mind is set on things unworthy. But she has skill. I am refreshed all over. When we reach the lower hills I shall be yet stronger. The *hakim* spoke truly to me this morn when he said a breath from the snows blows away twenty years from the life of a man. We will go up into the Hills—the high hills—up to the sound of snow-waters and the sound of the trees—for a little while. The *hakim* said that at any time we may return to the Plains, for we do no more than skirt the pleasant places. The *hakim* is full of learning; but he is in no way proud. I spoke to him—when thou wast talking to the Sahiba—of a certain dizziness that lays hold upon the back of my neck in the night, and he said it rose from excessive heat—to be cured by cool air. Upon consideration, I marvelled that I had not thought of such a simple remedy.'

'Didst thou tell him of thy Search?' said Kim, a little jealously. He preferred to sway the lama by his own speech—not through the wiles of Hurree Babu.

'Assuredly. I told him of my dream, and of the manner by which I had acquired merit by causing thee to be taught wisdom.'

'Thou didst not say I was a Sahib?'

'What need? I have told thee many times we be but two souls seeking escape. He said—and he is just herein—that the River of Healing will break forth even as I dreamed—at my feet, if need be. Having found the Way, seest thou, that shall free me from the Wheel, need I trouble to find a way about the mere fields of earth—

which are illusion? That were senseless. I have my dreams, night upon night repeated; I have the *Jâtaka*; and I have thee, Friend of all the World. It was written in thy horoscope that a Red Bull on a green field—I have not forgotten—should bring thee to honour. Who but I saw that prophecy accomplished? Indeed, I was the instrument. Thou shalt find me my River, being in return the instrument. The Search is sure!'

He set his ivory-yellow face, serene and untroubled, towards the beckoning Hills; his shadow shouldering far before him in the dust.

Chapter 13

Who hath desired the Sea—the immense and contemptuous surges?
The shudder, the stumble, the swerve ere the star-stabbing bowsprit emerges—
The orderly clouds of the Trades and the ridged roaring sapphire thereunder—
Unheralded cliff-lurking flaws and the head-sails' low-volleying thunder?
His Sea in no wonder the same—his Sea and the same in each wonder—
 His Sea that his being fulfils?
So and no otherwise—so and no otherwise hill-men desire their hills!
 The Sea and the Hills.

'Who goes to the hills goes to his mother.'

They had crossed the Sewaliks and the half-tropical Doon, left Mussoorie behind them, and headed north along the narrow hill-roads. Day after day they struck deeper into the huddled mountains, and day after day Kim watched the lama return to a man's strength. Among the terraces of the Doon he had leaned on the boy's shoulder, ready to profit by wayside halts. Under the great ramp to Mussoorie he drew himself together as an old hunter faces as well-remembered bank, and where he should have sunk exhausted swung his long draperies about him, drew a deep double-lungful of the diamond air, and walked as only a hillman can. Kim, plains-bred and plains-fed, sweated and panted astonished. 'This is *my* country,' said the lama. 'Beside Such-zen, this is flatter than a rice-field'; and with steady, driving strokes from the loins he strode upwards. But it was on the steep downhill marches, three thousand feet in three hours, that he went utterly away from Kim, whose back ached with holding back, and whose big toe was nigh cut off by his grass sandal-string. Through the speckled shadow of the great deodar-forests; through oak feathered and plumed with ferns; birch, ilex, rhododendron, and pine, out on to the bare hill-sides' slippery sunburnt grass, and back into the woodlands' coolth again, till oak gave way to bamboo and palm of the valley, the lama swung untiring.

Glancing back in the twilight at the huge ridges behind him and the faint, thin line of the road whereby they had come, he would lay out, with a hillman's generous breadth of vision, fresh marches for the morrow; or, halting in the neck of some uplifted pass that gave on Spiti and Kulu,[1] would stretch out his hands yearningly towards the high snows of the horizon. In the dawns they flared windy-red above stark blue, as Kedarnath and Badrinath[2]—kings of that wilderness—took the first sunlight. All day long they lay like molten silver under the sun, and at evening put on their jewels again. At first they breathed temperately upon the travellers, winds good to meet when one crawled over some gigantic hog's-back, but in a few days, at a height of nine or ten thousand feet, those breezes bit; and Kim kindly allowed a village of hillmen to acquire merit by giving him a rough blanket-coat. The lama was mildly surprised that any-one should object to the knife-edged breezes which had cut the years off his shoulders.

'These are but the lower hills, *chela*. There is no cold till we come to the true Hills.'

'Air and water are good, and the people are devout enough, but the food is very bad,' Kim growled; 'and we walk as though we were mad—or English. It freezes at night, too.'

'A little, maybe; but only enough to make old bones rejoice in the sun. We must not always delight in soft beds and rich food.'

'We might at least keep to the road.'

Kim had all a plainsman's affection for the well-trodden track, not six feet wide, that snaked among the mountains; but the lama, being Tibetan, could not refrain from short cuts over spurs and the rims of gravel-strewn slopes. As he explained to his limping disciple, a man bred among mountains can prophesy the course of a mountain-road, and though low-lying clouds might be a hin-drance to a short-cutting stranger, they made no earthly difference to a thoughtful man. Thus, after long hours of what would be reckoned very fair mountaineering in civilized countries, they would pant over a saddle-back, sidle past a few landslips, and drop through forest at an angle of forty-five on to the road again. Along their track lay the villages of the hill-folk—mud and earth huts, timbers now and then rudely carved with an axe—clinging like swallows' nests against the steeps, huddled on tiny flats half-way down a three-thousand-foot glissade;[3] jammed into a corner between cliffs that tunnelled and focused every wandering blast; or, for the sake of summer pasture, cowering down on a neck that in winter would be ten feet deep in snow. And the people—the sal-

1. Valleys in northwest India between the Punjab and Tibet.
2. Mountain peaks over twenty thousand feet.
3. Slide.

low, greasy, duffle-clad people, with short bare legs and faces
almost Esquimaux[4]—would flock out and adore. The Plains—
kindly and gentle—had treated the lama as a holy man among holy
men. But the Hills worshipped him as one in the confidence of
all their devils. Theirs was an almost obliterated Buddhism, over-
laid with a nature-worship fantastic as their own landscapes, elab-
orate as the terracing of their tiny fields; but they recognized the
big hat, the clicking rosary, and the rare Chinese texts for great
authority; and they respected the man beneath the hat.

'We saw thee come down over the black Breasts of Eua,' said a
Betah[5] who gave them cheese, sour milk, and stone-hard bread one
evening. 'We do not use that often—except when calving cows stray
in summer. There is a sudden wind among those stones that casts
men down on the stillest day. But what should such folk care for the
Devil of Eua!'

Then did Kim, aching in every fibre, dizzy with looking down,
footsore with cramping desperate toes into inadequate crannies,
take joy in the day's march—such joy as a boy of St Xavier's who had
won the quarter-mile on the flat might take in the praises of his
friends. The hills sweated the *ghi* and sugar suet off his bones; the
dry air, taken sobbingly at the head of cruel passes, firmed and built
out his upper ribs; and the tilted levels put new hard muscles into
calf and thigh.

They meditated often on the Wheel of Life—the more so since,
as the lama said, they were freed from its visible temptations.
Except the grey eagle and an occasional far-seen bear grubbing and
rooting on the hillside; a vision of a furious painted leopard met at
dawn in a still valley devouring a goat; and now and again a bright-
coloured bird, they were alone with the winds and the grass singing
under the wind. The women of the smoky huts over whose roofs the
two walked as they descended the mountains, were unlovely and
unclean, wives of many husbands, and afflicted with goitre.[6] The
men were wood-cutters when they were not farmers—meek, and of
an incredible simplicity. But that suitable discourse might not fail,
Fate sent them, overtaking and overtaken upon the road, the cour-
teous Dacca physician, who paid for his food in ointments good for
goitre and counsels that restore peace between men and women. He
seemed to know these hills as well as he knew the hill dialects, and
gave the lama the lie of the land towards Ladakh and Tibet. He said
they could return to the Plains at any moment. Meantime, for such as
loved mountains, yonder road might amuse. This was not all revealed
in a breath, but at evening encounters on the stone threshing-

4. Eskimo.
5. A hill-tribesman.
6. A reference to the tradition of polyandry and to a disease of the thyroid gland.

floors, when, patients disposed of, the doctor would smoke and the lama snuff, while Kim watched the wee cows grazing on the house-tops, or threw his soul after his eyes across the deep blue gulfs between range and range. And there were talks apart in the dark woods, when the doctor would seek herbs, and Kim, as budding physician, must accompany him.

'You see, Mister O'Hara, I do not know what the deuce-an'-all I shall do when I find our sporting friends; but if you will kindly keep within sight of my umbrella, which is fine fixed point for cadastral survey,[7] I shall feel much better.'

Kim looked out across the jungle of peaks. 'This is not my country, *hakim*. Easier, I think, to find one louse in a bear-skin.'

'Oah, thatt is my strong points. There is no hurry for Hurree. They were at Leh not so long ago. They said they had come down from the Karakorum with their heads and horns and all. I am onlee afraid they will have sent back all their letters and compromising things from Leh into Russian territoree. Of course they will walk away as far to the East as possible—just to show that they were never among the Western States. You do not know the Hills?' He scratched with a twig on the earth. 'Look! They should have come in by Srinagar or Abbottabad. *Thatt* is their short road—down the river by Bunji and Astor. But they have made mischief in the West. So'—he drew a furrow from left to right—'they march and they march away East to Leh (ah! it is cold there), and down the Indus to Hanlé (I know that road), and then down, you see, to Bushahr and Chini valley. That is ascertained by process of elimination, and also by asking questions from people that I cure so well. Our friends have been a long time playing about and producing impressions. So they are well known from far off. You will see me catch them some-where in Chini valley. Please keep your eye on the umbrella.'

It nodded like a wind-blown harebell down the valleys and round the mountain sides, and in due time the lama and Kim, who steered by compass, would overhaul it, vending ointments and powders at eventide. 'We came by such and such a way!' The lama would throw a careless finger backward at the ridges, and the umbrella would expend itself in compliments.

They crossed a snowy pass in cold moonlight, when the lama, mildly chaffing Kim, went through up to his knees, like a Bactrian camel—the snow-bred, shag-haired sort that came into the Kashmir Serai. They dipped across beds of light snow and snow-powdered shale, where they took refuge from a gale in a camp of Tibetans hur-rying down tiny sheep, each laden with a bag of borax.[8] They came

7. Maps used as the basis for property taxes.
8. A mild disinfectant.

out upon grassy shoulders still snow-speckled, and through forest, to grass anew. For all their marchings, Kedarnath and Badrinath were not impressed; and it was only after days of travel that Kim, uplifted upon some insignificant ten-thousand-foot hummock, could see that a shoulder-knot or horn of the two great lords had—ever so slightly—changed outline.

At last they entered a world within a world—a valley of leagues where the high hills were fashioned of a mere rubble and refuse from off the knees of the mountains. Here one day's march carried them no farther, it seemed, than a dreamer's clogged pace bears him in a nightmare. They skirted a shoulder painfully for hours, and, behold, it was but an outlying boss in an outlying buttress of the main pile! A rounded meadow revealed itself, when they had reached it, for a vast tableland running far into the valley. Three days later, it was a dim fold in the earth to southward.

'Surely the Gods live here!' said Kim, beaten down by the silence and the appalling sweep and dispersal of the cloud-shadows after rain. 'This is no place for men!'

'Long and long ago,' said the lama, as to himself, 'it was asked of the Lord whether the world were everlasting. To this the Excellent One returned no answer . . . When I was in Ceylon, a wise Seeker confirmed that from the gospel which is written in Pali.[9] Certainly, since we know the way to Freedom, the question were unprofitable, but—look, and know illusion, *chela*! These are the true Hills! They are like my hills by Such-zen. Never were such hills!'

Above them, still enormously above them, earth towered away towards the snow-line, where from east to west across hundreds of miles, ruled as with a ruler, the last of the bold birches stopped. Above that, in scarps and blocks upheaved, the rocks strove to fight their heads above the white smother. Above these again, changeless since the world's beginning, but changing to every mood of sun and cloud, lay out the eternal snow. They could see blots and blurs on its face where storm and wandering wullie-wa[1] got up to dance. Below them, as they stood, the forest slid away in a sheet of blue-green for mile upon mile; below the forest was a village in its sprinkle of terraced fields and steep grazing-grounds. Below the village they knew, though a thunderstorm worried and growled there for the moment, a pitch of twelve or fifteen hundred feet gave to the moist valley where the streams gather that are the mothers of young Sutluj.[2]

As usual, the lama had led Kim by cow-track and by-road, far from the main route along which Hurree Babu, that 'fearful man',

9. Buddhists' sacred language.
1. A wind-blown, delicate snowdrift.
2. The Sutlej River flows from Tibet through the Punjab to join the Chenab.

had bucketed three days before through a storm to which nine Englishmen out of ten would have given full right of way. Hurree was no game-shot—the snick of a trigger made him change colour—but, as he himself would have said, he was 'fairly effeecient stalker', and he had raked the huge valley with a pair of cheap binoculars to some purpose. Moreover, the white of worn canvas tents against green carries far. Hurree Babu had seen all he wanted to see when he sat on the threshing-floor of Ziglaur, twenty miles away as the eagle flies, and forty by road—that is to say, two small dots which one day were just below the snow-line, and the next had moved downward perhaps six inches on the hillside. Once cleaned out and set to the work, his fat bare legs could cover a surprising amount of ground, and this was the reason why, while Kim and the lama lay in a leaky hut at Ziglaur till the storm should be over-past, an oily, wet, but always smiling Bengali, talking the best of English with the vilest of phrases, was ingratiating himself with two sodden and rather rheumatic foreigners. He had arrived, revolving many wild schemes, on the heels of a thunderstorm which had split a pine over against their camp, and so convinced a dozen or two forcibly impressed baggage-coolies the day was inauspicious for farther travel that with one accord they had thrown down their loads and jibbed.[3] They were subjects of a Hill Rajah who farmed out their services, as is the custom, for his private gain; and, to add to their personal distresses, the strange Sahibs had already threatened them with rifles. The most of them knew rifles and Sahibs of old: they were trackers and *shikarris*[4] of the Northern valleys, keen after bear and wild goat; but they had never been thus treated in their lives. So the forest took them to her bosom, and, for all oaths and clamour, refused to restore. There was no need to feign madness or—the Babu had thought of another means of securing a welcome. He wrung out his wet clothes, slipped on his patent-leather shoes, opened the blue-and-white umbrella, and with mincing gait and a heart beating against his tonsils appeared as 'agent for His Royal Highness, the Rajah of Rampur, gentlemen. What can I do for you, please?'

The gentlemen were delighted. One was visibly French, the other Russian, but they spoke English not much inferior to the Babu's. They begged his kind offices. Their native servants had gone sick at Leh. They had hurried on because they were anxious to bring the spoils of the chase to Simla ere the skins grew moth-eaten. They bore a general letter of introduction (the Babu salaamed to it orientally) to all Government officials. No, they had not met any other

3. Stopped in their tracks.
4. Hunters.

shooting-parties *en route*. They did for themselves. They had plenty
of supplies. They only wished to push on as soon as might be. At this
he waylaid a cowering hillman among the trees, and after three min-
utes' talk and a little silver (one cannot be economical upon State
service, though Hurree's heart bled at the waste) the eleven coolies
and the three hangers-on reappeared. At least the Babu would be a
witness to their oppression.

'My royal master, he will be much annoyed, but these people are
onlee common people and grossly ignorant. If your honours will
kindly overlook unfortunate affair, I shall be much pleased. In a lit-
tle while rain will stop and we can then proceed. You have been
shooting, eh? That is fine performance!'

He skipped nimbly from one *kilta*[5] to the next, making pretence
to adjust each conical basket. The Englishman is not, as a rule,
familiar with the Asiatic, but he would not strike across the wrist a
kindly Babu who had accidentally upset a *kilta* with a red oilskin
top. On the other hand, he would not press drink upon a Babu were
he never so friendly, nor would he invite him to meat. The strangers
did all these things, and asked many questions—about women
mostly—to which Hurree returned gay and unstudied answers.
They gave him a glass of whitish fluid like to gin, and then more;
and in a little time his gravity departed from him. He became thickly
treasonous, and spoke in terms of sweeping indecency of a
Government which had forced upon him a white man's education
and neglected to supply him with a white man's salary. He babbled
tales of oppression and wrong till the tears ran down his cheeks for
the miseries of his land. Then he staggered off, singing love-songs
of Lower Bengal, and collapsed upon a wet tree-trunk. Never was so
unfortunate a product of English rule in India more unhappily
thrust upon aliens.

'They are all just of that pattern,' said one sportsman to the other
in French. 'When we get into India proper thou wilt see. I should
like to visit his Rajah. One might speak the good word there. It is
possible that he has heard of us and wishes to signify his good-will.'

'We have not time. We must get into Simla as soon as may be,' his
companion replied. 'For my own part, I wish our reports had been
sent back from Hilás, or even Leh.'

'The English post is better and safer. Remember we are given all
facilities—and Name of God!—they give them to us too! Is it unbe-
lievable stupidity?'

'It is pride—pride that deserves and will receive punishment.'

'Yes! To fight a fellow-Continental in our game is something.
There is a risk attached, but these people—bah! It is too easy.'

5. Basket carried on the head and strapped to the forehead.

'Pride—all pride, my friend.'

'Now what the deuce is good of Chandernagore being so close to Calcutta and all,' said Hurree, snoring open-mouthed on the sodden moss, 'if I cannot understand their French? They talk so particularly fast! It would have been much better to cut their beastly throats.'

When he presented himself again he was racked with a headache—penitent, and volubly afraid that in his drunkenness he might have been indiscreet. He loved the British Government—it was the source of all prosperity and honour, and his master at Rampur held the very same opinion. Upon this the men began to deride him and to quote past words, till step by step, with deprecating smirks, oily grins, and leers of infinite cunning, the poor Babu was beaten out of his defences and forced to speak—truth. When Lurgan was told the tale later, he mourned aloud that he could not have been in the place of the stubborn, inattentive coolies, who with grass mats over their heads and the raindrops puddling in their footprints, waited on the weather. All the Sahibs of their acquaintance—rough-clad men joyously returning year after year to their chosen gullies—had servants and cooks and orderlies, very often hillmen. These Sahibs travelled without any retinue. Therefore they were poor Sahibs, and ignorant; for no Sahib in his senses would follow a Bengali's advice. But the Bengali, appearing from somewhere, had given them money, and could make shift with their dialect. Used to comprehensive ill-treatment from their own colour, they suspected a trap somewhere, and stood by to run if occasion offered.

Then through the new-washed air, steaming with delicious earth-smells, the Babu led the way down the slopes—walking ahead of the coolies in pride; walking behind the foreigners in humility. His thoughts were many and various. The least of them would have interested his companions beyond words. But he was an agreeable guide, ever keen to point out the beauties of his royal master's domain. He peopled the hills with anything they had a mind to slay—thar, ibex, or markhor[6] and bear by Elisha's allowance.[7] He discoursed of botany and ethnology with unimpeachable inaccuracy, and his store of local legends—he had been a trusted agent of the State for fifteen years, remember—was inexhaustible.

'Decidedly this fellow is an original,' said the taller of the two foreigners. 'He is like the nightmare of a Viennese courier.'

'He represents in little India in transition—the monstrous hybridism of East and West,' the Russian replied. 'It is *we* who can deal with Orientals.'

6. A dark, heavy animal with corkscrew-like horns up to four feet long. Thar is a reddish goat with horns; ibex is a short-legged, heavy animal with curved horns.
7. See 2 Kings 2.24: "and there came forth two she bears out of the wood."

'He has lost his own country and has not acquired any other. But he has a most complete hatred of his conquerors. Listen. He confides to me last night,' etc.

Under the striped umbrella Hurree Babu was straining ear and brain to follow the quick-poured French, and keeping both eyes on a *kilta* full of maps and documents—an extra-large one with a double red oil-skin cover. He did not wish to steal anything. He only desired to know what to steal, and, incidentally, how to get away when he had stolen it. He thanked all the Gods of Hindustan, and Herbert Spencer, that there remained some valuables to steal.

On the second day the road rose steeply to a grass spur above the forest; and it was here, about sunset, that they came across an aged lama but they called him a bonze[8]—sitting cross-legged above a mysterious chart held down by stones, which he was explaining to a young man, evidently a neophyte, of singular, though unwashen, beauty. The striped umbrella had been sighted half a march away, and Kim had suggested a halt till it came up to them.

'Ha!' said Hurree Babu, resourceful as Puss-in-Boots.[9] 'That is eminent local holy man. Probably subject of my royal master.'

'What is he doing? It is very curious.'

'He is expounding holy picture—*all* hand-worked.'

The two men stood bareheaded in the wash of the afternoon sunlight low across the gold-coloured grass. The sullen coolies, glad of the check, halted and slid down their loads.

'Look!' said the Frenchman. 'It is like a picture for the birth of a religion—the first teacher and the first disciple. Is he a Buddhist?'

'Of some debased kind,' the other answered. 'There are no true Buddhists among the Hills. But look at the folds of the drapery. Look at his eyes—how insolent! Why does this make one feel that we are so young a people?' The speaker struck passionately at a tall weed. 'We have nowhere left our mark yet. Nowhere! *That*, do you understand, is what disquiets me.' He scowled at the placid face, and the monumental calm of the pose.

'Have patience. We shall make your mark together—we and you young people. Meantime, draw his picture.'

The Babu advanced loftily; his back out of all keeping with his deferential speech, or his wink towards Kim.

'Holy One, these be Sahibs. My medicines cured one of a flux, and I go into Simla to oversee his recovery. They wish to see thy picture—'

'To heal the sick is always good. This is the Wheel of Life,' said

8. The Japanese term for a Buddhist priest was "bonzo."
9. The wily and daring cat from the French children's tale by Charles Perrault (1628–1703).

the lama, 'the same I showed thee in the hut at Ziglaur when the rain fell.'

'And to hear thee expound it.'

The lama's eyes lighted at the prospect of new listeners. 'To expound the Most Excellent Way is good. Have they any knowledge of Hindi, such as had the Keeper of Images?'

'A little, maybe.'

Hereat, simply as a child engrossed with a new game, the lama threw back his head and began the full-throated invocation of the Doctor of Divinity ere he opens the full doctrine. The strangers leaned on their alpenstocks and listened. Kim, squatting humbly, watched the red sunlight on their faces, and the blend and parting of their long shadows. They wore un-English leggings and curious girt-in belts that reminded him hazily of the pictures in a book in St Xavier's library: *The Adventures of a Young Naturalist in Mexico* was its name. Yes, they looked very like the wonderful M. Sumichrast[1] of that tale, and very unlike the 'highly unscrupulous folk' of Hurree Babu's imagining. The coolies, earth-coloured and mute, crouched reverently some twenty or thirty yards away, and the Babu, the slack of his thin gear snapping like a marking-flag in the chill breeze, stood by with an air of happy proprietorship.

'These are the men,' Hurree whispered, as the ritual went on and the two whites followed the grass-blade sweeping from Hell to Heaven and back again. 'All their books are in the large *kilta*, with the reddish top—books and reports and maps—and I have seen a King's letter that either Hilás or Bunár has written. They guard it most carefully. They have sent nothing back from Hilás or Leh. That is sure.'

'Who is with them?'

'Only the *beegar*-coolies. They have no servants. They are so close they cook their own food.'

'But what am I to do?'

'Wait and see. Only if any chance comes to me thou wilt know where to seek for the papers.'

'This were better in Mahbub Ali's hands than a Bengali's,' said Kim scornfully.

'There are more ways of getting to a sweetheart than butting down a wall.'

'See here the Hell appointed for avarice and greed. Flanked upon the one side by Desire and on the other by Weariness.' The lama warmed to his work, and one of the strangers sketched him in the quick-fading light.

1. M. Francis E. Sumichrast wrote books on the reptiles of Mexico and on the native birds of Vera Cruz.

'That is enough,' the man said at last brusquely. 'I cannot under-
stand him, but I want that picture. He is better artist than I. Ask
him if he will sell it.'

'He says "No, sar,"' the Babu replied. The lama, of course, would
no more have parted with his chart to a casual wayfarer than an
archbishop would pawn the holy vessels of his cathedral. All Tibet
is full of cheap reproductions of the Wheel; but the lama was an
artist, as well as a wealthy abbot in his own place.

'Perhaps in three days, or four, or ten, if I perceive that the Sahib
is a Seeker and of good understanding, I may myself draw him
another. But this was used for the initiation of a novice. Tell him so,
hakim.'

'He wishes it now—for money.'

The lama shook his head slowly and began to fold up the Wheel.
The Russian, on his side, saw no more than an unclean old man
haggling over a dirty piece of paper. He drew out a handful of
rupees, and snatched half-jestingly at the chart, which tore in the
lama's grip. A low murmur of horror went up from the coolies—
some of whom were Spiti[2] men and, by their lights, good Buddhists.
The lama rose at the insult; his hand went to the heavy iron pencase
that is the priest's weapon, and the Babu danced in agony.

'Now you see—you see why I wanted witnesses. They are highly
unscrupulous people. Oh, sar! sar! You must *not* hit holy man!'

'*Chela!* He has defiled the Written Word!'

It was too late. Before Kim could ward him off, the Russian struck
the old man full on the face. Next instant he was rolling over and over
downhill with Kim at his throat. The blow had waked every unknown
Irish devil in the boy's blood, and the sudden fall of his enemy did the
rest. The lama dropped to his knees, half-stunned; the coolies under
their loads fled up the hill as fast as plainsmen run across the level.
They had seen sacrilege unspeakable, and it behoved them to get
away before the Gods and devils of the hills took vengeance. The
Frenchman ran towards the lama, fumbling at his revolver with some
notion of making him a hostage for his companion. A shower of cut-
ting stones—hillmen are very straight shots—drove him away, and a
coolie from Ao-chung snatched the lama into the stampede. All came
about as swiftly as the sudden mountain-darkness.

'They have taken the baggage and all the guns,' yelled the
Frenchman, firing blindly into the twilight.

'All right, sar! All right! Don't shoot. I go to rescue,' and Hurree,
pounding down the slope, cast himself bodily upon the delighted
and astonished Kim, who was banging his breathless foe's head
against a boulder.

2. A valley near Kulu.

'Go back to the coolies,' whispered the Babu in his ear. 'They have the baggage. The papers are in the *kilta* with the red top, but look through all. Take their papers, and specially the *muraslu* (King's letter). Go! The other man comes!'

Kim tore uphill. A revolver-bullet rang on a rock by his side, and he cowered partridge-wise.

'If you shoot,' shouted Hurree, 'they will descend and annihilate us. I have rescued the gentleman, sar. This is particularly dangerous.'

'By Jove!' Kim was thinking hard in English. 'This is dam'-tight place, but *I* think it is self-defence.' He felt in his bosom for Mahbub's gift, and uncertainly—save for a few practice shots in the Bikanir desert, he had never used the little gun—pulled the trigger.

'What did I say, sar!' The Babu seemed to be in tears. 'Come down here and assist to resuscitate. We are all up a tree, I tell you.'

The shots ceased. There was a sound of stumbling feet, and Kim hurried upward through the gloom, swearing like a cat—or a country-bred.

'Did they wound thee, *chela?*' called the lama above him.

'No. And thou?' He dived into a clump of stunted firs.

'Unhurt. Come away. We go with these folk to Shamlegh-under-the-Snow.'

'But not before we have done justice,' a voice cried. 'I have got the Sahibs' guns—all four. Let us go down.'

'He struck the Holy One—we saw it! Our cattle will be barren—our wives will cease to bear! The snows will slide upon us as we go home. . . . On top of all other oppression too!'

The little fir-clump filled with clamouring coolies—panic-stricken, and in their terror capable of anything. The man from Ao-chung clicked the breech-bolt of his gun impatiently, and made as to go downhill.

'Wait a little, Holy One; they cannot go far. Wait till I return,' said he.

'It is this person who has suffered wrong,' said the lama, his hand over his brow.

'For that very reason,' was the reply.

'If this person overlooks it, your hands are clean. Moreover, ye acquire merit by obedience.'

'Wait, and we will all go to Shamlegh together,' the man insisted.

For a moment, for just so long as it needs to stuff a cartridge into a breech-loader, the lama hesitated. Then he rose to his feet, and laid a finger on the man's shoulder.

'Hast thou heard? *I* say there shall be no killing—I who was Abbot of Such-zen. Is it any lust of thine to be re-born as a rat, or a snake

under the eaves—a worm in the belly of the most mean beast? Is it
thy wish to—'

The man from Ao-chung fell to his knees, for the voice boomed
like a Tibetan devil-gong.

'Ai! ai!' cried the Spiti men. 'Do not curse us—do not curse him.
It was but his zeal, Holy One! . . . Put down the rifle, fool!'

'Anger on anger! Evil on evil! There will be no killing. Let the
priest-beaters go in bondage to their own acts. Just and sure is the
Wheel, swerving not a hair! They will be born many times—in tor-
ment.' His head drooped, and he leaned heavily on Kim's shoulder.

'I have come near to great evil, *chela*,' he whispered in that dead
hush under the pines. 'I was tempted to loose the bullet; and truly,
in Tibet there would have been a heavy and a slow death for them
. . . He struck me across the face . . . upon the flesh . . .' He
slid to the ground, breathing heavily, and Kim could hear the over-
driven heart bump and check.

'Have they hurt him to the death?' said the Ao-chung man, while
the others stood mute.

Kim knelt over the body in deadly fear. 'Nay,' he cried passion-
ately, 'this is only a weakness.' Then he remembered that he was a
white man, with a white man's camp-fittings at his service. 'Open
the *kiltas*! The Sahibs may have a medicine.'

'Oho! Then I know it,' said the Ao-chung man with a laugh. 'Not
for five years was I Yankling Sahib's *shikarri* without knowing that
medicine. I too have tasted it. Behold!'

He drew from his breast a bottle of cheap whisky—such as is sold
to explorers at Leh—and cleverly forced a little between the lama's
teeth.

'So I did when Yankling Sahib twisted his foot beyond Astor. Aha! I
have already looked into their baskets—but we will make fair division
at Shamlegh. Give him a little more. It is good medicine. Feel! His
heart goes better now. Lay his head down and rub a little on the chest.
If he had waited quietly while I accounted for the Sahibs this would
never have come. But perhaps the Sahibs may chase us here. Then it
would not be wrong to shoot them with their own guns, heh?'

'One is paid, I think, already,' said Kim between his teeth. 'I kicked
him in the groin as we went downhill. Would I had killed him!'

'It is well to be brave when one does not live in Rampur,' said one
whose hut lay within a few miles of the Rajah's rickety palace. 'If we
get a bad name among the Sahibs, none will employ us as *shikarris*
any more.'

'Oh, but these are not Angrezi Sahibs—not merry-minded men
like Fostum Sahib or Yankling Sahib. They are foreigners—they can-
not speak Angrezi as do Sahibs.'

Here the lama coughed and sat up, groping for the rosary.

'There shall be no killing,' he murmured. 'Just is the Wheel! Evil on evil—'

'Nay, Holy One. We are all here.' The Ao-chung man timidly patted his feet. 'Except by thy order, no one shall be slain. Rest awhile. We will make a little camp here, and later, as the moon rises, we go to Shamlegh-under-the-Snow.'

'After a blow,' said a Spiti man sententiously, 'it is best to sleep.'

'There is, as it were, a dizziness at the back of my neck, and a pinching in it. Let me lay my head on thy lap, *chela*. I am an old man, but not free from passion . . . We must think of the Cause of Things.'

'Give him a blanket. We dare not light a fire lest the Sahibs see.'

'Better get away to Shamlegh. None will follow us to Shamlegh.' This was the nervous Rampur man.

'I have been Fostum Sahib's *shikarri*, and I am Yankling Sahib's *shikarri*. I should have been with Yankling Sahib now but for this cursed *beegar* (the *corvée*). Let two men watch below with the guns lest the Sahibs do more foolishness. *I* shall not leave this Holy One.'

They sat down a little apart from the lama, and, after listening awhile, passed round a water-pipe whose receiver was an old Day and Martin[3] blacking-bottle. The glow of the red charcoal as it went from hand to hand lit up the narrow, blinking eyes, the high Chinese cheek-bones, and the bull-throats that melted away into the dark duffle folds round the shoulders. They looked like kobolds[4] from some magic mine—gnomes of the hills in conclave. And while they talked, the voices of the snow-waters round them diminished one by one as the night-frost choked and clogged the runnels.

'How he stood up against us!' said a Spiti man admiring. 'I remember an old ibex, out Ladakh-way, that Dupont Sahib missed on a shoulder-shot, seven seasons back, standing up just like him. Dupont Sahib was a good *shikarri*.'

'Not as good as Yankling Sahib.' The Ao-chung man took a pull at the whisky-bottle and passed it over. 'Now hear me—unless any other man thinks he knows more.'

The challenge was not taken up.

'We go to Shamlegh when the moon rises. There we will fairly divide the baggage between us. I am content with this new little rifle and all its cartridges.'

'Are the bears only bad on thy holding?' said a mate, sucking at the pipe.

'No; but musk-pods[5] are worth six rupees apiece now, and thy women can have the canvas of the tents and some of the cooking-

3. An English firm of blacking manufacturers for whom Charles Dickens worked as a child.
4. Goblins or dwarfs.
5. Perfumed glands of musk deer.

gear. We will do all that at Shamlegh before dawn. Then we all go
our ways, remembering that we have never seen or taken service
with these Sahibs, who may, indeed, say that we have stolen their
baggage.'

'That is well for thee, but what will our Rajah say?'

'Who is to tell him? Those Sahibs, who cannot speak our talk, or
the Babu, who for his own ends gave us money? Will *he* lead an
army against us? What evidence will remain? That we do not need
we shall throw on Shamlegh-midden, where no man has yet set
foot.'

'Who is at Shamlegh this summer?' The place was only a grazing
centre of three or four huts.

'The Woman of Shamlegh. *She* has no love for Sahibs, as we
know.[6] The others can be pleased with little presents; and here is
enough for us all.' He patted the fat sides of the nearest basket.

'But—but—'

'I have said they are not true Sahibs. *All* their skins and heads
were bought in the bazar at Leh. I know the marks. I showed them
to ye last march.'

'True. They were all bought skins and heads. Some had even the
moth in them.'

That was a shrewd argument, and the Ao-chung man knew his
fellows.

'If the worst comes to the worst, I shall tell Yankling Sahib, who
is a man of a merry mind, and he will laugh. We are not doing any
wrong to any Sahibs whom we know. *They* are priest-beaters. They
frightened us. We fled! Who knows where we dropped the baggage?
Do ye think Yankling Sahib will permit down-country police to wan-
der all over the hills, disturbing his game? It is a far cry from Simla
to Chini, and farther from Shamlegh to Shamlegh-midden.'

'So be it, but I carry the big *kilta*. The basket with the red top that
the Sahibs pack themselves every morning.'

'Thus it is proved,' said the Shamlegh man adroitly, 'that they are
Sahibs of no account. Who ever heard of Fostum Sahib, or Yankling
Sahib, or even the little Peel Sahib that sits up of nights to shoot
serow[7]—I say, who ever heard of these Sahibs coming into the hills
without a down-country cook, and a bearer, and—and all manner of
well-paid, high-handed and oppressive folk in their tail? How can
they make trouble? What of the *kilta*?'

'Nothing, but that it is full of the Written Word—books and
papers in which they wrote, and strange instruments, as of worship.'

'Shamlegh-midden will take them all.'

6. Called Lispeth in the story of that name, the Woman of Shamlegh had once fallen in love
 with a Sahib who betrayed her. See p. 247ff.
7. A mountain goat with horns.

'True! But how if we insult the Sahibs' Gods thereby! I do not like to handle the Written Word in that fashion. And their brass idols[8] are beyond my comprehension. It is no plunder for simple hill-folk.'

'The old man still sleeps. Hst! We will ask his *chela*.' The Aochung man refreshed himself, and swelled with pride of leadership.

'We have here,' he whispered, 'a *kilta* whose nature we do not know.'

'But I do,' said Kim cautiously. The lama drew breath in natural, easy sleep, and Kim had been thinking of Hurree's last words. As a player of the Great Game, he was disposed just then to reverence the Babu. 'It is a *kilta* with a red top full of very wonderful things, not to be handled by fools.'

'I said it; I said it,' cried the bearer of that burden. 'Thinkest thou it will betray us?'

'Not if it be given to me. I can draw out its magic. Otherwise it will do great harm.'

'A priest always takes his share.' Whisky was demoralizing the Aochung man.

'It is no matter to me,' Kim answered, with the craft of his mother-country. 'Share it among you, and see what comes!'

'Not I. I was only jesting. Give the order. There is more than enough for us all. We go our way from Shamlegh in the dawn.'

They arranged and re-arranged their artless little plans for another hour, while Kim shivered with cold and pride. The humour of the situation tickled the Irish and the Oriental in his soul. Here were the emissaries of the dread Power of the North, very possibly as great in their own land as Mahbub or Colonel Creighton, suddenly smitten helpless. One of them, he privately knew, would be lame for a time. They had made promises to Kings. Tonight they lay out somewhere below him, chartless, foodless, tentless, gunless— except for Hurree Babu, guideless. And this collapse of their Great Game (Kim wondered to whom they would report it), this panicky bolt into the night, had come about through no craft of Hurree's or contrivance of Kim's, but simply, beautifully, and inevitably as the capture of Mahbub's *faquir*-friends by the zealous young policeman at Umballa.

'They are there—with nothing; and, by Jove, it is cold! I am here with all their things. Oh, they will be angry! I am sorry for Hurree Babu.'

Kim might have saved his pity, for though at that moment the Bengali suffered acutely in the flesh, his soul was puffed and lofty. A mile down the hill, on the edge of the pine-forest, two half-frozen men—one powerfully sick at intervals—were varying mutual

8. Survey instruments.

recriminations with the most poignant abuse of the Babu, who
seemed distraught with terror. They demanded a plan of action. He
explained that they were very lucky to be alive; that their coolies, if
not then stalking them, had passed beyond recall; that the Rajah,
his master, was ninety miles away, and, so far from lending them
money and a retinue for the Simla journey, would surely cast them
into prison if he heard that they had hit a priest. He enlarged on this
sin and its consequences till they bade him change the subject.
Their one hope, said he, was unostentatious flight from village to
village till they reached civilization; and, for the hundredth time dis-
solved in tears, he demanded of the high stars why the Sahibs 'had
beaten holy man'.

Ten steps would have taken Hurree into the creaking gloom
utterly beyond their reach—to the shelter and food of the nearest
village, where glib-tongued doctors were scarce. But he preferred to
endure cold, belly-pinch, bad words, and occasional blows in the
company of his honoured employers. Crouched against a tree-
trunk, he sniffed dolefully.

'And have you thought,' said the uninjured man hotly, 'what sort
of spectacle we shall present wandering through these hills among
these aborigines?'

Hurree Babu had thought of little else for some hours, but the
remark was not to his address.

'We cannot wander! I can hardly walk,' groaned Kim's victim.

'Perhaps the holy man will be merciful in loving-kindness, Sar,
otherwise—'

'I promise myself a peculiar pleasure in emptying my revolver into
that young bonze when next we meet,' was the unchristian answer.

'Revolvers! Vengeance! Bonzes!' Hurree crouched lower. The war
was breaking out afresh. 'Have you no consideration for our loss?
The baggage! The baggage!' He could hear the speaker literally
dancing on the grass. 'Everything we bore! Everything we have
secured! Our gains! Eight months' work! Do you know what that
means? "Decidedly it is we who can deal with Orientals!" Oh, you
have done well.'

They fell to it in several tongues, and Hurree smiled. Kim was
with the *kiltas*, and in the *kiltas* lay eight months of good diplomacy.
There was no means of communicating with the boy, but he could
be trusted. For the rest, Hurree could so stage-manage the journey
through the hills that Hilás, Bunár, and four hundred miles of hill-
roads should tell the tale for a generation. Men who cannot control
their own coolies are little respected in the Hills, and the hillman
has a very keen sense of humour.

'If I had done it myself,' thought Hurree, 'it would not have been
better; and, by Jove, now I think of it, of course I arranged it myself.

How quick I have been! Just when I ran downhill I thought it! Thee outrage was accidental, but onlee me could have worked it—ah—for all it was dam'-well worth. Consider the moral effect upon these ignorant peoples! No treaties—no papers—no written documents at all—and *me* to interpret for them. How I shall laugh with the Colonel! I wish I had their papers also: but you cannot occupy two places in space simultaneously. Thatt is axiomatic.'

Chapter 14

> My brother kneels (so saith Kabir)
> To stone and brass in heathen wise,
> But in my brother's voice I hear
> My own unanswered agonies.
> His God is as his Fates assign—
> His prayer is all the world's—and mine.[1]
> *Kabir.*

At moonrise the cautious coolies got under way. The lama, refreshed by his sleep and the spirit, needed no more than Kim's shoulder to bear him along—a silent, swift-striding man. They held the shale-sprinkled grass for an hour, swept round the shoulder of an immortal cliff, and climbed into a new country entirely blocked off from all sight of Chini valley. A huge pasture-ground ran up fan-shaped to the living snow. At its base was perhaps half an acre of flat land, on which stood a few soil and timber huts. Behind them—for, hill-fashion, they were perched on the edge of all things—the ground fell sheer two thousand feet to Shamlegh-midden, where never yet man has set foot.

The men made no motion to divide the plunder till they had seen the lama bedded down in the best room of the place, with Kim shampooing his feet,[2] Mohammedan fashion.

'We will send food,' said the Ao-chung man, 'and the red-topped *kilta*. By dawn there will be none to give evidence, one way or the other. If anything is not needed in the *kilta*—see here!'

He pointed through the window—opening into space that was filled with moonlight reflected from the snow—and threw out an empty whisky-bottle.

'No need to listen for the fall. This is the world's end,' he said, and

1. Also titled "A Song of Kabir" in *Songs from Books*, the poem celebrates the ecumenical leadership of the fifteenth-century religious reformer Kabir. Although he taught the unity of godhead, condemned idol-worship, and criticized both Hindu and Muslim priests, he had a following of Hindus, Muslims, and Jains, and he was particularly influential on the founder of Sikhism, Guru Nanak.
2. Massaging, a gesture of affection and respect.

went out. The lama looked forth, a hand on either sill, with eyes
that shone like yellow opals. From the enormous pit before him
white peaks lifted themselves yearning to the moonlight. The rest
was as the darkness of interstellar space.

'These,' he said slowly, 'are indeed my Hills. Thus should a man
abide, perched above the world, separated from delights, consider-
ing vast matters.'

'Yes; if he has a *chela* to prepare tea for him, and to fold a blan-
ket for his head, and to chase out calving cows.'

A smoky lamp burned in a niche, but the full moonlight beat it
down; and by the mixed light, stooping above the food-bag and cups,
Kim moved like a tall ghost.

'*Ai!* But now I have let the blood cool, my head still beats and
drums, and there is a cord round the back of my neck.'

'No wonder. It was a strong blow. May he who dealt it—'

'But for my own passions there would have been no evil.'

'What evil? Thou hast saved the Sahibs from the death they
deserved a hundred times.'

'The lesson is not well learnt, *chela*.' The lama came to rest on a
folded blanket, as Kim went forward with his evening routine. 'The
blow was but a shadow upon a shadow.[3] Evil in itself—my legs
weary apace these latter days!—it met evil in me: anger, rage, and a
lust to return evil. These wrought in my blood, woke tumult in my
stomach, and dazzled my ears.'[4] Here he drank scalding block-tea
ceremonially, taking the hot cup from Kim's hand. 'Had I been pas-
sionless, the evil blow would have done only bodily evil—a scar, or
a bruise—which is illusion. But my mind was *not* abstracted, for
rushed in straightway a lust to let the Spiti men kill. In fighting that
lust, my soul was torn and wrenched beyond a thousand blows. Not
till I had repeated the Blessings' (he meant the Buddhist Beatitudes)
'did I achieve calm. But the evil planted in me by that moment's
carelessness works out to its end. Just is the Wheel, swerving not a
hair! Learn the lesson, *chela*.'

'It is too high for me,' Kim muttered. 'I am still all shaken. I am
glad I hurt the man.'

'I felt that, sleeping upon thy knees, in the wood below. It disqui-
eted me in my dreams—the evil in thy soul working through to
mine. Yet on the other hand'—he loosed his rosary—'I have
acquired merit by saving two lives—the lives of those that wronged
me. Now I must see into the Cause of Things. The boat of my soul
staggers.'

'Sleep, and be strong. That is wisest.'

3. Illusion.
4. A rough compressed tea made of the powdered grounds rather than the finer tea leaves.

'I meditate. There is a need greater than thou knowest.'

Till the dawn, hour after hour, as the moonlight paled on the high peaks, and that which had been belted blackness on the sides of the far hills showed as tender green forest, the lama stared fixedly at the wall. From time to time he groaned. Outside the barred door, where discomfited kine[5] came to ask for their old stable, Shamlegh and the coolies gave itself up to plunder and riotous living. The Ao-chung man was their leader, and once they had opened the Sahibs' tinned foods and found that they were very good they dared not turn back. Shamlegh kitchen-midden took the dunnage.[6]

When Kim, after a night of bad dreams, stole forth to brush his teeth in the morning chill, a fair-coloured woman with turquoise-studded headgear drew him aside.

'The others have gone. They left thee this *kilta* as the promise was. I do not love Sahibs, but thou wilt make us a charm in return for it. We do not wish little Shamlegh to get a bad name on account of the—accident. I am the Woman of Shamlegh.' She looked him over with bold, bright eyes, unlike the usual furtive glance of hillwomen.

'Assuredly. But it must be done in secret.'

She raised the heavy *kilta* like a toy and slung it into her own hut.

'Out and bar the door! Let none come near till it is finished,' said Kim.

'But afterwards—we may talk?'

Kim tilted the *kilta* on the floor—a cascade of Survey-instruments, books, diaries, letters, maps, and queerly scented native correspondence. At the very bottom was an embroidered bag covering a sealed, gilded, and illuminated document such as one King sends to another. Kim caught his breath with delight, and reviewed the situation from a Sahib's point of view.

'The books I do not want. Besides, they are logarithms—Survey, I suppose.' He laid them aside. 'The letters I do not understand, but Colonel Creighton will. They must all be kept. The maps—they draw better maps than me—*of* course. All the native letters—oho!—and particularly the *murasla*.' He sniffed the embroidered bag. 'That must be from Hilás or Bunár, and Hurree Babu spoke truth. By Jove! It is a fine haul. I wish Hurree could know . . . The rest must go out of the window.' He fingered a superb prismatic compass and the shiny top of a theodolite.[7] But after all, a Sahib cannot very well steal, and the things might be inconvenient evidence later. He sorted out every scrap of manuscript, every map, and the native letters. They made one softish slab. The three locked ferril-backed books, with five worn pocket-books, he put aside.

5. Restless cows.
6. Garbage.
7. A heavy, cumbersome instrument used by survey teams to measure angles.

'The letters and the *murasla* I must carry inside my coat and under my belt, and the hand-written books I must put into the food-bag. It will be very heavy. No. I do not think there is anything more. If there is, the coolies have thrown it down the *khud*,[8] so *thatt* is all right. Now you go too.' He repacked the *kilta* with all he meant to lose, and hove it up on to the window-sill. A thousand feet below lay a long, lazy, round-shouldered bank of mist, as yet untouched by the morning sun. A thousand feet below that was a hundred-year-old pine-forest. He could see the green tops looking like a bed of moss when a wind-eddy thinned the cloud.

'No! I don't think any one will go after *you!*'

The wheeling basket vomited its contents as it dropped. The theodolite hit a jutting cliff-ledge and exploded like a shell; the books, inkstands, paint-boxes, compasses, and rulers showed for a few seconds like a swarm of bees. Then they vanished; and, though Kim, hanging half out of the window, strained his young ears, never a sound came up from the gulf.

'Five hundred—a thousand rupees could not buy them,' he thought sorrowfully. 'It was verree wasteful, but I have all their other stuff—everything they did—I hope. Now how the deuce am I to tell Hurree Babu, and *whatt* the deuce am I to do? And my old man is sick. I must tie up the letters in oilskin. That is something to do first—else they will get all sweated. . . . And I am all alone!' He bound them into a neat packet, swedging down the stiff, sticky oil-skin at the corners, for his roving life had made him as methodical as an old hunter in matters of the road. Then with double care he packed away the books at the bottom of the food-bag.

The woman rapped at the door.

'But thou hast made no charm,' she said, looking about.

'There is no need.' Kim had completely overlooked the necessity for a little patter-talk. The woman laughed at his confusion irreverently.

'None—for thee. Thou canst cast a spell by the mere winking of an eye. But think of us poor people when thou art gone. They were all too drunk last night to hear a woman. Thou art not drunk?'

'I am a priest.' Kim had recovered himself, and, the woman being aught but unlovely, thought best to stand on his office.

'I warned them that the Sahibs will be angry and will make an inquisition and a report to the Rajah. There is also the Babu with them. Clerks have long tongues.'

'Is that all thy trouble?' The plan rose fully formed in Kim's mind, and he smiled ravishingly.

'Not all,' quoth the woman, putting out a hard brown hand all covered with turquoises set in silver.

8. Precipice.

'I can finish that in a breath,' he went on quickly. 'The Babu is the very *hakim* (thou hast heard of him?) who was wandering among the hills by Ziglaur. I know him.'

'He will tell for the sake of a reward. Sahibs cannot distinguish one hillman from another, but Babus have eyes for men—and women.'

'Carry a word to him from me.'

'There is nothing I would not do for thee.'

He accepted the compliment calmly, as men must in lands where women make the love, tore a leaf from a note-book, and with a patent indelible pencil wrote in gross Shikast[9]—the script that bad little boys use when they write dirt on walls: '*I have everything that they have written: their pictures of the country, and many letters. Especially the* murasla. *Tell me what to do. I am at Shamlegh-under-the-Snow. The old man is sick.*'

'Take this to him. It will altogether shut his mouth. He cannot have gone far.'

'Indeed no. They are still in the forest across the spur. Our children went to watch them when the light came, and have cried the news as they moved.'

Kim looked his astonishment; but from the edge of the sheep-pasture floated a shrill, kite-like trill. A child tending cattle had picked it up from a brother or sister on the far side of the slope that commanded Chini valley.

'My husbands are also out there gathering wood.' She drew a handful of walnuts from her bosom, split one neatly, and began to eat. Kim affected blank ignorance.

'Dost thou not know the meaning of the walnut[1]—priest?' she said coyly, and handed him the half-shells.

'Well thought of.' He slipped the piece of paper between them quickly. 'Hast thou a little wax to close them on this letter?'

The woman sighed aloud, and Kim relented.

'There is no payment till service has been rendered. Carry this to the Babu, and say it was sent by the Son of the Charm.'

'*Ai*! Truly! Truly! By a magician—who is like a Sahib.'

'Nay, a Son of the Charm: and ask if there be any answer.'

'But if he offer a rudeness? I—I am afraid.'

Kim laughed. 'He is, I have no doubt, very tired and very hungry. The Hills make cold bed-fellows. *Hai*, my'—it was on the tip of his tongue to say Mother, but he turned it to Sister—'thou art a wise and witty woman. By this time all the villages know what has befallen the Sahibs—eh?'

9. Disconnected letters, as in print.
1. The sexual implication of the two halves of a walnut are particular to the hills and to Shamlegh, even as almonds are to the plains (p. 214).

'True. News was at Ziglaur by midnight, and by tomorrow should be at Kotgarh. The villages are both afraid and angry.'

'No need. Tell the villages to feed the Sahibs and pass them on, in peace. We must get them quietly away from our valleys. To steal is one thing—to kill another. The Babu will understand, and there will be no after-complaints. Be swift. I must tend my master when he wakes.'

'So be it. After service—thou hast said?—comes the reward. I am the Woman of Shamlegh, and I hold from the Rajah. I am no common bearer of babes. Shamlegh is thine: hoof and horn and hide, milk and butter. Take or leave.'

She turned resolutely uphill, her silver necklaces clicking on her broad breast, to meet the morning sun fifteen hundred feet above them. This time Kim thought in the vernacular as he waxed down the oilskin edges of the packets.

'How can a man follow the Way or the Great Game when he is so-always pestered by women? There was that girl at Akrola of the Ford; and there was the scullion's wife behind the dovecot—not counting the others—and now comes this one! When I was a child it was well enough, but now I am a man and they will not regard me as a man. Walnuts, indeed! Ho! ho! It is almonds in the Plains!'

He went out to levy on the village—not with a begging-bowl, which might do for down-country, but in the manner of a prince. Shamlegh's summer population is only three families—four women and eight or nine men. They were all full of tinned meats and mixed drinks, from ammoniated quinine to white vodka, for they had taken their full share in the overnight loot. The neat Continental tents had been cut up and shared long ago, and there were patent aluminium saucepans abroad.

But they considered the lama's presence a perfect safeguard against all consequences, and impenitently brought Kim of their best—even to a drink of *chang*—the barley-beer that comes from Ladakh-way. Then they thawed out in the sun, and sat with their legs hanging over infinite abysses, chattering, laughing, and smoking. They judged India and its Government solely from their experience of wandering Sahibs who had employed them or their friends as *shikarris*. Kim heard tales of shots missed upon ibex, serow, or markhor, by Sahibs twenty years in their graves—every detail lighted from behind like twigs on tree-tops seen against lightning. They told him of their little diseases, and, more important, the diseases of their tiny, sure-footed cattle; of trips as far as Kotgarh, where the strange missionaries live, and beyond even to marvellous Simla, where the streets are paved with silver, and anyone, look you, can get service with the Sahibs, who ride about in two-wheeled carts and spend money with a spade. Presently, grave and aloof, walking

very heavily, the lama joined himself to the chatter under the eaves, and they gave him great room. The thin air refreshed him, and he sat on the edge of precipices with the best of them, and, when talk languished, flung pebbles into the void. Thirty miles away, as the eagle flies, lay the next range, seamed and channelled and pitted with little patches of brush—forests, each a day's dark march. Behind the village, Shamlegh hill itself cut off all view to southward. It was like sitting in a swallow's nest under the eaves of the roof of the world.

From time to time the lama stretched out his hand, and with a little low-voiced prompting would point out the road to Spiti and north across the Parungla.

'Beyond, where the hills lie thickest, lies De-ch'en' (he meant Han-lé), 'the great Monastery. s'Tag-stan-ras-ch'en built it, and of him there runs this tale.' Whereupon he told it: a fantastic piled narrative of bewitchment and miracles that set Shamlegh a-gasping. Turning west a little, he speered for the green hills of Kulu, and sought Kailung under the glaciers. 'For thither came I in the old, old days. From Leh I came, over the Baralachi.'

'Yes, yes; we know it,' said the far-faring people of Shamlegh.

'And I slept two nights with the priests of Kailung. These are the Hills of my delight! Shadows blessed above all other shadows! There my eyes opened on this world; there my eyes were opened to this world; there I found Enlightenment; and there I girt my loins for my Search. Out of the Hills I came—the high Hills and the strong winds. Oh, just is the Wheel!' He blessed them in detail—the great glaciers, the naked rocks, the piled moraines and tumbled shale; dry upland, hidden salt-lake, age-old timber and fruitful water-shot valley one after the other, as a dying man blesses his folk; and Kim marvelled at his passion.

'Yes—yes. There is no place like our Hills,' said the people of Shamlegh. And they fell to wondering how a man could live in the hot terrible Plains where the cattle run as big as elephants, unfit to plough on a hillside; where village touches village, they had heard, for a hundred miles; where folk went about stealing in gangs, and what the robbers spared the Police carried utterly away.

So the still forenoon wore through, and at the end of it Kim's messenger dropped from the steep pasture as unbreathed as when she had set out.

'I sent a word to the *hakim*,' Kim explained, while she made reverence.

'He joined himself to the idolaters? Nay, I remember he did a healing upon one of them. He has acquired merit, though the healed employed his strength for evil. Just is the Wheel! What of the *hakim*?'

'I feared that thou hadst been bruised and—and I knew he was
wise.' Kim took the waxed walnut-shell and read in English on the
back of his note: *Your favour received. Cannot get away from present
company at present, but shall take them into Simla. After which, hope
to rejoin you. Inexpedient to follow angry gentlemen. Return by same
road you came, and will overtake. Highly gratified about correspon-
dence due to my forethought.* 'He says, Holy One, that he will escape
from the idolaters, and will return to us. Shall we wait awhile at
Shamlegh, then?'

The lama looked long and lovingly upon the hills and shook his
head.

'That may not be, *chela*. From my bones outward I do desire it,
but it is forbidden. I have seen the Cause of Things.'

'Why? When the Hills give thee back thy strength day by day?
Remember we were weak and fainting down below there in the
Doon.'

'I became strong to do evil and to forget. A brawler and a swash-
buckler upon the hillsides was I.' Kim bit back a smile. 'Just and per-
fect is the Wheel, swerving not a hair. When I was a man—a long
time ago—I did pilgrimage to Guru Ch'wan among the poplars' (he
pointed Bhotanwards), 'where they keep the Sacred Horse.'

'Quiet, be quiet!' said Shamlegh, all arow. 'He speaks of Jam-lin-
nin-k'or, the Horse That Can Go Round The World In A Day.'

'I speak to my *chela* only,' said the lama, in gentle reproof, and
they scattered like frost on south eaves of a morning. 'I did not seek
truth in those days, but the talk of doctrine. All illusion! I drank the
beer and ate the bread of Guru Ch'wan. Next day one said: "We go
out to fight Sangor Gutok down the valley to discover" (mark again
how Lust is tied to Anger!) "which Abbot shall bear rule in the val-
ley and take the profit of the prayers they print at Sangor Gutok." I
went, and we fought a day.'

'But how, Holy One?'

'With our long pencases as I could have shown . . . I say, we
fought under the poplars, both Abbots and all the monks, and one
laid open my forehead to the bone. See!' He tilted back his cap and
showed a puckered silvery scar. 'Just and perfect is the Wheel!
Yesterday the scar itched, and after fifty years I recalled how it was
dealt and the face of him who dealt it; dwelling a little in illusion.
Followed that which thou didst see—strife and stupidity. Just is the
Wheel! The idolater's blow fell upon the scar. Then I was shaken in
my soul: my soul was darkened, and the boat of my soul rocked
upon the waters of illusion. Not till I came to Shamlegh could I
meditate upon the Cause of Things, or trace the running grass-roots
of Evil. I strove all the long night.'

'But, Holy One, thou art innocent of all evil. May I be thy sacrifice!'

Kim was genuinely distressed at the old man's sorrow, and Mahbub Ali's phrase slipped out unawares.

'In the dawn,' the lama went on more gravely, ready rosary clicking between the slow sentences, 'came enlightenment. It is here . . . I am an old man . . . hill-bred, hill-fed, never to sit down among my Hills. Three years I travelled through Hind, but—can earth be stronger than Mother Earth? My stupid body yearned to the Hills and the snows of the Hills, from below there. I said, and it is true, my Search is sure. So, at the Kulu woman's house I turned hillward, over-persuaded by myself. There is no blame to the *hakim*. He—following Desire—foretold that the Hills would make me strong. They strengthened me to do evil, to forget my Search. I delighted in life and the lust of life. I desired strong slopes to climb. I cast about to find them. I measured the strength of my body, which is evil, against the high Hills, I made a mock of thee when thy breath came short under Jamnotri. I jested when thou wouldst not face the snow of the pass.'

'But what harm? I *was* afraid. It was just. I am not a hillman; and I loved thee for thy new strength.'

'More than once I remember'—he rested his cheek dolefully on his hand—'I sought thy praise and the *hakim's* for the mere strength of my legs. Thus evil followed evil till the cup was full. Just is the Wheel! All Hind for three years did me all honour. From the Fountain of Wisdom in the Wonder House to'—he smiled—'a little child playing by a big gun—the world prepared my road. And why?'

'Because we loved thee. It is only the fever of the blow. I myself am still sick and shaken.'

'No! It was because I was upon the Way—tuned as are *sinen* (cymbals) to the purpose of the Law. I departed from that ordinance. The tune was broken: followed the punishment. In my own Hills, on the edge of my own country, in the very place of my evil desire, comes the buffet—here!' (He touched his brow.) 'As a novice is beaten when he misplaces the cups, so am I beaten, who was Abbot of Such-zen. No word, look you, but a blow, *chela*.'

'But the Sahibs did not know thee, Holy One?'

'We were well matched. Ignorance and Lust met Ignorance and Lust upon the road, and they begat Anger. The blow was a sign to me, who am no better than a strayed yak, that my place is not here. Who can read the Cause of an act is halfway to Freedom! "Back to the path," says the Blow. "The Hills are not for thee. Thou canst not choose Freedom and go in bondage to the delight of life."'

'Would we had never met that cursed Russian!'

'Our Lord Himself cannot make the Wheel swing backward. And for my merit that I had acquired I gain yet another sign.' He put his

hand in his bosom, and drew forth the Wheel of Life. 'Look! I considered this after I had meditated. There remains untorn by the idolater no more than the breadth of my fingernail.'

'I see.'

'So much, then, is the span of my life in this body. I have served the Wheel all my days. Now the Wheel serves me. But for the merit I have acquired in guiding thee upon the Way, there would have been added to me yet another life ere I had found my River. Is it plain, *chela*?'

Kim stared at the brutally disfigured chart. From left to right diagonally the rent ran—from the Eleventh House where Desire gives birth to the Child (as it is drawn by Tibetans) across the human and animal worlds, to the Fifth House—the empty House of the Senses. The logic was unanswerable.

'Before our Lord won Enlightenment'—the lama folded all away with reverence—'He was tempted. I too have been tempted, but it is finished. The Arrow fell in the Plains—not in the Hills. Therefore, what make we here?'

'Shall we at least wait for the *hakim*?'

'I know how long I shall live in this body. What can a *hakim* do?'

'But thou art all sick and shaken. Thou canst not walk.'

'How can I be sick if I see Freedom?' He rose unsteadily to his feet.

'Then I must get food from the village. Oh, the weary Road!' Kim felt that he too needed rest.

'That is lawful. Let us eat and go. The Arrow fell in the Plains . . . but I yielded to Desire. Make ready, *chela*.'

Kim turned to the woman with the turquoise headgear who had been idly pitching pebbles over the cliff. She smiled very kindly.

'I found him like a strayed buffalo in a cornfield—the Babu; snorting and sneezing with cold. He was so hungry that he forgot his dignity and gave me sweet words. The Sahibs have nothing.' She flung out an empty palm. 'One is very sick about the stomach. Thy work?'

Kim nodded, with a bright eye.

'I spoke to the Bengali first—and to the people of a near-by village after. The Sahibs will be given food as they need it—nor will the people ask money. The plunder is already distributed. The Babu makes lying speeches to the Sahibs. Why does he not leave them?'

'Out of the greatness of his heart.'

'Was never a Bengali yet had one bigger than a dried walnut. But it is no matter . . . Now as to walnuts. After service comes reward. I have said the village is thine.'

'It is my loss,' Kim began. 'Even now I had planned desirable things in my heart which'—there is no need to go through the com-

pliments proper to these occasions. He sighed deeply . . . 'But my master, led by a vision—'

'Huh! What can old eyes see except a full begging-bowl?'

'—turns from this village to the Plains again.'

'Bid him stay.'

Kim shook his head. 'I know my Holy One, and his rage if he be crossed,' he replied impressively. 'His curses shake the Hills.'

'Pity they did not save him from a broken head! I heard that thou wast the tiger-hearted one who smote the Sahib. Let him dream a little longer. Stay!'

'Hillwoman,' said Kim, with austerity that could not harden the outlines of his young oval face, 'these matters are too high for thee.'

'The Gods be good to us! Since when have men and women been other than men and women?'

'A priest is a priest. He says he will go upon this hour. I am his *chela*, and I go with him. We need food for the Road. He is an honoured guest in all the villages, but'—he broke into a pure boy's grin—'the food here is good. Give me some.'

'What if I do not give it thee? I am the woman of this village.'

'Then I curse thee—a little—not greatly, but enough to remember.' He could not help smiling.

'Thou hast cursed me already by the down-dropped eyelash and the uplifted chin. Curses? What should I care for mere words?' She clenched her hands upon her bosom . . . 'But I would not have thee to go in anger, thinking hardly of me—a gatherer of cow-dung and grass at Shamlegh, but still a woman of substance.'

'I think nothing,' said Kim, 'but that I am grieved to go, for I am very weary; and that we need food. Here is the bag.'

The woman snatched it angrily. 'I was foolish,' said she. 'Who is thy woman in the Plains? Fair or black? I was fair once. Laughest thou? Once, long ago, if thou canst believe, a Sahib looked on me with favour. Once, long ago, I wore European clothes at the Mission-house yonder.' She pointed towards Kotgarh. 'Once, long ago, I was Ker-lis-ti-an[2] and spoke English—as the Sahibs speak it. Yes. My Sahib said he would return and wed me—yes, wed me. He went away—I had nursed him when he was sick—but he never returned. Then I saw that the Gods of the Kerlistians lied, and I went back to my own people . . . I have never set eyes on a Sahib since. (Do not laugh at me. The fit is past, little priestling.) Thy face and thy walk and thy fashion of speech put me in mind of my Sahib, though thou art only a wandering mendicant to whom I give a dole. Curse me? Thou canst neither curse nor bless!' She set her hands on her hips and laughed bitterly. 'Thy Gods are lies; thy works are

2. Christian. See "Lispeth," pp. 247–51.

lies; thy words are lies. There are no Gods under all the Heavens. I know it . . . But for awhile I thought it was my Sahib come back, and he was my God. Yes, once I made music on a *pianno* in the Mission-house at Kotgarh. Now I give alms to priests who are *heatthen*.' She wound up with the English word, and tied the mouth of the brimming bag.

'I wait for thee, *chela*,' said the lama, leaning against the door-post.

The woman swept the tall figure with her eyes. 'He walk! He cannot cover half a mile. Whither would old bones go?'

At this Kim, already perplexed by the lama's collapse and foreseeing the weight of the bag, fairly lost his temper. 'What is it to thee, woman of ill-omen, where he goes?'

'Nothing—but something to thee, priest with a Sahib's face. Wilt thou carry him on thy shoulders?'

'I go to the Plains. None must hinder my return. I have wrestled with my soul till I am strengthless. The stupid body is spent, and we are far from the Plains.'

'Behold!' she said simply, and drew aside to let Kim see his own utter helplessness. 'Curse me. Maybe it will give him strength. Make a charm! Call on thy great God. Thou art a priest.' She turned away.

The lama had squatted limply, still holding by the door-post. One cannot strike down an old man that he recovers again like a boy in the night. Weakness bowed him to the earth, but his eyes that hung on Kim were alive and imploring.

'It is all well,' said Kim. 'It is the thin air that weakens thee. In a little while we go! It is the mountain-sickness. I too am a little sick at stomach,' . . . and he knelt and comforted with such poor words as came first to his lips. Then the woman returned, more erect than ever.

'Thy Gods useless, heh? Try mine. *I* am the Woman of Shamlegh.' She hailed hoarsely, and there came out of a cow-pen her two husbands and three others with a *dooli*, the rude native litter of the Hills, that they use for carrying the sick and for visits of state. 'These cattle'—she did not condescend to look at them—'are thine for so long as thou shalt need.'

'But we will not go Simla-way. We will not go near the Sahibs,' cried the first husband.

'They will not run away as the others did, nor will they steal baggage. Two I know for weaklings. Stand to the rear-pole, Sonoo and Taree.' They obeyed swiftly. 'Lower now, and lift in that holy man. I will see to the village and your virtuous wives till ye return.'

'When will that be?'

'Ask the priests. Do not pester me. Lay the food-bag at the foot, it balances better so.'

'Oh, Holy One, thy Hills are kinder than our Plains!' cried Kim,

relieved, as the lama tottered to the litter. 'It is a very king's bed—a place of honour and ease. And we owe it to—'

'A woman of ill-omen. I need thy blessings as much as I do thy curses. It is *my* order and none of thine. Lift and away! Here! Hast thou money for the road?'

She beckoned Kim to her hut, and stooped above a battered English cash-box under her cot.

'I do not need anything,' said Kim, angered where he should have been grateful. 'I am already rudely loaded with favours.'

She looked up with a curious smile and laid a hand on his shoulder. 'At least, thank me. I am foul-faced and a hillwoman, but, as thy talk goes, I have acquired merit. Shall I show thee how the Sahibs render thanks?' and her hard eyes softened.

'I am but a wandering priest,' said Kim, his eyes lighting in answer. 'Thou needest neither my blessings nor my curses.'

'Nay. But for one little moment—thou canst overtake the *dooli* in ten strides—*if* thou wast a Sahib, shall I show thee what thou wouldst do?'

'How if I guess, though?' said Kim, and putting his arm round her waist, he kissed her on the cheek, adding in English:

'Thank you verree much, my dear.'

Kissing is practically unknown among Asiatics, which may have been the reason that she leaned back with wide-open eyes and a face of panic.

'Next time,' Kim went on, 'you must not be so sure of your heathen priests. Now I say good-bye.' He held out his hand English-fashion. She took it mechanically. 'Good-bye, my dear.'

'Good-bye, and—and'—she was remembering her English words one by one—'you will come back again? Good-bye, and—thee God bless you.'

Half an hour later, as the creaking litter jolted up the hill path that leads south-easterly from Shamlegh, Kim saw a tiny figure at the hut door waving a white rag.

'She has acquired merit beyond all others,' said the lama. 'For to set a man upon the way to Freedom is half as great as though she had herself found it.'

'Umm,' said Kim thoughtfully, considering the past. 'It may be that I have acquired merit also . . . At least she did not treat me like a child.' He hitched the front of his robe, where lay the slab of documents and maps, re-stowed the precious food-bag at the lama's feet, laid his hand on the litter's edge, and buckled down to the slow pace of the grunting husbands.

'These also acquire merit,' said the lama after three miles.

'More than that, they shall be paid in silver,' quoth Kim. The Woman of Shamlegh had given it to him; and it was only fair, he argued, that her men should earn it back again.

Chapter 15

I'd not give room for an Emperor—
 I'd hold my road for a King.
To the Triple Crown I'd not bow down—
 But this is a different thing!
I'll not fight with the Powers of Air—
 Sentry, pass him through!
Drawbridge let fall—He's the Lord of us all—
 The Dreamer whose dream came true!
 The Siege of the Fairies.[1]

Two hundred miles north of Chini, on the blue shale of Ladakh, lies Yankling Sahib, the merry-minded man, spy-glassing wrathfully across the ridges for some sign of his pet tracker—a man from Aochung. But that renegade, with a new Männlicher rifle and two hundred cartridges, is elsewhere, shooting musk-deer for the market, and Yankling Sahib will learn next season how very ill he has been.

Up the valleys of Bushahr—the far-beholding eagles of the Himalayas swerve at his new blue-and-white gored umbrella—hurries a Bengali, once fat and well-looking, now lean and weather-worn. He has received the thanks of two foreigners of distinction, piloted not unskilfully to Mashobra tunnel, which leads to the great and gay capital of India. It was not his fault that, blanketed by wet mists, he conveyed them past the telegraph-station and European colony of Kotgarh. It was not his fault, but that of the Gods, of whom he discoursed so engagingly, that he led them into the borders of Nahan, where the Rajah of that State mistook them for deserting British soldiery. Hurree Babu explained the greatness and glory, in their own country, of his companions, till the drowsy kinglet smiled. He explained it to everyone who asked—many times—aloud—variously. He begged food, arranged accommodation, proved a skilful leech for an injury of the groin—such a blow as one may receive rolling down a rock-covered hillside in the dark—and in all things indispensable. The reason of his friendliness did him credit. With millions of fellow-serfs, he had learned to look upon Russia as the great deliverer from the North. He was a fearful man. He had been afraid that he could not save his illustrious employers from the anger of an excited peasantry. He himself would just as lief hit a holy man as not, but . . .

1. After this stanza was added for the *Collected Edition*, the poem was titled "The Fairies Siege." The Triple Crown is the papal tiara and therefore a powerless symbol. The dreamer could refer to either the spiritual lama or the material imperialist. Kipling's friendship with "the dreamer of empires," Cecil Rhodes, developed after his 1898 visit to South Africa, during which (he writes in his autobiography) Rhodes would ask him "disconcerting" and childlike questions such as "'What's your dream?' I answered that he was part of it" (*Something of Myself and Other Autobiographical Writings*, ed. Thomas Pinney [Cambridge: Cambridge University Press, 1990] 142).

He was deeply grateful and sincerely rejoiced that he had done his 'little possible' towards bringing their venture to—barring the lost baggage—a successful issue; he had forgotten the blows; denied that any blows had been dealt that unseemly first night under the pines. He asked neither pension nor retaining fee, but, if they deemed him worthy, would they write him a testimonial? It might be useful to him later, if others, their friends, came over the Passes. He begged them to remember him in their future greatnesses, for he 'opined subtly' that he, even he, Mohendro Lal Dutt, MA of Calcutta, had 'done the State some service.'

They gave him a certificate praising his courtesy, helpfulness, and unerring skill as a guide. He put it in his waist-belt and sobbed with emotion; they had endured so many dangers together. He led them at high noon along crowded Simla Mall to the Alliance Bank of Simla, where they wished to establish their identity. Thence he vanished like a dawn-cloud on Jakko.

Behold him, too fine-drawn to sweat, too pressed to vaunt the drugs in his little brass-bound box, ascending Shamlegh slope, a just man made perfect. Watch him, all Babudom laid aside, smoking at noon on a cot, while a woman with turquoise-studded headgear points south-easterly across the bare grass. Litters, she says, do not travel as fast as single men, but his birds should now be in the Plains. The holy man would not stay though Lispeth pressed him. The Babu groans heavily, girds up his huge loins, and is off again. He does not care to travel after dusk; but his days' marches—there is none to enter them in a book—would astonish folk who mock at his race. Kindly villagers, remembering the Dacca drug-vendor of two months ago, give him shelter against evil spirits of the wood. He dreams of Bengali Gods, University textbooks of education, and the Royal Society, London, England. Next dawn the bobbing blue-and-white umbrella goes forward.

On the edge of the Doon, Mussoorie well behind them and the Plains spread out in golden dust before, rests a worn litter in which—all the Hills know it—lies a sick lama who seeks a River for his healing. Villages have almost come to blows over the honour of bearing it, for not only has the lama given them blessings, but his disciple good money—full one-third Sahibs' prices. Twelve miles a day has the *dooli* travelled, as the greasy, rubbed pole-ends show, and by roads that few Sahibs use. Over the Nilang Pass in storm when the driven snow-dust filled every fold of the impassive lama's drapery; between the black horns of Raieng[2] where they heard the whistle of the wild goats through the clouds; pitching and strained on the shale below; hard-held between shoulder and clenched jaw

2. Twin peaks overlooking the travelers' northern route.

when they rounded the hideous curves of the Cut Road under Bhagirati; swinging and creaking to the steady jog-trot of the descent into the Valley of the Waters; pressed along the steamy levels of that locked valley; up, up and out again, to meet the roaring gusts off Kedarnath; set down of mid-days in the dun gloom of kindly oak-forests; passed from village to village in dawn-chill, when even devotees may be forgiven for swearing at impatient holy men; or by torchlight, when the least fearful think of ghosts—the *dooli* has reached her last stage. The little hill-folk sweat in the modified heat of the lower Sewaliks, and gather round the priests for their blessing and their wage.

'Ye have acquired merit,' says the lama. 'Merit greater than your knowing. And ye will return to the Hills,' he sighs.

'Surely. The high Hills as soon as may be.' The bearer rubs his shoulder, drinks water, spits it out again, and readjusts his grass sandal. Kim—his face is drawn and tired—pays very small silver from his belt, heaves out the food-bag, crams an oilskin packet—they are holy writings—into his bosom, and helps the lama to his feet. The peace has come again into the old man's eyes, and he does not look for the hills to fall down and crush him as he did that terrible night when they were delayed by the flooded river.

The men pick up the *dooli* and swing out of sight between the scrub clumps.

The lama raises a hand toward the rampart of the Himalayas. 'Not with you, O blessed among all hills, fell the Arrow of Our Lord! And never shall I breathe your airs again!'

'But thou art ten times the stronger man in this good air,' says Kim, for to his wearied soul appeal the well-cropped, kindly Plains. 'Here, or hereabouts, fell the Arrow, yes. We will go very softly, perhaps, a *koss* a day, for the Search is sure. But the bag weighs heavy.'

'Ay, our Search is sure. I have come out of great temptation.'

• • • • •

It was never more than a couple of miles a day now, and Kim's shoulders bore all the weight of it—the burden of an old man, the burden of the heavy food-bag with the locked books, the load of the writings on his heart, and the details of the daily routine. He begged in the dawn, set blankets for the lama's meditation, held the weary head on his lap through the noonday heats, fanning away the flies till his wrists ached, begged again in the evenings, and rubbed the lama's feet, who rewarded him with promise of Freedom—today, tomorrow, or, at furthest, the next day.

'Never was such a *chela*. I doubt at times whether Ananda more faithfully nursed Our Lord. And thou art a Sahib? When I was a man—a long time ago—I forgot that. Now I look upon thee often, and every time I remember that thou art a Sahib. It is strange.'

'Thou hast said there is neither black nor white. Why plague me
with this talk, Holy One? Let me rub the other foot. It vexes me.
I am not a Sahib. I am thy *chela*, and my head is heavy on my
shoulders.'

'Patience a little! We reach Freedom together. Then thou and I,
upon the far bank of the River, will look back upon our lives as in
the Hills we saw our days' marches laid out behind us. Perhaps I was
once a Sahib.'

'Was never a Sahib like thee, I swear it.'

'I am certain the Keeper of the Images in the Wonder House was
in past life a very wise abbot. But even his spectacles do not make
my eyes see. There fall shadows when I would look steadily. No mat-
ter—we know the tricks of the poor stupid carcass—shadow chang-
ing to another shadow. I am bound by the illusion of Time and
Space. How far came we today in the flesh?'

'Perhaps half a *koss*.' (Three quarters of a mile, and it was a weary
march.)

'Half a koss. Ha! I went ten thousand thousand in the spirit. How
we are all lapped and swathed and swaddled in these senseless
things.' He looked at his thin blue-veined hand that found the beads
so heavy. '*Chela*, hast thou never a wish to leave me?'

Kim thought of the oilskin packet and the books in the food-bag. If
someone duly authorized would only take delivery of them the Great
Game might play itself for aught he then cared. He was tired and hot
in his head, and a cough that came from the stomach worried him.

'No,' he said almost sternly. 'I am not a dog or a snake to bite
when I have learned to love.'

'Thou art too tender towards me.'

'Not that either. I have moved in one matter without consulting
thee. I have sent a message to the Kulu woman by that woman who
gave us the goat's milk this morn, saying that thou wast a little fee-
ble and wouldst need a litter. I beat myself in my mind that I did not
do it when we entered the Doon. We stay in this place till the litter
returns.'

'I am content. She is a woman with a heart of gold, as thou sayest,
but a talker—something of a talker.'

'She will not weary thee. I have looked to that also. Holy One, my
heart is very heavy for my many carelessnesses towards thee.' An
hysterical catch rose in his throat. 'I have walked thee too far: I have
not picked good food always for thee; I have not considered the
heat; I have talked to people on the road and left thee alone . . . I
have—I have . . . *Hai mai!* But I love thee . . . and it is all too
late . . . I was a child . . . Oh, why was I not a man? . . .'
Overborne by strain, fatigue, and the weight beyond his years, Kim
broke down and sobbed at the lama's feet.

'What a to-do is here!' said the old man gently. 'Thou hast never stepped a hair's breadth from the Way of Obedience. Neglect *me*? Child, I have lived on thy strength as an old tree lives on the lime of a new wall. Day by day, since Shamlegh down, I have stolen strength from thee. *Therefore*, not through any sin of thine, art thou weakened. It is the Body—the silly, stupid Body—that speaks now. Not the assured Soul. Be comforted! Know at least the devils that thou fightest. They are earth-born—children of illusion. We will go to the woman from Kulu. She shall acquire merit in housing us, and specially in tending me. Thou shalt run free till strength returns. I had forgotten the stupid Body. If there be any blame, I bear it. But we are too close to the Gates of Deliverance to weigh blame. I could praise thee, but what need? In a little—in a very little—we shall sit beyond all needs.'

And so he petted and comforted Kim with wise saws and grave texts on that little-understood beast, our Body, who, being but a delusion, insists on posing as the Soul, to the darkening of the Way, and the immense multiplication of unnecessary devils.

'*Hai! hai!* Let us talk of the woman from Kulu. Think you she will ask another charm for her grandsons? When I was a young man, a very long time ago, I was plagued with these vapours—and some others—and I went to an abbot—a very holy man and a seeker after truth, though then I knew it not. Sit up and listen, child of my soul! My tale was told. Said he to me, "*Chela*, know this. There are many lies in the world, and not a few liars, but there are no liars like our bodies, except it be the sensations of our bodies." Considering this I was comforted, and of his great favour he suffered me to drink tea in his presence. Suffer me now to drink tea, for I am thirsty.'

With a laugh across his tears, Kim kissed the lama's feet, and set about the tea-making.

'Thou leanest on me in the body, Holy One, but I lean on thee for some other things. Dost know it?'

'I have guessed maybe,' and the lama's eyes twinkled. 'We must change that.'

So, when with scufflings and scrapings and a hot air of importance, paddled up nothing less than the Sahiba's pet palanquin sent twenty miles, with that same grizzled old Oorya servant in charge, and when they reached the disorderly order of the long white rambling house behind Saharunpore, the lama took his own measures.

Said the Sahiba cheerily from an upper window, after compliments: 'What is the good of an old woman's advice to an old man? I told thee—I *told* thee, Holy One, to keep an eye upon the *chela*. How didst thou do it? Never answer me! *I* know. He has been running among the women. Look at his eyes—hollow and sunk—and

the Betraying Line from the nose down! He has been sifted out![3]
Fie! Fie! And a priest, too!'

Kim looked up, over-weary to smile, shaking his head in denial.

'Do not jest,' said the lama. 'That time is done. We are here upon
great matters. A sickness of soul took me in the Hills, and him a
sickness of the body. Since then I have lived upon his strength—eat-
ing him.'

'Children together—young and old,' she sniffed, but forbore to
make any new jokes. 'May this present hospitality restore ye! Hold
awhile and I will come to gossip of the high good Hills.' At evening
time—her son-in-law was returned, so she did not need to go on
inspection round the farm—she won to the meat of the matter,
explained low-voicedly by the lama. The two old heads nodded wisely
together. Kim had reeled to a room with a cot in it, and was dozing
soddenly. The lama had forbidden him to set blankets or get food.

'I know—I know. Who but I?' she cackled. 'We who go down to
the burning-ghats clutch at the hands of those coming up from the
River of Life with full water-jars—yes, brimming water-jars. I did
the boy wrong. He lent thee his strength? It is true that the old eat
the young daily. Stands now we must restore him.'

'Thou hast many times acquired merit—'

'*My* merit. What is it? Old bag of bones making curries for men
who do not ask "Who cooked this?" Now if it were stored up for my
grandson—'

'He that had the belly-pain?'

'To think the Holy One remembers *that*! I must tell his mother. It
is most singular honour! "He that had the belly-pain"—straightway
the Holy One remembered. She will be proud.'

'My *chela* is to me as is a son to the unenlightened.'

'Say grandson, rather. Mothers have not the wisdom of our years.
If a child cries they say the heavens are falling. Now a grandmother
is far enough separated from the pain of bearing and the pleasure of
giving the breast to consider whether a cry is wickedness pure or the
wind. And since thou speakest once again of wind, when last the
Holy One was here, maybe I offended in pressing for charms.'

'Sister,' said the lama, using that form of address a Buddhist monk
may sometimes employ towards a nun, 'if charms comfort thee—'

'They are better than ten thousand doctors.'

'I say, if they comfort thee, I who was Abbot of Such-zen, will
make as many as thou mayest desire. I have never seen thy face—'

'*That* even the monkeys who steal our loquats[4] count for a gain.
Hee! hee!'

3. Tested and found wanting.
4. Yellow apricotlike fruit.

'But as he who sleeps there said,'—he nodded at the shut door of the guest-chamber across the forecourt—'thou hast a heart of gold . . . And he is in the spirit my very "grandson" to me.'

'Good! I am the Holy One's cow.' This was pure Hinduism, but the lama never heeded. 'I am old. I have borne sons in the body. Oh, once I could please men! Now I can cure them.' He heard her armlets tinkle as though she bared arms for action. 'I will take over the boy and dose him, and stuff him, and make him all whole. *Hai! hai!* We old people know something yet.'

Wherefore when Kim, aching in every bone, opened his eyes, and would go to the cook-house to get his master's food, he found strong coercion about him, and a veiled old figure at the door, flanked by the grizzled manservant, who told him very precisely the things that he was on no account to do.

'Thou must have? Thou shalt have nothing. What? A locked box in which to keep holy books? Oh, that is another matter. Heavens forbid I should come between a priest and his prayers! It shall be brought, and thou shalt keep the key.'

They pushed the coffer under his cot, and Kim shut away Mahbub's pistol, the oilskin packet of letters, and the locked books and diaries, with a groan of relief. For some absurd reason their weight on his shoulders was nothing to their weight on his poor mind. His neck ached under it of nights.

'Thine is a sickness uncommon in youth these days: since young folk have given up tending their betters. The remedy is sleep, and certain drugs,' said the Sahiba; and he was glad to give himself up to the blankness that half menaced and half soothed him.

She brewed drinks, in some mysterious Asiatic equivalent to the still-room[5]—drenches that smelt pestilently and tasted worse. She stood over Kim till they went down, and inquired exhaustively after they had come up. She laid a taboo upon the forecourt, and enforced it by means of an armed man. It is true he was seventy odd, that his scabbarded sword ceased at the hilt; but he represented the authority of the Sahiba, and loaded wains,[6] chattering servants, calves, dogs, hens, and the like, fetched a wide compass by those parts. Best of all, when the body was cleared, she cut out from the mass of poor relations that crowded the back of the buildings—household dogs, we name them—a cousin's widow, skilled in what Europeans, who know nothing about it, call massage. And the two of them, laying him east and west, that the mysterious earth-currents which thrill the clay of our bodies might help and not hinder, took him to pieces all one long afternoon—bone by bone, muscle by

5. Storeroom for preserves and alcoholic beverages.
6. Wagons.

muscle, ligament by ligament, and lastly, nerve by nerve. Kneaded
to irresponsible pulp, half hypnotized by the perpetual flick and
readjustment of the uneasy *chudders*[7] that veiled their eyes, Kim slid
ten thousand miles into slumber—thirty-six hours of it—sleep that
soaked like rain after drought.

Then she fed him, and the house spun to her clamour. She
caused fowls to be slain; she sent for vegetables, and the sober,
slow-thinking gardener, nigh as old as she, sweated for it; she took
spices, and milk, and onion, with little fish from the brooks—anon
limes for sherbets, fat quails from the pits, then chicken-livers upon
a skewer, with sliced ginger between.

'I have seen something of this world,' she said over the crowded
trays, 'and there are but two sorts of women in it—those who take
the strength out of a man and those who put it back. Once I was
that one, and now I am this. Nay—do not play the priestling with
me. Mine was but a jest. If it does not hold good now, it will when
thou takest the road again. Cousin,'—this to the poor relation, never
wearied of extolling her patroness's charity—'he is getting a bloom
on the skin of a new-curried horse. Our work is like polishing jew-
els to be thrown to a dance-girl—eh?'

Kim sat up and smiled. The terrible weakness had dropped from
him like an old shoe. His tongue itched for free speech again, and
but a week back the lightest word clogged it like ashes. The pain in
his neck (he must have caught it from the lama) had gone with the
heavy dengue-aches[8] and the evil taste in the mouth. The two old
women, a little, but not much, more careful about their veils now,
clucked as merrily as the hens that had entered pecking through the
open door.

'Where is my Holy One?' he demanded.

'Hear him! Thy Holy One is well,' she snapped viciously.
'Though that is none of his merit. Knew I a charm to make him
wise, I'd sell my jewels and buy it. To refuse good food that I
cooked myself—and go roving into the fields for two nights on an
empty belly—and to tumble into a brook at the end of it—call you
that holiness? Then, when he has nearly broken what thou hast
left of my heart with anxiety, he tells me that he has acquired
merit. Oh, how like are all men! No, that was not it—he tells me
that he is freed from all sin. *I* could have told him that before he
wetted himself all over. He is well now—this happened a week
ago—but burn me such holiness! A babe of three would do better.
Do not fret thyself for the Holy One. He keeps both eyes on thee
when he is not wading our brooks.'

7. Coverings or veils.
8. Pains from a fever peculiar to the tropics.

'I do not remember to have seen him. I remember that the days and nights passed like bars of white and black, opening and shutting. I was not sick: I was only tired.'

'A lethargy that comes by right some few score years later. But it is done now.'

'Maharanee,' Kim began, but led by the look in her eye, changed it to the title of plain love—'Mother, I owe my life to thee. How shall I make thanks? Ten thousand blessings upon thy house and—'

'The house be unblessed!' (It is impossible to give exactly the old lady's word.) 'Thank the Gods as a priest if thou wilt, but thank me, if thou carest, as a son. Heavens above! Have I shifted thee and lifted thee and slapped and twisted thy ten toes to find texts flung at my head? Somewhere a mother must have borne thee to break her heart. What used thou to her—son?'

'I had no mother, my mother,' said Kim. 'She died, they tell me, when I was young.'

'*Hai mai!* Then none can say I have robbed her of any right if—when thou takest the road again and this house is but one of a thousand used for shelter and forgotten, after an easy-flung blessing. No matter. I need no blessings, but—but—' She stamped her foot at the poor relation. 'Take up the trays to the house. What is the good of stale food in the room, O woman of ill-omen?'

'I ha—have borne a son in my time too, but he died,' whimpered the bowed sister-figure behind the *chudder*. 'Thou knowest he died! I only waited for the order to take away the tray.'

'It is I that am the woman of ill-omen,' cried the old lady penitently. 'We that go down to the *chattris* (the big umbrellas above the burning-ghats where the priests take their last dues) clutch hard at the bearers of the *chattis* (water-jars—young folk full of the pride of life, she meant; but the pun is clumsy). When one cannot dance in the festival one must e'en look out of the window, and grandmothering takes all a woman's time. Thy master gives me all the charms I now desire for my daughter's eldest, by reason—is it?—that he is wholly free from sin. The *hakim* is brought very low these days. He goes about poisoning my servants for lack of their betters.'

'What *hakim*, mother?'

'That very Dacca man who gave me the pill which rent me in three pieces. He cast up like a strayed camel a week ago, vowing that he and thou had been blood-brothers together up Kulu-way, and feigning great anxiety for thy health. He was very thin and hungry, so I gave orders to have him stuffed too—him and his anxiety!'

'I would see him if he is here.'

'He eats five times a day, and lances boils for my hinds to save himself from an apoplexy. He is so full of anxiety for thy health that

he sticks to the cook-house door and stays himself with scraps. He will keep. We shall never get rid of him.'

'Send him here, mother'—the twinkle returned to Kim's eye for a flash—'and I will try.'

'I'll send him, but to chase him off is an ill turn. At least he had the sense to fish the Holy One out of the brook; thus, as the Holy One did *not* say, acquiring merit.'

'He is a very wise *hakim*. Send him, mother.'

'Priest praising priest? A miracle! If he is any friend of thine (ye squabbled at your last meeting) I'll hale him here with horse-ropes and—and give him a caste-dinner[9] afterwards, my son . . . Get up and see the world! This lying abed is the mother of seventy devils . . . my son! my son!'

She trotted forth to raise a typhoon off the cook-house, and almost on her shadow rolled in the Babu, robed as to the shoulders like a Roman emperor, jowled like Titus, bare-headed, with new patent-leather shoes, in highest condition of fat, exuding joy and salutations.

'By Jove, Mister O'Hara, but I *am* jolly-glad to see you. I will kindly shut the door. It is a pity you are sick. Are you very sick?'

'The papers—the papers from the *kilta*. The maps and the *murasla!*' He held out the key impatiently; for the present need on his soul was to get rid of the loot.

'You are quite right. That is correct Departmental view to take. You have got everything?'

'All that was hand-written in the *kilta* I took. The rest I threw down the hill.' He could hear the key's grate in the lock, the sticky pull of the slow-rending oilskin, and a quick shuffling of papers. He had been annoyed out of all reason by the knowledge that they lay below him through the sick idle days—a burden incommunicable. For that reason the blood tingled through his body, when Hurree, skipping elephantinely, shook hands again.

'This is fine! This is finest! Mister O'Hara! You have—ha! ha! swiped the whole bag of tricks—locks, stocks, and barrels. They told me it was eight months' work gone up the spouts! By Jove, how they beat me! . . . Look, here is the letter from Hilás!' He intoned a line or two of Court Persian, which is the language of authorized and unauthorized diplomacy. 'Mister Rajah Sahib has just about put his foot in the holes. He will have to explain offeecially how the deuce-an'-all he is writing love-letters to the Czar. And they are very clever maps . . . and there is three or four Prime Ministers of these parts implicated by the correspondence. By Gad, sar! The British Government will change the succession in Hilás and Bunár, and

9. A special dinner prepared in accordance with sacred Hindu ritual.

nominate new heirs to the throne. "Trea-son most base" . . . but you do not understand? Eh?'

'Are they in thy hands?' said Kim. It was all he cared for.

'Just you jolly-well bet yourself they are.' He stowed the entire trove about his body, as only Orientals can. 'They are going up to the office, too. The old lady thinks I am permanent fixture here, but I shall go away with these straight off—immediately. Mr Lurgan will be proud man. You are offeecially subordinate to me, but I shall embody your name in my verbal report. It is a pity we are not allowed written reports. We Bengalis excel in thee exact science.' He tossed back the key and showed the box empty.

'Good. That is good. I was very tired. My Holy One was sick, too. And did he fall into—'

'Oah yess. I am his good friend, I tell you. He was behaving very strange when I came down after you, and I thought perhaps he might have the papers. I followed him on his meditations, and to discuss ethnological points also. You see, I am verree small person here nowadays, in comparison with all his charms. By Jove, O'Hara, do you know, he is afflicted with infirmity of fits. Yess, I tell you. Cataleptic, too, if not also epileptic. I found him in such a state under a tree *in articulo mortem*,[1] and he jumped up and walked into a brook and he was nearly drowned but for me. I pulled him out.'

'Because I was not there!' said Kim. 'He might have died.'

'Yes, he might have died, but he is dry now, and asserts he has undergone transfiguration.' The Babu tapped his forehead knowingly. 'I took notes of his statements for Royal Society—*in posse*.[2] You must make haste and be quite well and come back to Simla, and I will tell you all my tale at Lurgan's. It was splendid. The bottoms of their trousers were *quite* torn, and old Nahan Rajah, he thought they were European soldiers deserting.'

'Oh, the Russians? How long were they with thee?'

'One was a Frenchman. Oh, days and days and days! Now all the hill-people believe all Russians are all beggars. By Jove! they had not one dam'-thing that I did not get them. And I told the common people—oah, *such* tales and anecdotes! I will tell you at old Lurgan's when you come up. We will have—ah—a night out! It is feather in both our caps! Yess, and they gave me a certificate. That is creaming joke. You should have seen them at the Alliance Bank identifying themselves! And thank Almighty God you got their papers so well! You do not laugh verree much, but you shall laugh when you are well. Now I will go straight to the railway and get out. You shall have all sorts of credits for your game. When do you come along?

1. He means *in articulo mortis* (Latin)—at the moment of death.
2. Within possibility (Latin), or with the hope that the Royal Society will publish his notes.

We are very proud of you though you gave us great frights. And especially Mahbub.'

'Ay, Mahbub. And where is he?'

'Selling horses in this vi-cinity, of course.'

'Here! Why? Speak slowly. There is a thickness in my head still.'

The Babu looked shyly down his nose. 'Well, you see, I am fearful man, and I do not like responsibility. You were sick, you see, and I did not know where deuce-an'-all the papers were, and if so, how many. So when I had come down here I slipped in private wire to Mahbub—he was at Meerut for races—and I tell him how case stands. He comes up with his men and he consorts with the lama, and then he calls me a fool, and is very rude—'

'But wherefore—wherefore?'

'That is what *I* ask. I only suggest that if anyone steals the papers I should like some good strong, brave men to rob them back again. You see, they are vitally important, and Mahbub Ali he did not know where you were.'

'Mahbub Ali to rob the Sahiba's house? Thou art mad, Babu,' said Kim with indignation.

'I wanted the papers. Suppose she had stole them? It was only practical suggestion, *I* think. You are not pleased, eh?'

A native proverb—unquotable—showed the blackness of Kim's disapproval.

'Well,'—Hurree shrugged his shoulders—'there is no accounting for thee taste. Mahbub was angry too. He has sold horses all about here, and he says old lady is *pukka* (thorough) old lady and would not condescend to such ungentlemanly things. *I* do not care. I have got the papers, and I was very glad of moral support from Mahbub. I tell you, I am fearful man, but, somehow or other, the more fearful I am the more dam'-tight places I get into. So I was glad you came with me to Chini, and I am glad Mahbub was close by. The old lady she is sometimes very rude to me and my beautiful pills.'

'Allah be merciful!' said Kim on his elbow, rejoicing. 'What a beast of wonder is a Babu! And that man walked alone—if he did walk—with robbed and angry foreigners!'

'Oah, thatt was nothing, after they had done beating me; but if I lost the papers it was pretty-jolly serious. Mahbub he nearly beat me too, and he went and consorted with the lama no end. I shall stick to ethnological investigations henceforwards. Now good-bye, Mister O'Hara. I can catch 4.25 p.m. to Umballa if I am quick. It will be good times when we all tell thee tale up at Mr Lurgan's. I shall report you offeecially better. Good-bye, my dear fallow, and when next you are under thee emotions please do not use the Mohammedan terms with the Tibetan dress.'

He shook hands twice—a Babu to his boot-heels[3]—and opened the door. With the fall of the sunlight upon his still triumphant face he returned to the humble Dacca quack.

'He robbed them,' thought Kim, forgetting his own share in the game. 'He tricked them. He lied to them like a Bengali. They give him a *chit* (a testimonial). He makes them a mock at the risk of his life—*I* never would have gone down to them after the pistol-shots—and then he says he is a fearful man . . . And he *is* a fearful man. I must get into the world again.'

At first his legs bent like bad pipe-stems, and the flood and rush of the sunlit air dazzled him. He squatted by the white wall, the mind rummaging among the incidents of the long *dooli* journey, the lama's weaknesses, and, now that the stimulus of talk was removed, his own self-pity, of which, like the sick, he had great store. The unnerved brain edged away from all the outside, as a raw horse, once rowelled, sidles from the spur. It was enough, amply enough, that the spoil of the *kilta* was away—off his hands—out of his possession. He tried to think of the lama—to wonder why he had tumbled into a brook—but the bigness of the world, seen between the forecourt gates, swept linked thought aside. Then he looked upon the trees and the broad fields, with the thatched huts hidden among crops—looked with strange eyes unable to take up the size and proportion and use of things—stared for a still half-hour. All that while he felt, though he could not put it into words, that his soul was out of gear with its sur-roundings—a cog-wheel unconnected with any machinery, just like the idle cog-wheel of a cheap Beheea sugar-crusher laid by in a corner. The breezes fanned over him, the parrots shrieked at him, the noises of the populated house behind—squabbles, orders, and reproofs—hit on dead ears.

'I am Kim. I am Kim. And what is Kim?' His soul repeated it again and again.

He did not want to cry—had never felt less like crying in his life—but of a sudden easy, stupid tears trickled down his nose, and with an almost audible click he felt the wheels of his being lock up anew on the world without. Things that rode meaningless on the eyeball an instant before slid into proper proportion. Roads were meant to be walked upon, houses to be lived in, cattle to be driven, fields to be tilled, and men and women to be talked to. They were all real and true—solidly planted upon the feet—perfectly comprehensible—clay of his clay, neither more nor less. He shook himself like a dog with a flea in his ear, and rambled out of the gate. Said the Sahiba,

3. Referring to the shrewd designs of Puss-in-Boots, Kim notes the discrepancy between Hurree Babu's timid façade and his actual bravery.

to whom watchful eyes reported this move: 'Let him go. I have done my share. Mother Earth must do the rest. When the Holy One comes back from meditation, tell him.'

There stood an empty bullock-cart on a little knoll half a mile away, with a young banyan tree behind—a look-out, as it were, above some new-ploughed levels; and his eyelids, bathed in soft air, grew heavy as he neared it. The ground was good clean dust—no new herbage that, living, is half-way to death already, but the hopeful dust that holds the seeds of all life. He felt it between his toes, patted it with his palms, and joint by joint, sighing luxuriously, laid him down full length along in the shadow of the wooden-pinned cart. And Mother Earth was as faithful as the Sahiba. She breathed through him to restore the poise he had lost lying so long on a cot cut off from her good currents. His head lay powerless upon her breast, and his opened hands surrendered to her strength. The many-rooted tree above him, and even the dead man-handled wood beside, knew what he sought, as he himself did not know. Hour upon hour he lay deeper than sleep.

Towards evening, when the dust of returning kine made all the horizons smoke, came the lama and Mahbub Ali, both afoot, walking cautiously, for the house had told them where he had gone.

'Allah! What a fool's trick to play in open country!' muttered the horse-dealer. 'He could be shot a hundred times—but this is not the Border.'

'And,' said the lama, repeating a many-times-told tale, 'never was such a *chela*. Temperate, kindly, wise, of ungrudging disposition, a merry heart upon the road, never forgetting, learned, truthful, courteous. Great is his reward!'

'I know the boy—as I have said.'

'And he was all those things?'

'Some of them—but I have not yet found a Red Hat's charm for making him overly truthful. He has certainly been well nursed.'

'The Sahiba is a heart of gold,' said the lama earnestly. 'She looks upon him as her son.'

'Hmph! Half Hind seems that way disposed. I only wished to see that the boy had come to no harm and was a free agent. As thou knowest, he and I were old friends in the first days of your pilgrimage together.'

'That is a bond between us.' The lama sat down. 'We are at the end of the pilgrimage.'

'No thanks to thee thine was not cut off for good and all a week back. I heard what the Sahiba said to thee when we bore thee up on the cot.' Mahbub laughed, and tugged his newly dyed beard.

'I was meditating upon other matters that tide. It was the *hakim* from Dacca broke my meditations.'

'Otherwise'—this was in Pushtu[4] for decency's sake—'thou wouldst have ended thy meditations upon the sultry side of Hell— being an unbeliever and an idolater for all thy child's simplicity. But now, Red Hat, what is to be done?'

'This very night,'—the words came slowly, vibrating with triumph—'this very night he will be as free as I am from all taint of sin—assured as I am, when he quits this body, of Freedom from the Wheel of Things. I have a sign'—he laid his hand above the torn chart in his bosom—'that my time is short; but I shall have safeguarded him throughout the years. Remember, I have reached Knowledge, as I told thee only three nights back.'

'It must be true, as the Tirah priest said when I stole his cousin's wife, that I am a *Sufi* (a free-thinker); for here I sit,' said Mahbub to himself, 'drinking in blasphemy unthinkable . . . I remember the tale. On that, then, he goes to *Jannatu l'Adn* (the Gardens of Eden). But how? Wilt thou slay him or drown him in that wonderful river from which the Babu dragged thee?'

'I was dragged from no river,' said the lama simply. 'Thou hast forgotten what befell. I found it by Knowledge.'

'Oh, ay. True,' stammered Mahbub, divided between high indignation and enormous mirth. 'I had forgotten the exact run of what happened. Thou didst find it knowingly.'

'And to say that I would take life is—not a sin, but a madness simple. My *chela* aided me to the River. It is his right to be cleansed from sin—with me.'

'Ay, he needs cleansing. But afterwards, old man—afterwards?'

'What matter under all the Heavens? He is sure of Nibban[5]— enlightened—as I am.'

'Well said. I had a fear he might mount Mohammed's Horse and fly away.'

'Nay—he must go forth as a teacher.'

'Aha! Now I see! That is the right gait for the colt. Certainly he must go forth as a teacher. He is somewhat urgently needed as a scribe by the State, for instance.'

'To that end he was prepared. I acquired merit in that I gave alms for his sake. A good deed does not die. He aided me in my Search. I aided him in his. Just is the Wheel, O horse-seller from the North. Let him be a teacher; let him be a scribe—what matter? He will have attained Freedom at the end. The rest is illusion.'

'What matter? When I must have him with me beyond Balkh in six months! I come up with ten lame horses and three strong-backed

4. The language of Pathans and Afghans, which Mahbub Ali uses because the lama can't understand it.
5. Nirvana.

men—thanks to that chicken of a Babu—to break a sick boy by force out of an old trot's[6] house. It seems that I stand by while a young Sahib is hoisted into Allah knows what of an idolater's Heaven by means of old Red Hat. And I am reckoned something of a player of the Game myself! But the madman is fond of the boy; and I must be very reasonably mad too.'

'What is the prayer?' said the lama, as the rough Pushtu rumbled into the red beard.

'No matter at all; but now I understand that the boy, sure of Paradise, can yet enter Government service, my mind is easier. I must get to my horses. It grows dark. Do not wake him. I have no wish to hear him call thee master.'

'But he *is* my disciple. What else?'

'He has told me.' Mahbub choked down his touch of spleen[7] and rose laughing. 'I am not altogether of thy faith, Red Hat—if so small a matter concern thee.'

'It is nothing,' said the lama.

'I thought not. Therefore it will not move thee, sinless, new-washed and three parts drowned to boot, when I call thee a good man—a very good man. We have talked together some four or five evenings now, and for all I am a horse-coper I can still, as the saying is, see holiness beyond the legs of a horse. Yea, can see, too, how our Friend of all the World put his hand in thine at the first. Use him well, and suffer him to return to the world as a teacher, when thou hast—bathed his legs, if that be the proper medicine for the colt.'

'Why not follow the Way thyself, and so accompany the boy?'

Mahbub stared stupefied at the magnificent insolence of the demand, which across the Border he would have paid with more than a blow. Then the humour of it touched his worldly soul.

'Softly—softly—one foot at a time, as the lame gelding went over the Umballa jumps. I may come to Paradise later—I have workings that way—great motions—and I owe them to thy simplicity. Thou hast never lied?'

'What need?'

'O Allah, hear him! "What need" in this Thy world! Nor ever harmed a man?'

'Once—with a pencase—before I was wise.'

'So? I think the better of thee. Thy teachings are good. Thou hast turned one man that I know from the path of strife.' He laughed immensely. 'He came here open-minded to commit a *dacoity* (a house-robbery with violence). Yes, to cut, rob, kill, and carry off what he desired.'

6. Old woman's.
7. Emotional response, because the spleen was considered the source of passion.

'A great foolishness!'

'Oh! black shame too. So he thought after he had seen thee—and a few others, male and female. So he abandoned it; and now he goes to beat a big fat Babu man.'

'I do not understand.'

'Allah forbid it! Some men are strong in knowledge, Red Hat. Thy strength is stronger still. Keep it—I think thou wilt. If the boy be not a good servant, pull his ears off.'

With a hitch of his broad Bokhariot belt the Pathan swaggered off into the gloaming, and the lama came down from his clouds so far as to look at the broad back.

'That person lacks courtesy, and is deceived by the shadow of appearances. But he spoke well of my *chela*, who now enters upon his reward. Let me make the prayer! . . . Wake, O fortunate above all born of women. Wake! It is found!'

Kim came up from those deep wells, and the lama attended his yawning pleasure; duly snapping fingers to head off evil spirits.

'I have slept a hundred years. Where—? Holy One, hast *thou* been here long? I went out to look for thee, but'—he laughed drowsily—'I slept by the way. I am all well now. Hast thou eaten? Let us go to the house. It is many days since I tended thee. And the Sahiba fed thee well? Who shampooed thy legs? What of the weaknesses—the belly and the neck, and the beating in the ears?'

'Gone—all gone. Dost thou not know?'

'I know nothing, but that I have not seen thee in a monkey's age. Know what?'

'Strange the knowledge did not reach out to thee, when all my thoughts were theeward.'

'I cannot see the face, but the voice is like a gong. Has the Sahiba made a young man of thee by her cookery?'

He peered at the cross-legged figure, outlined jet-black against the lemon-coloured drift of light. So does the stone Bodhisat sit who looks down upon the patent self-registering turnstiles of the Lahore Museum.

The lama held his peace. Except for the click of the rosary and a faint *clop-clop* of Mahbub's retreating feet, the soft, smoky silence of evening in India wrapped them close.

'Hear me! I bring news.'

'But let us—'

Out shot the long yellow hand compelling silence. Kim tucked his feet under his robe-edge obediently.

'Hear me! I bring news! The Search is finished. Comes now the Reward . . . Thus. When we were among the Hills, I lived on thy strength till the young branch bowed and nigh broke. When we came out of the Hills, I was troubled for thee and for other matters

which I held in my heart. The boat of my soul lacked direction; I could not see into the Cause of Things. So I gave thee over to the virtuous woman altogether. I took no food. I drank no water. Still I saw not the Way. They pressed food upon me and cried at my shut door. So I removed myself to a hollow under a tree. I took no food. I took no water. I sat in meditation two days and two nights, abstracting my mind; inbreathing and outbreathing in the required manner . . . Upon the second night—so great was my reward— the wise Soul loosed itself from the silly Body and went free. This I have never before attained, though I have stood on the threshold of it. Consider, for it is a marvel!'

'A marvel indeed. Two days and two nights without food! Where was the Sahiba?' said Kim under his breath.

'Yea, my Soul went free, and, wheeling like an eagle, saw indeed that there was no Teshoo Lama nor any other soul. As a drop draws to water, so my Soul drew near to the Great Soul which is beyond all things. At that point, exalted in contemplation, I saw all Hind, from Ceylon in the sea to the Hills, and my own Painted Rocks at Such-zen; I saw every camp and village, to the least, where we have ever rested. I saw them at one time and in one place; for they were within the Soul. By this I knew the Soul had passed beyond the illusion of Time and Space and of Things. By this I knew that I was free. I saw thee lying in thy cot, and I saw thee falling downhill under the idolater—at one time, in one place, in my Soul, which, as I say, had touched the Great Soul. Also I saw the stupid body of Teshoo Lama lying down, and the *hakim* from Dacca kneeled beside, shouting in its ear. Then my Soul was all alone, and I saw nothing, for I was all things, having reached the Great Soul. And I meditated a thousand thousand years, passionless, well aware of the Causes of all Things. Then a voice cried: "What shall come to the boy if thou art dead?" and I was shaken back and forth in myself with pity for thee; and I said: "I will return to my *chela*, lest he miss the Way." Upon this my Soul, which is the Soul of Teshoo Lama, withdrew itself from the Great Soul with strivings and yearnings and retchings and agonies not to be told. As the egg from the fish, as the fish from the water, as the water from the cloud, as the cloud from the thick air, so put forth, so leaped out, so drew away, so fumed up the Soul of Teshoo Lama from the Great Soul. Then a voice cried: "The River! Take heed to the River!" and I looked down upon all the world, which was as I had seen it before—one in time, one in place—and I saw plainly the River of the Arrow at my feet. At that hour my Soul was hampered by some evil or other whereof I was not wholly cleansed, and it lay upon my arms and coiled round my waist; but I put it aside, and I cast forth as an eagle in my flight for the very place of the River. I pushed aside world upon world for thy

sake. I saw the River below me—the River of the Arrow—and, descending, the waters of it closed over me; and behold I was again in the body of Teshoo Lama, but free from sin, and the *hakim* from Dacca bore up my head in the waters of the River. It is here! It is behind the mango-tope here—even here!'

'*Allah kerim!* Oh, well that the Babu was by! Wast thou very wet?'

'Why should I regard? I remember the *hakim* was concerned for the body of Teshoo Lama. He haled it out of the holy water in his hands, and there came afterwards thy horse-seller from the North with a cot and men, and they put the body on the cot and bore it up to the Sahiba's house.'

'What said the Sahiba?'

'I was meditating in that body, and did not hear. So thus the Search is ended. For the merit that I have acquired, the River of the Arrow is here. It broke forth at our feet, as I have said. I have found it. Son of my Soul, I have wrenched my Soul back from the Threshold of Freedom to free thee from all sin[8]—as I am free, and sinless! Just is the Wheel! Certain is our deliverance! Come!'

He crossed his hands on his lap and smiled, as a man may who has won salvation for himself and his beloved.

8. The lama describes his arrival at the threshold of nirvana, from which he returns (as befits a Bodhisattva) to lead Kim to salvation. See Zohreh T. Sullivan, "What Happens at the End of *Kim*?" in this volume.

BACKGROUNDS

North India 1857

From R. C. Majumdar, ed., *The History and Culture of the Indian People*, vol. 9, *British Paramountcy and Indian Renaissance* (Bombay: Bharatiya Vidya Bhaven, 1963), endpiece.

MODERN
INDIA

The Grand Trunk Road

The Grand Trunk Road was the great communications route constructed by the East India Company, running from Calcutta in east Bengal into northwest India and then south through Agra (see the text of the novel, p. 41).

Short Stories

Lispeth[†]

> Look, you have cast out Love! What Gods are these
> You bid me please?
> The Three in One, the One in Three? Not so!
> To my own gods I go.
> It may be they shall give me greater ease
> Than your cold Christ and tangled Trinities.
> <div align="right">*The Convert*[1]</div>

She was the daughter of Sonoo, a Hill-man of the Himalayas, and Jadéh his wife. One year their maize failed, and two bears spent the night in their only opium poppy-field just above the Sutlej Valley on the Kotgarh side;[2] so, next season, they turned Christian, and brought their baby to the Mission to be baptized. The Kotgarh Chaplain christened her Elizabeth, and 'Lispeth' is the Hill or *pahari* pronunciation.

Later, cholera came into the Kotgarh Valley and carried off Sonoo and Jadéh, and Lispeth became half servant, half companion, to the wife of the then Chaplain of Kotgarh. This was after the reign of the Moravian missionaries[3] in that place, but before Kotgarh had quite forgotten her title of 'Mistress of the Northern Hills'.

Whether Christianity improved Lispeth, or whether the gods of her own people would have done as much for her under any circumstances, I do not know; but she grew very lovely. When a Hill-girl grows lovely, she is worth travelling fifty miles over bad ground to look upon. Lispeth had a Greek face—one of those faces people paint so often, and see so seldom. She was of a pale, ivory colour, and, for her race, extremely tall. Also, she possessed eyes that were wonderful; and, had she not been dressed in the abominable print-cloths affected by Missions, you would, meeting her on the hillside

† First published in the *Civil and Military Gazette*, November 29, 1886. Collected in *Plain Tales from the Hills* (1888).

1. The poem glosses the failure of Christianity to give the love it professes to the Indian convert who prefers to return to her own, warmer, gods.

2. From its source in Tibet, the Sutlej River flows west through the Himalayas; the Kotgarh "side" is above the river, northeast of Simla, on the road to Tibet.

3. Members of a Protestant sect that originated in central Czechoslovakian Moravia in the eighteenth century.

unexpectedly, have thought her the original Diana of the Romans[4] going out to slay.

Lispeth took to Christianity readily, and did not abandon it when she reached womanhood, as do some Hill-girls. Her own people hated her because she had, they said, become a white woman and washed herself daily; and the Chaplain's wife did not know what to do with her. One cannot ask a stately goddess, five feet ten in her shoes, to clean plates and dishes. She played with the Chaplain's children and took classes in the Sunday School, and read all the books in the house, and grew more and more beautiful, like the Princesses in fairy tales. The Chaplain's wife said that the girl ought to take service in Simla[5] as a nurse or something 'genteel'. But Lispeth did not want to take service. She was very happy where she was.

When travellers—there were not many in those years—came in to Kotgarh, Lispeth used to lock herself into her own room for fear they might take her away to Simla, or out into the unknown world.

One day, a few months after she was seventeen years old, Lispeth went out for a walk. She did not walk in the manner of English ladies—a mile and half out, with a carriage-ride back again. She covered between twenty and thirty miles in her little constitutionals, all about and about, between Kotgarh and Narkunda.[6] This time she came back at full dusk, stepping down the break-neck descent into Kotgarh with something heavy in her arms. The Chaplain's wife was dozing in the drawing-room when Lispeth came in breathing heavily and very exhausted with her burden. Lispeth put it down on the sofa, and said simply, 'This is my husband. I found him on the Bagi Road. He has hurt himself. We will nurse him, and when he is well your husband shall marry him to me.'

This was the first mention Lispeth had ever made of her matrimonial views, and the Chaplain's wife shrieked with horror. However, the man on the sofa needed attention first. He was a young Englishman, and his head had been cut to the bone by something jagged. Lispeth said she had found him down the hillside, and had brought him in. He was breathing queerly and was unconscious.

He was put to bed and tended by the Chaplain who knew something of medicine; and Lispeth waited outside the door in case she could be useful. She explained to the Chaplain that this was the man she meant to marry; and the Chaplain and his wife lectured her severely on the impropriety of her conduct. Lispeth listened quietly,

4. Virgin goddess of hunting.
5. Simla, summer headquarters for the government of India, was a popular hill station to which the English retreated from the summer heat of the plains.
6. Narkunda is twelve miles south of Simla on the road to Tibet.

and repeated her first proposition. It takes a great deal of Christianity to wipe out uncivilised Eastern instincts, such as falling in love at first sight. Lispeth, having found the man she worshipped, did not see why she should keep silent as to her choice. She had no intention of being sent away, either. She was going to nurse that Englishman until he was well enough to marry her. This was her programme.

After a fortnight of slight fever and inflammation, the Englishman recovered coherence and thanked the Chaplain and his wife, and Lispeth—especially Lispeth—for their kindness. He was a traveller in the East, he said—they never talked about 'globe-trotters' in those days, when the P. & O. fleet[7] was young and small—and had come from Dehra Dun[8] to hunt for plants and butterflies among the Simla hills. No one at Simla, therefore, knew anything about him. He fancied that he must have fallen over the cliff while reaching out for a fern on a rotten tree-trunk, and that his coolies must have stolen his baggage and fled. He thought he would go back to Simla when he was a little stronger. He desired no more mountaineering.

He made small haste to go away, and recovered his strength slowly. Lispeth objected to being advised either by the Chaplain or his wife; therefore the latter spoke to the Englishman, and told him how matters stood in Lispeth's heart. He laughed a good deal, and said it was very pretty and romantic, but, as he was engaged to a girl at Home, he fancied that nothing would happen. Certainly he would behave with discretion. He did that. Still he found it very pleasant to talk to Lispeth, and walk with Lispeth, and say nice things to her, and call her pet names while he was getting strong enough to go away. It meant nothing at all to him, and everything in the world to Lispeth. She was very happy while the fortnight lasted, because she had found a man to love.

Being a savage by birth, she took no trouble to hide her feelings, and the Englishman was amused. When he went away, Lispeth walked with him up the Hill as far as Narkunda, very troubled and very miserable. The Chaplain's wife, being a good Christian and disliking anything in the shape of fuss or scandal—Lispeth was beyond her management entirely—had told the Englishman to tell Lispeth that he was coming back to marry her. 'She is but a child, you know, and, I fear, at heart a heathen,' said the Chaplain's wife. So all the twelve miles up the Hill the Englishman, with his arm round Lispeth's waist, was assuring the girl that he would come back and

7. The Peninsular and Oriental Steamship Company, which offered regular travel between England and India.
8. A military post southeast of Kotgarh; he would not have traveled through Simla, southwest of Kotgarh.

marry her; and Lispeth made him promise over and over again. She wept on the Narkunda Ridge till he had passed out of sight along the Muttiani path.[9]

Then she dried her tears and went in to Kotgarh again, and said to the Chaplain's wife, 'He will come back and marry me. He has gone to his own people to tell them so.' And the Chaplain's wife soothed Lispeth and said, 'He will come back.' At the end of two months Lispeth grew impatient, and was told that the Englishman had gone over the seas to England. She knew where England was, because she had read little geography primers; but, of course, she had no conception of the nature of the sea, being a Hill-girl. There was an old puzzle-map of the World in the house. Lispeth had played with it when she was a child. She unearthed it again, and put it together of evenings, and cried to herself, and tried to imagine where her Englishman was. As she had no ideas of distance or steamboats her notions were somewhat wild. It would not have made the least difference had she been perfectly correct; for the Englishman had no intention of coming back to marry a Hill-girl. He forgot all about her by the time he was butterfly-hunting in Assam. He wrote a book on the East afterwards. Lispeth's name did not appear there.

At the end of three months Lispeth made daily pilgrimage to Narkunda to see if her Englishman was coming along the road. It gave her comfort, and the Chaplain's wife finding her happier thought that she was getting over her 'barbarous and most indelicate folly.' A little later the walks ceased to help Lispeth, and her temper grew very bad. The Chaplain's wife thought this a profitable time to let her know the real state of affairs—that the Englishman had only promised his love to keep her quiet—that he had never meant anything, and that it was wrong and improper of Lispeth to think of marriage with an Englishman, who was of a superior clay, besides being promised in marriage to a girl of his own people. Lispeth said that all this was clearly impossible because he had said he loved her, and the Chaplain's wife had, with her own lips, asserted that the Englishman was coming back.

'How can what he and you said be untrue?' asked Lispeth.

'We said it as an excuse to keep you quiet, child,' said the Chaplain's wife.

'Then you have lied to me,' said Lispeth, 'you and he?'

The Chaplain's wife bowed her head, and said nothing. Lispeth was silent too for a little time; then she went out down the valley, and returned in the dress of a Hill-girl—infamously dirty, but without the nose-stud and ear-rings. She had her hair braided into the long pigtail, helped out with black thread, that Hill-women wear.

9. Twelve miles beyond Narkunda on the way to Simla.

'I am going back to my own people,' said she. 'You have killed Lispeth. There is only left old Jadéh's daughter—the daughter of a *pahari* and the servant of *Tarka Devi*.[1] You are all liars, you English.'

By the time that the Chaplain's wife had recovered from the shock of the announcement that Lispeth had 'verted to her mother's gods the girl had gone; and she never came back.

She took to her own unclean people savagely, as if to make up the arrears of the life she had stepped out of; and, in a little time, she married a woodcutter who beat her after the manner of *paharis*, and her beauty faded soon.[2]

'There is no law whereby you can account for the vagaries of the heathen,' said the Chaplain's wife, 'and I believe that Lispeth was always at heart an infidel.' Seeing she had been taken into the Church of England at the mature age of five weeks, this statement does not do credit to the Chaplain's wife.

Lispeth was a very old woman when she died. She had always a perfect command of English, and when she was sufficiently drunk could sometimes be induced to tell the story of her first love-affair.

It was hard then to realise that the bleared, wrinkled creature, exactly like a wisp of charred rag, could ever have been 'Lispeth of the Kotgarh Mission'.

1. Hindu goddess of dawn.
2. *Kim* describes a very different future for Lispeth as the beautiful and seductive Woman of Shamlegh (see pp. 211–21).

To Be Filed for Reference[†]

By the hoof of the Wild Goat up-tossed
From the Cliff where she lay in the Sun,
 Fell the Stone
To the Tarn where the daylight is lost;
So she fell from the light of the Sun,
 And alone.

Now the fall was ordained from the first,
With the Goat and the Cliff and the Tarn,
 But the Stone
Knows only her life is accursed,
As she sinks from the light of the Sun,
 And alone.

Oh, Thou who hast builded the World!
Oh, Thou who hast lighted the Sun!
Oh, Thou who hast darkened the Tarn!
 Judge Thou
The sin of the Stone that was hurled
By the Goat from the light of the Sun,
As she sinks in the mire of the Tarn,
 Even now—even now—even now!
 From the Unpublished Papers of McIntosh Jellaludin[1]

'Say is it dawn, is it dusk in thy Bower,
Thou whom I long for, who longest for me?
Oh, be it night—be it——'[2]

Here he fell over a little camel-colt that was sleeping in the Serai[3]
where the horse-traders and the best of the blackguards from Central
Asia live; and, because he was very drunk indeed and the night was
dark, he could not rise again till I helped him. That was the beginning
of my acquaintance with McIntosh Jellaludin. When a loafer, and
drunk, sings 'The Song of the Bower,' he must be worth cultivating.
He got off the camel's back and said, rather thickly, 'I—I—I'm a bit
screwed, but a dip in Loggerhead[4] will put me right again; and, I say,
have you spoken to Symonds[5] about the mare's knees?'

Now Loggerhead was six thousand weary miles away from us,
close to Mesopotamia,[6] where you mustn't fish and poaching is
impossible, and Charley Symonds' stable a half mile farther across
the paddocks. It was strange to hear all the old names, on a May

† Originally published in *Plain Tales from the Hills* (1888).
1. McIntosh has chosen a Muslim surname.
2. From "The Song of the Bower," by Dante Gabriel Rossetti (1828–1882).
3. Caravanserai, where travelers rest.
4. A men's bathhouse in Oxford; *screwed*: drunk.
5. Owner of an Oxford stable.
6. A walk beside the Cherwell River, in England.

night, among the horses and camels of the Sultan Caravanserai. Then the man seemed to remember himself and sober down at the same time. He leaned against the camel and pointed to a corner of the Serai where a lamp was burning.

'I live there,' said he, 'and I should be extremely obliged if you would be good enough to help my mutinous feet thither; for I am more than usually drunk—most—most phenomenally tight. But not in respect to my head. "My brain cries out against"—how does it go? But my head rides on the—rolls on the dunghill I should have said, and controls the qualm.'

I helped him through the gangs of tethered horses, and he collapsed on the edge of the verandah in front of the line of native quarters.

'Thanks—a thousand thanks! O Moon and little, little Stars! To think that a man should so shamelessly . . . Infamous liquor too. Ovid in exile drank no worse.[7] Better. It was frozen. Alas! I had no ice. Good-night. I would introduce you to my wife were I sober—or she civilised.'

A native woman came out of the darkness of the room and began calling the man names, so I went away. He was the most interesting loafer that I had had the pleasure of knowing for a long time; and later on, he became a friend of mine. He was a tall, well-built, fair man, fearfully shaken with drink, and he looked nearer fifty than the thirty-five which, he said, was his real age. When a man begins to sink in India, and is not sent Home by his friends as soon as may be, he falls very low from a respectable point of view. By the time that he changes his creed, as did McIntosh, he is past redemption.

In most big cities natives will tell you of two or three *Sahibs*, generally low-caste, who have turned Hindu or Mussulman, and who live more or less as such. But it is not often that you can get to know them. As McIntosh himself used to say, 'If I change my religion for my stomach's sake, I do not seek to become a martyr to missionaries, nor am I anxious for notoriety.'

At the outset of acquaintance McIntosh warned me. 'Remember this. I am not an object for charity. I require neither your money, your food, nor your cast-off raiment. I am that rare animal, a self-supporting drunkard. If you choose, I will smoke with you, for the tobacco of the bazars does not, I admit, suit my palate; and I will borrow any books which you may not specially value. It is more than likely that I shall sell them for bottles of excessively filthy country-liquors. In return, you shall share such hospitality as my house affords. Here is a charpoy[8] on which two can sit, and it is possible

7. Ovid's poem "Tristia" describes his boring, difficult exile.
8. Floor mat or bedding.

that there may, from time to time, be food in that platter. Drink, unfortunately, you will find on the premises at any hour; and thus I make you welcome to all my poor establishment.'

I was admitted to the McIntosh household—I and my good tobacco. But nothing else. Unluckily, one cannot visit a loafer in the Serai by day. Friends buying horses would not understand it. Consequently, I was obliged to see McIntosh after dark. He laughed at this, and said simply, 'You are perfectly right. When I enjoyed a position in society, rather higher than yours, I should have done exactly the same thing. Good Heavens! I was once'—he spoke as though he had fallen from the Command of a Regiment—'an Oxford Man!' This accounted for the reference to Charley Symonds' stable.

'You,' said McIntosh slowly, 'have not had that advantage; but, to outward appearance, you do not seem possessed of a craving for strong drinks. On the whole, I fancy that you are the luckier of the two. Yet I am not certain. You are—forgive my saying so even while I am smoking your excellent tobacco—painfully ignorant of many things.'

We were sitting together on the edge of his bedstead, for he owned no chairs, watching the horses being watered for the night, while the native woman was preparing dinner. I did not like being patronised by a loafer, but I was his guest for the time being, though he owned only one very torn alpaca coat and a pair of trousers made out of gunny-bags.[9] He took the pipe out of his mouth, and went on judicially, 'All things considered, I doubt whether you are the luckier. I do not refer to your extremely limited classical attainments, or your excruciating quantities, but to your gross ignorance of matters more immediately under your notice. That, for instance.' He pointed to a woman cleaning a samovar near the well in the centre of the Serai. She was flicking the water out of the spout in regular cadenced jerks.

'There are ways and ways of cleaning samovars. If you knew why she was doing her work in that particular fashion, you would know what the Spanish Monk meant when he said—

> I the Trinity illustrate,
> Drinking watered orange-pulp—
> In three sips the Arian frustrate,
> While he drains his at one gulp—[1]

and many other things which now are hidden from your eyes. However, Mrs. McIntosh has prepared dinner. Let us come and eat

9. Sackcloth made of rough jute or hemp.
1. From Robert Browning's "Soliloquy of the Spanish Cloister."

after the fashion of the people of the country—of whom, by the way, you know nothing.'

The native woman dipped her hand in the dish with us. This was wrong. The wife should always wait until the husband has eaten. McIntosh Jellaludin apologised, saying—

'It is an English prejudice which I have not been able to overcome; and she loves me. Why, I have never been able to understand. I forgathered with her at Jullundur, three years ago, and she has remained with me ever since. I believe her to be moral, and know her to be skilled in cookery.'

He patted the woman's head as he spoke, and she cooed softly. She was not pretty to look at.

McIntosh never told me what position he had held before his fall. He was, when sober, a scholar and a gentleman. When drunk, he was rather more of the first than the second. He used to get drunk about once a week for two days. On those occasions the native woman tended him while he raved in all tongues except his own. One day, indeed, he began reciting *Atalanta in Calydon*,[2] and went through it to the end, beating time to the swing of the verse with a bedstead-leg. But he did most of his ravings in Greek or German. The man's mind was a perfect rag-bag of useless things. Once, when he was beginning to get sober, he told me that I was the only rational being in the Inferno into which he had descended—a Virgil in the Shades,[3] he said—and that, in return for my tobacco, he would, before he died, give me the materials of a new *Inferno* that should make me greater than Dante. Then he fell asleep on a horse-blanket and woke up quite calm.

'Man,' said he, 'when you have reached the uttermost depths of degradation, little incidents which would vex a higher life are to you of no consequence. Last night my soul was among the Gods; but I make no doubt that my bestial body was writhing down here in the garbage.'

'You were abominably drunk, if that's what you mean,' I said.

'I *was* drunk—filthily drunk. I who am the son of a man with whom you have no concern—I who was once Fellow of a College whose buttery-hatch you have not seen—I was loathsomely drunk. But consider how lightly I am touched. It is nothing to me—less than nothing; for I do not even feel the headache which should be my portion. Now, in a higher life, how ghastly would have been my punishment, how bitter my repentance! Believe me, my friend with

2. Poetic drama (1865) by Algernon Charles Swinburne, who outraged society with his poetry of transgression, excess, and violence.
3. In Dante Alighieri's *Divine Comedy*, Virgil's spirit guides Dante through the "shades" of hell (inferno) and purgatory before leading him to paradise.

the neglected education, the highest is as the lowest—always sup-
posing each degree extreme.'

He turned round on the blanket, put his head between his fists
and continued—

'On the Soul which I have lost and on the Conscience which I
have killed, I tell you that I cannot feel! I am as the Gods, knowing
good and evil, but untouched by either. Is this enviable or is it not?'

When a man has lost the warning of 'next morning's head' he
must be in a bad state. I answered, looking at McIntosh on the blan-
ket, with his hair over his eyes and his lips blue-white, that I did not
think the insensibility good enough.

'For pity's sake, don't say that! I tell you it *is* good and most envi-
able. Think of my consolations!'

'Have you so many, then, McIntosh?'

'Certainly. Your attempts at sarcasm, which is essentially the
weapon of a cultured man, are crude. First, my attainments, my
classical and literary knowledge, blurred, perhaps, by immoderate
drinking—which reminds me that before my soul went to the Gods
last night I sold the Pickering Horace[4] you so kindly lent me. Ditta
Mull the clothesman has it. It fetched ten annas, and may be
redeemed for a rupee—but still infinitely superior to yours.
Secondly, the abiding affection of Mrs. McIntosh, best of wives.
Thirdly, a monument, more enduring than brass, which I have built
up in the seven years of my degradation.'

He stopped here, and crawled across the room for a drink of
water. He was very shaky and sick.

He referred several times to his 'treasure'—some great possession
that he owned—but I held this to be the raving of drink. He was as
poor and as proud as he could be. His manner was not pleasant, but
he knew enough about the natives, among whom seven years of his
life had been spent, to make his acquaintance worth having. He
used actually to laugh at Strickland[5] as an ignorant man—'ignorant
West and East'—he said. His boast was, first, that he was an Oxford
Man of rare shining parts, which may or may not have been true—
I did not know enough to check his statements; and secondly, that
he 'had his hand on the pulse of native life'—which was a fact. As
an Oxford man, he struck me as a prig: he was always throwing his
education about. As a Mahommedan *faquir*—as McIntosh
Jellaludin—he was all that I wanted for my own ends. He smoked
several pounds of my tobacco, and taught me several ounces of
things worth knowing; but he would never accept any gifts, not even
when the cold weather came, and gripped the poor thin chest under

4. William Pickering (1796–1854), English publisher of the works of Horace.
5. The policeman-detective, who knows India better than the Indians, appears in *Kim* and
 in five stories.

the poor thin alpaca coat. He grew very angry, and said that I had insulted him, and that he was not going into hospital. He had lived like a beast and he would die rationally, like a man.

As a matter of fact, he died of pneumonia; and on the night of his death sent over a grubby note asking me to come and help him to die.

The native woman was weeping by the side of the bed. McIntosh, wrapped in a cotton cloth, was too weak to resent a fur coat being thrown over him. He was very active as far as his mind was concerned, and his eyes were blazing. When he had abused the Doctor who came with me so foully that the indignant old fellow left, he cursed me for a few minutes and calmed down.

Then he told his wife to fetch out 'The Book' from a hole in the wall. She brought out a big bundle, wrapped in the tail of a petticoat, of old sheets of miscellaneous notepaper, all numbered and covered with fine cramped writing. McIntosh ploughed his hand through the rubbish and stirred it up lovingly.

'This,' he said, 'is my work—the Book of McIntosh Jellaludin, showing what he saw and how he lived, and what befell him and others; being also an account of the life and sins and death of Mother Maturin.[6] What Mirza Murad Ali Beg's book[7] is to all other books on native life, will my work be to Mirza Murad Ali Beg's!'

This, as will be conceded by any one who knows Mirza Murad Ali Beg's book, was a sweeping statement. The papers did not look specially valuable; but McIntosh handled them as if they were currency-notes. Then said he slowly—

'In despite the many weaknesses of your education, you have been good to me. I will speak of your tobacco when I reach the Gods. I owe you much thanks for many kindnesses. But I abominate indebtedness. For this reason I bequeath to you now the monument more enduing than brass—my one book—rude and imperfect in parts, but oh, how rare in others! I wonder if you will understand it. It is a gift more honourable than . . . Bah! where is my brain rambling to? You will mutilate it horribly. You will knock out the gems you call Latin quotations, you Philistine, and you will butcher the style to carve into your own jerky jargon; but you cannot destroy the whole of it. I bequeath it to you. Ethel . . . My brain again! . . . Mrs. McIntosh, bear witness that I

6. The title of a book about an outcast Eurasian woman that Kipling worked on for many years in India. In an 1885 letter to his aunt Edith Macdonald, Kipling wrote of the novel: "It's not one bit nice or proper but it carries a grim sort of a moral with it and tries to deal with the unutterable horrors of lower class Eurasian and native life as they exist outside reports and reports and reports." For other references, see his letters, pp. 268 and 271.
7. Mirza Murad Ali Beg's "Lalun, the Beragun" (1884) was described at the time as one of the world's great short stories (see *Kipling Journal*, July 1955).

give the *Sahib* all these papers. They would be of no use to you,
Heart of my Heart; and I lay it upon you,' he turned to me here,
'that you do not let my book die in its present form. It is yours
unconditionally—the story of McIntosh Jellaludin, which is *not* the
story of McIntosh Jellaludin, but of a greater man than he, and of
a far greater woman. Listen now! I am neither mad nor drunk!
That book will make you famous.'

I said, 'Thank you,' as the native woman put the bundle into my
arms.

'My only baby!' said McIntosh, with a smile. He was sinking fast,
but he continued to talk as long as breath remained. I waited for the
end; knowing that, in six cases out of ten, a dying man calls for his
mother. He turned on his side and said—

'Say how it came into your possession. No one will believe you,
but my name, at least, will live. You will treat it brutally, I know you
will. Some of it must go; the public are fools and prudish fools. I
was their servant once. But do your mangling gently—very gently. It
is a great work, and I have paid for it in seven years' damnation.'

His voice stopped for ten or twelve breaths, and then he began
mumbling a prayer of some kind in Greek. The native woman cried
very bitterly. Lastly, he rose in bed and said, as loudly as slowly—
'Not guilty, my Lord!'

Then he fell back, and the stupor held him till he died. The native
woman ran into the Serai among the horses, and screamed and beat
her breasts; for she had loved him.

Perhaps his last sentence in life told what McIntosh had once
gone through; but, saving the big bundle of old sheets in the cloth,
there was nothing in his room to say who or what he had been.

The papers were in a hopeless muddle.

Strickland helped me to sort them, and he said that the writer was
either an extreme liar or a most wonderful person. He thought the
former. One of these days you may be able to judge for yourselves.
The bundle needed much expurgation, and was full of Greek non-
sense at the head of the chapters, which has all been cut out.

If the thing is ever published, some one may perhaps remember
this story, now printed as a safeguard to prove that McIntosh
Jellaludin and not I myself wrote the Book of Mother Maturin.

I don't want *The Giant's Robe*[8] to come true in my case!

8. The title of an 1884 novel by Thomas Anstey Guthrie (F. Anstey) about a man who pub-
lishes his dead friend's novel as his own, and afterward finds he cannot write a work that
equals it. In a letter to Anstey dated July 9, 1900, Kipling expressed his thanks "from the
depths of my liver," his blessing, and his envy for Anstey's recently published novel *The
Brass Bottle*: "It's beautiful. It's Royal, and it's entirely and gravely true. Bayswater I know
more or less and Djinns I know more or less—but you've put the two together so that I
see how Djinns behave . . ." (*The Letters of Rudyard Kipling*, ed. Thomas Pinney [Iowa
City: University of Iowa Press, 1996] 3:25).

Poems

Recessional[†]

God of our fathers, known of old,
 Lord of our far-flung battle-line,
Beneath whose awful[1] Hand we hold
 Dominion over palm and pine—
Lord God of Hosts,[2] be with us yet, 5
Lest we forget[3]—lest we forget!

The tumult and the shouting dies;
 The Captains and the Kings depart:
Still stands Thine ancient sacrifice,
 An humble and a contrite heart.[4] 10
Lord God of Hosts, be with us yet,
Lest we forget—lest we forget!

Far-called, our navies melt away;
 On dune and headland sinks the fire:
Lo, all our pomp of yesterday 15
 Is one with Nineveh and Tyre![5]
Judge of the Nations,[6] spare us yet,
Lest we forget—lest we forget!

[†] First published July 17, 1897, in *The Times* and reprinted in many other newspapers. The poem, written the morning after, and first titled "After," was Kipling's fearful reaction to the celebrations of Queen Victoria's Diamond Jubilee by a people "drunk with sight of power." In his autobiography, Kipling describes the poem as "in the nature of a *muzzur-wattu* (an averter of the Evil Eye)" (*Something of Myself and Other Autobiographical Writings*, ed. Thomas Pinney [Cambridge: Cambridge University Press, 1990] 86). The letter that accompanied the poem's first printing reveals a hope that others shared his feelings: "Enclosed please find my sentiments on things—which I hope are yours. We've been blowing up the Trumpets of the New Moon a little too much for White Men, and it's about time we sobered down." The poem draws extensively on the Old Testament. A recessional is the hymn sung while the clergy and choir file out after a church service. See 1 Chronicles 29.10–18 for a passage similar in tone and content.

1. Awe-inspiring.
2. Similar phrases occur throughout the Bible.
3. A variant of this phrase appears in Deuteronomy 4.9: "Only take heed to thyself, and keep thy soul diligently, lest thou forget the things which thine eyes have seen, and lest they depart from thy heart all the days of thy life: but teach them thy sons, and thy sons's sons."
4. Psalms 51.17: "The Sacrifices of God are a broken spirit: a broken and a contrite heart, O God, thou wilt not despise."
5. The Bible describes the destruction of Nineveh; Isaiah 23 foretells the destruction of Tyre.
6. Isaiah 2.4: "And he shall judge among the nations."

If, drunk with sight of power, we loose
 Wild tongues that have not Thee in awe, 20
Such boastings as the Gentiles[7] use,
 Or lesser breeds without the Law[8]—
Lord God of Hosts, be with us yet,
Lest we forget—lest we forget!

For heathen heart that puts her trust 25
 In reeking tube and iron shard,
All valiant dust that builds on dust,
 And guarding, calls not Thee to guard.
For frantic boast and foolish word—
Thy mercy on Thy People, Lord! 30

The White Man's Burden[†]

Take up the White Man's burden—
 Send forth the best ye breed—
Go bind your sons to exile
 To serve your captives' need;
To wait in heavy harness 5
 On fluttered folk and wild—
Your new-caught, sullen peoples,
 Half devil and half child.

Take up the White Man's burden—
 In patience to abide, 10
To veil the threat of terror
 And check the show of pride;
By open speech and simple,
 An hundred times made plain,
To seek another's profit, 15
 And work another's gain.

Take up the White Man's burden—
 The savage wars of peace—
Fill full the mouth of Famine
 And bid the sickness cease; 20
And when your goal is nearest
 The end for others sought,

7. Non-Jewish people.
8. The allusion is to Romans 2.14, "The Gentiles, which have not the law," and to unlawful
 imperial powers, not non-Europeans (see the essay by A. Michael Matin in this volume).
† First published February 4, 1899, in *The Times*, the poem was addressed to the United
 States in the wake of its 1898 war with Spain, which led to the acquisition of Cuba and
 the Philippines (both previously Spanish colonies). Kipling sent an advance copy to his
 friend Theodore Roosevelt.

Watch Sloth and heathen Folly
 Bring all your hope to nought.

Take up the White Man's burden— 25
 No tawdry rule of kings,
But toil of serf and sweeper—
 The tale of common things.
The ports ye shall not enter,
 The roads ye shall not tread, 30
Go make them with your living,
 And mark them with your dead!

Take up the White Man's burden—
 And reap his old reward:
The blame of those ye better, 35
 The hate of those ye guard—
The cry of hosts ye humour
 (Ah, slowly!) toward the light:—
'Why brought ye us from bondage,
 Our loved Egyptian night?'[1] 40

Take up the White Man's burden—
 Ye dare not stoop to less—
Nor call too loud on Freedom
 To cloak your weariness;
By all ye cry or whisper, 45
 By all ye leave or do,
The silent, sullen peoples
 Shall weigh your Gods and you.

Take up the White Man's burden—
 Have done with childish days— 50
The lightly proffered laurel,
 The easy, ungrudged praise.
Comes now, to search your manhood
 Through all the thankless years,
Cold-edged with dear-bought wisdom, 55
 The judgment of your peers!

1. See Exodus 16.2–3, the wandering Israelites' complaint against Moses.

Letters

To Margaret Burne-Jones, [27] September 1885[†]

<div style="text-align: right">Lahore. / Sept. 26th. 1885.</div>

* * *

Oh! about that sentence you couldn't quite follow. Maybe I wrote at Random but what I meant was this. You[1] see in our best of all possible worlds—read India—there are whole hosts of abuses oppressions and unthinking wrongs that may one of these days be set right if you hammer long enough. Understand clearly that I don't mean the sort of Indian wrongs that Crom Price writes to me about—the extended employment of natives out of Hindustan etc.—because my views on that subject would shock you a good deal and C.P. bless him doesn't know that any native of any caste would flatly refuse to cross the "black water" unless he had received a purely English education and had been *outcasted*. What I mean is that the population out here die from purely preventible causes; are starved from purely preventible causes; are in native states hideously misgoverned from their rulers' own folly and so on. Let me make my meaning clearer by an instance. Say that a district as big as Yorkshire near Delhi lies out of the reach of the regular rains and that consequently for three years out of seven the villagers are face to face with starvation. A system of what we call *bunds*, dams, channels and embankments would at least store water and stave off drought for a year. Well that means saving so many men and so many cattle, easing the work of the Deputy Commissioner and improving the land. Find out, if you can, how many bunds could be raised for how much money; where retrenchment or an extra cess elsewhere could raise that money: consult

† The following are from *The Letters of Rudyard Kipling*, ed. Thomas Pinney (Iowa City: University of Iowa Press and Macmillan Press Ltd., 1996) 1:88, 91–93, 97–101, 126–27, 130. Rudyard Kipling's letters, © 1990 by The National Trust for Places of Historic Interest or Natural Beauty. Reprinted by permission of the publisher.

1. Margaret Burne-Jones, Rudyard's favorite cousin, sometimes addressed as "wop," was the daughter of his uncle Edward Burne-Jones and Georgie (his mother's sister), at whose home, "The Grange," he stayed every December during his breaks from the miserable "House of Desolation" at Southsea (1871–77).

specialists and nearly every Civilian in India is strong either in set-
tlement work, crime repression, canals, public buildings or some-
thing of the kind[;] get all your information into a taking form—
never mind if you have to delay a month or even two, and then
begin to hammer away about this district through the paper as
hard as you know how. Keep on hammering. Get good men to
write you leaders about it: get lesser men to write letters about it;
get statistics and drive ahead. Ten to one nothing will be done at
first but other papers take up the matter; the Deputy
Commissioner of the District is asked first, tentatively, by the
Provincial Government if he thinks anything can be done and
whether these suggestions of yours are any good. Perhaps he can
perhaps he can't. Maybe he'll raise one *bund* to see how it works.
Then as soon as the villagers begin to realize that a *bunded* tehsil
(parish) turns out better crops than an unbunded one they'll go
into the business with a will. Same thing with drains; supply of
horses for the Punjab; village debts; prevention of fever; outstation
dispensaries and a thousand thousand other things. Just now Lady
Dufferin's fund for the Medical education of native women is
exciting a good deal of comment. A Bengal native paper, whose
editor I should like to lick till he couldn't stand, begins talking a
lot of nonsense about "we should have preferred an extended
movement on a national basis dealing with the primary education
of womenkind" and discounting the scheme all it knows. We might
wait till Doomsday till the Bengalis educated their native women:
meantime they are rotting in the zenanas, for sheer want of med-
ical attendance; English docs you know aren't allowed to see a
zenana woman in her last agonies. Well, that's a piece of flatulent
wind baggery that might do mischief to a notion that if properly
carried out will do infinitely more good than all the "Associations
for advancement" [of] "National Progress" (that is national foot
and mouth disease) in the Empire. Your duty clearly is to combat
that paper with all your power. Rake it with statistics; tall writing;
appeals, and finally "chaff"—no Asiatic understands "chaff." If
prose doesn't go home hack out some verses with a lilting refrain
that will take and catch the public ear and you have helped to
scotch a snake. Same with "widow remarriage." Thank Goodness
you haven't any notion of the horrors of enforced widow hood out
here. The agitation is as old as the hills but our progressive Aryan
brother, the Oxford B.A. who'll eat with you, ride with you and
talk to your wife won't *dare* to fly in the face of his "custom."
Hammer away at that in prose and verse and see what comes of
it. The danger of course specially with a young writer lies in over-
stating the case. This must be guarded against by rigorous check-
ing and pruning; for however powerful the press may be at home,

it is infinitely more powerful out here where a paper can be sup-
pressed at any moment. Queer Paradox ain't it? But it is so.
Personally I'm death on Drains and water supply—that doesn't
lend itself to verse—and every now and again I have a chance of
wiring in to some municipality where the cholera returns are
higher than they should be. People won't stir quickly for abstracts
of reports. Go down and look at the place yourself and write all
you know on the running pen. Serve hot and something is sure to
come of it. I had a rare chance the other day, though it didn't con-
cern men as much as horses. I left Simla by an "ordinary" mail
cart in company with a lot of natives. Well, the native officials
treated those passengers like pigs and turned out, in the darkness,
chafed, galled and bleeding horses. I went round with a lantern
and inspected the whole lot quietly and explained my views to the
native contractor. Got in to Lahore and gave an unimpassioned
account of the whole journey in the paper. Ten days later comes
a Government letter to the contractor with my account cut out
and an intimation for him to "explain his conduct in writing".
Better still, the Vet whose duty it is to inspect the line woke up to
a sense of his duties and made things extra lively for the contrac-
tor. Result not a single galled horse on the road and more con-
sideration for native passengers. That's a small business of course
and not half so important as the bunded district. If we can get
that really forced into the public (or rather the Supreme Govt's
notice) we shall have done something worth the doing and I shall
chortle like a Boojum. You see, if you once set the ball a rolling
you can generally get two or three men infinitely better than your-
self with twenty years' experience to help it along. They only want
the prodding and therefore it is your bounden duty, for the per-
formance or nonperformance of which your conscience holds you
answerable, that you shall keep your pen-point sharp and *clean*
and try all you know to get a style that commands attention and
the power of writing facilely. It mayn't be literature (there's ample
time for that in the next world, where one of the delights of
Paradise will be printing your poems on rubbed rough edged paper
and reading laudatory reviews of 'em in the *Celestial Intelligencer*)
but it may save men and cattle alive and lead to really tangible
results. There's no finer feeling in life than the knowledge that a
year's work has really done some living good, besides amusing and
interesting people, for a Province that you are genuinely interested
in and love. Then again there's nothing more sobering than the
knowledge of the enormous mass of work that remains to be done
and the utter hopelessness of doing one tithe of it. Also the knowl-
edge that you have been entrusted with the control—for an assis-
tant editor has far more real control over his paper than an edi-

tor—on the same principal that a first mate navigates a P and O
steamer—of a big power that can make even Lieutenant Governors
and Viceroys "sit up" to use a vile *slangerie*. Curiously enough I
have written to you more freely, my sister, than I have *even spo-
ken* to any one I know. * * *

 * * *

To Margaret Burne-Jones, 28 November 1885–11 January 1886

 Lahore. / November. 28th / 85.

Noble, fluent-penned, Excellent wop of Albion!

 * * *

When you write "native" who do you mean? The Mahommedan
who hates the Hindu; the Hindu who hates the Mahommedan; the
Sikh who loathes both; or the semi-anglicized product of our Indian
colleges who is hated and despised by Sikh, Hindu, and
Mahommedan. Do you mean the Punjabi who will have nothing to
do with the Bengali; the Mahrattha to whom the Punjabi's tongue
is as incomprehensible as Russian to me; the Parsee who controls
the whole trade of Bombay and ranges himself on all questions as
an Englishman; the Sindee who is an outsider; the Bhil or the Gond
who is an aborigine; the Rajput who despises everything on God's
earth but himself; the Delhi traders who control trade to the value
of millions; the Afghan who is only kept from looting these same
merchants by dread of English interference. Which one of all the
thousand conflicting tongues, races, nationalities and peoples
between the Khaibar Pass and Ceylon do you mean? There is no
such thing as the natives of India, any more than there is the
"People of India" as our friends the Indian delegates would have you
believe. You may rest assured Wop that if we didn't hold the land in
six months it would be one big cock pit of conflicting princelets.
Now "do the English as a rule feel the welfare of the natives much
at heart." Oh Wop! If you had met some of the men I know you
would cross out the sentence and weep. What else are we working
in the country for. For what else do the best men of the Commission
die from overwork, and disease, if not to keep the people alive in the
first place and healthy in the second. We spend our best men on the
country like water and if ever a foreign country was made better
through "the blood of the martyrs" India is that country. I couldn't
now tell you what the men one knows are doing but you can read

for yourself if you will how Englishmen have laboured and died for the peoples of the country. Wop dear have you ever heard of a "demoralized district"; when tens of thousands of peoples are panic stricken say, with an invasion of cholera—or dying from famine? Do you know how Englishmen, Oxford men expensively educated, are turned off to "do" that district—to make their own arrangements for the cholera camps; for the prevention of disorder; or for famine relief, to pull the business through or die—whichever God wills. Then another man, or may be boy takes his place. Yes the English in India do do a little for the benefit of the natives and small thanks they get.

* * *

But to return to our cousins I have endeavoured to put forward feebly the fact that the English have the welfare of the natives at heart. One year out here would show you how much truth I have *not* written. Then you demand:—Have we any interests in common? *Werry* few dear old Wop—the bulk of us—d——d few. And 'faith if you knew in what inconceivable filth of mind the peoples of India were brought up from their cradle; if you realized the views—or one tenth of the views—they hold about women and their absolute incapacity for speaking the truth as we understand it—the immeasurable gulf that lies between the two races in all things you would see how it comes to pass that the Englishman is prone to despise the natives—(I *must* use that misleading term for brevity's sake)—and how, except in the matter of trade, to have little or nothing in common with him. Now this is a wholly wrong attitude of mind but it's one that a Briton who washes, and don't take bribes, and who thinks of other things besides intrigue and seduction most naturally falls into. *When he does*—goodbye to his chances of attempting to understand the people of the land. (It's rather a Pott and Slurkian thing to do but I send you herewith my "East and West" an almost verbatim repro. of my confab with an Afghan gentleman (who by the way is an old friend of mine) on my way up from Rajputana the other day. It may bear on what we are talking about). Underneath our excellent administrative system; under the piles of reports and statistics; the thousands of troops; the doctors; and the civilian runs wholly untouched and unaffected the life of the peoples of the land—a life as full of impossibilities and wonders as the Arabian nights. I don't want to gush over it but I do want you to understand Wop dear that, immediately outside of our own English life, is the dark and crooked and fantastic, and wicked, and awe inspiring life of the "native". Our rule, so long as no one steals too flagrantly or murders too openly, affects it in no way whatever—only fences it

around and prevents it from being disturbed. I have done my little
best to penetrate into it and have put the little I have learnt into the
pages of "Mother Maturin"—Heaven send that she may grow into a
full blown novel before I die—My experiences of course are only a
queer jumble of opium-dens, night houses, night strolls with
natives; evenings spent in their company in their own homes (in the
men's quarter of course) and the long yarns that my native friends
spin me, and one or two queer things I've come across in my own
office experience. The result of it all has been to interest me
immensely and keenly in the people and to show me how little an
Englishman can hope to understand 'em. I would that you could see
some of the chapters of Mother Maturin and you would follow more
plainly what I mean. But this is a digression. Again you want to
know whether the natives feel "affectionately" towards Europeans.
No, they don't take to a European 'cos he *is* a European—but when
they take to a man because they like him their attachment is rather
striking. In this country every thing is done by personal influence—
the personal influence of the Englishman. Only our government
doesn't recognize the fact and goes centralizing and centralizing at
Simla until the District officers—the little kings of the counties—
are reduced simply to machines for compiling statistics and lose
touch with the people. A man who has the confidence of the natives
can do *anything*, whether he is Civilian or Unofficial. Let me give
two humble examples. The Mahommedans in the city know my
Pater and almost worship him in many ways, for things he's done—
'specially for his kindness towards poor Mahommedans (frankly
both he and I prefer Mussalmans to Hindus; they're a better lot
roughly speaking). Pater is collecting exhibits for the Indo Colonial
Exhibition and can get through about twice as much work as other
men simply because he knows the people, they know him and he
handles 'em properly. Beyond a certain point however they refuse to
go. They won't send valuables for exhibit across the black water
unless they know my Pater goes with 'em. If he did they'd send *lakhs*
worth on his simple assurance that they would be returned unin-
jured. But the Pater can't go and to his assurances that everything
will be safe in the hands of the other Sahibs they simply reply:—
"Ah! but what do those Sahibs know about us or we about them. Go
you yourself Sahib and you can take anything you like". Pater can't
go: so much the worse therefore for the Exhibition as far as the
Punjab is concerned. They (the peoples of this country) are by birth
and training suspicious but if you get their confidence they'll do
anything. With a few exceptions all the Englishmen who have to
deal with 'em get their confidence and to do that they have to be
handled like children or young horses. Another small very small
instance. My own men, about 170 altogether, have rather a belief in

me—primarily because I am my father's son (and in this country everyone is the son of some father—and writes his father's name down when he writes his own) and nextly because I've laid myself out to try and understand 'em. The last three years have just shown me how hopeless and how interesting the task is, but also how my *wish*—*not* my order—can make the whole gang buckle to and work double tides or overtime for nothing so long as they understand it was for the Chota Sahib. And yet, if these men weren't paid for an extra half hour's work, under ordinary circumstances, they'd *cry* like children. A queer people indeed. Touchy as children; obstinate as men; patient as the High God's themselves; vicious as Devils but always loveable if you know how to take 'em. And so far as I know, the proper way to handle 'em is not by looking on 'em "as excitable masses of barbarism" (I speak for the Punjab only) or the "down trodden millions of Ind groaning under the heel of an alien and unsympathetic despotism", but as men with a language of their own which it is your business to understand; and proverbs, which it is your business to quote (this is a land of proverbs) and bywords and allusions which it is your business to master; and feelings which it is your business to enter into and sympathize with. Then they'll believe in you and do things for you, and let you do things for them. *But* (and here you will think me wrong perhaps) never lose sight of the fact that so long as you are in this country you will be looked to by the natives round in [*sic*] you as their guide and leader if anything happens. Therefore comport yourself as such. This is a solemn fact. If anything goes wrong from a quarrel to an accident the natives *instantly* fly to a European for "orders." If a man's dying in the road they won't touch him unless they have an Englishman to order 'em. If there's a row in the city the native policeman will take his orders from the first wandering white man he sees and so on *ad infinitum*. This is only the sober truth. They will go to their own District officer first and if they can't get him to the nearest Englishman. I had almost forgotten another instance of "confidence." The financial management of the funds of the "Durbar Sahib"—the big temple at Amritsar which is the centre of the Sikh religion was till recently "bossed" by an Englishman on the urgent request of the Sikhs' priests. Now I believe they have a native treasurer but that Englishman is always called in if there's any hitch. It comes to this then—The natives aren't "affectionate" to Englishmen *qua* Englishmen but they have a belief that they can be trusted implicitly to speak truth and keep accounts straight—all of 'em. When they believe in any particular Englishman affection is a mild word for their feelings. They worship him almost. At the same time they'd perjure their immortal souls to cheat him to the extent of d/1/2 English money. You can reconcile these manifold contradictions

Wop as you please. But they are all pretty near the truth. Have I answered your questions at sufficient length think you?

* * *

To E. K. Robinson, 30 April 1886

Lahore. / April 30th. 86

Dear Kay,[1]

* * *

Would you be astonished if I told you that I look forward to nothing but an Indian journalist's career? Why should I? My home's out here; my people are out here; all the friends etc. I know are out here and all the interests I have are out here. Why should I go home. Any fool can put up rhymes and the market is full of boys who could undersell me as soon as I put foot in it. Recollect that at present I serve in my own stud for Rs 400 a month. Where would a colt get Rs 400 for his services on a home farm? Besides I was bought out of the stockyard on trust. Bitted, mouthed and broken to saddle polo and harness on spec. Very well. I shall begin to pay for my breaking in a few years. Then it will take some time to refund that expenditure. Then there is my personal and purely unprofessional gratitude to the gang who selected me, which gives the gang a further right to my services—for as long a time in fact as they may choose to retain them. London journalism—you have some years of it behind you—is a great and grand thing but it seems to me, I speak in ignorance; that out here one lives and writes more in the centre of history with one's hands on everything than in a land where by reason of its hugeness every one is on the outskirts of everything; watching ministers, policies and financiers from afar. What do *you* think?

However if I live I'm young enough to change my opinions many times over; but I shall have to go through a rough time of it if I prefer a life that I don't know to the broad margins, uncut edges and pleasant type of my daily existence in this land.

For another thing I am deeply interested in the queer ways and works of the people of the land. I hunt and rummage among 'em; knowing Lahore City—that wonderful, dirty, mysterious ant hill—blind fold and wandering through it like Haroun Al-Raschid in

1. Edward Kay Robinson, Kipling's lifelong friend, was editor of two newspapers for which Rudyard wrote: the *Pioneer* and the *Civil and Military Gazette*.

search of strange things. "Section 420. I.P.C."[2] (originally called "in the House of Suddhoo") is the outcome of some of these researches but the bulk of my notes and references goes to enrich a bruised tin tea box where lies—350 f.cp. pages thick—my "Mother Maturin." The novel that is always being written and yet gets no furrarder.

You—I know—don't care for this sort of thing and I daresay you wonder what's the good of "perugin'" among bunnias and prostitutes (the aliteration would be coarse). Naturally. You made your mark at home and you want to go and chalk it over again. I'm in love with the country and would sooner write about her than anything else. Wherefore let us depart our several ways in amity? You to Fleet Street (where I shall come when I die if I'm good) and I to my own place where I find heat and smells of oil and spices, and puffs of temple incense, and sweat, and darkness, and dirt and lust and cruelty, and, above all, things wonderful and fascinating innumerable. Give me time Kay—Give me seven years and three added to them and abide the publishment of "*Mother Maturin.*" Then you shall sit down in your gas lit, hotwater pipe warmed office, at midnight, and shall indite a review saying that the book ought never to have been written. And perhaps I shall agree with you then.

To Margaret Burne-Jones, 3 May–24 June 1886

Lahore. / May. 3rd. 6. P.M. Grey twilight / 1886

Dear Wop,

It's very sickening and if I weren't ashamed of myself as it is I'd throw up my head and howl. The Mother and the Maid have just left the house for Simla—gone till the 15th of October and Trix covered herself with glory by weeping. Pater's gone with 'em to the Station. I've got office work coming on in half an hour so I can't go—can't do anything but sit down in the half emptied house with the punkah creaking and the thermantidote throbbing and pour out my woes to you. Yah! how I loathe and abominate the hot weather and the necessity of sending away one's women folk for six months of the twelve. Here's the Pater and me thrown back on bachelor life again; dining at Clubs, knocking about alone with never a lady at the head of the table or Trix to make fun of us, or anything decent at all. You don't know—for which thank your God—the sinking when the heat shuts in and the women folk go off. I like it less each year. 1883 was moderate; 1884 was not nice, for Trix and the

2. An early story, first published in 1886 in the *Civil and Military Gazette*, collected in *Plain Tales from the Hills* (1888).

Mother were at Dalhousie; '85 was all right because I was only
adrift for two months and three weeks. This year is horrid—I shall
be all right in a day or so when I've returned to the desolate free-
dom of the wild ass and linked on to the hot weather group of men
who talk of nothing but their work and go to sleep directly after din-
ner. But oh Lord! Lord! how bad I feel now.

That's a manly way of shutting up under discomfort. It was
Trixie's fault. She sat down and yowled and the Mother was nearly
as bad. Pater didn't mind. He joins 'em in six weeks, I hope and pray
for his sake. * * *

* * *

Autobiography and Biography

RUDYARD KIPLING

From Something of Myself[†]

[Written when he was seventy, during the last few months of his life, Kipling's unfinished autobiography, *Something of Myself for My Friends Known and Unknown* (1937), looks back on his childhood in India and in the House of Desolation; his return to India as a journalist and writer; his obsession with finding his "very own house"; his travels from India to England, Japan, America, Canada, South Africa, New Zealand, and Australia; and finally, his writing life at Bateman's. In his last chapter, "Working-Tools," Kipling acknowledges writing both as a craft and as an irrational activity inspired by the "Daemon" who, he claimed, came to him in his finest works—the Jungle Books, *Kim*, and both Puck books—"and good care I took to walk delicately, lest he should withdraw." The following passages concern the birth and evolution of *Kim*.]

[*On the Origins of* Kim]

* * * It[1] stood in a sort of little island behind flint walls which we then thought were high enough, and almost beneath some big ilex trees. It was small, none too well built, but cheap, and so suited us who still remembered a little affair at Yokohama. Then there grew up great happiness between 'The Dene,' 'North End House,' and 'The Elms.' One could throw a cricket-ball from any one house to the other, but, beyond turning out at 2 A.M. to help a silly foxhound puppy who had stuck in a drain, I do not remember any violent alarms and excursions other than packing farm-carts filled with mixed babies—Stanley Baldwin's and ours—and despatching them into the safe clean heart of the motherly Downs for jam-smeared

[†] From *Rudyard Kipling: Something of Myself and Other Autobiographical Writings*, ed. Thomas Pinney (Cambridge: Cambridge University Press, 1990) 81–84, 122–23, 132–33. Copyright © 1990 by Thomas Pinney. Reprinted with the permission of Cambridge University Press.
1. "The Elms," a house Kipling rented in Rottingdean near his cousin Stanley Baldwin's and his Aunt and Uncle Burne-Jones's shortly after the birth of his son. Baldwin was a British statesman and prime minister (1923–24).

273

picnics. Those Downs moved me to write some verses called
'Sussex.' To-day, from Rottingdean to Newhaven is almost fully
developed suburb, of great horror.

When the Burne-Jones' returned to their own 'North End House,'
all was more than well. My Uncle's world was naturally not mine,
but his heart and brain were large enough to take in any universe,
and in the matter of doing one's own work in one's own way he had
no doubts. His golden laugh, his delight in small things, and the
perpetual war of practical jokes that waged between us, was refresh-
ment after working hours. And when we cousins, Phil, his son,
Stanley Baldwin and I, went to the beach and came back with
descriptions of fat bathers, he would draw them, indescribably
swag-bellied, wallowing in the surf. Those were exceedingly good
days, and one's work came easily and fully.

Now even in the Bliss Cottage I had a vague notion of an Irish
boy, born in India and mixed up with native life. I went as far as to
make him the son of a private in an Irish Battalion, and christened
him 'Kim of the 'Rishti'—short, that is, for Irish. This done, I felt
like Mr. Micawber[2] that I had as good as paid that I.O.U. on the
future, and went after other things for some years.

In the meantime my people had left India for good, and were
established in a small stone house near Tisbury, Wilts. It possessed
a neat little stone-walled stable with a shed or two, all perfectly
designed for clay and plaster of Paris works, which are not desired
indoors. Later, the Father put up a tin tabernacle which he had
thatched, and there disposed his drawing portfolios, big photo and
architectural books, gravers, modelling-tools, paints, siccatives, var-
nishes, and the hundred other don't-you-touch-'ems that every
right-minded man who works with his hands naturally collects.
(These matters are detailed because they all come into the story.)

Within short walk of him lay Fonthill, the great house of Arthur
Morrison, millionaire and collector of all manner of beautiful
things, his wife contenting herself with mere precious and sub-
precious stones. And my Father was free of all these treasures, and
many others in such houses as Clouds, where the Wyndhams lived,
a few miles away. I think that both he and my Mother were happy
in their English years, for they knew exactly what they did not want;
and I knew that when I came over to see them I had no need to sing:
'Backward, turn backward, O Time in thy flight.'[3]

In a gloomy, windy autumn *Kim* came back to me with insistence,
and I took it to be smoked over with my Father. Under our united
tobaccos it grew like the Djin released from the brass bottle, and the

2. The improvident character in Charles Dickens's *David Copperfield* (1850) who is always
 taking financial shortcuts.
3. Elizabeth Akers Allen, "Rock Me to Sleep, Mother" (1860), stanza 1.

more we explored its possibilities the more opulence of detail did we discover. I do not know what proportion of an iceberg is below water-line, but *Kim* as it finally appeared was about one-tenth of what the first lavish specification called for.

As to its form there was but one possible to the author, who said that what was good enough for Cervantes was good enough for him.[4] To whom the Mother: 'Don't you stand in your wool-boots hiding behind Cervantes with *me*! You *know* you couldn't make a plot to save your soul.'

So I went home much fortified and *Kim* took care of himself. The only trouble was to keep him within bounds. Between us, we knew every step, sight, and smell on his casual road, as well as all the persons he met. Once only, as I remember, did I have to bother the India Office, where there are four acres of books and documents in the basements, for a certain work on Indian magic which I always sincerely regret that I could not steal. They fuss about receipts there.

At 'The Elms,' Rottingdean, the sou'-wester raged day and night, till the silly windows jiggled their wedges loose. (Which was why the Committee vowed never to have a house of their own with up-and-down windows. Cf. Charles Reade on that subject.) But I was quite unconcerned. I had my Eastern sunlight and if I wanted more I could get it at 'The Gables,' Tisbury. At last I reported *Kim* finished. 'Did *it* stop, or you?' the Father asked. And when I told him that it was *It*, he said: 'Then it oughtn't to be too bad.'

He would take no sort of credit for any of his suggestions, memories or confirmations—not even for that single touch of the low-driving sunlight which makes luminous every detail in the picture of the Grand Trunk Road at eventide. The Himalayas I painted *all* by myself, as the children say. So also the picture of the Lahore Museum of which I had once been Deputy Curator for six weeks—unpaid but immensely important. And there was a half-chapter of the Lama sitting down in the blue-green shadows at the foot of a glacier, telling Kim stories out of the Jatakas,[5] which was truly beautiful but, as my old Classics master would have said, 'otiose,' and it was removed almost with tears.

But the crown of the fun came when (in 1902) was issued an illustrated edition of my works, and the Father attended to *Kim*. He had the notion of making low-relief plaques and photographing them afterwards. Here it was needful to catch the local photographer, who, till then, had specialised in privates of the Line with plastered hair and skin-tight uniforms, and to lead him up the strenu-

4. Kipling refers to the picaresque narrative of episodes on the road characteristic of *Don Quixote* and *Kim*.
5. Narratives of the many births of Buddha.

ous path of photographing dead things so that they might show a lit-
tle life. The man was a bit bewildered at first, but he had a teacher
of teachers, and so grew to understand. The incidental muck-heaps
in the stable-yard were quite noticeable, though a loyal housemaid
fought them broom-and-bucket, and Mother allowed messy half-
born 'sketches' to be dumped by our careless hands on sofas and
chairs. Naturally when he got his final proofs he was sure that 'it all
ought to be done again from the beginning,' which was rather how
I felt about the letterpress, but, if it be possible, he and I will do that
in a better world, and on a scale to amaze Archangels.

There is one picture that I remember of him in the tin taberna-
cle, hunting big photos of Indian architecture for some utterly triv-
ial detail in a corner of some plaque. He looked up as I came in and,
rubbing his beard and carrying on his own thought, quoted: 'If you
get simple beauty and naught else, You get about the best thing God
invents.'[6] It is the greatest of my many blessings that I was given
grace to know them at the time, instead of having them brought to
my remorseful notice too late.

I expect that is why I am perhaps a little impatient over the High
Cannibalism[7] as practised to-day.

And so much for *Kim* which has stood up for thirty-five years.
There was a good deal of beauty in it, and not a little wisdom; the
best in both sorts being owed to my Father.

* * *

[*On Writing with the Help of the "Daemon"*]

> But if he be utterly present, and they swerve not from his
> behest, The word that he gives shall continue, whether in
> earnest or jest.

Most men, and some most unlikely, keep him under an alias which
varies with their literary or scientific attainments. Mine came to me
early when I sat bewildered among other notions, and said: 'Take
this and no other.' I obeyed, and was rewarded. It was a tale in the
little Christmas Magazine *Quartette* which we four wrote together,
and it was called 'The Phantom Rickshaw.' Some of it was weak,
much was bad and out of key; but it was my first serious attempt to
think in another man's skin.

After that I learned to lean upon him and recognise the sign of
his approach. If ever I held back, Ananias fashion, anything of
myself (even though I had to throw it out afterwards) I paid for it by

6. Robert Browning, "Fra Lippo Lippi," lines 217–18.
7. The new vogue of memoir and biography that Kipling saw as a kind of cannibalistic
 devouring of the ancestor.

missing what I *then* knew the tale lacked. As an instance, many years later I wrote about a mediaeval artist, a monastery, and the premature discovery of the microscope. ('The Eye of Allah.') Again and again it went dead under my hand, and for the life of me I could not see why. I put it away and waited. Then said my Daemon—and I was meditating something else at the time—'Treat it as an illuminated manuscript.' I had ridden off on hard black-and-white decoration, instead of pumicing the whole thing ivory-smooth, and loading it with thick colour and gilt. Again, in a South African, post–Boer War tale called 'The Captive,' which was built up round the phrase 'a first-class dress parade for Armageddon,' I could not get my lighting into key with the tone of the monologue. The background insisted too much. My Daemon said at last: 'Paint the background first once for all, as hard as a public-house sign, and leave it alone.' This done, the rest fell into place with the American accent and outlook of the teller.

My Daemon was with me in the *Jungle Books*, *Kim*, and both Puck books, and good care I took to walk delicately, lest he should withdraw. I know that he did not, because when those books were finished they said so themselves with, almost, the water-hammer click of a tap turned off. One of the clauses in our contract was that I should never follow up 'a success,' for by this sin fell Napoleon and a few others. *Note here.* When your Daemon is in charge, do not try to think consciously. Drift, wait, and obey.

* * *

[On Kim]

Kim, of course, was nakedly picaresque and plotless—a thing imposed from without.

Yet I dreamed for many years of building a veritable three-decker out of chosen and long-stored timber—teak, green-heart, and ten-year-old oak knees—each curve melting deliciously into the next that the sea might nowhere meet resistance or weakness; the whole suggesting motion even when, her great sails for the moment furled, she lay in some needed haven—a vessel ballasted on ingots of pure research and knowledge, roomy, fitted with delicate cabinet-work below-decks, painted, carved, gilt and wreathed the length of her, from her blazing stern-galleries outlined by bronzy palm-trunks, to her rampant figure-head—an East Indiaman worthy to lie alongside *The Cloister and the Hearth*.

Not being able to do this, I dismissed the ambition as 'beneath the thinking mind.' So does a half-blind man dismiss shooting and golf.

CHARLES CARRINGTON

[The Origins of *Kim*]†

* * *

The valediction to [Kipling's] old life was the publication of *Kim*, his last word on India, so many times laid aside, so long on the anvil. Ten years had passed since he had been an Anglo-Indian by right of service, ten years in which much had happened in India which he never appreciated. Lord Curzon invited him to Simla as a guest in 1899, but viceroys, he said, were not much in his line. India remained, in his eyes, the unchanging East, as he remembered it from childhood, and so he described it, lovingly, in *Kim*.

The new book owed something to his youthful romance, *Mother Maturin*, but how much cannot be told since no one now living has read the earlier work. Mrs Hill gave the following account of it:

> *Mother Maturin* I have read, which was never published because John Lockwood Kipling was not satisfied with it. It is the story of an old Irishwoman who kept an opium den in Lahore but sent her daughter to be educated in England. She married a Civilian and came to live in Lahore—hence a story how Government secrets came to be known in the Bazaar and *vice versa*.[1]

In London Rudyard had turned to *Mother Maturin* again, and then perhaps realized that his father had judged rightly in condemning it. The manuscript remained for years in the safe at A. P. Watt's office until in 1899 Rudyard brought it down to Rottingdean to ransack it for notions which he could work into *Kim*. Thereafter *Mother Maturin* vanished, probably destroyed by the author, though many years later Kipling prepared a draft for a film scenario which contained episodes from the old story.

The second plan for an Indian Romance took shape at 'Naulakha' in 1894. Now it was to be the life-story of *Kim O'rishti*, an Irish soldier's orphan, living foot-loose in India. Three times begun and laid aside, it was abandoned in favour of *Captains Courageous*. In the fall of 1899, having finished with *Stalky*, he turned again to *Kim*. Many times he took the draft down to Tisbury to be smoked over

† We gratefully acknowledge permission to reprint from *Rudyard Kipling, His Life and Works* by Charles Carrington, pp. 422–28, published by Penguin, 1986. Originally published in 1955 by Macmillan & Co. Ltd., London.

1. *Catalogue of English and American Authors, issued by the American Art Association*, 30 April 1921.

with the 'Pater' until in August 1900 Carrie wrote triumphantly in her diary that it was pronounced complete by a family council, which included the 'Pater' and Sallie Norton.

* * *

Kim was published at the end of 1900 about the time of the 'Khaki Election',[2] when public opinion was sharply divided over the political views with which Kipling's name was linked, and so did not at first produce the chorus of applause which had greeted some of his earlier work. There was some hostile, and more of cool and grudging, criticism like that of Arnold Bennett, who said in an essay: '*Stalky* chilled me and *Kim* killed me.'[3] Since then the book has grown in stature and is often now selected as the Kipling book with the highest measure of artistry. It is, however, in the author's own words, not a novel but 'nakedly picaresque and plotless'.

Surely no other Englishman has written of India with such loving interest! Mr Forster's *Passage to India* is the only work which can be laid beside it, and in many respects *Kim* comes well out of the comparison. In this instance Forster, not Kipling, is the political writer, the observer of a passing phase. With his cool, sensitive regard Forster appraises the Indian character and the Indian scene, noting conscious and unconscious processes, analysing with a skill that Kipling did not and could not attempt to equal. In the cold light of Forster's observation all is clear and all unlovable.

Kim is not a political romance; the reader soon loses interest in a plot which the author does not trouble to elaborate. The education of a police spy—and that is what, superficially, *Kim* seems to be about—is hardly a subject for an *epos*; nor does it much matter. The hero, Kim, is thrown by this path into the vagabond life of India so that we may see, and smell, the hot scented dust and the people of the land. Here is a boy roving through India, loving it and causing us to love it. Politics, the Empire, the Law, are taken for granted. It is not 'Kim's' affair, nor the reader's, to question the credentials of the *Pax Britannica*, but to savour life within its borders. Nothing is explained or excused or justified.

Apart from a slight sketch of Lockwood Kipling ('the Keeper of the Wonder-house') in the opening chapter, Englishmen do not play a conspicuous part in the story. 'Bennett', the English Chaplain, is

2. The British Conservative government used the "Khaki election" of 1900 to overthrow the anti-imperial Liberal opponents to such colonial wars of expansion as the South African (or Boer) War of 1899–1902. This was also the time that Kipling's friend Theodore Roosevelt began to use the gun-slinging cowboy as an American emblem of individual enterprise [*Editor*].

3. A. Bennett, *Books and Persons*, 1917.

shown in an unfavourable light, and the Irish Chaplain, though less unpleasing, is merely a stock figure.[4] The drummer-boy who chums with 'Kim' in barracks is allowed none of the charm which, in spite of their depravity, was conceded to the 'Drums of the Fore and Aft'.[5] 'Lurgan, the healer of sick pearls,' is a nondescript, not a true *sahib*. Kim's kindly patron, 'Colonel Creighton', is kept in the background.

The interest is all concentrated upon Kim's relation with four natives of India: the Pathan horse-dealer, Mahbub Ali; the Bengali, Hurree Chunder; the old dowager *sahiba* from Saharunpore; and the Tibetan lama who steals the limelight to become hero of the book. The lean ferocious Pathan and the suave sophisticated Babu seem at first to be stock characters, until they burst into life by showing the contradictions of living persons. The faithless, cruel Mahbub is gradually revealed as true and even tender; the volatile, timid Babu as discreet and courageous when put to the test; and the interaction of these characters illumines Kim's slow adolescence. This is a display of the novelist's art which Kipling rarely achieved in his other works (unless perhaps in that juvenile *tour de force, The Story of the Gadsbys*). There was a real Mahbub Ali, as Kay Robinson put on record; Babus looking like Hurree Chunder are plentiful in Calcutta to this day, but the *sahiba* and the lama were original inventions, new in literature. The *sahiba* was the first full-length in Kipling's gallery of elderly women, a group worth examining. The lama has no literary ancestry or progeny; he is Kipling's final comment on Buddhist Asia.

The author dwells lovingly upon some minor characters, the Jat, the Ressaldar, the 'Woman of Shamlegh' (who had made an earlier appearance as 'Lispeth' in *Plain Tales*); but all disappear from the scene before the end, leaving the stage to Kim and the lama, the two principals. The lama withdraws his mind into the world of reality, having rejected all the appearances of the world of illusion, even such symbols of infinity as his beloved Hills. Kim, too, has reached a stage of maturity and must make a decision. No longer a ragamuffin of the bazaars, but a beautiful godlike youth, he must choose

4. Kipling's views on missionaries, when he was a young man, are expressed in a letter written from 'Naulakha' to the Rev J. Gillespie, on 16 October 1895. The original is in the Houghton Library.

 'It is my fortune to have been born and to a large extent brought up among those whom white men call "heathen"; and while I recognize the paramount duty of every white man to follow the teachings of his creed and conscience as "a debtor to the whole law", it seems to me cruel that white men, whose governments are armed with the most murderous weapons known to science, should amaze and confound their fellow creatures with a doctrine of salvation imperfectly understood by themselves and a code of ethics foreign to the climate and instincts of those races whose most cherished customs they outrage and whose gods they insult.'

5. A story about two drummer boys in the "Fore and Aft" regiment whose drunken bravado turns potential defeat in battle into victory [*Editor*].

between contemplation and action. Is he to follow the lama or to return to the chains which enslave the Pathan and the Babu to their material duties? Divided in loyalty, like Mowgli between the Village and the Jungle, living like the Brushwood Boy on two mental planes, he can be more conscious of the marriage of East and West than the Calcutta-trained Babu or the Pathan who has learned to outwit the English by their own devices.[6] In the last stage of the lama's pilgrimage Kim quite forgets his own task in the world, while absorbed in the humble duty of love and gratitude.

> He begged in the dawn, set blankets for the lama's meditation, held the weary head on his lap through the noonday heats, fanning away the flies till his wrists ached, begged again the evenings, and rubbed the lama's feet, who rewarded him with promise of Freedom—today, tomorrow, or, at furthest, the next day.

And when that day came, it was the lama who reminded Kim that he was a *sahib* with another course of life to pursue. Again the dilemma was presented, East or West, the Jungle or the Village, the world of dreams or the world of action; and, though it is not expressly stated, the reader is left with the assurance that Kim, like Mowgli, and like the Brushwood Boy, will find reality in action, not in contemplation.

> With an almost audible click, he felt the wheels of his being lock up anew on the world without. Things that rode meaningless on the eyeball an instant before slid into proper proportion. Roads were meant to be walked upon, houses to be lived in, cattle to be driven, fields to be tilled, and men and women to be talked to. They were all real and true.

The desire to penetrate the occult exercised a strong fascination over Rudyard throughout life, an attraction which he resisted, not altogether successfully. In this respect Rudyard was a man of his day, interested in what interested his contemporaries, a reader of the numerous novels and poems that touched on these themes. His youth was passed in a circle where Madame Blavatsky and the early Theosophists had made no small impression. Later he was a friend of William James and acquainted with the speculations which, in 1902, were to be formulated in the *Varieties of Religious Experience*, the book which made a rational analysis of Eastern and Western mysticism.

The study of the irrational, the subliminal, the supernormal made great strides after the Viennese psychologists had found the key to

6. Mowgli (in the *Jungle Books*) and Georgie (in "The Brushwood Boy") both experience Kiplingesque divisions between opposing worlds, values, desires, and demands [*Editor*].

the unconscious mind, with the consequence that many of the phenomena which the men of the eighteen-nineties regarded as supernatural were examined by the men of the nineteen-twenties in terms of the new psychology. Rudyard's later stories were to provide some evidence of his movement with this stream of thought.

Contemporary Reviews

J. H. MILLAR

[A 'New Kipling']†

In discussing a few of the novels of the last six months or so, it is right and proper, on many accounts, which it were superfluous to specify, that due precedence should be awarded to Mr. Kipling. *Kim* is in some respects his most ambitious and elaborate work, and having, we confess, 'shied' at *Stalky & Co.*, we fell with a double portion of alacrity upon a 'new Kipling' which held out hopes of proving equal to the old ones. Nor have we been disappointed. Mr. Kipling has decidedly 'acquired merit' by this his latest essay. There is fascination, almost magic, in every page of the delightful volume, whose attractiveness is enhanced by illustrations of (to our mind) superlative excellence.

* * *

The character of Kim is from first to last a masterly conception. As a study of adolescence—of the progress from boyhood to youth, and from youth to early manhood—it is incomparably fresh and true: full of the delight of the artificer in the work of his hands, of the joy that comes from nothing so much as from the sense of successful achievement. The pride of the labourer in a task well performed has always been a congenial and favourite theme with Mr. Kipling; and we know of no other which, once duly appreciated, is likely to do so much for the maintenance of our Empire in all its manifold interests. Over and above Kim, there is a portrait-gallery of unusual extent and interest. Mahbub Ali, the old Ressaldar, the Rajah's widow, and Baboo Hurree, are the chief of those who find a place in it. And in the background there is always the impressive figure of the lama, whose mysterious apophthegms about the Wheel and the most Excellent Law form a deep and solemn accompaniment, as it were, to the music of the whole composition. You do not

† From *Blackwood's Magazine*, December 1901, pp. 793–95.

stop to inquire whether he or any one else is true to life. You *know* they are; you accept them all without question or reservation or cavil. That absolute perfection, however, may not be predicated of his work, Mr. Kipling has been obliging enough to throw in a couple of characters of whom so much cannot be said. Both Mr. Bennett, the Anglican, and Father Victor, the Roman Catholic chaplain, strike us as being conventional and commonplace—just the sort of personages whom we have learned to expect from Mr. Kipling's imitators.

But it is neither in the fable (exciting and ingenious though it be) nor in the portrayal of character (however skilful and convincing) that the charm of *Kim* consists. Its secret lies in the wonderful panorama it unrolls before us of the life of the great Peninsula over whose government England has now presided for more than a century. We despair of giving our readers any adequate conception of the glorious variety of the feast here spread before them. The kaleidoscopic quality, if we may venture so to call it, of Mr. Kipling's genius, has never before been displayed on so extensive a scale or to such great advantage. Turn to the description of the wayfarers on the Grand Trunk Road (too long, unfortunately, for transcription here), and consider for a moment the patient industry, the protracted observation, the thorough knowledge, which go to the making of these three pages. The thought is merely astounding; and one feels inclined in one's bewilderment to fall back upon the convenient and plausible theory that Mr. Kipling knows everything by instinct. That he knew much of native life we were aware already, but how much he knew we had not—perhaps have not yet—fathomed. Take one of the Strickland series of his stories: expand it, strengthen it, add indefinite multiplicity of detail to it; and you have the formula for producing a *Kim*. But let the adventurous aspirant see that his hand is well 'in' before he tries it.

WILLIAM MORTON PAYNE

[Mr. Kipling's Enthralling New Novel]†

* * *

Mr. Kipling's new novel is a story of the India that he knows so well—a story entirely without love-making or other sentimental interest of the conventional sort, yet singularly enthralling. It is

† From "Recent Fiction," *The Dial* 31 (November 16, 1901): 368.

entitled "Kim," which is the name of the principal character. Kim is
a child of Irish parentage, cast as a waif upon the sea of Indian life
when an infant, and growing up under native influences. He is a
preternaturally shrewd little beggar, and has had to learn the lesson
of living by his wits from his earliest years. Although he speaks
English, he prefers Hindostanee, and the racial traits that are his by
inheritance seem to have been almost wholly submerged. They
reappear after it is discovered that he is Kimball O'Hara, the son of
a former soldier, and when his education is taken in hand by his
father's regiment. His unusual gifts are marked out by certain gov-
ernment officials, and he is put in training for the Secret Service, in
which department we feel quite sure that he will become distin-
guished, although the book ends when he is upon the threshold of
his new career. The story offers us a great variety of Oriental types
of race and character, including the winning personality of a
Thibetan holy man, seeking through long years and in strange lands
for the river of cleansing whereby he may gain the longed-for release
from the Wheel of Change. The Buddhist attitude toward life is very
sympathetically figured in this venerable character, who seems to us
quite as interesting as Kim himself. It is needless to say that few
Europeans understand the workings of the Oriental mind as Mr.
Kipling understands them, and far fewer have his gift of imparting
the understanding to their readers. Among English writers, he has
been matched by Mrs. Steel, but hardly by any other in our day.

* * *

ARTHUR BARTLETT MAURICE

Rudyard Kipling's *Kim*†

Probably every reader of THE BOOKMAN has at some time in the last
six months asked some other BOOKMAN reader, "Are you reading
Kim serially?" and the other has, of course, made the inevitable
reply, "I have tried to, but somehow I don't seem to be able to get
into it." And then the two have put their heads together and asked
each other confidentially what it was all about, finally coming to the
conclusion that they did not know, but that they might possibly be
able to decide when the story appeared in book form. And there, in
a nutshell, you have the whole case of Mr. Kipling's latest book. His
"last book" seems to have been written about three years ago.

† From "Seven Books of Some Importance," *The Bookman* 14 (October 1901): 146–49.

There are two ways in which a reviewer for THE BOOKMAN might write about *Kim*. It might be treated merely as one of the extraordinarily large crop of autumn novels, relegated to the department called Novel Notes, and dismissed with two or three hundred words of cursory explanation. In that case one would probably find some very pleasant words to say. The author would be applauded for his very minute and exact knowledge of Asiatic life and Oriental superstition. He would be told, perhaps with a certain bumptious impertinence, that he had not written a novel, and a large amount of advice would be ladled out to him in a few words. His style might have caused one to think twice about the book, but the chances are that it would have been "passed on" and then promptly forgotten, as are the general run of mediocre novels in the office of the literary magazine. However, one cannot very well do that. Whatever *Kim* may be, it is Mr. Kipling's.

There was, once upon a time—somehow it seems very many years ago—a young man who left his home in English India and came to Europe and America, bringing with him a dressing-case, filled with the manuscripts of marvellous tales about soldiers and civilians. He went through the conventional rough experience which befalls most literary aspirants. He knocked at editors' doors, and was kept waiting in the anteroom. His manuscripts were glanced at briefly and loftily. He was told that they were too short, or too long, or that they lacked "the love interest," or that nobody knew or cared anything about India anyway; and, worse still, many of them were probably very often handed back to him without any comment or criticism whatever. Occasionally, however, a story or a bit of stray verse found its way into print; and after a time a few discerning literary men began calling people's attention to the real promise and the remarkably original work being done by a young man by the name of Kipling. Some of his stories, which had appeared in obscure newspapers in India, were gathered together and made into books in England; and for one of these volumes an introduction was written by no less a literary personage than Mr. Andrew Lang, who prophesied that, although Rudyard Kipling would never make any great popular success, he would have the satisfaction of knowing that his work would always be appreciated by a select few.

Suddenly fame came. The Man from Nowhere began to be talked about everywhere; his books were passed from hand to hand, and people were telling one another that a new star had risen in the literary sky—a star of the first magnitude. All the English-reading world seemed to catch the mood, and Mrs. Hauksbee and Mrs. Reiver and Mulvaney and Ortheris and Lleroyd became by-words. Here was a young genius caught in the open and brought in to overturn the old order of things. He came defiantly and imperiously. He

scattered broadcast his treasures of wit and humour and observation. He laughed at tradition; began at the beginning or at the middle or at the end, as suited him; he flung before you descriptions of the East that made you smell its incense, hear its sounds and feel all its mystery and wonder. Everything seemed to be done without effort; there never was any straining after effect; words rushed, all hot and flaming and poignant, from his pen. He made you share with him the sheer joy and gaiety of life, or he led you, shuddering, to the very edge of some fearful abyss. That, in a word, was the Mr. Kipling of other days whom men deservedly called great. Unfortunately, it is not the Mr. Kipling of to-day.

It should be understood that mediocre and meaningless as *Kim* is, it is not to be classed with some of Mr. Kipling's other recent literary efforts—especially with some attempts at verse of which he has of late been guilty. For instance, there was "The Lesson," an alleged poem, which treated of England's political and military mistakes in the war in the Transvaal. Now, "The Lesson" was absolutely and flatly unspeakable bosh. We are quite serious and sincere when we say that as a poem it was as senseless as the average poetical effusion of Mr. J. Gordon Coogler. Of course, *Kim* is nothing like this. Here and there in the book there are little bits of dialogue, fragments of description, of which Mr. Kipling alone is capable. Only the virile spirit to give them life seems lacking. When we meet Kim of the Rishti he is sitting astride of a cannon outside the Lahore Museum; a brown-skinned, vernacular-speaking little Oriental, whose Caucasian blood shows only in the manner in which he reviles and tyrannises over his native comrades. His father had been Kimball O'Hara, a young colour sergeant of the Irish Regiment of the Mavericks, and his mother a nurse-maid in a colonel's family. She died of cholera, and O'Hara fell to drink, then drifted away to learn the taste of opium, and finally to die as poor whites die in India. His estate at his death consisted of three papers—one he called his "Ne varietur," because those words were written below his signature thereon, and the other his "clearance certificate." The third was Kim's birth certificate. And these were the things he used to say in his glorious opium hours that would yet make little Kimball a man. As we find Kim at first, we find him pretty much throughout the book. He is a typical Kipling boy, a gutter brother to Jakin and Lew, the little drummers, who marched to their death in the story of "The Drums of the Fore and Aft," who were in turn cousins to the Gavroche of *Les Misérables*. The most striking characteristic in the Kipling gamin is his spirit of insubordination. The expression, in some manner or other, of this spirit of insubordination seems to be his chief joy. If ladies pet him and make much of him, he waits until their backs are turned, and then finds huge delight in caustic criticism of their looks and morals. If he is attached

to the army in some capacity or other, he will obey explicit orders well enough, but it is purely a limited obedience, born of an innate *esprit de corps*. After his insubordination there is his intimate and precocious acquaintance with matters of which he ought to know nothing. Kim, like Jakin and Lew, had at his tongue's end a fund of the most astounding profanity. He was ready with strange oaths in English and stranger oaths in the vernacular. He had an easy and comfortable acquaintance with places, the very mention of which would have caused shudders of horror to have run up and down the spinal columns of his preceptors. But Kim, unlike Jakin and Lew, possessed a deep reverence, which came of his Oriental training. It was this reverence which caused him to desert the alleys and bazaars of Lahore, and, partly as guide and partly as servitor, to follow the fortunes of a wandering lama from Tibet. The story tells of a Buddhistic legend of how Buddha, making a trial of strength with the bow and arrow against all comers, overshot all other marks, the arrow passing far and far beyond sight. At last it fell; and, where it touched earth, there broke out a stream which presently became a river, whose nature is that whoso bathes in it washes away all taint and speckle of sin. It is of this river that the lama is in search, and together he and Kim wander about India, huddled in third-class railway carriages or sleeping in the open under the stars. In the course of time they stumble upon the Irish Regiment in which Kim's father, years before, had been a colour sergeant. By the three inherited papers which Kim carries in a bag, which he wears around his neck, the paternity of the boy is discovered; and, despite his strenuous objections, he is adopted by the regiment, and finally sent away to be educated at a school in Lucknow. There are in Kim wonderful natural talents for the work of the Indian Secret Service; and these talents, which have been sharpened in early years by his share in the intrigues of native life, are soon perceived by those who have taken charge of his career. In one of his vacations he is sent to stay for a time with an Englishman named Lurgan, whose business it is to train men, both English and natives, for the work of the Secret Service, and there his powers of observation are systematically developed.

Through the afternoons he and the Hindu boy would mount guard in the shop, sitting dumb behind a carpet bale or a screen, and watching the many and very curious visitors who came to buy curiosities. There were small Rajahs, their escorts coughing in the veranda, who came to buy curiosities—phonographs and French mechanical toys. There were ladies in search of necklaces, and men, it seemed to Kim—but his mind may have been vitiated by early training—in search of the ladies; natives from independent and feudatory courts, whose ostensible business was the repair of broken necklaces—rivers

of light poured out upon the table—but whose real end seemed
to be to raise money for angry Maharanees or young Rajahs.
There were Babus, to whom Lurgan Sahib talked with auster-
ity and authority, but at the end of each interview he gave them
money in coined silver and currency notes. There were occa-
sional gatherings of long-coated theatrical natives, who talked
metaphysics in English and Bengali, to Mr. Lurgan's great edi-
fication. He was always interested in religion. At the end of the
day Kim and the Hindu boy—whose name varied at Lurgan's
pleasure—were expected to give a detailed account of all that
they had seen and heard—their view of each man's character,
as shown in his face, talk and manner, and their notions of his
real business. After dinner Lurgan Sahib's fancy turned more to
what might be called dressing-up, in which game he took the
most informing interest. He could paint faces to a marvel; with
a brush dab here and a line there changing them past recogni-
tion. The shop was full of all manner of dresses and turbans,
and Kim was apparelled variously as a young Mohammedan of
good family, an oilman, and once—which was a joyous
evening—as the son of an Oudh landholder in the fullest of full
dress. Lurgan Sahib had a hawk's eye to detect the least flaw in
the make-up.

Throughout his school days Kim has kept up his friendship with
the lama—indeed, it was the lama who had furnished the money
that had enabled Kim's English guardians to send him to St.
Xavier's, instead of to a cheaper and inferior school—and when he
is thought to be fitted to begin work at the Great Game and receive
a minor official position, he and the lama begin again their wander-
ings about India, Kim to gather information and to communicate
with his fellow-workers of the Secret Service, and the lama to
search untiringly for the river of the arrow. A character who recalls
in a measure the Kipling of other days is Hurree Babu. In him we
have the deliciously pompous speech of the educated Asiatic.

Hurree Babu snapped his fingers with irritation. "Of
course I shall affeeliate myself to their camp in supernumerary
capacity as perhaps interpreter or person mentally impotent
and hungree, or some such thing. And then I must pick up
what I can, I suppose. That is as easy for me as playing Mister
Doctor to the old lady. Onlee—onlee—you see, Mister O'Hara,
I am, unfortunately, Asiatic, which is a serious detriment in
some respects. And *all*so I am Bengali—a fearful man."

"God made the hàre and the Bengali. What shame?" said
Kim, quoting the proverb.

"It was process of Evolution, *I* think, from Primal
Necessity, but the fact remains in all its *cui bono*. I am, oh,

awfully fearful—I remember once they wanted to cut off my head on the road to Lhassa. (No, I have never reached to Lhassa.) I sat down and cried, Mister O'Hara, anticipating Chinese tortures. I do not suppose these two gentlemen will torture me, but I like to provide for possible contingency with European assistance in emergency." He coughed, and spat out the cardamoms. "It is purely unoffeecial request, to which you can say 'No, Babu.' If you have no pressing engagement with your old man—perhaps you might divert him; perhaps I can seduce his fancies—I should like you to keep in Departmental touch with me—till I find those sporting coves. I have great opeenion of you since I met my friend at Delhi. And also I will embody your name in my offeecial report when matter is finally adjudicated. It will be a great feather in your cap. That is why I come really."

Hurree Babu is also employed in playing the Great Game; and he and Kim lay plans for the discomfiture of a Russian and a Frenchman, who were spying and conspiring in Northern India. They succeed in effectually worrying the strangers, in rousing their retinue of natives to mutiny, and in stealing the plans and papers which have been acquired after months of labour. In an outburst of passion the Russian strikes the venerable lama, and it is the shame of this blow that hastens the old man's death. With this death the story ends, and the history of Kim's later career is left to the imagi- nation of the reader. And there you have *Kim*, a jumble of native phrases, of extraneous conversations, of Eastern mysticism, redeemed and brought into a certain concrete form by that craft which Mr. Kipling could not fail to acquire in the years of his apprenticeship and of his genius. It is all so cold, so dead, so life- less. Mr. Kipling seems to have gone raking through the cinders of his youth in search of the bits of half-burned coals with which to make a little flame and warmth. The old spontaneous fire seems so irrevocably gone.

NOBEL PRIZE COMMITTEE

The Nobel Prize for Literature, 1907[†]

The suggestions for names of suitable recipients of this year's Nobel Prize in Literature have been numerous, and there has been no

† Written by C. D. of Wirsén, Permanent Secretary of the Swedish Academy. From *Nobel Lectures*, Literature 1901–1967.

dearth of exceedingly well-qualified candidates for this honourable and coveted distinction.

From these candidates, the Swedish Academy has selected for this occasion a writer who belongs to Great Britain. For centuries past the literature of England has flourished and blossomed with marvellous luxuriance. When Tennyson's immortal lyre was silenced forever, the cry which is so customary at the passing of literary giants was raised. With him the glorious reign of poetry is over; there is none to take up the mantle. Similar despairing notes were struck in this country on the demise of Tegnér, but it is not so with the fair goddess Poetry. She does not perish, is not deposed from her high estate; she but arrays herself in a fresh garb to suit the altered tastes of a new age.

In the works of Tennyson idealism is so pervasive that it meets the eye in a very palpable and direct form. Traits of idealism, however, may be traced in the conceptions and gifts of writers who differ widely from him, such writers who seem primarily concerned with mere externals and who have won renown especially for their vivid word-picturings of the various phases of the strenuous, pulsating life of our own times, that life which is often chequered and fretted by the painful struggle for existence and by all its concomitant worries and embarrassments. This description applies to Rudyard Kipling, to whom the Swedish Academy has awarded the Nobel Prize in Literature this year. Of him a French author, who has devoted much time and study to English literature, wrote more than six years ago: "He, Kipling, is undoubtedly the most noteworthy figure that has appeared within recent years in the domain of English literature."

Kipling was born in Bombay on December 30, 1865. At the age of six he was placed in the care of some relatives in England, but he returned to India on reaching the age of seventeen. He obtained a position on the staff of *The Civil and Military Gazette*, published at Lahore, and in his early twenties edited *The Pioneer* at Allahabad. In his capacity as a journalist, and for his own purposes, he travelled extensively throughout India. On those journeys he acquired a thorough insight into Hindu conceptions and sentiments and became intimately acquainted with the different Hindu groups, with their varying customs and institutions, and with the special features of English military life in India. This firm grasp of the true inwardness of all things Indian is abundantly reflected in Kipling's writings, so much so that it has even been said that they have brought India nearer home to the English nation than has the construction of the Suez Canal. Of his early works the satirical *Departmental Ditties* (1886) attracted notice by the audacity of the allusions it contained, and by the originality of its tone. Also among

the early productions are *Plain Tales from the Hills* (1888) and *Soldiers Three* (1888), collections of stories famous among other things for the three lovingly drawn soldier types: Mulvaney, Ortheris, and Learoyd. Other works in the same category are, for instance, *The Story of the Gadsbys* (1888), *In Black and White* (1888), and *Under the Deodars* (1889), all of which are concerned with society life in Simla. The series entitled *Life's Handicap*, embracing some stories of serious import, appeared in 1891. The same year saw the publication of *The Light that Failed*, a novel somewhat harsh in style but containing some strongly coloured descriptive passages of excellent effect.

As a poet Kipling was already full-fledged at the appearance of *Barrack Room Ballads* (1892), magnificent soldier-songs brimming over with virile humour and depicting realistically Tommy Atkins in all his phases, valiantly marching onward to encounter dangers and misery wherever it pleases "the Widow of Windsor", or her successor on the throne, to dispatch him. In Kipling the British Army has found a minstrel to interpret in a new, original, and tragicomical manner the toils and deprivations through which it has to pass, and to depict its life and work with abundant acknowledgment of the great qualities it displays, but without the least trace of meretricious embellishment. In his verses descriptive of soldiers and sailors he so happily expresses their own thoughts, often in the very language they themselves employ, that they appreciate him deeply and, as we are told, sing his song whenever they have a pause in the day's occupations. Surely, there is hardly any greater mark of honour that can be given to a poet than to be beloved by the lower orders.

In the cycle entitled *The Seven Seas* (1896) Kipling reveals himself as an imperialist, a citizen of a world-wide empire. He has undoubtedly done more than any other writer of pure literature to draw tighter the bonds of union between England and her colonies.

In Sweden, as elsewhere, "the jungle books" by Kipling, the first of which appeared in 1894, are much admired and beloved. A primordial type of imaginative power inspired the creator of these mythlike tales of the animals in whose midst Mowgli waxed in strength: Bagheera the Black Panther, Baloo the Bear, Kaa the cunning and mighty Rock-Python, Nag the White Cobra, and the chattering, foolish Monkeys. Some of the scenes are simply sublime; for instance, the one where Mowgli is resting in "the living armchair" Kaa, while the latter, who has witnessed so many generations of trees and animals, dreams of bygone ages; or again when Mowgli causes Hathi the Elephant to "let in the jungle" to take over the fields of men. These descriptions display an instinctive feeling for a poetry of nature which is quite phenomenal, and Kipling is far more in his true element in the primeval grandeur of these jungle stories

than, for instance, in "The Ship that Found Herself" (in *The Day's Work*, 1898), an interesting though eccentric personification of mechanical inventions. *The Jungle Book* tales have made Kipling a favourite author among children in many countries. Adults share the delight experienced by the young and relive their childhood while perusing these marvellously delightful, wonderfully imaginative fables of animals.

Among the large number of Kipling's creations, *Kim* (1901) deserves special notice, for in the delineation of the Buddhist priest, who goes on a pilgrimage along the banks of the stream that purifies from sin, there is an elevated diction as well as a tenderness and charm which are otherwise unusual traits in this dashing writer's style. There is, too, in the figure of the little rascal Kim, the priest's chela, a thorough type of good-humoured roguishness.

The accusation has occasionally been made against Kipling that his language is at times somewhat coarse and that his use of soldier's slang in some of the broadest of his songs and ballads verges on the vulgar. Though there may be some truth in such remarks, their importance is offset by the invigorating directness and ethical stimulus of Kipling's style. He has won immense popularity, not only in the Anglo-Indian world, which possesses in him a great literary master, but also far beyond the limits of the vast British Empire. During his serious illness in America in 1899, the American newspapers issued daily bulletins regarding his condition, and the German Emperor dispatched a telegram to his wife to express his earnest sympathy.

What is then the cause of this world-wide popularity that Kipling enjoys? Or, rather: In what way has Kipling shown himself to deserve it? How is it, too, that he has been deemed worthy of the Nobel Prize in Literature, for which a writer must especially show an idealism in his conceptions and in his art? The answer follows:

Kipling may not be eminent essentially for the profundity of his thought or for the surpassing wisdom of his meditations. Yet even the most cursory observer sees immediately his absolutely unique power of observation, capable of reproducing with astounding accuracy the minutest detail from real life. However, the gift of observation alone, be it ever so closely true to nature, would not suffice as a qualification in this instance. There is something else by which his poetical gifts are revealed. His marvellous power of imagination enables him to give us not only copies from nature but also visions out of his own inner consciousness. His landscapes appear to the inner vision as sudden apparitions do to the eye. In sketching a personality he makes clear, almost in his first words, the peculiar traits of that person's character and temper. Creativeness which does not rest content with merely photographing the temporary phases of

things but desires to penetrate to their inmost kernel and soul, is the basis of his literary activity, as Kipling himself says: "He draws the thing as he sees it for the God of things as they are." In these weighty words lies a real appreciation of the poet's responsibility in the exercise of his calling.

Rudyard Kipling's manly, at times brusque, energy does not preclude tenderness and delicacy of touch, though these qualities never clamour affectedly for recognition in his works. The simple "Story of Muhammad Din" is imbued with the poetry of genuine heartfelt emotion, and who can ever forget the little drummer boys in "The Taking of Lungtumpen" (in *Plain Tales*)?

In the innermost being of this indefatigable observer of life and human nature vibrate strings attuned to a lofty note. His poem "To the True Romance" reveals that yearning for a patiently sought, never to be attained ideal that resides in living form in the breast of every true poet, from where the scenes and impressions of the sensuous world can never dislodge it:

> *Enough for me in dreams to see*
> *And touch thy garment's hem:*
> *Thy feet have trod so near to God*
> *I may not follow them!*

This writer's philosophy of life is diffused with a piety characteristic of the Old Testament, or rather perhaps of Puritan times, wholly devoid of pretentiousness or wordiness, based upon a conviction that "the fear of the Lord is the beginning of wisdom" and that there exists a

> *God of our fathers, known of old,*
> *Beneath whose awful Hand we hold*
> *Dominion . . .*

If Kipling is an idealist from an aesthetic point of view by reason of poetical intuition, he is so, too, from an ethical-religious standpoint by virtue of his sense of duty, which has its inspiration in a faith firmly rooted in conviction. He is acutely conscious of the truth that even the mightiest states would perish unless they rested upon the sure foundation in the citizens' hearts of a loyal observance of the law and a reasoned self-restraint. For Kipling, God is first and foremost Almighty Providence, termed in *Life's Handicap* a "Greet Overseer". The English as a nation can well appreciate these conceptions, and Kipling has become the nation's poet, owing not only to his numerous highly prized soldier-songs, but perhaps quite as much to the brief lines of the hymn ("Recessional") which he composed on the occasion of Queen Victoria's Diamond Jubilee in 1897. Especially striking are these words expressing genuine and humble religious feelings:

The tumult and the shouting dies;
The Captains and the Kings depart:
Still stands Thine ancient sacrifice,
An humble and a contrite heart.

The recessional hymn voices the spirit of national pride, yet it also conveys a warning against the dangers of presumptuous pride . . .

Quite naturally, during the Boer War Kipling sided with his own nation, the English. He has, however, done full justice to the heroic courage of the Boers, for his imperialism is not of the uncompromising type that pays no regard to the sentiments of others.

Many and varied are the movements that have had their vogue in English literature, a literature unparalleled for wealth of output and adorned to surpass all others by the immortal figure of Shakespeare. In Kipling may be traced perhaps more of Swift and Defoe than of Spenser, Keats, Shelley, or Tennyson. Clearly, however, imagination is as strong in him as empirical observation. Though he does not possess the refined and sensuously beautiful style of Swinburne, yet he escapes, on the other hand, all tendency toward a pagan worship of pleasure for pleasure's sake. He avoids all morbid sentimentality in matter and Alexandrian superflorescence in form.

Kipling favours concreteness and concentration; empty abstractions and circumlocutionary descriptions are wholly absent from his works. He has a knack for finding the telling phrase, the characteristic epithet, with swift accuracy and certainty. He has been compared now to Bret Harte, now to Pierre Loti, now to Dickens; he is, however, always original, and it would seem that his powers of invention are inexhaustible. Nevertheless, the apostle of the imagination is likewise, as stated above, the standard-bearer of law-abidingness and discipline. The Laws of the Jungle are the Laws of the Universe; if we ask what their chief purport is, we shall receive the brief answer: "Struggle, Duty, Obedience". Kipling thus advocates courage, self-sacrifice, and loyalty; unmanliness and lack of self-discipline are abominations to him, and in the world order he perceives a nemesis before which presumption is constrained to surrender.

If Kipling is quite independent as a writer, it does not follow that he has learned nothing from others; even the greatest masters have done so. With Bret Harte, Kipling shares his appreciation of the picturesqueness of vagabond life, and with Defoe his accuracy in depicting every detail and his sense of the values of exactness in the use of terms and phrases. Like Dickens he feels a keen sympathy with those of low degree in the community, and like him he can perceive the humour in trifling traits and acts. But his style is distinctively original and personal. It accomplishes its ends by suggestion rather than by description. It is not quite uniformly brilliant but it

is always eminently expressive and picturesque. The series *From Sea to Sea* (1899) is a veritable model of graphic description, whether the scene is laid in the Elephant City governed by the Grand Divinity of Laziness, in Palm Island, or in Singapore, or whether the story deals with manners and customs of Japan. Kipling has at his command a large fund of irony—sometimes highly pungent—but he has abundant resources of sympathy, too, sympathy for the most part extended to those soldiers and sailors who have upheld the honour of England in far-distant lands. He has every right and reason to tell them: "I have eaten your bread and your salt, I have drunk your water and wine, I have lived your life, I have watched o'er your beds of death."

He attained fame and success as a very young man, but he has continued to develop ever since. One of his biographers has stated that there are three "notes" to be traced in his authorship. The satirical note is found in *Department Ditties*, *Plain Tales from the Hills*, *The Story of the Gadsbys*, with its amusing commendation of single blessedness, and in the much-debated novel, *The Light that Failed*. The second, the note of sympathy and human kindness, is most clearly marked in "The Story of Muhammad Din" and in "Without Benefit of Clergy" (in *Life's Handicap*), a gem of heartfelt emotion. The third, the ethical note, is clearly traceable in *Life's Handicap*. Whether there be much value or not in this classification which, as is usually the case in such matters, cannot be consistently applied to the whole of his production, one thing is certain: Kipling has written and sung of faithful labour, fulfilment of duty, and love of one's country. Love of one's country with Kipling does not mean solely devotion to the island kingdom of England, but rather an enthusiastic affection for the British Empire. The closer uniting of that Empire's separate members is a long and fervently cherished aspiration of the poet's. That is surely clear from his exclamation: "What should they know of England who only England know?"

Kipling has given us descriptions in vivid colours of many different countries. But the picturesque surface of things has not been the principal matter with him; he has always, in all places, had a manly ideal before him: ever to be "ready, ay ready at the call of duty" and then, when the appointed time comes, to "go to God like a soldier".

The Swedish Academy, in awarding the Nobel Prize in Literature this year to Rudyard Kipling, desires to pay a tribute of homage to the literature of England, so rich in manifold glories, and to the greatest genius in the realm of narrative that that country has produced in our times.

Historical Context

BLAIR B. KLING

Kim in Historical Context[†]

The events in *Kim* take place in the 1880s and 1890s, at the apex of the British Indian Empire. We know this because of a single reference early in the story to the "old soldier" who "told tales of the Mutiny and young captains thirty years in their graves." If we conclude that the Indian Mutiny of 1857–58 took place 30 years before the events in the novel, Kim would have been 13 in 1888 and 17 in 1892, when the story ends. This roughly corresponds to the period from 1882 to 1889, when Kipling lived in India as a young adult. We can assume that the India described in *Kim* is the India Kipling experienced during his five years as a newspaper reporter for the *Civil and Military Gazette* of Lahore and two years for the *Pioneer* of Allahabad. The India depicted in *Kim* is India viewed from the perspective of common people—villagers, soldiers, and urchins—rather than from the viewpoint of the relatively few upper-class Indians and British officials who usually fill the history books. The exceptions are a handful of Britishers whose role in the story is to train Kim to be a secret agent. The reader of *Kim* is given no hint of the momentous political events that were taking place in India during the 1880s and early '90s. True, at the time these events involved only a relatively small number of upper-class Indians and may not have appeared important to Kipling and his countrymen, but in retrospect they laid the foundations for Indian nationhood in the twentieth century.

At its apex, the British Indian Empire, with its population of 256 million, covered the entire subcontinent and included what are today the nations of India, Pakistan, and Bangladesh. About two-thirds of the empire was governed by a bureaucracy headed by fewer than 2,000 Britishers, members of the elite Indian Civil Service, who supervised the work of about 40,000 Indian clerks and admin-

[†] This is an original essay written for this Norton Critical Edition by Blair B. Kling, Professor of History, University of Illinois at Urbana-Champaign.

istrators. The other third of India was made up of native states gov-
erned through Indian princes under British supervision. Some of
these states, such as Hyderabad, Kashmir, and Mysore, were as
large as England while some were only a few square miles in area.
References to native states emerge in the pages of *Kim*—the maha-
rani who befriended the lama and Kim is the widow of the ruler of
a small state in the Kulu Valley, and, in one of his many disguises,
Babu Mookerjee poses as an emissary of the raja of Rampur. The
areas of the Indian Empire governed directly by the British included
the three giant provinces, called presidencies, of Bengal, Bombay,
and Madras. Through a series of military campaigns by the troops
of the East India Company these presidencies had grown in the late
eighteenth and early nineteenth centuries from coastal trading
towns into giant provinces that covered most of the subcontinent.
Each had its own governor and council, but these local officials
were subordinate to the governor-general or viceroy. New provinces
had been added by the 1880s—the Northwestern Provinces and
Oudh, the Punjab, the Central Provinces, Assam, and Burma. The
action in *Kim* takes place in the Northwestern Provinces and Oudh,
the Punjab, and in the natives states in the foothills of the
Himalayan Mountains.

As a colony India was governed by an authoritarian government.
British leaders of the latter nineteenth century rationalized the
authoritarian system by arguing that Indians were too backward to
govern themselves, that they were better off being governed by men
who, like Plato's "guardians," were properly educated and morally
suited to provide the best and most efficient government for the
poor and ignorant masses. Some British officials believed that in
time Indians would be mature enough to participate in their own
governance, but others thought they would never be able to over-
come the superstitions of Hinduism and the stultifying rigidity of
the caste system and that the British would have to remain in
charge permanently. Another argument made in support of British
control was that the British were there to act as impartial umpires
to decide disputes among the inhabitants of a subcontinent divided
by ethnicity, language, religion, caste, culture, and even race. With
Kim and the lama on the Grand Trunk Road we are given a glimpse
of that ethnic diversity.

In spite of the authoritarian framework of colonial India, there
seems to be no atmosphere of government oppression in *Kim* but,
on the contrary, evidence of a great deal of freedom—freedom of
movement, freedom of expression, and more or less easy relations
between the people and the police. Colonial authoritarianism was
limited by many factors: First, Britain itself was a democracy, and
the Liberals, led by Gladstone who was prime minister for much of

the 1880s and 1890s, believed in extending freedom and representative government in India. Second, the British were few in number and dependent on Indian cooperation and collaboration to manage their vast empire. Third, an ever-growing western-educated Indian middle class, particularly in the urban centers of Calcutta, Bombay, and Madras, was demanding the rights of Englishmen and participation in government. Their views were exchanged in the meetings of a large number of civil organizations and in a lively, virtually free press, whose roots went back to the late eighteenth century. Finally, the Indian Mutiny of 1857–58 was still fresh in the minds of many Britishers. In the reconstituted Indian Army Indians outnumbered Britishers two to one and British policy was to build up loyalty and encourage good relations between the British officers and their men. One could say that the British ruled India by employing their organizational skills and command of military technology, and by co-opting educated Indians and building alliances with various sectors of the Indian population, but certainly not by using brute force or even economic power.

One of the sectors of Indian society that strongly supported the British during the Mutiny were the western-educated classes. Beginning in the late eighteenth century, Bengalis had been the first Indians to grasp the importance of learning English and western sciences. They were the most politically active, professing loyalty to the queen and her viceroy and demanding the freedoms of British citizens. As early as the 1830s they had learned to organize for political action and to lobby Parliament in London. In 1867 a Bengali had gone to England and through examination had won admission into the elite Indian Civil Service. By the last decades of the nineteenth century the western-educated Indians began to pose a threat to British rule far more serious than the Mutiny. They mastered the very tools that had made British hegemony possible—western organizational skills, nationalism and national identity, and western science and technology. In Calcutta the educated Indians excelled in their knowledge of the English legal system and English language and literature, while in Bombay various traditional business communities competed with the British in international trade and, by the time of the Mutiny, had already begun to build modern textile mills.

In *Kim* these western-educated Indians are represented by the figure of the Bengali Babu, or "gentleman," Hurree Chunder Mookerjee. In his educational accomplishment Mookerjee personifies the 645 Indians who had earned an M.A. from Calcutta University by 1888. In addition, 3,032 of his fellow Bengalis had earned a bachelor's degree, 1,653 a law degree, 1,179 a medical degree, and 102 an engineering degree. Similar numbers had

received degrees from Bombay and Madras universities. Like Mookerjee, many Bengalis had left their native city, Calcutta, to seek their fortunes in other parts of India. Bengalis were spread over north India as teachers, lawyers, doctors, and government officials, teaching techniques of political organization to their less cosmopolitan brethren in the Punjab and Ganges plain. Some were employed in the governments of native states. As evidenced by Kipling's treatment of Mookerjee, the British Indian establishment had mixed feelings about the Bengalis. Before mid-century they had applauded the emergence of "brown Englishmen" as proof of the success of their civilizing mission. By the 1880s they perceived the Bengalis who had learned to play their game as a threat and attacked them with ridicule as well as racist legislation. To the British in India the Bengalis might be English educated, but they were still racially inferior and did not have the moral fiber, manliness, or common sense to warrant more than subordinate administrative appointments. The reader of *Kim* perceives some of this ambivalence in Kipling's treatment of Mookerjee, and even more in his other writings.

In the light of this emerging Indian middle class, we can understand the sociological basis of those important political events that are contemporaneous with the story of *Kim*. The first two events were precipitated by the Liberal viceroy sent to India by Gladstone in 1880, Lord Ripon. One of his first official moves was to enact the Ilbert Bill of 1883–84 which would allow any European to be tried by an Indian judge. The European non-official community in India reacted with angry protest meetings in which they denounced Lord Ripon and attacked the educated Indian class with abusive racial insults. The Indian community was aroused to counterattack and in 1885 united to support the formation of an all-India political organization, the Indian National Congress, as a platform for their views. It met first in Bombay, then in a different city each year on Christmas and New Year's Day. For its first 20 years the Congress passed resolutions critical of British policies and recommendations for improvement, always making sure to balance criticism with professions of loyalty. But after the turn of the century its meetings began to reflect the increasing radicalization of the educated youth, frustrated by poverty and unemployment, and after World War I the Indian National Congress, under the leadership of Mahatma Gandhi, became the spearhead for Indian independence.

Another equally momentous historical event of the *Kim* period was Ripon's enactment of the Local Self Government Acts of 1884, which introduced elections on a very limited franchise to local rural and municipal governing bodies. This was the foundation of local self-government in India and produced the first local elections not

only in India but in all of Asia. Eight years later another viceroy promulgated the Indian Councils Act of 1892, which allowed Indian representatives of the educated middle class to participate in the governing councils of the Indian Empire. Though inadequate even in its day, it was the embryo of parliamentary government in a free India. Thus, while Kim and his friends were working in the mountainous borderlands to save the British Indian Empire from Russian threats, the compatriots of Hurree Chunder Mookerjee and their counterparts in Bombay and Poona were moving in a direction that would culminate in the replacement of the British with Indian self-government within 60 years. There is no hint of any of these political landmarks in the pages of *Kim*. Perhaps Kipling, like his fellow Britishers, perceived of the real India in terms of its peasant masses and of themselves as their God-given protectors. In their minds the educated Indians were self-serving, untrustworthy, and incapable of impartiality.

For their part, the educated Indians lost no opportunity to blame the British government for its most obvious shortcoming—the pervasive poverty of the country, particularly in the rural areas where 75 percent of the population lived. In Kim's day, as in our own, India's poverty was its most striking feature. The impression is confirmed when the economy of India of 1882 is compared with that of the United States of the same year. Through a strenuous tax-collecting effort the imperial government of India was able to raise about $360 million from a population of 250 million, while the federal government of the United States effortlessly collected $400 million from a population of 50 million. Almost all federal revenue in the United States came from import duties and taxes on liquor and tobacco. In contrast, at least a quarter of the Indian revenues came from a peasantry who lived on the margins of existence and had to pay upward of one-third of the value of their harvests in taxes. To add to the burden, large areas of rural India were plagued by a series of devastating droughts in the last quarter of the nineteenth century.

The largest single expenditure in the Indian budget of the period, about 17 percent, was allocated to support the army. Given the acute shortage of funds for education, public health, and famine relief, the politically aware Indian elite criticized the government for spending so large a part of government resources on an army that was used primarily to secure the country's northwestern border—or, in other words, to play the "Great Game." The government felt history supported its policy, since from earliest times until the Europeans reached India by sea, the passes through the mountainous northwest were the only routes that invaders used to enter India. A list of successive invaders would include folk movements

such as the early Aryans and nomadic horsemen and empire builders from the Middle East and Central Asia, including the Persians, Bactrians, Kushans, Mongols, and Turks. Kipling seemed to have had a strong fascination for the northwest frontier as a place of high adventure, danger, and mystery. It was a place of intrigue and espionage, a place where empire builders, as in his story "The Man Who Would Be King," are destroyed by mountains, blizzards, and inscrutable tribesmen. At the same time, Kipling believed Europeans had a legitimate claim to the area. *Kim* opens with the lama's tour of the Lahore Museum and his ecstatic reaction to the classical Indo-Greek images of the Buddha from Gandhara, an ancient name for the northern Punjab. These were the legacy of the conquest of another European, Alexander the Great, in 327 B.C.E. Consciously or not, Kipling reminds us that Europeans had been conquering and introducing elements of their civilization into the area for many centuries.

The "Great Game" that plays a central part in the story of *Kim* refers to the contest for hegemony in the Middle East and Central Asia between Britain and Russia. The contest was carried on through diplomacy, alliances, client states, espionage, exploration, surveys, maps, and the out-positioning of each other along their border areas. The struggle was directed from London and St. Petersburg, and decisions were made in the broader framework of British strategic interests in the Near East as well as India. According to Peter Hopkirk, the term "the Great Game" was first used by a British officer, Arthur Conolly, who was sent in 1829 by the governor-general, Lord Ellenborough, to explore the terrain between the Caucasus and the Khyber Pass through which a Russian army might advance on India.[1] Conolly traveled through the area in disguise, lived by his wits, and, in the words of Hopkirk, was "the archetypal Great Game player." The British first began to fear an invasion of India from the northwest during the Napoleonic wars, even before they had established their own empire in India. During the nineteenth century they became increasingly obsessed with a possible Russian invasion because of the gradual Russian conquest of areas of Central Asia that had once been ruled by the Tatars. With each successive annexation, Russian troops came closer to India. As Hopkirk points out, at the beginning of the nineteenth century the Russian border was 2,000 miles from India, and by the end of the century as close as 20 miles. In the area northwest of India, Russia and British India were separated by the buffer states of Persia and Afghanistan, and

1. Peter Hopkirk, *The Great Game: The Struggle for Empire in Central Asia* (New York: Kodansha International, 1992) 123–24.

both players competed for alliances with or control over these two states.

The first involvement of the Indian Army in the Great Game was a total disaster. It occurred in Afghanistan where the ruler, Dost Muhammad, had turned to the Russians for help against incursions by both Persia on the west and the Sikh Kingdom on the east. Rather than permit Russian influence in a buffer state so close to India, Lord Auckland blundered into a campaign to invade Afghanistan and place a British candidate on the throne. He sent 16,000 troops to Kabul and replaced Dost Muhammad with an unpopular relative, but as winter set in and the snows blocked their return to India, the British Indian troops found themselves trapped. When they attempted to retreat they were decimated by Afghan tribesmen, and only a single Britisher and a handful of Indians escaped alive. The next governor-general tried to restore the British reputation by re-conquering Kabul and departing quickly, but the damage had been done. The British lost their mystique of invincibility and gained a healthy respect for the warrior tribes of the mountains of the northwest frontier. In 1878–1880, closer to the events in *Kim*, the British were again involved in an invasion of Afghanistan to establish a friendly ruler in Kabul, this time with better luck. In general, however, the British were more successful when they played the Great Game with diplomacy and espionage.

A second theater of competition between Russia and Britain was Tibet, whose foreign relations were in theory under Chinese control. As long as the Chinese were able to exercise some control the British could do little but try to negotiate for trade concessions. But at the turn of the century, with a much weaker Manchu dynasty, the Dalai Lama tried to free his country from Chinese control with Russian help arranged through his Russian tutor, Dorjieff, a professed Buddhist. The Russians claimed to have only a religious interest in Tibet, but the British feared religion was only a cover for political activity. The British countered with an expedition under Sir Francis Younghusband in 1904 that ended up massacring an army of poorly armed Buddhist monks. A trade agreement was forced on Tibet, but public opinion in Britain turned against the government's brutal behavior, and the terms were reduced.

In his book *Empire and Information*, C. A. Bayly puts the clandestine side of the Great Game into historical perspective.[2] He writes that India was covered with an intelligence network made up of various kinds of paid informants and information gatherers long before the British took over. Local rulers, landlords, and merchants

2. C. A. Bayly, *Empire and Information: Intelligence Gathering and Social Communication in India, 1780–1870* (Cambridge: Cambridge University Press, 1996).

all depended for information on *harkaras*, or intelligence agents. Heads of Indian states employed another group of informants called newswriters who were assigned to serve in distant courts and to report back on court gossip and intrigue. The identity of these newswriters was known to everyone at court and they were usually tolerated. In the eighteenth century when the British first began to govern large expanses of the subcontinent, their unfamiliarity with the languages, customs, power relationships, military resources, and capabilities of their opponents made them dependent on a variety of Indian informants. During military operations informants were essential as guides in unknown areas of the country. In the eighteenth and early nineteenth centuries every important British official had teams of informants, some high caste and some low, and some from communities that specialized in gathering and selling information. Women of certain occupations were employed to obtain information during sexual liaisons, and educated men who were skilled in languages were highly valued.

Because of the gap in language and culture between the British and their subjects, the entire operation of the government hinged on good communications between the officials and their teams of Indian informants. Bayly calls breakdowns in such communications "information panics." He attributes the Mutiny of 1857–58 to such a breakdown and suggests that one reason for the massive failure of intelligence in that period was the bureaucratization of information gathering after the mid-nineteenth century. The government had begun to place too much reliance on statistics instead of on the old-fashioned *harkaras*. After the Mutiny the government put much more effort into information gathering, hoping they would never again be caught off guard. A department of government was established to collect and translate extracts from the vernacular press, and the most important reason cited for inclusion of Indians in legislative councils and for the initial official encouragement given to the formation of the Indian National Congress was that it would help the government know the minds of its subjects.

Mapmaking and surveying, so central in *Kim*, could also be classified as a type of espionage and was an especially important prop of British rule. According to Hopkirk, the model for Colonel Creighton was a British captain of the Royal Engineers, Thomas Montgomerie, who was assigned to map northern Afghanistan, Turkestan, and Tibet in the 1860s and '70s.[3] Before Montgomerie the British surveyors and mapmakers had always confined Indians to the most menial jobs on both racist and cultural grounds.

3. Peter Hopkirk, *Quest for Kim: In Search of Kipling's Great Game* (London: John Murray, 1996) 120 ff.

Montgomerie, however, realized that Europeans could not do the job in dangerous and hostile areas and trained a group of Indians, called "pandits," to survey the areas disguised as Buddhist pilgrims. As in *Kim*, they used their prayer beads to keep track of their measured paces and hid their compasses in their prayer wheels. Their names were kept secret and they were referred to only by code numbers. Their exploits have been written up in many places and they are models for the fieldworkers of the modern Survey of India. Matthew H. Edney believes their actual importance in the grand scheme of the mapping of British India has been exaggerated.[4] They captured the popular imagination, however, and Kipling was the first to realize the fictional value of their exploits. They fit right in with his practice of making brave and loyal Indians the heroes of his stories and poems.

Another example of the "native hero" in *Kim* is the old soldier, a veteran of the Mutiny, who was ever after rewarded for his loyalty to the sahibs in their hour of greatest trial. More properly called the Rebellion of 1857, the Mutiny began with a revolt of the sepoys of the Bengal Army, but it soon involved disaffected native states, peasants, and landlords. Sepoys, Indian soldiers trained to fight by European military standards, were first used by the East India Company's army in 1748 during the wars with France. Each presidency was allowed to recruit and train its own army, which remained under separate command until the Mutiny. On the company level sepoys were commanded by Indian officers, but on the battalion level British officers controlled the troops. These sepoy armies did most of the fighting and conquering of the subcontinent, but occasionally Royal Army troops were sent from Britain to reinforce them and officers were sent from the Royal Army to command Indian troops. By the time of the Mutiny Sepoys were proud, professional, and well paid by Indian standards and loyal not so much to the British government as to their battalions. The Bengal Army that mutinied in 1857 was composed of high-caste Hindus from Bihar, Oudh, and Agra. It captured large areas of northern India, and Britishers, especially those scattered in the rural areas, were terrified. Both sides committed atrocities, and when the rebellion was defeated by troops brought in from Britain, the British took terrible revenge.

After the Mutiny the colonial government was streamlined and the army reconstituted. The British developed an ideology of army recruitment based on a theory of martial races—that certain "races" of India, because they were more loyal, braver, physically stronger,

4. Matthew H. Edney, *Mapping an Empire: The Geographical Construction of British India, 1765–1843* (Chicago: University of Chicago Press, 1997) 308–09.

and less arrogant, made better soldiers than others. The Punjab became the preferred recruitment ground, and Sikhs, Punjabi Muslims, and Hindu yeoman farmers, called Jats, formed the core of the post-Mutiny army. Other martial races were Rajputs, Gujars, Pathans, and specialized communities such as Gurkhas from Nepal and Coorgs from south India. Brahmins, Bengalis, and western-educated classes in the Bombay presidency were excluded. Kipling was fond of the Indian Army and believed that the relationship of mutual respect and loyalty that he thought to exist between the martial Indian and the British officer was the ideal relationship between subject and ruler. This theory of the martial races was part of the general ideology of racism that existed in western Europe and the United States in the last decades of the nineteenth century and well into the twentieth century—a concept that Kipling agreed with and expressed in his work. The British, French, Germans, and Americans used the theory of white supremacy to justify colonialism, racial discrimination, and economic exploitation. In India British racism infuriated the upper-caste, talented, western-educated leaders, who had remained loyal during the Mutiny, and it was a major factor in the radicalization of the nationalist movement that led to widespread antigovernment demonstrations and terrorist activity in the first decade of the twentieth century.

Another set of beliefs popular among the British in late Victorian India, and one that had some vogue in Britain itself toward the end of the century, was a belief in the power of the occult and magic. This seems an anomaly when paired with the belief that the British were superior because of their rationalist and scientific attitudes. Based on his study of British writers in India, including Kipling, Lewis D. Wurgaft notes "a preoccupation with native magic and superstition [and a] wide-ranging Anglo-Indian concern with the occult and the supernatural." Britishers appeared to be fascinated by the "Indian effort to manipulate the environment by magical means though spells, curses, or sacrifices . . ." To the Hindus, divinity was everywhere—in rivers and mountains, natural objects, animals, a bride and groom, and in holy men who could amass divine power through austerities. Peasants also attributed magical powers to the powerful British district officer, and many district officers had the uncanny experience of being treated as deities and possessors of magical powers.[5]

Other Britishers, like Kipling, were bewitched by the spectacular landscape of India, and in *Kim*, Kipling captures the magic of both the land—especially the mountainous area north of Simla—and the

5. Lewis D. Wurgaft, *The Imperial Imagination: Magic and Myth in Kipling's India* (Middletown, Conn.: Wesleyan University Press, 1983) 54–59, *passim*.

people. He also integrates magic into his espionage story through the figure of Lurgan Sahib and his shop of wonders. The direct influences on Kipling's own fascination with the magic of India probably derived initially from his early childhood in Bombay where he was raised until age 5 1/2 by servants, spoke in the vernacular, and experienced through a child's eyes the spectacle of daily life in India. If the childhood experiences of other Europeans who spent their first years in India are any indication, Kipling, without even leaving his home, would have explored his own "magic garden," bursting with flowers and scents, and observed in the ordinary street life outside his door snake charmers, fire eaters, and sword swallowers, thieving monkeys, wandering mendicants, musicians, and colorful religious processions. He would no doubt have taken part in throwing colored powder at the good-natured servants on Holi and lighting little lamps on Divali.[6] All these dormant childhood memories would have resurfaced in some form when he returned to India after 11 years in England.

The event most directly involving Kipling with the occult was the visit to India between 1879 and 1884 of Madame Helena Petrovna Blavatsky and Colonel Henry Steel Olcott, founders of the Theosophical Society in New York. Madame Blavatsky convinced her followers that she was able to communicate directly through her psychic powers with *mahatmas*, spiritual beings from Tibet who appeared in bodily form to her and Colonel Olcott in dreams and visions. Their message, transmitted by Madame Blavatsky, was a garbled mixture of Buddhist and Hindu theology. During their five years in India Blavatsky and Olcott crisscrossed the country a number of times, discussed their ideas with some important people, some of whom they converted to theosophy, and established the Theosophical Society headquarters at Adyar in Madras with a branch at Simla. Madame Blavatsky exchanged ideas with Dayananda Saraswati, founder of the important Hindu reform movement, the Arya Samaj, and with a number of prominent western-educated Indian leaders who were flattered that a European would become a devotee of Indian mysticism. Among her converts was A. P. Sinnett, owner and editor of the *Allahabad Pioneer* who employed Kipling from 1887 to 1889 and who, Kipling wrote, "used the paper for propaganda to an extent which got on the nerves not only of the public but of a proof-reader. . . ."[7] She also met Kipling's father, who considered her "one of the most interesting and unscrupulous impostors he had ever met," and she appears

6. Festival of lights celebrating the triumph of Khrishna and his wife Satyabhama over the demon Naraka [Editor].
7. Quoted from Kipling, *Something of Myself*, in Martin Seymour-Smith, *Rudyard Kipling: A Biography* (New York: St. Martin's Press, 1989) 331.

to have had a strong influence on Kipling's neurotic sister, Trix.[8] Her most important convert was Allan Octavian Hume, a maverick retired ICS officer who, as a bridge between the educated Indians and the British establishment, organized the first meeting of the Indian National Congress in 1885. Madame Blavatsky heightened British interest in India's mysterious neighbor, Tibet, and may have been a factor in Kipling's choice of a Tibetan monk as a major character in *Kim*.

Aside from its literary value, *Kim* enhances our understanding of modern Indian history by capturing the flavor of life in north India in the later nineteenth century. Reading about the Grand Trunk Road, the summer capital of Simla, Russophobia among the British Indian officials, Hindu-Muslim relations in the days before communal conflict, the Indian Army, rail travel, Buddhist philosophy and ethics, race relations, the system of private schools—and much more—helps us to visualize life in the Indian Empire in its heyday. What Kipling has omitted from his tale is equally important, for it reveals the limitations of the British Indian vision. His caricatures of the Christian clergy, the westernized Bengali, various rogues, the Pathan horse trader, the Brahmin priest, the Frenchman, and the Russian give us some notion of British Indian attitudes toward the people they lived among.

Another lesson that *Kim* teaches us is that the problems along India's northern and northwestern borders are perennial and deep-seated. Today's conflicts in the area appear to be variants of those discussed in *Kim*. The Great Game itself has echoes in the power struggles and military battles between India and Pakistan over control of Kashmir. Pakistan, which faces India on its east and Afghanistan on its west, plays both the Russian and the British roles. The old Northwest Frontier Province and Baluchistan, now part of Pakistan, are peopled by tough and shrewd men like Mahbub Ali, as well as by independent tribesmen who support separatist movements.[9] Afghanistan is still a troublesome neighbor, now controlled by the turbulent Islamic fundamentalist Taliban party that drove from power a moderate pro-Russian government. Russia itself is still sending troops to its own southern border, now trying to hold intact the empire they inherited from the czars through the Soviet Union. The plight of the Dalai Lama is an uncanny reminder of Kim's lama, and his refugee community in Dharmsala is near the area north of Simla where Kim, the lama, and Hurree Chunder Mookerjee discovered and thwarted the foreign intruders.

8. Martin Seymour-Smith, p. 331.
9. Ayesha Jalal, *The State of Martial Rule: The Origins of Pakistan's Political Economy of Defence* (Cambridge: Cambridge University Press, 1990) 90–93.

One reason for the enduring popularity of *Kim*, aside from its good writing and riveting story, may be its evocation of the lost empire, a sentiment labeled "empire nostalgia." *Kim* evokes a simpler era before the Grand Trunk Road was fouled by diesel fumes, the sacred rivers poisoned by industrial effluents, the forests in the Himalayan foothills clear-cut, and the air polluted by factory emissions, and when the population of India was 250 million compared to the present nearly one billion. In Kim's day one could travel freely across the length of northern India from the northwest frontier to Calcutta. Today the area is divided between India and Pakistan with armed soldiers facing each other along a desolate border. The sites where Kim lived in harmony with Muslim and Hindu friends are now rife with communal enmity and scarred with the memories of the thousands of refugees who were slaughtered during the partition of India at the time of its independence in 1947.

Kipling has succeeded better than any other writer in bringing to life an India of ordinary villagers, horse traders, pilgrims and holy men, rustic gentry, thieves, beggars, servants, mischievous boys, travelers who walked along the Grand Trunk Road or rode in third-class railway carriages, and an old soldier who had served in the sepoy army. The lives and achievements of just such ordinary people have been the primary focus of postcolonial, anti-imperialist historical scholarship in recent years. It is ironic that the master storyteller of imperialism writes with sympathy and affection for the ordinary people under British rule that historians can seldom match.

ANN PARRY

[Recovering the Connection Between *Kim* and Contemporary History][†]

* * *

The chronology of the action [in *Kim*], its type and the imperial discourses that they implicate prove to be an important factor. It has been suggested that, "on the basis of internal evidence . . . the dating of the action precedes by a generation or so the date of com-

† From "History and Artifice in Rudyard Kipling's *Kim*," *Q/W/E/R/T/Y: Arts, Litteratures and Civilization du Monde Anglophone* 4 (October 1994): 90–95. Reprinted by permission of Publications de l'Université de Pau. The author's notes have been edited, and bracketed page references to this Norton Critical Edition have been added following the original references.

position . . . Kim was born in 1865 and joined the Lama in 1878."[1] Page's line of reasoning here leads us to suppose that the text is dealing with the India of the past; and it supports all those readings that stress the nostalgic aspects of the narrative, linking it to Kipling's own years there as a child and in early manhood. The internal evidence of the text would suggest, however, that the main action derives from actual events of the 1890s and is, therefore, much more closely related to the time of its writing.

In the first few weeks of their wanderings Kim and the Lama meet a veteran soldier of the Indian Mutiny, who was awarded the Order of British India in 1887 at the Jubilee, when Victoria became Empress. He speaks of this as being some years past and his great age is stressed[2] [47]. A further clue suggests a contemporary location for the text. Kimbal O'Hara, "a young colour sergeant of the Mavericks," fought in the Second Afghan War between 1878 and 1880; he married "a nursemaid in a colonel's family" and stayed on in India to work on the railway [3]. It would be unlikely that Kim, his son, was born before the end of the Afghan campaign. Other internal evidence suggests that the novel is situated in the last decade of the nineteenth century. During Kim's school career at St Xavier's he is awarded, for his performance in mathematics, the *Life of Lord Lawrence* in 2 volumes (164) [139]. This exhaustive work by Reginald Bosworth was not published until 1885. Kim is thirteen when we first encounter him and if he were born around 1880 it seems reasonable to assume that the earliest point when the action of the novel might begin would be 1893. Beyond that the narrative covers about five years, the headmaster bids Kim farewell when he is seventeen years old and there then follows his re-union with the Lama and the adventure in the Himalayas with Hurree; this occupies the six months that Creighton decrees Kim has to serve under the tutelage of others. The earliest finishing point for the novel, therefore, would be 1898. If we now turn to the activities of the British in India during the 90s and compare them with the manoeuvres in the Great Game, which constitute the central action of the novel, a steady resemblance emerges; furthermore, their representation implicates the whole contemporary debate about imperial security in India.

Kipling, like many other imperialists, saw India as the hub of the Empire; it was the territorial base for Britain's Far and Middle Eastern policies and it played an increasingly important role in buttressing the home economy. Externally, therefore, threats were per-

1. Norman Page, *A Kipling Companion* (London: Macmillan, 1984) 150–52.
2. Rudyard Kipling, *Kim* (Oxford UP, 1987). Subsequent references to the novel appear in the text.

ceived to come from the ambitions of Russia along the North West Frontier, and along the northeast from France, which had a sphere of influence in China and thereby Tibet, which was a suzerain of China. Russian ambitions along the North West Frontier had been particularly in evidence since the 1860s, when, thwarted in designs on the Ottoman Empire, Russia had turned back towards Afghanistan. A boundary between Russia and Britain had been agreed in 1887; but Britain remained in a continual state of watchfulness about Russian activities amongst the volatile and war-like tribes of the North. During the 1890s Britain asserted authority over several tribes and the Durand line of 1893 included them within British territory; essentially, they were seen as a buffer against Afghanistan and the influence Russia periodically exerted there. However, feuds constantly arose amongst these peoples and Russian mischief-making was always suspected. A series of campaigns involving up to 40,000 men were required to maintain British authority amongst the tribes; the largest of these was the Chitral campaign of 1895 that led to the Pathan rising of 1897. Kipling's poem 'The Truce of the Bear', published first on October 1, 1898, warned of the need for constant vigilance against Russia and the danger of thinking that it ever accepted defeat on the North West Frontier.[3] Mahbub Ali's information gathering about the perfidious kings who change sides and who have to be brought to heel by the Army is more than reminiscent of actual campaigns and skirmishes of between 1890 and 1895. The function of the horse-dealer is to provide the British Army with early warnings about what is going on between the Russians and the leaders of the Northern tribes. At various points *Kim* voices the position of the forward school on the Frontier, that the need for recurrent campaigns was caused by "not smashing them thoroughly the first time" (37) [35] and pushing onwards to extend British suzerainty.

In the final adventure in *Kim* Great Britain is threatened on the Northern Frontier of India along both the west and the east. The text represents to a contemporary reader committed both to the maintenance and extension of British power in India the worst of all possibilities. The obvious parallel between the text's imaginings and actual events would have made it even more disturbing. In 1898 the Dalai Lama had assumed his majority, closed his country to Britain and had advisers from Russia around him. The two fake hunters who emerge over the passes of the North West Frontier carry surveying equipment and guns and they are heading for Tibet. They

3. As with many of his poems that made strong political statements, Kipling sought to give it maximum exposure; it appeared in *Literature* on October 1, in the *New York Tribune* on October 13, and in *The Critic* of December 1898. It was collected in *The Five Nations*, published in 1903.

also have with them important letters and as they go they map the
regions through which they travel. Moreover, one of them is a
Russian and "one Russian is a Frenchman" (236) [197]. The horror
is, therefore, compounded as the novel represents the co-operation
of Russia and France against Britain. The final comment that the
text offers on the frontier policy of the Government criticises the
new Viceroy Curzon, who made it one of his first concerns when he
arrived there in 1899. As Kim recovers after his return to Kulu
Hurree fills him in on the situation on the North West Frontier: "the
Government, anxious to avoid expense" is paying tribesmen to guard
the passes and the Army has been withdrawn (221) [186]. Curzon
too, as the following memorandum from him shows, had ordered a
"withdrawal of British forces from advanced positions, employment
of tribal forces in defence of tribal country, concentration of British
forces in British territory as a safeguard and a support, improvement
of communications in the rear."[4] Creighton and his spy network in
Kim express the opinion throughout that such a policy will run into
trouble repeatedly: it underrates the duplicity of the Russians and
the volatility of the tribesmen which will require constant attention
from the protaganists of the Great Game and the British Army.

The imperial discourse that underlies the main adventure action
of Kim, therefore, not only draws on actual events in Indian history,
it ties in with the 'songs' Kipling had been singing prior to, during,
and after the Boer War.[5] A constant threnody was the unwillingness
of the political establishment to shoulder its imperial destiny; the
Empire was falling apart because of the failure of the Government
where necessary to make territorial advances, subdue recalcitrant
'natives' ruthlessly and be aggressive in defence of its 'own' ground.
In the South African campaign one of the problems faced by the
British Army was that it had found itself campaigning without ade-
quate maps of the terrain on which it was to fight. Clearly, the sur-
veying activities of the Russian and the Frenchman suggested to the
contemporary that what had been a source of British weakness in
South Africa repeated itself in India; this is why so much stress is
laid on Kim's training as a 'chainman' at St Xavier's and Kim sug-
gests that India will be held in India; all that the Government will
do is waste the information provided by the spy network (cf. 221)
[186]. The restoration of the connection between the story of the
Great Game and the international power politics of the 1890s
inevitably raises questions about its "relational place in the dialogi-

4. Quoted in P. Spear, ed., *Oxford History of India*, 3rd ed. rev. V. A. Smith (Oxford: Oxford
 UP, 1958), 751.
5. These are seen at their most transparent in the poems included in *The Five Nations* pub-
 lished in 1903. An extended discussion of the volume is to be found in Ann Parry, *The
 Poetry of Rudyard Kipling* (Buckingham: Open UP, 1992).

cal system" of the text. How are the spy story and the quest story related; how does the imperial polemic shape the course of the narrative in the text as a whole; what ideological enunciations are represented by both major and minor protagonists?

The relationships between the spy story and that of the quest are more integral than has previously been recognized. The decision to focus the story about the Great Game on trouble on the North West Frontier had consequences for the literary form of the text and the interpretation of the internal history of India. The first of these consequences relates to the geographical setting of *Kim*, which, in terms of India at large, is parochial. Kim and the Lama travel to Benares and this is the furthest south that the novel extends. They then wander along the Grand Trunk Road, which would have taken them north again. Far, therefore, from hearing in this novel as it claims "The soul of all the East" (26) [25] both the quest and the spy story happen in, relatively speaking, a small northern area of the subcontinent. The obsession with the Frontier contracts the geographical limits of the book and in effect the Empire it was representing; in doing so it points also towards an unresolvable problem for the British in India which takes on a particular literary manifestation in *Kim*.

The pursuance of a forward policy in relation to the Frontier, which required the involvement of the Army in small or large excursions, was only possible if the British in India were unchallenged within the country. It is well known that relative to the number of indigenous peoples the British presence was tiny. Curzon in his memorandum stressed the importance of improving communications because this was the way to ensure the swift movement of the Army in times of trouble. The real nightmare for the British in India is the one of which *Kim* does not speak: pressure from other powers on the Frontier *and* from within the country. By this time Indian opposition to British rule was well under way, yet *Kim* not only ignores this, it falsifies the historical actuality by representing the internal state of India as a place that rejoices in its cosmopolitanism. In relation to the internal condition of India Mark Paffard was quite correct when he observed that "*Kim* wilfully ignores Indian politics."[6] The 'authenticity' of the spy story, in that it has a basis in an imperialist construction of actual events, is matched by an equally 'inauthentic' representation of the attitudes of indigenous peoples towards the Raj. The early meeting with the veteran from the Indian Mutiny stresses that a lesson was learnt in 1857, and that since British rule has been willingly accepted; the number of important characters in the novel who serve the Empire in order

6. Mark Paffard, *Kipling's Indian Fiction* (London: Macmillan, 1989), 80.

to perpetuate it strengthens and confirms this view. Kipling's por-
trayal of "the happy Asiatic disorder," this "diversity without strife"
in which there is "no neurotic polarization," these are qualities crit-
ics have commended about *Kim*.[7] Indeed, they form the grounds for
the claim that in this book the author "transcended his own ethno-
centric vision." But, in terms of other work that Kipling was pro-
ducing at that time "the uniquely multiple being" of *Kim* remains a
puzzle.[8] In *The Five Nations*, for example, Kipling had become
increasingly shrill on imperial matters.[9] The beneficence of *Kim* has
been most frequently explained in biographical terms: it is nostalgia,
a trip down memory lane to produce "an India of the imagination."[1]
Such a position omits to explain how a work produced in the midst
of the Boer War was not tempered by that experience, especially as
most Kipling scholars agree that it had a profound effect on the
writer and was, indeed, "a crisis" for him. The uncertainty about
Britain's imperial future, the desire that it should continue and be
carefully maintained, the fear that it would not, these were all a part
of Kipling's response to what had happened in South Africa. It was
a psychical state that produced an obsessive watchfulness about the
infringement of British territory by others, and such watchfulness
on the North West Frontier was only possible if all was at peace
within India. The representation of India that has so far only been
seen in literary terms [i.e. as "a pastoral" or "an idyll"] should also
be recognized as a historical necessity for a colonialist like Kipling
committed to a forward policy. Since the British in India could not
cope with a war on the Frontier *and* resistance from within, the
novel had not only to deny the latter, but invert the actual state of
affairs. Far from resistance existing the text suggests that there were
emerging at subaltern level amongst the country-born those like
Kim who could and would "borrow right and left-handedly from all
the customs of his country he knew and loved" (73) [65]. In the
story of the quest which 'reveals' the internal state of India a world
of the "magic" took over; India became a place which accepted
British rule as its best destiny.[2] The requirements of the imperial
present necessitated an inversion of Indian history. 'The False
Structure' that John Bayley has identified elsewhere in Kipling's
work operates here too; its effect is that "The weight of truth falls

7. Alan Sandison, "Introduction" to *Kim* (Oxford UP, 1987), xiv, xvi.
8. Benita Parry, "The Contents and Discontents of Kipling's Imperialism," *New Formations*
 6 (1988): 4.
9. See for example 'Et Dona Ferentes' or 'The White Man's Burden' or 'The Dykes'. The kind
 of training Kipling saw as necessary for the colonialist of the twentieth century is not far
 from the experience he constructs for Kim. What was necessary was "Each man . . .
 entered at youth to the game not to be mastered in haste, / But after trial and labour, by
 temperance, living chaste." See the poem 'The Islanders.'
1. Edward Said, "Introduction" to *Kim* (Penguin, 1987), 28.
2. *Ibid.*, 7.

on the area of contrivance; truth is palpably at one with artifice."[3] An obsession with the Frontier required an India that, in its internal condition, comprised a mass of peoples and faiths happily accepting British law and surveillance as the best way to contain their eternal tendency to fall into mayhem. Hence, those scenes on the train to Benares, or on the Grand Trunk Road, or later in Kulu of which we are told "This was seeing the world in real truth" (*Kim* 73) [65]. The indigenous peoples are represented as living in a world in which time has stood still, for "All hours of the twenty-four are alike to Orientals" (26) [26]. In fact, it was a world of magic and glamour that bore little resemblance to any historical actuality; with its peculiar mixture of nostalgia, tolerance, and condescension it is an example, to quote Bayley again, of the "Overkill of a kind" that in this phase of his career became a "Kipling landmark."[4] The "real truth" of which the text speaks is one, therefore, with 'artifice' and 'contrivance', and the effaced historical determinations that produced this "India of the imagination" in *Kim* make this apparent. The question that now remains is how well the 'contrivances' necessary to the maintenance of 'truth' conceal the dissonant ideological articulations in various areas of the text.

The essential 'artifice' of the novel is the pretence throughout that Kim can serve the Lama's quest and needs of the Great Game. It has been argued that Kipling refuses to compromise either narrative or to represent the Lama in a condescending way. This conviction amongst critics that the artifice is waterlight deserves examination.[5] From the outset the two narratives run together, but the demands of the Great Game are always more urgent and are from early on prioritised. Initially, the textual strategy that strives to efface this prioritisation is Kim's age. His being a child is an acceptable reason for his failure to understand the conflict there is between the renunciations demanded by the quest and the activities demanded of him by spying for British India. In the first adventure Kim's childlike pleasure in secrecy and his curiosity about the Kashmir Serai allow him to make use of the Lama in all innocence. Although the Lama wishes to begin his search at Benares his prime function on the train is as a cover to make Kim less noticeable as a possible courier of Mahbub's information. On their arrival the Lama is lodged quickly so that Creighton can be immediately sought and the language of the text frequently indicates just how the Lama is serving other ends: "Go! said Kim, pushing him lightly" and "The Lama rose obediently." While the boy's affection for the old man is

3. John Bayley, "The False Structure," *English Literature in Transition* 29 (1986), 20.
4. Bayley, 25.
5. Sandison, xxiv; Said, 15–16; Mark Kinkead-Weekes, "Vision in Kipling's Novels," in *Kipling's Mind and Art*, ed. A. Rutherford (Stanford UP, 1966), 233–34.

unquestionable the quest is of second importance for Kim com-
pared to the establishment of "the pedigree of the white stallion"
(20) [21].

Just as the conflict between the narratives can only be resolved by
strategies which struggle to efface the precedence of the one over
the other in the action, so there is an imbalance between the rever-
ence for the Lama as a learned and holy man, established in his
meeting with the curator, and the way in which he is regarded by
Kim and other major protaganists. Again, *from the outset*, he is rep-
resented as an object of amusement or curiosity. Kim is attracted to
the Lama because he is a novelty; he cannot place him in relation
to his own experience or knowledge: this is why he is treasure or
"trove" (12) [14]. The boy never detracts from his initial judgment
that "he is quite mad" and he often repeats it. Mahbub Ali holds the
same view as Kim, only without the same affection for the old man;
and the veteran of the Mutiny dubs him "a weaponless dreamer"
whose peace depends upon those who are willing to act against evil
in the world (19, 52) [47]. As Said admits, he is represented at times
as "stupefyingly innocent," while at others he appears to be frail and
senile, a creature of the decisions made by others. There are times,
however, when this eccentricity of the Lama serves a purpose within
the text. It becomes a justification for those moments when he is
required to become complicitous with the Great Game in British
India.[6] The "divine, spiritual idiocy of the Lama"[7] becomes a spuri-
ous explanation for an obvious plot contrivance. Such an instance
occurs over the issue of Kim's schooling. When Kim is 'captured' by
the Mavericks the plan is to send him to an orphanage after which
would have followed inevitably a military career. Kim is saved from
this fate by the Lama's intervention who pays for him to be taught
at St Xavier's. Why should he do this? Why should he hand Kim
over to an education in his originary culture that will most likely
alienate him from his own teachings and faith? The Lama says by
way of explanation, "Education is greatest blessing if of best sorts.
Otherwise no earthly use" (104) [90]. The cliché, like most clichés,
explains very little and the act remains a bizarre impulse.[8] What Kim
is taught at St Xavier's does prove to be of "no earthly use" as
regards seeking freedom from the Wheel. Kim will be trained there
in a role that will, ironically, require his fast attention to the earth
that the Lama seeks to transcend. It is Mahbub Ali and Hurree who

6. Said, 17.
7. Sandison, xxiv.
8. The representation of the Lama as senile is probably at its strongest in the final passages
 of the novel where all the other characters respond to the news that he has achieved
 Enlightenment. Kim himself puts it down to a lack of food and drink and worries whether
 the old man will have taken cold from his dousing in the stream.

provide the real reason why Kim has to attend St Xavier's: the Game urgently needs trained spies to stem the threat to British rule from outside.[9] If this requires the Lama at certain times to betray his own best interests and his essential beliefs and become complicitous with these needs, then the text will contrive the means for this to be so; and his 'stupefying innocence' may act as a feint to cover the imperial polemic that is driving the narrative at this point. The frontier paranoia that lies behind it all then produces different strategies, like the use of a child character or an eccentric foreign Holy Man, to manipulate the story of the quest to serve the needs of "the Ethnological Survey."[1] Any notion that it is only in the final adventure that the quest is betrayed, is, therefore, difficult to sustain. The ambivalent enunciations that emerge in the sequence of events that follow Kim's leaving school arise directly from his changed perceptions of both Game and Quest.

Most critics of *Kim* have agreed that "there is a teasing ambiguity . . . as regards Kim's final decision."[2] The novel ends with the Lama's invitation to Kim to "Come" and join him for "Certain is our deliverance" (289) [240]. The Lama has found the Way but has, altruistically, returned to collect Kim and take him with him; and there the novel ends. Kipling said it "stopped," but commentators have insisted that the exclusion of Kim's reply constitutes an ambivalence.[3] It is worth investigating perhaps the extent to which the abruptness of the ending is justified by what has already occurred in the final adventure. In terms of the literary structure of the novel the silence of Kim is necessary to the pretence of 'contrivance' of non-precedence between the two narratives. Silence ensures that a reader can imagine that the old man has not been rejected and, therefore, not been subordinated to the Great Game. Kim's boyhood early on played an important role in maintaining this credibility; here his youth, verging on adulthood, is equally important. He is seventeen and while he can no longer be credited with the naïveté of childhood neither is decisiveness about life's direction generally required of people of this age.

The "truth which is palpably at one with artifice"[4] in *Kim* has also, however, throughout struggled to efface an historically deter-

9. See *Kim* 167, 172 [141–42, 146] for instances in which Mahbub Ali and Hurree press on Creighton the need for Kim in the field.
1. *Kim* 109 [94], though the term is used throughout. The name signifies the main thrust of colonial discourse as the alliance of power and knowledge; and it is interesting to note that Creighton feels threatened as well as amused by Hurree's ethnological studies and his effort like himself to become F.R.S. See 174–75.
2. K. C. Behappa, "The Meaning of Rudyard Kipling's *Kim*," *Journal of Commonwealth Literature* 26 (1991): 156.
3. Sandison, Said, Kinkead-Weekes, Meyers, and Zohreh Sullivan all subscribe to this point of view.
4. Bayley, 20.

mined colonial discourse, and this is no less so at the end. In the last adventure and the terrible journey back to Kulu Kim is claimed as a trained man of the Ethnological Survey *almost* ready for a career in the Great Game; and that representation in itself excludes him from any intellectual participation in the Enlightenment the Lama seeks as well as raising questions about the supposed ambivalence of the ending. The final months are a rite of passage in which the young man's readiness is tested along with his understanding of the world he must enter. Hurree, the Babu, plays an important role in this final stage of Kim's life, a role that has significant implications within the colonial discourse of the text. A reader cannot but be struck by the contradiction between Hurree's representation as the stereotype of a Babu and his achievements as an agent for the British Government in India.[5] He is described throughout as a person whose Europeanization is only superficial; a follower of Herbert Spencer, he fears the evil eye Huneefa may cast on him; the 'typical' fat Bengali, he cleans his teeth like a "decently bred Babu and then stuffs his mouth with pan and betel" (191) [153]. But, as Lurgan Sahib acknowledges, Hurree's outstanding capacities as a spy call into doubt his stereotype; they fracture the stereotype and he escapes from it into a new definition: "From time to time, God causes men to be born . . . who have a lust to go abroad at the risk of their lives and discover news . . . these souls are very few; and of these few, not more than ten are of the best. Among these ten I count the Babu, and that is curious" (161) [136]. Hurree's European master Creighton is dependent for news on Hurree and in this displacement it is the Babu who holds power and knowledge. Bhabha's conjecture that power is not entirely possessed by the coloniser is borne out by the discursive formations in *Kim* which surround Hurree.[6] The man who claims in the final pages that he is "Unfortunately Asiatic . . . a Bengali, a fearful man" (223) [187], and must, therefore, have the support of Kim, nevertheless courageously ingratiates himself with the Russians and at great risk of discovery leads them on a deliberately circuitous journey to Simla to give Kim and the Lama time to escape. Hurree's courage and resourcefulness in the final adventure disrupt orientalist strategies, which normally guarantee the superiority of the Westerner vis-a-vis the Orient, and the inversion ensures that Kim comes to understand

5. Hurree Chunder Mukerjee is one of the four characters in *Kim* who appeared earlier in Kipling's work. The others are Mahbub Ali ('The Ballad of the King's Jest'), Strickland (stories in *Plain Tales* . . .), and the Woman of Shamlegh (*Plain Tales* . . .). Hurree's earlier manifestation was in 'What Happened' (*Departmental Ditties*) as a foolish Babu whose naïveté was used by the British Government to secure his defeat at the hands of his own people. In *Kim* both sides are less foolish and the change is an implicit recognition of what is happening in India.

6. Homi K. Bhabha, "Of Mimicry and Men," *October* 28 (1984): 125–33.

the nature of the true identity of the 'chainman' in British India. In these contradictory "hybrid" moments Hurree becomes not a copy of the colonial original but a qualitatively different kind of person who constitutes "a textual insurrection against the discourse of colonial authority."[7]

At the beginning of the sequence in which Kim learns of the new situation in the Great Game of which he is to be a part both he and Hurree appear to assume the stereotypes indicated by their racial positions. Hurree wordily obfuscates around the affair and is smartly reprimanded: "Babuji . . . I am a Sahib . . . And I hope to play the Great Game . . . why talk like an ape in a tree? . . . How can I do anything if you *bukh* (babble) all round the shop." The distinction breaks down however as Hurree reminds Kim that it is his authority which is to be proven; Kim is still "subordinate to me departmentally" (220) [185], and the reader knows that in spite of Hurree's protestations of fear it is Kim about whom uncertainty still exists; this is to be his trial, not the Babu's. This time the test he faces requires him *in all knowledge* to allow the Lama and his quest to become a subterfuge in the effort to capture the foreign spies. The injury and trauma to the Lama that result from this and the responsibility of getting him and the captured papers to safety causes the breakdown of the final pages, although it is important to note that he is successful in his mission and will be reported as such "departmentally" by Hurree. Furthermore, the decision to support Hurree and render help when necessary requires of Kim a rejection of the Way the Lama would have him go on the quest: "To those who follow the Way there is neither black nor white" (212) [178]. The *chela* must not be waylaid by the circumstances that arise out of conceptions of racial difference. It is a precept which undercuts the basis of British rule in India and it was totally at odds with the efficiency of the spy network there. Every adventure of the Great Game in *Kim* turns on disguise: escape is effected or information gathered by the agent assuming a caste or religious disguise. Earlier in the novel, as a boy, Kim asked, "What am I? Mussalman, Hindu, Jain, or Buddhist?" and was told by Mahbub Ali, "Each has merit in its own country." The boy's objection that the Lama had taught him "an altogether different thing" is met by the usual dismissal of him as "a dreamer of dreams." The realization that circumstances required him to become the Sahib in disguise to support Hurree's claimed inadequacies is a validation of Mahbub Ali's teaching that, for a player in the Great Game, what you are often depends on where you are "among Sahibs . . . among

7. Benita Parry, "Problems in Current Theories of Colonial Discourse," *Oxford Literary Review* 9 (1987): 41. Bhabha has further developed the concept of mimicry as one of hybridity. His theory and its strengths and limitations are discussed by Benita Parry, "Problems," 27–58.

the folk of Hind"; at different moments "both kinds of faces" may be necessary (143) [121]. For the spy in India racial difference is the stuff of existence, the contrivance on which his art is based, that was why disguise was one of the important things Kim learnt with Lurgan Sahib; and Kim's special virtue is being able to temper his soul so that he can enter another's (see Lurgan Sahib's comment, 160) [135]. To renounce difference, as the Lama instructs, is to disable yourself as a player in the Great Game. Kim in this last adventure learns that a lack of self-definition may be his most powerful professional weapon. This is why, as he recovers, no answer comes to the question "And what is Kim?" We are told quite clearly that he feels "the wheels of his being lock up anew on the world without" (282) [234] while the question remains unanswered. He must be content for circumstance and place to define his being. To be a spy is to be no-one, to have a ubiquity (Little Friend of all the World) founded on a fluidity of identity; achievement will depend upon the success of this artifice. Hurree again was his teacher; Kim is an admiring witness as the "hulking, obese Babu" becomes "lean and weather worn"; he watches with reverence as the "oily and effusive" stereotype becomes a "polished, polite, attentive . . . son of experience and adversity" (226) [189–90]. As Hurree departs to make his report to Creighton we are all asked to "Behold him, too fine drawn to sweat . . . a just man made perfect" (268) [223]. The Kim who is left to respond to the Lama's invitation knows what the Great Game demands of him, a purposeful rejection of self-definition and a continuing conservation of his powers of transformation. Any inferences about what his response might be must take this into account. But it is Hurree whose collusion with his stereotype has exposed the uncertainty at the heart of the colonial discourse in *Kim* and produced throughout a performance that undermines it. Acknowledgment of the threat that he poses is displaced to those other colonisers, the Russians. They describe him as "India in transition—the monstrous hybridism of East and West" (239) [199]. This expression of fear and revulsion is another sign of that "Overkill of a kind that is a Kipling landmark"[8] at this stage of his writing; and it is a recognition of Hurree's disruptive potential within colonial discourse.

The disappearance of the historical determinations within *Kim* and the production of a construct which emphasises the literary qualities of the text have had the effect of silencing a colonial discourse whose chief component in this instance was a preoccupation with the North West Frontier that necessitated an effacement of the resistance to British rule within India.

8. Bayley, 25.

CRITICISM

NOEL ANNAN

Kipling's Place in the History of Ideas[†]

Criticism has not yet come to terms with Kipling: the man and his works symbolise a part of British political and social history about which his countrymen have an uneasy conscience. Ever since the turn of the century when Max Beerbohm began to caricature him with loathing, he has been regarded as a strident geranium, red as a map of the colonies and the antithesis of the green carnations of the nineties;[1] and at the root of every assessment of Kipling lies the problem of his morality. In 1941 the two most famous critics in England and America chose quite independently to consider his status. T. S. Eliot, meditating among the bombs in war-time London, asked us to reconsider the fashionable verdict on the great imperialist.[2] He met with an unequivocal response. Raymond Mortimer, Peter Quennell, Graham Greene, G. W. Stonier, Hugh Kingsmill, and *Scrutiny* in the person of Boris Ford echoed each other's disgust; and in America Lionel Trilling denied that Eliot could claim Kipling for the Tory tradition, "a tradition which is honoured by Dr. Johnson, Burke, and Walter Scott. . . . he has none of the *mind* of the few great Tories. His Toryism had in it a lower middle-class snarl of defeated gentility" Auden and Orwell characteristically refused to sing in harmony but took as proved the usual charges against Kipling's social and moral philosophy; and Desmond MacCarthy's encomium at Kipling's death, though judicious, was restrained.[3]

On the other side of the Atlantic, however, Edmund Wilson, writing at the high-noon of American liberalism, gave a verdict which has become orthodoxy.[4] He found much to praise in the young

† From *Victorian Studies* 3 (1959–60): 323–24, 326–27, 342–44. Reprinted by permission of *Victorian Studies*, Indiana University Press.

1. Max Beerbohm, cartoonist and satirist, began a series of cartoons and parodies attacking Kipling in 1901; the green carnation means "effete" in reference to the flower associated with Oscar Wilde, the turn-of-the-century dramatist, poet, aesthete, and wit. In 1891, Wilde wrote an essay for *The Nineteenth Century* in which he said that reading *Plain Tales from the Hills* was like "reading life by superb flashes of vulgarity. . . . Mr Kipling is a man of talent who drops his aspirates. . . . From the point of view of life he is a reporter who knows vulgarity better than anyone has ever known it" [*Editor*].
2. *A Choice of Kipling's Verse* made by T. S. Eliot (London: 1941).
3. *Sunday Times*, 14 Sept. 1952; Quennell, *The Singular Preference* (London: 1952), pp. 159–66; Greene, *The Lost Childhood* (London: 1951), pp 74–75; *New Statesman and Nation* XXIII (1942), 10; Kingsmill, *Progress of a Biographer* (London: 1949), pp. 27–37; *Scrutiny* XI (1942), 23–33; Trilling, *The Liberal Imagination* (London: 1951), p. 125; Auden, "The Poet of the Encirclement" in *Literary Opinion in America*, ed. M. D. Zabel (New York: 1951), reprinted from the *New Republic*, CIX (1943), 579–581; Orwell, *Critical Essays* (London: 1951), pp. 113–128; MacCarthy, *Memories* (London: 1953), pp. 76–82.
4. Wilson, "The Kipling that Nobody Read," in *The Wound and the Bow* (London: 1941). First published in *Atlantic Monthly*, CLXVII (1941), 201–214, 340–354.

Anglo-Indian journalist and in the dark stories of Jamesian com-
plexity written in his last years—"the Kipling that nobody read." But
the praise was combined with a devastating judgment on the mature
man whose morality Wilson found repulsive. In a brilliant piece of
conjectural biography he reconciled the two Kiplings and explained
how this lively and sympathetic young man, who wrote with equal
understanding of Englishmen and Indians, became the champion of
authoritarian upper-middle-class rule: yet eventually with the loss of
his son in the first world war, which led to the collapse of Kipling's
ideal of Imperial Britain ruling the world, was purged of his sins
through suffering and emerged as an Oedipus Coloneus.

* * *

Nothing marks the break with Victorian thought more decisively
than modern sociology. The new sociologists in Europe broke with
philosophy and historicism, whether Positivist, Idealist, or Marxist.
They saw society as a nexus of groups; and the patterns of behav-
iour which these groups unwittingly established, rather than men's
wills or anything so vague as a class, cultural, or national tradition,
primarily determined men's actions. They asked how these groups
promoted order or instability in society whereas their predecessors
had asked whether certain groups helped society to progress. Weber
did not consider whether religion was true or good. He accepted it
as a social fact and argued that different religions produced differ-
ent codes of conduct which affected the politics and economy of the
society in which they flourished. Durkheim showed concretely how
people's behaviour was determined by the society in which they
lived. In his famous analysis of suicide he deduced which groups
constantly had the highest rate and argued that one important fac-
tor was the degree to which the individual was integrated within his
group and accepted the code of communal behaviour. He saw the
individual as a bolt which might snap if the nut of society held it too
tightly or too loosely. Excessive integration, as in the army officer
caste with its strict code of behaviour which sometimes ran counter
to the morality of the community as a whole, could be as dangerous
as imperfect integration. Institutions could never be explained
solely in terms of their utility: they could be understood only by dis-
covering how they corresponded to the general needs of society.
Durkheim thus explained in a new manner the existence of order
and of the deviations from the norms in society. Men did not so
much search for goals to pursue but accepted those which their
group or class in society chose for them. The dichotomy between
the individual and society he pronounced to be largely false; for
though men might act, and be judged to be acting rightly, against

the moral consensus of society, without such a moral consensus they could not act at all. A society without moral consensus or rituals and sacred objects would disintegrate.

These insights are commonplace today and indeed we are more aware of the questions which these great innovators left unanswered than of those they settled. But to an historian the striking fact is that for long they were virtually ignored in England. Paradoxically in the land which prides itself on approaching political problems empirically, society continued to be studied in terms of ethics and philosophy.[5] Kipling prided himself, however, on describing what Durkheim called social facts and on despising talk of individual rights, sanctions, and contracts. He did not, of course, analyse social processes in the manner of Durkheim and Weber: he was an artist working through his sensibilities and had no use for deductive systems of thought. While for most writers society is the background, or provides the interests for, or is a positive threat to their characters, for Kipling the very existence of society is a problem. Like the new sociologists he was fascinated by the problem of social order. His English contemporaries, living in a society untouched for generations by civil war or revolution or economic or spiritual disaster were never forced to consider why society still continued to hang together. But Kipling was forced to consider it. He had been born and began to work in India and belonged to one of the many groups, each with its own customs, conventions, and morality, that flourished on the sub-continent. Only thirty years before he began to write, the caste to which he belonged, Anglo-India, had faced annihilation in the days of the Mutiny. Like Maine or Fitzjames Stephen, Kipling perceived the contradictions between what Englishmen were taught to believe about society and what actually existed in India; and when he asked what forces kept the groups in this bewildering society together, he found the answer, as Durkheim had, in the forces of social control. Then again his notion of the "Law" is not an ordinary idea: it is the same as the anthropologists' *culture*. The impression which his work as a whole gives is that of a man who sees human beings moving in a definable network of social relationships which impose upon them a code of behaviour appropriate to their environment.

* * *

* * * [T]he real refutation of Edmund Wilson's essay lies in *Kim*.

5. I have suggested some reasons why this was so in my Hobhouse Memorial Lecture, *The Curious Strength of Positivism in English Political Thought*, London, 1958.

Wilson disposes of Kipling's novel by arguing that there must be
an inescapable conflict between the Indians and British. Kim, the
white orphan, has escaped into native life and becomes simultane-
ously a neophyte in the British secret service and the disciple of the
Lama. "Now what the reader tends to expect is that Kim will come
eventually to realise that he is delivering into bondage to the British
invaders those whom he has always considered his people" (Wilson,
p. 110). But, he complains, the conflict never materialises and the
discrepancy between the Lama's search for salvation and Kim's dis-
reputable mundane activities remains unresolved. No doubt this is
what a courageous liberal writing at a time when Gandhi and Con-
gress were struggling for Indian independence did expect, but such
a conflict is imposed by the critic on the novel. No doubt the future
life of a young agent would have entailed confounding Indian resis-
tance to the British, but this is an *ex post facto* judgment, and in the
novel such a career is depicted as the maintenance of that minimum
of order such as is necessary to prevent foreign intrigue, frontier
invasions, and injustice by native princes and to permit the joyous,
noisy, pullulating mess of India life on the Great Trunk Road to con-
tinue. Secret services in general since the rise of communist and
fascist regimes, and the British secret service in particular since
Buchan, Sapper, and other best-sellers for many weary years used it
as a vehicle, have little to recommend them in the eyes of the lib-
eral: unhappily they are necessary and in Kipling's India the secret
service formed part of that ideal of minimal government—of a hand-
ful of officials and a few brigades of troops—which is some degrees
better than a full-scale military occupation and a bureaucracy of
spies coming not as single sorrows but in M.V.D. battalions. This
conflict cannot arise within the terms of the book because the hier-
archy of religion and life which is implicit in every description of
Indian or English society allots a place to each character which he
is compelled to occupy. Born white, Kim can no more become an
Indian than the Lama can reverse the Wheel of Life and become a
merchant. Just as Tolstoy's characters in *War and Peace* find rest
when they realise their essential being and their place and duties, so
Kim has to discover the exact slot into which his own tiny person-
ality must fit in the bewildering variety of human beings who pass
their transitory lives in the Indian sub-continent.

There can then be no conflict in deciding what role to play in life.
Kim and the Lama each has his vocation, Kim to govern, the Lama
to achieve Nirvana. These vocations are not contradictory but com-
plementary. Kim and the Lama are the two sides of the coin of man's
duty on earth. Both are engaged on a search for reality through
knowledge, Kim to find his niche on earth and to discover what he
really is, the Lama to find the sacred river on whose banks he will

be freed from sin. Both have much to learn. Kim has to endure the humiliation and boredom of being transformed into an Englishman in cantonment and school and has then to master the mysteries of his craft. The Lama, who has realised that God cannot be approached solely through adherence to the reformed laws of his monastery in Tibet, has to experience what other people are and what position they occupy on the Wheel of Life; and whereas at the beginning of the story he blessed the Amritzar courtesan for her alms—"She has acquired merit. Beyond doubt it was a nun"—he has learnt much by the end.

The conflict lies elsewhere, and the fact that it materialises late and is not inevitable is the weakness of the book. The conflict is born of the loyalty of Kim and the Lama to their separate vocations and of their love for each other. When Kim and the Babu have thwarted the two foreign spies, Kim is faced with the dilemma on the one hand of being loyal to his trust, delivering the papers speedily and safely to his chiefs and helping his fellow agent the Babu; and on the other of succouring the Lama who is exhausted by the realisation that he has sinned through pride in his prowess in climbing among the hills and through anger against the Russian officer who struck him. Under this physical and mental strain Kim breaks down and weak with illness staggers out to sleep in the life-giving dust. When he wakes the cogwheel of his soul has fallen into place and connects with the Wheel of Life on which he and all other beings are bound. Meanwhile the Lama too has been torn with conflict. For while Kim was ill, he stumbled into a brook and found at last his sacred river. In a trance he left the illusions of Time and Space and saw the whole world within the Soul and drew near to the Great Soul. "'Then a voice cried: "What shall come to the boy if thou art dead?" and I was shaken back and forth in myself with pity for thee; and I said: "I will return to my *chela* lest he miss the Way." Upon this my Soul . . . withdrew itself from the Great Soul with strivings and yearning and retchings and agonies not to be told . . . I pushed aside world upon world for thy sake.'" At the moment of union with Nirvana, the Lama renounces for love his soul's desire.

Kim and the Lama each pursue different kinds of knowledge and neither desires or pretends to understand the other's mind. Both find enlightenment and freedom—the comprehension of the order of things—through love. Kim's love for the Lama makes the Sahiba, the woman of Shamlegh, and Mahbub Ali all love him; the Lama's love for Kim makes Mahbub Ali, who despises the Lama as an unbeliever and a madman, resist the temptation to pillage the Sahiba's household. But the Babu—the only babu whom Kipling drew with affection—does not know love: he is "too good Herbert Spencerian." For only those who are loyal to people, as distinct from ideas, can love.

Such was Kipling's scheme of things. It rests on a highly articulated functional analysis of society in which none but socialised individuals exist. From the analysis proceeds a conservative theory of human existence and political life. This in turn is modified by an awareness of spiritual facts such as repentance, forgiveness, love, and supernatural (or inexplicable) forces which can mitigate the harshness of existence, however little Kipling is willing to allow his readers to forget the harshness. Kipling is almost the sole analogue in England at the turn of the century to Durkheim and Weber and the German and Italian thinkers (whom H. Stuart Hughes treats in his book *Consciousness and Society*) who were in revolt against mid-nineteenth century constructs of the individual and society. He was not a social Darwinist as Wells argued; his understanding of social forces was original and was not as superficial as has been imagined. The charge that he has no mind must be mitigated.[6] He was one of the *cleverest* of Victorian writers.

IRVING HOWE

The Pleasures of *Kim*[†]

That sense of evil which for cultivated people has become a mark of wisdom and source of pride, indeed, the very sun of their sunless world, is not a frequent presence in the pages of *Kim*, and when it does appear it can rarely trouble us with either its violence or grasp. We are inclined these days to exalt the awareness of evil into a kind of appreciation. We find it hard to suppose that a serious writer could turn his back upon the malignity at the heart of things; we urge it as a criticism of writers like Emerson and Whitman that they are weak in the awareness of evil, as if nature had denied them a necessary faculty. But *Kim* is unsubdued by the malignity at the heart of things. Whatever evil it does encompass tends to be passed off onto a troop of bumbling Russian spies who muddle along on the northern borders of India, stage-comic Russians about as alarming as Laurel and Hardy. *Kim* is at ease with the world, that unregenerate place which is the only one most of us know, and because at ease, it can allow itself to slide toward another possible world, one that some of us may yet come to know. For readers trained in the

6. H. G. Wells, *The Outline of History* (London: 1924), p. 661. Cf. Auden, p. 262.
† From *Art, Politics, and Will: Essays in Honor of Lionel Trilling*, ed. Quentin Anderson, Stephen Donadio, and Steven Marcus (New York: Basic Books, 1977) 35–44. Copyright © 1977 by Basic Books, Inc. Reprinted by permission of Basic Books, a member of Perseus Books, L.L.C.

severities of Kafka and Sartre, all this may constitute a literary scandal, especially if one goes so far as to make a claim for the seriousness and greatness of the book; and precisely this scandal is what I propose here to cultivate.

There is greater scandal. *Kim* evokes and keeps returning to sensations of pleasure, a pleasure regarded as easy, natural, and merited. Our sophistication teaches us that all the literary works we esteem can be expected to yield pleasure; that the torments, dryness, and even boredom of certain exemplary twentieth-century texts can also be made to yield pleasure. Our sophistication muddies the issue. For the pleasure of *Kim* is of a more traditional and unproblematic sort, a pleasure in the apprehension of things as they are, in embracing a world as enchanting as it is flawed. Kipling's book accepts the world's body, undeterred by odors, bulges, wrinkles, scars. Life, in its final bearing, may prove to be absurd, but *Kim*, though far from an innocent book, has little commerce with this view, since it is a book that takes delight in each step of the journey bringing us closer to the absurd: delight in our clamor, our foolishness, our vanity, our senses, and—through the lumbering radiance of the lama who comes from and goes back to the hills of Tibet—delight in an ultimate joy of being which beckons from the other side of sensuous pleasure but which, implies Kipling, those of us not lamas would be advised to seek through pleasure.

Part of the pleasure that *Kim* engages is that of accepting, even venerating sainthood, without at all proposing to surrender the world, or even worldliness, to saints. *Kim* embraces both worlds, that of the boy and the lama, the senses and beyond, recognizing that anyone who would keep a foot, or even a finger, in both of these worlds must have some discipline in adjustment and poise—otherwise, what need would there be for the lama's or any other serious education? But never for a moment does the book propose to smudge the difference between the senses and beyond, or worse still, to contrive some facile synthesis. The "Wheel of Things," to which we are all bound in this world, and the "Search," by which we may penetrate another, have each their claim and dignity. The two speed along in parallel, but what they signify cannot readily be merged. There is earth, there is spirit, both are real. In any case, a writer open to the allurements of pleasure is more likely to explore the Many than strain toward the One.

And greater scandal still: *Kim* is the work of a man quite unable to evoke the admiration we give to culture heroes. He is a jingo and a bully, or defender of bullies; he swaggers in the style of an overgrown schoolboy; he is usually more talented than wise. That there was a "wound behind his bow" hardly excuses all that we find unattractive in Kipling: there is a wound behind every bow. He is not a writer we

take to heart, as one takes Hardy, or respect unreservedly, as one respects Chekhov. Yet this often small-spirited writer composed, once in his life, a book of the most exquisite radiance of spirit, breathing a love of creation such as few of his greater contemporaries could match. There is a puzzle here, and I propose to let it remain.

The story starts with noises of sociality. Kim is a thirteen-year-old darling of the streets, a fast-talking urchin, white by birth and dark from the sun, who awaits each day as an encounter with possibility. Trading amiable epithets with the bazaar merchants who call him "Little Friend of all the World," Kim is neither innocent nor naive. He has "known all evil since he could speak," but he does not let it determine or overwhelm him; he absorbs and then puts aside that knowledge, as if breaking a skin, for there is always something to see and experience in the streets of Lahore, that "wonderful walled city." In these streets he is as shrewd as his distant cousin Huck Finn is shrewd along the shore; like that cousin, he has learned "to avoid missionaries and white men of serious aspect," and also has learned the fine art of doing "nothing with an immense success." Whenever he sidles up to a booth, the men of the city smile, knowing they will hear something clever or mischievous and will enjoy his command of the Indian art of cursing. He is a young entrepreneur and apprentice con man, a quick-change artist who does not care for any fixed or even steadily emergent self because life offers so many selves to discover and try out. "Who is Kim?" he will ask himself later in the book, and each chapter will yield the happy answer that there are many answers. He loves "the game for its own sake"— the "game" standing here for both the British Secret Service, with which he will become enmeshed through his worldly self, and the entirely of the business of life. "The game" is not an adequate term, or concept, at all; it reflects the all-too-familiar side of Kipling's sensibility which is adolescent and stunted.

When Kim meets the lama, an ungainly rhapsodist who makes transcendence seem a familiar option, the two of them quickly find common ground. They share a meal, they bound their territory, they match prospects for the future. To the boy, the old man represents a new experience, a guru such as the mainland does not yield; for the old man, the boy is a guide through the bewilderments of India and a friend ripening into a *chela* or disciple. Kim is possessed by the evidence of his senses, the lama with a vision beyond, and the book will make as its central matter an unfolding of the love between the two, that thrill of friendship which in nineteenth-century literature comes to replace the grace of God.

At first Kim literally takes the old man in hand. He goes to beg food for him, charmingly vain in the confidence with which he can tap the city. "They ate together in great content"—so begin and end

half the great stories of mankind. Awakened after a sleep brought on by the meal, the old man looks for the boy and is bewildered to find Kim in one of his transmutations, "a Hindu urchin in a dirty turban." One thinks to compare this moment with the trick Huck plays on Jim, but only to reject the comparison, since everything is far gentler in Kipling's India than in Twain's America, and Kim need not go through torments of conscience in order to declare himself "thy chela," certainly need not declare himself ready, like Huck, for perdition. Because he is utterly fortified in his sense of being at home in the world and feels some mild superiority to the unworldliness of the old man, Kim can also begin to see, in an incipient way, that the lama represents other possibilities for him: "'I have never seen anyone like to thee in all this my life. I go with thee.'" It is not yet a spiritual discipleship; it is simply a companionship of the road. "Boy-like, if an acquaintance had a scheme, Kim was quite ready with one of his own." Perhaps, he smiles to himself, "they will make me a king" during the journey. To which the lama replies: "'I will teach thee other and better desires upon the road.'"

But not yet, not at the beginning. The first five chapters of the book form a picaresque entry into "the great good-tempered world," first on the "te-rain" and then along the Great Trunk Road (India's Mississippi). It is an India refracted through Kipling's adoring memory and in its relation to the "real" India complex beyond hope of disentangling. It is an India Kipling loves for its rough vivacity, its easy mixture of manners, its encompassing of gutter and cloud; and it is praised by him (as if to unsettle all those who declare settled views of his work) as the "only democratic land in the world"—by which he means, I gather, not the absence of rank or distinction but a readiness to live with and intermingle all ranks and distinctions. (At this point historical fact and imaginative vision may find themselves at considerable odds: a problem by no means confined to Kipling, indeed, common to all serious novelists.) In Kipling's India—Kim's playground—the boy is a trickster delighting in his tricks and expecting that his audiences will delight with him in seeing, and seeing through, them. A people raised with a sense of hazard appreciates the boy's virtuosity; shrewdly eyes his performance, an utterly this-worldly performance; yet looks tolerantly upon "holy men stammering gospels in strange tongues." The multiplicity of visions and ways that Kipling attributes to India becomes the ground of his delight.

Kim and the lama now move through a world that is like a vast, disorderly bazaar. People are quick to embrace and to anger. They speak suddenly from the heart, as if any traveler may be a friend. They curse with the expertness of centuries. ("Father of all the daughters of shame and husband of ten thousand virtueless ones,

thy mother was devoted to a devil, being led thereto by her mother.")
Their ripeness shows itself in a linked incapacity to be surprised and
readiness to enjoy the familiar. Running errands for Mahbub Ali,
the free-thinking Afghan horse trader who initiates him into the
British Secret Service, Kim charms a fierce-tongued old Indian lady
(straight in the line of Chaucer, from one pilgrimage to another)
into helping him and the lama. He trades stories with retired sol-
diers, jests with travelers, even pokes a little tender fun at his
lama—for this is Kim's world, a stage for his multiple roles as
urchin, beggar, raconteur, flirt, apprentice spy, and apprentice
chela, who is always eager, as Kipling shrewdly notes, for "the visi-
ble effect of action." Picked up by some British soldiers who pro-
pose to educate him ("sivilize," says Huck), Kim tells the lama:
"Remember, I can change swiftly." It is the motto of every youth try-
ing to evade the clamp of civilization.

And the world's evil? The poverty, injustice, caste rigidities which
must have been so grinding in the India of eighty years ago? If it
would be morally shameful to suppress these questions entirely, it
would also be foolish to let them deprive us of the pleasures of *Kim*.

There is a "literary" way of coping with these questions, but like all
merely "literary" ways, it seems to me finally unsatisfying. Kipling's
book releases a distinct, which is necessarily to say, a limited vision.
It seeks to give life a desirable look; it brushes past social misery as
more recent novels brush past personal happiness; it neglects the
shadows as others neglect the lights; it sees the world as fresh, allur-
ing, and young—young, in India! But *Kim* is not an idyll, not a retreat
from the world; it is a celebration of, a plunge into the world.

Let us try another tack. The book has no assured answers to the
questions of Indian poverty, injustice, and caste rigidity, partly
because it does not choose to give them priority, though we surely
know that it is not an evasive or willfully "positive" book. All the
wrongs and evils of India are there, steeped in the life of the people,
yet these do not keep them from grasping the sensations of their
moment, or from experiencing the appetites and ceremonies they
rightly take to be their due. What so wonderfully distinguishes
Kipling's characters is their capacity for shifting from treble to bass,
from pure spirit to gross earth, from "the Search" to "the Game." It
is as if their culture actually enables them to hold two ideas in their
heads at once. The India of Kipling is a place in which people live
by custom and caprice, fixed in ways given them yet ready to move
past those ways when they feel a need to. They make life for them-
selves, and it has its substance.

One great flaw in the reforming passion, as Ralph Ellison
reminded me during a polemic about black fiction a decade ago, is
that in its eagerness to remedy social wrongs it tends to neglect the

experience, certainly to undervalue the experience, of those whose
lives it wishes to improve. It does not weigh or honor fully enough the
life-hungers, the life-capacities of the oppressed. Now Kipling, it is
true, did not see India as particularly oppressed, and I am as ready as
the next liberal or radical to deplore this failure; but he did see the
people of India as vigorous, full of humor and energy, deeply worthy.
How are we to explain that in the pages of this apologist for imperial-
ism, the masses of India seem more alive, more autonomous than in
the pages of writers claiming political correctness?

Regarding Kipling's apparent indifference to the social evils of
India there remains another and more radical "answer." Though in
much of his work he shows a quite sufficient awareness of evil, even
at some points an obsessive concern, he seems really to want to per-
suade us through *Kim*, his most serious book, that in the freshness
of a boy's discoveries and the penetration of an old man's vision, evil
can become ultimately insignificant, almost as nothing before the
unsubdued elation of existence, almost as nothing before the idea
of moral beauty. Others in the West and the East, long before
Kipling, have said as much, though few have embodied it with the
plastic vividness that Kipling has. I will confess here to not entirely
grasping the import of this vision of ultimate goodness or harmony;
I find it a kind of moral slope, very slippery, very attractive. Yet in
reading *Kim* one may yield to this vision, just as one might for a
moment come to accept beatitude upon meeting a saint. Nor should
we try to get round the problem by remarking that *Kim* is a chil-
dren's book. For it seems intolerable that the best things in life
should be supposed available only to children. Old bones have their
rights too.

The middle portion of *Kim*, another five chapters, brings to an
end the rapturous picaresque of boy and old man: it must come to
an end. Kim is sent to the white man's school, to be trained as the
son of a *sahib* that he is; he will be prepared for the "Great Game,"
the world of power, rationality, governance. Who is Kim, he now
asks himself with an anxiety that is new to him. "He considered his
own identity, a thing he had never done before, till his head swam."
He submits to the disadvantages of the whites, though he is still per-
suaded in his heart that he is one of the blacks—"'when the *madris-
sah* [school] is shut, then I must be free and go among my people.'"
On vacations he "changes swiftly," drops his European being,
dresses as an Indian, returns to "my people." The lama fades out of
the picture, while still, in the style of a Dickens's benefactor, sup-
porting Kim in the white man's school. "Come to me! Come to me!
Come to me!" the boy writes to him in an outburst of longing, and
when they meet for a short while it is now in open love. " 'If I eat
thy bread,' cried Kim passionately, 'how shall I ever forget thee?'"

The old man consoles him: " 'Do not weep; for look you, all Desire
is illusion, and a new binding upon the Wheel. Go up to the Gates
of Learning. Let me see thee go. . . . Doest thou love me? Then
go, or my heart cracks.'" The boy goes, to learn his trade, to be
tested by other agents, British and Indian, to become part of the
Game, a man who can govern.

These chapters are beautifully done, with delicacy in shifting
from milieu to milieu, but they are minor Kipling rather than major:
the adventures here are more like those of Tom Sawyer than those
of Huck Finn. And they leave us somewhat uneasy. Edmund Wilson,
who thought *Kim* "almost a first-rate book," put his finger on the
source of this uneasiness: "What the reader tends to expect is that
Kim will come eventually to realize that he is delivering into
bondage to the British invaders those whom he has always consid-
ered his own people, and that a struggle between allegiances will
result. . . . We have been shown two entirely different worlds
existing side by side, with neither really understanding the other,
and we have watched the oscillations of Kim, as he passes to and fro
between them. But the parallel lines never meet; the alternating
attractions felt by Kim never give rise to a genuine struggle."

About Wilson's criticism Noel Annan remarks:

> No doubt this is what a courageous liberal writing at a time
> when Gandhi and Congress were struggling for Indian inde-
> pendence did expect, but such a conflict is imposed by the
> critic on the novel. No doubt the future life of a young agent
> would have entailed confounding Indian resistance to the
> British, but this is an *ex post facto* judgment, and in the novel
> such a career is depicted as the maintenance of that minimum
> of order such as is necessary to prevent foreign intrigue, fron-
> tier invasions, and injustices by native princes and to permit
> the joyous, noisy, pullulating mess of Indian life on the Great
> Trunk Road to continue.

Annan's reply is adequate as far as it goes, but we might try to go
a little farther. And oddly, it is Wilson who, in the very course of his
complaint, provides our answer. "The parallel lines [between what
the lama signifies and what the English require] never meet; the
alternating attractions felt by Kim never give rise to a genuine strug-
gle." Precisely so; indeed, that is Kipling's major theme—the paral-
lel lines *cannot* meet. For what impinges upon Kim's consciousness
are not two systems of political beliefs, or social orders, but two
ways of apprehending human existence, each of which is shown to
have its own irreducible claims. The dualism that Wilson deplores
yet keenly notices lies at the very heart of the book.

Would it, in any case, make much difference if Kim were to join

an incipient Indian nationalist movement instead of the British Secret Service? Would he still not have to undergo a similar training in the ways of the world, a similar apprenticeship in stratagems and devices? Would he still not be torn between the irreconcilable claims of this world and another? Would not the lama still remain before him as a loving apparition of a "Way" never to be accepted wholly but never to be abandoned wholly?

Most of us, I suppose, would be happier if Kim worked for a Gandhi or some forerunner of Gandhi rather than Colonel Creighton, the head of the British Secret Service, since that would ease our discomfort with the part of Kipling which, intellectually, we find insupportable. But for the dynamic of the novel itself, for the inner development of Kim, it would not matter decisively. The Secret Service, rather than a secret underground, is what Kipling's experience made available to him at a fairly superficial plane of consciousness; it is a given of the world in which he grew up, the India of his youth, and it is not, one notes with gratitude, subjected to any quick "purification" by virtue of Kim's service to the lama. All that the Game—the Secret Service and its prep-school hijinks—need really do is to embody the Wheel of Things, that terrestrial "illusion" which the first portion of the book has shown to be the substance of delight.

The parallel lines of the two main actions draw closer and closer in the concluding chapters, a soaring movement of ecstasy, one of the most beautiful set-pieces in the English language. It is Kipling's skill, but behind that skill, his easiness and poise as a juggler of worlds, which leads him to see that the two lines of action can indeed by brought very close together but that their meanings, their "ways" must remain beyond conciliation.

Kim's mission for the British service leads him toward Tibet, in a pleasantly exciting rigmarole about chasing off Russian spies; his mission as the lama's *chela* leads him toward Tibet, where the old man, as a mighty walker of the hills, takes on a new energy, but also sins through his lapse into anger when he is struck by one of the Russians. Everything comes finally into place, even that coarse-grained love for the world which the lama, here if nowhere else, finds himself sharing:

> "These are the hills of my delight! Shadows blessed above all other shadows! There my eyes opened on this world; there my eyes were opened to this world; there I found Enlightenment; and there I girt my loins for my Search. Out of the Hills I came—the high Hills and the strong winds. Oh, just is the Wheel." He blessed them in detail—the great glaciers, the naked rocks, the piled moraines and tumbled shale; dry,

upland, hidden salt-lake, age-old timber and fruitful water-shot valley one after the other, as a dying man blesses his folk, and Kim marvelled at his passion.

Both Kim and the lama suffer brief, sharp moments of crisis: the boy, his mission successful, is diverted into helping the old man and succumbs to a kind of breakdown of uncertainty, while the old man, though believing himself at the verge of nirvana, forces himself to return to this world out of his love for the boy:

> Then a voice cried: "What shall come to the boy if thou art dead?" and I was shaken back and forth in myself with pity for thee; and I said: "I will return to my *chela* lest he miss the Way." Upon this my Soul . . . withdrew itself from the Great Soul with strivings and yearnings and retchings and agonies not to be told. . . . I pushed aside world upon world for thy sake.

It is a climax of rhapsodic union, but only of the boy and the old man, not the two Ways. One of Kipling's best critics, J. M. S. Tompkins, notices that "the beauty of *Kim* lies largely in the figure of the lama. . . . Benign, courteous, humble and clean of heart, but a man of authority in his place and time, he draws Kim not to any mystical height—the boy remains firmly terrestrial and takes a very practical view of the lama's immersion in the River of the Arrow—but to a perception of these qualities in his master."

All through the last third of the book there run a series of anticipatory communions, moments of meeting between the two, in which all seems at peace in, and out of, the world. As they eat together, Kim recognizes: "'And we are beyond all castes.'" The old man speaks "as a Seeker walking in humility, as an old man, wise and temperate, illumining knowledge . . . till Kim, who had loved him without reason, now loved him for fifty good reasons." And "each long, perfect day rose behind Kim for a barrier to cut him off from his race and his mother-tongue."

There are moments of pure charm: "'These,'" says the lama, "'are indeed my Hills. Thus should a man abide, perched above the world, separated from delights, considering vast matters.'" And Kim answers: "'Yes, if he has a *chela* to prepare tea for him, and to fold a blanket for his head, and to chase out calving cows.'" There are moments of pure yielding, when they wearily make their way down from the hills, the lama weakens, and Kim "held the weary head on his lap through the noonday heats." The lama cannot help remarking how strange it is that a young sahib should serve him so, and Kim replies: "'Thou hast said there is neither black nor white. Why plague me with this talk, Holy One? Let me rub the other foot. It vexes me. I am not a Sahib, I am thy *chela*, and my head is heavy on my shoulders.'"

For all that *Kim* can be seen (not very profitably, I think) to strike a contrast between East and West, Buddhism and Christianity, it is far more harmonious and accepting, far more "organic," than *Huckleberry Finn*, the book to which it bears so many surface similarities. In Twain's story there is hardly a profitable, let alone pleasurable entry into the world; there can only be an escape from it, for a moment or two, on a floating raft. Nothing along the shores of the Mississippi seems as rich or refreshing as the mundane world into which Kim and the lama plunge at the outset of their journey, and finally Twain's book comes to be a much more otherworldly, much more despairing book than *Kim*, even though, or perhaps because, it has no lama, no religious atmosphere, no invocation of the Great Soul. For Kim, while yielding himself to the lama, also feels "with an almost audible click . . . the wheels of his being lock up anew on the world without. Things that rode meaningless on the eyeball of an instant before slid into proper proportion. Roads were meant to be walked upon, houses to be lived in, cattle to be driven, fields to be tilled, and men and women to be talked to."

The parallel lines, then, move endlessly into the future, without joining or reconcilement. Yet a mark of transfiguration has been stamped upon the book; whatever he may do, Kim will forever and beyond forgetting be the old man's *chela*. That mark of transfiguration is of course the print of love, and one can only wonder, in putting down this incomparable book, how strongly Kipling was aware that in guiding his two friends through pleasure and into the joy of being, he may also have been leaving pleasure behind.

EDWARD W. SAID

[*Kim* as Imperialist Novel][†]

* * *

* * * *Kim* is a work of great aesthetic merit; it cannot be dismissed simply as the racist imagining of one fairly disturbed and ultra-reactionary imperialist. George Orwell was certainly right to comment on Kipling's unique power to have added phrases and concepts to the language—East is East, and West is West; the white man's Burden; somewhere East of Suez—and right, also, to say that Kipling's concerns are both vulgar and permanent, of urgent interest. Now,

† From "Introduction" to *Kim*, ed. Edward W. Said (Harmondsworth, Eng.: Penguin Books, 1987) 30–46. Reprinted by permission.

one reason for Kipling's power is that he was an artist of enormous gifts; what he did in his art was to have elaborated ideas that would have had far less permanence, for all their vulgarity, without the art. But the other reason for his power is that he was also supported by (and therefore could make use of) the authorized monuments of nineteenth-century European culture, for whom the inferiority of non-white races, the necessity for them to be ruled by a superior civilization, and the absolute unchanging essence of Orientals, blacks, primitives, women were more or less undebatable, unquestioned axioms of modern life. The extraordinary status of racial theory, in which it was scientifically proven that the white man stood at the pinnacle of development and civilization, is a case in point.

It would be tedious here to run through the arguments and the names: I have discussed these notions in *Orientalism*.[1] Suffice it to say that Macaulay, Carlyle, Arnold, Ruskin, J. A. Froude, John Robert Seeley, even John Stuart Mill, plus every major novelist, essayist, philosopher, and historian of note accepted as fact the division, the difference and, in Gobineau's phrase, the inequality of the races. Moreover these views were regularly adduced as evidence for the desirability of European rule in less-developed regions of the world. Much the same situation obtains in France, Belgium, Germany, Holland, and the United States. True, there were debates about how the colonies were to be ruled, or whether some of them should be given up. Yet no one with any power to influence public discussion or policy demurred as to the basic superiority of the white European male, who should always retain the upper hand when dealing with natives. Statements like 'the Hindu is inherently untruthful and lacks moral courage' were the expression of wisdom from which very few, least of all the governors of Bengal, dissented; similarly when a historian of India like Sir H. M. Elliot planned his work, central to it was the notion of Indian barbarity.[2] An entire system of thought clustered around these conceptions. Climate and geography dictated certain character traits in the Indian; Orientals, according to Lord Cromer, one of their most redoubtable rulers, could not learn to walk on sidewalks, could not tell the truth, could not use logic; the Malaysian native was essentially lazy, the way the northern European was energetic and resourceful. V. G. Kiernan's book *The Lords of Human Kind* gives a remarkable picture of how widespread these views were.[3] Disciplines like colonial economics, anthropology, history and sociology were built out of these dicta, with the result that almost to a man and woman the Europeans who dealt with colonies such as India became

1. Edward W. Said, *Orientalism* (Penguin, 1985).
2. Sir H. M. Elliott, Preface to *India's History As Told By Its Own Historians*, ed. J. Dowson (1867).
3. V. G. Kiernan, *The Lords of Human Kind* (Columbia University Press, 1986).

insulated to the facts of change and nationalism. Even Karl Marx succumbed to thoughts of the changeless Asiatic village, or agriculture, or despotism. And as colonial work progressed in time it became specialized. A young Englishman sent to India would belong to a class whose national dominance over each and every Indian, no matter how aristocratic and poor, was absolute. He would have heard the same stories, read the same books, learned the same lessons, joined the same clubs as all the other young colonial officials. Ronnie Heaslop in E. M. Forster's *A Passage to India* is a well-known portrait of such an official.

All of this is absolutely relevant to *Kim*, whose main figure of worldly authority is Colonel Creighton. This ethnographer-scholar-soldier is no mere accidental creature of invention, sprung fully grown and ready from Kipling's imagination. He is almost certainly a figure drawn from Kipling's experiences in the Punjab, and he is most interestingly interpreted both as an evolution out of earlier figures of authority in colonial India as well as someone whose role answered to Kipling's own needs. In the first place, although Creighton is seen infrequently and his character is not as fully drawn as either Mahbub Ali's or the Babu's, he is nevertheless very much there, a point of reference for the action, a discreet director of events, a man whose power is eminently worthy of respect. Yet he is no crude martinet. He takes over Kim's life by persuasion, not by imposition of his rank. He can be flexible when it seems reasonable—who could have wished for a better boss than Creighton during Kim's footloose holidays?—and stern when events require it.

In the second place, what makes Creighton especially interesting is Kipling's rendition of him as a colonial official and scholar. This union of power and knowledge is contemporary with Conan Doyle's invention of Sherlock Holmes (whose faithful scribe, Doctor Watson, is a veteran of the North-West Frontier), also a man whose approach to life includes a healthy respect for, and protection of, the law, allied with a superior, specialized intellect. In both instances, Kipling and Conan Doyle represent for their readers men whose unorthodox style of operation is rationalized by relatively new fields of experience turned into quasi-academic specialities. Colonial rule and crime detection appear now to have almost the respectability and order of the classics and chemistry. When Mahbub Ali turns Kim in for his education, Creighton, overhearing their conversation, thinks 'that the boy mustn't be wasted if he is as advertised'. Creighton sees the world from a totally systematic viewpoint. Everything about India interests him, because everything in it is significant for his rule. The interchange between ethnography and colonial work in Creighton is fluent; he can study the talented boy both as a future spy and as an anthropological curiosity. Thus when Father Victor wonders whether

it might not be too much for Creighton to attend to a bureaucratic detail concerning Kim's education, the colonel dismisses the scruple. 'The transformation of a regimental badge like your Red Bull into a sort of fetish that the boy follows is very interesting.'

Two further points should be made about Creighton the anthropologist. Of all the modern social sciences, anthropology is the one historically most closely tied to colonialism, since it has often been the case that since the mid-nineteenth century anthropologists and ethnologists were also advisors to colonial rulers on the manners and mores of the native people to be ruled. Claude Lévi-Strauss's allusion to anthropological investigations in *The Scope of Anthropology* as 'sequels to colonialism' is a recognition of this fact;[4] the excellent collection of essays edited by Talal Asad, *Anthropology and the Colonial Encounter*, develops the connections still further.[5] And, finally, in Robert Stone's recent novel on United States imperialist involvement in Latin American affairs, *A Flag for Sunrise*,[6] its central character is Holliwell, an anthropologist with ambiguous ties to the CIA. Kipling was simply one of the first novelists to portray a logical alliance between Western science and political power at work in the colonies.

Secondly Creighton is always taken seriously by Kipling, which is one of the reasons the Babu is there. The native anthropologist is clearly a bright man whose reiterated ambitions to belong to the Royal Society are not entirely unfounded. Yet he is almost always funny, or gauche, or somehow caricatural not because he is incompetent or inept in his work—on the contrary, he is exactly the opposite—but because he is not white, that is, he can never be a Creighton. Kipling, I think, is very careful about this. Just as he could not imagine an India in historical flux *out of* British control, he could not imagine Indians who could be as effective and as serious in what Kipling and many others of the time considered to be exclusively Western pursuits. Hence, lovable and admirable though he may be, there remains in Kipling's portrait of him the grimacing stereotype of the ontologically funny native, hopelessly trying to be like 'us'.

I said above that the figure of Creighton, is, in a sense, the culmination of a change taking place over generations in the personification of British power in India. Behind Creighton are late eighteenth-century adventurers and pioneers like Warren Hastings and Robert Clive, men whose innovative rule and personal excesses required legislation in England to subdue the unrestricted authority of the Raj. What survives of Clive and Hastings in Creighton is their sense of freedom, their willingness to improvise, their preference for the

4. Claude Lévi-Strauss, *The Scope of Anthropology* (Cape, 1967).
5. Talal Asad, *Anthropology and the Colonial Encounter* (Ithaca Press, 1973).
6. Robert Stone, *A Flag for Sunrise* (Knopf, 1981).

informal over the formal. Standing behind Creighton, also, are the great scholar figures for whom service in India was an opportunity to study an alien culture—men like Sir William ('Asiatic') Jones, Sir Charles Wilkins, Nathaniel Halhed, Henry Colebrooke, Jonathan Duncan. But whereas such men belonged not to a national but to a principally commercial enterprise, they seemed never to have had what Creighton (and Kipling) had, the feeling that work in India was as patterned and as a economical (in the literal sense of the word) as running a total polity. What distinguishes Creighton from the Clives, the Colebrookes, and the Halheds, is that his norms are those of disinterested government, government based not upon whim, or personal preference, but upon laws, principles of order and control. Creighton embodies the notion that you cannot govern India unless you know India, and to know India means understanding the way it operates. This immediately sets the governor apart from the ordinary human being, for whom questions of right and wrong, of virtue and harm are both emotionally involving and important. To the government personality, the main prerogative is not whether something is good or evil, and therefore must be changed or kept, but whether something works or not, whether it helps or hinders one in ruling what is in effect an alien entity. Thus Creighton satisfies the Kipling who had imagined an ideal India, unchanging and attractive, as an eternally integral part of the Empire. *This* was an authority one could give in to.

In a celebrated essay, Noel Annan presented the notion that Kipling's vision of society in his novels was similar to that of the new sociology—as put forward by Durkheim, Weber and Pareto.

> [The new sociology] saw society as a nexus of groups; and the pattern of behaviour which these groups unwittingly established, rather than men's wills or anything so vague as a class, cultural or national tradition, primarily determined men's actions. They asked how these groups promoted order or instability in society, whereas their predecessors had asked whether certain groups helped society to progress.[7]

Annan goes on to say that Kipling was similar to the founders of modern sociological discourse to the extent that he believed efficient government in India depended upon 'the forces of social control [such as religion, law, custom, convention, morality] which imposed upon individuals certain rules which they broke at their peril'. In the late nineteenth century it had become almost a commonplace of British imperial theory that the British Empire was different from (and therefore better than) the Roman Empire in that

7. Noel Annan, 'Kipling's Place in the History of Ideas', *Victorian Studies*, vol. III, no. 4 (June 1960), p. 323. [See p. 324 in this volume—*Editor*.]

the latter was just robbery and profit, whereas the former was a rig-
orous system in which order and law prevailed. Cromer makes the
point in *Imperialism Ancient and Modern*,[8] and so does Conrad's
Marlow in *Heart of Darkness*. Creighton understands this perfectly,
which is why he works with Muslims, Bengalis, Afghans, Tibetans
without appearing ever to belittle their beliefs or slight their differ-
ences. It was, I think, a natural insight for Kipling, to have imagined
Creighton as a scientist whose speciality included the minute work-
ings of a complex society, rather than as either a colonial bureau-
crat, necessary but dull, or a rapacious profiteer. Creighton's
Olympian humour, his affectionate but detached attitude towards
people, his eccentric bearing, are Kipling's embellishments of an
ideal Indian official, whose genealogy is a long one, but whose pre-
sent state is the refinement of many costly antecedents, numerous
failures, and a fair number of major achievements.

But Creighton the organization man not only presides over the
Great Game (whose ultimate beneficiary is of course the Kaisar-i-
Hind, or Queen Empress, and her British people), he also works
hand-in-hand with the novelist himself. If there is a consistent point
of view to be ascribed to Kipling, it is in Creighton, more than any-
one else, that it can be found. Like Kipling, Creighton respects the
distinctions within Indian society. When Mahbub Ali tells Kim that
he must never forget that he is a sahib, we should remember that,
in a sense, he speaks as Creighton's trusted, experienced employee.
Creighton, again like Kipling, never tampers with the hierarchies,
the priorities and privileges of caste, religion, ethnicity and race;
neither do the men and women who work for him. By the late nine-
teenth century the so-called Warrant of Precedence which began,
according to Geoffrey Moorhouse in *India Britannica*,[9] by recogniz-
ing 'fourteen different levels of status' had expanded to 'sixty-one,
some reserved for one person, others shared by a number of people'.
Moorhouse speculates that the special 'love-hate' relationship
between the British and Indians derived from the complex hierar-
chical attitude present in each people—class for the British, caste
for the Indians. 'Each grasped the other's basic social premise and
not only understood it but subconsciously respected it as a curious
variant of their own.' One sees this everywhere in *Kim*—the
patiently detailed register of different races and castes, the accep-
tance by everyone (even the lama) of the doctrine of racial separa-
tion, the lines and the customs which cannot easily be traversed by
outsiders. Everyone in *Kim* is therefore equally an outsider to other
groups and an insider in his.

8. Evelyn Baring, 1st Earl of Cromer, *Ancient and Modern Imperialism* (J. Murray, 1910).
9. Geoffrey Moorhouse, *India Brittanica* (Paladin, 1983), p. 103.

Thus Creighton's almost instinctive appreciation of Kim's abilities, his quickness, his capacity for disguise and for getting into a situation as if it were native to him, is like the novelist's interest in a complex and chameleon-like character, who can dart in and out of adventure, intrigue, episode. The ultimate analogy is between the Great Game and the novel itself. To be able to see all India from the vantage of controlled observation: this is one great satisfaction. Another is to have at one's fingertips a character who can sportingly cross lines and invade territories, a little 'Friend of all the World', Kim O'Hara himself. It is as if by holding Kim at the centre of the novel (just as Creighton the spy master holds the boy in the Great Game) Kipling can *have* and enjoy India in a way that even imperialism never dreamed of. What does this mean in terms of so codified and organized a structure as the late nineteenth-century realistic novel?

III

Along with Conrad, Kipling is a writer of fiction whose heroes belong to a startling unusual world of foreign adventure and personal charisma. When we think of Kim or, say, Lord Jim and Kurtz, we immediately bring to mind creatures with a flamboyant will who presage later adventures like T. E. Lawrence in *The Seven Pillars of Wisdom* and Malraux's Perken in *La Voie royale*. Conrad's heroes, I said earlier, have been bitten by an unusual power of reflection and cosmic irony, but they remain in the memory as strong and often heedlessly daring men of action. Like Conrad, Kipling had difficulties with romantic love, with women, with domesticity.

The interesting thing about the two men is that although their fiction belongs to the genre of adventure-imperialism (along with Rider Haggard, Conan Doyle, Charles Reade, Vernon Fielding, G. A. Henty, and dozens of lesser writers) they are nevertheless writers with a claim on serious aesthetic and critical attention. True, their world was the world of heroes like 'Chinese' Gordon, Cecil Rhodes, Lord Curzon, Livingstone and Stanley, Richard Burton—a world brilliantly described in Martin Green's *Dreams of Adventure, Deeds of Empire*,[1] which he correctly traces back to *Robinson Crusoe*—and yet there is in the writing of Conrad and Kipling an additional complexity that makes them more interesting than all their other contemporaries, whom we only read today as sociological or perhaps historical exhibitions.

One way of grasping what is unusual about Kipling's best work of long fiction, *Kim*, is to recall briefly who his other great contemporaries were. We have become so used to seeing him alongside Hag-

1. Martin Green, *Dreams of Adventure, Deeds of Empire* (Basic Books, 1979).

gard and John Buchan that we have forgotten that, as an artist, he
can justifiably be compared with Thomas Hardy, with Henry James,
George Meredith, George Gissing, the later George Eliot, George
Moore, Samuel Butler. In France, Kipling's peers are Flaubert and
Zola, even Proust and the early Gide. Yet the major difference
between all these writers and Kipling is that their works are essen-
tially novels of disillusion and disenchantment, whereas *Kim*, for
instance, is not. Almost without exception the protagonist of the late
nineteenth-century novel is someone who realizes that his or her
life's project—the wish to be great, rich, or distinguished—is mere
fancy, illusion, dream. If we think of Frédéric Moreau in Flaubert's
Sentimental Education, or Isabel Archer in *The Portrait of a Lady*, or
Ernest Pontifex in Butler's *The Way of All Flesh*, we will bring to
mind a young man or woman bitterly awakened from a fancy dream
of accomplishment, action or glory, forced instead to come to terms
with a considerably reduced status, a betrayed love, and a hideously
bourgeois world of crass mammonism and philistine taste.

This awakening is by no means to be found in *Kim*. Nothing
brings the point home more powerfully than a comparison between
Kim and his nearly exact contemporary Jude Fawley, the 'hero' of
Thomas Hardy's *Jude the Obscure* (1896). Both are eccentric
orphans, objectively at odds with their environments: Kim is an
Irishman in India, Jude a minimally gifted rural English boy who is
more interested in Greek than he is in farming. Both imagine lives
of appealing attractiveness for themselves and both try to achieve
this life through apprenticeship of some sort, Kim as chela to the
wandering abbot-lama, Jude as a supplicant student at the univer-
sity. But there the comparisons stop, and the contrasts begin. Jude
is ensnared by one circumstance after the other; he marries the ill-
suited Arabella, falls in love disastrously with Sue Bridehead, con-
ceives children who commit suicide, ends his days dying as a
neglected man after years of pathetic wandering. Kim, on the other
hand, graduates from one brilliant success to the other. By the end
of the novel he is at the beginning of a new and satisfying life, hav-
ing helped the lama achieve his dream of redemption, the British to
foil a serious plot, the Indians to continue enjoying prosperity under
Britain.

Yet it is important to insist again on the similarities between *Kim*
and *Jude the Obscure* the better to appreciate the difference in tone
between these two striking novels by two great writers. In each case
we have an odd or somehow eccentric young man who is compelled,
like Robinson Crusoe or Tom Jones, to make his own way in the
world. Both boys, Kim and Jude, are singled out for their unusual
pedigree; neither is like 'normal' boys whose parents and family are
there to assure a smooth passage through life. Central to their

predicaments as individuals is the problem of identity—what to be, where to go, what to do. Since they cannot be like the others therefore, who are they? Impelled by these questions they are restless seekers and wanderers. In this they are like the archetypal hero of the novel form itself, Don Quixote, who, according to Georg Lukàcs in *The Theory of the Novel* decisively marks off the world of the novel in its fallen, unhappy state, its 'lost transcendence', from the world of the epic, which is happy, satisfied, full. Every novelistic hero, Lukàcs says, attempts to restore a lost world of his or her imagination which, particularly in the late nineteenth-century novel of disillusionment, is shown to be doomed everlastingly to wish unsuccessfully for an unrealized dream. Clearly Jude, like Frédéric Moreau, like Dorothea Brooke, like Isabel Archer, Ernest Pontifex, and all the others, is condemned to such a fate. The paradox of personal identity is that it is implicated in that unsuccessful dream. Jude would not be who he is were it not for his futile wish to become a scholar. What promises him relief from his mediocre existence, therefore, is an escape from his identity as a social nonentity. The structural irony that is basic to every late nineteenth-century realistic novel is precisely that very conjunction: what you wish for is exactly what you cannot have. Hence the utter poignancy and defeated hope that by the end of *Jude the Obscure* has become synonymous with Jude's very identity.

It is exactly in getting beyond this paralysing, dispiriting impasse that Kim O'Hara is so remarkably optimistic a novelistic character. Kim's search for an identity that he can be comfortable with by the end of the novel is successful. Like many of the other heroes of imperial fiction (as we read about their exploits in Conrad and Haggard, for example) Kim's actions result in victories not defeats. He restores India to health, as the invading foreign agents are apprehended and expelled. And, indeed, throughout *Kim* itself we are impressed with the boy's resilience, his capacity for standing up to extreme situations such as those trials of identity engineered for him by Lurgan Sahib. Part of the boy's strength is his deep knowledge, almost instinctive in its wellspring, of his difference from the Indians around him; after all he has a special amulet given him during infancy, and unlike all the other boys he plays with—this is established right at the novel's opening—he is endowed, through natal prophecy, with a unique fate of which he wishes to make everyone aware. Later this develops explicitly into his awareness of being a sahib, a white man, and whenever he wavers there is someone to remind him of the basic fact that he is indeed a sahib, with all the rights and privileges of that quite special rank. Even the saintly guru is made by Kipling to affirm the difference between a white man and a non-white.

But that fact about Kim does not by itself impart to the novel its curious sense of enjoyment and confidence. Compared to James or Conrad, Kipling was not an introspective writer, nor—from the evidence that we have—did he think of himself like Joyce, as an Artist. The force of his best writing comes from his ease and fluency, his seeming naturalness as narrator and master of characterization, where the sheer variousness of his creativity rivals Dickens and Shakespeare. Language for him was not, as it was for Conrad in particular, a resistant medium; it was transparent, capable of many tones and inflections without too much trouble, all of them directly representative of the world he explored. It is precisely this aspect of Kipling's writing that gives Kim his sprightliness and wit, his energy and attractiveness. In many ways Kim resembles a character who might have been drawn much earlier in the nineteenth century, by somebody like Stendhal, for example, whose vivid portrayals of Fabrice del Dongo and Julien Sorel have the same blend of adventure and occasional wistfulness, which Stendhal called *espagnolisme*. We can speculate, I think, that the reason Kim is so unlike Hardy's Jude is that for him, as for Stendhal's characters, the world is full of possibilities, much like Caliban's island, 'full of noises,/Sounds, and sweet airs that give delight and hurt not'. Certainly danger threatens from time to time, but we never seriously doubt that Kim will somehow wiggle out or that he will outsmart his opponents.

At times, that same world is restful, even idyllic. So not only do we get the bustle and vitality of the Grand Trunk Road, but also the welcoming, gentle pastoralism of that scene *en route* with the old soldier (Chapter 3) as the little group of travellers reposes peacefully:

> There was a drowsy buzz of small life in hot sunshine, a cooing of doves, and a sleepy drone of well-wheels across the fields. Slowly and impressively the lama began. At the end of ten minutes the old soldier slid from his pony, to hear better as he said, and sat with the reins round his wrist. The lama's voice faltered—the periods lengthened. Kim was busy watching a grey squirrel. When the little scolding bunch of fur, close pressed to the branch, disappeared, preacher and audience were fast asleep, the old officer's strong-cut head pillowed on his arm, the lama's thrown back against the tree-bole, where it showed like yellow ivory. A naked child toddled up, stared, and moved by some quick impulse of reverence, made a solemn little obeisance before the lama—only the child was so short and fat that it toppled over sideways, and Kim laughed at the sprawling, chubby legs. The child, scared and indignant, yelled aloud.

On all sides of this sort of Edenic composure there is the 'wonderful spectacle' of the Grand Trunk Road where, as the old soldier

puts it, 'all castes and kinds of men move here . . . Brahmins and chumars, bankers and tinkers, barbers and bunnias, pilgrims and potters—all the world coming and going. It is to me as a river from which I am withdrawn like a log after a flood.'

One especially fascinating index of Kim's way with this teeming and yet strangely hospitable world he lives in is his remarkable gift for disguise. We first see him perched on the ancient gun in a square in Lahore (where it still stands today), an Indian boy among other Indian boys. Kipling carefully differentiates the different religions and background of each boy (the Muslim, the Hindu, the Irish) but is just as careful to show us that none of these identities, though they may hinder each of the other boys, is a hindrance to Kim. He can pass from one dialect, from one set of values and beliefs, to the other. Throughout the book Kim takes on the dialects of numerous Indian communities, Muslim, Hindu, northern and southern. He speaks Urdu, English (Kipling does a superbly funny, but gentle, mockery of the boy's stilted Anglo-Indian, which he rather finely distinguishes from the Babu's orotund verbosity), Eurasian, Hindi, Bengali; Mahbub speaks Pashto, and Kipling, so to speak, gets that, as apparently does Kim; the lama speaks Chinese Tibetan, and he can be understood too. As orchestrator of this Babel of tongues, this veritable Noah's Ark of Sansis, Kashmiris, Akalis, Sikhs and many others, Kipling also manages Kim's progress through it all, chameleon-like in his gift for dancing in and out of it, like a great actor who passes through all situations, at home in each of them.

How very different this is from the dull, mediocre and lustreless world of the European bourgeoisie, whose ambiance as it is rendered by every novelist of importance reconfirms the utter debasement of all contemporary life, all dreams of passion, success and exotic adventure. Hence the antithesis offered by Kipling's fiction: his world, because it is set in an India dominated by Britain, appears to hold nothing back from the expatriate European. *Kim*, therefore, is expressly designed as a novel to show how a white sahib can enjoy life in this lush complexity; and, I would argue, the apparent absence of resistance to European intervention in it—symbolized by Kim's abilities to move relatively unscarred through India—is due precisely to the imperialist vision of the world. For what one cannot do in one's own Western environment, where to try to live out the grand dream of a successful quest is only to keep coming up against one's own mediocrity and the world's corruption and degradation, one can do abroad. Isn't it possible in India to do everything, be anything, go anywhere with impunity?

Consider, also, the pattern of Kim's wanderings as they affect the structure of the novel. Most of his voyages within the Punjab, occur

around the axis formed by Lahore and Umballa, an Indian Army
(hence British) garrison town on the frontier of the United
Provinces. The Grand Trunk Road, built by the great Muslim ruler
Sher Shah in the late sixteenth century, runs from Peshawar to Cal-
cutta, although the lama never goes further south and east than
Benares. There are excursions made by Kim to Simla, to Lucknow,
and later to the Kulu valley; with Mahbub Kim goes as far south as
Bombay and as far west as Karachi. But the overall impression cre-
ated by these voyages is that of a relatively carefree meandering.
Occasionally Kim's trips are punctuated by the requirements of the
school year at St Xavier's but the only serious agendas in the novel,
the only equivalents of temporal pressure on the characters, are,
firstly, the abbot-lama's Quest, which is fairly elastic and, secondly,
the pursuit and final expulsion of the foreign agents trying to stir up
trouble in the North-West Frontier region. There are no scheming
money-lenders here, no village prigs, no vicious gossips or unattrac-
tive and heartless *parvenus* as there are in the novels of Kipling's
major European contemporaries.

Now contrast *Kim's* rather loose structure based as it is on a lux-
urious geographical and spatial expansiveness, with the tight,
relentlessly unforgiving *temporal* structure of the European novels
contemporary with *Kim*. Time, says Lukàcs in *The Theory of the
Novel*, is the great ironist, almost a character in these novels, as it
both drives the protagonist further into illusion and derangement,
in that with the passing of time the illusions grow, and contact with
reality decreases, and at the same time reveals his or her illusions to
be groundless, empty, bitterly futile. In *Kim*, you have the impres-
sion that time is on your side, because, I think, its geography—to an
English reader as India might be to a modern Western tourist—is
yours to move about in more or less freely. Certainly Kim feels that,
and so, too, in his patience, and the sporadic, even vague way in
which he appears and disappears, does Colonel Creighton. The
opulence of India's space, the commanding British presence there,
the sense of freedom communicated by the interaction between
those two factors: this adds up to an overwhelmingly positive atmos-
phere irradiating the pages of *Kim*. This is not a driven world of has-
tening disaster, as in Flaubert and Zola.

Kipling's rather unique geographical and spatial preference in
Kim over the temporal element governing metropolitan European
fiction, is, of course, a privileged aesthetic fact. But I would want to
insist that it expresses an irreducible political judgement on
Kipling's part. It is as if he were saying that India is ours and there-
fore we can see it in this mostly uncontested, meandering and ful-
filling way, rather than as a narrow little site of class conflict and
hopelessly middle-class values. India is 'other' and, importantly, for

all its wonderful size and variety, it is safely held by Britain. There is, however, another aesthetically satisfying coincidence that Kipling arranges, and it, too, must be taken into account. This is the confluence between Creighton's Great Game and Kim's inexhaustibly renewed capacity for disguises and adventure. Kipling keeps the two things tightly connected in the novel. The first is the device of political surveillance and control; the second, at a much deeper and more interesting level, is the wish-fantasy of someone who would like to think that everything is possible, that one can go anywhere and be anything. T. E. Lawrence in *The Seven Pillars of Wisdom* expresses this fantasy over and over, as he reminds us how he—a blond and blue-eyed Englishman—moved among the desert Arabs as if he were one of them.

I call this a fantasy because, as both Kipling and Lawrence endlessly remind us, no one—least of all actual whites and non-whites in the colonies—ever forgets that 'going native' or playing the Great Game are facts built on rock-like foundations, those of European power. Was there ever a native fooled by the blue or green-eyed Kims and Lawrences who passed among the inferior races as agent adventurers? I doubt it, just as I doubt that there existed any white man or woman within the orbit of European imperialism who ever forgot that the discrepancy in power between the white rulers and the native subject was absolute, intended to be unchanging, rooted in cultural, political, and economic reality.

Kipling never lets us forget that Kim, the positive boy hero who travels in disguise all over India, across boundaries and rooftops, into tents and villages, is everlastingly responsible to British power, represented by Creighton's Great Game. The reason we can see that so clearly is that since *Kim* was published, India did become independent of Britain and was partitioned, just as since the publication of Gide's *The Immoralist* and Camus's *The Stranger*, Algeria became independent of France. To read these major works of the imperial period retrospectively, then, is to be obligated to read them in the light of decolonization, but, we must immediately add, it is neither to slight their great aesthetic force, nor to treat them reductively as imperialist propaganda. It is a much graver mistake, nevertheless, to read them stripped of their countless affiliations with the facts of power which inform and enable them, to interpret them as if the many inscriptions of race and class in the text were not there at all.

Thus, as I have been saying, *Kim* is a master work of imperialism: I mean this as an interpretation of a rich and absolutely fascinating, but nevertheless profoundly embarrassing novel. The device invented by Kipling, by which British control over India (the Great Game) coincides in detail with Kim's disguise fantasy to be

at one with India, is a remarkable one precisely because it would not have occurred without British imperialism. As such, then, we must read the novel as the realization of a great cumulative process, which in the closing years of the nineteenth century is reaching its last major moment before Indian independence. On the one hand, surveillance and control over India; on the other, love for and fascinated attention to its every detail. What Kipling also saw is what makes possible the overlap between the political hold of the one and the aesthetic and psychological pleasure of the other, British imperialism itself; yet many of his later readers have refused to see his implicit recognition of this troubling and embarrassing truth. And not just Kipling's recognition of British imperialism in general, but imperialism at that specific moment in its history when it had almost completely lost sight of the unfolding dynamics of its own human and secular truth: the truth that India was once independent, that control over it was seized by a European power, and that, over time, Indian resistance to that power had grown so much as inevitably to struggle out from under British subjugation.

The variously qualified pleasure we can derive from reading *Kim* today, therefore, is that in it we can watch a great artist blinded in a sense by his own insights about India, confusing the realities before him, which he saw with such colour and ingenuity, with the notion that these realities were permanent and essential. What Kipling takes and adopts from the novel form he tries to bend to this basically obfuscatory end. But it is surely one of the greatest of novelistic ironies that not only does he not truly succeed in this obfuscation, but his very attempt to use the novel for this purpose reaffirms the quality of his aesthetic integrity. *Kim* most assuredly is *not* a political tract. Kipling's choice of the novel form to express himself, and of Kim O'Hara to engage more profoundly with an India that Kipling obviously loved but could never properly have, this is what our reading should keep resolutely as its central strand. Only then will we be able to see *Kim* both as a great document of its historical moment, as well as an aesthetic milestone along the way to midnight 15 August, 1947,[2] a moment whose children have done so much to revise our sense of the past's richness and its enduring problems.

2. The independence of India [*Editor*].

IAN BAUCOM

[The Survey of India]†

The mapping of the subcontinent, officially known as the Survey of India and colloquially referred to as the "Great Game," was an immense, protracted, and varied task. The survey began in 1767, when Lord Clive appointed James Rennell surveyor general of Bengal, and continued without interruption until India's independence in 1947. In the earliest years of the survey, English cartographers concentrated on plotting serviceable roads, productive land, hill forts, and remarkable natural features. In 1806, William Lambton, armed with a theodolite, began the work of triangulating the entire subcontinent and reducing the surface of India to a comprehensive and rigorously accurate chart. In 1865, Thomas Montgomerie addressed the survey's most intractable problem: that of getting mapmakers into the forbidden territory of Tibet. Montgomerie alighted on the solution of training Indians in the use of the compass and sextant, disguising them as pilgrims, equipping them with an array of hidden instruments—including 100- rather than 108-bead rosaries with which they could count off their paces—and sending them across the border to advance the work of the survey.[1] It is among this group of costumed cartographers that Kipling places Kim.

In joining Kim to this band of wandering mapmakers, Kipling identifies the problem of refashioning Kim's identity with the dilemma of India's Montgomerie-era cartographers. The mapping of India, as Thomas Richards has demonstrated in the most intriguing sections of his essay on *Kim*,[2] was a vital element in the English attempt to control the empire less by occupying it than by knowing it, classifying it, and rendering it visible. Faced with possession of imperial territories too vast to be directly and continuously controlled, the English state had little choice but to exercise its power in the production of knowledge. That that knowledge could not always be retranslated into power was, if not irrelevant, frequently ignored. The accumulation of information in what Richards terms an "imperial archive" created the illusion of control for an imperial

† From *Out of Place: Englishness, Empire, and the Locations of Identity* (Princeton, N.J.: Princeton University Press, 1999) 93–99. Copyright © 1999 by Princeton University Press. Reprinted by permission of the publisher. Page references to *Kim* have been changed to correspond to this Norton Critical Edition.

1. For information on the Survey of India, I have relied on Mary Lynette Larsgaard's *Topographic Mapping of Africa, Antarctica, and Eurasia* (Provo, Utah: Western Association of Map Libraries, 1993) and John Noble Wilford's *The Mapmakers* (New York: Alfred A. Knopf, 1981) 161–73.
2. *The Imperial Archive: Knowledge and the Fantasy of Empire* (New York: Verso, 1993).

state incessantly dreaming the nervous dream of its own demise. Within that archive, the map occupies a position of privilege. Its fiction remains the one most seductive to the imperial state: the fiction of fixity, of ordered, visible, and bounded space. Kipling depicts Colonel Creighton, the Montgomerie-inspired figure of his novel, as a devotee of that fable. At once the director of the survey and the chief of Indian intelligence. Creighton understands that the security of the colonial state depends on his ability to render visible and to map the territory England purports to possess.

Creighton must, however, confront a vexing imperial dilemma. In order to chart—and so imaginatively discipline—the biggest blank on the subcontinental map, the cross-border territory of Tibet, he has to rely on a small band of costumed wanderers, a tribe of nomads whose activities seem to subvent the interests of imperial cartography. The object of the survey, as Creighton cannot fail to understand, was not the production of knowledge in a pure, disinterested state but the production of an ordered, demarcated, and fixed terrain. That object encompasses the policing of movement. It implies, in fact, the absence of movement. Maps represent roads, but not travelers; railways, but not passengers. More significant, maps adore boundaries, and the argument of the boundary is the argument of territorial fixity. Indeed, the promise of the survey is to fix India not only as a governed territory in space but as a permanent possession in time. The wanderings, displacements, and spatial uncertainties of nomadism seem, then, to articulate a direct threat to the spatial and temporal permanencies of cartography, to be the surplus that the map not only cannot represent but must repress. As Richards suggests, Creighton's genius lies in his recognition that the opposition between the nomad and the cartographer can be dissolved, that cartography depends in the moment of its production, if not in the moment of its consumption, on the wandering, exploratory movement of the surveyor. If the nomad could be induced to produce a record of his wanderings, then the colonial state, Creighton recognizes, could harness the nomad to the policing of movement and the ordering of space.

Creighton's value to Kipling resides in the neatness with which, in solving this problem of imperial cartography, he simultaneously solves the author's problem with Kim. In discovering a vocation in which waywardness ceaselessly converts itself into an act of policing, and in which the wanderer continuously exchanges identity with the theodolite, he introduces Kim's anxious parent and biographer to a career in which this most nettlesome of children can do the state some service. Recognizing this, Kipling hands Kim over to Creighton with almost unseemly—but understandable— haste. But the value of this gift is ambiguous. For while Kim

appears to be the perfect child for the marriage Creighton has fashioned between cartography and nomadism, he also represents a constant danger to Creighton's system. So culturally fluent that he can slip with ease into the unmapped spaces of Tibet disguised as a lama's acolyte, yet so nomadically fluid that he perpetually threatens to slip loose from Creighton's control, Kim constantly promises to embrace wandering as an end in itself, to become the very embodiment of a principle of uncertain movement that the colonial state exists to exterminate.

The importance of this imperial urge to extinguish the nomadic cannot be overestimated. Kipling's text hinges on it. If we follow Edward Said and Thomas Richards and read the novel as a minor specimen of the tragic, then we have no choice but to conclude that in tutoring Kim, and in teaching him to embrace the disciplinary imperatives of the Great Game, Creighton erases the little friend of all the world—until at last he exists as nothing other than a code name. Kipling, in directing the reader to construe the text as a rewriting of *Othello*, offers his support for this interpretation. According to the author, we are to identify Kim, like the Moor, as a character who has "done the state some service," and who completes that service by acceding to his self-annihilation. For this reading to succeed, we must regret Kim's fate; we must join Kipling in mourning what becomes of the little friend. This is why Kipling labors so diligently to elicit our sympathy for Kim. For that sympathy, or outrage, emerges as the condition of the state's triumph over Kim. As we curse Kim's disappearance, and his resurrection as the zombielike R17, we affirm that Kim, like India, has indeed been enumerated, and that the colonial state has at long last succeeded in its deadly work of subject-fashioning.

By identifying such a mournful reading of the novel as the only available reading of the text, however, we ignore the profound fragility of Colonel Creighton's system, deny the indebtedness of his police to the trespassive, and abandon those textual moments in which the subcontinent refuses to be mapped and Kim declines to be a sahib. A less partial reading of the text demands our recognition that, like the Victoria Terminus, Kim's sahibized identity resists closure, persistently indicates that "many different races have worked upon it. . . . [and exhibits] the traces of migrations, conquests, changes of style and other marks of difference,"[3] and our admission that Colonel Creighton's map of India suffers a similar scoring. When closely examined, the artifacts of imperial cartography that Creighton's agents have produced disclose themselves as

3. T. Roger Smith, "Architectural Art in India," *Journal of the Royal Society of Arts* 21 (1873): 278.

allegories of imperial Gothic.[4] Pretending to imprint onto paper, rather than marble, the signature of a confidently panoptic colonial state, these maps again write the text of the Raj's hybridization. They are the products of a system of rule that can sustain its fantasies of ubiquitous surveillance only by enlisting, or even inventing, a body of wandering, nativized, fifth columnists. To produce its disciplinary maps of the subcontinent, and so ensure that India remains English, the colonial state finds that it must not only consent to but cultivate its own tropicalization. In contributing to the Anglicization of India, Colonel Creighton finds himself in the odd position of Orientalizing England.

Creighton's embarrassment is not limited to the scandal of the Raj's tropicalization. Not only are his maps contaminated by the marks of difference; they are, at crucial points, blank. The cartographic model of imperial rule establishes a simple equivalence between power and knowledge. To govern India, Creighton suggests, is to know the subcontinent, a formula justifying that perilous dabbling in ethnography which threatens always to become the act of going native. Creighton holds to the conceit that he and his white subordinates can costume themselves in the fabrics of India while remaining resolutely English—an act that Ruskin would have told him was impossible. His gambit depends not only on his, and Kim's, ability to remain unpolluted by that India they are so constantly touching, but, more obviously, on the perpetual production of knowledge. To fail to know is to have risked the loss of Englishness and to have nothing to show for this gamble, to surrender both identity and rule. As Kipling admits, Creighton and his cohorts occasionally fail in this fundamental responsibility.

In the opening chapter of the text, as the curator of the Lahore Museum concludes his tour of the Wonder House, he opens "a mighty map" and shows it to the lama. For all the courtesy that the curator has heretofore shown the holy man, this primal scene of imperial instruction unfolds itself as an act of complacent arrogance, as less a sharing of information than an unveiling of England's ability to know the subcontinent, to order India's spaces, and to render them visible to its own inhabitants. Gesturing with his pencil, the curator draws the lama's eye "from point to point": "Here was Kapilavastu, here the Middle Kingdom, and here Mahabodhi, the Mecca of Buddhism; and here was Kusinagara, sad place of the

4. Patrick Brantlinger also uses the expression "imperial Gothic" in his *Rule of Darkness: British Literature and Imperialism, 1830–1914* (Ithaca: Cornell University Press, 1988); see especially 227–54. Brantlinger, however, uses the term to refer to an imperial manifestation, and refabrication, of the literary genre, whereas I am using it more in the sense of a Bourdieuvian habitus. [Pierre Bourdieu, the French sociologist, conceived of "habitus" as the internalized ways of knowing the world, or as "embodied" social structures through which people experience the world—*Editor*.]

Holy One's death." Gazing at this awesome artifact of imperial
power, the humbled lama responds as his pedagogue might have
expected: "The old man bowed his head over the sheets in silence
for a while, and the Curator lit another pipe" [11]. If Kipling's text
was solely an anatomy of imperial discipline, the scene would end
here; but it is not, and the scene does not. Moments later, after
explaining his quest for the River of the Arrow, the lama returns the
curator's attention to the map:

> The lama drew a long breath. "Where is that River? Foun-
> tain of Wisdom, where fell the arrow?"
> "Alas, my brother, I do not know," said the Curator.
> "Nay, if it please thee to forget—the one thing only that
> thou hast not told me. Surely thou must know? See, I am an
> old man! I ask with my head between my feet, O Fountain of
> Wisdom. We *know* He drew the bow! We *know* the arrow fell!
> We *know* the stream gushed! Where, then, is the River? My
> dream told me to find it. So I came. I am here. But where is the
> River?"
> "If I knew think you not I would cry it aloud?"
> "By it one attains freedom from the Wheel of Things," the
> lama went on, unheeding. "The River of the Arrow! Think
> again! Some little stream, maybe—dried in the heats? But the
> Holy One would never so cheat an old man."
> "I do not know. I do not know."
> The lama brought his thousand-wrinkled face once more a
> handsbreadth from the Englishman's. "I see thou dost not
> know. Not being of the Law, the matter is hid from thee." [12]

The enduring, almost uncanny, humility of the lama makes this an
exchange that can be easily misread; for in it the lama, however
briefly, translates the rhetoric of humility into an idiom of civil
insubordination and sly mockery. Bending his head to his feet,
addressing the curator as that fountain of wisdom which he has rep-
resented himself to be, investing his discourse with a tone of urgent
supplication, the lama plays the child to this mighty representative
of the Raj, repeating his "Where, where?" until he drives the cura-
tor to confess his own inadequacy. The curator, in fact, admits to
more than ignorance. He acknowledges that the empire has
founded itself on a bordered epistemology and confronts the limit of
colonial knowledge. In so doing, he, along with the reader, becomes
aware of the existence of the unmapped and the unmappable within
the cartography of imperialism. At the close of this brief exchange,
the curator is a shattered man, trapped within the agony of
mouthing over and again those words that the English in India
could not afford to utter: "I do not know. I do not know."

The curator is not the only figure so mocked in Kipling's narrative, nor the only individual whose faith in the power of the colonial state breaks. Kipling, who has labored so diligently to convince the reader that he can redeem the tragedy of Kim's annihilation through the victories of Englishness and the state, finds himself similarly mocked and disappointed. At the last he discovers that Colonel Creighton will sacrifice Kim's Englishness to the imperatives of imperial rule, and that India, governed as Creighton and his allies see fit to govern it, simply is not a place in which one can remain unalterably English to the backbone. His narrative emerges, then, as no less tragic; but what it finally represents as tragic is not the ransom paid for the recovery of Kim's Englishness but the betrayal of Englishness by the officers of the Raj.

Throughout the greater part of the text, we have been led to believe that Creighton, like Father Victor, Mr. Bennett, and Kipling himself, remains committed to Kim's sahibization, that, indeed, Kim's sahibization not only is consistent with Creighton's disciplining of India but will emerge as an offshoot of the colonel's policing labors. It is therefore something of a surprise to discover, fairly late in the novel, that Creighton has little interest in either Kim's sahibness or his Englishness. On yet another of those occasions on which he has made his break from St. Xavier's, Kim falls into the hands of Hurree Babu, another of Creighton's operatives. Hurree, rather than returning Kim to school, equips the boy with an array of passwords, undercover gimmicks, and disguises and sets Kim loose to wander, concluding his instructions to the astonished orphan with these rather startling words: "This half year . . . is to make you de-Englishized, you see" [155]. In the paragraphs that immediately follow this pronouncement, Kim, instead of reveling in this unexpected liberation, contemplates the implication of Hurree's words with something like horror:

> "Now I am alone—all alone," he thought. "In all India is no-one so alone as I . . . I, Kim."
> A very few white people, but many Asiatics, can throw themselves into amazement as it were by repeating their own name over and over again to themselves, letting the minds go free upon a speculation as to what is called personal identity. When one grows older, the power usually departs, but while it lasts it may descend upon a man at any moment.
> "Who is Kim—Kim—Kim?"
> He squatted in a corner of the clanging waiting-room, rapt from all other thoughts; hands folded in lap, and pupils contracted to pin-points. In a minute—in another half second—he felt he would arrive at the solution of the tremendous puzzle; but here, as always happens, his mind dropped away from those

heights with a rush of a wounded bird, and passing his hand
before his eyes, he shook his head. [150]

Kim's bewildered shock before the sudden sublimity of his identity
should not entirely surprise us. He has, once again, been aban-
doned—not by another adoptive parent but by a narrative of belong-
ing. However much Kim has rebelled against St. Xavier's, he has
come to understand the benefits of his reinvention as a white and a
sahib. To be "de-Englishized" is, before all else, to be expelled from
a history that he thought he had been invited to join. Kim, a more
subtle reader of the confusions of empire than most of the adults
who surround him, decodes Hurree's words as an invitation to cul-
tural loneliness. That loneliness, he understands, is the sole reward
for the freakishness that Colonel Creighton, through Hurree, has
offered him. Even Kipling, regarding Kim in this critical moment,
cannot avoid identifying him as something of a monster: a putatively
white but performatively Asiatic hybrid, cognitively trapped in that
maze where mythical monsters literally dwell. Kim translates this
loneliness and freakishness back into that question which we—and
he, and Kipling—had thought was already answered in favor of his
sahibization. "Who is Kim?" he demands of himself again, only to
discover himself as a dizzying and unnameable excess.

That excess, consonant with what Kipling will later call "the mon-
strous hybridism of East and West" [199], not only *produces* a pro-
found sense of cultural bewilderment and estrangement; it is *pro-
duced*, and, crucially, it is produced by the colonial state. As Kim
meets himself in this late episode, he encounters a self that has
been manufactured by the officers of the empire as a multiple per-
sonality, a self that has at once been elaborately sahibized and
meticulously de-Englishized. The immediate reason for this is obvi-
ous enough: Creighton cannot afford to have Kim move too far from
those worlds he must eventually infiltrate. Alternatively put,
Creighton's decision to re-Orientalize Kim reflects his decision to
guarantee English rule in India through the pursuit of knowledge
rather than the cultivation of Englishness. If Kim, on Creighton's
behalf, is ever to chart that unmapped space which the lama has
uncovered in the cartography of empire, then, Creighton recog-
nizes, he must be taught, not precisely to sacrifice his incipient Eng-
lishness, but to make it no more than one among a series of cultural
costumes. However pragmatic this decision looks to Colonel
Creighton, Kipling can view it as nothing but disastrous. For it
implies that the empire, advertised as a factory for the production
of English identity, can sustain itself only through a commitment
to tropicalization, that the immense project of imperial subject-
fashioning which Kipling has at once been describing and extolling

can succeed only by producing individuals who are stupefied, hybridized, and schizophrenic. If the Raj is a place that must remain British to the backbone, then, Kipling discovers in the shock of this moment, it will remain British only by subjecting the English to a rigorous regimen of de-Englishization.[5]

A. MICHAEL MATIN

Kim, Invasion-Scare Literature, and the Russian Threat to British India[†]

In an address to the Kipling Society in 1961, the renowned Kipling biographer Charles Carrington dismissed as an act of "impudence" a young scholar's recently published claim that Kim constitutes a "defence of the policy of British expansion," and he went on to quip that "[o]ne might as well say that Jane Eyre is a defence of polygamy."[1] Carrington's remarks on this issue clearly signal his less than disinterested outlook, yet for many years even critics who are not to be numbered among Kipling's apologists, such as Mark Kinkead-Weekes and Irving Howe, accorded Kim a privileged status in Kipling's oeuvre as a transcendent exception to his otherwise tendentious work, and demonstrations of the untenability of their claims—premised, for the most part, on moral grounds[2]—remained inchoate. It would not be until the rise of postcolonial studies that

5. For Kipling—who, from that moment in which he so warily introduced Kim, has been struggling to return "English" to the catalog of colonial identity-positions—this is all thoroughly intolerable. In the remaining chapters of the novel, he conspires to free Kim from Creighton's clutches, stages an overdetermined scene in which Kim abandons the implements of cartography, and, finally, as if to punish Creighton by exorbitantly de-Englishizing Kim, hands Kim over to the lama and accords the holy man the right to give the little friend of all the world an adult name. For a reading of how the lama's naming of Kim as "beloved" can be construed as yet another act of incarceration, see Sara Suleri, *The Rhetoric of English India* (Chicago: University of Chicago Press, 1992) 111–31.

† This essay is based on portions of the first half of "'The Hun Is at the Gate!': Historicizing Kipling's Militaristic Rhetoric, from the Imperial Periphery to the National Center," a two-part article in *Studies in the Novel* 31.3 (Fall 1999): 317–56 and 4 (Winter 1999): 432–70, which is adapted from a book in progress, *Securing Britain: Invasion-Scare Literature before the Great War*. Reprinted by permission of the author and the University of North Texas. Copyright © 1999 by the University of North Texas. Bracketed page references to this Norton Critical Edition have been added following the original references.

1. Charles Carrington, "Kipling and the Empire," *The Kipling Journal* 29.141 (1962): 8–13, p. 9.

2. When Noel Annan, surveying the criticism on Kipling's writings generally in his seminal 1960 essay "Kipling's Place in the History of Ideas," concluded that "at the root of every assessment of Kipling lies the problem of his morality," he identified not only an abundantly evident fact but also a practical limit for approaches to Kipling's fiction—a limit that he attempted to move beyond by interpreting that morality as an epiphenomenon of Kipling's radically sociological outlook on the human condition (in Andrew Rutherford, ed., *Kipling's Mind and Art* [Stanford: Stanford University Press, 1964], p. 97).

discussions of *Kim* identifying it as a polemical work, such as those of Edward Said and Sara Suleri, would undergo a shift of emphasis from denunciations of the moral vision presumed to underlie it to cogent analyses of the respects in which it is designed to legitimize British rule in subcontinental Asia: the Indians, the novel affirms, are better off governed by the British than they would be if governed either by themselves or by the covetous Russians. Ann Parry and Peter Hopkirk have analyzed the novel's treatment of the Russo-British imperial rivalry in particular, yet neither they nor the other critics who have explored this theme have sufficiently contextualized it in terms of literary history. *Kim*, which is generally characterized by conspicuous formal discontinuities,[3] is, in fact, imbued with the motifs of invasion-scare literature—a body of narratives, tracts, and treatises that warn of potential military attempts on the territories of the empire (especially India, the most profitable of British imperial possessions) and Great Britain itself. This pre-World-War-One genre was all but exclusively a product of Tory-Conservative political interests, and it was primarily geared towards stimulating public and Parliamentary support for increased military expenditures. The rhetorical techniques Kipling uses in *Kim* for representing the alleged menace of Russian aggression in India were entirely of a piece with those of the authors of invasion-scare literature, who consisted chiefly of opportunistic journalists and novelists as well as career army and navy officers with vested professional interests in heightening public concern over such issues. However, these affinities have been occluded by the traditionally selective vision of literary history that tends to filter out subcanonical forms. By situating *Kim* in the context of these narratives, tracts, and treatises, I will endeavor to make visible Kipling's role as a participant in a prevalent literary phenomenon and thereby deepen our understanding of how *Kim* functions as a polemical work.

After having been schooled in England, Kipling returned to India, the land of his birth, in 1882 to work as a subeditor and reporter on Lahore's *Civil and Military Gazette*, a position he was to occupy for the next five years. His residence near the primary British Army base in northwest India (an area widely viewed as the Achilles' heel of the empire) not only enhanced his already intense admiration for the martial life but also reinforced his view of the region's military situation, which had been established before his departure from England: a year before his return to India—likely prompted, Angus Wilson observes, by letters from his parents from northwest India,

3. As Zohreh T. Sullivan observes in *Narratives of Empire: The Fictions of Rudyard Kipling* (Cambridge: Cambridge University Press, 1993), "*Kim*'s complexity comes, in part, from [its] curious stacking up of various genres" (p. 148).

particularly those of his "frontier-conscious" father—he had
asserted during a school debate that "the advance of the Russians in
central Asia is hostile to the British Power."[4] The young Anglo-
Indian journalist was hardly alone in this conviction. Fictional nar-
ratives such as *The Great Russian Invasion of India* (1879, pseudo-
nymously published), contentious histories such as *Russia's March
towards India* (1894, anonymously published), and military analyses
and forecasts such as Major-General Sir Charles MacGregor's *The
Defence of India: A Strategical Study* (1884) and Colonel G. B.
Malleson's *The Russo-Afghan Question and the Invasion of India*
(1885) all warned of an imminent Russian "theft" of British terri-
tory. As MacGregor asserts in *The Defence of India*, "we must be
regarded as to all intents and purposes at present at war with Rus-
sia on the Russo-Indian question." If British forces are not deployed
"to defeat Russian attempts to seize certain commanding positions
in Afghanistan," he contends, summing up the position of so-called
Forward Policy advocates, "India will pass from our grasp."[5] Such
claims about India's vulnerability were similarly made during this
era in innumerable narratives warning of potential assaults by rival
European powers on England, many of which conclude with the
quasi-ritualistic spectacle of the British Empire torn apart as retri-
bution for British hubris and military unsoundness. For example, in
The Siege of London (1885), in which a French invasion of England
leads to a dismembering of the empire, Russia "swe[eps] with a hur-
ricane's wrath through the length and breadth of the land, and, as
it [i]s impossible for help to come from the Mother Country, India
bec[omes] Russian."[6] And in *The Sack of London in the Great
French War of 1901* (1901), which was published in the same year
as *Kim*, British power is menaced by "a Russian army of 800,000
men on the frontiers of India."[7]

It is important to recognize, however, that not only the Russo-
British contest for dominance in central Asia, but a variety of impe-
rial conflicts around the globe contributed to the making of *Kim*. As
the anti-imperialist poet and diplomat Wilfrid Scawen Blunt
summed up the tenor of British foreign relations and their possible
ramifications for the security of the empire in 1896, while the novel
was in its early stages, "We have now managed in the last six months
to quarrel violently with China, Turkey, Belgium, Ashanti, France,

4. Angus Wilson, *The Strange Ride of Rudyard Kipling: His Life and Works* (New York:
 Viking, 1978), p. 43.
5. Charles MacGregor, *The Defence of India: A Strategical Study* (Simla: Government Cen-
 tral Branch Press, 1884), pp. 106–07, 183.
6. "Posteritas," *The Siege of London* (London: Wyman and Sons, 1885), p. 68.
7. "One Who Saw It," *The Sack of London in the Great French War of 1901* (London: F. V.
 White, 1901), p. 94.

Venezuela, America, and Germany. This is a record performance, and if it does not break up the British Empire nothing will."[8] *Kim's* protracted gestation, in fact, began with the 1894 Russo-French Entente, which allied what were then generally considered to be Britain's two primary enemies, and its completion coincided with the disastrous beginnings of the 1899–1902 Anglo-Boer War, which left Britain bloodied and humiliated. Sandwiched between these events were Kaiser Wilhelm II's provocative 1896 telegram to Transvaal President Paul Kruger, which darkly hinted at German military support for the Boers against the British; the 1898 Fashoda Crisis, in which Britain and France (having already been at odds over various territories, most notably Egypt) came to the brink of war over their competing claims to the upper Nile region; and the *Reichstag's* passages in 1898 and 1900 of the First and Second Navy Laws, which, calling for battleship production on a massive scale, made clear Germany's imminent challenge to British control of the seas and hence to British imperial preeminence. It is in light of this constellation of imperial conflicts that the rivalry between Britain and Russia in *Kim* should be assessed.

The novel is constructed around the maturation of the boy-protagonist Kim O'Hara, who, in a lesson in British subjecthood, learns to play the "Great Game" of intelligence gathering and counter-espionage in service of the empire and is thus transformed from a parasitic street urchin into a useful imperial subject. In the text's first sentence, we see Kim sitting "astride the gun Zam-Zammah on her brick platform opposite . . . the Lahore Museum."[9] He is playing, and winning, a game of "king-of-the-castle" with a Muslim boy and a Hindu boy, and he envisions this activity as a reenactment of local history. "All Mussalmans fell off Zam-Zammah long ago," he boasts from his perch on the ornate cannon in response to the Muslim boy's demand to be allowed up. To the Hindu boy's similar request, he taunts that "[t]he Hindus fell off Zam-Zammah too. The Mussalmans pushed them off" (pp. 184–85) [6]. As the narrator puts it, making clear the implied connection between the children's game and the politico-military subtext, "There was some justification for Kim,—he had kicked Lala Dinanath's boy off the trunnions,—since the English held the Punjab and Kim was English" (p. 181) [3]. Yet while Kim is here identified as "English"—a role to which his success over the Indian boys with whom he plays the king-of-the-castle game effectively assigns

8. Wilfrid Scawen Blunt, *My Diaries: Being a Personal Narrative of Events 1888–1914*, 2 vols. (New York: Knopf, 1921), vol. 1, p. 212.
9. Rudyard Kipling, *The Collected Works of Rudyard Kipling* (New York: AMS Press, 1970), vol. 16, p. 181 [3]. All subsequent quotations from Kipling's works are from this edition and are cited parenthetically in the text.

Map from Major-General Sir Charles MacGregor's *The Defence of India: A Strategical Study* (1884). The space between the two thick lines in the southeast quadrant—the lower one runs southwest to northeast, and the upper one (which is less prominent here than in the color-coded original) runs roughly west to

east—marks the Afghan buffer zone that separates the British and Russian terri-
tories. Kipling lived from 1882 to 1887 in Lahore (on the eastern edge of the
southeast quadrant), the site of the principal British military base in northwest
India.

him—he is actually *Irish*, and a recognition of this fact is crucial to appreciating the subtlety with which Kipling manipulates categories of nationality in the service of his own political ends.[1] The significance of Kim's Irishness is implied in a later scene, when he fortuitously encounters his deceased father's army unit and is informed that "the Regiment will take care of you and make you as good a man as your—as good a man as can be" (p. 287) [78]. The suppressed term here is clearly *father*. Kim is the orphaned child of an alcoholic and opium-addicted Irishman named O'Hara, whom "[s]ocieties and chaplains, anxious for the child, tried to catch" in order to compel him to hand over his son to more responsible authorities (p. 182) [4]. And the fact that Kim flourishes when he is finally placed under British control and in a British school has an unmistakable rhetorical intention. Consider in this context how Ireland is represented in Kipling and C. R. L. Fletcher's 1911 collaborative project, *A School History of England*:

> It was . . . a misfortune for Britain that Rome never conquered [all of Great Britain and Ireland]. . . . So Ireland never went to school, and has been a spoilt child ever since; the most charming of children, indeed, full of beautiful laughter and tender tears, full of poetry and valour, but incapable of ruling herself, and impatient of all rule by others.[2]

What Kipling and Fletcher would a decade later depict *figuratively*, Kipling in *Kim* depicts *literally* in an encrypted allegorical version of this patronizing argument: the "spoilt child" of an unfit Irish parent is "adopted" by the British government and sent to school, where his talents are harnessed through his participation in the morally and spiritually edifying project of imperialism. The story of Kim's individual *Bildung*—which, having notably begun with a tussle with a

1. As Edward Said points out in *Culture and Imperialism* (New York: Knopf, 1993), the fact "[t]hat Kim . . . is both an Irish outcast boy and later an essential player in the British Secret Service Great Game suggests Kipling's uncanny understanding of the workings and managing control of societies" (p. 141). Said's contention is elucidated by Phillip E. Wegner, who observes that this co-optation of Kim should be glossed as a "utopian reconstruction of [an] increasingly restive Irish populace" (" 'Life as He Would Have It': The Invention of India in Kipling's *Kim*," *Cultural Critique* 26 [1993–94]: 129–59, p. 155).
2. C. R. L. Fletcher and Rudyard Kipling, *A School History of England* (Oxford: Clarendon Press, 1911), p. 21. A comparison of different copies of the volume discloses that the text was silently emended between printings, for the lines disparaging Irish Home Rule that follow the semicolon in the above quotation do not appear in all copies of the same edition. It should also be noted that while Kipling gets equal billing on the title page of *A School History of England*, presumably because of his fame, he did not have an equal share in the writing—he contributed twenty-three poems to Fletcher's prose text—but the work nonetheless represents the unified vision of the co-authors. Further, Fletcher would acknowledge in later years that "some of the most valuable prose suggestions" and "all the pretty little love poems in prose to England" were Kipling's (quoted in editor's introduction to J. J. Ross, "An English History: Kipling's Joint Authorship, with C. R. L. Fletcher, of *A School History of England*," *The Kipling Journal* 60.240 [1986]: 31–42, p. 31).

Church of England chaplain, concludes with the invocation and enlistment of "every unknown Irish devil in the boy's blood" (p. 469) [202] on behalf of the British cause during hand-to-hand combat with a Russian spy—thus microcosmically enacts the fantasy of an Ireland rendered disciplined, tractable, and, above all, *serviceable* for the British Empire during a period when Conservative imperialists such as Kipling were vociferously denouncing proposals for Irish Home Rule. Precisely such fantasies typify those invasion-scare narratives that were published during this era of so-called Splendid Isolation in which the empire is cast as a prosthetic alliance system, thereby enabling Britain simultaneously to maintain isolationism *and* have dependable allies. For example, in William Le Queux's novel *The Great War in England in 1897* (1894), a Russo-French assault on England leads to the shipping in of troops from all over the British Empire—including Ireland—to assist in expelling the invaders:

> Although the colonies had shown how zealously they were prepared to guard the interests of the Mother Country, their public spirit was eclipsed by the spontaneous outburst of patriotism which occurred in Ireland. . . .
>
> Whatever differences of political opinion had previously existed between them on the question of Home Rule, were forgotten by the people in the face of the great danger which threatened the Empire to which they belonged. The national peril welded the people together, and shoulder to shoulder they marched to lay down their lives, if necessary, in the work of driving back the invader.
>
> Within six days of this spontaneous outburst of patriotism, 25,000 Irishmen of all creeds and political opinions were on their way to assist their English comrades.[3]

Such assumptions of the ideological efficacy of British forms of imperialism over those of other powers subtend *Kim*'s representation of not only the nationality of its eponymous protagonist but also the competition between Britain and Russia over possession of India. In this respect, Kipling's novel engages in a common practice for colonial fictions of the period, many of which tendentiously thematize imperial rivalries. A pertinent example is August Niemann's novel *Der Weltkrieg: Deutsche Träume* (1904), a translation of which was widely read in Britain under the lurid title *The Coming Conquest of England*. (The numerous tales of invasion written by the British for the British were supplemented by translations of jingoistic French, Russian, and German narra-

3. William Le Queux, *The Great War in England in 1897* (1894; 11th ed., London: Tower Publishing, 1895), pp. 133–34.

tives that ostensibly corroborated Britons' worst fears about their competitors' intentions. As J. H. Freese asserts in his translator's introduction to *The Coming Conquest of England*, he has reproduced this German text "in the English language for English readers [for whom t]he meaning and the moral should be obvious and valuable."[4]) In this account, Britain, for its imperial successes, is depicted as having earned the animosity, and hence having incurred the combined military and naval might, of the major Continental powers. The dual themes of *The Coming Conquest of England*—which is as much a Great Game narrative as is *Kim*—are Russian espionage in, and ultimate invasion of, India and a naval war fought between the British fleet and the united French, Russian, and German fleets that is followed by an invasion of England. In the opening scene, representatives from the allied nations meet in Saint Petersburg in order to plot the destruction of Britain. At this meeting, the Russian secretary of state, who touts the accomplishment of having rendered much of central Asia "accessible to Russian civilisation," complains that "we have never taken a step, either east or south, without meeting with English opposition or English intrigues." Pointing out that "we are unable to reach the markets of the world," he asserts that "Russia must push her way down to the [Arabian] sea" (p. 4). His pronouncements are seconded by the Russian war minister, who, backed by an army four million men strong, endorses the strategic soundness of a plan for an invasion of India via Afghanistan and concludes that

> "If the English army is defeated, then India is lost to Great Britain; for the English are, in India, in the enemy's country. . . . They would be attacked on all sides by the Indian native chieftains, whose independence they have so brutally destroyed, at the very moment that their power is broken. We, on the other hand, should be received with open arms, as rescuers of the Indian people from their intolerable yoke." (pp. 6–7)

These contentions are substantiated later in the novel when a British professor, admiringly describing "the slow, steady advance of the Russians in Asia" (p. 165), chastises his own country for having ignored the "soul" of India (p. 167):

> "[T]he Russians have known how to win over the hearts of their subject races, and how to humour their religious views. The victors and the vanquished thus better assimilate. The English, on the other hand, have governed India purely from the politi-

4. August Niemann, *The Coming Conquest of England*, trans. of *Der Weltkrieg: Deutsche Träume*, trans. J. H. Freese (London: Routledge, 1904), p. vii.

cal side. The hearts of the various races in India have remained strange and hostile to us." (p. 165)

The argument of *The Coming Conquest of England*, in short, is that the British are unfit to possess colonies and therefore ought to be relieved of them. This imperative is fulfilled in the *dénouement*, as the coalition of European nations occupies England and dismantles the British Empire. Particularly featured is "the cession of British India to Russia" (p. 376).

Conversely, in *Kim* the status of the Russians as among the "lesser breeds without the Law"—the phrase is the pejorative epithet deployed by Kipling in the 1897 poem "Recessional" [p. 259] to denote unworthy imperial powers, not, as it is often misread, non-white peoples in need of imperial guidance—is entertainingly displayed in the novel's climax, when Kim and the Indian Secret Service agent Hurree Chunder Mookerjee not only foil the Russian plot but also orchestrate the situation in such a way that their opponents thoroughly earn the disrespect of the Indians whom they would presume to lead. Bemoaning to his French partner[5] that "[w]e [Russians] have nowhere left our mark yet. Nowhere!" the Slavic agent asserts his nation's claim to imperial entitlement: "It is *we* who can deal with Orientals," he contends (pp. 465–66) [199–200]. But through his ineptness and brutality, he exhibits his countrymen's incapacity for the project of empire. In fact, everything about the Russian signals his people's rank as a lesser breed without the Law, and hence their unfitness for the moral mission of imperialism; they are manifestly unqualified to carry the White Man's Burden. *Kim*'s depiction of the Russians as unsuited, on humanitarian grounds, to rule other peoples echoes a charge that was frequently leveled by proponents of British expansionism during this era, particularly when the fate of central and subcontinental Asia was at issue. Kipling's own pronouncements on the relative merits of British and Russian stewardship go back at least as far as 1885, when he asserted in a *Civil and Military Gazette* article,

> Reservoired, watered, drained and policed in the face of all opposition, and for the benefit of a proverbially thankless race, Peshawur as it now stands, is a city that could only have grown up under English care and English rule. Holy Russia would have tamed the wild beasts [i.e., the Indians] as effectually perhaps. [But t]hey would have died largely under the process.[6]

5. Although the novel suggests French complicity in the scheme to overthrow British rule in India, the contention is muted. The real foe in this context, Kipling makes clear, is Russia.
6. Rudyard Kipling, *Kipling's India: Uncollected Sketches, 1884–88*, ed. Thomas Pinney (London: Macmillan, 1986), p. 84.

The Coming Struggle for India (1885), by Arminius Vambéry, is replete with similar pronouncements. Having conducted a "comparative study of English and Russian civilisations in the East,"[7] Vambéry maintains that Britain, founded on "the solid rock of Anglo-Saxon character" (p. 208), "has bestowed rare blessings upon the peoples entrusted to her care" (p. 174), whereas Russia, "standing . . . on the verge of both [the European and Asian] cultural worlds" (pp. 166–67), is guilty of "wanton neglect" and "thinks least of ameliorating the condition of the life of the people entrusted to its care" (p. 172). Claiming that "at the appearance of the Russian coloniser the natives quickly disappear, . . . [for] the Government, instead of taking care of the cruelly oppressed subject, rather encourages the destructive work of the Russian Cossack" (p. 169), he contentiously queries "can the state of things created through Russian agency be really called civilisation, and does it represent even the faintest ray of that glorious light which we call the modern culture of the Christian West?" (p. 167).

Such charges as Kipling's and Vambéry's of Russian barbarism participate in what Christopher GoGwilt has termed, in *The Invention of the West*, the "discursive shift" that—emanating in part from "the increasingly important distinction between Russia and the West that came to dominate political, cultural, and historical articulations of the East-West division on the map of Europe" during the era of the New Imperialism—produced "a new European definition of the West as Western Europe distinct from Russia."[8] This rhetorical shift is also at work in Kipling's 1890 short story "The Man Who Was," which describes the events surrounding a Russian officer's mysterious arrival at a British Army base in northwest India. Behaving "distressingly European" as he ingratiates himself with the British soldiers whose begrudging hospitality he enjoys, the Russian claims to look forward to "the glorious future that await[s] the combined arms of England and Russia when their hearts and their territories should run side by side, and the great mission of civilising Asia should begin" (vol. 4, p. 92). But when he later gets drunk— and with his crude patriotism galvanized by the damning evidence presented by a British soldier who, having been taken prisoner of war during the Crimean conflict thirty years earlier, has only recently escaped from enslavement in Siberia—his disingenuous veneer is peeled away, and he openly boasts that the Russians will soon supplant the British in India. It is intimated in the tale's open-

7. Arminius Vambéry, *The Coming Struggle for India: Being an Account of the Encroachments of Russia in Central Asia, and of the Difficulties Sure to Arise Therefrom to England* (London: Cassell, 1885), p. 165.
8. Christopher GoGwilt, *The Invention of the West: Joseph Conrad and the Double-Mapping of Europe and Empire* (Stanford: Stanford University Press, 1995), pp. 27, 241.

Map depicting the progressive advancement of the Russian Empire towards British India, from Arminius Vambéry's *The Coming Struggle for India: Being an Account of the Encroachments of Russia in Central Asia, and of the Difficulties Sure to Arise Therefrom to England* (1885).

ing lines that the officer's Jekyll-and-Hyde-like dual nature is representative of the antinomies of Russian character generally:

> Let it be clearly understood that the Russian is a delightful person till he tucks in his shirt. As an Oriental he is charming. It is only when he insists upon being treated as the most easterly of Western peoples instead of the most westerly of Easterns that he becomes a racial anomaly extremely difficult to handle. The host never knows which side of his nature is going to turn up next. (p. 91)

In light of this story, the Russian spy's haughty allusion in *Kim* to the Bengali babu Hurree as typifying "the monstrous hybridism of East and West" (p. 465) [199] takes on a rich irony, as Kipling clearly implies that it is the ignoble Russians themselves who exemplify precisely this "monstrous hybridism."

Kim's role in the Great Game culminates in his battle with the Russian agent in the novel's climax—a scene that plays out in burlesque miniature the long-anticipated Russo-British military confrontation over India. But his involvement in the conflict has begun three years earlier, when, at the age of thirteen, he has unofficially been initiated into it by the Afghan Mahbub Ali, who has had him deliver to the British authorities a coded message warning of the cooperation with Russia of "five confederated Kings, who had no business to confederate" (p. 205) [21]. The political circumstances are cryptically related, but they are clarified later by Hurree: "There were Five Kings who prepared a sudden war three years ago. . . . Upon them, because of that news [i.e., the message Kim has delivered], and ere they were ready, fell our Army" (p. 444) [185]. Mahbub Ali remarks to Kim of this situation, "That war is done now, and the evil, we hope, nipped before the flower—thanks to me—and thee" (p. 340) [114]. His hope, however, is not matched by the reality, for the threat has been dealt with inadequately by the British and has therefore recurred. Depicting this recurrence as a typical consequence of British irresoluteness, Kipling delegates to Hurree the task of articulating to Kim—and to the reader—the politico-military situation as well as the propagandistic crux of the novel. He begins by describing the strategic blunders that followed the preemptive attack launched by the British three years earlier:

> " . . . [T]he war was not pushed. That is the Government custom. The troops were recalled because the Government believed the Five Kings were cowed; and it is not cheap to feed men among the high Passes. Hilás and Bunár—Rajahs with guns—undertook for a price to guard the Passes against all coming from the North [i.e., Russia]. They protested both fear

and friendship. . . . This pleased the Government, anxious to avoid expense. . . ." (p. 444) [185–86]

Kipling thus illustrates the British penny-wise-and-pound-foolish disposition towards defense spending that he finds so reprehensible and that he expresses as well in the narrator's assertion that "the Secret Service . . . is ludicrously starved" (p. 389)[148]. He had registered the same sentiment on the matter of short-sighted British parsimony in an 1885 *Civil and Military Gazette* article, in which he predicted how the British would comport themselves in the war that the Russian attack on the strategically important Afghan territory of Penjdeh seemed likely to trigger:

> We shall blunder horribly at the outset; and throw away many army corps and much money in our laudable efforts to do things "on the cheap." Then the oriental mind, yet unused to our eccentric methods of doing battle, will turn against us, and we shall have our hands unpleasantly full. . . . Eventually, of course, we shall emerge from the conflict victors and triumphant, to float new loans for the depleted Russian treasury, and to give back gracefully her broken sword into her weakened right arm. Once committed to actual war, we shall fight as the "mad Englishman" usually fights—with one hand tied behind his back, and the other ready to hoist up his enemy the moment he shows signs of having had "enough of it." (*Kipling's India*: *Uncollected Sketches, 1884–88*, pp. 107–08)

When he would voice these same opinions sixteen years later in *Kim*, it would be as perceived through the lens of one such "oriental mind . . . unused to our eccentric [i.e., incompetent] methods of doing battle"—that of Hurree, whose attempts to warn the British of the Russian threat have fallen on deaf ears: "I send word many times that . . . two Kings were sold to the North; and Mahbub Ali, who was yet farther North, amply confirmed it. Nothing was done." He proceeds to elucidate his meaning:

> "Over the Passes this year . . . come two strangers under cover of shooting wild goats. . . .
> "They are well received by Hilás and Bunár. They make great promises; they speak as the mouthpiece of a Kaisar with gifts. . . . The [British] Government knows, but does nothing. . . . When all the evil is done . . . —when these two strangers with the levels and the compasses make the Five Kings to believe that a great army will sweep the Passes to-morrow or the next day . . . —comes the order to me, Hurree Babu, 'Go North and see what those strangers do.' I say to Creighton Sahib, 'This is not a lawsuit, that we go about to collect evidence. . . . [W]hy the dooce do you not issue demi-

offeecial orders to some brave man to poison them, for an example? It is, if you permit the observation, most reprehensible laxity on your part.' And Colonel Creighton, he laughed at me! It is all your beastly English pride. You think no one dare conspire!" (pp. 444–46) [186–87]

What particularly irks Hurree is the casual and above-board way the British behave under circumstances that clearly call for ruthlessness. His agitated assertions are corroborated by the Russian and French spies, who, astonished at the ease with which they have been able to conduct their surveillance and espionage mission, note the enervating effects of British hubris on the imperial defense system:

> ". . . [W]e are given all facilities—and Name of God!—they give them to us too! Is it unbelievable stupidity?"
>
> "It is pride—pride that deserves and will receive punishment."
>
> "Yes! To fight a fellow-Continental in our game is something. There is a risk attached, but these people—bah! It is too easy." (p. 463) [198]

Such circumstances are depicted as well in the 1879 narrative *The Great Russian Invasion of India,* but with graver consequences. Published during the Second Anglo-Afghan War by a Lahore-based author (almost certainly a British Army officer), the tale, which is targeted at a home readership characterized as "indulging in complacent dreams of the invincibility of British arms in Asia,"[9] is primarily occupied with detailing a military conflict of precisely the sort that is narrowly averted in *Kim.* In *The Great Russian Invasion of India,* as in the case of *Kim,* the British government has ignored repeated warnings of malevolent Russian intentions:

> The authorities were warned over and over again that attacks would be made on cantonments, and that large numbers of men who had been serving in the Russian army had come back to the country. However, they did not altogether believe these reports, and did not like to show any signs of timidity in view of the disturbed state of the country; and therefore they did nothing towards putting the barracks into a state of defence. (p. 23)

Further, the requests of British officers—made in response to reports of Russian spy activities—that "measures . . . be taken to prevent foreigners from learning too much about the country" have been declined, as the government has been unwilling "to introduce regulations to prevent people from making any inquiries they pleased." Likewise, proposals for the construction of defenses

9. A. Dekhnewallah [pseud.], *The Great Russian Invasion of India: A Sequel to the Afghanistan Campaign of 1878–9* (London: Harrison, 1879), p. 42.

devised by an "engineer . . . [who] had drawn attention to the danger of leaving the large railway bridges in the Punjab entirely unprotected" have been rejected "on the score of expense" (p. 27). The result of such policies is that the work of saboteurs—who, as in *Kim*, have conducted their mission on the frontier while pretending to be on a hunting expedition—goes unanswered until it is too late, and Russian troops along with Russian-armed Afghans invade. The British forces are ill prepared and outnumbered, but they are skill-fully led by an unnamed major-general whose copious pre-invasion recommendations concerning "the need of securing our position in India" had been dismissed as the pronouncements of "a Russo-phobist" (p. 43). Thanks to this resourceful officer, the Russian forces are confounded, and, with the Russian-fomented native insurgents unable to coordinate their efforts, the British Army even-tually prevails. Further, not only is the enemy repelled from north-west India, but the opportunity is taken finally to do the job right. Recognizing that "[s]o long . . . as the Russians held Afghanistan there could be no hope of permanent peace for India" (p. 66), the British launch a full-scale offensive, and the narrative concludes with a glorious fulfillment of Forward Policy aspirations: having taken Afghanistan—which is "now as peaceful and as thriving as any *other* part of British India" (my emphasis)—the British are now "gradually extending [their] hold over Persia" (p. 69).

In *Kim* as well, despite the ample opportunities accorded to the enemy agents, the invasion plans are thwarted, although more qui-etly. Hurree informs Kim of the stellar success of their own counter-espionage mission in the novel's final meeting between them. The documents they have acquired include a political "love-letter . . . to the Czar," and "three or four Prime Ministers of these parts [are] implicated by the correspondence." Based on this information, "[t]he British Government will change the succession" in the disloyal terri-tories and, he euphemistically asserts, "nominate new heirs to the throne" (p. 512) [231–32]. Yet the novel's cheery tone on this matter masks a troubling implication, for although the government will take steps to preclude the immediate danger, all indications are that it will be business as usual so far as overall strategy goes. That is to say—as distinct from *The Great Russian Invasion of India*, in which the attempt on India stimulates redoubled vigilance and sweeping policy changes—at the end of *Kim*, in the absence of an actual invasion, we are left with a public that remains blissfully unaware of the Russian peril and a government whose response is geared towards merely *averting* rather than genuinely *eradicating* the danger. Indeed, Kipling implies, it has been because of the inefficacy, frugality, and complacency of the British authorities that the Russian threat has been permitted to recur at all. Twice in three years—in a figurative

anticipation of the reproach Kipling would level in the 1902 poem "The Islanders" that the British disgracefully relied on troops from colonial territories ("the Younger Nations [with] men who could shoot and ride") to fight their battles for them in the Anglo-Boer War—British hold on India has been sustained by the efforts of an Indian, an Afghan, and an Irish boy. And the fact that these victories have been enabled by a combination of individual ingenuity and sheer luck, as opposed to sound policy, is clear. Such dubious sources of protection, Kipling implies, are hardly the stuff to be counted on for the maintenance of a mighty empire. The polemical essence of *Kim* thus runs against the grain of the novel's optimistic surface and accords seamlessly with the position articulated by Colonel G. B. Malleson in *The Russo-Afghan Question and the Invasion of India* and maintained by all Forward Policy advocates: the British government is pursuing "a policy, born of infirmity of purpose and cowardice, which will lose for us our Indian Empire!"[1]

Written in an era when the principal threat to imperial possessions appeared to be rival powers rather than subjugated peoples, *Kim* is premised on a misapprehension about the direction history was to take. The seeds *were* being sown for the loss of India (and for the dismemberment of the empire as a whole), but this would not occur in the manner in which Kipling and the authors of invasion-scare literature feared most. Ironically, it was in 1885, the apex of post-Crimean-War Russo-British antagonism, while hawkish polemicists were preoccupied with the alleged Russian hazard, that the Indian National Congress was formed. Decried by Kipling as misguided and illegitimate although misjudged by him as a potential political force, this organization would be primarily responsible for marshaling the indigenous resistance to imperial rule that would ultimately lead to the expulsion of the British from India. We should not, however, overestimate the significance of *Kim*'s failures of prognostication or of the fact that its political agenda is irrelevant to today's readers. Further, to demonstrate that its politico-military content is largely derivative is by no means to suggest that the work as a whole is reducible to the status of its more crudely propagandistic counterparts. On the contrary, our awareness of the literary contexts from which *Kim* emerged enhances rather than diminishes our appreciation of this intricately textured novel by sharpening our focus on one of its most intriguing paradoxes: the fact that a work infused with the signal motifs and ideas of so unnuanced and ephemeral a genre is itself so complex and enduring.

1. G. B. Malleson, *The Russo-Afghan Question and the Invasion of India* (2nd ed., London: Routledge, 1885), p. 6.

JOHN A. McCLURE

[Kipling's Richest Dream]†

Kim is Kipling's richest dream. The "great and beautiful" India it depicts with a spirit of celebration dazzles the reader, especially if he comes to it across the bitter landscape of the earlier stories. In those, India is a grim realm of exile; in *Kim*, it is the very heart of life. Responding to this spirit in *Kim*, Mark Kinkead-Weekes offers the book as "the answer to nine-tenths of the charges levelled against Kipling and the refutation of most of the generalisations about him."[1]

This does not seem to me to be the case. Rather, I believe *Kim* represents at best only a partial victory for Kipling over the authoritarian elements in his own personality, a victory achieved not by grappling with these elements but by retiring into a fantasy world where they can exist side by side with finer ideals of fraternity and tolerance. Once again in *Kim*, though in a far more subtle fashion than in *The Jungle Book*, brotherhood and despotism keep uneasy company. Although Kipling finds a way to reconcile the Empire's need for bureaucratic chains of command with the imperialist's dream of autonomy, his method, that of making *Kim* a spy, raises important ethical and political questions.

The generous spirit animating *Kim* has been widely praised by Kipling's admirers. J. M. S. Tompkins, for instance, is pleased to note that "the sympathies of the book are inclusive not exclusive," and Kinkead-Weekes also finds in *Kim* a welcome change of spirit: "The eye is caught by a whole kaleidoscope of race, caste, custom, and creed, all seen with a warm affection that is almost unique in Kipling."[2] How Kipling, so long an advocate of caste distinctions and feudal hierarchies, achieves this atmosphere of affectionate inclusiveness reveals both *Kim*'s virtues and its weaknesses.

The structure of *Kim* contributes much to the impression of inclusiveness. Picaresque in its organization, the narrative follows Kim in his travels across India. Kim, himself of course, provides the thread of continuity, tying together the many distinct episodes just as he does the disparate worlds they illuminate. But cohesion

† From *Kipling and Conrad: The Colonial Fiction* (Cambridge, Mass.: Harvard University Press, 1981) 70–81. Copyright © 1981 by the President and Fellows of Harvard College. Reprinted by permission of the publisher. Bracketed page references to this Norton Critical Edition have been added following the original references.

1. Mark Kinkead-Weekes, "Vision in Kipling's Novels," in Andrew Rutherford, ed., *Kipling's Mind and Art* (Stanford, Calif.: Stanford University Press, 1964), p. 233.

2. J. M. S. Tompkins, *The Art of Rudyard Kipling* (London: Methuen, 1959), p. 23; Kinkead-Weekes, "Vision in Kipling's Novels," p. 216.

is basically taken for granted; the stress is on the variegated beauty of what is included. India lies before Kim and the reader like the plater of jewels in Lurgan Sahib's shop. This larger structural casualness is reflected in the many vivid catalogues Kipling presents in *Kim*.

The action of the book encompasses much of India, moving the reader from west to east along the Grand Trunk Road, and from the sweltering south to the superb Himalayan north. In both directions the roads reveal the plentitude of life. On the road north to Simla,

> it was all pure delight—the wandering road, climbing, dipping, and sweeping about the growing spurs; the flush of the morning laid along the distant snows; the branched cacti; tier upon tier on the stony hillsides; the voices of a thousand water-channels; the chatter of the monkeys; the solemn deodars, climbing one after another with down-drooped branches; the vista of the Plains rolled out far beneath them; the incessant twanging of the tonga-horns and the wild rush of the led-horses when a tonga swung round a curve.[3]

While the glories of the northern road are primarily natural, those of the Grand Trunk Road are exuberantly human: "'All castes and kinds of men move here. Look! Brahmins and chumars, bankers and tinkers, barbers and bunnyas, pilgrims and potters—all the world going and coming . . .' And truly the Grand Trunk Road is a wonderful spectacle. It runs straight, bearing without crowding India's traffic for fifteen hundred miles—such a river of life as nowhere else exits in the world" (p. 94) [51]. As the book continues, the metaphor of the road as river merges with the other great metaphor of inclusion, that of the lama's Wheel of Life on which all men are bound in their "thousand thousand shapes." The lama seeks to escape from road and wheel alike, but Kim finds both fascinating: "by the roadside trundled the very Wheel itself, eating, drinking, trading, marrying, and quarrelling—all warmly alive" (pp. 346–347) [177]. Kim's ambition, which he achieves, is to live at the very center of the wheel, in the heart of life.

Another image of inclusion in *Kim* is the family. Like Mowgli and Adam, Kim is freed from the exclusive bonds of his real family to become the "Little Friend of all the World" and "son" to "Half Hind." Lionel Trilling considers this expansion of the family to be one of the book's chief delights: "*Kim* . . . is full of wonderful fathers, all dedicated men in their different ways, each representing a different possibility of existence, and the charm of each is the greater because the boy need not commit himself to one

3. Rudyard Kipling, *Kim* (1901; reprint ed., New York: Charles Scribner's Sons, 1913), p. 238 [123]. Subsequent references to this edition appear in the text.

alone."[4] Almost all of us have grown up in some version of the
nuclear family, surrounded by an indifferent society, stunted, per-
haps, by the smallness of our intimate world. We have all been
forced, as we have matured, to make exclusive choices. Thus in
terms of our own society as well as that of the Indian Empire,
Kim's privilege is enormous.

Finally, from the perspective of this study, the most significant
inclusion in *Kim* is that of the alien imperialist in the culture he rules.
Kim's upbringing, so unconventional and so similar to that of Mowgli
and Adam, is the vehicle of this transformation; Kim emerges from
childhood as both son and father of a vast Indian family.

The plot of *Kim* parallels those of *The Jungle Book* and, to a lesser
extent, of "The Son of His Father." Like the heroes of these works,
and unlike most Anglo-Indian children, Kim is exiled not to an Eng-
lish world of hostile authority, but to the ready-made kingdom of
India. The loss of his parents, which cuts him off from the exclusive
world of the imperial community, saves him from the exile and
oppression that would ordinarily have been his lot, and catapults
him into the very heart of his homeland, India. Like Mowgli and
Adam, Kim enters this exotic world as a privileged member of the
superior race. Like them, he is soon surrounded by a protective ring
of fathers—Ali, the lama, Colonel Creighton, and others—who pro-
tect and educate him. With their support, Kim grows ever wiser,
freer, and more confident. At last he is ready to assume a place
among the imperial elite of the secret service. In assuming this role,
moreover, he transforms it, for he brings to it a set of skills and sym-
pathies not heretofore available in a white man. Like Mowgli and
Adam, he is the first of a new breed.

In *Kim*, however, Kipling resolves the question left unsettled in
"The Son of His Father." The notion of the country-born hero first
introduced in the earlier story now undergoes a final logical meta-
morphosis, and what emerges is the idea of the "country-born and
bred" hero who grows up entirely in India. Kim has the ultimate in
country breedings, but the youths he meets at St. Xavier's School
are also country-bred, and he approves of their ways: "Kim watched,
listened, and approved. This was not insipid, single-word talk of
[English] drummer-boys. It dealt with a life he knew and in part
understood. The atmosphere suited him" (p. 204) [106–07]. The
stories Kim hears reveal that the country-born posses a fearless
familiarity with India:

> There were boys of fifteen who had spent a day and a half on
> an islet in the middle of a flooded river, taking charge, as by

4. Lionel Trilling, "Kipling," in Rutherford, *Kipling's Mind and Art*, p. 88.

right of a camp of frantic pilgrims returning from a shrine;
there were seniors who had requisitioned a chance-met Rajah's
elephant, in the name of St. Francis Xavier, when the rains
once blotted out the cart-track that led to their father's estate,
and had all but lost the huge beast in a quicksand. There was
a boy who, he said, and none doubted, had helped his father to
beat off with rifles from the verandah a rush of Akas in the days
when those head-hunters were bold against lonely plantations.
(p. 203) [106]

Assumed superiority, eagerness for command, and familiarity with
India are the common denominators of these anecdotes; Kim's
schoolmates, like Adam Strickland, never ask permission of Indians.

Kipling wants us to approve of these boys, and to recognize their
superiority to English-born-and-bred imperialists. These are the
men, Kipling insists, who should be ruling India. As the Sahiba,
Kim's adopted mother, puts it, "These be the sort to oversee justice.
They know the land and the customs of the land. The others, all
new from Europe, suckled by white women and learning our
tongues from books, are worse than the pestilence. They do harm to
Kings" (p. 125) [67]. *Kim* is replete with such criticisms of the Eng-
lish-born imperial official, the "genuine imported Sahib from Eng-
land" (p. 248) [129]. Soldiers and administrators alike are ridiculed
for their "dull fat eyes," their blindness to India. Kim's young tor-
mentor during his brief stay with the Irish regiment is the type of all
such imperialists: "He did not care for any of the bazars which were
in bounds. He styled all natives 'niggers'; yet servants and sweepers
called him abominable names to his face, and, misled by their def-
erential attitude, he never understood" (p. 174) [92]. Ignorance
insures isolation; the same drummer-boy tells Kim all the English
soldiers agree that "in this bloomin' Injia you're only a prisoner at
large" (p. 168) [89]. Kim, forced to wear a uniform, finds that it
"crippled body and mind alike" and when he travels second class,
like an Englishman, he is lonely and longs for the pleasure of com-
pany in third class. The English-born-and-bred, Kipling suggests,
live desiccated lives in the very midst of India's living stream.

In *Kim*, then, the inclusion of the imperialist is made contingent
on his being country-born-and-bred. Kipling had distrusted certain
English liberal notions of imperial rule for years. He had, along with
the Orientalist group in the Indian Civil Service, resented the intru-
sion of English Members of Parliament and high civil servants in
local affairs. And he had hated his memories of persecution in an
English home and school. The calamities of the Boer War, in
progress while he was writing *Kim*, probably helped convince him
finally that the colonies should avoid contamination from England.

But *Kim* does not explore the exclusive and separatist implications of the celebration of the country-born. Instead, Kipling focuses on the country-born imperialist's inclusion in the society he rules. It is Kim's membership in this society that is kept constantly before our eyes.

The last chapters of *Kim* are filled with gestures of inclusion that affirm Kim's status as a privileged member of the Indian family. Perhaps the most dramatic of these is Kim's symbolic union with the Woman of Shamlegh. After the struggle with the Russian spies, Kim and the lama retire to the mountain village of Shamlegh. The head of this village is an impressive Indian woman whose fondness for Kim leads her first to try to seduce him and then, when she realizes that he is bound to save the ailing lama, to give him valuable assistance.

This episode does not reveal its full significance unless the reader recognizes the Woman of Shamlegh as Lispeth, the heroine of the early Kipling story of the same name. The Woman's history, which she relates to Kim, recapitulates the plot of the earlier story: " 'Once, long ago, if thou canst believe, a Sahib looked on me with favour. Once, long ago, I wore European clothes at the Mission-house yonder.' She pointed towards Kotgarh. 'Once, long ago, I was *Ker-lis-ti-an* and spoke English—as the Sahibs speak it. Yes. My Sahib said he would return and wed me—yes, wed me. He went away—I had nursed him when he was sick—but he never returned.'" (p. 431) [219]. Here is "Lispeth of the Kotgarh Mission," the heroine of the Kipling story most critical of imperial rule, reappearing after fourteen years.

Kipling reintroduces her at this time, I believe, in order to impress on us the superiority of country-bred rulers. Lispeth's pain, Kipling suggests in the earlier story, stems from the ignorance and aloofness of the English. Her lover does not recognize her as a fellow human being, nor does he accept the obligations such a recognition would entail. Instead, he takes her love and deludes her as to his own feelings, while all the time planning his return to England and to his English fiancée. His careless betrayal of a marriage pledge suggests the larger betrayal of the Indian people by their English rulers.

Kipling has Kim meet Lispeth to show that such betrayals are not inevitable. Kim's situation resembles that of the earlier European: he is aided and wooed by Lispeth in much the same way. But whereas the earlier figure, repaying kindness with deception, makes pledges he does not plan to keep, Kim deals with the Woman of Shamlegh frankly, fairly, and generously. She wants him as a lover, and he apparently refuses her, but he does reveal his true identity in an embrace and a kiss, for which she blesses him. And when she gives him money, he is careful to see it restored to her.

The full significance of their relationship emerges in the echoes set off by her last question, "you will come back again?" (p. 435)

[221]. These words, recalling the faithlessness of her first lover, suggest the difference between him and Kim. He was English-born, and had his heart set on a return to England. Kim, however, is deeply bound to India; he wants nothing more than to continue exploring its many roads. In a sense, he is already wed to the country, committed by his upbringing and his vocation to a life as a benevolent ruler of her people. His kiss seals this commitment, and symbolizes not only his inclusion but also that of his fellow country-born-and-bred Englishmen within the culture they are to rule.

For someone who has read through Kipling's Indian works, this episode is particularly moving and unexpected. It suggests that all along, as Kipling is praising his imperial heroes, depicting their sacrifices, exploring the weaknesses that make India hell for them, he is also thinking of how they fail their subjects, and looking for ways to mend this flaw as well as the others. Reference to the imperial breach of faith reemerges, perhaps for political reasons, only when Kipling has what he considers a solution to the problem, a mold that will form the ideal benevolent despot. Then, in an act of breathtaking inclusiveness, he reintroduces Lispeth and invites us to read *Kim* not alone, but in the context of all his Indian works—a history that ends in the achievement of social harmony.

Once again, however, there is a darker side to Kipling's gesture of inclusion. For if Kim will not desert the Indian peoples, neither will he leave their land and thus liberate them. The faithless Englishman of the early story at least does not impose himself on India for eternity; he has a home to go to. The country-born-and-bred Anglo-Indian, on the other hand, considers India his home. Kipling, praised by Tompkins for so generously including the Indians within the world he portrays with sympathy, is actually busy trying to make a permanent place for people like himself at the top of their social hierarchy.

In other ways as well, the spirit of inclusiveness in *Kim* is neither so ethically sound nor so universal as it may first appear. Kim's own commitment to inclusiveness lacks depth, and the inclusive spirit of the book is predicated on a primary exclusion of considerable magnitude. The exclusive tendencies in Kim's own personality emerge in his relation with Colonel Creighton of the espionage service. Kim, the "Friend of all the World" (p. 222) [112] takes immediately to Creighton as "a man after his own heart—a tortuous and indirect person playing a hidden game" (p. 191) [117]. In Creighton's presence he becomes a "queer, silent, self-possesed boy" (p. 209) [128]. Kim himself, then, is by no means entirely loving and inclusive. The model of human relations implicit in Creighton's personality and profession would, if universalized, render community, friendship, and openess shams and establish policy and power as the sole determinants of human contact. Yet when Kim is forced to choose

between his loving relation with the lama and his contract with
Creighton, he puts the contract and all it implies first. He employs
the lama as a screen in his engagement with the Russian spies,
deflecting the old man from his spiritual search and putting his life
in jeopardy. The lama continues to love Kim after this incident, and
Kim shows great affection for him. But the fact remains that Kim,
in choosing to manipulate the old man, expose him to danger, and
use him as an instrument, has made an important personal choice
for cold exclusiveness. This choice is further confirmed at the
book's end, when Kim decides to continue his work as a spy.

Another kind of exclusion provides the basis for the inclusive
atmosphere of *Kim* as a whole. For the book's inclusiveness is
achieved not through a vision that successfully reconciles the con-
tradictions at work in imperial India, but through primary acts of
exclusion that annihilate the troubling aspects of the Indian situa-
tion, preserving only those elements of Indian life of which Kipling
approves.

On the most accessible level, certain affects are clearly excluded
from the emotional climate of *Kim*, as several critics have noticed.
Kinkead-Weekes, for instance, observes that "Kim's junior version of
'the Great Game'—his stealthy commissions on the housetops—
involves danger, intrigue, and worldly knowledge of a sort, but it
hardly supports the claim that 'he had known all evil since he could
speak.' Indeed, the world is strangely disinfected as it passes
through Kim's eyes."[5] Kipling dramatizes elsewhere what it is like
for a child to know all evil—that is the theme of "Baa Baa, Black
Sheep"—but Kim certainly endures no such crushing experience. If
he knows all evil, he knows it in a very different way from Punch, a
way that, as Kinkead-Weekes suggests with a metaphor from medi-
cine, inoculates both him and the reader against its poison.

Herein lies the key to another form of exclusiveness in *Kim*. The
consciousness of the main character, in fact the very existence of
that character, is not human at all, but divine in the manner of the
pagan gods of mythology, who walked the earth enjoying human
pleasures but free from human travail. Kim never encounters evil
and pain in the same terrible, immediate way as the imperialists of
the earlier stories. And since the reader is invited to identify with
Kim, he, too, experiences India from this godlike vantage point.
Having precluded the possibility of pain and evil, Kipling can easily
create the impression of joyous all-inclusiveness.

Because Kim is a god, India is a kind of paradise. It has its dan-
gers, but only enough to keep things interesting. For the rest, the
country Kipling called a house of torment and compared with hell

5. Kinkead-Weekes, "Vision in Kipling's Novels," p. 217.

is described now as a "great good-tempered world" (p. 57) [32], a "great and beautiful land" (p. 222) [115], and "the kindly East" (p. 346) [177]. Part of this transformation is legitimate, for Kipling's theme is that to a country-born-and-bred European India is a familiar home, not a foreign prison. But much of the transformation involves a gigantic act of imaginative disinfection. Kipling simply wipes out, erases from his picture of India, all those groups and forces that were making life there in his time difficult for any imperialist, country-born or not.

The two social forces that most infuriated Kipling and his fellow imperial officials are nowhere to be found in *Kim*. These forces, the imperial administrative hierarchy and the emerging nationalist Indian bourgeoisie, appear frequently in the early stories as objects of exasperation and anger. But now the administrative hierarchy figures only tangentially, in a few references to its obtuseness, and the only Western-educated Indian is a gifted spy and aspiring member of the Royal Society.

In place of the bureaucratic hierarchy, the weight of which crushes many Kipling heroes in the stories of the eighties, there is in *Kim* the wonderful, mysterious abstraction called the Game, an espionage network "so large that one sees but a little at a time" (p. 277) [143]. The players follow orders, but share a common love of their dangerous vocation. Moreover, the very secrecy of their work confers a certain freedom, for between them and the visible government there can be little contact. "Cannot the Government protect?" asks Kim of a fellow agent. "We of the Game are beyond protection" is the reply (p. 328) [168]. But by the same token they are to a considerable extent beyond control.

And yet to treat the Game, as Kipling does, as if it were some utterly autonomous activity, with its own laws and life, is to distort reality. Here is another version of Kipling's old dream of autonomous despotism and licensed anarchy, only this time the confining geographical boundaries are down, and the middle-level imperial officer ranges over an entire Empire. In fact, however, the imperial bureaucracy remained, sending down assignments, defining larger goals, and undoubtedly checking, however fitfully, too independent subordinates. And the other team is rarely defeated quite so easily in life as Kim defeats them in Kipling's fiction. We know enough of the work of spies to realize that Kipling and the many popular writers since who make the world of espionage the last realm of heroic individualism are merely dreaming.

Finally, Kipling excludes from *Kim* not only the imperial antagonists of the official in the field but also his Indian enemies. In order to paint a picture of a harmonious India reconciled to imperial rule Kipling has no alternative but to exclude the Indian nationalists

entirely, and he does so. Hurree Chunder Mookerjee, the only
Western-educated Indian in *Kim*, betrays no nationalistic sentiments
whatsoever. Nor, as several critics have pointed out, are any of the
efforts of the Game directed against the nationalists. Indeed, all of
Kim's enemies come from beyond the border of British India. Within
these borders, all is amity. Such was not the case, of course, nor is
there any reason to conclude that Kipling's basic attitudes have
changed when, after writing numerous stories that criticize the
nationalists bitterly, he writes a book celebrating an India from which
they are completely missing. In fact, *Kim* achieves its inclusive spirit
by an imaginative annihilation of Kipling's perpetual enemies.

What Kipling excludes, ultimately, is history, the vital forces chang-
ing Indian society. He does so by focusing on either side of the his-
torical process, on the plentitude of the moment and the finality of
the eternal. The highways and bazaars are the locus of *Kim*'s world of
the moment; the great patterns of the Game and the Search provide
the eternal frame. Both realms are finally static, for a vision of the
moment may record motion, but it can hardly discover the dynamics
of that motion, the direction of change. And from the vantage point
of the eternal ("When every one is dead the Great Game is finished.
Not before" [p. 362] [185]), change loses much of its significance.
Only by means of this exclusion can Kipling evade the truth that the
British position in India is deteriorating rather than improving.

Only at one point, and then perhaps unconsciously, does Kipling
suggest the fragility of the world he celebrates in *Kim*. This is when
he writes of the ancient lama's passion for the mountains he is leav-
ing forever: "He blessed them in detail—the great glaciers, the
naked rocks, the piled moraines and tumbled shale; dry upland, hid-
den salt-lake, age-old timber and fruitful water-shot valley one after
the other, as a dying man blesses his folk" (p. 422) [215]. The lama's
style of prayer is Kipling's style of writing in *Kim*. The book, with its
many catalogues of wonders, is a blessing in detail of a dream of
India, a dream held by many men besides Kipling. Yet in this case it
is not the suppliant but the dream that is dying, and in this sense
Kim is as much an elegy as a prescription for change.

What the discovery of all these exclusions leads to, finally, is the
recognition that the generous inclusiveness of *Kim* is in the spirit of
wish fulfillment, not of hard-won victory or compromise. Kipling
has surrendered nothing; his "kindly East" is a land that accepts as
its natural rulers the very group to which he himself belongs—the
country-born Englishman. Nor has he resolved the contradictions
in the imperial system that crippled the imperialist's personality and
frustrated his longings for absolute, unchallenged authority. The
India of *Kim* is a world from which Kipling's enemies, and those of
his fellow imperialists, have been magically banished. Who could

not write generously about such a world? But we need not be surprised when in years to come, as the Empire begins to disintegrate, Kipling turns once again to polemic and invective, displaying the same authoritarian traits rendered largely invisible in *Kim*.

In his efforts to eliminate the flaws in the imperial mold, Kipling devises an educational program that depends on social inequality for its success and aims at making inequality permanent. Kim, Mowgli, Adam Strickland, and the thousands of country-born colonial children they represent achieve their invulnerability artificially, like the sons of feudal lords, by virtue of their race. Their childhood exercise of authority over adults of the subject community convinces them of their inherent superiority and of the naturalness of continued despotic rule. They grow, in other words, neither into submissive adults nor into cooperative ones but into the fundamentally dominating type of authoritarian described by Mannoni[6] as one product of imperialism.

But the bastions of racial privilege were already under attack when Kipling began to write, and the social system on which his new model depended was already slipping into the past. Thus Kipling arrives, at the turn of the century and the peak of his career, at the archetypal condition of the European colonialist as seen by Mannoni. He is a man projecting fantasies of omnipotence onto a world that bears less and less resemblance to his dream. This is at once a pathetic situation and a dangerous one, for while Kipling did his projecting with a pen, the men he idolized and encouraged more often used the sword. * * *

MICHAEL HOLLINGTON

[Storytelling in *Kim*]†

* * *

"Give a woman an old wife's tale and a weaver-bird a leaf and a thread and they will weave wonderful things," says the voice of a Sikh on the train in which Kim and the lama travel to Umballa.[1]

6. Ottave Mannoni, French psychologist whose *Prospero and Caliban: The Psychology of Colonization* (1950/56) theorized the relation between colonizer and colonized in terms of an Oedipal drama of competitive authority in search of perpetual dependency [*Editor*].
† From Michael Hollington, "*Kim* and Kipling: Concentration Camps and Their Sweet Opposites," *Q/W/E/R/T/Y: Arts, Litteratures and Civilization du Monde Anglophone* 4 (October 1994): 84–88. Reprinted by permission of Publications de l' Université de Pau. The author's notes have been edited, and bracketed page references to this Norton Critical Edition have been added following the original references.
1. Rudyard Kipling, *Kim*, ed. Edward Said (Harmondsworth: Penguin, 1987) 98 [00]. Subsequent references to the novel appear in the text.

This sounds like a routine example of the misogyny of anxiety in the novel, but it is followed by a surprising juxtaposition, in which the exercise of the imagination in storytelling is linked with the exalted: "all holy men dream dreams, and by following holy men their disciples attain power."

At any rate [Kipling] is introducing a nexus of imagery equating women and birds and storytelling. The association of women with birds, more particularly one woman, the Sahiba, with one bird, the parrot, is initially derogatory, in such references as "she chuckled like a contented parrot above the sugar lump" (263) [180] or, in a passage that vigorously restates the nexus of the dangers of transition and the open mouth: "Get her her pipe. In the name of the Gods, get her her pipe and stop her ill-omened mouth. She and the parrots are alike. They screech in the dawn" (122) [65]. But pipes also seem to promote storytelling, both in *Kim* itself and in Kipling's account of its making, and at other moments this is the note that is uppermost in this nexus: on page 112 [57] there is emphasis on specifically *female* storytelling birds, "the chattering, grey-backed Seven sisters, talking over the day's adventures." On page 214 [141], moreover, we have an image of the lama's sojourn as Saharunpore in which the terrors of women's narration are presented benignly, associated with shelter and the cooing of doves: "In an apartment of the forecourt overlooked by cooing doves he would sit, while she laid aside her useless veil and chattered of spirits and fiends of Kulu" (214) [141].

It is essential here to remember the *locus classicus* of oral narration for nineteenth-century writers (Dickens is only one great name to have acknowledged and explored his huge debt to it, and Kipling again clearly implicitly follows him when he compares the process of writing *Kim* to "the Djinn released from the brass bottle"[2]): the Arabian Nights. In that work, of course, the heroic central storyteller is a woman, and her oral powers are life-giving. Scheherezade practises storytelling as a means of surviving through the night: if she breaks down, so that gaps may appear in the cycle of 1001 nights, she will be beheaded. She is thus clearly a key reference for the vital Kipling theme of getting through the night, reflected in *Kim* at St Xavier's, for instance, that place where there are no mothers, but where the soothing remedy for night fears is the "womanly" practice of oral narration: "the boys threshed through the hot nights telling tales till the dawn" (171) [106]. You may also survive long railway journeys in a similar way, overcoming a similar orphaned state: "Kim did not feel so lonely after this, and ere he had sat out twenty miles in the crowded compartment, was cheering his neigh-

2. Rudyard Kipling, *Something of Myself* (Harmondsworth: Penguin, 1977), 116.

bours with a string of most wonderful yarns about his own and his master's magical gifts" (234) [157].

Traditional oral epic narration, of course, is in effect singing. It is therefore of interest that in *Kim* women are not only associated with storytelling but with the composition of song: "As a town-mouse well acquainted with the latest songs by the most fashionable composers—they are women for the most part—Kim had a distinct advantage over men from a little fruit-village behind Saharunpore" (124) [68]. And in *Kim* song is an ecstatic mode that accompanies journeying, an expression for instance of the "pure delight" of the sequence of bends in the road up to Simla: "all these things lifted Kim's heart to song within him" (194) [124].

It is within this discursive network that the old Sahiba—she too at the transition point between life and death—gradually comes to represent a wisdom that is an alternative to the lama's "wisdom beyond earthly wisdom—the high and lonely lore of meditation" (275) [189]. Two interconnected aspects of this wisdom are to be noted: first, that it is oral and explicitly contrasted with textual authority—the old lady only likes "divine" writing that can be easily rubbed off; and second, that its essence is a love of life: "She liked charms with plenty of ink that one could wash off in water, swallow, and be done with. Else what was the use of the Gods? She liked men and women, and she spoke of them . . . And Kim, as interested in the life of this world as she soon to leave it, squatted with his feet under the hem of his robe, drinking all in" (275) [190].

To follow this logic through is to ask whether this love of life, of the real world in general and India in particular (the frequent source of readers' admiration for *Kim*), which seems to motivate the oral narration, is essentially "feminine." Do West—equated with secular, practical knowing—and the non-spiritual "feminine" East here meet, at a fold in the road, in an unexpected way? The lama's journey to the hills and back again, at any rate, follows a suggestive itinerary. "Who goes to the hill goes to his mother" (279) [192] is the motto with which Chapter Thirteen opens, to suggest that the lama's urge to return there is not wholly ascetic. He is to realise this himself later in his interpretation of the Russian's aggression as a punishment for the complex selfishness of the desire to renounce self: he ends up renouncing hills instead, and descending from "the great height of speculation" to the plains again.

Once there, he treats the Sahiba with new respect, becoming much more accommodating to her requests for charms, and calling her "Sister," "using that form of address a Buddhist monk may sometimes employ towards a nun" (323) [227]. And Kim, too, though he foregoes the sensual delights offered him by the Woman of Shamlegh, now submits on the plains to other intense physical

pleasures administered by women. Two tantric *masseuses* are permitted to invade his defenses in no uncertain way—they "took him to pieces all one long afternoon" and "kneaded [him] to irresponsible pulp"—and the consequence is the precise equivalent of Scheherezade's storytelling: "Kim slid ten thousand miles into slumber—thirty-six hours of it—sleep that soaked like rain after drought." * * * The plains seem to symbolise matriarchy, the mother earth with whom Kim is now getting into deeper rhythm (even if his love of the material world already tends in its direction), as the two women lay him on a significant east-west axis "that the mysterious earth-currents which thrill the clay of our bodies might help and not hinder" (324) [228].

Time and Oral Narrative

If the benign dispeller of danger in the text is a storyteller, it is because she offers an effect of absolute seamless continuity, with no dangerous gaps: she can mediate all transitions. The appropriate imagery is liquid, for narrative at its best and most fluent is capable of reproducing that "broad, smiling river of life" (109) [54–55] that is the source of pleasure in *Kim*. It is to be noted how many chapters flow without a pause from one incident to the next: Chapter Three, for instance, ends, "they embraced as do father and son in the East," and Chapter Four commences, "Then, lowering their voices, they spoke together" (106–7) [52–53].

Here too at this bend in the road the lama's critique of life "bound upon the wheel"—contemporary western life, if you like * * *—as a lurching "from despair to despair—hot, uneasy, snatching" is vindicated. Even the male narrative voice is capable of approving of "the happy Asiatic disorder which, if you only allow time, will bring you everything that a simple man needs" (112) [57]. Of course Kim is not that—he likes Creighton because he is like himself, a complicated and not a simple person, needing to get into Paradise through the back door. But he can certainly transcend the Western anxiety of the clock. Echoing Milton's Adam and Eve in Paradise ("With thee conversing I forget all time") he says to the lama at one point: "It is less than three days since we took the road together, and it is as though it were a hundred years" (118) [63].

In this novel, indeed, there is a clear alternative to clock-time, a notion of a storytelling time linked to natural rhythm. On the road you tell time by the sun's position: "it was a very short march, and time lacked an hour to sundown" (126) [68]. Out in the open you can be happy, sleeping under the stars, with "a bed among brickbats and ballast-refuse on a damp night, between overcrowded horses and unwashed Baltis" (185) [116]; in this way you pass easily

through the terrifying gap of time that stretches to dawn. And if you slip into the rhythm of the Indian siesta, you don't need tantric massage: "at mid-day after talk and a little wayfaring, they slept; meeting the world refreshed when the air was cooler."

The Pleasures of Dissembling

Though the anxious male narrator may be at pains to make sharp distinctions between truth and lies—the "lying" Eastern World ("Kim could lie like an Oriental", 71 [23]; "the truth . . . is a thing a native on the road seldom presents to a stranger", 64 [17]) is habitually opposed to the truth-telling West—the tale once more undermines its teller, blurring the East-West axis. The lama, of course, is the most authoritative truth-teller of all in the novel, and by contrast Kim recognises the white authority-figure Creighton as *mon semblable, mon frère* in the business of lying: "here was a man after his own heart—a tortuous and indirect person playing a hidden game" (165) [100]. The capacity to lie is in fact the Open Sesame that enables Kim to penetrate the threshold of the Great Game as an equal with such as Mahbub Ali: "I tell thee he does not know how to lie—as we two know" (68) [20].

But Kim's lying is accompanied by disguise, and it is appropriate that the essential aiders and abettors of Kim in this version of storytelling are again women, and in particular prostitutes. They share with him (and Huckleberry Finn, another adolescent adept of lies and disguises) the experience of fundamental marginality. Brought up by "auntie," "never trained to consider them in any way improper" (168) [103], he knows that "ladies of that persuasion . . . were generous" (78) [29], and even in Lucknow he can readily make a bee-line to "frivolous ladies at upper windows in a certain street" (168) [103]. Once arrived at the brothel he makes a request for a rather unusual speciality—"I would go as a gardener's boy"—and his entertainer readily sets about helping him: "the girl worked busily, dabbing a twist of cloth into a little saucer of brown dye that holds longer than any walnut-juice" (174) [108]. But the main point to notice is how protean Kim's lying is—even here at ease with a fellow marginal and dissembler he's not willing simply to tell the truth. Chameleon-like, he must invent a fiction that blends in with the erotic setting in which he finds himself, pretending that his disguise is for the purpose of a seduction rather than a mundane flight from school.

And then, once in disguise, he boards the third-class compartment of a train and treats himself to an orgy of lies: "He explained to the company that he was assistant to a juggler who had left him behind sick with fever, and that he would pick up his master at

Umballa. As the occupants of the carriage changed, he varied this tale, or adorned it with all the shoots of a budding fancy, the more rampant for being held off native speech so long. In all India that night was no human being so joyful as Kim" (175) [109].

This kind of delight in playacting validates Richard Cronin's stress upon the ludic aspects of *Kim*.[3] It is not only the masculine "great game" with its worldwide scope ("the last ripple of the stone Kim had helped to heave was lapping against the steps of a mosque in far-away Roum," 258 [176]; there is also the "little game" of dressing up and putting on a histrionic performance, as in an earlier train where "Kim burst into a flood of tears, protesting that the lama was his father and his mother, that he was the prop of the lama's declining years, and that the lama would die without his care" (78) [29].

The Pleasures of the Craft

"We be craftsmen together, thou and I" (59) [13] is how the curator compliments the lama on his skills as a penman. The autobiographical sediment shows through quite strongly here—the curator is a portrait of John Lockwood Kipling and his enthusiasm for the Arts and Crafts Movement in England in the later nineteenth century. The word "craft" is dual, combining a reference to art with another to philosophy or belief, the "craft" of freemasonry reflected in his ready acceptance of the lama, the representative of another creed who himself combines the same two qualities of soul as he "went through the collection with the reverence of a devotee and the appreciative instinct of a craftsman" (56) [9].

"Craft" is a distinctive feature of the prose of *Kim*. It offers a virtuoso display of the "quick eyes" (in Pound's phrase) of the craftsman, passed on through inheritance to the "bright eyes" of Kim (109) [54] which take in the pleasures of the seeable world. These are very much painterly and even Aesthetic eyes, in the 1890s sense, as they observe, for instance, "the lama, very straight and erect, the deep folds of his yellow clothing slashed with black in the light of the *parao* fires precisely as a knotted tree-trunk is slashed with the shadow of the low sun, addressed a tinsel and lacquered *ruth* which burned like a many-coloured jewel in the same uncertain light" (119) [63], or again, at the end of the novel: "the cross-legged figure, outline jet-black against the lemon-coloured drift of light" (336) [238].

Men tell stories too in *Kim*: the old soldier is one good example, bringing out "his cavalry sabre and, balancing it on his dry knees,

3. Richard Cronin, "The Indian English Novel: *Kim* and Midnight's Children," *Modern Fiction Studies* (Summer 1987): 201–13.

[telling] tales of the Mutiny and young captains thirty years in their graves, till Kim dropped asleep" (98) [45]. The "craft" version of storytelling appears as a specifically male gift and inheritance. And (though there is not space here to explore "homosexual" elements in Kipling, handled crudely and exploitatively by Seymour-Smith,[4] and without feel for the much subtler naming strategies of this text) it seems to go together with a reverence for specifically masculine beauty. This appears to be less overtly sexual and therefore less polluting than female beauty, and can shine through dirt—Kim is glimpsed as "a neophyte, of singular, though unwashen, beauty" on page 288 [000]. Its aesthetic. Pre-Raphaelite quality is evident elsewhere in such passages as this on page 243 [164] where "he looked rather like the young saint of a stained-glass window."

Yet there is a sexual element there, expressed by the earthier Mahbub, who greets Kim idiomatically but ambivalently, seeming to wish him the energy for many nights of love: "May you never be tired, Pathan! Oh, the hearts to be broken! Oh, the eyes under the eyelashes, looking sideways!" (219) [145]. One of the hearts is clearly that of the lama—with an interlinear echo of *King Lear*, he says as much at one point: "Dost thou love me? Then go, or my heart cracks" (171) [105]. Following in the footsteps of David in his love for Jonathan or Socrates for Alcibiades, he too in Benares forsakes the written text and accepts for a while the humble role of story-teller: "he ceased for a while to mourn the loss of his River, or to draw wondrous pictures of the Wheel of Life, but preferred to talk of the beauty and wisdom of a certain mysterious *chela*" (213) [140]. Like any street entertainer, he summons his audience—"let all listen to the *Jâtaka*!"—and tells what is for him the supreme love story, of the Buddha for Ananda.

Storytelling and Translation

The constant need to consult footnotes in reading Kipling (we have to look up "Roum" above, for instance, to discover that it is Istanbul) is an index of an essential aspect of this text: the vital importance of translation. The perception of India as a place of "holy men stammering gospels in strange tongues" (80) [31] highlights the role of translation in this novel. Narrating the tale involves a ceaseless activity of translation between a host of disparate languages and their regional variants (the euphemism for sex is "walnuts" in the hills for instance and "almonds" in the plains [306] [214]).

But the point of this activity is not to control and master the otherness of foreign tongues by offering versions of them that smooth over

4. Martin Seymour-Smith, *Rudyard Kipling* (London, 1989).

differences and provide easy idiomatic consumption for the speaker of the language of reception. It is almost the reverse—a means of highlighting the weird and wonderful hybrids that bloom as a consequence of the overlaying of English upon the various vernaculars. * * *

The first thing to do is simply listen to the multiple voices, even without comprehension, as Kim does to the lama: "now and again he heard the sing-song cadence of a Chinese quotation" (77) [63].

Om mane pudme hum (81) is a constant refrain, accompanied by the clicking of rosary beads—it remains untranslated, for its effect does not depend upon recognition of its meaning. Nor are we to suppose that translation is a one-way process only, or that there are not equally unintelligible encoded aspects of Anglo-Indian culture, some of them highly strategic and ironic, using Kim as a kind of Candide.[5] "Kim did not know what bounds meant" (148) [86] is one example, or "'struck off the strength,' which conveyed no meaning to him till he was ordered to go off and play" (163) [98].

Kim's English is of course at all times a special idiom that the moments of faulty grammar (e.g. "every month I become a year more old," 185 [116]) serve to characterise. It is the unique instrument for expressing a very particular experience that couldn't be expressed in any other way. One should note the ubiquity of the phrase "as it were" in the notation of the impossible task of precise translation. "Few can translate the picture-parable" is the narrative commentary upon the lama's charts of the Great Wheel, and asking the mean of signs is endemic ("What colour ash is there in thy pipe-bowl . . . Was there raw turmeric among thy foodstuffs?" 250 [170]).

In fact, on many an occasion we are made conscious that the texts simply won't merge. The very ponderousness of some of the explanatory matter is a symptom of this, as in the notation of the Sahiba's jokes in Hindi: "We that go down to the *chattris* [the big umbrellas above the burning-ghats where the priests take their last dues] clutch hard at the bearers of the *chattis* [young folk full of the pride of life, she meant; but the pun is clumsy]" (326) [230]. The non-convergence of the separate languages that make up *Kim* is another fundamental manifestation of the essential palimpsest nature of this text, here seen at the synchronic rather than the diachronic level of language.

A Non-Teleological Ending

At least since Edmund Wilson, the rich and complex ending of *Kim* has often tended to leave readers with a feeling of dissatisfaction, either because (like Wilson) they feel that Kim is about to

5. The eponymous naive protagonist of Voltaire's satirical novel [*Editor*].

betray his lama, or more simply, because of its indeterminacy. It is this latter feature of the ending I shall focus upon here, hoping to show that it exemplifies the multilayered oral and palimpsestual nature of this text.

Of course from one perspective the ending looks simply absurd. In a kind of trance, believing that his sacred river is found, the lama stumbles into a brook and nearly drowns before being rescued by Hurree Babu. He appears indeed from a Western perspective as a kind of Don Quixote.

But to rest content with that or any other univocal version of the ending would be to display an unidiomatic appetite for conventional teleology. If the lama is a fool, he is unquestionably a holy fool, and has his own authority. It is his voice that dominates the concluding pages. Kim sleeps a second time in the arms of mother earth and awakes refreshed in the evening, content to remain silent and listen to a voice that appears rejuvenated, "like a gong." The lama's conviction that his search is over may not carry entire conviction: it may be almost as illusory as the earlier belief that Kim has found the "red bull on a green field" of his father's prophecy. This is certainly the way I read the last sentence: "he crossed his hands on his lap and smiled, as a man may who has won salvation for himself and his beloved" (338) [240]. There is sharp contradiction here, in the lama's own ascetic terms, between "salvation" and "the beloved," and the past tense of "has won" seems to jar with the implications of an immediately preceding sentence where it appears that the job of saving Kim has only just begun: "I have wrenched my Soul back from the Threshold of Freedom to free thee from all sin." But there is no final authoritative perspective from which to judge: his is one version, Hurree Babu's another. The text validates both.

Seen in this way, the essence of *Kim* is thus an attempt at finding ways of incorporating multiple conflicting realities into a unity, and finding metaphors to express the process. If in this essay we have concentrated chiefly on the figure of the palimpsest, it might be appropriate to conclude by highlighting another—the gamut. At one point we have an image of sleep-inducing contentment, of story-telling, of pipe-smoking, of voices blending, of high and low united, with the dancing-girl and her instrument at the top of the scale, that can serve as a concluding epiphany of the benign vision of the multiplicity of Indian life that this novel eventually manages to endorse and express: "The voices of early evening had settled down to one soothing hum whose deepest note was the steady chumping of the bullocks above their chopped straw, and whose highest was the tinkle of a Bengali dancing-girl's *sitar*. Most men had eaten and pulled deep at their gurgling, grunting hookahs, which in full blast sound like bull-frogs" (119) [63].

PARAMA ROY

[*Kim*, the Myth of the Nation, and National Identity]†

* * *

The novel, then, both invokes and rejects two apparently indigenous modes—the violence of the Mutiny and the civility of [Indian National] Congress demands—of conceiving nationalism and nationness. But what *Kim* does, above and beyond this uneasy and furtively represented engagement with available nationalisms, is to make the subject of nationalism its own; it seeks to generate a myth of the nation and of the national subject.

Let us consider for a moment the paradoxes that constitute the idea of nationness. In the classic essay, "What Is a Nation?" (1882), Renan identifies the nation as the most compelling and pervasive formation of modern western politics while systematically eliminating any "rational" or "natural" basis for national identity. Language, religion, race, geography, dynastic continuity, even a commonality of material interests—none of these can generate nationness or account for the sentimental charge of national identity. Renan delights, in fact, in the contradictions that not only inhere in the national idea but provide its very grounds of possibility. Thus nations originate in violence, conquest, and oppression, and a national memory and national unity in the nation's present can only be achieved if the citizen makes it a point to forget much of the past: "Forgetting, I would even go so far as to say historical error, is a crucial factor in the creation of a nation."[1] A nation nonetheless transcends its immanent contradictions in a collective will-to-nationness which is also a will-to-homogenization; it exists on a democratic, voluntaristic basis, being the result of a "daily plebiscite." Benedict Anderson's *Imagined Communities* (1991) plays upon some of the ambivalences in the idea of the nation, but his objective is explicitly *not* to supply or invent a principle of nationness. For him, the nation is not a principle of transcendence or reconciliation but the supreme fiction of modern politics.[2] There

† From *Indian Traffic: Identities in Question in Colonial and Postcolonial India* (Berkeley: University of California Press, 1998). Copyright © 1998 The Regents of the University of California. Reprinted by permission of the publisher. Page references to *Kim* have been changed to correspond to this Norton Critical Edition.

1. Ernest Renan, "What Is a Nation?" in *Nation and Narration*, ed. Homi K. Bhabha (London and New York: Routledge, 1990), 13.

2. Benedict Anderson, *Imagined Communities: Reflections on the Origin and Spread of Nationalism* (London: Verso, 1991 [1983]). Anderson's characterization of the nation as imagined community needs to be supplemented by Arjun Appadurai's caution in his

can be no objective definition of a nation, no authentic and inauthentic nations; a nation is an "imagined community" that can mean whatever its members want it to mean. The word *imagined* is key, because Anderson argues that the nation as political principle was conceived, historically, through certain forms of representation, most notably narrative fiction and print journalism. Anderson's study is salutary among other things for its refusal to dismiss nationalism as simply a pathology of contemporary political life. It aligns the nation with questions of religion, faith, kinship, and emotional allegiance; unlike others, it seeks to understand the *affect* of the nation through its splits, repressions, and ambivalences. It refuses to assume a true-false judgmentality and positivism in understanding the nation; the concept of imagination, of nation as representation, is at the heart of this analysis. The nation is never automatically there, even as a geographical, physical entity; as a place of mobility, migrancy, movement, it has to be literalized through pilgrimages and the travels of the indigenized bureaucracy of the colonial state. Nations must be *seen* as well as read as novels or newspapers.[3] In several ways, however, Anderson reproduces the affect he seeks to analyze and duplicates the homogenizing tendency of nationalisms in his conception of a "homogeneous empty time" of the nation that produces the normative citizen.

The essays in *Nation and Narration* offer implicit and explicit critiques of this, pointing to the internal contradictions of the nation, to its dialectical logic, to its status as a differential principle, and to the repressions that are necessary to produce the people as one. Geoff Bennington points to the ways in which the nation must necessarily be constructed from the outside in:

> It is tempting to try to approach the question of nation directly, by aiming for its centre or its origin. . . . [But] such access is in general illusory: the approach to the nation implies borders, policing, suspicion, and crossing (or refusal of entry)—try to enter a country at the centre (by flying in, say), and the border is still there to be crossed, the frontier shifted from periphery to centre. . . . The frontier does not merely close the nation in on itself, but also, immediately, opens it to an outside, to other nations.[4]

"Patriotism and Its Futures," *Public Culture* 5 (Spring 1993): 414: "The modern nation-state, in this view, grows less out of natural facts—such as language, blood, soil, and race—but is a quintessential cultural product, a product of the collective imagination. . . . In many of these theories of the nation as imagined, there is always a suggestion that blood, kinship, race, and soil are somehow less imagined, more natural than the imagination of collective interest or solidarity."

3. Anderson, *Imagined Communities*, passim.
4. Geoff Bennington, "Postal Politics and the Institution of the Nation," in *Nation and Narration*," 121.

While Renan had insisted on the nation's resolution or transcendence of its contradictions, tensions, and fissiparous tendencies through a gigantic act of collective will, Bennington argues that it is these very differences that make the idea of the nation fragmentary, contentious, and discontinuous. A nation therefore has to be narrated in order to exist; it requires a foundational fiction—which is always necessarily a fiction—to mark its legitimation and continuity.[5]

The instance of *Kim* provides a most productive illustration of and commentary upon the construction of nationness and nationness as construct. Though the action of the novel is set in the 1880s (Kim encounters the old Rissaldar after the Golden Jubilee of Victoria's coronation in 1887) it was conceived in Vermont in the mid-1890s and finished in Sussex about six years later.[6] Kipling, as we might know, was born in India (in 1865) and spent his first six years there, years that were, in his recall, idyllic to a degree. Raised by Indian servants, he claims to have been familiar with the bazaars and temples and Indian neighborhoods of Bombay and to have thought in Hindustani. When he was sent to school in England at the age of six, he was apparently traumatized in ways he never forgot. This was a common enough experience for Anglo-Indian children as young inhabitants of an "invaded colony" rather than a "settler colony."[7] Angus Wilson points to the numerous reasons that made such a separation of the English child from India seem necessary:

> Ostensibly the reason that parents sent their children at an early age back to England was the care of their health, the avoidance of the Indian climate which, particularly given the limitations of nineteenth-century medicine, was perilous, especially in the hot seasons. . . . The children of English people in the lower echelons of the Anglo-Indian hierarchy stayed there and went to boarding schools like Kim's at Lucknow or up in the hill stations. . . . Those children who went there, however, would share their lives with boys of "dubious" social origin and with those Portuguese names that so sprinkle Kipling's stories of half-caste life. To health, then, were added social and racial reasons. Anyone who was anyone would send his children home. Children speaking an Indian tongue more easily than English, or recounting Hindu fables, or mouthing the names of outlandish gods and goddesses, were charming up to, at the most, six years. . . . Ayahs, native servants of all

5. For a useful elaboration of this idea, see Doris Sommer, *Foundational Fictions: The National Romances of Latin America* (Berkeley: University of California Press, 1991).

6. J. M. S. Tompkins, *The Art of Rudyard Kipling* (London: Methuen, 1959), 21.

7. The terms to mark this distinction—a common enough one—are borrowed from Bill Ashcroft, Gareth Griffiths, and Helen Tiffin, eds., *The Empire Writes Back: Theory and Practice in Post-Colonial Literatures* (London and New York: Routledge, 1989).

kinds were "wonderful with children", but they spoiled them.
. . . Then the standards of all natives were not ours—in mat-
ters of truth-telling, of hard work, of hygiene, and . . . in sex-
ual life where, as the terrible child marriages showed, they were
notoriously precocious.[8]

Kipling returned to India when he was sixteen, to resume residence
with his parents in Lahore, and he served on the staff of the *Pioneer*
and the *Civil and Military Gazette* for a few years. This was also the
period when he established his fame (more fully perhaps in England
than in Anglo-India) as the writer of *Plain Tales from the Hills* as
well as other fictions of Anglo-Indian life. In his midtwenties he left
for an extended tour of the world that took him to England (which,
once again, he hated) and then to the United States, to the home of
his new bride, Carrie. Kipling was then writing his great novel about
India after his permanent departure from the country of his birth
and early childhood (he was to return only once, for a brief visit); he
was writing it from the outside, as an exile (exiled at one point from
both India and England). It is precisely this placement, I will argue,
that allows him to conceive of a national horizon for the geograph-
ical space designated doubly as "India" and as "colony." It is this dis-
tance, too, and the sense of India as a totality that this distance
enables, that gives the novel its distinctly monumental, if not epic,
flavor.

If liminality is central to the construction of the nation, then
Kipling's India is certainly produced and reproduced at its borders.
Who, after all, are the primary Indian characters of the nation that
names itself India? The central Indian character is of course the
Buddhist lama from Tibet; indeed, Kipling has been sometimes crit-
icized (by patriotic Indian critics) for making Buddhism, which was
exported out of India in the third and fourth centuries B.C. and
which in any event has been a minor presence in the country for
centuries, representative of Indian spirituality.[9]

The Pathan Mahbub Ali, who is at home in Kabul and border
towns like Peshawar, is another player on the Indian scene, and he
too is exorbitant to colonial space and to Indian national space. In
the 1840s and once again in the 1880s, the colonial government in
India had fought two bloody and humiliating wars over the control
of Afghanistan, which marked the point at which British and Russ-
ian colonialisms encountered each other. Despite the energetic exe-
cution of a British "Forward Policy," Afghanistan remained unas-
similable into the British Empire, and the North-West Frontier

8. Angus Wilson, *The Strange Ride of Rudyard Kipling* (Harmondsworth: Penguin Books,
 1979), 20–21.
9. Cited in ibid., 132.

Province (from which Mahbub Ali apparently hails) remained in a stormy and contested relationship with the government in Delhi.[1] The third Indian, Hurree Babu, evokes not geographical but—as we have seen—political and ideological liminality (as well as centrality) in colonial discourse. He is thus a character in whom very specific cultural meanings are vested. He himself is well aware of them, and even as he *is* the typical Bengali, verbose, cowardly, superstitious, he also knows how to *play* the boastful Bengali babu or the malcontent babu to perfection.

If India in this novel is represented best by liminal figures, much of its action also occurs in the margins of the nation. Its narrative takes place not in central or southern India, though Kim travels widely, as far south as Bombay, and so apparently does the lama. Much of what happens happens in northern India, in Lahore, Ambala, and the hills that mark the point of contact between India and its northern neighbors—and other imperial powers. This of course was the India most familiar and beloved to Kipling. He spent most of his adult years in India in Lahore and Allahabad; he saw southern India only through the window of a train, and he seems to have had little physical contact with the country's eastern reaches, despite "The City of Dreadful Night" (1888) which is one of the most famous literary indictments of Calcutta.[2] English officials in his stories ("William the Conqueror" is but one example) pride themselves on being "Punjabis."[3] But, more important, for India to be invoked as a totality, as a nation, it must be constructed at its borders; a boundary has to be invoked in order to construct a center. As Bhabha points out in "DissemiNation," liminality is at the very heart of the national idea.[4]

In a very real sense, the nation in the novel is also created quite literally out of the very fact of travel. Benedict Anderson speaks of the ways in which travel by administrators literalized the imagined community, as did the travel undertaken by ordinary people on the new railway systems.[5] In late-nineteenth-century India the civil service, which had been partially indigenized, may also have produced the nation as an effect of travels, territorializations, and contextualizations. The trope of pilgrimage in *Kim*, pilgrimage without a spe-

1. R. C. Majumdar, H. C. Raychaudhuri, and Kalikinkar Dutta, *An Advanced History of India* (London and Delhi: Macmillan, 1967), 2:823–32. We might recall that in the Sherlock Holmes stories, Dr. Watson's wound (acquired at the battle of Miani) is always painfully present.

2. Rudyard Kipling, "The City of Dreadful Night," in *From Sea to Sea: Letters of Travel* (New York: Charles Scribner's Sons, 1906 [1899]), 2:287–363.

3. See Lewis Wurgraft, *The Imperial Imagination: Magic and Myth in Kipling's India* (Middletown, Conn.: Wesleyan University Press, 1983), for British psychic investment in the frontier and in the myth of the "Punjabi" as the architect of British greatness in India.

4. Bhabha, "DissemiNation," in *Nation and Narration*, 305.

5. Anderson, *Imagined Communities*, 55–56.

cific local object—the River of the Arrow is, like the idea of the
nation, mythical and internal and therefore necessitates travel to all
places—serves to concretize and make visible the form of the
nation. What this evokes is the spectacle of Gandhi's endless pere-
grinations (in Richard Attenborough's film), both on foot and by
train, through a geographical space that assumes the lineaments of
a nation through this very process. (To this end Indian political lead-
ers practice *padayatras* [an elevated term for "traveling on foot" that
does not translate easily—*yatra* for instance is not simply travel, it is
also pilgrimage] for political ends. In the last decade the Bharatiya
Janata Party has undertaken numerous *yatras* in a bid to assert
"national unity," a fairly transparent code for the expression of anti-
Muslim sentiment.

If the nation has always to be coaxed into existence, if the idea of
the nation is not native, is always imported, then who or what con-
stitutes the national subject? This is a critical question for *Kim*. It
is in its engagement with this question that we see Kipling's implicit
dialectic with the idea of (Indian) nationalism. If nationalism's pro-
ject is to locate and name a native self and an alien self, then
Kipling too must make such discriminations. It has been said by
John McClure that the project of this novel is to naturalize the Eng-
lishman in India, or at least to naturalize British control of India.[6]
How is rule presented as something else? How does one belong and
not belong? I would argue that this emphasis is quite literally relo-
cated in *Kim*; it is far more ambitious in its reach than other novels
about India. The Anglo-Indian for Kipling becomes the site of the
dissolution and reconfiguration of the native-alien opposition. *Kim*
distinguishes between Indian Englishness and English Englishness;
it incorporates and co-opts the anticolonial argument about foreign
rule by making the Anglo-Indian (almost) an unhyphenated Indian.
Kipling knew very well that the best defense of colonialism was to
argue its self-reflexive and self-monitoring capacity, as well as its
faculty for internal reform, and it is his privileging of the Anglo-
Indian as the true insider that allows him both to criticize British
India and to ensure its permanence. Thus the Sahiba can say, of
Strickland and his ilk: "'These be the sort to oversee justice. They
know the land and the customs of the land. The others, all new from
Europe, suckled by white women and learning our tongues from
books, are worse than the pestilence. They do harm to Kings'" [67].
Kim, too, gives his assent to the Anglo-Indian boys who are his com-
patriots at St. Xavier's:

6. This is the thrust of John McClure's argument in *Kipling and Conrad: The Colonial Fic-
tion* (Cambridge, Mass.: Harvard University Press, 1981). I am indebted to this insight,
though the trajectory of my argument is obviously different from McClure's.

> The mere story of their adventures, which to them were no adventures, on their road to and from school would have crisped a western boy's hair. . . . And every tale was told in the even, passionless voice of the native-born, mixed with quaint reflections, borrowed unconsciously from native foster-mothers, and turns of speech that showed they had been that instant translated from the vernacular. Kim watched, listened, and approved. This was not the insipid, single-word talk of drummer-boys. [106]

Kipling must have been well aware that his target audience for such a philosophy was not just the Indian (who might require persuasion of the Anglo-Indian's indigeneity) but also Anglo-Indians themselves. As Angus Wilson puts it,

> The English remained, throughout their rule in India, as transient in their final image of themselves, despite all the home-making of the memsahibs, as they had been in the East India Company days of "make your lakhs of rupees and come home". It was to be Kipling's chief difficulty, when he later dreamed of an Anglo-Saxon Empire, of fitting India, his beloved, into the sisterhood of Canada, Australia, New Zealand and South Africa. However miserable, however made impotent by retirement to Bognor or Torquay or Eastbourne, "home" was not just a name for the mother country for Anglo-Indians, as it continued to be for Australians or New Zealanders or English South Africans until the Second War; England was their real home. . . . The English as a whole were dug into India to stay as long as the mind could imagine, and yet individual English men and women, although their families might have served India for generations, were there not to settle but to serve their time.[7]

It is Kipling's task, then, to make the Anglo-Indian perform as first citizen of a country named India. The Strickland of the stories may have been caught up in trying to solve the problem of how one can be inside and outside at the same time. The issues are not extraneous to *Kim*, but what this novel takes on is the figuring of the colony as nation. If Anderson had spoken of the nation as an imagined community, Kipling speaks of the colony in the same terms. He in fact collapses the oppositions between colony and nation. In such an arrangement, it is not the "Indian" Indian who features as the

7. A. Wilson, *Strange Ride*, 22. Ali Behdad uses the term *self-exoticization* to describe the situation of the Anglo-Indian: "The British colonizers spent long periods, sometimes their entire lives, in India, and so they often felt alienated from 'home' (and in that sense inclined to identify themselves as 'Indians') while simultaneously remaining alienated (as 'English') with respect to the Indians as 'natives'" (*Belated Travelers: Orientalism in the Age of Colonial Dissolution* [Durham, N.C., and London: Duke University Press, 1994], 77–78).

primary national subject but the Anglo-Indian, who is carefully dis-
tinguished from the Englishman and who in a sense may be said to
"choose" India in a manner not available to the native.[8] B. J. Moore-
Gilbert, however uncritically he might read Anglo-India's represen-
tation of itself, nonetheless usefully reminds us that "the growing
community of foreigners in India was to produce its own quite dis-
tinctive contributions to . . . [Orientalist] discourse. . . . It
would be a mistake to assume that Anglo-Indians were simply the
British abroad."[9] He points to a distinctively Anglo-Indian literary
and journalistic tradition going as far back as the 1830s, a tradition
that generates and reflects the community's sense of its specific
audience and its unique locational and experiential identity.[1] Anglo-
Indians like Kim and Strickland and presumably Creighton and
Lurgan (and, of course, Kipling himself), who have been born and
raised in India and who have what is certainly represented as a
native's access to indigenous language and culture, are an entirely
different breed from the despised and alien English, whose awk-
wardness, intolerance, and ignorance justifies Kim's contempt for
them. These Anglo-Indians are also different, and better educated
in citizenship and nationness, than are the teeming but transparent
masses that populate the pages of the novel, the masses that have
no capacity to transcend their differences in order to imagine the
nation. They are superior above all to the Eurasians, those dis-
turbingly visible rem(a)inders of the illegitimate, because
(hetero)sexual traffic across the racial divide, a traffic that can only
produce hyphenated Indians. Kipling is particularly revulsed by the
"half-caste," the Eurasian (known in postcolonial India as Anglo-
Indian!) who is neither flesh nor fowl. The Anglo-Indian (that is, the
India-raised white man), because he is an (almost) unhyphenated
Indian, becomes the native of the Indian nation.

8. Sara Suleri astutely remarks about Kim's putative freedom that "[despite] his ostensible
 mobility and cultural dexterity . . . Kim is an imperial casualty of more tragic propor-
 tions than he is usually granted. It is not as though Kim stands outside the colonial sys-
 tem called the Great Game and—as Edmund Wilson implies—has the luxury of choosing
 whether or not to play it: instead, Kim *is* the game, and finally is unable to separate it from
 the parameters of his own history. Kim's collaboration is therefore emblematic of not so
 much an absence of conflict as the terrifying absence of choice in the operations of colo-
 nialism" (*The Rhetoric of English India* [Chicago and London: University of Chicago
 Press, 1992], 116). Thomas Richards describes the use of the Great Game's agents in
 similar terms: "the state constitutes a kind of infra-individual implant detached from the
 active consciousness of its subjects yet, at the same time, an activating part of them"
 ("Archive and Utopia," *Representations* 37 [Winter 1992]: 113).
9. B. J. Moore-Gilbert, *Kipling and "Orientalism"* (London and Sydney: Croom Helm,
 1986), 5–6.
1. It is difficult, however, to sympathize with his fetishization of residence in India in "Intro-
 duction: Writing India, Reorienting Colonial Discourse Analysis," in *Writing India,
 1757–1990: The Literature of British India*, ed. Bart Moore-Gilbert (Manchester and
 New York: Manchester University Press, 1996), 1–29; in this essay he insists that the fact
 of Indian residence placed Anglo-Indian writers outside the circuit of Orientalist racism.

And yet Kim's own whiteness is never something that can be taken as given; it must also be learned, demonstrated, and defended. His whiteness is never a fully secure inheritance; his racial identity is always interstitial and contested. He is, after all, Irish, an ethnic-national category often conflated with the Indian and in many instances affiliated with Indian nationalism;[2] it is surely of some interest to remember Kipling's own Scottish, Irish, and Welsh ancestry on his mother's side.[3] He is, besides, the son of an alcoholic and degraded private, and is "a poor white of the very poorest" [3]. He is only tenuously connected with the whiteness of Colonel Creighton and Lurgan Sahib, and the novel oscillates between defining sahibness as a property that is biological and as something that must be carefully cultivated. Gyan Prakash is surely right to point to the doubleness that marks the production of Kim's whiteness (and he also notes that it may be possible to see Kim's mother as ethnically unmarked):

> Obvious and easy though it is to see how *Kim* asserts racial polarities, it is equally significant to observe that these oppositions are rendered profoundly enigmatic in the process of their formulation. Thus Kim's whiteness does not stand separate from his blackness but is bleached from his "burned as black" skin. So immersed is the formation of Kim's racial identity and authority in difference—whiteness formed on the borderlines of black and white, fact and fable, English and the vernacular—that liminality marks the emergence of a powerful colonizer-colonized hierarchy.[4]

2. It is striking to observe how many of the non-Indian figures most sympathetic to India and to Indian nationalist demands have been Irish. Radha Kumar mentions the Freedom for India and Ireland group in the United States in the early twentieth century, in *The History of Doing: An Illustrated Account of Movements for Women's Rights and Feminism in India, 1800–1990* (New Delhi: Kali for Women; London and New York: Verso, 1993), 66. See also V. G. Kiernan, *The Lords of Humankind* (London: Century Hutchinson, 1969). Abdul JanMohamed describes quite persuasively Kim's "*personal* and *emotional* allegiance to the Indians . . . and, on the other, his *impersonal* and *rational* relation to the Englishmen" ("The Economy of Manichean Allegory: The Function of Racial Difference in Colonialist Literature," in *"Race," Writing, and Difference,* ed. Henry Louis Gates [Chicago and London: University of Chicago Press, 1986], 99). I am not in disagreement with this reading of Kim's alignments, though I will point to the ways in which the emotional charge of his "Indian" relationships is not outside the calculus of the Great Game, which uses everything that is at hand.
3. Charles Carrington, *Rudyard Kipling: His Life and Work* (London: Macmillan, 1986), 34.
4. Prakash, "Science 'Gone Native,'" 154. Joseph Bristow also remarks that the "slippage between his 'Englishness' and 'Irishness' indicates how Kim variously represents white superiority *and* white subordination" (*Empire Boys: Adventure in a Man's World* [London: HarperCollins, 1991], 198). Finally, see Christopher Lane: "If the meaning of race is disputable in *Kim*, the text also designates a split between racial identity and political identification that leads it into potential crisis even as it insists that each is finally commensurate" (*The Ruling Passion: British Colonial Allegory and the Paradox of Homosexual Desire* [Durham, N.C., and London: Duke University Press, 1995], 42).

When "discovered" by Father Victor and the Reverend Arthur Ben-
nett, he speaks very much in the accents of the Eurasian from
whom he is careful, later, to distinguish himself in caste terms:
"Their eyes are blued and their nails are blackened with low-caste
blood, many of them. Sons of *mehteranees*—brothers-in-law to the
bhungi [sweeper]" [122]. When Kim contemplates his racial iden-
tity, it is often, significantly, in terms of what must be learned—"I
must needs go to a *madrissah* [school] and be turned into a Sahib"
[78]—and what must be remembered: "One must never forget that
one is a Sahib, and that some day, when examinations are passed,
one will command natives" [107].

The (Anglo-Indian) nation thus conceived also has its other citi-
zens, and certainly Mahbub Ali and Hurree Babu are among them
by virtue of their training for and participation in the Great Game.
Indeed, the Great Game, which employs the most liminal subjects,
which conceives of India as a unified field upon which actions, trav-
els, and exchanges must occur ceaselessly, becomes the institution
that tropes the nation. And if Anglo-Indians are the founding fathers
and representative citizens of the Indian nation, how do they guar-
antee, consolidate, and reproduce this Indianness? What ensures
that their Indianness will be persuasive and uncontested? How do
the "Indian" Indians signify national identity? What are the rituals
of nationness that the national institution of the Great Game
demands?

Mimicry and exchange are key to the Great Game: the exchange
of messages and information, the exchange of clothing, and the
mimicry of "Indian" identities (and "English"/"Anglo-Indian" ones).
These exchanges must be continually performed; paradoxically, this
continual movement between identities is necessary to fix iden-
tity/Indianness. Hence the extraordinary gratuitousness that often
seems to attend the rituals of impersonation and nationness. There
is no point at which Kim's identity becomes stabilized; making him
Indian, and keeping him Indian, is an ongoing process. The signs of
national life must always be kept visible through miming the various
modalities of national identity. What can or must be represented is
not the insurgent subject, who is always outside the circuits of
exchange mandated by the Great Game. Instead the players must
mimic themselves and each other as "Indians"; what results in this
continuous representation of the nation is a mirroring dynamic in
which all players are implicated in a circuit of (reciprocally consti-
tutive) desire.

Note that the various encounters between the members of the
Game are organized around a semiotic of dressing and undressing.
It is not surprising that perhaps the proudest moment for Kim in the
novel is when he transforms the Maratha agent into a sadhu: "Kim

had been trained by Lurgan Sahib; E23, by virtue of his business, was no bad actor. In place of the tremulous, shrinking trader there lolled against the corner an all but naked, ash-smeared, ochre-barred, dusty-haired Saddhu, his swollen eyes . . . luminous with insolence and bestial lust" [171–72]. This is Kim's masterpiece, a performance/production that produces two mimic subjects in the same process: himself as *chela* with magical powers, E23 as half-naked sadhu. This process of ceaseless mimicry is obviously not without its (homo)erotic charge. What Kim receives as a gift from Mahbub Ali at the end of his apprenticeship is, first, a gift of clothing which not only (re)produces Kim as Indian but quite specifically names him as an eroticized body ("Oh, the hearts to be broken! Oh, the eyes under the eyelashes, looking sideways!" [145]). What this chain of impersonations does is (re)produce the bond that exists within the members of the fraternity. The national polity, as numerous scholars have noted, is typically constituted through the marginalization of women as symbolic figures; it is troped as a passionate brotherhood or as, in Jonathan Goldberg's words, an "ideal of union between men."[5] Citizenship and nationness are generated and consolidated in this endless circuit of exchange and impersonation between Anglo-Indian and other Indian men.

Does the nation have a gender? Does the national subject? The motherland model of nationness is familiar from Indian and other nationalisms: woman becomes that which represents the nation, the culture, and her purity, integrity, and seclusion are the concepts that are foregrounded in the struggle for possession. Many nationalist movements have bought into this masculinism and have conceived of themselves in virilized terms, a situation that of course requires enactment at the expense of women. The ideology of cultural restoration assumes the guise of radical nationalism; women are the revered objects of the collective act of national deliverance and the role model for the new nationalist collective which was analogous to the patriarchal family. Women as the carriers of culture have represented the nation, which must be saved and restored; at the same time they have existed in an oppositional relation to the nation, because in order to conceive of itself as one, the nation has to suppress internal difference.

If citizenship is only available for and between men, then what is the relation of woman to men in these personifications of the nation? The marginalization of women in *Kim* has been noted by more than one reader. Edward Said says of it:

5. Jonathan Goldberg, "Bradford's 'Ancient Members' and 'A Case of Buggery . . . amongst Them,'" in *Nationalisms & Sexualities*, ed. Andrew Parker et al. (New York and London: Routledge, 1992), 63.

It is an overwhelmingly male novel. . . . The women in the
novel are remarkably few in number by comparison, and all are
somehow debased or unsuitable for male attention: . . . to be
always pestered by women, Kim believes, is to be hindered in
playing the Great Game, which is best played by men alone. So
not only are we in a masculine world dominated by travel,
trade, adventure and intrigue, we are in a celibate world, in
which the common romance of fiction and the enduring insti-
tution of marriage have been circumvented, avoided, all but
ignored.[6]

In this novel, women seem precluded even from a symbolic role in
the (re)production of the nation. In the various nationalist dis-
courses that circulated in nineteenth- and twentieth-century India,
the nation had to be imagined as the great mother—Mother
Indian—as a prelude to any conceptualization of the national sub-
ject.[7] This (re)production of the (male) citizen by the symbolic
mother is marvelously literalized in a novel like Salman Rushdie's
Midnight's Children (1981); though this Mother India is (misogy-
nistically) transformed into a monstrous figure by the end of the
novel, becoming the widow Indira Gandhi (about whom the syco-
phantic slogan—"India is Indira and Indira is India"—is generated),
who devours her children.

Some of this sense of the monstrosity of the mother—or of the
female—is certainly anticipated in *Kim*, which seeks rather desper-
ately to erase the motherland model of nationness. Kim himself
betrays no interest either in his dead mother or in the Eurasian
woman who apparently stands in loco parentis to him until his ado-
lescence; the latter represents the repulsive fact of interracial sex-
ual relations that Kim must scrupulously forego and, further, may in
fact be held (partially) responsible for the death of the Father. He
spends his energies attaching himself to actual and symbolic fathers
throughout the novel: the lama, Mahbub Ali, Creighton, Lurgan,
Hurree Babu, all of whom compete rather jealously for his time and
loyalty. Is Mother India then abolished from the Anglo-Indian
national imagination? I would argue that the maternal model is dis-
placed in a number of ways. If there is a positive maternal figure at
all in the novel, and one who may be said to provide a partial rep-
resentation of a good Mother India, it is the lama.[8] In interesting
ways he anticipates the epicene figure of Gandhi, who also occupied

6. Edward W. Said, "Introduction" to *Kim* (Harmondsworth, Eng.: Penguin Books, 1987),
 12.
7. Ashis Nandy speaks of "the mythography of India as a powerful mother" in *The Intimate
 Enemy: Loss and Recovery of Self under Colonialism* (Delhi: Oxford University Press,
 1983), 92.
8. Many readers have seen him, not surprisingly, as a "feminized" figure.

a space of ambivalent gendering, especially in relation to the discourse of nationalism.[9]

Though *Kim* attempts to excise women from the performance of nationness, it is at the same time curiously dependent upon women—often prostitutes—for innumerable services, particularly the mechanics of the impersonation that induces nationness. It is through prostitutes like the Flower of Delight that the enemies of the colonial state attempt to obtain information from Mahbub Ali; it is a generous prostitute from Amritsar who pays for Kim's and the lama's train tickets; and it is to the courtesans of Lucknow that Kim goes when he wishes to convert from whiteness to Indianness for his travels through India. When Kim is finally initiated into the Great Game by Mahbub Ali, the initiation involves a visit to the prostitute Huneefa, who produces spiritual protection and a disguise for Kim simultaneously. Significantly, his visit to a prostitute upon reaching symbolic manhood does not involve any form of (hetero)sexual initiation. Kim is of course a figure of significant sexual attractiveness to women, and his sexual attentions are continually solicited by women through the novel. These must repeatedly be disavowed: "How can a man follow the Way or the Great Game when he is so-always pestered by women?" thinks Kim. "There was that girl at Akrola of the Ford; and there was the scullion's wife behind the dovecot—not counting the others. . . . When I was a child it was well enough, but now I am a man and they will not regard me as a man" [214]. This disavowal is most explicit in the instance of the Woman of Shamlegh, where Kipling will not permit a cross-racial heterosexual union despite the ethical claim the Woman is said to have on Kim's sexual regard.

The prostitute is, obviously, the most literal figure of exchange in a sexual economy which is also intimately linked to an economy of disguise and mimicry. She becomes one of the primary counters in the circulation of information, identity, and homosocial power. It is her presence—that of the carnal and completely embodied female figure—that facilitates the overt disavowal of all femininity in national space, including the maternal model of femininity and nationness (the mother, of course, signifying a disembodied but nonetheless gendered subject). Thus, through the prostitute, the domain of heterosexuality is also invoked and repudiated.

It is, of course, noteworthy that no Anglo-Indian or English women—whether as mothers, prostitutes or (potential) citizens—feature in this performative model of the nation; in fact, they find no place in the narrative at all.[1] What novel inflections are accu-

9. My thanks to Sandhya Setty for suggesting this to me.
1. Patrick Williams ("*Kim* and Orientalism," in *Kipling Considered*, ed. Phillip Mallet [London: Macmillan, 1989], 45–49) speaks of their absence as function[ing] as a potential

mulated in this new definition of nationness? Women (including mothers) are, as we have seen, both necessary and superfluous to the staging of citizenship; they are the source of a certain unease in the novel's conception of an alternative national polity. The reproductive paradigm of nationness, which is embodied in the maternal model, is (dis)embodied in *Kim* through the mimicry of identities—rather than the duplication of bodies—the mimicry that (re)produces the nation. In the absence of Mother India, the men who would be Indian must always keep performing.

SARA SULERI

[Kim's Colonial Education][†]

* * * At what point does the love affair of *Kim* cease to become a colonial joke? When does a reader learn that the tragic erotics of the story have less to do with the lama and Kim than with imperial narrative and an emblem of cultural mobility? Let us return to the passion that informs the separation of the Road from the River; the young from the venerable: " 'The Gates of Learning' shut with a clang."

Kipling assiduously omits to describe the education that the lama buys for Kim, and furthermore draws the reader's attention to his omission. In the quick elision of Kim's experiences within the "gates of learning," the narrative makes an unmistakable indication concerning the location of its audience, which by implication is situated far from the "country-born" quality of India and thus requires cultural description in order to understand the machinery of a colonized culture:

> The country-born and bred boy has his own manners and customs, which do not resemble those of any other land; and his teachers approach him by roads which an English master would not understand. Therefore, you would scarcely be interested in Kim's experiences as a St. Xavier's boy. . . . His quickness would have delighted an English master, but at St.

escape clause by allowing, within the terms of the text, the unspoken displacement of the condemnation of women from women in general to Indian women in particular, since the latter are the only ones we see. . . . Racial superiority was, by the end of the century, one of the few remaining justifications for British rule, and the perceived threat from uncontrolled female sexuality (here rendered as uncontrolled *Indian* female sexuality, the truth [of white women's desire for Indian males] being literally unspeakable), was a grave one indeed. [See Williams's essay in this volume.]

† From *The Rhetoric of English India* (Chicago: University of Chicago Press, 1992) 127–31. Copyright © 1992 The University of Chicago Press. All rights reserved. Reprinted by permission of the publisher. Page references to *Kim* have been changed to correspond to this Norton Critical Edition.

Xavier's they know the first rush of minds developed by sun and surroundings, as they know *the half-collapse that sets in at twenty-one or twenty-three*. (emphasis added) [105–07].

Here, Kipling supplies a casual but crucial anticipation of the collapsibility of Kim: in keeping his institutional education a secret from the reader, moreover, the narrative suggests that Kim's real instruction lies in the hands of Colonel Creighton, Mahbub Ali, Lurgan Sahib, and Hurree Babu, who train their "colt" for the Great Game. The jest at hand, of course, indicates the futility of the lama's intervention, which—far from saving Kim—physically secures him for his role in the Game.

As Kim is inexorably reduced to the sum of his utility, his power as a cultural reader is simultaneously curtailed. The magical quality of his hybridity, of his ability to be one with each disguise that he assumes, is modified by the nature of the disguises that the Game requires he adopt. Much as a Macaulayan interpreter, Kim is trained to gather bureaucratically useful facts: his access to cultural "wisdom" must necessarily be reduced to the acquisition of pragmatic information. In this context, the lama's commitment to "acquiring knowledge" assumes the fatigued irony that is Kim's undoing, for within the parameters of the Game of colonialism, all epistemologies reduce to utilitarianism.

While it would certainly be erroneous to imply that *Kim* is intentionally an allegory of imperial education in the subcontinent, the text indeed lends itself to such an analogy. Kim's tutors fall into Orientalist and Anglicist camps, with the Anglicists clearly winning over the Orientalism that the lama represents. The text thus fictionally embodies the questions raised by Gauri Viswanathan's cogent reading of the interconnectedness between literary study and British rule in India, particularly when she observes, "The fact that English literary study had its beginnings as a strategy of containment raises the question, Why literature? . . . What accounts for the British readiness to turn to a disciplinary branch of knowledge to perform the task of administering their colonial subjects? What was the assurance that a disguised form of authority would be more successful in quelling potential rebellion among the natives than a direct show of force?"[1] *Kim* unwittingly aligns itself to such questions by posing, in the first place, the possibility of disguise as an enchantment of cultural mobility, but then grimly collapsing such youthful fantasy into "a disguised form of authority." The longer Kim serves the needs of the Great Game, the more circumscribed are his abilities to interpret.

1. Gauri Viswanathan, *Masks of Conquest: Literary Study and British Rule in India* (New York: Columbia UP, 1989), p. 11.

The figure of education in *Kim* thus becomes synonymous with the tautology of colonial encounter, in which the child who is already culturally fluent must be caught in order that he may learn the far more alienating idiom of cultural description. Where cultural authority was once disparate and as dialogical as Kim's delight in his various disguises, the very excesses of the Game render it localized within a colonizer's bureaucracy. Here, Edward Said's reading of Colonel Creighton as the emblem of the dialogue between anthropology and colonial chronology deserves attention: "Creighton embodies the notion that you cannot govern India unless you know India," claims Said. "And to know India means understanding the way it operates. . . . To the government personality the main consideration is not whether something is good or evil, and therefore must be changed or kept, but whether something works or not, whether it hinders one in ruling what is in effect an alien entity. Thus Creighton satisfies the Kipling who had imagined an ideal India, unchanging and attractive, as an eternally integral part of the Empire."[2] The stasis of such a model of cultural epistemology is in complete contrast with the readership embodied in the preeducated manifestation of Kim, and calls for further attention to his ability to transmogrify from adolescent mobility into the inflexibility represented by colonial knowledge.

What, however, of the anthropologist as journalist, of a mind ravished by the immediacy of all that colonial knowledge may signify? Under such a rubric, are the attractions of empire further reduced to an adolescent intransigence toward education, pointing to Kipling's interest in a discourse of cessation that proleptically images the language of partition at the historical moment of the most established colonial strength? Which is the idiom in which adolescence must die before it is allowed to attain the colonial maturity that Burke[3] devotedly desired? *Kim* suggests that the anthropology undertaken by the narrative requires even closer scrutiny than does the figure of Colonel Creighton, for Kipling in the guise of anthropologist locates highly novel forms for the moment of cultural extinction that it is his business to record. Once Kim has been released from St. Xavier's, the narrative assumes an oddly deferential tone toward the child who thus far has supplied the tale with an abundance of energy. Even though Kim continues to play the Game, he is increasingly represented in the third person: in the opening chapters of the book, the reader sees the subcontinent through Kim's eyes, but in the conclud-

2. Edward Said, "*Kim:* The Pleasures of Imperialism," *Raritan* 2 (Fall 1987): 53.
3. Edmund Burke (1729–1797), conservative statesman and politician known for his unrestrained and ill-tempered speeches on political control of India. He opposed government interference in the commercial activities of the British East India Company and led the move to impeach Warren Hastings, governor-general of Bengal in 1787 [*Editor*].

ing sections of the narrative, the reader is forced to cast an anthropologist's eye upon the figure of Kim.

The crucial crossing of the text consists in its swerve from the mode of journalism into anthropology, allowing for the journalistic present tense to assume a more elegiac recognition of its protagonist's unavoidable extinction. If a submerged homoeroticism impelled the initial love of surprise between the lama and Kim the latter sections of the novel redirect that passion to the relation between narrator and protagonist. As Kim learns to play the Great Game, the narrative forces us to conceive of him as a third person: "The pallor of hunger suited Kim very well as he stood, tall and slim, in his sad-coloured, sweeping robes, one hand on his rosary and the other in the attitude of benediction, faithfully copied from the lama. An English observer might have said that he looked rather like the young saint of a stained-glass window, whereas he was but a growing lad faint with emptiness" [164].

In such a visual reconfiguration, Kim has become the image of the colonizer, but one that is elegiacally mourned as passing in its prematurity. Even though the final "adventure" of the novel returns the disciple to the alternative knowledge of his tutelary status with the lama, the passion for Kim is curiously displaced into the narrative's desire to hold him as a nonverbal object that is somewhat exempt from its subjugation to the transmittal of colonial information. After having established Kim as the inevitable victim of imperial education, in other words, Kipling seems drawn to an anthropologist's farewell to the emblem that finally reveals the classifiability of cultural dexterity. The impishness of Kim's ingenuity drops away from the verbal into the visual, so that the reader is continually reminded of his bodily presence. Whereas the preeducated Kim was both a voice and a body that commanded comfort wherever it found itself, the posteducated Kim is suddenly vulnerable to the pains of mind and body. Rather than dictate the energy of the narrative, posteducated Kim becomes the focus of the narrative's futile compassion. It is no surprise, therefore, when the crucial scene that allows the Russian spies to destroy the lama's map is envisioned from perspectives that Kim could not possibly see: "They came across an aged lama . . . sitting cross-legged above a mysterious chart held down by stones, which he was explaining to a young man, evidently a neophyte, of singular, though unwashen, beauty" [200]. Until this moment, Kim's beauty has been manifested by his linguistic range, or his ability to read cultures rapidly and well. His sudden elevation into an aesthetic icon, therefore, dangerously anticipates the third-person silence imposed by the education that signifies the playing of the Great Game.

The loneliness of Kim's adolescent question "Who is Kim?" is

thus transferred to the reader, who must now picture the marvelous boy as an analogy for colonial casualty. Whatever may be the journalistic enthusiasm for the present tense of colonialism, *Kim* darkly illustrates its epistemological ill-proportion. Nothing indicates its astonishing obfuscation more than the conclusion of the text, where an Anglicist narrative and an Orientalist lama collide in vying for the affections of the protagonist. The surprise of *Kim* inheres in such a battle, which the text conducts for the fealty of its protagonist: is Kim loved more by the lama or the narrator, or who more totally frames him in colonial imprisonment? As an allegory of colonial education, the conclusion of *Kim* extracts significance at the very point where it appears to confer imperial meaning.

The narrator knows that Kim must be killed. He hands the deed over to the otherworldly lama, however, with whom he remains in perpetual contestation for Kim's love. In the chilling conclusion of the book, Kim's recuperation is necessarily followed by the lama's claim that he alone constitutes the salvation of the boy: "I meditated a thousand things, passionless, well aware of the Causes of all Things. Then a voice cried: 'What shall become of the boy if thou art dead?' and I was shaken back and forth in myself with pity for thee; and I said: 'I will return to my *chela*, lest he miss the way'" [239]. Such intervention, however, is hardly passionless. Neither is the concluding sentence of the text, which once again images Kim in a magnificent moment of uncontrol: "[The lama] crossed his hands on his lap and smiled, as a man may who has won Salvation for himself and his beloved" [240]. Here, Kim is envisioned as the absent other that indicates the silence of classical Urdu poetry, in which the beloved has no voice at all. But it is colonial education that has silenced his voice, and demonstrated that in its adolescence is its end.

PATRICK WILLIAMS

Kim and Orientalism[†]

* * *

There are * * * other important reasons for choosing to write on *Kim*, foremost among which is the fact that it has been and contin-

† From "*Kim* and Orientalism," in *Kipling Considered*, ed. Phillip Mallett (London: Macmillan, 1989) 33–55. Copyright © 1989 Phillip Mallett. Reprinted with permission of St. Martin's Press, LLC. Page references to *Kim* have been changed to correspond to this Norton Critical Edition.

ues to be regarded as in some way central, special, even unique, not
only within Kipling's *oeuvre*, but also within the entire range of colo-
nial literature. * * * What is more interesting is that recent crit-
ics, even radical ones, are prepared to accord it special status. (Not
that Kipling's attraction for the Left is a recent phenomenon: Gram-
sci—to whom we shall return later—was an admirer of Kipling's
work and wanted his sons to read it.) John McClure is representa-
tive of recent critics when he argues that *Kim* not only repudiates
racist modes of characterisation, but also dramatises the repudia-
tion, that it is a Utopian portrayal of future racial harmony, and that
it is perhaps a more effective antidote to racial antipathies than any
of Conrad's works (which he has already praised for their attacks on
racist forms of representation).[1] A more radical critic, Abdul Jan-
Mohamed, in a recent article on colonial (or as he prefers to call it,
colonialist) fiction, sees *Kim* as the novel which, above all others,
explores the possibilities of bridging the gap which separates
coloniser and colonised. More than this,

> We are thus introduced to a positive, detailed and nonstereo-
> typic portrait of the colonized that is unique in colonialist lit-
> erature. . . . What may initially seem like a rapt aesthetic
> appreciation of Indian cultures turns out, on closer examina-
> tion, to be a positive acceptance and celebration of difference.[2]

The force of this assessment lies in the fact that [Edward] Said and
those critics who have followed him, such as JanMohamed and Homi
Bhabha, have located the stereotype as perhaps the principal mecha-
nism in ideologies of discrimination and domination at work in colo-
nialism. To assert, therefore, that *Kim* offers the representation free
of stereotypes is to make a very large claim indeed. It is claims of this
nature which the present essay intends to examine. Another reason
for continuing to scrutinise works such as *Kim* is that, although
clearly neither Kipling the author nor the range of positions offered
by his texts is reducible to the merely imperialist, it is nevertheless
important to achieve as precise a notion as possible of the ways in
which the texts were involved in the process of the Empire. As Said
reminds us, texts may have very substantial material effects, be they
social, political or economic, and nowhere, one might argue, is this
more the case than within imperialism. Said also talks about the

> rather complex dialetic of reinforcement by which the experi-
> ences of readers in reality are determined by what they have

1. John McClure, "Problematic Presence: The Colonial Other in Kipling and Conrad," in
 The Black Presence in English Literature, ed. David Dabydeen (Manchester, 1985) pp.
 154–67.
2. Abdul JanMohamed, "The Economy of Manichean Allegory: The Function of Racial Dif-
 ference in Colonialist Literature," *Critical Inquiry* 12 (Autumn 1985) p. 78.

read, and this in turn influences writers to take up subjects defined in advance by readers' experiences. . . . Most important, such texts can *create* not only knowledge but also the very reality they appear to describe.[3]

* * *

The theoretical assumptions behind this essay are partly those elaborated in Pierre Macherey's *A Theory of Literary Production*,[4] and partly those of Said in *Orientalism*. Macherey says, among other things, that we need to look both at the text and beyond it: at it, in order to see how it attempts to create its own unity, to establish the 'class of truth' which determines its meaning; beyond it, because it is not an isolated object, but part, and product, of a combination of socio-historical forces. Regarding the latter point, he says that the (inevitable) incorporation of ideology into a text results in certain textual silences, contradictions and inconsistencies which allow the reader to perceive the workings of that ideology, and that what ideology remains silent about is the reality of the historical situation.

Orientalism as defined by Said is:

the corporate institution for dealing with the Orient—dealing with it by making statements about it, authorizing views of it, describing it, by teaching it, settling it, ruling over it; in short, Orientalism is a Western style for dominating, restructuring and having authority over the Orient.[5]

It is particularly concerned with the production of knowledge as power, and with the representation of the Orient and its inhabitants as static, unchanging, incapable of change. With these points in mind, I hope to be able to interrogate some of the impressive claims made for *Kim*, and also to show something of the way in which the text relates to the larger Orientalist and imperialist projects. In doing so, I am aware that I am reading somewhat against the grain of critical consensus on *Kim*.

Turning to look at the text in more detail, I propose to examine three positions which it offers, attitudes which may be taken as exemplary by virtue of being held by characters to which the text gives credence, and through them to reveal the ways in which ideology works in the text.

3. Edward Said, *Orientalism* (London, 1985) p. 94.
4. Pierre Macherey, *A Theory of Literary Production* (London, 1978).
5. Said, *Orientalism*, p. 3.

I

but thou art a Sahib and the son of a Sahib. Therefore do not at
any time be led to contemn the black man
(Colonel Creighton to Kim)

One of the principal reasons for the large amounts of praise be-
stowed on the book is its perceived sympathy for the Indians * * *
Within the context of Kipling's *oeuvre*, there is some truth in this:
there would, for instance, appear to be nothing in *Kim* to equal the
overt racism with which 'Beyond the Pale' opens. In addition, there
is a significant increase in the proportion of the work devoted to
Indians, and there are even a number of derogatory remarks made
about white men. Demands for the fair treatment of Indians, such
as that made by Creighton, are, however, undermined by what hap-
pens in the text, as are both the apparently improved representa-
tions of the Indians and the anti-British sentiments. Indeed, there
is a sense in which the attitude is undermined before it is voiced:
Creighton's command occurs half way through the book, but there
have already been a number of opposing actions or assertions, one
of which forms the opening to the story. Here, Kim has just kicked
his Hindu and Muslim playmates off the cannon outside the Lahore
Museum. This is justified, we are told, because whoever holds the
cannon holds the Punjab; Kim is English (*sic*) and holds the can-
non, and the English hold the Punjab. It is also acceptable for Kim
to kick Chota Lal off the cannon, because, even though his father
is worth half a million sterling, India is 'the only democratic land in
the world' [6]. Given Kipling's unflattering views on democracy, this
is a strange sort of compliment, carrying as it does the added impli-
cation that democracy is a licence for the poor to kick the rich, but
in essence it is simply one more restatement of the (democratic)
right of the white man to kick the native, however rich he may be.

More insidious than this, because less immediately visible, and
more damning because more all-pervasive, is the depiction of Indi-
ans. While it is true that some—Hurree, the Sahiba, and, above all,
Mahbub—are treated with a certain amount of sympathy, particu-
larly as individuals, the cumulative picture, operating as it does
almost subliminally, makes any stated intent not to 'contemn' look
rather hollow. The ability of texts and larger discourses to cope with
this particular type of apparent contradiction between the individ-
ual and the general is by no means unusual, and, as Said points out,
the disparity in no way disrupts the certainties of Orientalism:

> For the general category in advance offers the specific instance
> a limited terrain in which to operate: no matter how deep the

specific exception, no matter how much a single Oriental can escape the fences placed around him, he is *first* an Oriental, *second* a human being, and *last* again an Oriental.[6]

<p style="text-align:center">* * *</p>

<p style="text-align:center">II</p>

'The more one knows about natives the less one can say what they
 will or won't do.'
'That's consolin'—from the head of the Ethnological Survey.'
 (Colonel Creighton to Father Victor)

This is an interesting exchange: Creighton utters what seems a classic formulation of Kipling-style Orientalism, but Father Victor's rejoinder adds a curious note of ambiguity. Is Father Victor in fact consoled that, like himself, the head of the Ethnological Survey cannot understand Indians, or is he ironically observing that the summation of the knowledge of the head of the Survey amounts to no more than this? Also, are we to assume that Creighton's ignorance is merely a function of his Ethnological persona, rather than his (undisclosed) Secret Service one? Regardless of how we interpret the conversation, Creighton's authoritative statement of one of the basic tenets of the white man's creed is contradicted by the events of the book.

In both of his guises, Creighton is in charge of collecting information, and it is obviously no small irony that the Survey, which is supposed to be concerned with scientific—and therefore, it would be claimed, disinterested—information, is in fact a spy network, and that the 'disinterested' information which is collected about the country is used for improved political control. Even such knowledge as is gathered by Creighton and Hurree and not specifically used in the maintenance of British power can hardly be said to be disinterested, since for both of them it represents the possibility of prestige in future membership of the Royal Society. (The slightly desperate air surrounding Hurree's efforts to succeed indicates the presence of yet another inadequate Indian attempt to emulate the British.) Further, the idea that, regardless of the way in which they operated in conjunction with colonialism, the new nineteenth-century sciences of ethnology and anthropology might aspire to a 'pure', impartial form will not stand scrutiny. * * *

However much it may represent acceptable, and accepted, ideology, Creighton's assertion must be wrong, especially in the case of those like himself whose Secret Service operations are to a large extent predicated on the use of acquired knowledge precisely to

6. Said, *Orientalism*, p. 102.

anticipate and forestall the various plots and contemplated treacheries. Like Creighton, then, the statement plays a double game (and perhaps more than one). On the one hand, it is a gesture of disavowal and concealment; it is Creighton in disguise, Creighton 'the father of fools', and as such is a lie; yet it is also one of the great (ideological) 'truths' of Empire, with the power to determine innumerable decisions and actions. At the same time, while it suggests the pointlessness of acquiring knowledge about natives—made famous in the lines like these from 'One Viceroy Resigns':

> You'll never plumb the Oriental mind,
> And if you did, it isn't worth the toil,[7]

—it also identifies that apparent resistance of Indians to Western attempts to 'know' them, which makes it all the more imperative that such attempts be repeated and extended.

As well as being contradicted by what Creighton is and does, this position is undercut by the forms of knowledge circulated in the text. Orientalism, as adjunct of colonial control, is preeminently involved in the production of various categories of knowledge about 'the native': historical, linguistic, religious, moral, political. This knowledge is most frequently presented in the form of bold syntheses, universal norms, invariant truths about Orientals, and one of its most obvious effects is the ability to say with enormous certainty exactly how they will or will not behave, which, being products of their eternally unchanging Oriental society, is exactly the same as the way they have behaved for centuries. If it is not already so, such knowledge is all too easily converted into stereotypes, and it is in this form that it most easily circulates in colonial literature. Interestingly enough, it is this fault which, as mentioned earlier, Abdul JanMohamed feels that Kipling spectacularly avoids, managing to produce 'a positive, detailed, nonstereotypic portrait of the colonized that is unique in colonialist literature'. However, despite the apparent air of benevolence which envelops the text, the more one reads it, the more derogatory stereotypes come to light, and although the narrative voice which enunciates them speaks as if from personal experience, thereby lending added weight to the condemnation, there is no sense of individualised observation, rather the mere reiteration of the already-known truths of Oriental degeneracy.

Foremost among such truths is that of the duplicitous, perpetually untruthful Oriental. It is no doubt a measure of the effect of India on him that 'Kim could lie like an Oriental' [23] and that he

7. Kipling, "One Viceroy Resigns," in *Rudyard Kipling's Verse: Definitive Edition* (London, 1942) p. 69.

and Mahbub Ali lie to everyone except one another. We also learn that natives never tell the truth to strangers—unlike their rulers, who are 'open-spoken English folk' [126]. This opposition occurs more than once: 'The English do eternally tell the truth,' he said, 'therefore we of this country are eternally made foolish' [119]. Even the westernised Hurree finds the English habit of demanding a straight and honest answer very unsettling. (It is perhaps worth setting beside these 'truths' the fact that in the book it is the English who are involved in the perpetration of deception and lies on a massive scale, in the shape of the Secret Service.)

According to Orientalist categorisation, one of the principal attributes of Orientals is that they are deficient or abnormal vis-à-vis the English, no matter what the context. In *Kim* we are told that Indians lack a proper sense of time: 'All hours of the twenty four are alike to Orientals' [26]. 'Even an Oriental, with an Oriental's views of the value of time' [22]; of motion: 'Swiftly—as Orientals understand speed' [121]; of order: 'the happy Asiatic disorder' [57]; of sound: 'he had all the Oriental's indifference to mere noise' [119]—no doubt because they make so much of it; of organisation: 'so he abandoned the project and fell back, Oriental fashion, on time and chance' [91]; and of correct speech, so that when they are not using 'what to a European would have been bad language' [58], they are indulging in 'the usual aimless babble that every low-caste native must raise on every occasion' [116]. The list is very long, but these may serve as an indication of just how stereotypically Indians are represented.

There are other ways in which knowledge functions in the text. One of the staples of Orientalism is that it is Europeans who provide Orientals with the first accurate descriptions and proper explanations of their history, religion, language, and so on. Despite infrequent remarks such as 'The Sahibs have not *all* the world's wisdom' [161] their control of its knowledge is so undisputed that a great Buddhist sage (Teshoo is one of only three men alive who can both draw and explicate the Wheel of Life) must come to an English museum curator for information about his own religion. He also appeals to the curator as the 'Fountain of Wisdom' and is astonished at how much white men know about Buddhism. Also, it is another white man, Lurgan, who teaches Kim the little he does not already know about things Indian.

Kim himself represents the apogee of a particular incarnation of Orientalism—the Englishman who has such a mastery of Oriental culture that he can pass for one of 'them'. This figure has its origins in travellers like Sir Richard Burton and Edward William Lane, whose accounts of their exploits beget a textual lineage particularly gratifying to the English sensibility. It was obvious at the time that

England's technological and military superiority could forcibly sub-
due other countries, but Burton and Lane were proof that an Eng-
lishman could meet the Orient on its own terms and outwit it. The
ideological power of the figure is no doubt also a function of its
compensatory force, given that the English in India were aware of
the fact that they were extraordinarily visible, culturally ignorant
and linguistically maladroit.

It is noticeable that when this figure makes its appearance in
Kipling's fiction, as it does in stories like 'Miss Youghal's Sais' and
'The Mark of the Beast' in the shape of Strickland, the mastery and
the knowledge it provides are specifically used for the purpose of
social and political control. Kim, of course, is more than Strickland:
like the almost mythical and unnamed individual on whom Strick-
land models himself, Kim can pass for a member of any religion,
class or caste, and when Strickland makes his guest appearance in
Kim, his part in the Great Game seems very much that of a white
man in contrast to Kim's role. Despite the characterisation of Kim
and Strickland as anti-authoritarian figures, or at least disturbers of
official procedures by their individualism, their abilities serve to
maintain British rule just as surely as if they did everything by the
book, perhaps even more so.

* * *

III

> How can a man follow the Way or the Great Game when he is eter-
> nally pestered by women? . . . When I was a child it was well
> enough, but now I am a man and they will not regard me as a man.
>
> (Kim to himself)

* * *

Certainly, the position of women in Kim is unusual. The first
thing to notice is that, apart from a disembodied voice telling
Creighton that the commander-in-chief has arrived, and a soldier's
wife who asks Kim if he thinks her husband will come back from the
war, there are no white women in the book at all. Although Kipling,
in a letter, attributed the absence to a reluctance to portray the
memsahibs who, he felt (and current ideology concurred), were
responsible for unsatisfactory racial relations, it is possible, as we
shall see later, to regard such an absence as ideologically deter-
mined in other ways. The lack of white women may, for example,
function as a potential escape clause by allowing, within the terms
of the text, the unspoken displacement of the condemnation of

women from women in general to Indian women in particular, since the latter are the only ones we see. Certainly, too, the text preaches 'the old doctrine of the nuisance of women' with great consistency. Whatever path a man chooses for himself in life, whether action (the Great Game) or contemplation (the Way), women are there to hinder him, we are told, with their ceaseless talk, or their sexual importuning, or both.

It may at first sight seem incongruous, in a book where all the major male characters are celibate, to lay as much stress as the text does on Kim's sexual attractiveness. * * * This world of male celibacy inscribes rejection of women in the very form of the text, and creates the value-laden opposition: female = uncontrolled language (chatter, babble) = uncontrolled sexuality (prostitution, sexual propositioning) vs male = control of language (silence, secrets) = sexual control (abstention, celibacy).

Also, although Kim, the lama, and others may say that women are a nuisance and a hindrance, this is belied by the way that, throughout the book, Kim actively seeks them out, generally in order to manipulate or exploit them in some fashion. As Kim has discovered, 'few could resist' his charms, and he uses them on the Mohammedan girl (to get cigars), the vegetable seller (to get food), the Amritsar courtesan (to get money and a ticket), the cultivator's wife (to get food, and later, a bed for the night), the Sahiba on pilgrimage (to get money and food), the prostitute in Lucknow (for the means of disguise), and the Woman of Shamlegh (for information-carrying, food, money, porters)—apart, that is, from 'the girl at Akrola of the Ford and . . . the scullion's wife behind the dovecot—not counting the others' [214]. It is no doubt a measure both of Kim's powers of attraction and her own preternatural powers of perception that the magic-working Huneefa declares—before we realise that she is blind—that he 'is very good to look upon' [150]— a sentiment echoed by Mahbub Ali and those women characters who call him a heart-breaker.

'[T]here are but two sorts of women . . . those who take the strength out of a man and those who put it back' [229], says the Sahiba, acknowledging that she was previously one of the former, as—the inference is plain—are all the other women encountered in the book, with their endless wearying chatter and their exhausting sexuality. Even though this does at least allow the possibility of there being good women, its dichotomy can no more stand up to scrutiny in the face of the evidence already cited than can Kim's simple denunciation. For, once again, how far would Kim have got in his travels or in the Great Game without the strength that these supposedly debilitating women put into him in the shape of food, shelter, money and numerous forms of assistance? This is particularly

true in the case of the Woman of Shamlegh, without whose help Kim and the lama (both exhausted, it should be noted, not through the fault of women, but through following their respective manly pursuits) could not possibly have returned to the safety of the Sahiba's house; and the crisis which she, the Woman of Shamlegh, represents helps to elucidate the type of ideology at work in the text.

Critics like John McClure have pointed to the importance of the fact that the Woman of Shamlegh is in fact Lispeth, from the story of that name, the first of the *Plain Tales from the Hills*, making a reappearance, but the conclusions they draw are in general unsatisfactory. It is clear—as she herself points out—that Lispeth is not like other women. Hitherto, it has hardly seemed to matter how many hearts Kim breaks, since their owners are doubly insignificant, being not only female but too old, like the Sahiba and her cousin, or too young, like the girls in the rissaldar's village; socially unacceptable—scullion's wives, and so on; morally unacceptable—a variety of prostitutes; or totally unacceptable—the hill women are 'unlovely and unclean, wives of many husbands, and afflicted with goitre' [194]. Now, however, we have a woman with power who is 'aught but unlovely' [212], 'no common bearer of babes' [214], and who calmly and boldly propositions Kim, offering not only herself but the village and all it contains. She is thus revealed as Kim's last and greatest temptation, and the anomaly of Kim's being the only white character who is obviously sexual is resolved: Kim is allowed sexuality so that he may triumph over it, in the unacceptable shape in which it presents itself, as part of his rites of passage to (proper) manhood.

McClure suggests that the situation of Kim and Lispeth parallels that in the earlier story, but that, unlike the first Englishman who deceives and rejects Lispeth, 'Kim deals with the Woman of Shamlegh frankly, fairly and generously'.[8] It is difficult to see how such an interpretation can be justified however, when Kim knowingly deceives her (since despite the clearly acknowledged understanding between them, he presumably has no intention of sleeping with her as the reward for her work as messenger), and then, when she asks for what he has promised, rejects her. The fact that Lispeth, having been not only rejected but also insulted by Kim as a 'woman of ill-omen' [221], still provides Kim and the lama with all manner of assistance, makes her all the more remarkable, and in many ways superior to Kim. Twice now, however, she has been sufficiently foolish or forgetful of her position to harbour designs on a Sahib, and twice she has been spurned. The lesson to be learned from her

8. John McClure, *Kipling and Conrad: The Colonial Fiction* (Cambridge, Mass., 1981) p. 75.

treatment is clearly that what Kim has to avoid is not the tedious
timewasting of chattering women, but the snares of inter-racial sex.
Far from there being, as McClure says, a 'symbolic union' between
Kim and Lispeth, there is, I would suggest, what in the text's terms
is a properly irrevocable sundering. Lispeth's final question, 'you
will come back again?' [221], which McClure sees as somehow
marking the difference between Kim and the first Englishman, nev-
ertheless—and significantly—goes unanswered. No doubt Kim has
had enough of perjuring himself for one day.

As well as carrying reminders of the cautionary tales of Trejago
and Bisesa, and Holden and Ameera in *Plain Tales* and *Life's Hand-
icap*, this situation helps to explain a certain silence or omission in
one of the remarks quoted earlier. When Creighton tells Kim not to
'contemn the black man', he neglects to say anything about people
of mixed race—the Eurasians—and it is these whom Kim most
viciously 'contemns', as in the following, oddly tautological, remark
on his schoolfellows, which manages to cast a slur on both Indians
and Eurasians:

> 'Their eyes are blued and their nails are blackened with low-
> caste blood, many of them. Sons of *metheeranees* [sweeper
> women]—brothers-in-law to the *bhungi* [sweeper].'
> We need not follow the rest of the pedigree, but Kim made
> his little point clearly and without heat, chewing a piece of sug-
> arcane the while. [122]

Also, in the 'do not be led to contemn' conversation, Kim attrib-
utes racist attitudes in the school solely to Eurasian boys, and yet he
accounts for this by making a racist remark himself. The silence on
the question of Eurasians is paralleled by that on the Western-
educated Indian middle class, a group which, like the Eurasians,
was deliberately created by the British and then systematically
denounced and discriminated against by them.

Although the dangers of sexual contact form a recurrent theme in
Kipling's work, particularly in the early stories, the way in which the
point is re-made here, using the repetition of Lispeth for added
emphasis, can be seen as an indication of the current state of racial
ideology. In the final years of the century, the pressures to avoid mis-
cegenation were greater than ever. Particularly during Curzon's
viceroyalty (1899–1905), the penalties for taking a native wife or
mistress included not only loss of social position, but also frequently
the loss of professional position too, and this applied even more in
India itself than in other parts of the greater Indian empire such as
Burma. Curzon became especially worried about the dangers of
contact between white women and Indian men, and for this reason
often refused permission for Indian princes to go to Britain. The

original justification for this was so that the princes could not corrupt Englishwomen, but it was later changed, this time in order that the princes might not be corrupted by white women. The official view of the situation is given in the correspondence of Curzon and Lord George Hamilton:

> Strange as it may seem, English women of the housemaid class, and even higher, do offer themselves to these Indian soldiers, attracted by their uniforms, enamoured of their physique, and with a sort of idea that the warrior is also an oriental prince.
> *(Curzon to Hamilton)*[9]

* * *

Once again, then, the purity of the race was in danger, but that this time it was the ideologically most sensitive element—English womanhood, which had been the most powerful rallying cry ever since the Indian Mutiny in 1857 (and was not to stop being so now)—which posed the threat, called for a correspondingly forceful ideological counter-offensive in terms of the condemnation of interracial sex, and of blaming female sexuality for a supposedly deteriorating situation. Racial superiority was, by the end of the century, one of the few remaining justifications for British rule, and the perceived threat from uncontrolled female sexuality (here rendered as uncontrolled *Indian* female sexuality, the truth being literally unspeakable), was a grave one indeed.

The problem of race is also posed by the text in another way—in Kim himself, his search for personal identity being also a realisation of racial identity. On the surface at least, there is a fascinating amount of playing with the boundaries of race and of mixing of categories: for example, much is made of Kim's apparent racial indefiniteness; as he says to Mahbub Ali, 'What am I? Mussulman, Hindu, Jain, or Buddhist?' [121], and people he meets never seem to suspect that he is other than he wishes to appear. At the same time, running through the text as a sort of counterpoint, is the statement 'Once a Sahib, always a Sahib'. The situation is nevertheless presented as if there were a choice for Kim, in which case a determining factor would no doubt be the nature of the races he might elect to join. We have already seen something of the available knowledge about Indians. Juxtaposed to this we are given a (restrained) amount of information about what it means to be a Sahib: Sahibs tell the truth; Sahibs cannot steal; Sahibs must act; Sahibs must obey; no Sahib would follow a Bengali's advice; Sahibs

9. Curzon-Hamilton correspondence, quoted in K. Ballhatchet, *Race, Sex and Class under the Raj* (London, 1981) pp. 119–20.

are a strong-backed breed who never grow old; Sahibs are the right
ones to oversee justice because they know the land.

Apart from any racial determinism implied in 'Once a Sahib,
always a Sahib', it would be astonishing, given these two sets of
'knowledge' about the races, if Kim chose to be an Indian. And of
course he does not. The real problem in textual terms is how to
make him black enough to fool everyone, but white enough to be
recuperable as a Sahib—a recurrent difficulty for those colonial
texts which wished to appear to question racial norms without really
doing so. The usual unsophisticated solution was to allow the reader
to assume that a particular character was black and then, by way of
denouement, discover a respectable white parentage for them, as,
for instance, in E. M. Hull's *The Sheik*. Here, the problem is
resolved by making Kim *culturally* Indian and *naturally* British, and
in such a contest the power of Nature is bound to win. Although,
therefore, *Kim* gives the appearance of greater honesty in this
respect, we might wish to question just how honest such an over-
determined 'choice' or contest really is.

Another related but perhaps more genuine choice is not made
until late in the book. Although Kim's fate as a Sahib might appear
to be sealed from the time he enters St Xavier's, it is not until his
second identity crisis at the end of the book that he opts for the
'real' world of materiality and common sense, which is *par excel-
lence* that of the Englishman, rather than the morally superior but
practically useless world of the lama.

The revealing/significant silence of the text in this respect concerns
the extent to which Kim can really be a Sahib, even after his choice.
It is not at all clear how far Kim, as 'a poor white of the very poorest'
[3] and Irish to boot, fits the image of the Sahib, which is very much
more that of Colonel Creighton, *pukka* Englishman of the ruling class.
There is a sense in which Kim's masters are playing a deceitful (great)
game with him—much as the text plays with the readers—in suggest-
ing that someone of his background can truly be a Sahib, other than
in the spuriously levelling context of simple racial categories.

As a poor white, Kim is the inheritor of the most contradictory
attitudes to the Indians—which may go some way towards explain-
ing his being the Little Friend of all the World, but also being so
unsuccessful at not 'contemning'. Along with the working class, the
Irish were the group most frequently conflated with blacks by impe-
rialists, as, for example, in the remark by Lord Salisbury, three times
Prime Minister between 1886 and 1902, that the Irish were as fit-
ted for self-government as the Hottentots. Both Irish and working
class were held to be responsible for the worst excesses of racism,
but they also showed the greatest solidarity with other oppressed
groups—as when Irish people working in Scotland Yard helped

Indian nationalists to smuggle documents. (The fact that this represents one of the best examples of collaboration shows how limited a scope the solidarity of the oppressed had.)[1]

Although there has been a certain amount of blurring of racial distinctions in the book—in Kim's relationship with the lama and with Mahbub Ali; in the figure of Strickland; in Kim himself—the effect is of *reculer pour mieux sauter*: distinctions are blurred in order to be more strickly redefined, in the same way that Kim is offered temptation so that correct sexual behaviour may be reasserted. Whatever doubts are created, whatever edges temporarily blurred, the central tenet, that Sahibs can and must continue to rule India, goes unquestioned, and it is only in Kim's contradictory relation to his status as Sahib, of which the text does not/cannot speak, that any questioning of whether the nature and function of Sahibs are such self-evident things can begin.

Another issue which the text treats in a less than straightforward manner is that of British political power in India. It is sufficiently present not to constitute one of the textual silences, the 'not-said' in Macherey's terms, but it is subject to another ideological operation, the attempt to make it appear as much a part of the natural order of things as possible. Thus, it is simply taken for granted that foreigners are wicked and must be kept out of India, since any actual discussion of the rightness of British rule would risk exposing its shaky foundations (not to mention its foreignness). Similarly, the political reasons for opposition to the Russians are shifted to the 'natural' plane of the racial and/or personal: they are not proper white men because they follow the advice of a Bengali, because they do not understand natives or treat them correctly as 'we' do, and because they are not merry slaughterers of animals like Yankling Sahib. British control is similarly naturalised by the fact that spying (on Indians) is done by Indians, making it seem as if it were done in their interests, even as if they might be controlling their own political destiny. Linked to this is the way in which much of the pro-British propaganda—about the Sahibs being a strong-backed breed, the proper overseers of justice, and so on—is put in the mouths of Indian characters, making it seem, once again, more right and natural.

It remains, by way of conclusion, to suggest in a little more detail how *Kim* as aesthetic object forms part of the socio-historical processes of its period, in line with the second part of Macherey's approach. In the context of Orientalism, Said talks of the way in which the discourse aspires to the production of a vision of a static,

1. On this, see V. G. Kiernan, *The Lords of Humankind* (London, 1969) ch. 1 and Christine Bold, "Race and Victorians," in C. C. Eldridge, *British Imperialism in the 19th Century* (London, 1984).

unchanging Orient, for which its truths would have permanent validity, and of how this state is disturbed by narrative, the representation of historical process. In *Kim* there is the contradiction between the movement of the picaresque form and the stasis of the dehistoricised vision of an India free of internal conflict and about which the classic Orientalist generalisations can be uttered. This contradiction may be more apparent than real, however, since we are presented with a curiously circumscribed and non-disruptive picaresque, the end of whose journeyings is to uphold rather than to disturb the existing order. In the struggle between action and contemplation, it would seem that Kim's choice of the former is vindicated, but it is an action whose aim is stasis, the maintenance of the status quo, rather than change of any sort. As Lord Salisbury said a year or two previously:

> Whatever happens will be for the worse, and therefore it is in our interests that as little should happen as possible.[2]

In aesthetic terms, this relates to the way in which the text produces the state of the Empire as an object for contemplation, a defused, dehistoricised spectacle, in much the same way as, for example, contemporary showmen were producing elements of imperial history as spectacle, with conflict contained and contradictions removed.[3] Empire as spectacle is also the appropriate aesthetic object for the period of Victoria's Jubilee celebrations, whose central message—we are all one big happy imperial family—finds its echo in Kim's India, where everyone would coexist so peacefully were it not for the trouble-making of foreigners jealous of Britain's achievements.

Finally, in producing this vision of the happy imperial family, *Kim* can be seen as both registering and participating in an important historical development. McClure makes the interesting suggestion that the book is a plea on behalf of the country-born Englishman (that is, born and bred in India), as the rightful ruler, rather than the 'genuine imported Sahib from England']. However, far from being, as McClure then goes on to describe it, an elegy for imperial power about to decay, *Kim*, I would suggest, is a refracted image of political realignment, the ruling class in the process of transition, but manoeuvring to strengthen its hold rather than bidding farewell to its power; in other words, nothing less than the change from a form of government based on domination to one which used those

2. Quoted in B. Porter, *The Lion's Share: A Short History of British Imperialism, 1850–1983* (London, 1984) p. 153.
3. See Ben Sheperd, "Showbiz Imperialism," in *Imperialism and Popular Culture*, ed. J. MacKenzie (Manchester, 1986) pp. 94–112.

strategies of hegemony (leadership and consent) which characterise more complex, essentially bourgeois, political systems.

According to Gramsci, in order for a class to become hegemonic it has to create a 'collective national-popular will', to take into account (to a certain extent) the needs of other classes, and to exercise power based on a series of strategic alliances with the other classes or elements within them. This is very much the situation both within Britain and in the Empire towards the end of the nineteenth century. In the wake of the electoral reforms of 1867, the Tory government, worried that the extended franchise would result in 'anarchy'—loss of power for the Tory government—set out deliberately to make itself more 'national-popular' and to create alliances, and the Empire was of central importance in both of these. The coincidence of ruling class and working class interests, which, according to the Tories, the Empire represented, became such a powerful force in late nineteenth-century politics that a change of government did not result in a change of policy, and thus, for example, the Liberal retreat from Empire, which was expected to occur with Gladstone's fourth ministry in 1892, did not materialise.

In India, different sorts of alliances had to be created to meet the changing conditions. Why the suggestion from McClure mentioned above is interesting is that it implicitly recognises one of the important aspects of *Kim*, the production of a new version of rulers and ruled. It is noticeable that this no longer consists of the old favourite of prince and peasant as the natural and proper combination; indeed, the princes in *Kim* are disaffected and rebellious. Instead, we have the country-born Englishman (as close to a mixture of English and Indian as racial ideology would permit), and the good Indian (more or less all of them, in the text's rosy vision). McClure's suggestion carries the unspoken but intriguing implication of the country-born English working to become a more autonomous colonial ruling class, like the *pieds noirs* in Algeria, and to that end attempting to forge an alliance with the Indians they would continue to rule. A text which not only figures such an alliance but also provides (a convincing illusion of) the sort of improved representations which might generate consent among the ruled is clearly at the heart of such a hegemonic project. It is entirely in keeping with what we have already seen of the visionary strategies at work within *Kim* that it says nothing of the real realignments occurring in Indian politics—for example, the admitting of Indian politicians to consultative positions in the 1890s—and instead offers this hypothetical alliance as not only right and natural but already in place, a combination which inevitably reveals it for the ideological construct it is.

SUVIR KAUL

Kim, or How to Be Young, Male, and British in Kipling's India[†]

Rudyard Kipling's Kim is arguably the most complex of the late nineteenth- and early twentieth-century English novels of empire, and one that reminds us forcefully of the "how-to" aspects of such story-telling. In particular, these novels show how best to be a man, or rather, how to be a man well suited to further imperial interests. Male protagonists are defined by their appropriate or inappropriate management of colonial affairs, a process that requires that they restrain both the natives and their own proclivities toward activities that might embarrass or threaten the legitimacy of empire. Whether these natives are cooperative, resentful, or resistant, whether they are portrayed empathetically or with suspicion, they serve—with rare exceptions—to demonstrate the ineluctable necessity of colonial rule and to frame the equally impressive flowering of a white imperial masculinity adequate to that mission. Central to such creative definitions of masculinity are of course questions of sexuality, of the relations between men and women, as indeed those between men and men. Thus, women in these novels exist either as diversions to the protagonist's commitment to the noble way of empire, or they play maternal or other roles that enable his progress. To that extent, even if they do not find much space in the novel, women are crucial to its idealization of masculinity; indeed they are the anvil and the whetstone necessary to forge and sharpen the young blade.

The novel of colonial adventure sharpens each of these oppositions till they are inescapable: not simply the structuring divide between imperialist and colonized, but that between good and not-so-good colonizer, between colonizers who are "man" enough to know their business and to do the duty they believe demanded of them, and those who fail the test of duty, as they do of masculinity. The point is simply that in the colonial novel, including one as textured and unusual as Kim, the exigencies of empire, and of its governance, dictate the way masculinity is modelled. Thus, as Kim grows into his adult identity, the challenges he faces, as well as the guidance and help that benefit him, all derive their forms from Kipling's search for an exemplar of duty and of masculinity who would legitimize British imperialism in India by making the question itself redundant: Kim represents the search for a British pro-

† This is an original essay written for this Norton Critical Edition by Suvir Kaul, Professor of English, University of Illinois at Urbana-Champaign.

tagonist Indian enough to cause the most visible divide of colonial power to—almost—disappear. But that "almost" is crucial, for at no time in his immersion into India must Kim forget that he is British (Irish in his genes and English in his training and affiliation). Thus, as Kim grows into his imperial responsibilities (and this novel is a *bildungsroman*) much that defines him is guided by this "almost": British/almost Indian//Indian/but still British; child/almost man//man/but still child. As this is the case, the figuration of sexualities, and of gender relations, in *Kim* are all factors of Kipling's contouring of Kim's masculinity.

Kim is, of course, a novel of male derring-do. To put it thus, however, is already to note a crucial difference between Kim and the typical protagonist of such tales of adventure: Kim is younger, and his tale has him growing between early and late adolescence (from perhaps thirteen to seventeen years of age). This means that even as Kim travels effortlessly in adult ways, and proves himself adept at activities that challenge men much older than himself, he remains a boy, one whose "rebirth" at the end of the novel (an idea to which I will return) reminds us that he has not quite crossed the threshold into adulthood. This is not a story of arrested development though, far from it—Kim's adventures are largely adult in their form and significance, and the roles he is called upon to play, and the competencies he must develop, are ordinarily those of men, particularly those intrepid sorts who would master the Great Game. That Kim remains, in the course of the novel, pre-adult, a colt still rather than the fully grown polo pony Mahbub Ali thinks he will one day become [98],[1] is important to the world Kipling forges for a number of reasons which I will address below. But most important of all is the need to preserve in Kim a radical innocence that will outlast his immersion into the cynical and manipulative world of adults, which is the world of imperialist intrigue. The ideological fantasy at the heart of *Kim* (Kim as white Sahib who is at once brown native) can be preserved only if Kim is a part of the world of colonial authority and apart from it, white and British in his affiliations but not quite white and certainly not British in his everyday ways.

If Kim represents a fantasy of fusion, it is worth specifying that his character does not so much combine opposed cultural or ethical ideals as represent a particular form of the imperialist will to

1. One way to contextualize this concern with age and "adulthood" is to note the exchange between Colonel Creighton and Mahbub Ali when they weigh the pros and cons of letting Kim begin work as a spy. "But he is so young, Mahbub," asks the Colonel, "not more than sixteen—is he?" "When I was fifteen," Mahbub Ali answers, "I had shot my man and begot my man, Sahib" [145]. Mahbub Ali's answer frames precisely the play between adolescence and adulthood that defines Kim. Like Mahbub Ali, Kim is precociously able to play the Great Game, but unlike this "impenitent old heathen!" (which is what Creighton calls him—affectionately to be sure—in response to his sally above), Kim is denied a similar sexual maturity. I will suggest reasons for this later in the argument.

power and control. Kim is the fantasy of absolute, effortless surveillance, because he solves the problem of the secret agent and the ethnographer—in him the colonial agent who surveys native geographies and cultures is at home in and indistinguishable from them. He travels light, shows no trace of his Irish ancestry or of his connections to Colonel Creighton's establishment, and is able to insinuate himself into any community of Indians he comes across. Yet there is never any danger that he will, as it were, "turn Turk," and betray either his racial or his national allegiances. In the novel, this is a real fear, for British India offers evidence of Britishers going native, or at least leaving behind a trail of children who are like— but, in the terms of the novel, very different from—Kim. The novel in fact opens by differentiating Kim from the children of miscegenation: "Kim was white," we are told, and though the "half-caste woman" who looks after him tells interfering missionaries that Kim's mother was her sister in order that he be left alone, Kim is in fact the product of two white parents [3]. Kim's views of this adoptive mother or caretaker are made clear later, while he is being interrogated by Father Victor and Reverend Bennett. When he mentions her and is asked if she is his mother, his reaction is a sharp "*No!*" accompanied "with a gesture of disgust" [76].

This theme, as is only to be expected in an English novel set in a colony, is of some consequence in the novel. The embarrassment of miscegenation, of sexual liaisons outside those permitted by the self-image of the imperial ruler, takes the form of racial and class prejudice: when Mahbub Ali, jealous of Teshoo Lama's paternal hold over Kim, suggests that it will be embarrassing for Kim if the Lama visits him at his school in the presence of other young Sahibs, Kim cuts him off by saying:

> Not all! . . . Their eyes are blued and their nails are black-
> ened with low-caste blood, many of them. Sons of *mehtera-
> nees*—brothers-in-law to the *bhungi* [sweeper].

Kim makes his point about their "pedigree," we are told, "clearly and without heat, chewing a piece of sugarcane the while" [122]. The sugarcane anchors his fulminations—chewing on it, squatting alongside Mahbub, he is of India in a way that those other "young Sahibs" will never be, for they have to work to repress their bloodlines, and to do so by identifying so totally with white colonial society that they educate themselves into ignorance of their surroundings.

Thus, Kim represents a very precise model of imperial belonging— one intimate with India but in no danger of being contaminated by its racial difference. In this he is of a type with a character who appears briefly, but with all the force of a normative ideal, the English District Superintendent of Police who rides up to the old Rani from Kulu

while she, Kim, and the Lama are on the Grand Trunk Road together. He addresses her with a flattering familiarity, and in an idiom so local that she demands of him: "*Hai*, my son, thou hast never learned all that since thou camest from *Belait* [Europe]. Who suckled thee?" "A *pahareen*—a hillwoman of Dalhousie," he answers, and thus confirms the Sahiba's intuitive assumption. The force of her intuition is however, more than personal: "These be the sort," she says to Kim, "These be the sort to oversee justice. They know the land and the customs of the land. The others, all new from Europe, suckled by white women and learning our tongues from books, are worse than the pestilence" [67]. (Not surprisingly, Kim discovers three years later that this District Superintendent of Police, Strickland Sahib, is "the greatest" of those who play the Great Game [175]). This parable of surrogate maternity is central to the play of gender, sexuality, masculinity and the making of the ideal imperial administrator in *Kim*: as there are no doubts about Kim's bloodlines, he is free to suckle, as it were, on Indian breasts. There is much colonial learning to be imbibed there, and much ideal sustenance.[2]

India as sustaining maternal body is contrasted, as we have seen, with the sexual possibilities that it makes available to the English child-who-would-be-administrator. As we might expect in a *bildungsroman* like *Kim*, growing up requires some articulation of sexuality, some experience of sexual attraction, if not actually of sex. The narrative does render Kim heterosexual, though it does not actually allow him to engage in sex—here his youth and the urgent demands of the Great Game preserve him—but before we get to that discussion, it is important to note the somewhat unexpected presence of homosexual desire in the novel. I say unexpected because necessary to the confident representation of the consistently male and often homosocial worlds of most novels of high colonial adventure is the repression of homoerotic sentiment. Repression of course entails coding in another key, and such tales of male adventure rarely succeed in keeping at bay all figurations of homosexual desire, but *Kim* is different in making visible what other texts strive to keep secret. Oddly, the secret of homosexuality is part of the entire mystique surrounding Lurgan Sahib, the man who teaches Kim the tradecraft of a spy, and whose hypnotic urging and suggestions Kim must resist in order to demonstrate his ability to be a player in the Great Game.

Kim is sent to Lurgan Sahib's curiosity shop in Simla by Colonel

2. Critics have noted that *Kim*, in spite of all of Kipling's empathy for India and things Indian, is full of slighting references to "Indian" or "Oriental" ways. Kim complicates this relation between such perceptions of "Indianness" and unacceptable cultural and ethical practices because he must, at the very least, mimic them effortlessly in order to pass unnoticed. When, for instance, Kim dissimulates, as he does when he suggests that he has no particular interest in the "*kilta* with the red top" that contains the notebooks of the Russian spies, the narrative notes that Kim assumes successfully "the craft of his mother country" [203].

Creighton, and almost instantly becomes embroiled in a drama of sex-
ual jealousy. Lurgan keeps a boy servant whose "scarlet lips" and soft
flesh Kim notices [127], and then, the very next morning, Lurgan tells
Kim that the boy is determined to kill him with a "knife or poison. He
is jealous," Lurgan explains, "almost too jealous to trust, just now"—
the boy has in fact attempted to lace Lurgan's breakfast with arsenic
that morning. Kim is more impressed with Lurgan's matter-of-fact
manner than with anything else: "a genuine imported Sahib from
England would have made a great to-do over this tale. Lurgan Sahib
stated it as simply as Mahbub Ali was used to record his little affairs
in the North" [129]. Lurgan's sexuality is as unmistakable as his pro-
fession is covert, and each is encoded as a species of going native. It
is tempting to read what comes next—Lurgan Sahib's attempt to
hypnotize Kim in order to test his powers of endurance—as a brief
allegory of (homo)sexual seduction and resistance. Kipling's prose cer-
tainly suggests such homoerotic overtones: "Lurgan Sahib laid one
hand gently on the nape of his neck, stroked it twice or thrice," and
whispered instructions. Kim freezes under Lurgan's touch: it "held
him as a vice, and his blood tingled pleasantly through him." He feels
he is about to lose consciousness, and as Lurgan moves his hand
again, "another wave of prickling fire" races down his neck. But just
when Kim is about to give in to Lurgan's post-hypnotic suggestion that
a broken jar, now lying in pieces on the floor, is fashioning itself into
a whole again, he takes refuge in the verities of "the multiplication-
table in English" (he has so far been "thinking in Hindi").

As he repeats these tables, the shift in language and logic clears
his head, and he recovers from Lurgan's "magic." When Kim asks
Lurgan if that was what he had been subjected to, Lurgan replies
elliptically and suggests his need to test the full range of Kim's
responses: "No, that was not magic. It was only to see if there was—
a flaw in a jewel. Sometimes very fine jewels will fly all to pieces if
a man holds them in his hand, and knows the proper way. That is
why one must be careful before one sets them" [131]. The "setting,"
of course, is the fieldwork of the Great Game, and all varieties of
vulnerability must be checked on beforehand. Kim passes his test,
so much so that Lurgan can enlist him in returning his servant boy
to favor. Within earshot of the boy, he asks Kim: "Suppose you were
fond of someone, and you saw someone come, and the man you
were fond of was more pleased with him than he was with you, what
would you do?" Kim, wise now to the blinding power of Lurgan's
touch, fashions an answer that reassures the boy-servant, who then
flings himself "passionately at Lurgan Sahib's feet," and begs for-
giveness [132]. In his interlude in Simla, Kim learns valuable
lessons from Lurgan, not least among which is this lesson about the
murky, bewildering power of sexual compulsion.

This is a lesson that comes in handy when Kim, high in the Himalayas in pursuit of Russian spies, meets the Woman of Shamlegh. But before he encounters her, Kim is put through another experience that parallels his meeting with Lurgan. Before Kim takes to the road, Mahbub Ali conducts him to Huneefa the courtesan, and as he does so, gives Kim "much the same sort of advice as his mother gave to Lemuel, . . . and . . . Mahbub was exact to point out how Huneefa and her likes destroyed kings." (The reference is to Proverbs 31.1–9, particularly to verse 3: "Give not thy strength unto women, nor thy ways to that which destroyeth kings.") Kim is off to spy for Creighton, and Mahbub Ali's warning is particular: "Most true it is in the Great Game, for it is by means of women that all plans come to ruin and we lie out in the dawning with our throats cut" [150]. Mahbub's advice is emphatic that "Huneefa and her likes" are seductresses to be feared, but once Kim is with the blind Huneefa, we realize that her function is not to initiate Kim into the mysteries of heterosexual union in order to prepare him for the women that he might encounter.

Instead, she assumes a strangely maternal function, and performs a mystic ceremony upon him, praying for his safety on the road. This time it is Mahbub who holds Kim's neck, and Huneefa's "horrible soft fingers" which touch him, till he loses his senses. She speaks in tongues, and then crumples by Kim's side: "Huneefa's crisis passed, as these things must, in a paroxysm of howling, with a touch of froth at the lips. She lay spent and motionless beside Kim, and the crazy voices ceased" [152]. While he is asleep, Mahbub Ali and Hurree Babu tint Kim's skin a lasting shade of brown, and thus prepare him for his immersion into Indian life. Kim is reborn into a new avatar (as he is so often in this novel), and this time it is Huneefa and Mahbub Ali who parent him safely into his new life. While Huneefa is both mother and midwife to the born-again brown and Indian Kim (which rebirth also bloods him into the Secret Service), we must notice the *frisson* of sexual tension that renders turgid Kipling's descriptions of Huneefa's voices and performance. This is scarcely surprising in that Mahbub Ali introduces Huneefa to Kim in precisely those terms. But sex is here sublimated into the mysteries of Huneefa's invocations, and as she and Kim lie spent on the floor, we witness once again Kim's exposure to, but protection from, the "means of women" that unman men.[3]

Thus, when Kim meets the Woman of Shamlegh, he is well

3. While it does not help to try and make sense of Huneefa's incantations, we should note that she invokes "Zulbazan, son of Eblis, who lives in bazars and *paraos*, making all the sudden lewd wickedness of wayside halts," and Dulhan, "invisible about mosques, the dweller amongst the slippers of the faithful, who hinders folks from their prayers" [151]. "Dulhan" is the Hindustani word for bride.

equipped to hold her at arm's length. As is well known, the Woman of Shamlegh is a carry-over from one of Kipling's earliest short stories, "Lispeth" (from *Plain Tales from the Hills*), where, as Lisbeth, a girl brought up in a mission in Kotgarh, she falls in love with an Englishman while nursing him back to health. He returns her affection but eventually abandons her. (Kipling first calls attention to Lisbeth's story when he has one of the porters pointedly say of her: "*She* has no love for Sahibs, as we know" [206], and then the Woman herself describes her unfortunate relationship with the Englishman and indeed with the "Englishness" and Christianity she learns at Kotgarh [219]). In Kipling's oeuvre, Lisbeth is memorable as a reminder of the damage that can result from relationships that cross colonial divides of race and power; that she reappears in *Kim* suggests the enduring fear and fascination such a figure had for Kipling in particular and perhaps the colonial imagination in general. Lisbeth is of course also important for her English education and exposure to European ways—this is how she and her Englishman can even think of "falling in love," although her racial identity remains an insuperable obstacle. Now, back to her Hill ways, her polyandrous community, and her property, she is the older Woman of Shamlegh, no longer vulnerable, and thus a different kind of challenge to Kim, himself now returned to his Indian disguise as *chela* to the Lama.

The Woman of Shamlegh is "fair-coloured," with "bold, bright eyes" and a forthright manner [211]. She has no hesitation in expressing her attraction to Kim, though he helps precipitate her declaration by smiling "ravishingly" at her. He does so because he needs her help to communicate with Hurree Babu, but once she says that there is nothing she would not do for him, he accepts her "compliment calmly, as men must do in lands where women make the love" [213]. She makes her intentions even clearer when she draws "a handful of walnuts from her bosom" and shares them with Kim, a gesture which causes him to first pretend that he does not understand her overture, and then, when this distresses her, to promise her "payment" only once she renders him service. Kim is here portrayed as master of the situation, in control of the moves and counter-moves of flirtation, but he still needs to make the rhetorical move that defines gender relations in the novel; he changes the form of his address to her: "it was on the tip of his tongue to say Mother, but he turned it to Sister" [213]. His attempt to dissipate sexual tension into the proprieties of kinship is made in the face of mounting offers from the Woman of Shamlegh, who reminds him that she is mistress of her property and of her person, and offers him all of Shamlegh. When she leaves, Kim, in the half-adolescent, half-adult manner that typifies him, returns to the fears Mahbub Ali had instilled in him:

How can a man follow the Way or the Great Game when he is so-always pestered by women? There was that girl in Akrola of the Ford; and there was the scullion's wife behind the dove-cot—not counting the others—and now comes this one! When I was a child it was well enough, but now I am a man and they will not regard me as a man. Walnuts, indeed! Ho! Ho! It is almonds in the Plains! [214]

His desire to be thought a man is expressed as a desire to be left alone, to be celibate, for that state is appropriate both to his discipleship to the Lama and to his apprenticeship to the Game. That is Kim then, man enough to know the forms of sexual desire, but child enough to need to distance them. Or perhaps simply man-child enough to want to be treated as an adult even while he believes he is one: when he finally looks back on the Woman of Shamlegh, his summary comment on her is "At least she did not treat me like a child" [221].

Or perhaps the better way to think about Kim's status as man-child is to see in that uneasy persona the only tenable form of the fantasy of colonial subjectivity that is enacted in the novel. Not a state of chronological limbo, as it were, but a supple way of being in the colonial world, such that Kim as (native) child is entitled to the protection and nurturance of all that is maternal in the Indian communities he passes through,[4] and Kim as (white) adult cleaves to the political tasks dictated by Colonel Creighton and his other spymasters. Any one—any woman—who interferes with the delicate balance between childlike entitlement and adult priorities must be distanced. But not before such a woman has allowed Kim to know himself as desirable and masculine, indeed enough so as to make the Woman of Shamlegh throw a jealous fit once her advances are gently rebuffed: "I was foolish. . . . Who is thy woman in the Plains? Fair or black? I was fair once" [219]. That Kim's hybrid identity, his identity in disguise, is precisely the issue at such moments is made clear to us when the Woman of Shamlegh tells him why she was attracted to him: "Thy face and thy walk and thy fashion of speech put me into mind of my Sahib, though thou art only a wandering mendicant. . . . But for awhile I thought it was my Sahib come back, and he was my God" [220]. There is enough of the Sahib in Kim the *chela* to let the Woman of Shamlegh intuit his origins, and such forbidden knowledge is exactly the threat that intimacy of this kind presents to Kim the British/Indian, colonial/native, man/child creature of espionage. And yet, once he is about to leave, Kim is confident enough to perform for her as she knows a Sahib would. He kisses her chastely on

4. Late in the novel, when the Lama tells Mahbub Ali, who has come searching for Kim, that he is being cared for in his illness by the Sahiba, who "looks upon him as a son," Mahbub Ali snorts his reply: "Hmph! Half Hind seems that way disposed" [235].

the cheek ("Kissing is practically unknown among Asiatics," the narrative adds gratuitously [221], but in order to make clear the cultural and racial dynamics of Kim's act), and lapses into English: "Thank you veree much my dear" [221].

Virginity and disguise preserved (after a fashion), Kim travels his long route with his Lama. Exhausted in mind and body, they meet once again the old woman from Kulu, who takes one look at Kim's condition and cackles: "How dids't thou do it? Never answer me! *I* know. He has been running among the women. Look at his eyes—hollow and sunk—and the Betraying Line from the nose down! He has been sifted out!" [226–27]. Her jocularity—and her inaccuracy—must not cause us to forget that being "sifted out" by women is a recurrent male fear in the novel, nor should we be surprised that Kim's recovery is a return to maternal care. There "are but two sorts of women" in this world, the Sahiba says, "those who take the strength out of a man and those who put it back. Once I was that one, and now I am this" [229], and she, true to her word, supervises Kim's return to health, feeding him and drugging him and arranging for therapeutic massages (by a cousin's widow who lives in her household). She restores him, but Kim's final recovery comes within the bosom of yet another mother. He falls into a "deeper than sleep" trance on a newly ploughed field, and we are told that

> Mother Earth was as faithful as the Sahiba. She breathed through him to restore the poise he had lost lying so long on a cot cut off from her good currents. His head lay powerless upon her breast, and his opened hands surrendered to her strength. [235]

This is the way, and the function, of the "mother country" in *Kim*: to restore to health and poise a colonial Antaeus. As Edward Said suggests, this is the moment in which Kipling "renders a powerful, almost instinctive desire to restore the child to its mother in a preconscious, undefiled, asexual relationship."[5] Instinctive perhaps, but the timing is also crucial: this match of the Great Game has been won, and Kim can be returned to his status as child in need of succor and sustenance.

Celibacy is appropriate, however, not only to Kim the spy, but, as he says so himself, to Kim the disciple ("How can a man follow the Way or the Great Game when he is so-always pestered by women?" [214]. In terms of sexuality, Kim's identification with the Lama places him at one pole, the other of which is defined by Mahbub Ali's sexual swagger. The Lama is of course a strange figure to loom as large as he does in a novel of colonial adventure—indeed his gentle otherworld-

5. Edward Said, "Introduction" to *Kim* (New York: Penguin Books, 1987) 21.

liness is far removed from the craft, and the world-view, that Kim must learn in order to be a good spy or indeed a good Sahib. Yet he does offer Kim lessons in fortitude and caring, and a model of masculinity unlike any other in the novel. He thus functions as a crucial pivot for Kim's shifts between childhood and adulthood in the novel—because the Lama is as he is, Kim can be both son and father to him, at once *chela* and protector. More important perhaps, given the world he and Kim travel in, is the radical innocence that he embodies, and to which Kim can return. Indeed, when Kim awakens from his trance—is reborn once again—at the very end of the novel, it is the Lama who awaits him, and who offers him a vision of spiritual transcendence. That this free-wheeling vision of "all Hind, from Ceylon in the sea to the Hills, and my own Painted Rocks at Such-zen" mimics the panoptic vision that is the ideal of colonial surveillance- and knowledge-systems is not incidental: if Kim is to return to his status as *chela* and as child without giving up on the priorities established for him by the Great Game, only the Lama's vision—of this world and not of it—will suffice.

And this is in fact the political import of the spectacular other-worldliness of the Lama. Teshoo Lama's impressive lack of knowledge about, or interest in, British colonialism in India or of British-Indian relations is in part derived from his spiritual quest and in part from his origins—he is Tibetan, possibly outside the purview of the empire (though large sections of Tibet were in fact included in its boundaries), and in India only to follow the footsteps of the Buddha. Of all Kim's mentors he is the only one unaware of, and without an opinion on, the British in India—he takes their presence for granted, and he reacts to those of them he meets no differently than he does to the Indians he encounters. They are for him a part of the human geography of India in a way that they are not, and cannot be, for even their collaborators like Mahbub Ali or Hurree Babu. In the novel then, Teshoo Lama, as someone who stands uncomprehending outside the political circuits of British India, "naturalizes" this India in a way that no other character can. At the end of the novel it is his all-seeing vision—that must note nothing about him—and his deep love for his *chela* that return the novel, and Kim, to a model of innocence destabilized by the travails of espionage in the high mountains.

It is worth noting too that the Lama is for Kim a model of the "enlightened" male subject who is single-minded in the pursuit of his duty, and who will let little or nothing dissuade him from his chosen way. Similarly, Teshoo Lama's commitment to non-violence (though he does reach for his heavy iron pencase to defend himself from the Russian [202]) is exemplary for Kim, and indeed for the novel itself. *Kim* is a remarkable colonial novel in that it features virtually no violence, even as Kim ranges the length and breadth of

colonial North India. For all of Mahbub Ali's potential for violent action, and even the presence of an injured spy, the method of the novel abjures violence, for any violence is a threat to the legitimacy of empire, and India is here being ruled not by military methods (although the army is on call) but by those who know it so well that they face no resistance, or perhaps preempt resistance before it can turn violent.[6] In *Kim*, the heroes of colonial governance are not members of the military but civilians, members of the Secret Service, gatherers of information and of local knowledge, those who use their intellect, and not their brawn, to effect their ends. In many ways, the Lama is their anti-type, but there are crucial parallels, and Kim inherits his way of being in the world—a Searcher and a Seeker after Knowledge—from both. And that is indeed the suture between the world of transcendent spirit and the world of colonial men that Kipling effects via the character of the Lama, who is father, with Creighton, of the man-child who would inherit the empire without boundaries, and live in a time without end.

MARK KINKEAD-WEEKES

[The Ending of *Kim*][†]

* * *

Questions of perspective are vital as the novel reaches its climactic scene.

> At last they entered a world within a world—a valley of leagues where the high hills were fashioned of the mere rubble and refuse from off the knees of the mountains. Here one day's march carried them no farther, it seemed, than a dreamer's clogged pace bears him in a nightmare. . . .
> "Surely the Gods live here!" said Kim, beaten down by the silence and the appalling sweep and dispersal of the cloud-shadows after rain. "This is no place for men!"

6. The novel's commitment to the settled, orderly, non-violent rule of the British may explain the terms used to describe the Revolt of 1857 (which some historians consider the First War of Indian Independence) by the old Indian soldier who had fought on the British side then: "A madness ate into the Army, and they turned against all their officers" [47]. Political and armed opposition to the British is here understood as irrational and insane. The old soldier's vehement telling of this tale is contrasted with the Lama's impassivity—in Tibet, the Lama heard only a "rumour" about 1857, and its events or politics mean little to him.
† From "Vision in Kipling's Novels," in *Kipling's Mind and Art*, ed. Andrew Rutherford (Stanford, Calif.: Stanford University Press, 1964; rpt. 1966) 228–34.

Kipling makes the Himalayas serve the same function Forster
wanted from his Marabar Caves; they make manifest a vision of the
world as inhuman, incredible, unintelligible, utterly dwarfing man.
Yet to the Lama it is the mountains that are ultimately illusion. As
he instructs Kim in his vision of a deeper reality there is re-enacted
"the birth of a religion—the first teacher and the first disciple"; and
instead of looking down on tiny dwarfs, we come with the "Rus-
sians" and the Babu *up* a steep spur to watch "bareheaded in the
wash of the afternoon sunlight low across the gold-coloured grass."
It is a moment of deep beauty, if unwashed, and also of great rever-
ence, if unintentional. Yet the strangers respond to it from other
perspectives still. The Frenchman sees the beauty and reverence,
but only as picturesque—to be sketched rather than questioned.
The Russian is the more, not the less, sensitive. What he feels is
spiritual authority, but he reacts to the implication of his own inad-
equacy in pride and passion, seeing the Lama's eyes as "insolent"
because he senses what their verdict on him would be, and insisting
on making *his* mark, as against the religion of the extinction of self.
When the Lama speaks, in Hindi so that all can understand, nobody
listens. They are blind to him and his meaning; they can see only a
"picture" to sketch, another picture on a "dirty piece of paper" and
an "unclean old man" haggling. Kipling now knows, moreover, that
blindness, the failure of human imagination, leads to brutality of
attitude and behaviour; and that failure to care about and respect
human beings results in a world of power and violence. So we get
the brutal assault on the old man, and one brutality releasing
another: strangling, kicking in the genitals, a head battered against
a rock, stoning, shooting, lynching only just averted. The "picture of
the birth of a religion" becomes a picture of blind hatred and blood-
lust in which even the Lama is momentarily tempted to revenge.

It is the surest sign of the new vision of *Kim* that the creator of
Dick Heldar and the publisher should now be able to make us know
on our pulses, and understand, how brutal and brutalising the blow
at the Lama is. Yet if one's first reaction is at all like Kim's—anger
and horror so intense as to demand a violent satisfaction—the Lama
has not been seen or understood. His greatest suffering is not
caused by the blow, but by the huge effort to rid himself of the vio-
lence it taps in him. Even as a response to unquestionable evil, the
very existence of violence in the soul is wholly evil and can only
beget more evil. The cobra scene has been re-orchestrated in a far
more difficult context. Kipling is not dewy-eyed about it: there is an
exaggeration in the Lama's remorse that is meant to raise half a
smile; and his attitude is saved from the charge of empty idealism
only by the emotional and physical cost of attaining it, which nearly
amounts to his life. Yet the Lama has real authority now, paid for in

effort and suffering; and though we can see why Kim feels his val-
ues are "too high," there can be no shrugging them off. Yet if we do
take this seriously—as we surely must—then it is not only the "Rus-
sians" who stand condemned. There is a clear correspondence
between Their attitudes and Ours. Our Players of the Game also
convert the Lama's truth into "interesting" theory, and his holiness
into the "curious"; they, too, subject human beings to their pur-
poses, and fail in human vision, affection, and respect. The Game
itself is a Hobbesian war of all on all, which may start as a battle of
wits but must end in violence—for its laws are kill or be killed, strike
or be struck, take or have taken from you. If They are responsible
for the death of E23, We create the pool of blood on the railway
line. While the "Russians" are sketching, the Babu is playing the
Game with Kim; and we ought to be able to measure what is
involved in his delight at the outcome. "'Thee outrage was acciden-
tal, but onlee me could have worked it—ah—for all it was dam'-well
worth. Consider the moral effect upon these ignorant peoples!'"

Kim really becomes a *chela* in the agonising escape from the
Hills, and begins to deserve the comparison with Ananda, living the
role he has acted so long. There is no longer any conflict; he angrily
rejects the least reference to his sahib-hood, and, if once he could
rid himself of the documents, "the Great Game might play itself for
all he then cared." The only realities left are those the game
denies—love, and the responsibility of love. The Lama fills his
whole horizon. Again, however, there is no sentimentality; what
Kipling wishes to bring home to the imagination is the tremendous
cost of such dedication. Kim wears himself out to the point of col-
lapse, but he is always chokingly aware of the failure to love and
care enough. "I have—I have . . . *Hai mai!* But I love thee . . .
and it is all too late . . . I was a child . . . Oh, why was I not a
man?" Given the exhaustion and hysteria (and the Lama's gentle
affection restores perspective), there yet speaks in this a new matu-
rity, the coming of age of the Little Friend. At the Maharanee's, too,
the whole emphasis is on tending others, as the old lady's loving
care pulls Kim back to life, and the Lama grows strong again.

In this world the Babu can only be an intrusion; his attitude to
the Lama and his notes for the Royal Society a stupidity; his readi-
ness to commit a "dacoity"—the word is deliberately loaded—on the
Maharanee's home a matter for Kim's "black disapproval." He
remains a great "character," full of imaginative vitality, but there can
be no doubt of the disabling criticism that has been directed at the
Game through him.[1] Even Mahbub Ali (who has been consorting

1. The Babu does of course rescue the Lama from drowning—which could be emblematic
of the need for protection that justifies Secret Services and Armies. The curious fact
remains however that after the Ressaldar passage Kipling never makes such a case in *Kim*.

with the Lama "no end") sees this on their last encounter. The scene is suffused with the Pathan's humorous response to the Lama's unwordly simplicity; but a new affection and respect shine through. Mahbub Ali has entered a different world; and though he will continue the Game and expect Kim to do so too, it could hardly be played in the same way.

We should need very strong evidence, however, to support the idea that Kim could return to the Game, against the whole current of the book's disabling criticism—and there is no such evidence. We must not mistake the last direction of the novel's imaginative exploration; for the remaining conflicts of Kim and the Lama are essentially complementary, and the issue leaves them finally united. When Kim staggers from his sickroom with the last and worst loss of his sense of his own identity, it is because as *chela* he has been involved not only with the old man's loving soul, but also with his Buddhist ideology. It is because of an essentially inhuman strain that he

> felt, though he could not put it into words, that his soul was out of gear with its surroundings . . . the parrots shrieked at him, the noises of the populated house behind . . . hit on dead ears. "I am Kim. I am Kim. And what is Kim?" His soul repeated it again and again. He did not want to cry . . . but of a sudden easy, stupid tears trickled down his nose, and with an almost audible click he felt the wheels of his being lock up anew on the world without. Things that rode meaningless on the eyeball an instant before slid into proper proportion. Roads were meant to be walked upon, houses to be lived in, cattle to be driven, fields to be tilled, and men and women to be talked to. They were all real and true—solidly planted upon the feet— clay of his clay, neither more nor less.

So his restoration is completed full-length on the earth, drawing strength from it. As the "gear" imagery makes clear, this is commitment not to the Game, with which we are no longer concerned, but, at a far more fundamental level, to the Wheel of earthly and human life, against the view which holds that all these things are illusion, and one must keep oneself apart from them. Yet this means no final conflict with the Lama, because in the end the Lama rejects apartness too. At the moment of achieving the final extinction of his humanity within the world-soul, he turns back "with strivings and yearnings and retchings and agonies not to be told." At the very last moment, love and human relationship are more important than Nirvana for oneself, and the images Kipling uses are all creative, active, fructifying. "As the egg from the fish, as the fish from the water, as the water from the cloud, as the cloud from the thick air; so put forth, so leaped out, so drew away, so fumed up the Soul of the Teshoo Lama

from the Great Soul." It is only then that he sees the River which can cleanse him from a sin still with him; and when one has reached this point, any old river will do. The "sin" can only be the element of self-ishness in the search for the perfection of self by turning away from others. It is by giving up self-perfection—"I pushed aside world upon world for thy sake"—that he finds it. Greater love hath no man than this, than that he lay down his after-life for his friend. The eyes that lock home on the Wheel and the eyes that look down on the Beloved and the River still see on very different levels, but they share the same kind of human commitment. The reconciliation can be put in an image, and Kipling's father does so, with exact sensitivity, in the last and finest of his illustrations of the book. In the foreground Kim half-reclines on the earth, but our eyes move past and through him to the Lama who confronts us in the classic attitude of meditation. But the tree that arches over him is not the Buddha's Bodhi Tree, and the Wheel of the bullock-cart is between him and it. Behind it again, dis-tanced, but still part of the same world because he has begun to share its loving vision, is Mahbub Ali. The Lama's head is in the centre of the Wheel: he defines its hub, it gives him a kind of halo. Perhaps at this moment we might remember that the Miracle of the Arrow was performed by a Buddha not "apart," indeed, in the act of proving him-self strong enough to love.

Once again it must be said that limitations remain. Kipling took refuge too easily in his theory of daemonic creation when he told his father that the novel stopped by itself, as a thing complete. For he doesn't finally face up to the problem of what Kim is to become in the world; the problem of working out the reconciliation of the book's deepest values with involvement in society—or, indeed, with the pro-tection of society. Oddly for Kipling, one can see that the Game is given less than justice because there is no powerful enough experi-ence of evil. Kim's eyes do disinfect the world, and we get the nota-tion of evil without its stench. The blow of course has deep symbolic significance, and it does raise the problem of how the world's evil is to be met, but without more agonised experience of the sort of thing the Ressaldar has known, the Little Friend and his Lama are not perhaps sufficiently tested. On a more technical level one also notices a ten-dency to abstraction in the final movement. Faced with a man of inaction and inner life like the Lama, Kipling's ability to render value concretely in terms of action cannot fully operate, and he hasn't the ability to convey the experience of inner conflict. Consequently he has to resort to direct exposition on several occasions, so that a quo-tation can sound like a sermon, and the critic who wishes to discuss it can seem to indulge in straight moral debate. Even at the great final *cruces* one experiences narrative and image rather than inner drama. Nevertheless *Kim* as a whole is a triumph of exploratory vision.

* * * Only in one respect, the attitude to women, does myopia remain, and it is marginal.[2] *Kim* is the answer to nine-tenths of the charges levelled against Kipling and the refutation of most of the generalisations about him. Yet it is not the result of a change in his personality or his thought, and it is by no means permanent. It is the product of a peculiar tension between different ways of seeing: the affectionate fascination with the kaleidoscope of external reality for its own sake; the negative capability getting under the skin of attitudes different from one another and one's own; and finally, a product of this last, but at its most intense and creative, the triumphant achievement of an anti-self so powerful that it became a touchstone for everything else—the creation of the Lama. This involved imagining a point of view and a personality almost at the furthest possible remove from Kipling himself; yet it is explored so lovingly that it could not but act as a catalyst towards some deeper synthesis. Out of this particular challenge—preventing self-obsession, probing deeper than a merely objective view of reality outside himself, enabling him now to see, think, and feel *beyond* himself—came the new vision of *Kim*, more inclusive, complex, humanised, and mature than that of any other work. The sad thing is that we cannot equate this vision with "Kipling" either. It is an artistic triumph that occurs only by virtue of its own conditions, and it never happened again.

ZOHREH T. SULLIVAN

What Happens at the End of *Kim*?[†]

* * *

Kim is the product of seven years wandering through Africa, Australia, New Zealand, once again India (1891), and the United

2. Lispeth has thematic relevance: she makes manifest the warping effect of failure in love, and tolerance, and truth. Her betrayal at Kotgarh mission—the story appears in *Plain Tales from the Hills*—has embittered her whole life, and the bitterness spurts out in "Thy Gods are lies; thy works are lies; thy words are lies. There are no Gods under all the heavens." Yet she is redeemed by an act of selfless charity.
 The trouble is that Kipling insists on grafting onto this another flirtation with exotic sex experience, and then draws back with unpleasantly prissy condescension. He has oddly, because so irrelevantly, touched once or twice on Kim's sexual attractiveness, and several times preached the old doctrine of the nuisance of women. On the one hand, the irrelevance shows how marginal the fault is; on the other, the fact that he is driven to put it all in, in spite of its irrelevance, points to the persistence of the old pressures * * *.

† From *Narratives of Empire: The Fictions of Rudyard Kipling* (Cambridge: Cambridge University Press, 1993) 148–49, 170–80. Reprinted with the permission of Cambridge University Press. Page references to *Kim* have been changed to correspond to this Norton Critical Edition.

States. It came after the *Jungle Books*, after his marriage (1892), his children, and the death of Josephine (1899). It captures both the fear of loss and the nostalgia for a lost Indian past, a lost dream of possibility for an eternal childhood in an imagined India, a fantasy of integration between the oppositional roles of colonizer and colonized and of the master who rules and the child who desires. It is also the result of a profound alienation from an England in which he had not yet found what he was to call "a very-own house"—that ultimate home which was to be Bateman's in Sussex. Yet ironically *Kim* announces, even as it laments, Kipling's choice of England over India.

At once a spy thriller, a picaresque adventure story, a maturation story, and a quest romance, *Kim*'s complexity comes, in part, from the curious stacking up of various genres: as spy thriller, it intermittently pursues the problem of whether or not Kim and his lama will stop the Russians; as picaresque adventure, it follows Kim's pursuits of "the Great Game" along the Grand Trunk Road of life; as maturation story it offers a variation on the familiar nineteenth-century theme of the search for a father in its embodiment of a fragmented culture in multiple father-figures; and as quest story, it involves two antithetical searches—Kim's for the Red Bull on a Green Field, and the lama's for the River of the Arrow. But even more important, its complexity results from its efforts to negotiate the effects of the death of the Father and to mediate the contrary but entangled demands of power and love.

The major problems and contradictions in the novel are informed and shaped by Kipling's divided sense of self, its multiple loyalties to the power of empire during a time of intensified authority, and his love for a lost India that blurred distinctions between the ruler and the ruled. The inner quest, the search for an identity ("Who is Kim—Kim—Kim?" [101, 121, 156, 234]), suggests the possibility of self-discovery and integration of his many selves, the arrival at an identity mediated by the lama Kim learns to love. But this search collides with his outer quest, the journey and the insistent pursuit for definition in a search for a father (the Red Bull on a Green Field) who will free him from some of the anxieties and problems involved in such a search. Kim's love for the lama and his search for identity, in other words, are consistently mediated by ruling structures of power, and finally come under the control of the colonial system.

* * *

The last part of *Kim*, chapters 11–15, Kim's double journey for which we have been prepared from the start, carries forward the

plot of the Great Game and brings to an ending the plot of the lama's search for the River of the Arrow. But the ending also returns us to the problem of Kim's origins and identity. Kim is born again after his illness, but he is reborn to a cry that returns from the past: "I am Kim. I am Kim. And what is Kim?" [234]. He returns to life "powerless" upon the breast of the Sahiba who breathes life into him. Kim's fall into the Law of the Father, into the Symbolic order of colonial civilization, circles around the problem of unconscious desire by appropriating desire into the field of power, by refusing to admit to his lama that he is a Sahib and not merely his "chela" ("Why plague me with this talk, Holy One? . . . It vexes me. I am *not* a Sahib. I am thy *chela*" [225]); and, finally, by giving the lama the last word in the story.

The completion of Kim's education is marked by his preparation of a report with a map of a "wild," "walled," "mysterious city . . . where the wells are four hundred feet deep, and lined throughout with camel bone" [143]. The geography of the landscape to be mastered recalls other hidden and mysterious cities in Kipling's early short stories that trapped ("The Strange Ride of Morrowbie Jukes") or threatened English protagonists ("In the House of Suddhoo," "The City of Dreadful Night," "Beyond the Pale"). The difference is that here there is less fear of the unknown because it is now only a space to be colonized and mapped into knowledge. For his "graduation," upon completing this report, he is rewarded with two symbolic gifts—a costume and a gun. It is Mahbub Ali who presents him with this "dress of honour," a gold embroidered Pathan garment and a mother of pearl, nickel-plated, self-extracting .450 revolver that completes the splendor and takes "Kim's delighted breath away" [145]. Once again, we are reminded of the opening scene and the announced opposition between the museum and the gun with its implications of control and knowledge over the native. And here again, native India can be contained (or tricked) by an English boy in Pathan disguise so long as he has the gun.

During the final and crucial journey to the north, Kim is accompanied again by split fathers who represent past desire and future order—the lama and Hurree Babu. These antithetical figures cluster around polarities established early in the novel by the English father with his emblem of the Red Bull on a Green Field and the Eastern father with his spiritual search. The political and the spiritual father fit the antithetical expectations of the Symbolic and the Imaginary. The lama as the Imaginary parent belongs to an earlier stage of development that precedes later consciousness of political categories and social power. The relationships with Symbolic fathers, however, are determined, as Lacan would have us understand, by a social organization so abstract and intangible that it is

known only through such symbolic terms as the Game, or the Great Game, or the flag of the Red Bull on a Green Field. It also involves a mode of human interaction that, determined by isolation, uniformity and "statistical anonymity," is serial rather than unified by a group.[1] * * * In such serial situations, individuals act only to intensify their serial helplessness, causing what they most fear against themselves. Thus Kim, though he is most afraid of being alone and isolated from his life in the native bazaars, commits actions that progressively alienate him from the group of natives with whom he has enjoyed an easy camaraderie.

That the last three chapters conflate not only the Search and the Game, but the Imaginary and the Symbolic, Indian dream and English reality, is part of the oppositional strategy of the text in which colonial order appropriates native desire. * * * The figurative conflation is prepared for at the opening of chapter 13: "Who goes to the Hills goes to his mother." The basic configuration of landscape involves an ascent into the hills followed by a descent onto the plains and into the river. The hills—overdetermined as feminine and spiritual "home" and as masculine, political testing ground—seem, at first, to provide a way out of the world of work into an idealized space where the lama and Kim can meditate on the problems of entrapment in the wheel of life, "the more so since, as the lama said, they were freed from its visible temptations" [194]. Kim's love for the lama and his declared devotion to his cause seem unconsciously to denounce the ideology that negates the lama's value. On the other hand, the hills are a place of business for Kim, the workplace of spies from both the British and Russian secret services who aim to turn the garden into a map, to structure, to colonize, and to contain the Indian within European structures. Yet, although the two meanings of the hills appear to contradict each other, in effect, the first tends to idealize and legitimize the second. The spiritual geography of the hills lends its luster to the political geography of imperialist intent.

Kim's oscillation between the Sahibs and the lama, the school and the road is a movement between the need for mechanical anonymity and competition and the opposing need for dependence and bonds of kinship with all the responsibility those bonds entail. The life of a Sahib in school, or out of it, is inevitably a life of cold competition whose final reward will be Kim's function as a cog in the imperial machine. His life on the road with the lama, on the contrary, is a carnival that inverts and democratizes the imperial hierarchy of class, creed, color, and race. By begging for the lama and serving as his eyes,

1. "Seriality is a vast optical illusion, a kind of collective hallucination projected out of individual solitude onto an imaginary being thought of as 'public opinion' or simply 'they.'"
Fredric Jameson, *Marxism and Form* (Princeton: Princeton UP, 1971), 248.

he supports him, fathers him, and becomes his guide. So intensely does Kim need that sense of bonding, dependence, and indispensable service that he is willing to lie for its privilege. Thus he tells the lama that he is a scribe and that he is "all free" [161], which of course he is not; he is as clearly bound to the "serial" hierarchy of Sahibs Creighton and Lurgan and the British Secret Service as is the lama to his wheel. And finally he pretends he has returned in order to pursue their original search when in fact he has returned to use the lama as a cover for his mission to the northern hills. The lama's subsequent words to Kim prepare us for the boundary confusion between the spiritual search and the English Game: "Thou wast sent for an aid. That aid removed, my Search came to naught. Therefore we go out again together, and our Search is sure" [162]. Their searches are of course contrary. The lama, used to aloneness and autonomy, wishes freedom from his remaining fraction of attachment to life and illusion, whereas Kim's search is for the opposite; what he wants is ever more binding attachments to fathers, Sahibs, and secret services. Although Kim creates the illusion of a free spirit, attachments far outweigh his autonomy. Even his deception of the lama seems forgivable because of his repeated declarations of love: "Kim, who had loved him without reason, now loved him for fifty good reasons" [179]. Love, then, serves both as an oppositional discourse opening a possibility of an alternate method of negotiation with the Other and also as an excuse to transcend personal betrayals.

Because Kim is made to seem unaware of his oscillation between dependence and autonomy, his meditations on his actions frequently seem forced and arbitrary. Neither he nor his creator appears entirely in control of motivations which seem to be energized by a variety of wish-fulfilling impulses. That perhaps accounts too for the frequent changes in narrative voice from the certain, omniscient, and distant narrator, to the insecure and involved subjective narrator. Such changes in voice create a characteristic indecisiveness and glide in the Kipling voice, a kind of evasiveness that raises issues and problems it does not intend to resolve. Kim's characteristic moments of introspection, for instance, are curiously depersonalized by shifts in voice and perspective:

> "Well is the Game called great! I was four days a scullion at Quetta, waiting on the wife of the man whose book I stole. And that was part of the Great Game! From the South—God knows how far—came up the Mahratta, playing the Great Game in fear of his life. Now I shall go far and far into the North playing the Great Game. Truly, it runs like a shuttle throughout all Hind. And my share and my joy"—he smiled to the darkness— "I owe to the lama here. Also to Mahbub Ali—also to Creighton

> Sahib, but chiefly to the Holy One. He is right—a great and a
> wonderful world—and I am Kim—Kim—Kim—alone—one
> person—in the middle of it all." [188]

As with his other freely associated meditations, this sequence of
thoughts runs not in English, but in Hindustanee. Yet the leaps and
shifts are characteristic of his deflective narrative strategy. Even
though this is presumably fragmented thought, its sequential logic
is self-contradictory. After Kim lists his adventures and his function
in the Game, and after the lengthy list of fathers to whom he owes
his joy, the reader is hard put to believe Kim's subsequent declara-
tion of aloneness. Kipling never allows Kim to be alone. Yet the cry
reproduces the opposition submerged at the beginning that the nar-
rative of Kim's quest intends to, but never does, resolve.

But because the recognition of aloneness appears so unexpect-
edly at unusual spaces in the text, it deserves more attention. The
opposition between aloneness and belonging, like the other opposi-
tions between the values of Kim and the values of the lama, create
social and ideological contradictions that structure not only the
entire text, but the everyday life of the colonial. Kim's illusion and
excuse for being, the justification for his mode of activity, is that he
had appropriated the power that accompanies his familial bonding
to Mahbub Ali, to the Sahiba, to the lama, and indeed to half of
India. If that is true, then his lament belongs to a grief and loss out-
side this plot, a grief without a specific object, one perhaps
repressed and denied by the author that returns to haunt the narra-
tive repeatedly with no change regardless of the situation or context.
But the opposing movement in the text, Kim's identity as a Sahib,
generates a contradiction: he cannot be a Sahib and friend, child,
and son to Indians simultaneously; and that unacknowledged con-
tradiction with its embedded loss is associated, through metonymy,
to the recurring cry of Kim "all alone." The figural construction of
the "great and wonderful" India of which Kim can be an ecstatic
part belongs to the Imaginary mode of understanding, an ahistoric
time when Kim's life could safely ignore social and political hierar-
chies. And because such a time never existed, it is necessarily a cre-
ation of Kipling's childhood Indian imagination. "Kim-all-alone,"
however, is a consequence of his "fall" into what Lacan calls "The-
name-of-the-Father," the discovery of his colonial identity which
awakens him to a sense of his function in a larger abstract machine
and which is a creation of Kipling's adult Symbolic and conse-
quently, alienated imagination.[2] The submerged problem of Kim's

2. Jacques Lacan theorizes the formation of identity in terms of a "fall" from the Imaginary
 phase of oneness with a mother prior to language into the Symbolic phase of the "law of
 the father," which, in marking sexual difference (male and not-male, self and Other), priv-
 ileges phallocentric power and defines maleness in terms of fear of phallic "lack."

aloneness ("In all India is no one so alone as I! If I die today, who shall bring the news—and to whom?" [156]) is confronted in the last two chapters not on a social but on the individual and personal level in terms of the lama's self-sacrificial love for his "chela." Thus, although the question of Kim's aloneness is raised on the Symbolic level of the text, its resolution will be found on the wish-fulfilling (or Imaginary) level of action. The combined forces of the lama and the hills ("Who goes to the hills goes to his mother" [192]) provide Kim with pre-Oedipal paternal and maternal forces on which to project his yearnings to belong to a primal family—the last consolation before he must truly part from the lama and enter as an alienated adult into the bitter heritage of his dead father—the British Secret Service.

The journey to the hills, like the rest of the book, operates on twin symbolic levels. It is both a fantasy of regression and a fantasy of realized ideology. Whereas on the first level, the lama is triumphant as lone discoverer of his river within and as lover of the "chela" for whom he renounces freedom from the wheel, on the second level, the lama is a museum piece, a nonviolent, nonactive absurdity in a world of guns, Russian spies, and violence. If on the private and Imaginary level, the lama gains strength, youth, and prestige, on the Symbolic and social level he is finally advised to recognize his own helplessness in a world where only the strong survive, and, further, to accept his need for the likes of Sahibs like Kim to ensure his continued saintliness. But on both levels, the ending transfigures the events that lead up to the conclusion.

The descent from the hills into Shamlegh takes Kim to a further stage of his fantasy of omnipotence: here he will meet the legendary Lispeth, from the story after her name in *Plain Tales from the Hills*. In the earlier story, Lispeth is seduced and abandoned by her English lover whom she has nursed to life. Here, Kim will be favorably compared to the earlier Sahib because he will evade her past role as the sexually submissive "Oriental" female by recasting and confirming his more enduring friendship with her present and newly empowered identity. The Woman of Shamlegh and the woman from Kulu help to conclude the series of women that appear marginally in the text. If it is through her sexuality that she has been allowed power in the past, Kim will deny her that power, yet will accept and invite her friendship. Lispeth's past relationship with Sahibs has been bitter. Sexually exploited and abandoned, she suggests the larger betrayal of the Indians by their colonizers.[3] Kim will refuse her sexual invitation, not only to show his moral superiority over cal-

3. See John McClure, *Kipling and Conrad: The Colonial Fiction* (Cambridge: Harvard UP, 1981), 75–76.

lous Sahibs, but also to prove that he has passed a crucial test of colonial manhood—the denial of sexuality. Though country born, he will not be a Jellaludin McIntosh or a Kimball O'Hara, prey to native women, sex, and drugs. Rather he will transcend such weaknesses and in so doing become a type of super-colonialist, simultaneously of the people and yet above them. The woman from Kulu, the widow, beyond sexuality, is the mother who gives Kim and the lama relief in the form of food and shelter when they most need it. Her division of women into two types echoes Kipling's fears in other Indian stories: "I have seen something of this world . . . and there are but two sorts of women in it—those who take the strength out of a man and those who put it back. Once I was that one, and now I am this" [229]. There are in fact no women in this book who "take the strength out of a man"; even the courtesan we met earlier in the train is "a kindly nun" who gives charity to the lama. And the women in the brothel who help disguise Kim all treat him as a son. Just as there are no sexual women in the book, there are also no nationalists, or natives who would prefer to be freed from imperialist control. The desexualizing and disembodying effect in Kim's attitudes towards his own sexuality is a sort of colonization of the self and of one's own desires. And the rigid definition and circumscribing of the roles of women as supporters or destroyers of men colonizes, controls, and marginalizes their function in the larger culture. So too the splitting of natives into such oppositions as the active and the contemplative prepares us for the privileging of the first over the second category, which will, in effect, be colonized and turned into a museum piece in order to be preserved.

Kim is about a child's discovery and recovery of identity and agency built upon a series of losses within an India he is about to lose, a child whose primary identification is with a lama whose parentage he must also lose if he is to enter the colonial order. By alienating him from his first (Indian) objects of desire, Kim's search for the Red Bull on a Green Field dooms him to endless disappointment, aloneness, and alienation. His collaboration with the lama's search, however, blurs and transfigures the limits of Kim's search for origins, his identity, and his end. Although Kim has been transformed from a youthful, reckless, happy adventurer into a cog in the imperialist wheel, the ending blesses and sacramentalizes this change by investing it with the displaced glow of the lama's transformation.

But the scene of closure appears to transcend the issues of identity and origins raised at each stage of Kim's initiation to the colonial order he inherits from his father. The last words of the novel belong not to Kim but to the lama. And it is this final evasion that gives me the greatest problems as a reader: part of the concluding

irony is that the powers earlier allotted to the lama—the powers of contemplation, meditation, vision, repose, and nonaction—are subverted at the end of the novel by the plot, by the ideology, and by the lama's final act. By choosing freely to return from Nirvana for the sake of Kim, the lama commits an action that is at once human, loving, sacrificial and also supportive of official ideology. By choosing love for the Sahib Kim over freedom from the Wheel of Life, the lama is appropriated into the values of action associated with such warriors as Mahbub and the colonial Sahibs. But of course, the lama also commits an act of self-sacrifice characteristic of the Boddhisatva—the holy figure who postpones his own entry into Nirvana to help others find the way; so here Kipling conflates two previously antithetical ideologies (the Christian/Western and the Buddhist) in valorizing the world of action, will, and choice over the renunciation and austerity that dominated traditional Hindu thought. Kim, however, has obfuscated: is he deluding the lama into thinking that as his "chela," he too is ready to be delivered from the Wheel of Life? That he enters such a bargain in the name of love is part of the problematic emotional field in which Kim operates all through his fictional life. Split by irreconcilable loyalties and loves and doomed to progressive alienation from the objects of his desire, Kim will eventually have to deny the lama, to whom the author gives the last, ironic, and materially false words in the novel: "'Son of my Soul, I have wrenched my soul back from the Threshold of Freedom to free thee from all sin—as I am free, and sinless. Just is the Wheel! Certain is our deliverance. Come!' He crossed his hands on his lap and smiled, as a man may who has won Salvation for himself and his beloved" [240].

A luminous freeze-frame on which to end a novel, the scene leaves Kim and the reader hanging in mid-air, as all that has been solid (in terms of constructing an idealized community in which Kim is a small part of a larger Indian whole) melts into the air of visionary illusion and prayer. Yet, this end is also a beginning, or rather a colonial fantasy that suggests an impossible origin for a new colonialist, one with a split sense of the constitution of self, who disavows difference from the native, yet knows otherwise.

A novel that ends in the glow of such ironic certainty suggests not only the deeply divided ambivalence of colonial discourse but also the contextual radiance of turn-of-the-century arrogance and self-doubt. Certainly, 1897–1901 were watershed years whose glorified celebrations of jubilees, as fragile as crystal, were constructed on the abyss of contradiction between rhetoric and reality, fantasy and defense. But more immediately, at the heart of Kim's ambivalence is a profound moment of personal and historical anguish—to be a Sahib he must allow the "two sides" of his head to evolve and internalize the

contradictions of what Bhabha calls the "colonial moment." One side accepts (along with power and knowledge) the myth of Kim as beloved child of India and the other articulates difference, separation, and division from the fantasy of connection with India. It is the moment, too, of Kim's entry into the Symbolic and into history as a subject, as a knowledgeable agent whose actions will turn him towards surveillance and power. The age of empire too, as so many historians, most recently and eloquently Eric Hobsbawm, have observed, is marked by a curious self-destructiveness, "victim of the very contradictions inherent in its advance."[4] The energy and ambition of those dreamers of empire sprang from the pressures and strains of an impossibly confined life in a threatened island desperate for the release and exploitation of colonization.

J. A. Hobson, Lenin, Cecil Rhodes and Kipling all knew the same story—that control of information and the "policing" of daily life were essential to power, that far from being a moral agency, the imperial state (like the capitalist state) relies on exploitation to protect the interests of a dominant class, and that it therefore violates the interests of the majority in both England and its empires. They merely orchestrated it differently: Hobson focused on the economic roots of imperialism and on the desire of financial capitalists to develop, at public expense, foreign markets for surplus goods and capital; Lenin's famous definition of imperialism as the monopoly stage of capitalism implied an insidious scenario where private cartels dominate world markets; Rhodes energized his campaigns, companies, and colonies with megalomaniacal dreams of a global political and economic empire controlled by Britain as the road to salvation. Kipling, less idealistic than Rhodes, more aware of the fragility of individuals and the societies they construct, wished to deny the economic basis of imperial dreams by constructing synthetic world orders, the day's work of bridge building and self-sacrifice as justification for colonization. The cost of such defense was the splitting of the self and its empire into the private or Imaginary, and the public or the Symbolic. Kipling's moral and familial universalism depended on the existence of the Other and yet marginalized and eventually negated its significance. His dream of empire would turn the world into a friendly jungle to protect Mowgli and his animal friends. The problem in the dream, of course, is that for the jungle to turn friendly, it must first be conquered; and that too is what Sandison would call the crisis of empire where the "subject" or "principal is at once aggressive and embattled in a foreign and menacing world which he nevertheless seeks to appropriate."[5]

4. *The Age of Empire: 1875–1914* (New York: Vintage, 1989), 10.
5. Alan Sandison, *The Wheel of Empire* (New York: St. Martin's Press, 1967), 62.

Such contradictions are still part of the dreams of empire, alive today in the rhetoric and actions of world powers: ethnic idealization now serves, as George Kennan once wrote of Marxist idealism, as "the fig leaf" covering the violence of national practice. After the second World War, the centers of imperial control shifted mainly to North America where the imperial system, no longer directly responsible to the colony, is now controlled by multinational corporations and "world managers." The principal resources of the world are voraciously exploited by invisible international corporations whose demands for oil, bananas, and other raw materials dictate the contradictory policies of the United States whose languages of "democracy" support counter-democratic forces in countries from the Middle East to South and Central America.

The poet of empire is also the Indian child whose fear of the abyss is turned into poetry, whose fundamental relationship to the outside world, mediated through language, presents a program of survival to the outside world of readers. That personal program (like the program of imperialism itself) must rest on deep ambivalence towards its obscure object of desire. And if Kipling has anything to say to us today, it is a way to see the contradictions and the costs of such programs of survival. The cost in his novels, stories, and poems—however defensive and facetious the armor—is horrendous because it dehumanizes, alienates, and destroys the dream jungle home of Kipling's underground, Indian, childhood self. The face that haunts him, blind and weeping, that can never wipe its eyes,[6] the anguished image of inexpressible private loss, is also an image of the source for empire, and by extension, of the self denied, abused, and victimized by the rigorous deeds of Englishmen in quest of dreams of empire. And the blindness is produced and inflicted by a culture that must be blind to its own ideological contradictions. As in his well-known, oft anthologized and misread poem "If," where the narrator assumes a social system built on nightmare contradictions, the ambivalence of Kipling's stories also lies in their paradoxical reaction against and affirmation of power and imperialism.

In drawing attention to the forms that contained the anxiety of one particular writer of empire, Rudyard Kipling, I suggest that the history of empire and of personalities produced by empire repeats itself, and that Kipling constructs a pathology of selves that illuminates the pathology of empire. Understanding Kipling's stories

6. Images of damaged perception, mutilation, and blindness haunt such stories as "They," "The Wish House," "A Matter of Fact," "In the Same Boat," and "At the End of the Passage," and the poem "La Nuit Balance":

> Then a Face came, blind and weeping,
> And It couldn't wipe its eyes,
> And It muttered I was keeping
> Back the moonlight from the skies. (*Verse* 28–9)

requires us to reread their representations of self in terms of the culture of empire, and then again, of representations of empire in terms of the self. The continual lesson of Kipling (and other colonial writers) is that our own views of otherness and Others are also grounded in psychohistory, that the anxieties of empire *are* the anxieties of family. Our creation of new world orders, our ways of synthesizing and ordering ourselves and others are an extension of the psychopathology of everyday life, and also a defense and antidote to the anxieties of division. The anxiety of imperial systems is still intact, its appetite displaced on to the "free" market. The dates and subjects may have changed, but the racist heritage, the compulsion to unify, centralize, and master society, nature, and world economies, the voracious rapacity that veils itself in multinational garbs, the confusion between public disguise and inner reality (as in American presidential performance or in wars of "liberation"), and the greater questions of economic inequalities between fenced world and unfenced jungle, between the first and third world, have not changed. The third world is still judged in terms of its adoption of first world political, cultural, and economic values, Kim must learn the multiplication tables in English, and the Bander-Log (the Monkey-People in the *Jungle Books*)—Indian, Irish, Arab, Central or Native American—must learn to respect and adopt the rule of power, law, and government represented by neo-imperialism's consistently insidious forms of surveillance and control.

Rudyard Kipling: A Chronology

1865 Born in Bombay on December 30. His father, John
 Lockwood Kipling, artist, craftsman, and instructor at
 the Jeejeebhoy School of Art in Bombay, emigrated to
 India in 1864 shortly after his marriage to Alice
 Macdonald, whose sister, Georgiana, had married the
 painter Edward Burne-Jones in 1860.

1871 Rudyard and his sister, Alice (Trix, born 1868), are left
 in England to board at Lorne Lodge, Southsea (which
 Rudyard later calls "The House of Desolation");
 Rudyard's eyesight and emotional health deteriorate.

1877 Alice Kipling returns from India to rescue the children
 from Lorne Lodge, through Trix returns to stay until
 1880.

1878 Enters the United Services College at Westward Ho! in
 Devon where he meets Lionel Dunsterville (the model
 for Stalky) and George Beresford (the model for M'Turk
 in *Stalky & Co.*). His father, who organizes the Indian
 section of the arts display at the International
 Exposition, takes him to Paris that summer.

1880 Falls in love with Florence Garrard (Flo), the model for
 Maisie in *The Light That Failed*.

1881 Edits the *United Services College Chronicle*. His par-
 ents publish his poems, *Schoolboy Lyrics*, for private
 circulation.

1882 Sails for India and works as assistant editor of the *Civil
 and Military Gazette*, a newspaper in Lahore, where his
 father is principal of the Mayo College of Art and the
 curator of the Lahore Museum. His summer holidays
 are spent in Simla.

1884 *Echoes*, a series of verse and skits, by Rudyard and Trix.

1885 *Quartette*, by Rudyard, Trix, and their parents, published
 at Christmas, includes early versions of Rudyard's "The
 Strange Ride of Morrowbie Jukes" and "The Phantom
 Rickshaw."

1886 *Departmental Ditties*; admitted to Lodge Hope and
 Perseverance, no. 782, EC, in Lahore, as a Freemason.

1887	Moves to Allahabad where he works at the newspaper, the *Pioneer*, and writes a series of articles about trips to Rajputana (Rajastan) published in *Letters of Marque*. Begins his life-long friendship with Professor "Aleck" Hill and his American wife, Edmonia, whose garden becomes the home of Rikki-tikki-tavi of *The Jungle Book*.
1888	*Plain Tales from the Hills*.
1888–89	*Soldiers Three*; *The Story of the Gadsbys*; *In Black and White*; *Under the Deodars*; *The Phantom Rickshaw*; *Wee Willie Winkie*.
1889	Leaves India in March; visits Rangoon, Singapore, Hong Kong, and Japan en route to the United States, where he meets Mark Twain and falls in love, briefly, with Caroline Taylor, sister of Professor and Mrs. Hill, his old friends from India. The articles about his travels across the United States are later collected in *From Sea to Sea*. Arrives in London that fall and enters its literary scene.
1890	*The Light That Failed*. Starts close friendship with American literary agent Wolcott Balestier. Visits Italy. Suffers depression and a nervous breakdown.
1891	Travels to South Africa, New Zealand, Australia, India, and Ceylon. Death of Wolcott Balestier.
1892	Marries Wolcott's sister Caroline (Carrie); the bride is given away by Henry James. Daughter Josephine born in December. *The Naulahka*, written with Wolcott Balestier. *Barrack-Room Ballads*.
1893	*Many Inventions*.
1894	*The Jungle Book*.
1895	*The Second Jungle Book*.
1896	*The Seven Seas*. Birth of second daughter, Elsie. Quarrels with brother-in-law, Beatty; returns to England.
1897	Birth of son John. *Captains Courageous*.
1898	*The Day's Work*.
1899	Tragic last visit to the United States: death of Josephine. *Stalky & Co.*, *From Sea to Sea*. Declines offer of knighthood.
1900	Travels to South Africa where he contributes to the army newspaper *The Friend*; befriends Cecil Rhodes, Jameson, and Baden-Powell.
1901	*Kim*.
1902	*Just So Stories*. Buys final house at Burwash in Sussex, "Bateman's."
1903	*The Five Nations*. Refuses offer of knighthood a second time.
1904	*Traffics and Discoveries*.

1906	*Puck of Pook's Hill.*
1907	Nobel Prize for Literature. *Collected Verse.*
1908	*Letters to the Family: Notes on a Recent Trip to Canada*
1909	*Actions and Reactions; Abaft the Funnel.*
1910	*Rewards and Fairies.* Death of Rudyard's mother.
1911	Death of Rudyard's father.
1913	Visits Egypt. *Songs from Books.*
1914–18	World War I. John enlists a week short of his seventeenth birthday. *The New Army in Training, France at War*, and other war writings.
1915	John reported missing, believed killed, in France.
1917	*A Diversity of Creatures.*
1919	*The Years Between; Rudyard Kipling's Verse: Inclusive Edition.*
1920	*Letters of Travel.*
1921	Visits France and accepts honorary degrees. Refuses offer of the Order of Merit from King George V.
1923	*The Irish Guards in the Great War; Land and Sea Tales for Scouts and Guides.*
1926	*Debits and Credits.*
1928	*A Book of Words.*
1930	*Thy Servant a Dog.*
1932	*Limits and Renewals.*
1936	Dies, January 18.
1937	*Something of Myself for My Friends Known and Unknown.*
1937–39	*The Complete Works of Rudyard Kipling*, Sussex Edition: the definitive edition prepared by Kipling during his last years.

Selected Bibliography

EDITIONS

Of the numerous editions of *Kim*, the standard is the Sussex Edition, 35 vols., 1937–39. The Burwash Edition, 28 vols., published in New York in 1941, generally follows the text of the Sussex Edition.

UNPUBLISHED MATERIALS

Kipling Papers, University of Sussex, England.
Kipling Collection, Houghton Library, Harvard University, Cambridge, Mass.
Berg Collection, New York Public Library, Main Branch, New York City.
Kipling ms. 44840, British Museum, London.

SELECTED OTHER WORKS

The Day's Work. Ed. Thomas Pinney. Oxford: Oxford UP, 1987.
The Letters of Rudyard Kipling. Ed. Thomas Pinney. 3 vols. Iowa City: U of Iowa P, 1996.
Life's Handicap. Ed. A. O. J. Cockshut. Oxford: Oxford UP, 1987.
The Man Who Would Be King and Other Stories. Ed. Louis Cornell. Oxford: Oxford UP, 1987.
The Jungle Book & The Second Jungle Book. Ed. W. W. Robson. Oxford: Oxford UP, 1987.
Plain Tales from the Hills. Ed. Andrew Rutherford. Oxford: Oxford UP, 1987.
Rudyard Kipling: A Critical Edition of the Major Works. Ed. Daniel Karlin. Oxford: Oxford UP, 1999.
Rudyard Kipling's Verse: Definitive Edition. New York: Doubleday, 1940.
Something of Myself and Other Autobiographical Writings. Ed. Thomas Pinney. Cambridge: Cambridge UP, 1990.
Stalky & Co. Ed. Isabel Quigly. Oxford: Oxford UP, 1987.

CRITICISM

• indicates works excerpted in this Norton Critical Edition.

• Annan, Noel. "Kipling's Place in the History of Ideas." *Victorian Studies* 3 (1959–60): 323–48.
• Baucom, Ian. "The Survey of India." In *Out of Place: Englishness, Empire, and Locations of Identity*. Princeton, N.J.: Princeton UP, 1999.
Beloff, Max. *Imperial Sunset: Britain's Liberal Empire, 1897–1921*. New York: Knopf, 1970.
Birkenhead, Lord. *Rudyard Kipling*. London: Weidenfeld and Nicholson, 1978.
Bivona, Daniel. *Desire and Contradiction: Imperial Visions and Domestic Debates in Victorian Literature*. Manchester: Manchester UP, 1990.
Bloom, Harold, ed. *Rudyard Kipling: Modern Critical Views*. New York: Chelsea House, 1987.
Bodelsen, C. A. *Aspects of Kipling's Art*. Manchester: Manchester UP, 1964.
Brantlinger, Patrick. *Rule of Darkness: British Literature and Imperialism, 1830–1914*. Ithaca, N.Y.: Cornell UP, 1988.
Bristow, Joseph. *Empire Boys: Adventure in a Man's World*. London: HarperCollins, 1991.
• Carrington, Charles. *Rudyard Kipling: His Life and Work*. London: Penguin, 1986 [1955].
Cornell, Louis L. *Kipling in India*. London: Macmillan, 1966.
Feeley, Margaret Peller. "The *Kim* That Nobody Reads." *Studies in the Novel* 13.3 (Fall 1981): 266–81.
Gilbert, Elliot L. *The Good Kipling: Studies in the Short Story*. Oberlin: Ohio UP, 1970.
———, ed. *Kipling and the Critics*. New York: New York UP, 1965.

Green, Martin. *Dreams of Adventure, Deeds of Empire*. New York: Basic Books, 1979.

Harbord, R. E., Roger Lancelyn Green, Alec Mason, eds. *The Reader's Guide to Rudyard Kipling's Work*. 8 vols. Canterbury: Gibbs & Sons; Bournemouth: Boscombe Printers, 1961–72.

• Hollington, Michael. "*Kim* and Kipling: Concentration Camps and Their Sweet Opposites." *Q/W/E/R/T/Y: Arts, Litteratures and Civilization du Monde Anglophone* 4 (Oct. 1994): 175–88.

• Howe, Irving. "The Pleasures of *Kim*." In *Art, Politics, and Will: Essays in Honor of Lionel Trilling*. Ed. Quentin Anderson, Stephen Donadio, and Steven Marcus. New York: Basic Books, 1977. 33–44.

Hutchins, Francis G. *The Illusion of Permanence: British Imperialism in India*. Princeton, N.J.: Princeton UP, 1967.

Islam, Shamsul. *Kipling's "Law."* London: Macmillan, 1975.

Jarrell, Randall. "On Preparing to Read Kipling." In *Kipling and the Critics*. Ed. Elliot L. Gilbert. New York: New York UP, 1965.

Kemp, Sandra. *Kipling's Hidden Narratives*. Oxford: Basil Blackwell, 1988.

———, and Lisa Lewis, eds. *Writings on Writing by Rudyard Kipling*. Cambridge: Cambridge UP, 1996.

Kiernan, V. G. *The Lords of Human Kind: Black Man, Yellow Man, and White Man in an Age of Empire*. Boston: Little, Brown, 1969.

• Kinkead-Weekes, Mark. "Vision in Kipling's Novels." In *Kipling's Mind and Art*. Ed. Andrew Rutherford. Stanford, Calif: Stanford UP, 1964. 228–34.

Lowe, Gail Ching-Liang. *White Skins, Black Masks: Representation and Colonialism*. London & New York: Routledge, 1996.

• McClure, John A. *Kipling and Conrad: The Colonial Fiction*. Cambridge, Mass.: Harvard UP, 1981.

Mallet, Phillip, ed. *Kipling Considered*. New York: St. Martin's Press, 1989.

• Matin, A. Michael. "'The Hun is at the Gate!': Historicizing Kipling's Militaristic Rhetoric, from the Imperial Periphery to the National Center." *Studies in the Novel* 31.3 (Fall 1999): 317–56 and 4 (Winter 1999): 432–70.

Meyers, Jeffrey. *Fiction and the Colonial Experience*. Ipswich: The Boydell Press, 1973.

Mohanty, S. P. "Kipling's Children and the Colour Line." *Race & Class* 31.1 (1989): 21–40.

Moore-Gilbert, B. J. *Kipling and "Orientalism."* London: Croom Helm, 1986.

Morris, James. *Pax Britannica: The Climax of an Empire*. Middlesex: Penguin, 1968.

Orel, Harold, ed. *Critical Essays on Rudyard Kipling*. Boston: G. K. Hall and Co., 1989.

• Parry, Ann. "History and Artifice in Kipling's *Kim*." *Q/W/E/R/T/Y: Arts, Litteratures and Civilization du Monde Anglophone* 4 (Oct. 1994):189–95.

Parry, Benita. *Delusions and Discoveries: Studies on India in the British Imagination 1880–1930*. Berkeley: U of California P, 1972.

———. "The Contents and Discontents of Kipling's Imperialism." *New Formations* 6 (Winter 1988): 49–63.

Randall, Don. "Ethnography and the Hybrid Boy in Rudyard Kipling's *Kim*." *Ariel* 27.3 (July 1996): 79–104.

Raskin, Jonah. *The Mythology of Imperialism*. New York: Random House, 1971.

Rosenthal, Michael. *The Character Factory: Baden-Powell's Boy Scouts and the Imperatives of Empire*. New York: Pantheon, 1984.

• Roy, Parama. *Indian Traffic: Identities in Question in Colonial and Postcolonial India*. Berkeley: U of California P, 1998.

Rutherford, Andrew, ed. *Kipling's Mind and Art: Selected Critical Essays*. Stanford, Calif.: Stanford UP, 1964,

Said, Edward W. *Orientalism*. New York: Vintage, 1979.

———. *Culture and Imperialism*. New York: Knopf, 1993.

• ———, ed. *Kim*. Harmondsworth, England: Penguin Books, 1987.

Sandison, Alan. *The Wheel of Empire*. New York: St. Martin's Press, 1967.

Shahane, Vasant A. *Rudyard Kipling: Activist and Artist*. Carbondale: Southern Illinois UP, 1973.

• Suleri, Sara. *The Rhetoric of English India*. Chicago: U of Chicago P, 1992.

• Sullivan, Zohreh T. *Narratives of Empire: The Fictions of Rudyard Kipling*. Cambridge: Cambridge UP, 1993.

Tompkins, J. M. S. *The Art of Rudyard Kipling*. London: Methuen, 1959.

• Williams, Patrick. "*Kim* and Orientalism." In *Kipling Considered*. Ed. Phillip Mallet. London: Macmillan, 1989. 33–55.

Wilson, Angus. *The Strange Ride of Rudyard Kipling: His Life and Work*. New York: Penguin, 1979.

Wilson, Edmund. *The Wound and the Bow*. New York: Farrar, Straus and Giroux, 1978.

Wurgaft, Lewis D. *The Imperial Imagination: Magic and Myth in Kipling's India*. Middletown, Conn.: Wesleyan UP, 1983.